# English

## For UGC-NET/JRF/SLET (Paper II and III) and Other Competitive Examinations

**Objective Type Questions with Solutions**

**Fifth Edition**

R.S. Malik
M.A., Ph.D.
Former Head, Postgraduate Dept. of English
C.R.A. College, Sonepat (Haryana)

ATLANTIC
PUBLISHERS & DISTRIBUTORS (P) LTD

7/22, Ansari Road, Darya Ganj, New Delhi
Tel.: +91-11-4077 5252, 2327 3880
E-mail: orders@atlanticbooks.com
Web: www.atlanticbooks.com

This edition published in 2025 by Atlantic Publishers & Distributors (P) Ltd.



First Edition 2013, Second Edition 2013
Third Edition 2015, Fourth Edition 2016
Fifth Edition 2019, 2020, 2021, 2022, 2023, 2024, 2025, 2026



Printed & bound in India by Atlantic Print Services

# English

## For
## UGC-NET/JRF/SLET
## (Paper II and III) and Other
## Competitive Examinations

**Objective Type Questions with Solutions**

Fifth Edition

***Dedicated to***

My wife Kamlesh

and

daughters

Meghna and Mimansa

and

to

my grandson, Abhiudaya

# General Information

## About the NET

The National Educational Testing Bureau of University Grants Commission (UGC) conducts National Eligibility Test (NET) to determine eligibility for lectureship and for award of Junior Research Fellowship (JRF) for Indian nationals in order to ensure minimum standards for the entrants in the teaching profession and research. The Test is conducted in Humanities (including languages), Social Sciences, Forensic Science, Environmental Sciences, Computer Science and Applications and Electronic Science.

The Council of Scientific and Industrial Research (CSIR) conducts the UGC-CSIR NET for other Science subjects, namely, Life Sciences, Physical Sciences, Chemical Sciences, Mathematical Sciences and Earth Atmospheric Ocean & Planetary Sciences jointly with the UGC. The tests are conducted twice in a year, generally in the months of June and December. For candidates who desire to pursue research, the Junior Research Fellowship (JRF) is available for five years subject to fulfillment of certain conditions. UGC has allocated a number of fellowships to the universities for the candidates who qualify the test for JRF. The JRFs are awarded to the meritorious candidates from among the candidates qualifying for eligibility for lectureship in the NET. JRFs are available only to the candidates who opt for it in their application forms.

The test for Junior Research Fellowship is being conducted since 1984. The Government of India, through its notification dated 22nd July, 1988 entrusted the task of conducting the eligibility test for lectureship to UGC. Consequently, UGC conducted the first National Eligibility Test, common to both eligibility for Lectureship and Junior Research Fellowship in two parts, that is, in December 1989 and in March, 1990.

## NET Schedule

UGC conducts NET twice a year, i.e. in the months of June and December. The notifications announcing the June and December examinations are published in the months of March and September respectively in the weekly journal of nation-wide circulation, viz. *Employment News*.

## NET Results Declaration Schedule

The result of June, UGC-NET is declared generally in the month of October. Similarly December, UGC-NET result is usually declared in the month of April. The UGC-NET results published in the Employment News are also available on UGC website.

## UGC-NET Pattern from July 2018 Onwards

The Test will consist of two papers. Both the papers will consist of only objective type questions.

| Session | Paper | Marks | Number of Questions | Duration |
|---|---|---|---|---|
| First | I | 100 | 50 questions all are compulsory | 1 Hours (09:30 A.M. to 10:45 A.M.) IST |
| Second | II | 200 | 100 questions all are compulsory | 1 Hours (11:00 A.M. to 01:00 P.M.) IST |

**Paper-I** shall consist of 50 objective type compulsory questions each carrying 2 marks. The questions which will be of general nature, intended to assess the teaching/research aptitude of the candidate. It will primarily be designed to test reasoning ability, comprehension, divergent thinking and general awareness of the candidate.

**Paper-II** shall consist of 100 objective type compulsory questions each carrying 2 marks which will be based on the subject selected by the candidate.

All the questions of Paper-II will be compulsory, covering entire syllabi of earlier Paper II and Paper-III (including all electives, without options).

The candidate will have to mark the responses for questions of Paper-I and Paper-II on the Optical Mark Reader (OMR) Sheet provided along with the test booklet.

## SYLLABUS FOR ENGLISH

## PAPER–II

1. Chaucer to Shakespeare
2. Jacobean to Restoration Periods
3. Augustan Age : 18th Century Literature
4. Romantic Period
5. Victorian Period
6. Modern Period
7. Contemporary Period
8. American and Other Non-British Literatures
9. Literary Theory and Criticism
10. Rhetoric and Prosody

## PAPER–III (A)
## (Core group)

1. British Literature from Chaucer to the Present Day
2. Criticism and Literary Theory.

**Unit–I** : Literary Comprehension (with internal choice of poetry stanza and prose passage; four comprehension questions will be asked carrying 4 marks each).

| | | |
|---|---|---|
| **Unit–II** | : | Up to the Renaissance |
| **Unit–III** | : | Jacobean to Restoration Periods |
| **Unit–IV** | : | Augustan Age : 18th Century Literature |
| **Unit–V** | : | Romantic Period |
| **Unit–VI** | : | Victorian and Pre-Raphaelites |
| **Unit–VII** | : | Modem British Literature |
| **Unit–VIII** | : | Contemporary British Literature |
| **Unit–IX** | : | Literary Theory and Criticism up to T.S. Eliot |
| **Unit–X** | : | Contemporary Theory |

## PAPER–III (B)
## (ELECTIVE/OPTIONAL)

| | | |
|---|---|---|
| **Elective–I** | : | History of English Language, English Language Teaching |
| **Elective–II** | : | European Literature from Classical Age to the 20th Century |
| **Elective–III** | : | Indian Writing in English and Indian Literature in English Translation |
| **Elective–IV** | : | American and Other Non-British English Literatures |
| **Elective–V** | : | Literary Theory and Criticism |

# Preface

Frankly speaking, I have not much to say by way of Preface except to quote F.R. Leavis: "It is usual in prefacing a book to express indebtedness to various persons for help and advice. The debt that I wish to acknowledge is to those whom I have, during the past dozen years, discussed literature as a teacher. If I have learnt anything about the methods of profitable discussion, I have learnt in collaboration with them." (Preface to *Revaluation*). During my teaching career of about fifty years, I have come to believe in the adage: "Students are the best teachers". My students taught me what to teach and how to teach. The present book is a product of my interaction with those students whom I have been teaching for the NET for the past some time.

After the encouraging response from the readers to the first three editions of the book, this latest edition has been brought out. In it, UGC-NET Question Papers II and III (with Answers) have been included up to January 2017. Since the NET pattern has been changed from 2018 onwards, merging two Papers II and III as one Paper II, this latest edition contains Paper II conducted by CBSE in July 2018, with answers, as per latest pattern. Besides, General Information contains the new 2018 exam pattern.

My grateful thanks are to Atlantic Publishers and Distributors (P) Ltd., New Delhi, especially Dr. K.R. Gupta, for bringing out the book in such a short time and promoting it for the benefit of students.

As there is always scope for improvement, suggestions will not only be welcomed but also highly appreciated.

**R.S. Malik**

# Contents

## Paper III

# PAPER-II

# 1

# Chaucer to Shakespeare

1. Which of the four chief dialects that flourished in the Pre-Chaucerian period became the standard English in Chaucer's time?
   (a) The Northern
   (b) The Southern
   (c) The East Midland
   (d) The West Midland
2. "He found English a dialect and left it a language". Who estimates Chaucer's greatness in this respect?
   (a) William Ker
   (b) Lowes
   (c) Ward
   (d) Mandeville
3. Which of the following poems of Chaucer is considered the first novel in English?
   (a) The House of Fame
   (b) The Parliament of Fowls
   (c) The Book of the Duchess
   (d) Troilus and Criseyde
4. There is something common between Boccaccio's "Filostrato" and Chaucer's
   (a) "Legende of Goode Wommen"
   (b) "Troilus and Criseyde"
   (c) "Prologue to Canterbury Tales"
   (d) "Roman de la Rose"
5. The plan of Chaucer's "Canterbury Tales" takes on
   (a) *Decameron*
   (b) *Filostrato*
   (c) *Roman de la Rose*
   (d) *Divinde Comedy*
6. Which of the following tales of Chaucer deals with the Chivalric romance of Palamon and Arcite?
   (a) *The Miller's Tale*
   (b) *The Merchant's Tale*
   (c) *The Knight's Tale*
   (d) *The Franklin's Tale*
7. Chaucer was called, "The earliest of the great moderns" and was also called, "The morning star of the Renaissance." Who initiated these remarks?
   (a) Kittredge
   (b) Hudson
   (c) Albert
   (d) Pope
8. Which of the following works of Chaucer presents the picture of a strong united nation?
   (a) "The House of Fame"
   (b) "Knight"
   (c) "Merchant"
   (d) "Canterbury Tales"
9. "When Adam delved and Eve span, who was then the gentleman." Who told this to the people?

(a) An agitator from peasants
(b) A Romantic Poet
(c) A Reformer
(d) An author of prose work

10. How many tales are to be told by each pilgrim?
(a) Two
(b) Three
(c) Four
(d) One

11. The pilgrims are going to visit the tomb of
(a) Thomas Acquinas
(b) Saint Mary
(c) Saint John
(d) Thomas Becket

12. Where is the tomb of the Saint situated?
(a) Warwickshire
(b) Shaftesbury
(c) Canterbury
(d) Stratford-upon-Avon

13. In which poem did Chaucer use the heroic couplet for the first time?
(a) "Canterbury Tales"
(b) "House of Fame"
(c) "The Legende of Goode Wommen"
(d) "Troilus and Criseyde"

14. How many tales in all were written by Chaucer?
(a) Thirty-two
(b) Twenty-four
(c) Sixty-four
(d) One hundred and twenty-eight

15. "Amor Vincit Omnia" in Chaucer's Prologue which means
(a) Love is blind
(b) Love is fatal
(c) Love conquers nothing
(d) Love conquers all

16. Which of the following comes forth with the story of "the infinite incredible patience of Griselda under the tests imposed by her husband Walter."
(a) Clerk of Oxford
(b) Prioress
(c) Wife of Bath
(d) Franklin

17. How many pilgrims are there in Prologue to "Canterbury Tales" including the poet?
(a) Thirty-one
(b) Thirty
(c) Twenty-nine
(d) Twenty-eight

18. Chaucer dedicated his "Troilus" to
(a) John Gower
(b) William Langland
(c) John Wycliff
(d) King Edward II

19. Who tells the last tale in Chaucer's "Canterbury Tales"?
(a) The Prioress
(b) The Nun
(c) The Parson
(d) The Monk

20. Which of the following tales is in prose?
(a) "The Parson's Tale"
(b) "The Tale of Melibeus"
(c) Both (a) and (b)
(d) None of the above

21. Who among the following said about Chaucer's Prologue to the "Canterbury Tales" that "here indeed is God's plenty"?
(a) Dryden
(b) Pope
(c) Ben Jonson
(d) Dr. Johnson

22. Who is known as the connecting link between Chaucer and Spenser?

(a) Henry Howard
(b) Thomas Sackville
(c) Roger Ascham
(d) Sir Thomas Wyatt

23. The works of Wyatt and Surrey were published in *Tottel's Miscellany* in
(a) 1553
(b) 1557
(c) 1563
(d) 1568

24. The Licencing Act for closing of all theaters except Drury Lane and Covent Garden was passed in
(a) 1734
(b) 1735
(c) 1736
(d) 1737

25. The first English playhouse called 'The Theatre' was founded in
(a) 1574
(b) 1575
(c) 1576
(d) 1577

26. *Gorboduc*, the first regular comedy in English, was written by
(a) Nicholas Udall
(b) John Heywood
(c) Thomas Norton
(d) Sackville and Norton

27. When were theatres closed in England?
(a) 1623
(b) 1642
(c) 1616
(d) 1650

28. When did the great fire of London take place?
(a) 1610
(b) 1606
(c) 1640
(d) 1666

29. Who among the following is/are the English Chaucerians?
(a) Thomas Occleve
(b) Alexander Barclay
(c) John Lydgate
(d) All the above

30. Who among the following is not the English Chaucerian
(a) Robert Henryson
(b) William Dunbar
(c) Stephen Howes
(d) Both (a) and (b)

31. Which work of the Scottish Chaucerians imitates Chaucer's "House of Fame"?
(a) Douglas' "King Hart"
(b) Douglas' "The Palace of Honour"
(c) Dunbar's "The Thistle and the Rose"
(d) Henryson's "Testament of Cresseid"

32. Caxton's printing press was set up in
(a) 1475
(b) 1476
(c) 1477
(d) 1478

33. Which is the first book in English in poetic prose?
(a) *Confessio Amantis*
(b) *Nun's Priest's Tale*
(c) *Morte d' Arthur*
(d) *Vox Clamantis*

34. Which work is considered to be the true prologue to the Renaissance?
(a) *Tottel's Miscellany*
(b) More's *Utopia*
(c) Aschem's *The Schoolmaster*
(d) None of the above

35. Chaucer wrote the "Romance of the Rose" under the influence of
(a) De Lorris and De Meun
(b) Dante and Boccaccio
(c) Blanche and De Lorries
(d) Blanche and Meung

36. Which war resulted in bringing Tudor Rule in England?
    (a) The Anglo-French Wars
    (b) The Battle of Hastings
    (c) The War of Roses
    (d) The Battle of Agincourt
37. *The Travels of Sir John Mandeville* is believed to be the English translation of a certain French writer named as
    (a) John of Trevisa
    (b) Meun
    (c) Jean de Bourgane
    (d) De Lorris
38. Gower is represented as a figure of old poetic authority in Shakespeare's play:
    (a) *Pericles*
    (b) *Venus and Adonis*
    (c) *Cymbeline*
    (d) *Titus Andronicus*
39. The Spanish Armada was defeated in
    (a) 1488
    (b) 1496
    (c) 1540
    (d) 1588
40. The literary genre, the ecologue, is attributed to
    (a) John Skelton
    (b) Alexander Barclay
    (c) William Dunbar
    (d) Stephen Hawes
41. "La Male Regale" by Thomas Occleve is a satire on
    (a) Poverty
    (b) Superstition
    (c) Fanaticism
    (d) Morality
42. *Tottel's Miscellany* contained the songs and sonnets of
    (a) Wyatt and Surrey
    (b) Wyatt and Raleigh
    (c) Sidney and Surrey
    (d) Sidney and Raleigh
43. Roger Ascham's *Toxophilus* is a dialogue in praise of
    (a) Fencing
    (b) Archery
    (c) Wrestling
    (d) Horse-riding
44. *The Schoolmaster* by Roger Ascham is a/an
    (a) morality play
    (b) human ideal
    (c) educational treatise
    (d) All of the above
45. Who is known as the Chaucer of Scotland?
    (a) William Dunbar
    (b) Robert Henryson
    (c) John Lydgate
    (d) Gavin Douglas
46. Which of Chaucer's work has the Trojan War as its background?
    (a) "The Parliament of Fowls"
    (b) "Troilus and Cryseyde"
    (c) "The Book of the Duchess"
    (d) "The House of Fame"
47. Chaucer lived during the reigns of
    (a) Edward III and Richard II
    (b) Edward III and Henry IV
    (c) Richard II and Henry IV
    (d) Edward III, Richard II and Henry IV
48. Chaucer has used the technique of mock-heroic in
    (a) "The Pardoner's Tale"
    (b) "Miller's Tale"
    (c) "Nun's Priest's Tale"
    (d) "Franklin's Tale"
49. The influence of Dante's "Divine Commedia" is apparent in which of Chaucer's works?
    (a) "The House of Fame"
    (b) "The Parliament of Fowls"

(c) "The Book of Duchess"
(d) "Troilus and Cryseyde"

50. 'The Peasant's Revolt' resulted in the
(a) Dethroning of the king
(b) Demolition of Church as an institution
(c) End of serfdom
(d) Rise of nationalism

51. The Wife of Bath in the Canterbury Tales tells about her ______ marriages.
(a) Three
(b) Four
(c) Two
(d) Five

52. "The Book of the Duchess" was written on the death of
(a) Simon de Monfort
(b) Edward the Confessor
(c) John of Gaunt
(d) Henry-II

53. What was the prize for the best story teller among the pilgrims in "The Canterbury Tales"?
(a) A free horse ride
(b) A free supper
(c) A free stay in the inn
(d) The Bible

54. In which tale of Chaucer, a daughter is killed by her father?
(a) "The Monk's Tale"
(b) "The Physician's Tale"
(c) "The Friar's Tale"
(d) "The Clerk's Tale"

55. In Chaucer's "The Canterbury Tales", which of the following deals with two young Theban Warriors?
(a) "The Knight's Tale"
(b) "The Squire's Tale"
(c) "The Miller's Tale"
(d) "The Friar's Tale"

56. The writer who gave the first full expression of the English sense of humour was
(a) Gower
(b) Langland
(c) Chaucer
(d) Wycliffe

57. In whose story, the character of Griselda appear?
(a) "The Clerk's Tale"
(b) "The Reeve's Tale"
(c) "The Miller's Tale"
(d) "The Friar's Tale"

58. In the Prologue to "The Canterbury Tales", Chaucer used
(a) Tercets
(b) Rhyme-royal
(c) Eight-Syllabic line
(d) Ten-syllabic line

59. In "The Book of the Duchess", Chaucer made use of
(a) Tercets
(b) Rhyma-royal
(c) Eight-Syllabic line
(d) Ten-syllabic line

60. Who called the Prologue to "The Canterbury Tales" "The Prologue to modern fiction"?
(a) Pope
(b) Long
(c) Arnold
(d) Spenser

61. Dream Allegory was a popular poetic form during the
(a) Medieval Period
(b) Renaissance
(c) Latin, English
(d) Puritan Age

62. John Gower's "Vox Clamantis and Confessio John Amantis" are written in

(a) French, Latin
(b) Latin and French
(c) Latin and English
(d) None of the above

63. Who translated the Bible into English?
(a) Gower
(b) Langland
(c) Wyclif
(d) Chaucer

64. What does the word "Lollard" mean?
(a) priests
(b) peasants
(c) rubble
(d) mumbling of prayers

65. Who is the author of *Piers the Plowman*?
(a) Lydgate
(b) Henryson
(c) Gower
(d) Langland

66. Who among the following is called the morning star of the Reformation?
(a) Calvin
(b) Bacon
(c) Luther
(d) Wycliffe

67. Langland's *Piers the Plowman* is a satire on
(a) Aristocracy
(b) Peasant's revolt
(c) Clergy
(d) Society

68. Who said that Chaucerians' inferiority is well marked in satire as in anything else?
(a) Saintsbury
(b) Hugh Walker
(c) A.C. Ward
(d) Dryden

69. In Chaucer's characters who is shown to be in love for gold?
(a) The monk
(b) The merchant
(c) Doctor of physic
(d) Man of law

70. Who called Chaucer, "The Well of English Undefiled"?
(a) Spenser
(b) Arnold
(c) Sidney
(d) Eliot

71. "The Well of English Undefiled" means Chaucer's
(a) Realism
(b) Art of characterization
(c) Humour
(d) Avoidance of foreign influence

72. William Blake said that their traits are universal, "their lineaments are of universal human, life beyond which Nature never steps." Here, who are theirs?
(a) English Chaucerians
(b) Scottish Chaucerians
(c) Chaucer's Characters
(d) Lollards

73. In 1388, Wycliffe's translation of the Bible was revised by
(a) Chaucer
(b) John Purvey
(c) Vulgate
(d) John Trevisa

74. Which poem celebrates the betrothal of Richard II and Anne of Bohemia?
(a) "The Book of Duchess"
(b) "The Parliament of Fowls"
(c) "The House of Fame"
(d) "Faerie Queene"

75. The Thrissil and the Rois celebrates the marriage of James IV to Margaret Tudor. Who wrote this allegory?
(a) Donne
(b) Dunbar

(c) King James I
(d) None of the above

76. Dunbar's *The Two Married Women and the Window* is
(a) A love allegory
(b) A ballad
(c) A novel
(d) About conjugal relationships

77. Michael Drayton's *The Shepherd's Garland* is a series of
(a) Lyric poems
(b) Eclogues
(c) Ballads
(d) Sonnets

78. "Why Come Ye Not to Court?" is a satire on
(a) Cromwell
(b) More
(c) Sidney
(d) Wolsey

79. Match the plays and their authors
1. *The Goldyn Targe*
2. *Why Come Ye Not to Court?*
3. *The Fall of Princes*
4. *The Ship of Fools*
(a) Alexander Barclay
(b) Lydgate
(c) John Skelton
(d) Dunbar
(a) 1-c, 2-d, 3-a, 4-b
(b) 1-d, 2-c, 3-b, 4-a
(c) 1-b, 2-d, 3-a, 4-c
(d) 1-a, 2-b, 3-c, 4-d

80. Which of the following poems of Skelton is not a satire?
(a) "The Book of the Laurel"
(b) "Colin Clout"
(c) "Speak Parrot"
(d) "Why Come Ye Not to Court"

81. "Ralph Roister Doister", the first regular English Comedy, is modelled after
(a) French
(b) Seneca
(c) Terence
(d) Plautus

82. Philip Sidney's *Astrophel and Stella* is addressed to
(a) Penelope
(b) Lady Rich
(c) Queen Elizabeth
(d) Both (a) and (b)

83. In *The School of Abuse* (1579), Stephen Gosson attacked as a Puritan, the art of the age, especially the drama. What form of literature is it?
(a) Satirical poem
(b) Drama
(c) Pamphlet
(d) Novel

84. Who wrote in prose "The Historie of Richard III"?
(a) Spenser
(b) Marlowe
(c) More
(d) Shakespeare

85. "The Shepherd's Calender", a series of twelve pastoral poems, is written by
(a) Chaucer
(b) Gower
(c) Spenser
(d) Sidney

86. Spenser's satirical poem is
(a) "The Faerie Queene"
(b) "Epithalamion"
(c) "Prothalamion"
(d) "Mother Hubberd's Tale"

87. To whom has Spenser addressed his introductory letter in "The Faerie Queene"?

(a) Virgil
(b) Sidney
(c) Raleigh
(d) Queen Elizabeth

88. Match the knights and the qualities they represent in “The Faerie Queene”
(a) Sir Calidore
(b) Sir Artegal
(c) Cambel and Telamond
(d) Sir Guyan
(e) Britomart
(f) Red Cross knight
1. Courtesy
2. Justice
3. Friendship
4. Chastity
5. Temperance
6. Holiness
(a) a - 1, b - 2, c - 3, d - 4, e - 5, f - 6
(b) a - 3, b - 4, c - 5, d - 6, e - 2, f - 1
(c) a - 4, b - 5, c - 6, d - 2, e - 1, f - 3
(d) a - 2, b - 3, c - 6, d - 5, e - 1, f - 4

89. Edmund Spenser's “The Fairie Queene” was modelled after an Italian prototype. Identify
(a) Virgil's *Aeneid*
(b) Boccaccio's *Decameron*
(c) Boccaccio's *Filostrato*
(d) Ariosto's *Orlando Furioso*

90. What is Spenser's sonnet series called?
(a) *Shepherd's Calender*
(b) *Amoretti*
(c) *Complaints*
(d) *Hymns*

91. Who wrote “Polyolbion”, a huge poem in Alexandrines, containing a descriptive geography of England?
(a) William Warner
(b) John Davies
(c) Michael Drayton
(d) Samuel Daniel

92. Match the sonnet volumes and their poets
(a) Daniel
(b) Drayton
(c) Lodge
(d) Constable
1. Phyllis
2. Diana
3. Idea
4. Delia
(a) a - 2, b - 3, c - 4, d - 1
(b) a - 4, b - 3, c - 1, d - 2
(c) a - 3, b - 1, c - 4, d - 2
(d) a - 1, b - 2, c - 3, d - 4

93. Who completed Christopher Marlowe's *Hero and Leader*?
(a) Ben Jonson
(b) Shakespeare
(c) Chapman
(d) Heywood

94. Christopher Marlowe's ‘mighty line’ first came into Elizabethan drama with
(a) *Tamburlaine*
(b) *Arden of Feversham*
(c) *The Spanish Tragedy*
(d) None of the above

95. Thomas Kyd was the founder of
(a) Romantic comedy
(b) Romantic tragedy
(c) Satire
(d) Dramatic romance

96. The first picaresque novel which is written by Thomas Nash was
(a) *Anatomy of Absurdity*
(b) *Terrors of Night*
(c) *The Life of Jack Wilton*
(d) None of the above

97. Which work of Robert Greene gave the plot to Shakespeare's “The Winter's Tale”?
(a) *Groats-Worth of Wit*
(b) *Pandosto*

(c) *Orlando Furioso*
(d) *Friar Bacon*

98. *Life of Shakespeare* is written by
(a) Sidney Lee
(b) Philip Sidney
(c) Marlowe
(d) Spencer

99. Shakespeare's *First Folio* was published in
(a) 1600
(b) 1610
(c) 1620
(d) 1623

100. Which play by Shakespeare is considered autobiographical?
(a) *The Winter's Tale*
(b) *The Tempest*
(c) *Pericles*
(d) *Cymbeline*

101. Who said?

"It is the stars,

The stars above us, govern our conditions."
(a) King Lear
(b) Edgar
(c) Kent
(d) Fool

102. Which play of Shakespeare is a dramatization of a story told by Chaucer in "Knight's Tale"?
(a) *The Merchant of Venice*
(b) *As You Like It*
(c) *The Two Noble Kinsmen*
(d) *The Tempest*

103. In which play of Shakespeare are all guilty?
(a) *Measure for Measure*
(b) *Twelfth Night*
(c) *As You Like It*
(d) *All's Well That Ends Well*

104. Boccaccio's "Decameron" is echoed in Shakespeare's
(a) *All's Well That Ends Well*
(b) *Troilus and Cressida*
(c) *Cymbeline*
(d) *Twelfth Night*

105. Sidney's *Arcadia* is drawn by Shakespeare in
(a) *King Lear*
(b) *Macbeth*
(c) "The Winter's Tale"
(d) *The Tempest*

106. Lyly's *Endymion* is an elaborate compliment to Queen Elizabeth. Who appears in the character of
(a) Elizabeth
(b) Helen
(c) Mary
(d) Cynthia

107. Which was Marlowe's first play?
(a) *Jew of Malta*
(b) *Dr. Faustus*
(c) *Tamburlaine*
(d) *Edward II*

108. Was this the face that launched a thousand ships / And burnt the topless towers of Ilium?

Where do these lines appear?
(a) *Edward II*
(b) *Dr. Faustus*
(c) *Jew of Malta*
(d) *Tamburlaine*

109. Who is the Jew of Malta?
(a) Falstaff
(b) Antonio
(c) Shylock
(d) Barabas

110. The credit for introducing "Poulter's Measure" in English Poetry goes to

(a) Spenser
(b) Chaucer
(c) Surrey
(d) Wyatt

111. *Mirror for Magistrates* (1563) is the work of
(a) Robert Henryson
(b) David Lindsay
(c) Thomas Shadwell
(d) Thomas Sackville

112. The term "Poulter's Measure" was coined by
(a) Surrey
(b) Sidney
(c) Gascoigne
(d) Shakespeare

113. Sidney's *Arcadia* is similar to
(a) More's *Utopia*
(b) Spenser's *Epithalamion*
(c) Drayton's *Poly-Olbion*
(d) Shakespeare's *Cymbeline*

114. Which of the following works of Daniel is a romance
(a) Certaine Epistles
(b) Hymen's Triumph
(c) Delia
(d) The Complaynt of Rosamond

115. The "Marlowian Hero" is known for his hunger for
(a) Knowledge
(b) Power
(c) Gold
(d) Peace

116. Which of the following plays of Marlowe is based on a German legend?
(a) *Edward II*
(b) *The Jew of Malta*
(c) *Doctor Faustus*
(d) *Tamburlaine the Great*

117. Which of the following plays of Robert Greene is an imitation of Marlowe's *Tamburlaine*?
(a) *Frier Bacon and Frier Bungay*
(b) *Menaphon*
(c) *Alphonsus, King of Aragon*
(d) *The Triumph of Time*

118. Which of the following Theatres was pulled down and rebuilt as
(a) The Globe
(b) Blackfriars
(c) The Theatre
(d) Avon

119. In which play of Shakespeare does Hippolyta appear?
(a) *The Tempest*
(b) *A Midsummer Night's Dream*
(c) *Titus Andronicus*
(d) *Much Ado About Nothing*

120. Shakespeare's *Julius Caesar* was modelled after
(a) Thomas North's Translation of Plutarch
(b) Holinshed's Chronicles
(c) Historical Truth
(d) Boccaccio's Decameron

121. Who said that Shakespeare knew "little Latin and less Greek"?
(a) Samuel Johnson
(b) Dryden
(c) Ben Jonson
(d) Marlowe

122. Which of the following plays of Shakespeare is not a Roman play?
(a) *Julius Caesar*
(b) *Antony and Cleopatra*
(c) *Coriolanus*
(d) *Timon of Athens*

123. Which play of Shakespeare is a "Conversation play"?

(a) *Much Ado About Nothing*
(b) *Comedy of Errors*
(c) *Two Gentlemen of Verona*
(d) *Love's Labour's Lost*

124. In which play Beatrice and Benedick appear?
(a) *All's Well That Ends Well*
(b) *Twelfth Night*
(c) *Much Ado About Nothing*
(d) *Measure for Measure*

125. *An Apology for Poetry* was in response to the *School of Abuse* by
(a) Michael Drayton
(b) Thomas Norton
(c) Stephen Gosson
(d) John Lyly

126. What does Shakespeare refer to in the following lines

"This royal throne of kings, the sceptred isle

This earth of Majesty, this seat of Mars.

This other Eden, demi Paradise".

(a) France
(b) London
(c) Denmark
(d) England

127. Who coined the phrase "Marlowe's mighty line"?
(a) Samuel Jonson
(b) Ben Jonson
(c) Matthew Arnold
(d) Richard Steele

128. Mephistopheles is a character in
(a) *Dr. Faustus*
(b) *The Jew of Malta*
(c) *The Massacre of Paris*
(d) *Edward II*

129. Shakespeare's *Venus and Adonis* is based on Marlowe's
(a) *The Tragedy of Dido*
(b) *The Passionate Shepherd*
(c) *Hero and Leander*
(d) *The Massacre of Paris*

130. Who is called the Dickens of Elizabethan age?
(a) Thomas Heywood
(b) John Marston
(c) Thomas Dekker
(d) George Chapman

131. Which of the following is considered to be the best play of Thomas Heywood?
(a) *The English Traveller*
(b) *The Captives*
(c) *A Woman Killed With Kindness*
(d) *King Edward the Fourth*

132. Who is the writer of *The Shoemaker's Holiday*?
(a) Middleton
(b) Thomas Dekker
(c) Thomas Hobbes
(d) Francis Beaumont

133. Who regards Shakespeare's early comedies as "joyous, refined, romantics"?
(a) Morris
(b) Swinburne
(c) Dowden
(d) Beardsley

134. The love-affair of Silivius and Phebe takes place in the play
(a) *The Merchant of Venice*
(b) *As You Like It*
(c) *A Midsummer Night's Dream*
(d) *The Tempest*

135. Which play of Shakespeare has been regarded as

"One of Shakespeare's most assured artistic successes" by T.S. Eliot?

(a) *Coriolanus*
(b) *Hamlet*

(c) *The Tempest*
(d) *The Comedy of Errors*

136. Match the heroines and their plays
(a) Portia
(b) Viola
(c) Rosalind
(d) Miranda
1. *As You Like It*
2. *The Tempest*
3. *Twelfth Night*
4. *The Merchant of Venice*
(a) a - 4, b - 3, c - 1, d - 2
(b) a - 3, b - 4, c - 2, d - 1
(c) a - 1, b - 2, c - 3, d - 4
(d) a - 2, b - 1, c - 4, d - 3

137. In which Shakespearean play do we come across Rosencrantz and Guildenstern?
(a) *A Midsummer Night's Dream*
(b) *Hamlet*
(c) *The Tempest*
(d) *King Lear*

138. Match the Protagonists and their tragic flaws
(a) *King Lear*
(b) *Hamlet*
(c) *Othello*
(d) *Macbeth*
1. Arrogance
2. Indecision
3. Jealousy
4. Ambition
(a) a - 1, b - 2, c - 3, d - 4
(b) a - 3, b - 3, c - 4, d - 1
(c) a - 4, b - 2, c - 1, d - 4
(d) a - 2, b - 1, c - 2, d - 3

139. What is the Subtitle of *Pericles*?
(a) *Prince of Princes*
(b) *Prince of Arden*
(c) *The Great Prince*
(d) *Prince of Tyre*

140. Whom did Charles Lamb call "a prose Shakespeare"?
(a) Thomas Heywood
(b) Thomas Middleton
(c) Thomas Dekker
(d) Thomas Kyd

141. What is the first collected edition of Shakespearean plays called?
(a) *First Edition*
(b) *First Folio*
(c) *Folio One*
(d) *First Collection*

142. Match the Protagonists and their beloveds
(a) *Hamlet*
(b) *Othello*
(c) *Bassanio*
(d) *Titania*
1. Ophelia
2. Desdemona
3. Portia
4. Oberon
(a) a - 1, b - 2, c - 3, d - 4
(b) a - 4, b - 3, c - 2, d - 1
(c) a - 3, b - 1, c - 4, d - 2
(d) a - 2, b - 4, c - 1, d - 3

143. "Full Fathom five thy father lies."
Where do we find these line?
(a) *A Midsummer Night's Dream*
(b) *A Winter's Tale*
(c) *The Taming of the Shrew*
(d) *The Tempest*

144. "Ripeness is all" occurs in
(a) *Hamlet*
(b) *King Lear*
(c) *Macbeth*
(d) *Othello*

145. "Readiness is all" occurs in
(a) *Julius Caesar*
(b) *Othello*
(c) *Macbeth*
(d) *Hamlet*

146. "There is providence in the fall of a sparrow" occurs in
   (a) *A Farewell to Arms*
   (b) *War and Peace*
   (c) *King Lear*
   (d) *Hamlet*

147. "Uneasy lies the head that wears the crown" occurs in
   (a) *Edward II*
   (b) *Richard III*
   (c) *Henry IV*
   (d) *Henry V*

148. Who made the study of imagery in Shakespeare?
   (a) Caroline Spurgeon
   (b) William Empson
   (c) I.A. Richards
   (d) T.S. Eliot

149. A distinguishing feature of the Shakespearean sonnet is that it has
   (a) an octave rhyming abcd abcd.
   (b) trochaic metre.
   (c) a variable number of lines.
   (d) a couplet at the end.

150. "But the Lear of Shakespeare cannot be acted." Who said it?
   (a) Lamb
   (b) Coleridge
   (c) Hazlitt
   (d) Dr. Johnson

151. *Hamlet* is a
   (a) Historical play
   (b) Romance
   (c) Revenge tragedy
   (d) Comedy of humours

152. Shakespeare's *Cymbeline* draws on
   (a) Plutarch's Lives
   (b) Boccaccio's Decameron
   (c) Historical truth
   (d) Holinshed's Chronicles

153. Which Shakespearean character asks to be remembered as one who "loved not wisely but too wise"?
   (a) Macbeth
   (b) Hamlet
   (c) King Lear
   (d) Othello

154. The subtitle of Shakespeare's *Othello* is
   (a) *The Prince of Denmark*
   (b) *The Mad Man*
   (c) *The Moor of Venice*
   (d) *Jealousy Incarnate*

155. In which of the following plays of Shakespeare appears an "Indian boy"?
   (a) *A Midsummer Night's Dream*
   (b) *As You Like It*
   (c) *Merry Wives of Windsor*
   (d) *Love's Labour's Lost*

156. Who among the following said that in Shakespeare's great tragedies "Character is destiny"?
   (a) S.T. Coleridge
   (b) Samuel Johnson
   (c) T.S. Eliot
   (d) A.C. Bradley

157. Who has made a Freudian interpretation of *Hamlet*?
   (a) Iris Murdoch
   (b) G. Wilson Knight
   (c) Ernest Jones
   (d) C.S. Lewis

158. Richard Hooker is the author of which of the following works?
   (a) *Of Love and Marriage*
   (b) *Of Books*
   (c) *Of Truth*
   (d) *Of the Laws of Ecclesiastical Polity*

159. The subtitle of the *White Devil* is
   (a) *The Duchess of Florence*
   (b) *A Classic Tragedy*

(c) *Death of a Pure Soul*
(d) *Vittoria Corombona*

160. "My soul, like to a ship in a black storm, Is driven, I know not whither."

These words are said by
(a) *The Duchess of Malfi*
(b) *Vittoria Corombona*
(c) *Helen of Troy*
(d) *Dr. Faustus*

161. John Webster wrote two clever comedies Westward HO, Northward HO in collaboration with
(a) Beaumont and Fletcher
(b) Ben Jonson
(c) Thomas Dekker
(d) Thomas Middleton

162. The Plot of which of the following tragedies is derived from William Painter's "Palace of Pleasure"?
(a) *The Duchess of Malfi*
(b) *The Spanish Tragedy*
(c) *The White Devil*
(d) *The Changeling*

163. Which of the following is a dark comedy?
(a) *The Taming of the Shrew*
(b) *All's Well That Ends Well*
(c) *The Merry Wives of Windsor*
(d) *Measure for Measure*

164. Where do we find the clown Feste?
(a) *Two Gentlemen of Verona*
(b) *Twelfth Night*
(c) *A Winter's Tale*
(d) *The Taming of the Shrew*

165. Match the following
A. *Antony and Cleopatra*
B. *As You Like It*
C. *Othello*
D. *Measure for Measure*
1. Promos and Cassandra
2. Plutarch's Lives
3. Rosalind
4. Hecatommithi

| **Codes:** | A | B | C | D |
|---|---|---|---|---|
| (a) | 2 | 3 | 4 | 1 |
| (b) | 1 | 2 | 3 | 4 |
| (c) | 4 | 3 | 2 | 1 |
| (d) | 3 | 4 | 1 | 2 |

166. Who asserted, "Unmarried men are best friends, best masters, best servants"?
(a) Pope
(b) Bacon
(c) Blake
(d) Shakespeare

167. Who died of cold?
(a) Plato
(b) Shakespeare
(c) Dryden
(d) Bacon

168. Who said, "A friend is another himself"?
(a) Lamb
(b) Bacon
(c) Pope
(d) Addison

169. Who said, "We are the fortunes of the human race"?
(a) Addison
(b) Pope
(c) Bacon
(d) Dryden

170. Who is known as the father of inductive philosophy?
(a) Aristotle
(b) Plato
(c) Bacon
(d) Homer

171. Which of the following books of Bacon is incomplete?
(a) *The Advancement of Learning* (1605)
(b) *The History of Henry VII* (1622)
(c) *Apophthegms* (1625)
(d) *The New Atlantis* (1627)

172. Which of the following Latin books of Bacon is on "the new logic or inductive method of reasoning"?
   (a) *De Augmentis Scientiarum* (1623)
   (b) *Novum Organum* (1620)
   (c) *Instauratio* (1623)
   (d) *Sylva Sylvarum* (1627)

173. The third and the final edition of Bacon's Essays came out in
   (a) 1597
   (b) 1612
   (c) 1625
   (d) 1631

174. Who wrote the following: "Crafty men condemn studies, simple men admire them, and wise men use them ________"?
   (a) Shakespeare
   (b) George Chapman
   (c) Robert Burton
   (d) Francis Bacon

175. The inhabitants of New Atlantis owe their happiness to
   (a) operation of reason.
   (b) equality for all.
   (c) study and research.
   (d) None of the above.

176. Solomon's House in *The New Atlantis* is the name of
   (a) A learned academy.
   (b) Parliament house.
   (c) Where money is stored.
   (d) None of the above.

**ANSWERS**

| | | | | | |
|---|---|---|---|---|---|
| 1. (c) | 2. (b) | 3. (d) | 4. (b) | 5. (a) | 6. (c) |
| 7. (c) | 8. (d) | 9. (a) | 10. (c) | 11. (d) | 12. (c) |
| 13. (c) | 14. (b) | 15. (d) | 16. (a) | 17. (c) | 18. (a) |
| 19. (c) | 20. (c) | 21. (a) | 22. (b) | 23. (b) | 24. (d) |
| 25. (c) | 26. (d) | 27. (b) | 28. (d) | 29. (d) | 30. (d) |
| 31. (b) | 32. (b) | 33. (c) | 34. (b) | 35. (a) | 36. (c) |
| 37. (c) | 38. (a) | 39. (d) | 40. (b) | 41. (a) | 42. (a) |
| 43. (b) | 44. (c) | 45. (a) | 46. (b) | 47. (d) | 48. (c) |
| 49. (a) | 50. (c) | 51. (d) | 52. (c) | 53. (b) | 54. (b) |
| 55. (a) | 56. (c) | 57. (a) | 58. (d) | 59. (c) | 60. (b) |
| 61. (a) | 62. (c) | 63. (c) | 64. (d) | 65. (d) | 66. (d) |
| 67. (c) | 68. (b) | 69. (c) | 70. (a) | 71. (d) | 72. (c) |
| 73. (b) | 74. (b) | 75. (b) | 76. (d) | 77. (b) | 78. (d) |
| 79. (b) | 80. (a) | 81. (d) | 82. (d) | 83. (c) | 84. (c) |
| 85. (c) | 86. (d) | 87. (c) | 88. (a) | 89. (d) | 90. (b) |
| 91. (c) | 92. (b) | 93. (c) | 94. (a) | 95. (a) | 96. (c) |
| 97. (b) | 98. (a) | 99. (d) | 100. (b) | 101. (a) | 102. (c) |
| 103. (a) | 104. (a) | 105. (a) | 106. (d) | 107. (c) | 108. (b) |

| | | | | | |
|---|---|---|---|---|---|
| 109. (d) | 110. (c) | 111. (d) | 112. (c) | 113. (a) | 114. (d) |
| 115. (b) | 116. (c) | 117. (c) | 118. (a) | 119. (b) | 120. (a) |
| 121. (c) | 122. (d) | 123. (d) | 124. (c) | 125. (c) | 126. (d) |
| 127. (b) | 128. (a) | 129. (c) | 130. (c) | 131. (d) | 132. (b) |
| 133. (c) | 134. (b) | 135. (a) | 136. (a) | 137. (b) | 138. (a) |
| 139. (d) | 140. (a) | 141. (b) | 142. (a) | 143. (d) | 144. (b) |
| 145. (d) | 146. (d) | 147. (c) | 148. (a) | 149. (d) | 150. (a) |
| 151. (c) | 152. (d) | 153. (d) | 154. (c) | 155. (a) | 156. (d) |
| 157. (c) | 158. (d) | 159. (d) | 160. (b) | 161. (c) | 162. (a) |
| 163. (c) & (d) | 164. (b) | 165. (a) | 166. (b) | 167. (d) | 168. (b) |
| 169. (c) | 170. (c) | 171. (d) | 172. (b) | 173. (c) | 174. (d) |
| 175. (c) | 176. (a) | | | | |

# 2

# Jacobean to Restoration Period

1. Who said "England emerged as a noble and puissant nation, arousing herself like a strong man after sleep"?
   (a) Shakespeare
   (b) Milton
   (c) Arnold
   (d) Dryden
2. The seventeenth century 'Political Arithmetic' is today known as—
   (a) Algebra
   (b) Statistics
   (c) Statics
   (d) Trigonometry
3. Who ruled England during the Jacobean Age?
   (a) James I
   (b) James II
   (c) Charles I
   (d) Queen Elizabeth
4. Who wrote the lyric "Drink to me only with thine eyes"?
   (a) William Shakespeare
   (b) Andrew Marvell
   (c) Ben Jonson
   (d) Beaumont and Fletcher
5. Which one is a famous tragedy written by Jonson?
   (a) *Sejanus*
   (b) *The Silent Woman*
   (c) *Catiline*
   (d) Both (a) and (c)
6. Whom did Ben Jonson attack in *The Poetaster?*
   (a) Thomas Middleton
   (b) Thomas Heywood
   (c) Thomas Dekker
   (d) John Donne
7. Shakespeare acted in which of the following plays of Ben Jonson?
   (a) *Every Man Out of His Humour*
   (b) *The Poetaster*
   (c) *Every Man in His Humour*
   (d) *Cynthia's Revels*
8. Who among the following is called the father of classical comedy in England?
   (a) Webster
   (b) John Lyly
   (c) Ben Jonson
   (d) William Shakespeare
9. *The Alchemist* (1610) is a play by
   (a) Ben Jonson
   (b) Shelley
   (c) H.G. Wells
   (d) Ariosto
10. The subtitle of Jonson's *Volpone* (1605) is
    (a) *The Vulture*
    (b) *The Fox*

(c) *The Crow*
(d) *The Tiger*

11. *The Silent Woman* is the subtitle of which of the following plays of Ben Jonson?
(a) *The Mosque of Beauty*
(b) *The Staple of News*
(c) *The Devil is an Ass*
(d) *Epicone*

12. Jonson's *Timber or Discoveries* (1640) is a
(a) Collection of notes and reflections
(b) Comic play
(c) Philosophic treatise
(d) Tragic Drama

13. Who said that "the moving of laughter" was not essential to comedy whereas "equity, truth, perspicuity, and candour" were?
(a) John Dryden
(b) Samuel Jonson
(c) Ben Jonson
(d) Alexander Pope

14. To which kind of comedy do we best associate Ben Jonson?
(a) Comedy of manners
(b) Comedy of humours
(c) Satire
(d) Dramatic monologue

15. What special human trait is hit upon by Ben Jonson in the Alchemist?
(a) Greed
(b) Gullibility
(c) Garrulity
(d) Grumbling

16. Corvino is a character in the play
(a) *The Alchemist*
(b) *Bartholomew Fair*
(c) *Volpone*
(d) *Sejanus*

17. Jonson wrote a volume of short reflections upon life and art. What is its title?
(a) *Timber*
(b) *Reflections*
(c) *Musings*
(d) *Temperament*

18. Who invented "antimasque"?
(a) Thomas Middleton
(b) Ben Jonson
(c) John Webster
(d) John Milton

19. Identify the play which contains this song: "Queen and huntress, chaste and fair"?
(a) *Every Man in His Humour*
(b) *Volpone*
(c) *Cynthia's Revels*
(d) *The Silent Woman*

20. Who was the lord of the "tavern-wits"?
(a) Shakespeare
(b) John Lyly
(c) Ben Jonson
(d) Dryden

21. Who among the following wrote the following as his objective? "I'll strip the ragged follies of time naked, as at their birth and with a whip of steel, print wounding lashes in their iron ribs."
(a) John Donne
(b) John Milton
(c) John Dryden
(d) Ben Jonson

22. Whom does Ben Jonson ridicule in his play *The Poetaster*?
(a) The poets who posed to be critics
(b) The inferior poets of his day
(c) The poets who tried to write plays also
(d) The playwrights who wrote humour comedies after his style

23. "It is he who in his own time and ever afterwards provided a typical antithesis to Shakespeare."

Identify the writer for whom this statement has been made?

(a) Christopher Marlowe
(b) Ben Jonson
(c) Philip Sidney
(d) George Chapman

24. Jonson's drama which is an unfinished pastoral drama is
(a) *The Sad Shepherd*
(b) *A Tale of a Tub*
(c) *The Staple of News*
(d) *The New Inn*

25. A play jointly written by Jonson, Marston, and Chapman is
(a) *Eastward Hoe*
(b) *The Silent Woman*
(c) *Volpone*
(d) *The Poetaster*

26. Comparison of a pair of lovers to a pair of compass is an example of
(a) Neo-classical simile
(b) Romantic irony
(c) Metaphysical conceit
(d) Petrarchan conceit

27. "For God's sake hold your tongue and let me love" appears in a poem by
(a) Lord Byron
(b) Robert Browning
(c) John Donne
(d) John Keats

28. Who among the following practised "Baroque Style"?
(a) Chaucer
(b) Donne
(c) Dryden
(d) Coleridge

29. "Songs and Sonnets" (1633) by Donne came out
(a) When Donne was Dying
(b) In Donne's Youth
(c) In Donne's Old age
(d) Posthumously

30. "One short sleep past, We wake eternally,

And death shall be no more, Death thou shalt die."

Whose poem are we talking about?
(a) Andrew Marvell
(b) Henry Vaughan
(c) John Donne
(d) Richard Crashaw

31. Which was the famous prose work written by Donne?
(a) Devotions
(b) Musings
(c) Sermons
(d) Reflections

32. "No man is an island.... Therefore send not to know/For whom the bell tolls. It tolls for thee."

Where do we find these famous lines?
(a) Donne's *Devotions*
(b) Butler's *Hudibras*
(c) Milton's *Paradise Lost*
(d) Dryden's *Religio Laici*

33. "She is all states, and all princes, Nothing else is!"

Which Donne poem is this?
(a) "Sweetest Love I Do Not Go"
(b) "The Sun Rising"
(c) "Twickenham Garden"
(d) "The Good Morrow"

34. Which famous poet managed to preach his last sermon dressed in his shroud?
(a) Chaucer
(b) Milton
(c) Donne
(d) Wordsworth

35. Who said that Donne "affects the metaphysics" in his love poems?

(a) Dr. Samuel Johnson
(b) John Dryden
(c) Ben Jonson
(d) T.S. Eliot

36. With Donne, it may be said Caroline Poetry
(a) Flourishes
(b) Declines
(c) Begins
(d) Closes

37. Donne's "The Progress of the Soul" is an illustration of his
(a) amorous poems
(b) metaphysical poems
(c) satirical poems
(d) religious poems

38. Which work of John Donne was highly approved by James I as a contribution to anti-Catholic controversy?
(a) *The Progress of the Soul*
(b) *Epithalamium*
(c) *An Anatomy of the World*
(d) *Pseudo Martyr*

39. John Donne was imprisoned for his
(a) clandestine marriage
(b) financial corruption
(c) obscene writing
(d) rebellious writing

40. In which poem Donne compares Mrs. Herbert's wrinkles to love's graves?
(a) "Twickenham Garden"
(b) "The Anniversary"
(c) "Autumnal"
(d) "Valediction"

41. Which one is not a work by Donne?
(a) *Divine Poems*
(b) *Holy Sonnets*
(c) *Songs and Sonnets*
(d) *Dramatic Poems*

42. The name of Aesop is connected with
(a) Supernatural Stories
(b) Fables
(c) Ballads
(d) Satire

43. Herbert's collection of religious poems "The Temple", "Sacred Poems" and "Private Ejaculations" was published in
(a) 1620
(b) 1630
(c) 1633
(d) 1635

44. Who is known as the saint of the Metaphysical poets?
(a) Donne
(b) Herbert
(c) Vaughan
(d) Cowley

45. Who was the only puritan among the Metaphysical poets?
(a) Vaughan
(b) Donne
(c) Marvell
(d) Cowley

46. Who observes, "Intensity is the keynote of Donne's career"?
(a) Eliot
(b) Dowden
(c) Fausset
(d) Grierson

47. *Silex Scintillans* is a collection of poems by
(a) Vaughan
(b) Donne
(c) Tennyson
(d) Browning

48. Silex Scintillans was written in ________ parts.
(a) 21
(b) 3
(c) 2
(d) 5

49. "Pilgrimage" is a poem from the collection
    (a) *Step to the Temple*
    (b) *The Temple*
    (c) *Poems*
    (d) *Silex*
50. Abraham Cowley's *The Davideis* is an epic on
    (a) King Hart
    (b) James I
    (c) King David
    (d) James II
51. The biographies of Donne, Hooker and Herbert were written by
    (a) Dryden
    (b) Cowley
    (c) Izaac Walton
    (d) None of the above
52. The first periodical Gazette first appeared in the city
    (a) Venice
    (b) London
    (c) New York
    (d) None of the above
53. The origin of the Comedy of Manners is in
    (a) Italy
    (b) France
    (c) Rome
    (d) Greece
54. Who has been regarded as the monarch of wit?
    (a) Johnson
    (b) Pope
    (c) Donne
    (d) Addison
55. Which one of the following is not a metaphysical characteristic?
    (a) Wit
    (b) Striking opening of the poem
    (c) Optimism
    (d) Far-fetched metaphors
56. Metaphysical School of Poetry was against
    (a) Satirical poetry
    (b) Religious poetry
    (c) Emotional poetry
    (d) Lyrical poetry
57. "Sweetest Love I Do Not Go" is a famous poem by
    (a) Larkin
    (b) Browning
    (c) Donne
    (d) Shakespeare
58. The Mistress is a poem written by
    (a) Marvell
    (b) Lovelace
    (c) Carew
    (d) Cowley
59. "To His Coy Mistress" is cavalier poem by
    (a) Marvell
    (b) Lovelace
    (c) Carew
    (d) Herrick
60. The legend of "King Arthur and His Knights of the Round Table" was first of all recounted in English in
    (a) Layaman's Brut
    (b) Tennyson's Idylls of the Kings
    (c) Macaulay's History of England
    (d) Lyly's Eupheus
61. *The Davideis* (1956) and *Pindarique Odes* were written by
    (a) Donne
    (b) Cowley
    (c) Lovelace
    (d) Herrick
62. Who called Donne and his followers "The Metaphysical Poets"?

(a) John Milton
(b) John Dryden
(c) Ben Jonson
(d) Dr. Samuel Johnson

63. "But at my back I always hear/ Time's winged chariot hurrying near".

Which poem boasts of these immortal lines?

(a) *Sweetest Love I Do Not Go*
(b) *The Cannonization*
(c) *Twickenham Garden*
(d) *To His Coy Mistress*

64. Who is the writer of *The Temple* (1633)?

(a) George Herbert
(b) Henry Vaughan
(c) Andrew Marvell
(d) Robert Herrik

65. Who wrote about Donne—

"Here lies a king,/ That ruled as he thought fit,/ The Universal monarchy of Wit".

(a) Henry Crashaw
(b) Andrew Marvell
(c) Thomas Carew
(d) George Herbert

66. The Subtitle given to *The Temple* was

(a) *Sacred Poems and Private Ejaculations*
(b) *Poems by a Holy Spirit*
(c) *Thoughts of a Private Poet*
(d) *Sacred Poems with Other Delights of the Muses.*

67. What is the title of Crashaw's English religious poems?

(a) "Steps to the Temple"
(b) "Carmen Deo Nostro"
(c) "Delights of the Muses"
(d) "Epigrammatum Sacrorum Liber"

68. Giles Fletcher and Phinease Fletcher were from the school of—

(a) Jonson
(b) Donne
(c) Spenser
(d) None of the above

69. Christ's Victory was written by

(a) Phineas Fletcher
(b) Giles Fletcher
(c) Thomas Browne
(d) John Milton

70. Match the following works and their poets

A. The Purple Island
B. Britannia's Pastorals
C. Mistress of Phil'arete
D. Coelum Britannicum

1. William Browne
2. Phineas Fletcher
3. George Wither
4. Thomas Carew

| **Codes:** | A | B | C | D |
|---|---|---|---|---|
| (a) | 1 | 2 | 3 | 4 |
| (b) | 2 | 1 | 4 | 3 |
| (c) | 3 | 4 | 1 | 2 |
| (d) | 2 | 1 | 3 | 4 |

71. "Assert Eternal Providence

And Justify the ways of God to men." Where do we find there lines?

(a) "Paradise Lost"
(b) "Paradise Regained"
(c) "Lycidas"
(d) "Samson Agonistes"

72. "Paradise Lost" (1667) is written in

(a) iambic pentameter
(b) heroic couplets
(c) blank verse
(d) terza rima

73. Who wrote *Life of Milton*?
 (a) David Masson
 (b) James Boswell
 (c) Matthew Arnold
 (d) Izaak Walton

74. Milton's *Epitaphium Damonis* written in Latin was in memory of
 (a) Henry Lawes
 (b) Edward King
 (c) Charles Diodati
 (d) None of the above

75. Who contended that in *Paradise Lost* Milton "was of the Devil's party without knowing it"?
 (a) Addison
 (b) Keats
 (c) Marvell
 (d) Blake

76. Who has been charged with being the corruptor of our language?
 (a) Chaucer
 (b) Pope
 (c) Eliot
 (d) Milton

77. Who called Milton "The mighty mouthed inventer of harmonies"?
 (a) Dr. Johnson
 (b) T.S. Eliot
 (c) Alfred Tennyson
 (d) Matthew Arnold

78. Match the following

| | |
|---|---|
| (a) *Areopagitica* | 1. 1633 |
| (b) *Lycidas* | 2. 1644 |
| (c) *Comus* | 3. 1637 |
| (d) *L' Allegro* | 4. 1634 |

 (a) a - 2, b - 3, c - 4, 2 - 1
 (b) a - 4, b - 1, c - 2, d - 2
 (c) a - 1, b - 2, c - 4, d - 3
 (d) a - 1, b - 4, c - 3, d - 2

79. "When I consider how my light is spent" appears in
 (a) Milton
 (b) Wordsworth
 (c) Donne
 (d) Browning

80. *Paradise Lost* began in 1658, and issued in 1667, had how many books?
 (a) 14
 (b) 12
 (c) 18
 (d) 10

81. In *Paradise Lost* who advises Adam against thirst for knowledge and 'scientific' truth?
 (a) God
 (b) Satan
 (c) Raphael
 (d) Michael

82. The "Infernal Debate" in *Paradise Lost* takes place in
 (a) Book I
 (b) Book II
 (c) Book IX
 (d) Book III

83. *Samson Agonistes* (1671) by Milton is a
 (a) Masque
 (b) Elegy
 (c) Comedy
 (d) Tragedy

84. "A mind not to be changed by place or time/The mind in its own place and in itself/Can make a Heaven of Hell, a Hell of Heaven."

 Who said these lines in Milton's *Paradise Lost*?
 (a) Satan
 (b) Adam
 (c) God
 (d) Eve

85. "Just are the ways of God,/And Justifiable to man/Unless there be who think not God at all."

Which work of Milton contains the above lines?

(a) *Comus*
(b) *Samson Agonistes*
(c) *Ode on Christ's Nativity*
(d) *Lycidas*

86. Milton was nick-named as 'The Lady of Christ's' because:

(a) he was shy like a dame
(b) he was extremely modest and polite
(c) he was most fashionably dressed
(d) he had an exceedingly fair complexion

87. Compared to *Paradise Lost*, *Paradise Regained* is less significant and more

(a) Liberal
(b) Puritan
(c) Religious
(d) Secular

88. How many books are there in Paradise Regained?

(a) Twelve
(b) Four
(c) Eight
(d) Ten

89. In which work of Milton does the following line appear?

"That with no middle flight intends to soar."

(a) *L'Allegro*
(b) *II Penseroso*
(c) *Paradise Lost*
(d) *Lycidas*

90. What is the meaning of L' Allegro?

(a) A melancholy man
(b) A happy man
(c) A man pining for love
(d) A God fearing man

91. "To scorn delights and live laborious days." This line is from Milton's *Lycidas* who is the poet referring to

(a) His friend Edward King on whose death this elegy is written
(b) To himself
(c) To his patron, Cromwell
(d) To the King of England

92. The main plank of *Aeropagitica's* argument was for the freedom of

(a) Movement
(b) Worship
(c) Press
(d) Forming a political party

93. Milton's 'Comus' is a/an

(a) Elegy
(b) Masque
(c) Ballad
(d) Epic

94. *The Bill of Rights* was passed in the year

(a) 1776
(b) 1676
(c) 1689
(d) 1705

95. Theatres were closed in England in the year

(a) 1616
(b) 1623
(c) 1642
(d) 1649

96. Which is not a heroic play by Nicholas Rowe?

(a) *Tamerlane* (1701)
(b) *The Fair Penitent* (1703)
(c) *Jane Shore* (1714)
(d) *Thystes* (1681)

97. Which is not a heroic play by Nathaniel Lee?

(a) *Sophonisba* (1676)
(b) *The Rival Queens* (1677)

(c) *Nero* (1674)
(d) *Mithridates* (1673)

98. The name of Aesop is connected with
(a) Fables
(b) Supernatural Stories
(c) Ballads
(d) Satire

99. *Incognito* (1692) is a brief novel by
(a) Sarah Fielding
(b) Lawrence
(c) Congreve
(d) Barclay

100. Which is not a play by Mrs. Centlivre (1680-1722)?
(a) *The Busie Body*
(b) *A Bold Stroke for a Wife*
(c) *The Gamester*
(d) *False Delicacy*

101. The first periodical—a manuscript newspaper—that figured in Europe (Venice) was—
(a) *Times Supplement*
(b) *Gazette*
(c) *The Rambler*
(d) *Paston Letters*

102. John Evelyn (1620-1706) and Samuel Pepys (1633-1703) are known as
(a) Dramatists
(b) Poets
(c) Story-tellers
(d) Diarists

103. How many scholars were appointed for preparing the Authorised version of The Bible (1611)?
(a) 40
(b) 47
(c) 32
(d) 41

104. Essay concerning *Human Understanding* (1690) was written by
(a) Jeremy Collier
(b) John Locke
(c) Butler
(d) Dryden

105. Butler's *Hudibras* is an attack on
(a) Female Sex
(b) Puritanism
(c) Aristocracy
(d) Male dominated society

106. Which one of the following is not a play by Thomas Otway (1651-1685)?
(a) *The Orphan*
(b) *Don Carlos*
(c) *Tyrannic Love*
(d) *Venice Preserved*

107. Royal society of London was founded in the year
(a) 1642
(b) 1658
(c) 1660
(d) 1678

108. *Love's Last Shift* and *Provoked Husband* are two plays by
(a) Colley Cibber
(b) Dryden
(c) Steele
(d) Sheridan

109. Which one of the following is not written by Thomas Browne?
(a) *Vulgar Errors*
(b) *Urn Burial*
(c) *Grace Abounding*
(d) *Anatomy of Melancholy*

110. "Anatomy of Melancholy" was written by
(a) Browne
(b) Burton
(c) Gray
(d) Robert Blair

111. Butler's Hudibras has been modelled on
  (a) *Euphues*
  (b) *Brut*
  (c) *Don Quixote*
  (d) *Pilgrim's Progress*

112. 'Mother' was written by
  (a) Plutarch
  (b) Bondello
  (c) Wilson Knight
  (d) Maxim Gorky

113. Who is the author of *The Mother*?
  (a) Pearl S. Buck
  (b) De Quincey
  (c) R.L. Stevenson
  (d) Swift

114. *Charles II* was written by
  (a) Halifax
  (b) Flecknoe
  (c) Richard Head
  (d) Goldsmith

115. The character sequence the *Microcosmography* (1628) was written by
  (a) Butler
  (b) Dryden
  (c) John Earle
  (d) None of the above

116. *The English Rogue* was written by
  (a) Richard Head
  (b) Halifax
  (c) Both (a) and (b)
  (d) None of the above

117. Which one of the following is not a play by Wycherley?
  (a) *Love in a Wood* (1671)
  (b) *The Country Wife* (1675)
  (c) *The Plain Dealer* (1677)
  (d) *The Man of Mode* (1676)

118. *The Man of Mode* is a play by
  (a) Congreve
  (b) Wycherley
  (c) Etherege
  (d) Jonson

119. Which one of the following is not a comedy by Etherege?
  (a) *Old Bachelor* (1693)
  (b) *The Double Dealer* (1693)
  (c) *The Plain Dealer* (1677)
  (d) *Love for Love* (1695)

120. Which poet expressed surprise at his having loved one woman for 'three whole days together'?
  (a) Lovelace
  (b) Suckling
  (c) Donne
  (d) Carew

121. The Authorised version of the *Bible* came out in
  (a) 1629
  (b) 1539
  (c) 1611
  (d) 1616

122. "*Why so Pale and Wan, Fond Lover*" is a Cavalier poem by
  (a) Waller
  (b) Suckling
  (c) Herrick
  (d) Lovelace

123. The Cavalier Poets were steeped into
  (a) gaiety and triviality
  (b) preaching
  (c) dignified morality
  (d) religious ceremonies

124. Massinger and Ford wrote _______ plays
  (a) morality
  (b) licentious
  (c) mystery
  (d) revenge

125. The result of Edmund Burke's *Reflection on the French Revolution* was
   (a) French Victory
   (b) Puritan dominance
   (c) War with France
   (d) Spiritual death of the English

126. Who among the following poets is/are the Cavalier poet(s)?
   (a) Carew
   (b) Lovelace
   (c) Suckling
   (d) All of the above

127. Sir John Suckling is famous for his short lyrics which are composed in
   (a) Heroic Couplet
   (b) Spenserian Stanza
   (c) Petrarchan Style
   (d) Anti-Petrarchan Style

128. The most popular Cavalier lyricist was
   (a) Anglicans
   (b) Lovelace
   (c) Independents
   (d) Herrick

129. "Stone Walls do not a prison make, Nor Iron bars a cage."

   Who wrote the above lines?
   (a) George Herbert
   (b) Richard Lovelace
   (c) Thomas Carew
   (d) John Heywood

130. Robert Herrick authored which of the following?
   (a) *Hesperides*
   (b) *Lucasta*
   (c) *Song and Sonnets*
   (d) *Pindareque Odes*

131. Which of the following is a revenge tragedy by Middleton
   (a) *The Changeling*
   (b) *The Roaring Girl*
   (c) *A Trick to Catch the Old One*
   (d) None of the above

132. *If You Know Not Me, You Know Nobody* (1605-06) a history play by Thomas Heywood deals with life of
   (a) James I
   (b) Henry IV
   (c) Elizabeth I
   (d) Henry VI

133. Charles Lamb called Heywood a prose Shakespeare for his
   (a) *The Captives*
   (b) *The Fair Maid of the West*
   (c) *A Woman Killed With Kindness*
   (d) *If You Know Not Me*

134. Sir Fapling Flutter is the subtitle of the play
   (a) *Comical Revenge*
   (b) *The Man of Mode*
   (c) *She Would If She Could*
   (d) *The Plain Dealer*

135. Marston, Jonson and Chapman joined hands to write
   (a) *All Fools*
   (b) *Eastward Ho*
   (c) *The Malcontent*
   (d) *Volpone*

136. Which is not a play by John Vanbrugh (1664-1726)?
   (a) *The Way of the World* (1700)
   (b) *The Relapse* (1696)
   (c) *The Provoked Wife* (1697)
   (d) *Confederacy* (1705)

137. Manly is a character in the play
   (a) *The Critic*
   (b) *The Plain Dealer*
   (c) *The Alchemist*
   (d) *School for Scandal*

138. The biographies of Donne, Hooker and Herbert were written by
   (a) Dryden
   (b) Cowley
   (c) Izaak Walton
   (d) None of the above

139. Match the following

| | | | |
|---|---|---|---|
| A Dryden | | 1. *Love's Labour* | |
| B Newton | | 2. *All for Love* | |
| C Congreve | | 3. *Love for Love* | |
| D John Ford | | 4. *Principia* | |

| **Codes:** | **A** | **B** | **C** | **D** |
|---|---|---|---|---|
| (a) | 1 | 2 | 3 | 4 |
| (b) | 2 | 4 | 3 | 1 |
| (c) | 4 | 3 | 2 | 1 |
| (d) | 3 | 2 | 1 | 4 |

140. Match the following

| | |
|---|---|
| A John Tillotson | 1. *Advice to a Daughter* |
| B Nathaniel Lee | 2. *Sermons* |
| C Sir William Temple | 3. *Nero* |
| D Lord Halifax | 4. *Memoirs* |

| **Codes:** | **A** | **B** | **C** | **D** |
|---|---|---|---|---|
| (a) | 2 | 3 | 4 | 1 |
| (b) | 3 | 4 | 2 | 1 |
| (c) | 4 | 2 | 3 | 1 |
| (d) | 1 | 2 | 3 | 4 |

141. Who prefixed verses to Ben Jonson's *Volpone* (1607) in honour of his dear friend The Author?
   (a) Francis Beaumont
   (b) Giles Fletcher
   (c) Shakespeare
   (d) John Ford

142. The collaboration of Beaumont and Fletcher lasted for
   (a) Five years
   (b) Six years
   (c) Seven years
   (d) Eight years

143. Which of the following plays of Beaumont was not written by him under collaboration with Fletcher?
   (a) *The Knight of the Burning Pestle*
   (b) *The Maid's Tragedy*
   (c) *Philaster*
   (d) *A King and No King*

144. *The Wild-Goose Chase* was written by
   (a) John Fletcher
   (b) Philip Massinger
   (c) Beaumont and Fletcher
   (d) John Ford

145. Thomas Dekker attacked which literary personality in his play 'Satiromastix'?
   (a) John Ford
   (b) Ben Jonson
   (c) Francis Beaumont
   (d) John Fletcher

146. *A Short View of the Immorality and Profaneness of the English Stage* published in 1698 is written by
   (a) William Congreve
   (b) John Dryden
   (c) Jeremy Collier
   (d) William Wycherley

147. Whose contemporaries called his plays "Manly"?
   (a) George Elherege
   (b) Thomas Shadwell
   (c) George Farquhar
   (d) William Wycherley

148. *The Provoked Wife* (1697) is a comedy by
   (a) William Congreve
   (b) Thomas Shadwell
   (c) Sir John Vanbrugh
   (d) John Crowne

149. *Grace Abounding* (1666) is a kind of religious autobiography of

(a) Lord Halifax
(b) Samuel Butler
(c) John Bunyan
(d) John Tillotson

150. Flamino, is a character in
(a) Cyril Tourneur's *The Atheist Tragedy*
(b) John Webster's *The White Devil*
(c) John Milton's *Comus*
(d) None of the above

151. Luke Frugal is a famous character in
(a) John Ford's *Perkin Warbeck*
(b) Philip Massinger's *The City Madam*
(c) Philip Massinger's *The Duke of Milan*
(d) John Ford's *The Broken Heart*

152. Name the first daily newspaper that began in 1702
(a) *The Examiner*
(b) *The Jockey's Intelligencer*
(c) *The Daily Courant*
(d) *The Chronicle*

153. Which of the following books is written in the form of a dialogue between Piscator (fisherman) and Venator (hunter)?
(a) Izaak Walton's *The Complete Angler*
(b) Thomas Fuller's *Worthies of England*
(c) John Selden's *Table Talk*
(d) Clarendon's *History of Rebellion*

154. 'Holy and Profane State' is one of the greatest works of character-sketch. Who wrote it?
(a) John Earl
(b) Robert Burton
(c) Thomas Overbury
(d) Thomas Fuller

155. How many characters does George Herbert's *The Country Parson* deal within its thirty-seven essays?
(a) Three
(b) One
(c) Fifteen
(d) Thirty seven

156. Who is the Squire of Sir Hudibras in *Hudibras?*
(a) Ralpho
(b) Don Quixote
(c) Ronaldo
(d) Sancho Panza

157. Which one of the following is written by John Heywood?
(a) *Love's Sacrifice*
(b) *The Silent Woman*
(c) *A Priest to the Temple*
(d) *The Four P's*

158. *The Four P's* is a/an
(a) Dialogue
(b) Romance
(c) Elegy
(d) Satire

159. The three characters out of four, in the *Four P's* are a Pedlar, a Pardoner, an Apothecary. Who is the fourth one?
(a) A Priest
(b) A Palmer
(c) A Parson
(d) A Philosopher

160. Name the writer of "Tis a Pity She's a Whore"
(a) John Heywood
(b) Philip Massinger
(c) John Ford
(d) John Herbert

161. Which movement is considered as the second and greater Renaissance?
(a) Aesthetic Movement
(b) Puritan Movement
(c) Oxford Movement
(d) Romantic Movement

162. What became popular in the beginning of the 17th century?

(a) Pepy's Diary
(b) Dryden's Drama
(c) Shakespeare's Sonnets
(d) Milton's Sonnets

163. Who among the following belongs to the "Correct School" of poetry?
(a) Donne
(b) Milton
(c) Cowley
(d) Dryden

164. About whom did Dr. Johnson say that he did to English literature what Augustus did to Rome, which he "found of brick and left of marble"?
(a) Dryden
(b) Pope
(c) Shakespeare
(d) Milton

165. In which of the following poems of Dryden is there a reference to the great fire of London?
(a) "Absalom and Achitophel"
(b) "The Medal"
(c) "Annus Mirabilis"
(d) "Mac Flecknoe"

166. In his *The Medal* Dryden Satirised—
(a) Monmouth
(b) Shadwell
(c) Shaftesbury
(d) Grand Jury

167. *The Medal of Jon Bayes* is a reply to *The Medal*. Who wrote it?
(a) Shadwell
(b) Monmouth
(c) Butler
(d) Pope

168. Dryden attacked Shadwell in his
(a) *Absalom and Achitophel*
(b) *The Medal*
(c) *Mac Flecknoe*
(d) None of the above

169. Dryden makes a comparison between Shakespeare and Ben Jonson in—
(a) The Essay of Dramatic Poetry
(b) The Medal
(c) Preface to the Fables
(d) The Hind and the Panther

170. In *Absalom and Achitophel*, Dryden directed the satire on
(a) Monmouth
(b) Shadwell
(c) Marvell
(d) Shaftesbury

171. The line, "Much malice mingled with a little wit." is from
(a) *The Medal*
(b) *The Hind and the Panther*
(c) *Hudibras*
(d) *The Dunciad*

172. Who is the first to make use of the historical method of criticism?
(a) Sidney
(b) Pope
(c) Dryden
(d) Arnold

173. Dryden's *All for Love* is a blank verse tragedy. It is based on Shakespeare's play
(a) *Love's Labour's Lost*
(b) *The Comedy of Errors*
(c) *Antony and Cleopatra*
(d) *The Merchant of Venice*

174. Who set the style for modern English prose?
(a) Chaucer
(b) Dryden
(c) Richardson
(d) Ben Jonson

175. Satire is a prose work by
(a) Pope
(b) Dr. Johnson
(c) Ben Jonson
(d) Dryden

176. "Great wits are sure to madness near allied", appear in which of the following poems?
  (a) Absalom and Achitophel
  (b) The Dunciad
  (c) Mac Flecknoe
  (d) The Rape of the Lock

177. Dryden's "Song for St. Cecilia's Day" and "Alexander's Feast" are
  (a) Dramatic poems
  (b) Narrative poems
  (c) Dramatic monologues
  (d) Lyrical poems

178. Which of the following is discussed at length in Dryden's Essay?
  (a) *The Silent Woman*
  (b) *Hamlet*
  (c) *The Alchemist*
  (d) *Volpone*

179. Dryden's prose is remarkable for his use of
  (a) Mysticism
  (b) Adoption of heroic couplet
  (c) Realism
  (d) Short sentences and concise expression

180. The story of *Absalom & Achitophel* has been taken from
  (a) *The Bible*
  (b) *The Roman History*
  (c) *Greek Legend*
  (d) *The English History*

181. In Dryden's "Mac Flecknoe" Mac means
  (a) Father of
  (b) Son of
  (c) Teacher of
  (d) None of the above

182. What was the relationship between Flecknoe and Shadwell?
  (a) Flecknoe was the natural father of Shadwell
  (b) Shadwell was the natural father of Flecknoe
  (c) Flecknoe and Shadwell are the same person
  (d) Flecknoe was the intellectual father of Shadwell

183. In Dryden's "Mac Flecknoe": "The mantle fell to the young prophet's part", "young prophet" refers to
  (a) Dryden
  (b) Richard Flecknoe
  (c) Heywood
  (d) Shadwell

184. In Dryden's "Mac Flecknoe" "Shadwell alone my perfect image bears", here 'my' refers to
  (a) Shadwell
  (b) Heywood
  (c) Richard Flecknoe
  (d) Dryden

## ANSWERS

| | | | | | |
|---|---|---|---|---|---|
| 1. (b) | 2. (b) | 3. (a) | 4. (c) | 5. (d) | 6. (c) |
| 7. (c) | 8. (c) | 9. (a) | 10. (b) | 11. (d) | 12. (a) |
| 13. (c) | 14. (b) | 15. (b) | 16. (c) | 17. (a) | 18. (b) |
| 19. (c) | 20. (c) | 21. (d) | 22. (b) | 23. (b) | 24. (a) |
| 25. (a) | 26. (c) | 27. (c) | 28. (b) | 29. (d) | 30. (c) |
| 31. (a) | 32. (a) | 33. (b) | 34. (c) | 35. (b) | 36. (c) |
| 37. (b) | 38. (d) | 39. (a) | 40. (c) | 41. (d) | 42. (b) |

| | | | | | |
|---|---|---|---|---|---|
| 43. (c) | 44. (b) | 45. (c) | 46. (c) | 47. (a) | 48. (c) |
| 49. (a) | 50. (c) | 51. (c) | 52. (a) | 53. (b) | 54. (c) |
| 55. (b) | 56. (c) | 57. (c) | 58. (d) | 59. (a) | 60. (a) |
| 61. (b) | 62. (d) | 63. (d) | 64. (a) | 65. (c) | 66. (a) |
| 67. (b) | 68. (c) | 69. (b) | 70. (d) | 71. (a) | 72. (c) |
| 73. (a) | 74. (c) | 75. (d) | 76. (d) | 77. (c) | 78. (a) |
| 79. (a) | 80. (d) | 81. (c) | 82. (b) | 83. (d) | 84. (a) |
| 85. (b) | 86. (d) | 87. (b) | 88. (b) | 89. (c) | 90. (b) |
| 91. (a) | 92. (c) | 93. (b) | 94. (c) | 95. (c) | 96. (d) |
| 97. (b) | 98. (a) | 99. (c) | 100. (d) | 101. (b) | 102. (d) |
| 103. (b) | 104. (b) | 105. (b) | 106. (c) | 107. (c) | 108. (a) |
| 109. (d) | 110. (b) | 111. (c) | 112. (d) | 113. (a) | 114. (a) |
| 115. (c) | 116. (a) | 117. (d) | 118. (c) | 119. (c) | 120. (b) |
| 121. (c) | 122. (b) | 123. (a) | 124. (b) | 125. (c) | 126. (d) |
| 127. (d) | 128. (d) | 129. (b) | 130. (a) | 131. (a) | 132. (c) |
| 133. (c) | 134. (b) | 135. (b) | 136. (a) | 137. (b) | 138. (c) |
| 139. (b) | 140. (a) | 141. (a) | 142. (c) | 143. (a) | 144. (a) |
| 145. (b) | 146. (c) | 147. (d) | 148. (c) | 149. (c) | 150. (b) |
| 151. (b) | 152. (c) | 153. (a) | 154. (d) | 155. (b) | 156. (a) |
| 157. (d) | 158. (a) | 159. (b) | 160. (c) | 161. (b) | 162. (a) |
| 163. (d) | 164. (a) | 165. (c) | 166. (c) | 167. (b) | 168. (c) |
| 169. (a) | 170. (a) | 171. (b) | 172. (c) | 173. (c) | 174. (b) |
| 175. (d) | 176. (a) | 177. (d) | 178. (a) | 179. (d) | 180. (a) |
| 181. (b) | 182. (d) | 183. (d) | 184. (c) | | |

3

# Augustan Age : 18th Century Literature

1. Which age is considered to be the Golden Age of political pamphleteering?
   (a) Restoration
   (b) Victorian
   (c) Augustan
   (d) None of the above
2. Who is the author of the following?
   "Learn hence for ancient rules a just esteem;/ To copy Nature is to copy them".
   (a) Wordsworth
   (b) Blake
   (c) Dryden
   (d) Pope
3. The following statement comes from:
   "Those Rules of Old discovered, not devised,/ Are Nature still, but Nature methodized".
   (a) Wordsworth
   (b) Pope
   (c) Dryden
   (d) Coleridge
4. The statement, "True wit is nature to advantage dressed/ What oft was thought, but never so well expressed," appears in
   (a) Pope
   (b) Dryden
   (c) Johnson
   (d) Butler
5. "This casket India's glowing gems unlocks,/ And all Arbia breathes from yonder box". These lines appear in which of the following poems?
   (a) "Mac Flecknoe"
   (b) "The Dunciad"
   (c) "The Medal"
   (d) "The Rape of the Lock"
6. Pope's "An Essay on Man" discusses
   (a) Human relations
   (b) History of man
   (c) Man's morality
   (d) Man's place in the universe
7. Pope's portrait of Addison as Atticus appears in which of the following?
   (a) "The Rape of the Lock"
   (b) "The Dunciad"
   (c) "Epistle to Arbuthnot "
   (d) "An Essay on Man"
8. Which one of the following is a characteristic of the Augustan Age?
   (a) Tolerance
   (b) Moderation
   (c) Common sense
   (d) All of the above
9. In which work of Pope, the following line appears:
   "A little knowledge is a dangerous thing"?
   (a) "Windsor Forest"
   (b) "An Essay on Criticism"
   (c) "Pastorals"
   (d) None of the above

10. Who is known as the high priest of a rationalistic and social age?
    (a) Ben Jonson
    (b) Dr. Johnson
    (c) Pope
    (d) Goldsmith
11. "Here thou, great Anna! whom three realms obey,/ Dost sometimes counsel take—and sometimes tea."

    Where do we find these lines?
    (a) "Absalom and Achitophel"
    (b) "Mac Flecknoe"
    (c) "The Rape of the Lock"
    (d) "The Dunciad"
12. "To err is human, to forgive divine".

    Where do we find these lines?
    (a) "Essay on Criticism"
    (b) "Essay on Man"
    (c) "Moral Epistles"
    (d) "The Dunciad"
13. How many epistles does "Essay on Man" contain?
    (a) Four
    (b) Eight
    (c) Six
    (d) Twelve
14. "For fools rush in where angels fear to tread."

    Where do we find this epigram?
    (a) "The Rape of the Lock"
    (b) "Essay on Man"
    (c) "Essay on Criticism"
    (d) "Epistle to Arbuthnot"
15. Which eighteenth century figure was no more than 4 ft 6 in tall?
    (a) Jonathan Swift
    (b) Henry Fielding
    (c) Daniel Defoe
    (d) Alexander Pope
16. Pope's *The Dunciad* is a satire on
    (a) Too much wit
    (b) Dullness
    (c) Avarice
    (d) Honesty
17. Who became the victim of Pope's attack in the final version of "The Dunciad"?
    (a) Lewis Theobald
    (b) Colley Cibber
    (c) John Arbuthnot
    (d) Ambrose Philips
18. In "The Dunciad", the subject of Pope's attack was
    (a) Lewis Theobald
    (b) John Dennis
    (c) William Browne
    (d) Colley Cibber
19. Which of the following arrangements of Alexander Pope's poems is chronologically correct in sequence?
    (a) "The Rape of the Lock" - "Windsor Forest" - "Shakespeare Restored" - "Epistle to Dr. Arbuthnot"
    (b) "Windsor Forest" - "Epistle to Dr. Arbuthnot" - "The Rape of the Lock" - "Shakespeare Restored"
    (c) "Shakespeare Restored" - "Windsor Forest" - "Epistle to Dr. Arbuthnot" - "The Rape of the Lock"
    (d) "Epistle to Dr. Arbuthnot" - "The Rape of the Lock", "Windsor Forest" - "Shakespeare Restored"
20. The Act of Settlement was passed in 1701 during the reign of
    (a) Mary II
    (b) James II
    (c) George I
    (d) Queen Anne
21. "True ease in writing comes from art, not chance, / As those move easiest who have learned to dance."

This statement expresses the critical credo of

(a) The Romantic poets
(b) The Metaphysical poets
(c) The Elizabethan poets
(d) The neo-classical poets

22. "If Pope be not a poet, where is poetry to be found?"

Who made this observation?

(a) Hazlitt
(b) Dryden
(c) Dr. Johnson
(d) M. Arnold

23. In which poem, Pope wanted to "vindicate the ways of God to man"?

(a) "An Essay on Man"
(b) "The Dunciad"
(c) "The Windsor Forest"
(d) "The Rape of the Lock"

24. Who said,

"Yes I am proud : I must be proud to see men not afraid of God, afraid of me"?

(a) Pound
(b) Swift
(c) Steele
(d) Pope

25. Who has been regarded by Voltaire as "the best poet of England and at present of all the world"?

(a) Shakespeare
(b) Swift
(c) Pope
(d) Goldsmith

26. Who said, "The proper study of mankind is man"?

(a) Shakespeare
(b) Pope
(c) Johnson
(d) Steele

27. Pope's "Essay on Criticism" was influenced by

(a) Horace
(b) Boileau
(c) Plato
(d) Both (a) and (b)

28. Who said that Pope's was "a prose style twisted into verse"?

(a) Arnold
(b) Eliot
(c) Johnson
(d) Rossetti

29. Who said, "All our knowledge is ourselves to know"?

(a) Eliot
(b) Bacon
(c) Shakespeare
(d) Pope

30. Who found Pope's "An Essay on Man" "arbitrary and unmethodical."

(a) Arnold
(b) T.S. Eliot
(c) Johnson
(d) Walter Pater

31. Whom did Swift Praise for "sweetness and light"?

(a) Shakespeare
(b) Ancients
(c) Moderns
(d) Christian faith

32. "Bickerstaff" pamphlets are associated with

(a) Charles Dickens
(b) Jonathan Swift
(c) Richard Steele
(d) Joseph Addison

33. Which of Swift's satire was designed "to vex the world rather than divert it"?

(a) *A Tale of a Tub*
(b) *A Modest Proposal*

(c) *Battle of the Books*
(d) *Gulliver's Travels*

34. Which of the following books was written by Jonathan Swift?
(a) *The Battle of the Books*
(b) *A Modest Proposal*
(c) *A Tale of A Tub*
(d) *Gulliver's Travels*
(e) All of the above

35. Match the following

| I | II |
|---|---|
| A. Pigmies | 1. Laputans |
| B. Giants | 2. Lilliputians |
| C. Moonstruck Philosophers | 3. Hovyhnhums |
| D. Race of Horses | 4. Brobdingnagians |

| Codes: | A | B | C | D |
|---|---|---|---|---|
| (a) | 2 | 4 | 3 | 1 |
| (b) | 2 | 1 | 4 | 3 |
| (c) | 2 | 4 | 1 | 3 |
| (d) | 3 | 2 | 1 | 4 |

36. Which book of Swift suggests that "This book was ______ an outlet for the author's own bitterness against Fate and Human Society"?
(a) *A Tale of a Tub*
(b) *A Modest Proposal*
(c) *The Battle of the Books*
(d) *Gulliver's Travels*

37. Who said, "I heartily hate and detest that animal called man"?
(a) Pope
(b) Swift
(c) Eliot
(d) Orwell

38. "In the growing polish and decency of society he saw only a mask for hypocrisy." Here, who is he?
(a) Shakespeare
(b) Chaucer
(c) Swift
(d) Tennyson

39. Who wrote *An Argument Against Abolishing Christianity*?
(a) Pope
(b) Swift
(c) Gosson
(d) Collier

40. Once Swift said, "Good God! What a genius I had when I wrote that book!" Here what is 'that book'?
(a) *The Battle of the Books*
(b) *A Tale of a Tub*
(c) *Gulliver's Travels*
(d) None of the above

41. The subject of the *Battle of the Books* is the comparative merit of
(a) Classical and neoclassicals
(b) Whigs and Tories
(c) Poets and Poetasters
(d) Ancients and Moderns

42. "Far from the madding crowd's ignoble strife."

Where do we find this famous line?
(a) "Elegy Written in a Country Churchyard"
(b) "The Deserted Village"
(c) "Night Thoughts"
(d) "Seasons"

43. Which of the following was not a member of the Kit-Cat Club?
(a) Joseph Addison
(b) Richard Steele
(c) William Congreve
(d) John Dryden

44. Who wrote verses on the "Death of Dr. Swift"?
(a) John Dryden
(b) Alexander Pope
(c) Jonathan Swift
(d) Daniel Defoe

45. In which of the following works would we find the fable of the coat?
   (a) *A Tale of a Tub*
   (b) *A Tale of Mystery*
   (c) *The Tale of Gamelyn*
   (d) *A Tale of Two Cities*

46. Swift wrote in one of his works: "A Young heathy Child, well nursed, is, at a year old, a most delicious, nourishing, and wholesome food, whether stewed, roasted, baked, or boiled." Where does he make this observation?
   (a) *A Modest Proposal*
   (b) *Journal to Stella*
   (c) *The Drapier's Letters*
   (d) *Gulliver's Travels*

47. "Pope can fix in one couplet more sense than I can do in six." Who said this?
   (a) Johnson
   (b) Dryden
   (c) Swift
   (d) Matthew Prior

48. Which of Swift's work is in support of the Irish cause of freedom?
   (a) *The Conduct of the Allies*
   (b) *The Drapier's Letters*
   (c) *The Public Spirit of the Whigs*
   (d) *Some Remarks on the Barrier Treaty*

49. Swift's *A Tale of a Tub* (1704) is a
   (a) Political treatise
   (b) Treatise on art
   (c) Social document
   (d) Religious allegory

50. *A Journal to Stella* by Swift is addressed to
   (a) Esther Johnson
   (b) Queen Anne
   (c) Swift's wife
   (d) Swift's daughter

51. Who said, "I shall endeavour to enliven morality with wit, and to temper wit with morality"?
   (a) Pope
   (b) Jonathan Swift
   (c) Steele
   (d) Joseph Addison

52. Who wrote the *Coverley Papers*?
   (a) Swift
   (b) Richard Steele
   (c) Addison
   (d) Alexander Pope

53. The Spectator was issued
   (a) Thrice a week
   (b) Daily
   (c) Twice a week
   (d) Weekly

54. Match the following

|  |  |
|---|---|
| (a) The Vision of Mirza | 1. Tragedy |
| (b) Rosamond | 2. Political allegory |
| (c) The Drummer | 3. Opera |
| (d) Cato | 4. Prose - Comedy |

| **Codes:** | A | B | C | D |
|---|---|---|---|---|
| (a) | 2 | 3 | 4 | 1 |
| (b) | 1 | 2 | 3 | 4 |
| (c) | 2 | 1 | 3 | 4 |
| (d) | 4 | 3 | 2 | 1 |

55. "Night Thought on Life, Death and Immortality" is the subtitle of the poem which is written in blank verse.
   (a) "The Last Day"
   (b) "The Force of Religion"
   (c) "The Complaint"
   (d) "The Love of Fame"

56. Which one of the following was inspired by the death of the poet's wife?
   (a) "The Last Day"
   (b) "The Complaint"
   (c) "The Force of Religion"
   (d) "The Love of Fame"

57. How many essays were published in *The Spectator*?
(a) 290
(b) 455
(c) 360
(d) 555

58. Out of 555 essays, how many were written by Addison?
(a) 209
(b) 274
(c) 360
(d) 475

59. Who aimed at pointing out "those vices which are too trivial for the chastisement of the law...and to assault the vice without hurting the person"?
(a) Jonathan Swift
(b) Pope
(c) Joseph Addison
(d) Steele

60. "Public Credit" is a political allegory by
(a) Addison
(b) Swift
(c) Steele
(d) Johnson

61. Which poem is known as a "rhymed gazette"?
(a) "The Campaign"
(b) "The Waste Land"
(c) "London"
(d) None of the above

62. The hero of the poem "The Campaign" is
(a) Steele
(b) Marlborough
(c) Neander
(d) Bolingbroke

63. At the age of 26 "__________ was the secretary for war in the Tory government."
(a) Arbuthnot
(b) Addison
(c) Steele
(d) Lord Bolingbroke

64. Match the following

| I | II |
|---|---|
| (a) The Spectator | 1. Sir Andrew Freeport |
| (b) Merchant | 2. The man of fashion |
| (c) Will Honeycomb | 3. Joseph Addison |
| (d) Country gentleman | 4. Roger de Coverley |

| **Codes:** | A | B | C | D |
|---|---|---|---|---|
| (a) | 1 | 2 | 3 | 4 |
| (b) | 2 | 1 | 3 | 4 |
| (c) | 3 | 1 | 2 | 4 |
| (d) | 3 | 2 | 1 | 4 |

65. The object of which periodical was to "observe upon the pleasurable as well as the busy part of mankind"?
(a) *The Spectator*
(b) *The Tatler*
(c) *Journal to Stella*
(d) *Bickerstaff Pamphlets*

66. *The Tatler* appeared
(a) Once a week
(b) Thrice a week
(c) Fortnightly
(d) Monthly

67. How many reports in all formed part of *The Tatler*?
(a) 162
(b) 271
(c) 190
(d) 296

68. *The Tatler* was founded by
(a) Richard Steele
(b) Joseph Addison
(c) Jonathan Swift
(d) Samuel Johnson

69. *The Beggar's Opera* was written by
   (a) James Thomson
   (b) John Gay
   (c) Edward Young
   (d) William Collins

70. The writer of the *Vicar of Wakefield* is
   (a) Thomas Hardy
   (b) Jane Austen
   (c) Charles Dickens
   (d) Oliver Goldsmith

71. Oliver Goldsmith's first successful poem was
   (a) "The Deserted Village"
   (b) "The Good - Natured Man"
   (c) "The Citizen of the World"
   (d) "The Traveller"

72. "Who, born for the universe, narrowed his mind,/ And to party gave up what was meant for mankind."

   Who wrote these lines?
   (a) Edward Gibbon
   (b) Edmund Burke
   (c) Oliver Goldsmith
   (d) Oscar Wilde

73. Who is the Vicar of Wakefield in Goldsmith's novel of the same name?
   (a) Thornhill
   (b) Primrose
   (c) Burchell
   (d) Jenkinson

74. Which of the following poems is not by Goldsmith?
   (a) "The Hermit"
   (b) "The Unfortunate Traveller"
   (c) "Elegy on the Death of a Mad Dog"
   (d) "When Lovely"

75. What is the name of the Vicar's daughter in Goldsmith's *The Vicar of Wakefield*?
   (a) Barbara
   (b) Catherine
   (c) Olivia
   (d) Helen

76. The Subtitle of *She Stoops to Conquer* (1773) is
   (a) *Journey's End*
   (b) *Ways to Win*
   (c) *Mistakes of a Night*
   (d) *The Story of a Maid*

77. Goldsmith's novel *The Vicar of Wakefield* (1766) is marked by the qualities of
   (a) Irony and satire
   (b) Valour and bravery
   (c) Ambiguity and paradox
   (d) Humour and pathos

78. Who is the author of *The Citizen of the World* (1759)?
   (a) Addison
   (b) Goldsmith
   (c) Swift
   (d) Steele

79. Who says about Johnson, "He has nothing of the bear but his skin"?
   (a) Arnold
   (b) T.S. Eliot
   (c) Goldsmith
   (d) Ruskin

80. The essay on "An Inquiry into the Present State of Polite Learning in Europe" (1759) against sentimental comedy was written by
   (a) Collier
   (b) Gosson
   (c) Addison
   (d) Goldsmith

81. Whose essays were originally published as "Chinese Letters"?
   (a) Goldsmith's
   (b) Steele's
   (c) Addison's
   (d) Johnson's

82. Fielding's *Joseph Andrews* (1742) has a direct link with Richardson's
    (a) Clarissa
    (b) Pamela
    (c) Sir Charles Grandison
    (d) The Apprentice's Vade Mecum

83. Abraham (Parson) Adams figures in which of the following works?
    (a) *Robinson Crusoe*
    (b) *Tom Jones*
    (c) *Joseph Andrews*
    (d) *Clarissa*

84. Who among the following is a foundling?
    (a) Robinson Crusoe
    (b) Pamela
    (c) Joseph Andrews
    (d) Tom Jones

85. The girl Tom Jones loves and marries is
    (a) Amelia
    (b) Sophia
    (c) Fanny
    (d) Pamela

86. Squire Alworthy is similar to
    (a) Uncle Toby
    (b) King Lear
    (c) Gradgrind
    (d) Parson Adams

87. Which of the following is a comic epic in prose?
    (a) Dicken's *Great Expectations*
    (b) Richardson's *Clarissa*
    (c) Fielding's *Joseph Andrews*
    (d) Defoe's *Moll Flanders*

88. Match the characters and the novels in which they appear

|  |  |
|---|---|
| A. Pipes | 1. Roderick Random |
| B. Bowling | 2. Amelia |
| C. Booth | 3. Peregrine Pickle |
| D. Blifil | 4. Tom Jones |

| **Codes:** | A | B | C | D |
|---|---|---|---|---|
| (a) | 3 | 1 | 2 | 4 |
| (b) | 1 | 2 | 4 | 3 |
| (c) | 3 | 4 | 1 | 2 |
| (e) | 2 | 3 | 1 | 4 |

89. How was Sarah Fielding related to Henry Fielding?
    (a) Wife
    (b) Mother
    (c) Daughter
    (d) Sister

90. Which novel begins with the sentence, "It is trite but true observation that examples work more forcibly on the mind than precepts"?
    (a) *Pamela*
    (b) *Joseph Andrews*
    (c) *Tristram Shandy*
    (d) *Humphry Clinker*

91. To whom Henry Fielding's *Tom Jones* is dedicated?
    (a) George Lytton
    (b) Richardson
    (c) Sterne
    (d) Pope

92. Henry Fielding's last work was a diary the name of which is
    (a) A Journey from the World to the Next
    (b) Amelia
    (c) Voyage to Lisbon
    (d) None of the above

93. Which of the following are novels by Henry Fielding?
    (a) *Joseph Andrews*
    (b) *Jonathan Wild, the Great*
    (c) *A Journey from this world to the Next*
    (d) All of the above

94. Which one of the following is the last novel by Fielding?

(a) *Joseph Andrews*
(b) *Amelia*
(c) *Tom Jones*
(d) None of the above

95. Who, among the following, is called the father of the English Novel?
(a) Defoe
(b) Richardson
(c) Fielding
(d) Sterne

96. Smollett is best known by which of the following novels he wrote?
(a) *Peregrine Pickle* (1751)
(b) *Humphry Clinker* (1771)
(c) *Roderick Random* (1748)
(d) *Sir Lancelot Greaves*

97. Which one of Smollett's novels was published shortly before his death?
(a) *Roderick Random*
(b) *Peregrine Pickle*
(c) *Humphry Clinker*
(d) None of the above

98. Who has been dubbed as "Smollett in Petticoats"?
(a) Fanny Burney
(b) Jane Austen
(c) George Eliot
(d) Virginia Woolf

99. Howser Trunnion is a character from
(a) *Tom Jones*
(b) *Roderick Random*
(c) *Humphry Clinker*
(d) *Peregrine Pickle*

100. Smollett's novel *The Expedition of Humphry Clinker* is a ________ novel.
(a) Victorian
(b) Stream-of-consciousness
(c) Picaresque
(d) Idealistic

101. Tom Bowling in *Roderick Random* is a
(a) Painter
(b) Artist
(c) Seaman
(d) Rogue

102. Mathew Bramble and Tabitha are the characters in
(a) *Humphry Clinker*
(b) *Pamela*
(c) *Tom Jones*
(d) *Tristram Shandy*

103. Which of the following was a physician apart from being a novelist?
(a) Henry Fielding
(b) Lawrence Sterne
(c) Samuel Richardson
(d) Tobias Smollett

104. Whom did Laurence Sterne satirize as "the learned Smelfungus" who "set out with the spleen and jaundice and every object he passed by was discoloured and distorted" in his novel *Sentimental Journey*?
(a) Daniel Defoe
(b) Samuel Richardson
(c) Tobias Smollett
(d) Henry Fielding

105. Where would we find the characters commodore Trunnion and Pipes?
(a) *Humphry Clinker*
(b) *Tom Jones*
(c) *Roxana*
(d) *Peregrine Pickle*

106. *Ferdinand, Count Fathom* (1753) is a novel by
(a) Laurence Sterne
(b) Daniel Defoe
(c) Henry Fielding
(d) Tobias Smollett

107. Richardson's *Pamela* is a
   (a) Picaresque novel
   (b) Sentimental novel
   (c) Psychological novel
   (d) Epistolary novel

108. The subtitle of *Pamela* is
   (a) *The Generous Lady*
   (b) *A Pure Woman*
   (c) *Virtue Rewarded*
   (d) *The Symbol of Chastity*

109. Which of the following writers was nicknamed as "Serious" and "Gravity" by his school fellows?
   (a) Henry Fielding
   (b) Daniel Defoe
   (c) Samuel Richardson
   (d) Laurence Sterne

110. Which novel is considered to begin the first great flowering to the English novel
   (a) *Clarissa*
   (b) *Pamela*
   (c) *Tom Jones*
   (d) *Joseph Andrews*

111. Who is known as not only "the first novelist of character but also the first novelist of feminine character"?
   (a) Richardson
   (b) James Joyce
   (c) Fielding
   (d) Eliot

112. Who among the following is not one of 'four wheels' of the English novel?
   (a) Richardson
   (b) Sterne
   (c) Smollett
   (d) Scott

113. The real novel form came into existence with the novel
   (a) *Pamela*
   (b) *Joseph Andrews*
   (c) *Clarissa*
   (d) *Amelia*

114. How many novels did Richardson write?
   (a) Two
   (b) Three
   (c) Five
   (d) Four

115. Richardson's Pamela marries
   (a) Monsieur Calbrand
   (b) Mr. Jewkes
   (c) Mr. B
   (d) Mr. Andrews

116. Which novel of Richardson was labelled by him as a dramatic narrative"?
   (a) *Pamela*
   (b) *Sir Charles Grandison*
   (c) *Clarissa*
   (d) None of the above

117. Richardson's novels are known for
   (a) Satire
   (b) Sentimentality
   (c) Songs
   (d) Realism

118. Which of the following is not a character in *The School for Scandal*?
   (a) Lady Teazle
   (b) Sir Oliver
   (c) Joseph Surface
   (d) Lydia Languish

119. Mrs. Malaprop is a character from
   (a) *The School for Scandal*
   (b) *She Stoops to Conquer*
   (c) *The Good-Natured Man*
   (d) *The Rivals*

120. "No caparisons, miss, if you please—". Which 18th century character would we expect to speak thus?
   (a) Pamela
   (b) Mrs. Malaprop

(c) David Simple
(d) Tristram Shandy

121. Sheridan's farcical play *St. Patrick's Day*, or *The Scheming Lieutenant* appeared in
(a) 1780
(b) 1785
(c) 1775
(d) 1770

122. In Sheridan's play *The School for Scandal*, Charles Surface is in love with
(a) Lady Teazle
(b) Maria
(c) Mrs. Candour
(d) Lady Sneerwell

123. Who has been called "a dramatic star of the first magnitude"?
(a) G.B. Shaw
(b) Shakespeare
(c) Sheridan
(d) Ibsen

124. Which of the following plays of Sheridan is best known?
(a) *The Rivals* (1774)
(b) *St. Patrick's Day*, or, *The Scheming Lieutenant*
(c) *The School for Scandal* (1777)
(d) *The Critic*, or, *A Tragedy Rehearsed* (1779)

125. Sterne's *Tristram Shandy* (1760-67) is known for its
(a) Fine Prose style
(b) Eccentricities
(c) Well-known plot
(d) High Seriousness

126. Who is the funniest character in *Tristram Shandy*?
(a) Uncle Toby
(b) Tristram
(c) Susannah
(d) Corporal Trim

127. Which of the following works were written by Laurence Sterne?
(a) *The Sermons of Mr. Yorick*
(b) *Tristram Shandy*
(c) *A Sentimental Journey*
(d) All of the above

128. Mr. Yorick features in
(a) *A Sentimental Journey*
(b) *Roderick Random*
(c) *Tom Jones*
(d) *Tristram Shandy*

129. *A Sentimental Journey* __________ complete the title of the novel.
(a) *Through France and Germany*
(b) *Through England and Scotland*
(c) *Through France and Italy*
(d) *Through Europe*

130. Who regarded *Tristram Shandy* as "a very insipid, tedious performance"?
(a) Horace Walpole
(b) Johnson
(c) Pope
(d) Arnold

131. Which one of the following is Sterne's quasi-autobiographical work?
(a) *Tristram Shandy*
(b) *271*
(c) *Journal to Eliza*
(d) None of the above

132. Who says that Lawrence Sterne is the freest writer of all time?
(a) Arnold
(b) Nietzsche
(c) F.R. Leavis
(d) Horace Walpole

133. Strene's visit to France influenced his work
(a) *Journal to Eliza*
(b) *A Sentimental Journey*
(c) Both (a) and (b)
(d) None of the above

134. The full title of *Robinson Crusoe* (1719) is
   (a) *The Life and Strange Adventures of Robinson Crusoe*
   (b) *The Life and Adventures of Robinson Crusoe*
   (c) *The Life of Robinson Crusoe*
   (d) *The Life and Strange Surprising Adventures of Robinson Crusoe*

135. What did Robinson name the man whose life he saved on the island?
   (a) John
   (b) Willy
   (c) Friday
   (d) Alexander

136. *David Simple* was written by
   (a) Jonathan Swift
   (b) Sarah Fielding
   (c) Fanny Burney
   (d) Mrs. Manley

137. "Far from the madding crowd's ignoble strife."

   This is from
   (a) "Night Thoughts"
   (b) "Seasons"
   (c) "Elegy Written in a Country Churchyard"
   (d) "The Deserted Village"

138. Who was known as "the Man of Feeling"?
   (a) Henry Mackenzie
   (b) Walpole
   (c) Sterne
   (d) None of the above

139. *The Man of Feeling* (1771) is a work by
   (a) Sterne
   (b) Mackenzie
   (c) Walpole
   (d) None of the above

140. Which one of the following novels is a story of one man on a deserted island?
   (a) *Pamela*
   (b) *Robinson Crusoe*
   (c) *Joseph Andrews*
   (d) None of the above

141. For how many years Crusoe stayed on the island.
   (a) 12
   (b) 20
   (c) 5
   (d) 26

142. Defoe's periodical 'Review' was put to an end in
   (a) 1721
   (b) 1722
   (c) 1712
   (d) 1710

143. The name of the first fiction by Daniel Defoe is
   (a) *Moll Flanders*
   (b) *Roxana*
   (c) *Robinson Crusoe*
   (d) *Duncan Campbell*

144. *Roxana* (1724) is a fiction by
   (a) Steele
   (b) Johnson
   (c) Defoe
   (d) Sterne

145. Who has been hailed as 'the master illusionist'?
   (a) Richardson
   (b) Sterne
   (c) Fielding
   (d) Daniel Defoe

146. Whose experiences inspired Defoe to write *Robinson Crusoe*?
   (a) Gulliver
   (b) Swift
   (c) Pope
   (d) Alexander Selkirk

147. Which of the following works of Johnson was written to pay for his mother's funeral?
    (a) *A Journey to the Western Islands of Scotland* (1775)
    (b) *The Lives of the Poets* (1777-81)
    (c) *Dictionary of the English Language* (1765)
    (d) *Rasselas, Prince of Abyssinia* (1759)

148. "There mark what ills the scholars life assail,/ Toil, envy, Want, the Patron, and the jail."

    These lines appear in Johnson's
    (a) "London"
    (b) "Dictionary"
    (c) "The Vanity of Human Wishes"
    (d) "Rasselas"

149. Which of the following periodical contains Johnson's best essays?
    (a) *The Rambler*
    (b) *The Idler*
    (c) *Universal Chronical*
    (d) *The Gentleman's Magazine*

150. Who considers Shakespeare "the poet of nature"?
    (a) Pope
    (b) Johnson
    (c) Wordsworth
    (d) Coleridge

151. Boswell's *Life of Johnson* was published in
    (a) 1771
    (b) 1781
    (c) 1800
    (d) 1791

152. Dr. Johnson's claim to be called a first-rate writer rests on his
    (a) Epics
    (b) Dramas
    (c) Poetry
    (d) Prose works

153. Dr. Johnson formed the Literary Club with the help of
    (a) Goldsmith
    (b) Addison
    (c) Steele
    (d) Pitt

154. Who says about Johnson, "He has nothing of the bear but his skin"?
    (a) Arnold
    (b) Goldsmith
    (c) Eliot
    (d) Ruskin

155. Who said, "A book should help us either to enjoy like or to endure it"?
    (a) Dr. Johnson
    (b) Bacon
    (c) Pope
    (d) Wordsworth

156. Who said, "What is fit for every thing can fit nothing well"?
    (a) Pope
    (b) Johnson
    (c) Eliot
    (d) Arnold

157. Johnson's *Dictionary* was published in
    (a) 1744
    (b) 1745
    (c) 1755
    (d) 1765

158. How many poets were treated in Johnson's *Lives of the Poets?*
    (a) 48
    (b) 42
    (c) 52
    (d) 59

159. Who exonerated Shakespeare for not abiding by the unities of timc and place?

(a) Pope
(b) Jonson
(c) Johnson
(d) Dryden

160. "Patriotism is the last refuse of a scoundrel." Who said this?
(a) Samuel Johnson
(b) James Boswell
(c) Oliver Goldsmith
(d) Thomas Hardy

161. Who criticises *Paradise Lost* for its lack of human interest?
(a) Pope
(b) Johnson
(c) Arnold
(d) Eliot

162. "Pope's is a velvet lawn, shaven by the scythe and levelled by the roller."
This quotation is from
(a) Dr. Johnson
(b) Bolingbroke
(c) Milton
(d) Cowley

163. Which one of the following was not written by George Berkeley
(a) *A Treatise Concerning the Principles of Human Knowledge*
(b) *Three Dialogues between Hylas and Philonous*
(c) *Characteristics of Men, Manners, Opinions and Times*
(d) *Alciphron, or the Minute Philosopher*

164. *Characteristics of Men, Manners, Opinions and Times* (1711) was written by
(a) Steele
(b) Goldsmith
(c) George Berkley
(d) Earl of Shaftesbury

165. Sir Samuel Garth's only work *The Dispensary* was published in the year
(a) 1680
(b) 1699
(c) 1705
(d) 1711

166. "The Scriblerus Club" was associated with
(a) Whig Wits
(b) Tory Wits
(c) Pope and Swift
(d) Queen Anne and William

167. Who among the following was not a member of "The Scriblerus Club".
(a) Addison
(b) Swift
(c) Arbuthnot
(d) Bolingbroke

168. Union of England and Scotland took place in the year
(a) 1701
(b) 1707
(c) 1731
(d) 1727

169. Who was the king when the terms 'Whig' and 'Tory' came into existence?
(a) Cromwell
(b) Charles II
(c) James I
(d) Queen Victoria

170. Whig party was in favour of
(a) Purposelessness
(b) Love at first sight
(c) Pre-eminence of personal freedom
(d) Dictatorship

171. 'Royal divine right' was supported by
(a) Dryden
(b) Whig Party
(c) Tory Party
(d) None of the above

172. Which one of the following was not written by John Arbuthnot?
(a) *Memoir of Martinus Scriblerus*
(b) *A New Voyage Round the World*
(c) *The History of John Bull*
(d) *The Art of Political*

173. Which one of the following was not written by Lord Bolingbroke?
(a) *Letter to Sir William Wyndham*
(b) *The Vision of Mirza*
(c) *A Letter on the Spirit of Patriotism*
(d) *The Idea of a Patriot King*

174. Which one of the following was written by Matthew Prior?
(a) *The Chameleon*
(b) *The Thief and the Cordelier*
(c) *To Chloe*
(d) *Alma*

175. The heroic tragedy was introduced by
(a) Thomas Otway
(b) Sir William Davenant
(c) Corneille
(d) Dryden

176. Who among the following is not a member of the Graveyard School of Poetry?
(a) Thomas Parnell
(b) Robert Blair
(c) Ward Young
(d) Bishop Percy

177. Which of the following novels is about a clothier's trade?
(a) *Jack of Newberie*
(b) *Thomas of Reading*
(c) *The Gentle Craft*
(d) None of the above

178. Which of the following novels is not a novel by Deloney?
(a) *Jack of Newberie*
(b) *Thomas of Reading*
(c) *The Gentle Craft*
(d) *The Horse's Mouth*

179. *Jack of Newberie* is a novel about
(a) A washerman
(b) A farmer
(c) The weaver's craft
(d) Shoemaker's trade

180. *The Gentle Craft* is about
(a) The art of farming
(b) Craftsmanship
(c) The shoemaker's trade
(d) None of the above

181. Who among the following is not a terror novelist?
(a) Clara Reeve
(b) Horace Walpole
(c) William Beckford
(d) Virginia Woolf

182. Which one is not a comedy by George Farquhar
(a) *Love and a Bottle*
(b) *The Recruiting Officer*
(c) *The Beaux Stratagem*
(d) *The Old Bachelor*

183. Which one is not a reason for the rise of the novel form
(a) Rise of the Middle class
(b) Rise of poetry
(c) Decline of drama
(d) Rise of the periodical essays

184. Which one of the following was written by Robert Burns?
(a) *The Holy Fair*
(b) *The Jolly Beggars*
(c) *The Cotter's Saturday Night*
(d) All of the above

185. *O My Love's Like a Red, Red Rose* was written by
(a) Crabbe
(b) Pope
(c) Larkin
(d) Robert Burns

186. Which one of the following was written by Robert Burns?
   (a) *A Fond Kiss*
   (b) *A Man's Man for all That*
   (c) *My Heart's in the Highlands*
   (d) All of the above

187. The Ossianic poems are associated with
   (a) Samuel Johnson
   (b) Henry Mackenzie
   (c) James Macpherson
   (d) Oliver Goldsmith

188. M.G. Lewis was also known as
   (a) Mott Lewis
   (b) Mac Lewis
   (c) Meg Lewis
   (d) Monk Lewis

189. M.G. Lewis' novel *The Monk* appeared in
   (a) 1776
   (b) 1796
   (c) 1786
   (d) 1799

190. Who considered M.G. Lewis as the "greatest master in the art of freezing the blood" after Ann Radcliffe?
   (a) S.T. Coleridge
   (b) William Hazlitt
   (c) Walter Scott
   (d) Ann Radcliffe

191. Who wrote the *Siege of Troy* (1707)?
   (a) Richard Savage
   (b) Elkanah Settle
   (c) Joseph Addison
   (d) None of these

192. "The Act of Walking the Streets of London" is the subtitle of the poem.
   (a) "London"
   (b) "Trivia"
   (c) "Liberty"
   (d) None of the above

193. Who wrote the above poem?
   (a) Dr. Johnson
   (b) James Thomson
   (c) John Gay
   (d) None of these

194. Which of the following works of Aphra Behn is a novel?
   (a) *Oroonoko, or the History of the Royal Slave*
   (b) *The Forced Marriage*
   (c) *The Feign'd Courtesans*
   (d) *The Roundheads*

195. Mary Astell is best known by which of the following?
   (a) *A Serious Proposal to the Ladies for the Advancement of their True and Greatest Interest*
   (b) *Some Reflections upon Marriage*
   (c) *Moderation Truly Stated*
   (d) *A Fair Way with the Dissenters and their Patrons*

196. Who among the following influenced Shelley on the philosophy of political justice?
   (a) Adam Smith
   (b) William Godwin
   (c) Gilbert White
   (d) Edmund Burke

197. Edward Young's, *The Complaint* is better known as
   (a) *Night Thoughts*
   (b) *The Brothers*
   (c) *The Foreign Address*
   (d) *Resignation*

198. The above work is divided into
   (a) Four parts
   (b) Nine parts
   (c) Six parts
   (d) Twelve parts

199. *Caleb Williams* was written by
   (a) Mary Godwin
   (b) William Godwin
   (c) Matthew Lewis
   (d) William Beckford

200. In whose version of *King Lear*, Cordelia's life is spared and is bethroned to Edgar in a happy ending?
   (a) Nahum Tate
   (b) David Garrick
   (c) William Hazlitt
   (d) Charles Lamb

201. Who observed, "Dryden and Pope are the classics of not our poetry,/ They are classics of our prose"?
   (a) Leavis
   (b) Arnold
   (c) A.R. Humphrey
   (d) Richards

202. Who remarked, "the age of prose and reason, our excellent and indispensable eighteenth century"?
   (a) Pope
   (b) Arnold
   (c) Dr. Johnson
   (d) Steele

203. Who poisoned himself with arsenic when he was only eighteen?
   (a) Thomas Chatterton
   (b) Burns
   (c) Macpherson
   (d) None of the above

204. Who said, "The wife bolts out her husband. She shuts herself in Eden with Satan. Adam is left outside"?
   (a) Dr. Johnson
   (b) Horace Walpole
   (c) Coleridge
   (d) Victor Hugo

205. Who is known as the "Ploughman Poet"?
   (a) Wordsworth
   (b) James Thomson
   (c) Robert Burns
   (d) Arnold

206. *Fingal* (1762) and *Timora* (1763) were written by
   (a) Macpherson
   (b) Pope
   (c) Crabbe
   (d) Smart

207. Match the works and the writers

| | |
|---|---|
| A. *The Castle of Indolence* | 1. Thomson |
| B. *The Castle of Otranto* | 2. Walpole |
| C. *The Castle* | 3. Kafka |
| D. *Castle Rackrent* | 4. Edgeworth |

| **Codes:** | A | B | C | D |
|---|---|---|---|---|
| (a) | 1 | 2 | 3 | 4 |
| (b) | 2 | 3 | 4 | 1 |
| (c) | 4 | 3 | 1 | 2 |
| (d) | 3 | 4 | 1 | 2 |

208. Which one of the following is written by Fergusson
   (a) *A King's Birthday in Edinburgh*
   (b) *To the Tron-Kirk Bell*
   (c) *The Farmer's Ingle*
   (d) All of the above

209. Which poet was lamented by William Collins in his poem "In Yonder Grave a Druid Lies"?
   (a) Pope
   (b) James Thomson
   (c) George Crabbe
   (d) Richard Steele

210. Who wrote the famous *The Rise and Fall of the Roman Empire*?
   (a) Edward Gibbon
   (b) Tom Paine
   (c) Edmund Burke
   (d) David Hume

211. Who is the author of *The Decline and Fall of the Romantic Ideal*?
   (a) C.S. Lewis
   (b) F.L. Lucas
   (c) L.C. Knights
   (d) A.C. Bradley

212. Who among the following was not a historian?
   (a) Edward Gibbon
   (b) Edmund Burke
   (c) David Hume
   (d) William Robertson

213. Thomas Percy is known for his collection of ballad poetry under the title
   (a) *Golden Treasury*
   (b) *Tottel's Miscellany*
   (c) *Reliques of Ancient English Poetry*
   (d) *The Phoenix Nest*

214. Aphra Behn was a contemporary of
   (a) Johnson
   (b) Pope
   (c) Fielding
   (d) Dryden

215. Who is considered to be the first of the women novelists?
   (a) Francis Burney
   (b) George Eliot
   (c) Virginia Woolf
   (d) Jane Austen

216. Which one of the following is a novel by Francis Burney?
   (a) *Evelina* (1778)
   (b) *Cecilia* (1782)
   (c) *Camilla* (1796)
   (d) *The Wanderer* (1814)
   (e) All of the above

217. Which of the following was written by David Hume?
   (a) *A Treatise of Human Nature* (1739-40)
   (b) *Essays, Moral and Political* (1741-42)
   (c) *The History of England* (1754-1761)
   (d) All of the above

218. Who pictured Boswell as being a knavish buffoon?
   (a) Arnold
   (b) Macaulay
   (c) Ruskin
   (d) Rossetti

219. *A Vindication of Natural Society* (1756) and *A Philosophical Inquiry into the Origin of Our Ideas of the Sublime and Beautiful* (1756), philosophical prose works are by
   (a) Bolingbroke
   (b) Smith
   (c) Arbuthnot
   (d) Edmund Burke

220. *The Wealth of Nations* (1776) is a prose work on economics, written by
   (a) Burke
   (b) Adam Smith
   (c) Gibbon
   (d) Addison

221. Match the following

| | |
|---|---|
| A. Otway | 1. Good Thoughts in Bad Times |
| B. John Fisher | 2. Don Carlos |
| C. John Ford | 3. The Ways to Perfect Religion |
| D. Thomas Fuller | 4. 'Tis Pity She's a Whore |

| Codes: | A | B | C | D |
|---|---|---|---|---|
| (a) | 4 | 3 | 2 | 1 |
| (b) | 1 | 2 | 3 | 4 |
| (c) | 2 | 3 | 4 | 1 |
| (d) | 3 | 4 | 2 | 1 |

222. *The Rights of Man* (1791-92) was written by

(a) Dr. Johnson
(b) Coleridge
(c) Thomas Paine
(d) Robert Clive

223. Whose poetry was known as 'namby - pamby'
(a) Pope
(b) John Gay
(c) Rossetti
(d) Ambrose Philips

224. Falkland is a character in
(a) *Nightmare Abbey*
(b) *Ruth*
(c) *Caleb Williams*
(d) *Vathek*

225. Mr. Knightley is a character from
(a) *Emma*
(b) *Jane Eyre*
(c) *Coolie*
(d) *Cranford*

226. Richard Saunders was the pseudonym of
(a) J.S. Mill
(b) Benjamin Franklin
(c) Thomas Paine
(d) Edmund Burke

## ANSWERS

| | | | | | |
|---|---|---|---|---|---|
| 1. (c) | 2. (d) | 3. (b) | 4. (a) | 5. (d) | 6. (d) |
| 7. (c) | 8. (d) | 9. (b) | 10. (c) | 11. (c) | 12. (a) |
| 13. (a) | 14. (c) | 15. (d) | 16. (b) | 17. (b) | 18. (a) |
| 19. (b) | 20. (d) | 21. (d) | 22. (c) | 23. (a) | 24. (d) |
| 25. (c) | 26. (b) | 27. (d) | 28. (d) | 29. (d) | 30. (c) |
| 31. (b) | 32. (b) | 33. (d) | 34. (e) | 35. (c) | 36. (d) |
| 37. (b) | 38. (c) | 39. (b) | 40. (b) | 41. (d) | 42. (a) |
| 43. (d) | 44. (c) | 45. (a) | 46. (a) | 47. (c) | 48. (b) |
| 49. (d) | 50. (a) | 51. (d) | 52. (c) | 53. (b) | 54. (a) |
| 55. (c) | 56. (b) | 57. (d) | 58. (b) | 59. (c) | 60. (a) |
| 61. (a) | 62. (b) | 63. (b) | 64. (c) | 65. (b) | 66. (b) |
| 67. (b) | 68. (a) | 69. (b) | 70. (d) | 71. (a) | 72. (c) |
| 73. (b) | 74. (b) | 75. (c) | 76. (c) | 77. (d) | 78. (b) |
| 79. (c) | 80. (d) | 81. (a) | 82. (b) | 83. (c) | 84. (d) |
| 85. (b) | 86. (d) | 87. (c) | 88. (a) | 89. (d) | 90. (b) |
| 91. (a) | 92. (c) | 93. (d) | 94. (b) | 95. (c) | 96. (b) |
| 97. (c) | 98. (a) | 99. (d) | 100. (b) | 101. (c) | 102. (a) |
| 103. (d) | 104. (d) | 105. (d) | 106. (d) | 107. (d) | 108. (c) |
| 109. (c) | 110. (b) | 111. (a) | 112. (d) | 113. (a) | 114. (b) |
| 115. (c) | 116. (c) | 117. (b) | 118. (d) | 119. (d) | 120. (b) |
| 121. (c) | 122. (b) | 123. (c) | 124. (c) | 125. (b) | 126. (a) |

| | | | | | |
|---|---|---|---|---|---|
| 127. (d) | 128. (d) | 129. (c) | 130. (a) | 131. (c) | 132. (b) |
| 133. (a) | 134. (d) | 135. (c) | 136. (b) | 137. (c) | 138. (a) |
| 139. (b) | 140. (b) | 141. (d) | 142. (c) | 143. (c) | 144. (c) |
| 145. (d) | 146. (d) | 147. (d) | 148. (c) | 149. (a) | 150. (b) |
| 151. (d) | 152. (d) | 153. (d) | 154. (b) | 155. (a) | 156. (b) |
| 157. (c) | 158. (c) | 159. (b) | 160. (a) | 161. (b) | 162. (a) |
| 163. (c) | 164. (d) | 165. (b) | 166. (b) | 167. (a) | 168. (b) |
| 169. (b) | 170. (c) | 171. (c) | 172. (b) | 173. (b) | 174. (c) |
| 175. (b) | 176. (d) | 177. (b) | 178. (d) | 179. (c) | 180. (c) |
| 181. (d) | 182. (d) | 183. (b) | 184. (d) | 185. (d) | 186. (d) |
| 187. (c) | 188. (d) | 189. (b) | 190. (b) | 191. (b) | 192. (b) |
| 193. (c) | 194. (a) | 195. (a) | 196. (b) | 197. (a) | 198. (b) |
| 199. (b) | 200. (a) | 201. (b) | 202. (b) | 203. (a) | 204. (d) |
| 205. (c) | 206. (a) | 207. (a) | 208. (d) | 209. (b) | 210. (a) |
| 211. (b) | 212. (b) | 213. (c) | 214. (d) | 215. (a) | 216. (e) |
| 217. (d) | 218. (b) | 219. (d) | 220. (b) | 221. (c) | 222. (c) |
| 223. (d) | 224. (c) | 225. (a) | 226. (b) | | |

4

# The Romantic Period

1. Theodore Watts Duntan gives the title 'The Renaissance of Wonder' to the
   (a) Elizabethan Age
   (b) Romantic Period
   (c) Restoration Age
   (d) None of the above
2. Who says, "The romantic movement was the expression of individual genius rather than of established rules"?
   (a) W.J. Long
   (b) Charles Lamb
   (c) Walter Pater
   (d) John Keats
3. "To me the meanest flower that blows can give thoughts that do often lie too deep for tears."

   Which poem are we talking about?
   (a) Wordsworth's "The Daffodils"
   (b) Keat's "Endymion"
   (c) Wordsworth's "Ode: Intimations of Immortality"
   (d) P.B. Shelley's "Ode to the West Wind"
4. Who is the lost leader in Browning's poem "The Lost Leader"?
   (a) Shelley
   (b) Shakespeare
   (c) Milton
   (d) Wordsworth
5. About whom Arnold said, "His poetry is the reality, his philosophy...is the illusion"?
   (a) F.R. Leavis
   (b) Wordsworth
   (c) Hazlitt
   (d) T.S. Eliot
6. *The Borderers* is a blank verse tragedy was written by
   (a) Coleridge
   (b) Southey
   (c) Wordsworth
   (d) Keats
7. Who said that "The child is father of the Man"?
   (a) Wordsworth
   (b) Pope
   (c) Milton
   (d) Shakespeare
8. Who wrote for Spenser

   "And that gentle Bard, Chosen by the Muses for their Page of state, Sweet Spenser.... I called him brother, Englishman and friend"?
   (a) Pope
   (b) Eliot
   (c) Wordsworth
   (d) Shelley

9. In which poem do the lines, "We have given our hearts away" and "We are out of tune" appear
   (a) Tintern Abbey
   (b) Dover Beach
   (c) Daffodils
   (d) The World is Too Much With Us
10. Who is of the view that "Our birth is but a sleep and a forgetting"?
    (a) Browning
    (b) Shelley
    (c) Wordsworth
    (d) Keats
11. "Bliss was it in that dawn to be alive/ But to be young was very heaven"?
    Here Wordsworth is referring to
    (a) Commonwealth period
    (b) French Revolution
    (c) Augustus Age
    (d) Elizabethan Age
12. "Resolution and Independence" is a famous poem by
    (a) Byron
    (b) Keats
    (c) Leigh Hunt
    (d) Wordsworth
13. Who said, "My heart leaps up when I behold a rainbow in the sky"?
    (a) Pope
    (b) Byron
    (c) Wordsworth
    (d) Coleridge
14. About whom Tennyson said, "He is often too diffuse and didactic for me"?
    (a) Coleridge
    (b) Keats
    (c) Eliot
    (d) Wordsworth
15. Who is of the view that "All things that love the sun are out of doors"?
    (a) Shelley
    (b) Keats
    (c) Wordsworth
    (d) Coleridge
16. Who called Wordsworth a 'moral eunuch'?
    (a) Arnold
    (b) Coleridge
    (c) Shelley
    (d) Browning
17. "Michael" of Wordsworth was
    (a) not included in Lyrical Ballads
    (b) included later in Lyrical Ballads
    (c) included in Lyrical Ballads
    (d) never included in Lyrical Ballads
18. Keats's statement that "We hate poetry that has palpable design upon us" is said in relation to
    (a) Wordsworth
    (b) Southey
    (c) Black
    (d) Coleridge
19. "And never turned a stone" appears in which of the following poems?
    (a) Leech Gatherer
    (b) Ode to Duty
    (c) Michael
    (d) Tintern Abbey
20. Wordsworth's first publication was
    (a) *Descriptive Sketches*
    (b) *Lyrical Ballads*
    (c) *Ecclesiastical Sonnets*
    (d) *Poetical Sketches*
21. For whom did Browning say, "For a handful of silver he left us"?
    (a) Tennyson
    (b) Wordsworth
    (c) Byron
    (d) Coleridge
22. Who defined poetry as "spontaneous overflow of powerful feelings" and "emotion recollected in tranquility"?

(a) Emerson
(b) Edgar Allen Poe
(c) Wordsworth
(d) Tennyson

23. *Lyrical Ballads* came out in
(a) 1797
(b) 1798
(c) 1800
(d) 1802

24. The first poem in *Lyrical Ballads* is
(a) "The Rime of the Ancient Mariner"
(b) "Christabel"
(c) "Tintern Abbey"
(d) "The Idiot Boy"

25. The title of Wordsworth's imitations ode is
(a) *Ode : Intimations of Immortality from Childhood Memories*
(b) *Intimations of Immortality*
(c) *Ode : Intimations of Immortality from Recollections of Early Childhood*
(d) *Intimations of Immortality : An Ode*

26. This line occurs in: "Our noisy years seem moments in the being of the eternal silence.""
(a) "Resolution and Independence"
(b) "Michael"
(c) "The Prelude"
(d) "Intimations of Immortality"

27. The subtitle of "The Prelude" is
(a) "Emotions Recollected in Tranquility"
(b) "Reflections of an Age Past"
(c) "Beliefs of a Poet"
(d) "Growth of a Poet's Mind"

28. Which of Wordsworth's poems is autobiographical?
(a) "The Prelude"
(b) "Michael"
(c) "The Solitary Reaper"
(d) "Lucy poems"

29. The subtitle of Michael is
(a) "The Lonely Boy"
(b) "The Child of Nature"
(c) "The Story of a Boy's Childhood"
(d) "A Pastoral Poem"

30. "All good poetry is the spontaneous overflow of powerful feelings."

Where did Wordsworth say this?
(a) In *The Edinburgh Review*
(b) In the Introduction to "The Prelude"
(c) In the Preface to "Lyrical Balads"
(d) In a letter to Coleridge

31. Which of the following works influenced Wordsworth the most?
(a) William Godwin's *Political Justice*
(b) Shelley's "Queen Mab"
(c) Byron's "English Bards and Scotch Reviewers"
(d) None of the above

32. "Water, water, every where,/ Nor any drop to drink." We find these lines in
(a) *Three Years She Grew in Sun and Shower*
(b) *Westminster Bridge*
(c) *The Rime of the Ancient Mariner*
(d) *Tintern Abbey*

33. Dejection : An Ode is autobiographical which is originally intended as a letter in verse to......
(a) Sara Fricker
(b) Sara Coleridge
(c) Wordsworth
(d) Sara Hutchinson

34. "A sadder and wiser man/ He rose the morrow morn"

Who is the wiser man?
(a) Kubla Khan
(b) The Ancient Mariner
(c) Dejection: An Ode
(d) Christabel

35. Of the following who is the poet of supernaturalism?
    (a) Coleridge
    (b) Wordsworth
    (c) Shelley
    (d) Southey
36. "The Rime of the Ancient Mariner" was one of four poems Coleridge contributed to *Lyrical Ballads*. How many poems did Wordsworth contribute to the volume?
    (a) 17
    (b) 19
    (c) 22
    (d) 4
37. Which of the following poems of Coleridge uses the myths of Lamia and Vampire?
    (a) "The Rime of the Ancient Mariner"
    (b) "Frost at Midnight"
    (c) "Christabel"
    (d) "Dejection: An Ode"
38. The phrases "Starlit Dome" and "Road to Xanadu" appear in which of the following poems?
    (a) "The Ancient Mariner"
    (b) "Christabel"
    (c) "Kubla Khan"
    (d) "Frost at Midnight"
39. Which work of Coleridge, among the following, is on the subject of Philosophy?
    (a) Biographia Literaria
    (b) Table Talk
    (c) Aids to Reflection
    (d) Christabel
40. *Lectures on Shakespeare* by Coleridge was published
    (a) The year he died
    (b) Posthusmously
    (c) In his lifetime
    (d) In his mature years
41. Coleridge discusses the difference between fancy and imagination in his
    (a) "Biographia Literaria"
    (b) "Aids to Reflection"
    (c) "Kubla Khan"
    (d) "The Friend"
42. Which poem did Coleridge compose in the presence of his sleeping, infant son, Hartley?
    (a) "The Rime of the Ancient Mariner"
    (b) "Frost at Midnight"
    (c) "Kubla Khan"
    (d) "Christabel"
43. Which bird is killed by the Mariner in Coleridge's "The Rime of the Ancient Mariner"?
    (a) Ostrich
    (b) Penguin
    (c) Peacock
    (d) Albatross
44. The number of lectures delivered by Coleridge on Shakespeare is
    (a) 45
    (b) 43
    (c) 48
    (d) 46
45. Who said, "I never thought as a child, never had the language of a child"?
    (a) Wordsworth
    (b) Coleridge
    (c) Keats
    (d) Shelley
46. Who defines elegy as the form of poetry natural to the reflective mind which may use any subject so long as it is related to the poet himself.
    (a) Coleridge
    (b) John Keats
    (c) P.B. Shelley
    (d) Thomas Gray

47. Who composed these lines: "He prayeth best, who loveth best/

    All things both great and small;/ For the dear God who loveth us,/ He made and loveth all"?
    (a) Cowper's "God Made the Country"
    (b) Coleridge's "Kubla Khan"
    (c) Blake's "Holy Thursday"
    (d) Coleridge's "Ancient Mariner"
48. The phrase, "Wonderful philosophical impartiality" was used by
    (a) Tennyson
    (b) Coleridge
    (c) Blake
    (d) Arnold
49. Who is an opium-addict?
    (a) Coleridge
    (b) De Quincey
    (c) Shelley
    (d) Blake
50. Who wrote:

    "O Lady : we receive but what we give, And in our life alone does nature live"?
    (a) Keats
    (b) Coleridge
    (c) Wordsworth
    (d) Rousseau
51. The phrase "the high road of life" was used by
    (a) Wordsworth
    (b) Kipling
    (c) T.S. Eliot
    (d) Coleridge
52. *Thalaba the Destroyer* was written by Robert Southey which was based on
    (a) Hindu Mythology
    (b) Muslim Legend
    (c) South Indian Myth
    (d) Christian Faith
53. "The Curse of Kehama" was written by Robert Southey which was based on
    (a) Hindu Mythology
    (b) Muslim Lagend
    (c) South Indian Myth
    (d) Christian Faith
54. About whom is it said, "My Days Among the Dead are Past"?
    (a) Walter Scott
    (b) P.B. Shelley
    (c) Southey
    (d) Coleridge
55. Whom did Wordsworth succeed as the Poet Laureate?
    (a) Lord Byron
    (b) Robert Southey
    (c) S.T. Coleridge
    (d) William Blake
56. Byron directed his satire mainly against
    (a) Shelley
    (b) Pope
    (c) Southey
    (d) Wordsworth
57. Which of the following poems of Southey is not long?
    (a) "Joan of Arc"
    (b) "Thalaba the Destroyer"
    (c) "The Curse of Kehama"
    (d) "The Battle of Blenheim"
58. Who said "...if poetry comes not as naturally as the leaves to a tree, it had better not come at all."
    (a) Keats
    (b) Coleridge
    (c) Wordsworth
    (d) Spenser
59. Who is of the view that "Beauty is truth and truth beauty."

(a) Keats
(b) Wordsworth
(c) Shelley
(d) Blake

60. The subtitle of "Endymion" is
(a) "A Dream"
(b) "A Poetic Romance"
(c) "The Lover of Lovers"
(d) "The Shepherd's Story"

61. Keats' statement that "We hate poetry that has palpable design upon us" is said in relation to
(a) Coleridge
(b) Blake
(c) Southey
(d) Wordsworth

62. "On First Looking into Chapman's Homer" is about Keats praise of
(a) Homer
(b) Chapman
(c) Chapman's Translation of Homer
(d) Art of poetry

63. Byron's "English Bards and Scotch Reviewers" is about
(a) The survey of English poetry
(b) The contemporary literacy scene
(c) A satire against poetry
(d) Both (a) and (b)

64. Who said that Byron was "mad, bad and dangerous to know"?
(a) Arnold
(b) Lady Lamb
(c) Eliot
(d) Tennyson

65. Shelley's *The Cenci* is a
(a) Masque
(b) Tragedy
(c) Comedy
(d) Prose Romance

66. Who married Mary Wollstonecraft in 1797?
(a) Godwin
(b) Horace Walpole
(c) Shelley
(d) None of these

67. "Don Juan" was written by
(a) Tennyson
(b) Pound
(c) Eliot
(d) Byron

68. The above work is a
(a) Heroic tragedy
(b) Elegy
(c) Romance
(d) Epic satire

69. Which tragedy of Lord Byron was not produced in 1821
(a) "Manfred"
(b) Marino Faliero
(c) The Two Foscari
(d) Cain

70. In style and structure, which poem of Keats is modeled on Paradise Lost?
(a) Endymion
(b) Isabella
(c) Hyperion
(d) Lamia

71. Who said, "first in beauty should be first in might"?
(a) Frost
(b) Shelley
(c) Keats
(d) Coleridge

72. "A thing of beauty is a joy for ever."

In which poem of Keats the above line appears:
(a) "Lamia"
(b) "Endymion"
(c) "When I Have Fears"
(d) "I Had a Dove"

73. "Here lies one whose name was writ in water" is the epitaph on whose tombstone in Rome?
   (a) Sidney
   (b) Byron
   (c) Shelley
   (d) Keats

74. Which one of the following works of Keats is a story of the elopement of two lovers?
   (a) Isabella
   (b) Hyperion
   (c) The Eve of St. Agnes
   (d) Lamia

75. Which work of Keats is based on Burton's *The Anatomy of Melancholy*?
   (a) Endymion
   (b) Lamia
   (c) Isabella
   (d) Hyperion

76. Keats took the "Endymion" story from
   (a) Greek Mythology
   (b) Italian Folk Tale
   (c) Irish legends
   (d) Roman myths

77. Who says, "I am certain of nothing but the holiness of the heart's affection and truth of imagination"?
   (a) Coleridge
   (b) Keats
   (c) Wordsworth
   (d) Cowper

78. Which work of Keats deals with the murder of a lady's lover by her two wicked brothers?
   (a) Endymion
   (b) Isabella
   (c) Hyperion
   (d) Lamia

79. The term 'Negative Capability' was given by
   (a) Coleridge
   (b) Eliot
   (c) Wordsworth
   (d) Keats

80. Who died of Tuberculosis?
   (a) Coleridge
   (b) Southey
   (c) Keats
   (d) Shelley

81. Which one of Keats's work is based on Drayton's *The Man in the Moon* and Fletcher's *The Faithful Shepherdess*?
   (a) Isabella (1818)
   (b) Endymion (1818)
   (c) Hyperion (1819)
   (d) The Eve of St. Agnes (1819)

82. Which one of the following works of Samuel Rogers is a Byronic tale?
   (a) *The Pleasures of Memory* (1792)
   (b) *Columbus* (1822)
   (c) *Jacqueline* (1814)
   (d) *Italy* (1922)

83. Who said, "I awoke one morning and found myself famous"?
   (a) Shelley
   (b) Byron
   (c) Pound
   (d) More

84. Which play of Byron is about an outcast who defies the censure of the world?
   (a) *Manfred*
   (b) *Cain*
   (c) *Marino*
   (d) *The Deformed Transformed*

85. A Byronic hero is he who is
   (a) Vain and melancholy
   (b) Cynical
   (c) Finds no good in life or love or anything
   (d) All of the above

86. Who wrote:

"It is strange but true; for truth is always strange; stranger than fiction"?

(a) Keats
(b) Shelley
(c) Blake
(d) Byron

87. "She walks in Beauty like the night" appears in
(a) Keats
(b) Shelley
(c) Browning
(d) Byron

88. Shelley was influenced by the book
(a) *The Medal*
(b) *Political Justice*
(c) *The Seasons*
(d) *Songs of Innocence*

89. Who wrote the following lines—"The desire of the month for the star,/ Of the might for the morrow/ The devotion to something afar/ From the sphere of our sorrow"?
(a) Coleridge
(b) Arnold
(c) Donne
(d) Shelley

90. For which book was Shelley expelled from Oxford?
(a) *Queen Mab*
(b) *The Necessity of Atheism*
(c) *Alaster*
(d) *The Cenci*

91. On which work was Shelley working when he died?
(a) *Queen Mab*
(b) *Alaster*
(c) *The Cenci*
(d) *The Triumph of Life*

92. Shelley's 'Adonais' in a/an _____ on Keats
(a) satire
(b) defense
(c) elegy
(d) lyric

93. The only instance of comedy during the Romantic period is *Oedipus Tyrannous* or *Swellfoot the Tyrant*. Who wrote it?
(a) Keats
(b) Shelley
(c) Coleridge
(d) Wordsworth

94. *Intellectual Beauty* is a composition by
(a) Keats
(b) Yeats
(c) Shelley
(d) Coleridge

95. Who was of the view that "hell is a city much like London"?
(a) Tennyson
(b) Wordsworth
(c) Keats
(d) Shelley

96. "Our Sweetest songs are those that tell us of saddest thoughts" comes from
(a) Keats
(b) Shelley
(c) Hardy
(d) Arnold

97. Which of the following poems of Shelley represents Byron through a character?
(a) "The Mask of Anarchy"
(b) "Epipsychidion"
(c) "Julian and Maddalo"
(d) "Adonais"

98. Shelley's "The Defence of Poetry" (1821) was provoked by
(a) Godwin
(b) Burke
(c) Peacock
(d) Byron

99. The prophetic words, "If winter comes, can spring be far behind," are from
    (a) Arthur Clough
    (b) Keats
    (c) Browning
    (d) Shelley

100. Who thinks of the poet as "the unacknowledged legislator of the world"?
    (a) Shelley
    (b) Keats
    (c) Coleridge
    (d) Arnold

101. Which is Shelley's autobiographical poem?
    (a) "Adonais"
    (b) "Alaster"
    (c) "Queen Mab"
    (d) "The Cenci"

102. Who considers Shelley as a "beautiful and ineffectual angel beating in the void his luminous wings in vain"?
    (a) Johnson
    (b) Eliot
    (c) Arnold
    (d) Pater

103. *Alastor* (1816) was written by
    (a) Keats
    (b) Browning
    (c) Shelley
    (d) Arnold

104. Who considers Jane Austen "a writer of serious domestic comedy, a mode in which she has attained something like perfection?"
    (a) Forster
    (b) Graham Hough
    (c) Joyce
    (d) I.A. Richards

105. John Thorpe is a character in the novel
    (a) *Pride and Prejudice*
    (b) *Emma*
    (c) *Northanger Abbey*
    (d) *Mansfield Park*

106. Whose novels can be considered as domestic or 'the tea table' novels
    (a) Eliot
    (b) Jane Austen
    (c) Henry Fielding
    (d) Walter Scott

107. Match the characters and their novels

| | |
|---|---|
| (a) Harriet Smith | 1. *Mansfield Park* |
| (b) Captain Wentworth | 2. *Pride and Prejudice* |
| (c) Fanny Price | 3. *Emma* |
| (d) Elizabeth Bennet | 4. *Persuasion* |

| **Codes:** | A | B | C | D |
|---|---|---|---|---|
| (a) | 3 | 4 | 1 | 2 |
| (b) | 1 | 4 | 2 | 3 |
| (c) | 4 | 2 | 3 | 1 |
| (d) | 1 | 2 | 3 | 4 |

108. Which of the following novels has a Gothic touch to it?
    (a) *Persuasion*
    (b) *Sense and Sensibility*
    (c) *Northanger Abbey*
    (d) *Emma*

109. Jane Austen's first novel was
    (a) *Emma*
    (b) *Persuasion*
    (c) *Pride and Prejudice*
    (d) *Sense and Sensibility*

110. Which of the following novels of Jane Austen was posthumously published?
    (a) *Northanger Abbey* (1818)
    (b) *Mansfield Park* (1814)
    (c) *Emma* (1816)
    (d) *Persuasion* (1815-16)

111. Which of Austen's following novels deals with elopement?
    (a) *Emma*
    (b) *Pride and Prejudice*
    (c) *Mansfield Park*
    (d) None of the above

112. Mr. Collins is a character in which of the following?
   (a) *Persuasion*
   (b) *Sense and Sensibility*
   (c) *Pride and Prejudice*
   (d) *Emma*

113. Miss Bates in *Emma* is
   (a) Shy
   (b) Servile
   (c) Garrulous
   (d) Discreet

114. In which Jane Austen's novel do we find the Dashwood sisters?
   (a) *Pride and Prejudice*
   (b) *Mansfield Park*
   (c) *Northanger Abbey*
   (d) *Sense and Sensibility*

115. "Sense is the foundation on which everything good may be based". Who said it?
   (a) Thomas Carlyle
   (b) Charles Lamb
   (c) Jane Austen
   (d) William Wordsworth

116. Which novel of Jane Austen was published last of all?
   (a) *Pride and Prejudice*
   (b) *Persuasion*
   (c) *Sense and Sensibility*
   (d) *Northanger Abbey*

117. Jane Austen died of
   (a) Consumption
   (b) Amnesia
   (c) Depression
   (d) Addison's disease

118. Catherine Morland is the heroine of which Austen's novel?
   (a) *Pride and prejudice*
   (b) *Emma*
   (c) *Northanger Abbey*
   (d) *Persuasion*

119. "It is a truth universally acknowledged that a single man in possession of a good fortune must be in want of a wife."

   Which Austen's novel begins this way?
   (a) *Emma*
   (b) *Pride and Prejudice*
   (c) *Mansfield Park*
   (d) *Sense and Sensibility*

120. "She was nobody with either father or sister: her word had no weight : her convenience was always to give away ; she was only Anne."

   Identify the novel
   (a) *Persuasion*
   (b) *Mansfield Park*
   (c) *Emma*
   (d) *Pride and Prejudice*

121. Fanny Price figures in
   (a) *Pride and Prejudice*
   (b) *Persuasion*
   (c) *Mansfield Park*
   (d) *Sense and Sensibility*

122. Mr. Flosky in *Nightmare Abbey* is
   (a) *Shelley*
   (b) *Wordsworth*
   (c) *Coleridge*
   (d) *Byron*

123. Who is the master of *Nightmare Abbey*?
   (a) *Mr. Glory*
   (b) *Mr. Hilary*
   (c) *Mr. Asterias*
   (d) *Mr. Flosky*

124. Who wrote *Nightmare Abbey* (1818)?
   (a) P.B. Shelley
   (b) Mary Shelley
   (c) Thomas Love Peacock
   (d) Jane Austen

125. Who were the "Lake Poets"?
   (a) Wordsworth, Coleridge, Southey
   (b) Tennyson, Arnold, Browning

(c) Gray, Collins, Burns
(d) Dryden, Pope, Arnold

126. The Romantic age was the age of
(a) Prose Fiction
(b) Drama
(c) Epic
(d) Lyric

127. Who wrote, "Long Poem in the Age of Wordsworth"?
(a) A.C. Swinburne
(b) A.C. Bradley
(c) S.T. Coleridge
(d) T.S. Eliot

128. The Waverley Novels are associated with
(a) Thomas Hardy
(b) Jane Austen
(c) W.M. Thackeray
(d) Walter Scott

129. Which of the following is not a Waverley Novel?
(a) *Ivanhoe*
(b) *The Black Dwarf*
(c) *The Antiquary*
(d) *Guy Mannering*

130. Match the characters and their novels

| | |
|---|---|
| A. Bailie Jarvie | 1. *The Heart of Midlothian* |
| B. Peter Peebles | 2. *Guy Mannering* |
| C. Madge Wildfire | 3. *Rob Roy* |
| D. Meg Merrilies | 4. *Redgauntlet* |

| **Codes:** | A | B | C | D |
|---|---|---|---|---|
| (a) | 3 | 4 | 1 | 2 |
| (b) | 1 | 2 | 3 | 4 |
| (c) | 2 | 3 | 3 | 4 |
| (d) | 3 | 2 | 4 | 1 |

131. The subtitle of Waverley is
(a) *Tis Sixty Year Since*
(b) *Sixty Years Later*
(c) *It is Sixty Years Hence*
(d) *After Sixty Years*

132. Which of the following works was written by Walter Scott?
(a) *Tales of a Grandfather*
(b) *Lay of the Last Minstrel*
(c) *Woodstock*
(d) All of the above

133. Lochinvar has been taken from the larger poetic work
(a) *The Lay of the Last Minstrel*
(b) *Marmion*
(c) *The Lady of the Lake*
(d) None of the above

134. Who said about Scott that he (Scott) "can not construct" and he has "a trivial mind and a heavy style"?
(a) E.M. Forster
(b) George Eliot
(c) Jane Austen
(d) Hazlitt

135. Who said that Scott "has neither artistic detachment nor passion"?
(a) Forster
(b) Joyce
(c) I.A. Richards
(d) F.R. Leavis

136. Walter Scott brought out his novel *A Legend of Montrose* in the year
(a) 1817
(b) 1818
(c) 1819
(d) 1821

137. The History of England is "a theme of Scott's novel"
(a) *Old Morality*
(b) *The Antiquary*
(c) *Waverley*
(d) *Ivanhoe*

138. In *Ivanhoe*, what is the name of the disguised Robin Hood?
(a) Brian de Bois-Guilbert
(b) Katherine

(c) William Breck
(d) Robert Louis Basselt

139. Who is considered to be the founder of historical novel?
(a) Richardson
(b) Walter Scott
(c) Virginia Woolf
(d) James Joyce

140. Scott's novels *Anne of Grierstein* and *Kenilworth* are based on ______ history.
(a) British
(b) Roman
(c) Latin
(d) French

141. Who regarded *Waverley* as one of the best things that has been written in the world.
(a) Gaskell
(b) Goethe
(c) Godwin
(d) Thackeray

142. Walter Scott's *The Minstrelsy of the Scottish Border* is a work
(a) Of his own poems
(b) Of Scott and his contemporaries
(c) Of editing old material
(d) Edited by several hands including Scott

143. Which of the following novels of Scott deals with the murder of Lady Leicester?
(a) *The Pirate*
(b) *Kenilworth*
(c) *The Fair Maid*
(d) *Ivanhoe*

144. The title of Scott's novel *The Heart of Midlothian* (1818) is derived from a
(a) Palace in London
(b) Castle in Windsor
(c) Prison in Edinburgh
(d) School in London

145. Samuel Johnson wrote the *Lives of the Poets*. Who wrote the *Lives of the Novelists*?
(a) Jane Austen
(b) Maria Edgeworth
(c) Walter Scott
(d) George Eliot

146. "Say Not, the Struggle Naught Availeth" is a poem by
(a) Leigh Hunt
(b) A.H. Clough
(c) Robert Browning
(d) William Shakespeare

147. *Virginibus Pureisque* a collection of essays was written by
(a) Hazlitt
(b) Goldsmith
(c) R.L. Stevenson
(d) Dr. Johnson

148. "Rejected Addresses" (1812) was written by
(a) James Smith
(b) Horace Smith
(c) Both (a) and (b)
(d) None of the above

149. *The Rehearsal* was written by
(a) Sheridan
(b) Congreve
(c) Goldsmith
(d) Duke of Buckingham

150. Who attacked the immorality of the English stage
(a) Stephen Gosson
(b) Sidney
(c) Jeremy Collier
(d) Love Peacock

151. Who came to be known as the "Corn law Rhymer"?
(a) Spenser
(b) Leigh Hunt
(c) James Hogg
(d) Ebenezer Elliot

152. Sir Leslie Stephen, an eminent critic, is the father of

(a) Jane Austen
(b) George Eliot
(c) Virginia Woolf
(d) Sarah Fielding

153. Walter De La Mare (1873-1956) wrote the poem -
(a) "The Listeners"
(b) "Lycidias"
(c) "Thyrsis"
(d) "Say Not the Struggle Nought Availeth"

154. The poem "Abu Ben Adhem" was written by
(a) Robert Browning
(b) P.B. Shelley
(c) Leigh Hunt
(d) Robert Southey

155. Who claimed that "my love is like a red, red rose"?
(a) Lord Byron
(b) John Keats
(c) Robert Burns
(d) Christopher Smart

156. Who wrote "A Vindication of the Rights of Women"?
(a) Mary Shelley
(b) Mary Wollstonecraft
(c) Mary Ann Evans
(d) Mary Lamb

157. *Imaginary Conversations of Literary Men and Statesmen* was written by
(a) Savage Landor
(b) Hazlitt
(c) De Quincey
(d) Charles Lamb

158. "Confessions of an English Opium—Eater" was written by
(a) Hazlitt
(b) De Quincey
(c) Coleridge
(d) Walter Savage Landor

159. "Confessions of an English Opium-Eater" is a/an
(a) Autobiographical poem
(b) Collection of essays
(c) Collection of articles
(d) Autobiographical narrative

160. The sequel to confessions was called
(a) More Confessions of an Opium Eater
(b) Suspiria de Profundis
(c) Confessions Part II
(d) English Mail-Coach

161. Which of the following claims to be a "Hibernian tale taken from facts and from the manners of the Irish squires before the year 1782"?
(a) Castle Rackrent
(b) Castle of Indolence
(c) The Monk
(d) Mysteries of Udolpho

162. Who wrote *The Age of Reason* (1793)?
(a) Rousseau
(b) Thomas Paine
(c) William Godwin
(d) Edmund Burke

163. Who wrote the Oriental tale "Lalla Rookh" (1817)?
(a) Leigh Hunt
(b) Walter Scott
(c) Thomas Moore
(d) Robert Southey

164. The subtitle of "Lalla Rookh" is
(a) The Veiled Prophet of Khorassan
(b) An Oriental Romance
(c) Paradise and the Peri
(d) The Light of the Harem

165. Which of the following is not a part of "Lalla Rookh"?
(a) *The Fire-Worshippers*
(b) *The Mermaid*
(c) *The Light of the Harem*
(d) *Paradise and the Peri*

166. Who wrote under the name of Christopher North
   (a) James Hogg
   (b) John Gibson Lockhart
   (c) John Wilson
   (d) None of the above

167. "Noctes Ambrisianae" (1822-35) is a series of imaginary conversations. Who was not a 'contributor to this work'?
   (a) John Wilson
   (b) James Hogg
   (c) John Gibson
   (d) None of the above

168. Which romantic author's boisterous manner and short temper were caricatured by Dickens in the character of Boythorn in his *Bleak House*?
   (a) S.T. Coleridge
   (b) P.B. Shelley
   (c) Walter Savage Landor
   (d) William Hazlitt

169. Who wrote the *Life of Byron*?
   (a) Robert Southey
   (b) Thomas Moore
   (c) Samuel Rogers
   (d) Thomas Campbell

170. Thomas Hood is better known by which of the following?
   (a) *The Song of the Shirt*
   (b) *Whims and Oddities*
   (c) *The Bridge of Sighs*
   (d) *Hero and Leander*

171. Who among the following is known as a peasant poet?
   (a) Thomas Moore
   (b) Thomas Hood
   (c) James Hogg
   (d) John Clare

172. John Clare is best known for which of the following?
   (a) *Poems Descriptive of Rural Life and Scenery*
   (b) *The Shepherd's Calendar*
   (c) *The Rural Muse*
   (d) *The Village Minstrel*

173. "On Murder Considered as One of the Fine Arts" by De Quincey is about
   (a) Shakespearean tragedy
   (b) Black humour
   (c) Elizabethan comedy
   (d) Jacobean tragedy

174. "On Knocking at the Gate in Macbeth" was written by
   (a) L.C. Knights
   (b) C.S. Lewis
   (c) De Quincey
   (d) A.C. Bradley

175. Who gave the slogan 'Back to Nature'?
   (a) Wordsworth
   (b) Cowper
   (c) Rousseau
   (d) Pope

176. Peterloo massacre took place in
   (a) 1891
   (b) 1890
   (c) 1819
   (d) 1765

177. Peninsular war began in
   (a) 1798
   (b) 1808
   (c) 1882
   (d) 1782

178. *Sybil*, a novel, is a powerful exposure of the abuses related to "capital and labour". Who wrote it?
   (a) Tennyson
   (b) Benjamin Disraeli
   (c) Mrs. Gaskell
   (d) Charles Dickens

179. Which one of the following works of Thomas Campbell is a tale of Pennsylvania?
(a) *Pleasures of Hope*
(b) *The Pilgrim of Glencoe*
(c) *The Battle of the Baltic*
(d) *Gertrude of Wyoming*

180. Which novel of James Cooper deals with the sea?
(a) *Precaution* (1820)
(b) *The Spy* (1821)
(c) *The Pilot*
(d) *The Pathfinder* (1840)

181. *Essays on Education, Manners and Literature* was written by
(a) Dryden
(b) Pope
(c) Johnson
(d) William Godwin

182. William Godwin brought out his *The Inquiry Concerning Political Justice* in the year
(a) 1784
(b) 1793
(c) 1795
(d) 1799

183. Who called Heywood "a sort of prose Shakespeare"?
(a) Evelyn Waugh
(b) Gibbons
(c) Pope
(d) Bacon

184. The second creative period of English Literature is the
(a) Neo-Classicism
(b) Romantic Period
(c) Victorian Age
(d) Puritan Age

185. *Melmoth, the Wanderer* is a Gothic novel by
(a) Lewis
(b) Clara Reeve
(c) Robert Maturin
(d) Robert Bage

186. Which of the following was Blake's first volume of poems?
(a) *Songs of Innocence*
(b) *Songs of Experience*
(c) *Poetical Sketches*
(d) *The Book of Thel*

187. "Tyger, Tyger, burning bright" appears in
(a) *Songs of Experience*
(b) *Songs of Innocence*
(c) *The Book of Urizen*
(d) *Poetical Sketches*

188. Blake's dictum that Milton was "a true poet and of the Devil's party without knowing it" appears in
(a) *The Marriage of Heaven and Hell*
(b) *Europe*
(c) *Jerusalem*
(d) *Milton*

189. "Without contraries there is no progression" appears in
(a) Milton
(b) Keats
(c) Blake
(d) Shelley

190. "To generalize is to be an idiot" comes from
(a) Johnson
(b) Byron
(c) Blake
(d) Pope

191. Who said that "ruins of time build mansions in eternity"?
(a) Pope
(b) Arnold
(c) Tennyson
(d) Blake

192. Who does not belong to "Satanic School" of criticism?
   (a) W.B. Yeats
   (b) W.H. Auden
   (c) T.S. Eliot
   (d) William Blake
193. Blake's Prophetic Books does not include the poem
   (a) "The Marriage of Heaven and Hell"
   (b) "Milton and Jerusalem"
   (c) "Songs of Innocence"
   (d) "The First Book of Urizen"
194. Who believes that "A tyrant is the worst, disease, and the cause of the all others"?
   (a) Pope
   (b) Bacon
   (c) Blake
   (d) Eliot
195. Who wrote the following lines:

   "And their sun does never shine/ And their fields are bleak and bare/ And their ways are fill'd with thorns

   It is eternal winter there"?
   (a) Blake
   (b) Arnold
   (c) Swift
   (d) Eliot
196. Who believes that "the tigers of wrath are wiser than the horses of instruct"?
   (a) Pope
   (b) Swift
   (c) Blake
   (d) Shelley
197. Who said, "Pity would be no more, if we did not make somebody poor"?
   (a) Shelley
   (b) Wordsworth
   (c) Blake
   (d) De Quincey
198. Who postulated the 'noble savage'?
   (a) Southey
   (b) Blake
   (c) Hazlitt
   (d) Rousseau
199. Who else besides Lamb studied at Christ's Hospital?
   (a) Hazlitt
   (b) Coleridge
   (c) Keats
   (d) Leigh Hunt
200. "Specimens of English Dramatic Poets, who lived about the Time of Shakespeare," by Charles Lamb, represents
   (a) Major dramatists
   (b) Minor dramatists
   (c) Classic dramatists
   (d) Romantic dramatists
201. "Tales from Shakespeare" was written by Lamb in collaboration with
   (a) William Hazlitt
   (b) Thomas de Quincey
   (c) Leigh Hunt
   (d) Mary Lamb
202. "Essays of Elia" was written by
   (a) Mary Lamb
   (b) Charles Lamb
   (c) William Hazlitt
   (d) De Quincey
203. Who wrote *Mr. H* (1806)?
   (a) Mary Shelley
   (b) P.B. Shelley
   (c) Charles Lamb
   (d) Thomas Moore
204. *Mr. H* is a
   (a) Satire
   (b) Drama
   (c) Farce
   (d) Novel

205. Which of the following are written by Charles Lamb?
(a) *The Adventures of Ulysses* (1808)
(b) *Mrs. Leicester's School* (1809)
(c) *Prince Dorus* (1811)
(d) All of the above

206. Who wrote the essay *On the Character and Genius of Hogarth*?
(a) Leigh Hunt
(b) Thomas De Quincey
(c) William Hazlitt
(d) Charles Lamb

207. Who is known as, "the prince of English Essayists"?
(a) Lamb
(b) Addison
(c) Eliot
(d) Steele

208. Who wrote, "For thy sake, tobacco, I would do anything but die"?
(a) Keats
(b) Lamb
(c) Coleridge
(d) Shelley

209. What is the subtitle of *Frankenstein* which is written by Mary Shelley?
(a) *The Man-Eating Monster*
(b) *The Cannibal*
(c) *The Modern Prometheus*
(d) *The Giant of Olympia*

210. *Frankenstein* was dedicated to
(a) Mary Wollstonecraft
(b) William Godwin
(c) P.B. Shelley
(d) Claire Clairmont

## ANSWERS

| | | | | | |
|---|---|---|---|---|---|
| 1. (b) | 2. (a) | 3. (c) | 4. (d) | 5. (b) | 6. (c) |
| 7. (a) | 8. (c) | 9. (d) | 10. (c) | 11. (b) | 12. (d) |
| 13. (c) | 14. (d) | 15. (c) | 16. (c) | 17. (b) | 18. (a) |
| 19. (c) | 20. (a) | 21. (b) | 22. (c) | 23. (b) | 24. (a) |
| 25. (c) | 26. (d) | 27. (d) | 28. (a) | 29. (d) | 30. (c) |
| 31. (a) | 32. (c) | 33. (d) | 34. (b) | 35. (a) | 36. (b) |
| 37. (c) | 38. (c) | 39. (c) | 40. (b) | 41. (a) | 42. (b) |
| 43. (d) | 44. (b) | 45. (b) | 46. (a) | 47. (d) | 48. (b) |
| 49. (a) | 50. (b) | 51. (d) | 52. (b) | 53. (a) | 54. (c) |
| 55. (b) | 56. (a) | 57. (d) | 58. (a) | 59. (a) | 60. (b) |
| 61. (d) | 62. (c) | 63. (d) | 64. (b) | 65. (b) | 66. (c) |
| 67. (d) | 68. (d) | 69. (a) | 70. (c) | 71. (c) | 72. (b) |
| 73. (d) | 74. (c) | 75. (b) | 76. (a) | 77. (b) | 78. (b) |
| 79. (d) | 80. (c) | 81. (b) | 82. (c) | 83. (b) | 84. (b) |
| 85. (d) | 86. (d) | 87. (d) | 88. (b) | 89. (d) | 90. (b) |
| 91. (d) | 92. (c) | 93. (b) | 94. (c) | 95. (d) | 96. (b) |
| 97. (c) | 98. (c) | 99. (d) | 100. (a) | 101. (b) | 102. (c) |
| 103. (c) | 104. (b) | 105. (c) | 106. (b) | 107. (a) | 108. (c) |

| | | | | | |
|---|---|---|---|---|---|
| 109. (d) | 110. (a) | 111. (b) | 112. (c) | 113. (c) | 114. (d) |
| 115. (c) | 116. (b) | 117. (d) | 118. (c) | 119. (b) | 120. (a) |
| 121. (c) | 122. (c) | 123. (a) | 124. (c) | 125. (a) | 126. (d) |
| 127. (b) | 128. (d) | 129. (a) | 130. (a) | 131. (a) | 132. (d) |
| 133. (b) | 134. (a) | 135. (a) | 136. (c) | 137. (d) | 138. (a) |
| 139. (b) | 140. (d) | 141. (b) | 142. (c) | 143. (b) | 144. (c) |
| 145. (c) | 146. (b) | 147. (c) | 148. (c) | 149. (d) | 150. (c) |
| 151. (d) | 152. (c) | 153. (a) | 154. (c) | 155. (c) | 156. (b) |
| 157. (a) | 158. (b) | 159. (d) | 160. (b) | 161. (a) | 162. (b) |
| 163. (c) | 164. (b) | 165. (b) | 166. (c) | 167. (d) | 168. (c) |
| 169. (b) | 170. (a) | 171. (d) | 172. (a) | 173. (b) | 174. (c) |
| 175. (c) | 176. (c) | 177. (b) | 178. (b) | 179. (d) | 180. (c) |
| 181. (d) | 182. (b) | 183. (a) | 184. (b) | 185. (c) | 186. (c) |
| 187. (a) | 188. (a) | 189. (c) | 190. (c) | 191. (d) | 192. (d) |
| 193. (c) | 194. (c) | 195. (a) | 196. (c) | 197. (c) | 198. (d) |
| 199. (b) | 200. (b) | 201. (d) | 202. (b) | 203. (c) | 204. (c) |
| 205. (d) | 206. (d) | 207. (a) | 208. (b) | 209. (c) | 210. (b) |

# 5

# The Victorian Period

1. Queen Victoria reigned from
   (a) 1836-1900
   (b) 1837-1901
   (c) 1832-1901
   (d) 1837-1900
2. Tennyson's "In Memoriam" (1850) was written to commemorate the death of
   (a) Arthur Hugh Clough
   (b) Arthur Hallam
   (c) Matthew Arnold
   (d) Robert Browning
3. Whom did Tennyson succeed as Poet Laureate in 1850?
   (a) Keats
   (b) Byron
   (c) P.B. Shelley
   (d) Wordsworth
4. Which work by Tennyson is the story of a fisherman, who is shipwrecked, and after spending 10 years on a desert island, returns home to discover, that his beloved wife, believing him dead has remarried and has a new child?
   (a) "Ulysses"
   (b) "The Lady of Shalott"
   (c) "Maud"
   (d) "Enoch Arden" (1864)
5. Which of the following is not a drama by Tennyson?
   (a) *Queen Mary*
   (b) *Harold*
   (c) *Becket*
   (d) *The Princess*
6. Which of the following pairs of Tennyson's poems is appropriate?
   (a) "Ulysses" and "The Palace of Art"
   (b) "The Lotos-Eaters" and "The Lady of Shalott"
   (c) "Ulysses" and "The Lotos-Eaters"
   (d) "Locksley Hall" and "The Palace of Art"
7. Who is the most representative poet of the Victorian age?
   (a) Swinburne
   (b) Browning
   (c) Tennyson
   (d) Arnold
8. Which of Tennyson's poems is called a "Monodrama"?
   (a) "The Princess"
   (b) "Maud"
   (c) "Ulysses"
   (d) "The Lotos Eaters"
9. Who is the author of the following lines?
   "Break, Break, Break,
   On thy cold gray stones, O Sea!"
   (a) Byron
   (b) Shelley

(c) Tennyson
(d) Browning

10. "Men may come and man may go/ But I go on for ever" comes from
(a) Tennyson
(b) Byron
(c) Arnold
(d) Browning

11. "Knowledge comes but wisdom lingers" appears in the work of
(a) Shakespeare
(b) Milton
(c) Wordsworth
(d) Tennyson

12. "It is better to have loved and lost/ Than to have never loved at all" Who is the author of the above lines?
(a) Keats
(b) Tennyson
(c) Shelley
(d) Browning

13. The Battle of Balaclava in the Crimean War finds its reference in the poem
(a) "Crossing the Bar"
(b) "Passing of Arthur"
(c) "Charge of the Light Brigade"
(d) "Maud"

14. Who informed King Arthur of the Queen's unfaithfulness to him in a poem of Tennyson?
(a) Sir Tristram
(b) The King's Nephew Modred
(c) Merlin
(d) Morgan le Faye

15. Queen Guinevere is a character in a poem of Tennyson. The name of the poem is
(a) "Maud"
(b) "Crossing the Bar"
(c) "Passing of Arthur"
(d) "In Memoriam"

16. Tennyson's lifelong ideal is expressed in
(a) "Maud"
(b) "Merlin"
(c) "Merlin and the Gleam"
(d) "The Princess"

17. Who asserted that "There remains more faith in honest doubt,/ Believe me than in half the creeds."
(a) Tennyson
(b) Pope
(c) Wordsworth
(d) Browning

18. What is the message of Tennyson's poetry
(a) Optimism
(b) Faith and trust
(c) Pessimism
(d) Frustration

19. In "The Passing of Arthur", the name of one knight of the Round Table, who was alive, is
(a) Galahad
(b) Lancelot
(c) Merlin
(d) Bedivere

20. Tennyson's *Idylls of the King* began in 1842 with the poem 'Morte' D 'Arthur'. Which is the last poem of the Idylls?
(a) Balin and Balan
(b) Gerant Enid
(c) Merlin Vivein
(d) None of the above

21. Which one of the following plays of Tennyson is a comedy based on a story from Boccaccio?
(a) *Queen Mary* (1875)
(b) *Harold* (1876)
(c) *The Falcon* (1879)
(d) *Becket* (1884)

22. Which one of the following plays of Tennyson is based on a story from Plutarch?
    (a) *The Falcon*
    (b) *The Cup*
    (c) *Becket*
    (d) *The Foresters*
23. About whom G.M. Hopkins said, "Come what may he will be one of our greatest poets"?
    (a) Arnold
    (b) Browning
    (c) Tennyson
    (d) A.H. Hallam
24. Who considered Nature as "Red in tooth and claw"?
    (a) Tennyson
    (b) Arnold
    (c) Blake
    (d) Ruskin
25. Which Browning's poem is loosely based on the life of a Florentine painter?
    (a) "My Last Duchess"
    (b) "Fra Lippo Lippi"
    (c) "Rabbi Ben Ezra"
    (d) "Andrea Del Sarto"
26. Which of the following poem contains the metaphor of life as a pot that is fashioned by the master's hand?
    (a) "Men and Women"
    (b) "Aurora Leigh"
    (c) "The Ring and the Book"
    (d) "Rabbi Ben Ezra"
27. Which dramatic poem is about an impoverished young winder of silk, who sings as she wanders aimlessly?
    (a) "Pippa Passes"
    (b) "Aurora Leigh"
    (c) "Evelyn Hope"
    (d) "Christina"
28. Which of the following has sections called "Morning", "Noon", "Evening", "Night"?
    (a) "Men and Women"
    (b) "Aurora Leigh"
    (c) "Casa Guidi Windows"
    (d) "Pippa Passes"
29. Which day is Pippa's only holiday for the entire year?
    (a) Christmas Eve
    (b) New Year Morn
    (c) Valentine's day
    (d) Easter Sunday
30. How many poems are there in Men and Women?
    (a) 21
    (b) 51
    (c) 41
    (d) 31
31. Which poem of Browning is addressed to his wife?
    (a) "My Last Duchess"
    (b) "One Word More"
    (c) "Love Among the Ruins"
    (d) "The Last Ride Together"
32. Which work of Browning is based on the proceedings of a murder trial in Rome in 1698?
    (a) "The Ring and the Book"
    (b) "Sordello"
    (c) "Men and Women"
    (d) "Bells and Pomegranates"
33. Which work of Mrs. Browning has been aptly called "a woman's love-making with a nation"?
    (a) "Aurora Leigh"
    (b) "Casa Guidi Windows"
    (c) "Seraphim and Other Poems"
    (d) "Sonnets from the Portuguese"
34. "A Fragment of a Confession" was the subtitle of

(a) "Men and Women"
(b) "The Ring and the Book"
(c) "Pauline"
(d) "Sordello"

35. Which of the following works of Browning was published first of all?
(a) "Pauline"
(b) "Paracelsus"
(c) "Sordello"
(d) "Pippa Passes"

36. "What I aspired to be/ And was not, comforts me."

These lines reveal the optimism of
(a) Robert Burns
(b) Robert Graves
(c) Robert Browning
(d) Robert Southey

37. Love is a predominant theme in the best poems of
(a) Browning
(b) Thomas Hardy
(c) Tennyson
(d) Arnold

38. "The Ring and the Book" is the most ambitious and complex work by
(a) Browning
(b) Philip Larkin
(c) Pater
(d) Oscar Wilde

39. Robert Browning eloped and married with Elizabeth Barrett in the year
(a) 1844
(b) 1846
(c) 1856
(d) 1848

40. Which public hero did Browning have in mind while writing "Patriot"?
(a) Prince Arthur
(b) Arnold of Brescia
(c) Hercules
(d) Adam

41. Browning's "Pauline" is
(a) A novel
(b) An essay
(c) A tribute to Shelley and his poetry
(d) Lament over his wife's death

42. In which work of Browning the following lines appears "God's in His Heaven And all is right with the world"?
(a) "Pauline" (1833)
(b) "Stafford" (1837)
(c) "Sordello" (1840)
(d) "Pippa Passes" (1837)

43. Which work of Browning is the story of the murder of a young wife, Pompilia, by her worthless husband in 1698?
(a) "The Ring and the Book"
(b) "Asolando"
(c) "One Word More"
(d) "Men and Women"

44. Who wrote, "...we fall to rise, are baffled to fight better, sleep to wake"?
(a) Browning
(b) Walter Pater
(c) Oscar Wilde
(d) Tennyson

45. "On Heroes and Hero Worship" was written by
(a) Thomas Carlyle
(b) Matthew Arnold
(c) J.S. Mill
(d) John Ruskin

46. "Teufelsdrockh" is a character in
(a) "Ulysses"
(b) "Amours de Voyage"
(c) "Sartor Resartus"
(d) "Aurora Leigh"

47. The theme of *Sartor Resartus* is
(a) Religion
(b) Books
(c) Clothes
(d) Feudalism

48. "Chartism" (1840) was written by
    (a) Newman
    (b) Ruskin
    (c) Macaulay
    (d) Carlyle

49. Which of the following works was written by Carlyle?
    (a) *Past and Present* (1843)
    (b) *Sartor Resartus* (1833-34)
    (c) *The French Revolution* (1837)
    (d) *On Heroes, Hero-Worship and the Heroic in History* (1841)
    (e) All of the above

50. "Seven Lamps of Architecture" was written by
    (a) William Empson
    (b) Matthew Arnold
    (c) John Ruskin
    (d) Charles Darwin

51. Which of the following is not one of the Lamps of Architecture?
    (a) Sacrifice
    (b) Power
    (c) Truth
    (d) Nature

52. Which figurative term did John Ruskin give to English Literature?
    (a) *Intentional Fallacy*
    (b) *Affective Fallacy*
    (c) *Pathetic Fallacy*
    (d) *Apathetic Fallacy*

53. Ruskin's *Unto this Last* is about
    (a) political economy
    (b) spiritual values
    (c) good conversation
    (d) painting and architecture

54. Which of the following works was written by John Ruskin?
    (a) *Sesame and Lilies* (1862)
    (b) *Munera Pulveris* (1872)
    (c) Both (a) and (b)
    (d) None of the above

55. Who regards Ruskin as "one of the greatest teachers of the age"?
    (a) George Eliot
    (b) Henry James
    (c) Arnold
    (d) Pater

56. *Praeterita* (1885-90) is an autobiography of
    (a) Walter Pater
    (b) Oscar Wilde
    (c) John Ruskin
    (d) Thomas Hardy

57. Which of the following works of Elizabeth Barrett Browning is best known (also autobiographical, covering her affair with Browning)?
    (a) *An Essay on Mind; With Other Poems* (1826)
    (b) *Prometheus Bound* (1833)
    (c) *The Seraphim and Other Poems* (1838)
    (d) *Sonnets From the Portuguese* (1847)

58. The play, *The Barretts of Wimpole Street*, is about the family of
    (a) The Barrett Brothers
    (b) The Barrett Barristers
    (c) The Barrett Bishops
    (d) The family of Elizabeth Barrett Browning

59. Sketches by 'Boz' was written by
    (a) Henry James
    (b) George Eliot
    (c) Charles Dickens
    (d) W.M. Thackeray

60. Match the characters and the novels in which they appear.

| | |
|---|---|
| A. Mr. Jingle | 1. *Our Mutual Friend* |
| B. Mr. Micawber | 2. *The Pickwick Papers* |

C. Mr. Podsnap 3. *David Copperfield*

D. Miss Havisham 4. *Great Expectations*

| Codes: | A | B | C | D |
|---|---|---|---|---|
| (a) | 1 | 3 | 4 | 2 |
| (b) | 2 | 3 | 1 | 4 |
| (c) | 3 | 2 | 4 | 1 |
| (d) | 4 | 1 | 3 | 2 |

61. Match the following

A. Heathcliff 1. *Jane Eyre*

B. Becky Sharp 2. *Wuthering Heights*

C. Rochester 3. *Vanity Fair*

D. Pip 4. *Pickwick Papers*

| Codes: | A | B | C | D |
|---|---|---|---|---|
| (a) | 2 | 3 | 1 | 4 |
| (b) | 1 | 4 | 3 | 2 |
| (c) | 3 | 2 | 4 | 2 |
| (d) | 1 | 2 | 3 | 4 |

62. Match the following

A. Maggie Tulliver 1. Charles Dickens

B. Martin Thackeray 2. W.M. Chuzzlewit

C. Henry Esmond 3. George Eliot

D. Paul Clifford 4. Edward Bulwer -Lytton

| Codes: | A | B | C | D |
|---|---|---|---|---|
| (a) | 3 | 1 | 2 | 4 |
| (b) | 4 | 2 | 1 | 3 |
| (c) | 2 | 1 | 3 | 4 |
| (d) | 1 | 3 | 4 | 2 |

63. Which novelist's father was confined for debt in the Marshalsea Prison?

(a) Benjamin Disraeli
(b) Charles Dickens
(c) W.M. Thackeray
(d) Bulwer-Lytton

64. Which famous character is always "waiting for something to turn up"?

(a) Mme Defarge
(b) Quilp
(c) Pecksniff
(d) Micawber

65. Dickens has attacked some legal or social evil in most of his novels, Identify.

A. Oliver Twist 1. *Imprisonment for Debt*

B. Bleak House 2. *Workhouse*

C. Little Dorrit 3. *Chancery Courts*

D. Nicholas Nickleby 4. *Exploitation of Pupils*

| Codes: | A | B | C | D |
|---|---|---|---|---|
| (a) | 2 | 3 | 1 | 4 |
| (b) | 4 | 1 | 3 | 2 |
| (c) | 3 | 2 | 1 | 4 |
| (d) | 1 | 4 | 2 | 3 |

66. We find the character of Mr. Bumble in

(a) *Oliver Twist*
(b) *Nicholas Nickleby*
(c) *Martin Chuzzlewit*
(d) *David Copperfield*

67. Which Dickensian novel was left unfinished at the time of his death?

(a) *The Cricket on the Hearth*
(b) *The Mystery of Edwin Drood*
(c) *Martin Chuzzlewit*
(d) *Hard Times*

68. Which novel was Dickens's favourite child?

(a) *Nicholas Nickleby*
(b) *Great Expectations*
(c) *David Copperfield*
(d) *Oliver Twist*

69. Matthew Arnold preached the value of

(a) Hebraism
(b) Hellenism
(c) Philistinism
(d) None of the above

70. The Predominant mood in Arnold's poetry is that of
    (a) Joy
    (b) Melancholy
    (c) Optimism
    (d) Pessimism
71. "Empedocles on Etna" (1852) by Arnold is a poem on a
    (a) Roman theme
    (b) English theme
    (c) Greek theme
    (d) Love theme
72. "Sohrab and Rustum" by Arnold is on
    (a) An Irish theme
    (b) An Indian theme
    (c) A Persian theme
    (d) A Puritan theme
73. Arnold's *Memorial Verses* mourns the deaths of
    (a) Wordsworth, Goethe, Byron
    (b) Wordsworth, Byron, Shelley
    (c) Byron, Shelley, Keats
    (d) Wordsworth, Keats, Shelley
74. *Thyrsis* by Arnold is an elegy on the death of
    (a) Tennyson
    (b) Browning
    (c) Wordsworth
    (d) A.H. Clough
75. "We mortal millions live alone" figures in
    (a) *Dover Beach*
    (b) *Immortality Ode*
    (c) *To Marguerite*
    (d) *To a Skylark*
76. "Literature and Dogma" (1873) deals with
    (a) Literary dogmas
    (b) Religious dogmas
    (c) Poetry and politics
    (d) Poetry and religion
77. Arnold's "The Function of Criticism at the Present Time" makes out a case for
    (a) the importance of critical activity for the creative output.
    (b) the value of criticism for market economy.
    (c) the function of criticism as aesthetic experience.
    (d) the function of criticism as "touch-stone".
78. Arnold's "touch-stone" method values
    (a) All literary pieces
    (b) Only the best writing
    (c) Only English Writers
    (d) Only Greek classics
79. Arnold's view of culture is best described by
    (a) Light and dark
    (b) Sweet and dark
    (c) Light and sweetness
    (d) Dark and sweet
80. Arnold's *Scholar Gypsy* is largely based on the life of
    (a) Clough
    (b) Wordsworth
    (c) Sidney
    (d) Shelley
81. Arnold read which of the following Indian book most?
    (a) *Ramayana*
    (b) *Mahabharata*
    (c) *Akbarnama*
    (d) *Bhagvad Gita*
82. Matthew Arnold took story from ______ for his "Sohrab and Rustam."
    (a) *Canterbury Tales*
    (b) *Panchtantra*

(c) *Arabian Nights*
(d) *Shah Namah*

83. Who regards Hebraism as the "strictness of conscience" and Hellenism as the "spontaneity of consciousness"?
(a) Pope
(b) Wordsworth
(c) Arnold
(d) T.S. Eliot

84. In which chapter of Culture and Anarchy does Arnold mention Hebraism and Hellenism?
(a) III
(b) IV
(c) IV
(d) VII

85. The name of Arnold Bennett's autobiography is
(a) *The Truth About an Author*
(b) *My Story*
(c) *What I Think of Me*
(d) *My Life's Story*

86. Who defined criticism to be "sincere, flexible, ardent, ever widening its knowledge."
(a) T.S. Eliot
(b) F.R. Leavis
(c) I.A. Richards
(d) Arnold

87. How many lyrics are there in "In Memoriam"?
(a) 100
(b) 131
(c) 135
(d) 145

88. Who says that "man must begin where nature ends"?
(a) Wordsworth
(b) Arnold
(c) Coleridge
(d) Keats

89. Who found himself "Between two worlds, one dead, The other powerless to be born"?
(a) Eliot
(b) Carlyle
(c) Arnold
(d) Auden

90. Who originated the term 'Grand Style'?
(a) Milton
(b) Alexander Pope
(c) T.S. Eliot
(d) Matthew Arnold

91. Who said about Matthew Arnold, "Poor Matt. He is gone to Heaven, no doubt-but he won't like God!"?
(a) Tennyson
(b) Charles Dickens
(c) R.L. Stevenson
(d) None of the above

92. Which movement in poetry originated in Russia early in the 20th century?
(a) Futurism
(b) Expressionism
(c) Dadaism
(d) Acmeism

93. Which play, though by some coincidence, ascribed to Oscar Wilde, was written by Chambers Haddon
(a) *The Importance of Being Earnest*
(b) *The Tyranny of Tears*
(c) *Salome*
(d) None of the above

94. Oscar Wilde was by birth
(a) English
(b) Scottish
(c) American
(d) Irish

95. Who said, "Literature always anticipates life. It does not copy it but moulds its purpose"?

(a) T.S. Eliot
(b) Oscar Wilde
(c) John Keats
(d) William Wordsworth

96. Who wrote the play *An Ideal Husband*?
(a) G.B. Shaw
(b) James Barrie
(c) Oscar Wilde
(d) Ibsen

97. Oscar Wilde's *The Importance of Being Earnest* (1895) is a
(a) Classical comedy
(b) Romantic comedy
(c) Farcical comedy
(d) Pastoral comedy

98. Which book is condemned as "a poisonous book"?
(a) *The Picture of Dorian Gray*
(b) *The Waste Land*
(c) *Kim*
(d) *Jungle*

99. Which book is a "story of the soul"?
(a) *The Picture of Dorian Gray*
(b) *Pamela*
(c) *Huckleberry Finn*
(d) *Joseph Andrews*

100. The originator of the Oxford Movement is
(a) Newman
(b) Keble
(c) Pusey
(d) Ward

101. Who says, "The essential elements of the romantic spirit are curiosity and the love of beauty"?
(a) Byron
(b) Lamb
(c) Pater
(d) Keats

102. Who wrote Marius, the Epicurean
(a) T.S. Eliot
(b) Ezra Pound
(c) Matthew Arnold
(d) Walter Pater

103. Who says, "To feel the virtue of the poet or the painter, to disengage it, to set it forth—these are three stages of the critic's duty"?
(a) Joseph Addison
(b) S.T. Coleridge
(c) Walter Pater
(d) T.S. Eliot

104. Which play of Wilde has the subtitle *A Trivial Comedy for Serious People?*
(a) *The Importance of Being Earnest*
(b) *Lady Windermere's Fan*
(c) *A Woman of No Importance*
(d) None of the above

105. Who established "Old Mortality Club"?
(a) Keats
(b) Shelley and others
(c) Rossetti
(d) Pater and others

106. Who is of the view that "Great art has the soul of humanity in it"?
(a) Keats
(b) Shelley
(c) Coleridge
(d) Pater

107. "Studies in the History of the Renaissance" (1873) was written by
(a) D.G. Rosetti
(b) Oscar Wilde
(c) Walter Pater
(d) Thomas Hardy

108. "Art for Art's Sake" was advocated by
(a) Ruskin
(b) Pater
(c) Carlyle
(d) Newman

109. Which of the following is by Walter Pater?
   (a) *Imaginary Conversations*
   (b) *Imaginary Portraits*
   (c) *The Imaginary Invalid*
   (d) None of the above

110. The inspiration of which work did Oscar Wilde get in jail?
   (a) *Lady Windermere's Fan*
   (b) *The Importance of Being Earnest*
   (c) *The Ballad of Reading Gaol*
   (d) *A Woman of No Importance*

111. Which George Eliot's novel is woven around the year 1832, the eve of Reform Bill?
   (a) *Mill on the Floss*
   (b) *Felix Holt*
   (c) *Middlemarch*
   (d) *Daniel Deronda*

112. About which of her novels did Mary Ann Evans write to her publishers that "it was a story of old-fashioned village life which has unfolded itself, from the merest millet-seed of thought"?
   (a) *Adam Bede*
   (b) *Silas Marner*
   (c) *The Mill on the Floss*
   (d) *Middlemarch*

113. I began it a young woman—I finished an old woman. Which of her novels brought out this remark from George Eliot?
   (a) *Romola*
   (b) *Felix Holt*
   (c) *Daniel Deronda*
   (d) *Middlemarch*

114. George Eliot's first novel was
   (a) *Adam Bede*
   (b) *The Mill on the Floss*
   (c) *Silas Marner*
   (d) *Daniel Deronda*

115. George Eliot's *Middlemarch* (1871-72) is called an epic novel, comparable to War and Peace by which of the following critics?
   (a) Raymond Williams
   (b) F.R. Leavis
   (c) T.E. Hulme
   (d) I.A. Richards

116. *A Study of Provincial Life* is the subtitle to which of the following novels?
   (a) *Far From the Madding Crowd*
   (b) *The Woodlanders*
   (c) *The Mayor of Casterbridge*
   (d) *Middlemarch*

117. Which is the most perfect novel of George Eliot?
   (a) *Adam Bede*
   (b) *Silas Marner*
   (c) *Romola*
   (d) *Scenes From Provincial Life*

118. George Eliot's first story *Amos Barton* was first published in
   (a) 1857
   (b) 1865
   (c) 1862
   (d) 1877

119. Who is not a regional novelist of the 20th century?
   (a) Arnold Bennett
   (b) E.C. Booth
   (c) George Eliot
   (d) May Webb

120. G.B.S. stands for
   (a) George Bishop of Shaftesbury
   (b) Great Britain's Symphony
   (c) George Bernard Shaw
   (d) George Bacon of Strastford

121. The title of Hardy's *Under the Greenwood Tree* is derived from

(a) Shakespeare
(b) Wordsworth
(c) Chaucer
(d) Spenser

122. Hardy left writing fiction after hostile public response to his last novel, namely
(a) *Tess of the D'Urbervilles*
(b) *Jude the Obscure*
(c) *The Mayor of Casterbridge*
(d) *The Return of the Native*

123. "Happiness is but an occasional episode in the general drama of pain." Who said this?
(a) George Eliot
(b) George Meredith
(c) Thomas Hardy
(d) Charles Dickens

124. Anne Elliot is the heroine of which Victorian novel?
(a) *Persuasion*
(b) *Sense and Sensibility*
(c) *Middlemarch*
(d) *The Mill on the Floss*

125. To which poet does Hardy owe his title "Far from the Madding Crowd"?
(a) Thomas Gray
(b) Robert Browning
(c) John Donne
(d) Alexander Pope

126. In which Hardy's novel do we find "The President of the Immortals"?
(a) *Under the Greenwood Tree*
(b) *Tess*
(c) *Desperate Remedies*
(d) *A Pair of Blue Eyes*

127. Where would we find the Stonehenge?
(a) *The Mayor of Casterbridge*
(b) *Tess*
(c) *For From the Madding Crowd*
(d) *The Return of the Native*

128. "Wessex" forms the background to the novels of
(a) Henry James
(b) Thomas Hardy
(c) George Eliot
(d) Charles Dickens

129. Which of the following is written in verse?
(a) *A Pair of Blue Eyes*
(b) *The Dynasts*
(c) *Under the Greenwood Tree*
(d) *Desperate Remedies*

130. The subtitle of *The Dynasts* is
(a) *An Epic-Drama of The War With Napoleon*
(b) *The Story of the Oaks*
(c) *After the Civil War*
(d) *The Saga of a Royal Family*

131. How many acts does *The Dynasts* boast of?
(a) Three
(b) Five
(c) Seven
(d) Nineteen

132. "On Liberty" was written by
(a) Carlyle
(b) Rousseau
(c) Newman
(d) J.S. Mill

133. *The Origin of Species* came out in
(a) 1857
(b) 1859
(c) 1858
(d) 1860

134. *Life of Charlotte Bronte* was written by
(a) Emily Bronte
(b) George Eliot
(c) Elizabeth Gaskell
(d) Charlotte Bronte

135. The narrator of *Jane Eyre* is
   (a) Jane Eyre
   (b) Rochester
   (c) Charlotte Bronte
   (d) Geloe

136. *Wuthering Heights* is written by
   (a) Charlotte Bronte
   (b) Emily Bronte
   (c) Anne Bronte
   (d) W.M. Thackeray

137. *The Cloister and the Hearth* was written by
   (a) Anthony Trollope
   (b) Charles Reade
   (c) Charles Dickens
   (d) W.M. Thackeray

138. The subtitle of *Vanity Fair* is
   (a) *A Pure Woman*
   (b) *A Novel Without a Hero*
   (c) *The Story of an Ambitious Woman*
   (d) *A Novel of Struggle*

139. "Barchester Towers" (1857) was written by
   (a) Charles Reade
   (b) W.M. Thackeray
   (c) Anthony Trollope
   (d) Charles Kingsley

140. We find the couple Mr. and Mrs. Proudie in
   (a) Anthony Trollope's *Barchester Towers*
   (b) Thackeray's *Pendennis*
   (c) Charles Dicken's *Pickwick Papers*
   (d) George Eliot's *Middlemarch*

141. Charlotte Bronte dedicated *Jane Eyre* to
   (a) Mrs. Gaskell
   (b) Thomas Hardy
   (c) Dickens
   (d) Thackeray

142. How many novels in all George Eliot wrote?
   (a) Four
   (b) Five
   (c) Six
   (d) Seven

143. Where would one find "The Mad Hatter's Tea Party"?
   (a) *Tales from Shakespeare*
   (b) *The Jungle Book*
   (c) *Grimm's Fairy Tales*
   (d) *Alice in Wonderland*

144. "Diana of the Crossways" was written by
   (a) George Eliot
   (b) George Meredith
   (c) Charles Reade
   (d) Thomas Hardy

145. Who wrote *Memories and Confessions of a Justified Sinner*?
   (a) James Hogg
   (b) Wilkie Collins
   (c) Oscar Wilde
   (d) Samuel Butler

146. *Esther Waters* (1894) by George Moore is a
   (a) Sentimental novel
   (b) Satirical novel
   (c) Psychological novel
   (d) Naturalist novel

147. Who said: "A Woman is only a woman, But a good cigar is a smoke"?
   (a) A.E. Housman
   (b) Rudyard Kipling
   (c) Samuel Butler
   (d) Oscar Wilde

148. Kipling's "Recessional" was written for the occasion of Victoria's
   (a) birth anniversary
   (b) silver jubilee
   (c) diamond jubilee
   (d) wedding anniversary

149. Which town did Hardy rename as Casterbridge in his novel?

(a) Wessex
(b) Northamptonshire
(c) Dorchester
(d) Shropshire

150. Which novel deals with four generations of the Pontifex Family?
(a) *Jude the Obscure*
(b) *Romola*
(c) *The Way of all Flesh*
(d) *Daisy Miller*

151. "A Shropshire Lad" by A.E. Housman is
(a) picaresque novel
(b) satirical drama
(c) collection of poems
(d) autobiographical novel

152. Where would we find Akela, the Wolf, Bagheera, the Panther and Rikki-Tikki-Tavi, the mongoose?
(a) *The Jungle Book*
(b) *The Second Jungle Book*
(c) *Aesop's Fables*
(d) *Just So Stories*

153. Which novel consists of a vision of England in the year 2090 presented as a dream of William Guest?
(a) *Erewhon*
(b) *News from Nowhere*
(c) *A Clockwork Orange*
(d) *Lord of the Flies*

154. *Uncle Tom's Cabin* is a novel by
(a) Mark Twain
(b) Charles Dickens
(c) Harriet Beecher Stowe
(d) Joel Harris

155. The subtitle of *Uncle Tom's Cabin* is
(a) *A Mysterious Story*
(b) *Life among the Lowly*
(c) *A Place for All and Sundry*
(d) *Life in a Village*

156. *Twenty Thousand Leagues under the Sea* was written by
(a) Arthur Conan Doyle
(b) Wilkie Collins
(c) R.L. Stevenson
(d) Jules Verne

157. *Uncle Tom's Cabin* is a story of
(a) Slaves
(b) Peasants
(c) Prisoners
(d) Miners

158. Where would we find Bar'er Rabbit, Br'er Fox and Br'er Bear?
(a) *The Jungle Book*
(b) *Alice in Wonderland*
(c) *Uncle Remus*
(d) *Aesop's Fables*

159. Uncle Remus is a fictional character created by
(a) Harriet Beecher Stowe
(b) Joel Harris
(c) Rudyard Kipling
(d) Lewis Carroll

160. The name of the magazine concerning the cause of the Pre-Raphaelites is
(a) *Jenny*
(b) *The Germ*
(c) *Goblin Market*
(d) *The House of Life*

161. "Sister Helen" is a poem by
(a) John Ruskin
(b) Christina Rossetti
(c) D.G. Rossetti
(d) Matthew Arnold

162. The title *Vanity Fair* has been taken from
(a) *Euphues*
(b) *Paradise Lost*
(c) *Utopia*
(d) *Pilgrim's Progress*

163. Which one is Gaskell's first novel?
   (a) *Mary Barton*
   (b) *Ruth*
   (c) *Cranford*
   (d) *North and South*

164. Dunstan is a character from the novel
   (a) *Silas Marner*
   (b) *Hard Times*
   (c) *Emma*
   (d) *Adam Bede*

165. Which movement revived under Whitefield and Wesley?
   (a) Oxford Movement
   (b) Pre-Rephalite
   (c) Methodist
   (d) Chicago

166. "The Three Way Fairers" is a dramatization of a piece of fiction by Thomas Hardy. Which story is it?
   (a) *Far From the Madding Crowd*
   (b) *Tess*
   (c) *The Three Strangers*
   (d) *Jude the Obscure*

167. *Pendennis* is the name of a novel by
   (a) Elizabeth Gaskell
   (b) Thackeray
   (c) Charles Dickens
   (d) George Eliot

168. Which is the main feature of the Victorian age?
   (a) Ethical literature
   (b) Influence of science
   (c) Attack on materialism
   (d) All of the above

169. The Centennial edition of Palgrave's *The Golden Treasury*" was compiled and edited by
   (a) William Collins
   (b) Oscar Williams
   (c) Palgrave
   (d) Dorothy Sayers

170. This edition contained books
   (a) Book 1-4
   (b) Book 1-7
   (c) Book 1-9
   (d) Book 1-10

171. The Book 5-7 of the new edition of *The Golden Treasury* contains poems from
   (a) 1400-1600
   (b) 1500-1800
   (c) 1700-1800
   (d) 1526-1850

172. The essay "Idea of Comedy" was written by
   (a) Bergson
   (b) Lamb
   (c) George Meredith
   (d) Joseph Addison

173. The name of the only novel of Emily Bronte is
   (a) *Vanity Fair*
   (b) *Wuthering Heights*
   (c) *Jane Eyre*
   (d) *Hard Times*

174. "The Great Exhibition" took place in the year
   (a) 1850
   (b) 1851
   (c) 1861
   (d) 1871

175. "Prometheus Bound" was written by
   (a) P.B. Shelley
   (b) Elizabeth Barrett Browning
   (c) John Ruskin
   (d) Rudyard Kipling

176. The name of Swinburne's excellent work is
   (a) *Atlanta in Calydon*
   (b) *House of Life*
   (c) *The Life and Death of Jason*
   (d) *Love is Enough*

177. *Time Flies, a Reading Dial* (1883) was published by

(a) George Eliot
(b) Emily Zola
(c) Christina Rossetti
(d) Virginia Woolf

178. Huree Babu and Teshoo Lama are Characters in
(a) *Kim*
(b) *Man Eater of Malgudi*
(c) *Coolie*
(d) *Jungle Book*

179. Who remarks, "There is not better English anywhere than the English of the Bible."
(a) Saintsbury
(b) A.C. Ward
(c) Dryden
(d) Dr. Johnson

180. Who says, "Shakespeare's tragedies are dramas of physical action and psychological conflict, not ballets of bloodless images or ceremonial for a dying god."
(a) Bradley
(b) Coleridge
(c) Henry Levin
(d) Matthew Arnold

181. Who is known as "The Father of English Socialism".
(a) Robert Browning
(b) Robert Owen
(c) A. Cooper
(d) J.S. Mill

182. Who wrote the following lines: "Wealth I ask not, hope nor love/ Nor a friend to know me/ All I ask, the heaven above,/ And the road below me."
(a) R.L. Stevenson
(b) Browning
(c) Wordsworth
(d) S.T. Coleridge

183. What is the name of the uncle of David Balfour in *Kidnapped*?
(a) Louis
(b) Herriet
(c) Ebenezer
(d) Styris

184. *The House of Life* is a collection of sonnets by
(a) D.G. Rossetti
(b) Drayton
(c) Daniel
(d) Elizabeth Barret Browning

185. The underlying strain of George Eliot's *Silas Marner* is
(a) Jealousy
(b) Indecisiveness
(c) Depressing tragedy and suffering
(d) Morbidity of dreams

186. Who was called "Tusitala" by the South Sea Islanders?
(a) Mark Jwain
(b) Virginia Woolf
(c) R.L. Stevenson
(d) Bacon

187. The biography, *The Life of Charlotte Bronte* (1857) was written by
(a) Elizabeth Gaskell
(b) S.T. Coleridge
(c) William Godwin
(d) P.B. Shelley

188. Who is not an original member of Pre-Raphaelite Poetry?
(a) D.G. Rossetti
(b) Holman Hunt
(c) William Morris
(d) Thomas Woolner

189. Which is not a novel by Charlotte Bronte?
(a) *Jane Eyre*
(b) *Villete*
(c) *Two on a Tower*
(d) *Shirley*

190. "A Blot in the Scutcheon" is the best play by

(a) Dryden
(b) Browning
(c) Sheridan
(d) G.B. Shaw

191. Charles Reade's "The Cloister and the Hearth" resembles with George Eliot's novel
(a) *Scenes from Provincial Life*
(b) *Romola*
(c) *Adam Bede*
(d) None of the above

192. Who made a distinction between 'Literature of Knowledge' and 'Literature of Power' is an essay published in *The North British Review* (1848)?
(a) Charles Lamb
(b) John Keats
(c) De Quincey
(d) Byron

193. Oxford Movement is known as the
(a) Tractarian Movement
(b) Education Movement
(c) University Movement
(d) Pre-Raphealite Movement

**ANSWERS**

| | | | | | |
|---|---|---|---|---|---|
| 1. (b) | 2. (b) | 3. (d) | 4. (d) | 5. (d) | 6. (c) |
| 7. (c) | 8. (b) | 9. (c) | 10. (a) | 11. (d) | 12. (b) |
| 13. (c) | 14. (b) | 15. (c) | 16. (c) | 17. (a) | 18. (b) |
| 19. (d) | 20. (a) | 21. (c) | 22. (b) | 23. (c) | 24. (a) |
| 25. (b) | 26. (d) | 27. (a) | 28. (d) | 29. (b) | 30. (b) |
| 31. (b) | 32. (a) | 33. (b) | 34. (c) | 35. (a) | 36. (c) |
| 37. (a) | 38. (a) | 39. (b) | 40. (b) | 41. (c) | 42. (d) |
| 43. (a) | 44. (a) | 45. (a) | 46. (c) | 47. (c) | 48. (d) |
| 49. (e) | 50. (c) | 51. (d) | 52. (c) | 53. (a) | 54. (c) |
| 55. (a) | 56. (c) | 57. (d) | 58. (d) | 59. (c) | 60. (b) |
| 61. (a) | 62. (a) | 63. (b) | 64. (d) | 65. (a) | 66. (a) |
| 67. (b) | 68. (c) | 69. (b) | 70. (b) | 71. (c) | 72. (c) |
| 73. (a) | 74. (d) | 75. (c) | 76. (d) | 77. (a) | 78. (b) |
| 79. (c) | 80. (a) | 81. (d) | 82. (d) | 83. (c) | 84. (b) |
| 85. (a) | 86. (d) | 87. (b) | 88. (b) | 89. (c) | 90. (d) |
| 91. (c) | 92. (d) | 93. (b) | 94. (d) | 95. (b) | 96. (c) |
| 97. (c) | 98. (a) | 99. (a) | 100. (b) | 101. (c) | 102. (d) |
| 103. (c) | 104. (a) | 105. (d) | 106. (d) | 107. (c) | 108. (b) |
| 109. (b) | 110. (c) | 111. (b) | 112. (b) | 113. (a) | 114. (a) |
| 115. (b) | 116. (d) | 117. (b) | 118. (a) | 119. (c) | 120. (c) |
| 121. (a) | 122. (b) | 123. (c) | 124. (a) | 125. (a) | 126. (b) |
| 127. (b) | 128. (b) | 129. (b) | 130. (a) | 131. (d) | 132. (d) |

| | | | | | |
|---|---|---|---|---|---|
| 133. (b) | 134. (c) | 135. (a) | 136. (b) | 137. (b) | 138. (b) |
| 139. (c) | 140. (a) | 141. (d) | 142. (c) | 143. (d) | 144. (b) |
| 145. (a) | 146. (d) | 147. (b) | 148. (c) | 149. (c) | 150. (c) |
| 151. (c) | 152. (a) | 153. (b) | 154. (c) | 155. (b) | 156. (d) |
| 157. (a) | 158. (c) | 159. (b) | 160. (b) | 161. (c) | 162. (d) |
| 163. (a) | 164. (a) | 165. (c) | 166. (c) | 167. (b) | 168. (d) |
| 169. (b) | 170. (b) | 171. (d) | 172. (c) | 173. (b) | 174. (b) |
| 175. (b) | 176. (a) | 177. (c) | 178. (a) | 179. (a) | 180. (c) |
| 181. (b) | 182. (a) | 183. (c) | 184. (a) | 185. (c) | 186. (c) |
| 187. (a) | 188. (c) | 189. (c) | 190. (b) | 191. (b) | 192. (c) |
| 193. (a) | | | | | |

# 6

# The Modern Period

1. Chicago critics were critical of the
   (a) Movement poets
   (b) New Critics
   (c) Angry Young men
   (d) Futurism
2. Who is the chief of the Chicago critics?
   (a) I.A. Richards
   (b) T.S. Eliot and I.A. Richards
   (c) T.S. Eliot
   (d) R.S. Crane
3. How many plays are there in Shaw's *Pleasant and Unpleasant* (1898)?
   (a) 7
   (b) 8
   (c) 9
   (d) 10
4. Out of these seven plays, how many are pleasant plays?
   (a) 3
   (b) 4
   (c) 5
   (d) 6
5. Which one is not an unpleasant play by Shaw?
   (a) *Widower's House* (1892)
   (b) *Mrs. Warren's Profession* (1894)
   (c) *Candida* (1895)
   (d) *The Philanderer* (1893; 1905)
6. In which play of Shaw, the third act is entitled "Don Juan in Hell"?
   (a) *Man and Superman* (1903)
   (b) *Arms and the Man* (1894)
   (c) *Pygmalion* (1912)
   (d) None of the above
7. *Caesar and Cleopatra* is a play by
   (a) Shakespeare
   (b) Dryden
   (c) Eliot
   (d) G.B. Shaw
8. Which play of G.B. Shaw is the first of the truly Shavian and the first of the pleasant plays?
   (a) *Arms and the Man* (1894)
   (b) *Candida* (1895)
   (c) *The Man of Destiny* (1897-99)
   (d) *You Never Can Tell* (1897-99)
9. Which play of Shaw inspired Sean O' Casey to write plays?
   (a) *S. Joan*
   (b) *Caesar and Cleopatra*
   (c) *Man and Superman*
   (d) *Androcles and the Lion*
10. Shaw's play *Man and Superman* has ________ acts
    (a) 3
    (b) 4
    (c) 5
    (d) 6
11. The background of which play is the historic war between Bulgaria and Serbia?

(a) *Man and Superman*
(b) *The Rivals*
(c) *Arms and the Man*
(d) *Coriolanus*

12. "I deal with all periods but I never study any period but the present." Who said it?
(a) Ibsen
(b) Wilde
(c) Shaw
(d) Conrad

13. Who dared to say, "I write plays with the deliberate purpose to convert the nation to my opinion"?
(a) Ibsen
(b) Shaw
(c) Yeats
(d) Barrie

14. In Shaw's *Man and Superman*, who writes "The Revolutionary's Handbook"?
(a) Ramsden
(b) Octavious
(c) John Tanner
(d) Ann

15. Which problem play of G.B. Shaw abounds in humour and deals with the subject of marriage and its limitations?
(a) *Pleasant and Unpleasant*
(b) *The Hand of Destiny*
(c) *The Philanderer*
(d) *Arms and the Man*

16. In which play do we come across a chocolate cream soldier?
(a) *Man and Superman*
(b) *Arms and the Man*
(c) *The Man of Destiny*
(d) *Caesar and Cleopatra*

17. In which play does Shaw propound his philosophy of 'Life Force'?
(a) *The Devil's Disciple*
(b) *Major Barbara*
(c) *Caesar and Cleopatra*
(d) *Man and Superman*

18. Which play of G.B. Shaw deals with poverty and religious hypocrisy?
(a) *Candida*
(b) *Major Barbara*
(c) *Heartbreak House*
(d) None of the above

19. Which play of Shaw satirises European materialism?
(a) *The Apple Cart*
(b) *Back to Methuselah*
(c) *Captain Brassbound's Conversion*
(d) *Heartbreak House*

20. Bernard Shaw got the Nobel Prize for literature in
(a) 1905
(b) 1917
(c) 1925
(d) 1935

21. One of Shaw's plays deals with the problem of phonetics and pronunciation. Which of the following is that play?
(a) *Pygmalion*
(b) *Candida*
(c) *Captain Brassbound's Conversion*
(d) *Major Barbara*

22. In which of the following plays of Shaw do we get a false concept of hero and hero-worship?
(a) *John Bull's Other Island*
(b) *Major Barbara*
(c) *Caesar and Cleopatra*
(d) *Captain Brassbound's Conversion*

23. Who said, "All I want is to answer my blood, direct"?
(a) W.H. Davies
(b) D.H. Lawrence
(c) W.H. Auden
(d) W.H. Hudson

24. Which novel did D.H. Lawrence call a "thought adventure"?
    (a) *The White Peacock* (1911)
    (b) *The Trespasser* (1912)
    (c) *The Rainbow* (1922)
    (d) *Kangaroo* (1923)
25. Paul Morel is a character from the novel
    (a) *Kangaroo*
    (b) *Sons and Lovers*
    (c) *The Rainbow*
    (d) *Women in Love*
26. Which novel of D.H. Lawrence deals with the mother-son relationship?
    (a) *Sons and Lovers* (1913)
    (b) *Aaron's Road* (1922)
    (c) *The Boy in the Bush* (1924)
    (d) *The Plumed Serpent* (1926)
27. Which one of the following has the beginning as "Ours is essentially a tragic age"?
    (a) *Sons and Lovers*
    (b) *Lady Chatterley's Lover*
    (c) *Rainbow*
    (d) *Women in Love*
28. To D.H. Lawrence, which of his own novel is "very very moral"
    (a) *Sons and Lovers* (1913)
    (b) *The Rainbow* (1922)
    (c) *Kangaroo* (1923)
    (d) *Lady Chatterley's Lover* (1928)
29. D.H. Lawrence was a pioneer of
    (a) stream-of-consciousness novel
    (b) psycho-analytical fiction
    (c) realistic fiction
    (d) imagism in fiction
30. Which of the following is a critical writing of D.H. Lawrence?
    (a) *Sea and Sardinia*
    (b) *Phoenix*
    (c) *Touch and Go*
    (d) *Morning in Mexico*
31. A good number of Lawrence's best poems which were stark, concentrated and unrhymed appeared in the volume of 1923.
    (a) *Pansies*
    (b) *Peacock Pie*
    (c) *Birds, Beasts and Flowers*
    (d) *Georgian Poetry*
32. D.H. Lawrence was greatly influenced by
    (a) Freud
    (b) Marx
    (c) Darwin
    (d) Aristotle
33. Which of the following novels of D.H. Lawrence has an autobiographical note?
    (a) *The White Peacock*
    (b) *Sons and Lovers*
    (c) *The Trespasser*
    (d) *Mr. Noon*
34. Which of the following is not a work of D.H. Lawrence?
    (a) *The Prussian Officer*
    (b) *The Rainbow*
    (c) *The Captain's Doll*
    (d) *Between the Acts*
35. The phrase 'religion of the blood' is associated with
    (a) Virginia Woolf
    (b) E.M. Forster
    (c) D.H. Lawrence
    (d) James Joyce
36. Lawrence announced in one of his essays that the novelist is superior to the saint, the poet, the philosopher and the scientist. Which is that essay?
    (a) *Surgery for a Novel or a Bomb*
    (b) *The Man Who Died*

(c) *Victorian Prose*
(d) *Why the Novel Matters*

37. Which one is not a quality of Masefield's poem "The Everlasting Mercy"?
(a) Violence
(b) Crudeness
(c) Optimism
(d) Realism

38. Which work of John Masefield betrays the wonder and magic of the sea?
(a) *The Widow in the Bye Street* (1912)
(b) *The Daffodil Fields* (1913)
(c) *Dauber* (1913)
(d) *Lollingdon Downs* (1917)

39. Who is not a war poet?
(a) John Masefield
(b) Rupert Brooke
(c) Siegfried Sasoon
(d) Wilfred Owen

40. John Masefield was made Poet Laureate in
(a) 1927
(b) 1928
(c) 1930
(d) 1932

41. Which one is not a novel by John Masefield?
(a) *The Tragedy of Nun* (1908)
(b) *Sard Harker* (1924)
(c) *Odtaa* (1926)
(d) All of the above

42. Which one is not a play by John Masefield?
(a) *Good Friday* (1917)
(b) *Shakespeare* (1911)
(c) *The Trial of Jesus* (1925)
(d) *The Coming of Christ* (1928)

43. W.B. Yeats was born in
(a) Ireland
(b) Scotland
(c) America
(d) England

44. Which one is not a play by W.B. Yeats
(a) *The Hour-Glass* (1904)
(b) *The Resurrection* (1913)
(c) *If* (1921)
(d) *The Cat and the Moon* (1926)

45. W.B. Yeats did not believe in man's
(a) Imagination
(b) Intuition
(c) Scientific reasoning
(d) Primitive impulses

46. Who said, "Poetry makes nothing happen"
(a) Eliot
(b) Arnold
(c) Auden
(d) Yeats

47. Who introduced Rabindranath Tagore to European readers?
(a) Ezekiel
(b) Yeats
c) Pound
(d) Eliot

48. Yeat's "Easter 1916" is
(a) Occasional Verse
(b) Light Verse
(c) Madrigal
(d) Folk Ballad

49. Who founded the Irish National Literary Society?
(a) Sean O' Casey
(b) Butler
(c) W.B. Yeats
(d) Mary Sinclair

50. Yeat's "A Vision" is a/an
(a) One-act play
(b) Absurd play
(c) Prose work
(d) Love poem

51. Which one is not a collection of plays by Lady Gregory?
    (a) *Seven Short Plays* (1909)
    (b) *The Lost Leader* (1918)
    (c) *Three Wonder Plays* (1922)
    (d) *Three Last Plays* (1928)
52. *The Lost Leader* is a play by
    (a) Lennox Robinson
    (b) Yeats
    (c) Browning
    (d) John Arvine
53. "The Lost Leader" is a poem by
    (a) Wordsworth
    (b) Browning
    (c) Yeats
    (d) Synge
54. Lady Gregory was drawn to the theatre by
    (a) W.B. Yeats
    (b) G.H. Hopkins
    (c) J.M. Synge
    (d) G.B. Shaw
55. In *The Tower* written by W.B. Yeats, what is the name of the tower?
    (a) Eiffel Tower
    (b) Roman Tower
    (c) Norman Tower
    (d) None of the above
56. In which poem of T.S. Eliot, the following lines appear: "My nerves are bad tonight. Yes, bad,/ Stay with me Speak to me. Why do you never speak, speak."
    (a) "Prufrock" (1917)
    (b) "The Waste Land" (1922)
    (c) "Gerontion" (1917)
    (d) "Ash Wednesday" (1930)
57. How many sections are there in "The Waste Land"?
    (a) 5
    (b) 6
    (c) 7
    (d) 8
58. Who viewed "The Waste Land" as the "longest poem in the English language because of its profoundity, perplexity and density of poetic allusions, myths and meaning"?
    (a) I.A. Richards
    (b) Wyndham Lewis
    (c) William Empson
    (d) Ezra Pound
59. The theme(s) of T.S. Eliot's "Four Quartets" is
    (a) Artistic Consciousness
    (b) Time and Eternity
    (c) The Potential of Words
    (d) All of the above
60. Eliot's "The Waste Land" appeared first in the quarterly magazine
    (a) *The Criterion*
    (b) *The Review*
    (c) *The Critic*
    (d) *The Imagist*
61. T.S. Eliot dedicated "The Waste Land" to
    (a) Ezra Pound
    (b) Dolittle
    (c) Tiresias
    (d) Oedipus
62. In which poem, T.S. Eliot compares the evening to "a patient etherized upon a table"?
    (a) "The Waste Land"
    (b) "Four Quartets"
    (c) "The Hollow Men"
    (d) "The Love Song of Alfred J. Prufrock"
63. Who is known as "a classicist in literature, royalist in politics and anglo-catholic" in religion?
    (a) G.B. Shaw
    (b) T.S. Eliot

(c) Virginia Woolf
(d) Thomas Hardy

64. The essay "Hamlet and His Problems" was written by
(a) Shakespeare
(b) F.R. Leavis
(c) Lamb
(d) T.S. Eliot

65. Who said, "A thought to Donne was an experience. It modified his sensibility"?
(a) Dryden
(b) Dr. Johnson
(c) T.S. Eliot
(d) Grierson

66. T.S. Eliot got the title of his poem "The Waste Land" from Miss Weston's book
(a) *From Ritual to Romance*
(b) *The Golden Bough*
(c) *Inferno*
(d) *The Psyche*

67. In which of his essays has Eliot said, "...no poet, no artist of any art, has his complete meaning alone"?
(a) *The Metaphysical Poets*
(b) *The Use of Poetry and the Use of Criticism*
(c) *Twentieth Century Poetry*
(d) *Tradition and the Individual Talent*

68. T.S. was awarded the Nobel Prize for literature for his _______ in 1948.
(a) "Four Quartets"
(b) "Portrait of a Lady"
(c) "The Waste Land"
(d) "The Love Song of J. Alfred Prufrock"

69. What is meant by Eliot's poetic shorthand?
(a) Short sentences to convey a better poetic effect
(b) Eliot's use of musical device
(c) Shorthand used by Eliot while writing his long poems
(d) Eliot's use of complex symbolic techniques to link the past with the present.

70. Which one of the following works of Joseph Conrad is a tale of Russian revolutionaries?
(a) *Heart of Darkness*
(b) *Typhoon*
(c) *Youth*
(d) *Under Western Eyes*

71. Which work of W.H. Davies tells us about his loss of a leg while attempting to board a moving freight train?
(a) *Later Days* (1925)
(b) *The Poet's Pilgrimage* (1918)
(c) *The Autobiography of a Super Tramp* (1908)
(d) All of the above

72. Which novel of Huxley is a light-hearted satire on contemporary society?
(a) *Crome Yellow* (1921)
(b) *Antic Hay* (1923)
(c) *Those Barren Leaves* (1925)
(d) *Point Counter Point* (1928)

73. In which of his novel, Aldous Huxley imagines a world without disease, without pain, without emotion and without spiritual life?
(a) *Bravo New World* (1932)
(b) *After Many a Summer* (1939)
(c) *Time Must have a Stop* (1944)
(d) *Point Counter Point*

74. Sherlock Holmes was introduced to the reader in 1887 by Sir Arthur Conan Doyle in
(a) *The Exploits of Brigadier General*
(b) *Micah Clarke*

(c) *A Study in Scarlet*
(d) *The Lost World*

75. Who wrote the elegy "Wordsworth's Grave"?
(a) William Watson
(b) Sydney Dobell
(c) Alexander Smith
(d) Oscar Wilde

76. The Polish Mariner who presented colonialism as both brutal and brutalizing in many of his stories and novels was
(a) Oscar Wilde
(b) Joseph Conrad
(c) J.M. Barrie
(d) A.W. Pinero

77. This novel is Conrad's masterpiece, which is concerned with honour, courage and solidarity. Name the novel.
(a) *Youth*
(b) *Lord Jim*
(c) *The Secret Agent*
(d) *Heart of Darkness*

78. Which of the following is a novella?
(a) *Almayer's Folly*
(b) *Nostramo*
(c) *Under the Western Eyes*
(d) *The Nigger of the Narcissus*

79. In which of his novel, Aldous Huxley "attempts to musicalize fiction"?
(a) *Crome Yellow* (1921)
(b) *Antic Hay* (1923)
(c) *Those Barren Leaves* (1925)
(d) *Point Counter Point* (1928)

80. Who expressed a nostalgic regret for the disappeared culture?
(a) Eliot
(b) Masefield
(c) Huxley
(d) Edith Sitwell

81. *Rule Britannia* is a novel by
(a) Daphne Du Maurier
(b) Thomson
(c) Golding
(d) Dorothy Sayers

82. "Rule Britannia" is a poem by
(a) Henry James
(b) James Thomson
(c) Dylan Thomas
(d) James Joyce

83. Jim Corbett's poem "Robin" is about
(a) A tiger
(b) A cat
(c) A mouse
(d) A dog

84. Which one of the following novelists did not die in 1957?
(a) Joyce Cary
(b) Wyndham Lewis
(c) Lowry
(d) Henry Green

85. "Shakespeare" is a
(a) Poem
(b) Memoir
(c) Prose Work
(d) Novel of Ideas

86. Which one of the following works of John Masefield is not poetry
(a) *Reynard, the Fox* (1919)
(b) *Right Royal* (1920)
(c) *The Bird of Dawning* (1933)
(d) *Collected Poems* (1932)

87. *The Bird of Dawning* is a
(a) Novel
(b) Drama
(c) Essay
(d) Opera

88. Which one of the following works of John Masefield is a play?
(a) *Dead Ned*
(b) *The Midnight Folk*

(c) *Sard Harker*
(d) *The Campden Wonder*

89. Which of the following plays of John Masefield is a domestic play written in prose?
(a) *The Faithful*
(b) *The Tragedy of Nan*
(c) *The Tragedy of Pompey the Great*
(d) *The Midnight Folk*

90. Who wrote in the essay *The Celtic Twilight*: "I have desired like every artist to create a little world out of the beautiful, pleasant and significant things of this marred and clumsy world"?
(a) G.B. Shaw
(b) A.E. Housman
(c) Oscar Wilde
(d) W.B. Yeats

91. "Crossways" (1889) by W.B. Yeats include
(a) The Sad Shepherd
(b) The Stolen Child
(c) Ephemera
(d) All of the above

92. The members of the Aesthetic Movement shared their mystical sympathies through its public voice
(a) Red Book
(b) Blue Book
(c) Yellow Book
(d) Green Book

93. Identify the poem which begins thus "Things fall apart, the centre cannot hold".
(a) "The Second Coming"
(b) "Vacillation"
(c) "The Hound of Heaven"
(d) "Sailing to Byzantium"

94. W.B. Yeats was awarded the Nobel Prize for literature in
(a) 1921
(b) 1922
(c) 1923
(d) 1924

95. Whose disciples were Shaw, D.H. Lawrence, Somerset Maugham and Wells?
(a) Samuel Butler
(b) Rudyard Kipling
(c) John Millington Synge
(d) John Galsworthy

96. Which novel deals with the Butler's childhood and his relation with his father?
(a) *Erewhon and Erewhon Revisited* (1901)
(b) *The Authors of the Odyssey* (1897)
(c) *The Way of All Flesh* (1903)
(d) *On the Trapanese Origin of the Odyssey*

97. Which of the following is not Butler's Pamphlet?
(a) *Alps and Sanctuaries of Piedmont and the Canton Ticino* (1881)
(b) *Life and Habit* (1977)
(c) *Evolution Old and New* (1879)
(d) *Unconscious Memory* (1880)

98. Which is not Butler's travel book?
(a) *Shakespeare's Sonnets Reconsidered* (1899)
(b) *The Life and Letters of Dr. Samuel Butler* (1896)
(c) *The Notebooks of Samuel Butler* (1912)
(d) *Luck or Cunning as the Means of Organic Modification* (1887)

99. In which book did Butler translate *Iliad* and *Odyssey*?
(a) *Essay on Life, Art and Science* (1904)
(b) *The Authors of the Odyssey* (1804)
(c) *Ex Voto* (1888)
(d) *Unconscious Memory*

100. Rudyard Kipling got Nobel Prize in
(a) 1905
(b) 1906
(c) 1907
(d) 1908

101. Who was born in Bombay?
   (a) G.B. Shaw
   (b) Rudyard Kipling
   (c) Oscar Wilde
   (d) Harley Granville-Barker

102. Which book of Rudyard Kipling is a collection of articles?
   (a) *The Phantom Rickshaw* (1888)
   (b) *Kim* (1901)
   (c) *Debits and Credits* (1926)
   (d) *From Sea to Sea* (1900)

103. Oscar Wilde composed *Comedies of Manners* in the tradition of
   (a) Jonson
   (b) Sheridan
   (c) Johnson
   (d) Galsworthy

104. Which of the following is a farcical comedy?
   (a) *Lady Windermere's Fan* (1893)
   (b) *A Woman of No Importance* (1892)
   (c) *An Ideal Husband*
   (d) *The Importance of Being Earnest* (1895)

105. Which is the best novel of Maugham?
   (a) *Strictly Personal* (1942)
   (b) *Liza of Lambeth* (1897)
   (c) *Of Human Bondage* (1915)
   (d) *Cakes and Ale* (1930)

106. *A Modern Lover* is a novel by
   (a) Henry James
   (b) William Faulkner
   (c) George Moore
   (d) None of the above

107. Who is not a Marxist Critic?
   (a) Edmund Wilson
   (b) C. Kirkpatrick
   (c) Newton Arvin
   (d) Philip Rahu

108. Which novel of Arnold Bennet exposes the religious bigotry of the five towns?
   (a) *The Old Wives' Tale* (1908)
   (b) *Clayhanger* (1910)
   (c) *Hilda Lessways* (1911)
   (d) *These Twain* (1916)

109. Which one is not a realistic problem play by Allan Monkhouse
   (a) *Mary Broome* (1911)
   (b) *The Education of Mr. Surrage* (1913)
   (c) *The Grand Cham's Diamond* (1924)
   (d) *First Blood* (1926)

110. Who is well known for his father Brown detective stories?
   (a) G.K. Chesterton
   (b) W.H. Hudson
   (c) John Masefield
   (d) W.H. Auden

111. Who wrote *The Patriot's Progress* (1930)?
   (a) John Bunyan
   (b) C.W. Lewis
   (c) Henry Williamson
   (d) Robert Graves

112. Which one of the following novels of Virginia Woolf is known as a prose poem?
   (a) *The Voyage Out* (1915)
   (b) *Night and Day* (1919)
   (c) *Mrs. Dalloway* (1925)
   (d) *The Waves* (1931)

113. Which work of Woolf traces the life from Elizabethan to modern times?
   (a) *To the Lighthouse* (1927)
   (b) *Orlando: A Biography* (1928)
   (c) *Flush* (1933)
   (d) *The Years* (1937)

114. Which one is not a novel by Virginia Woolf?
   (a) *To the Lighthouse*
   (b) *Orlando: A Biography* (1928)
   (c) *Flush* (1933)
   (d) *The Years* (1937)

115. Which is not written by F. Scott Fitzgerald?
   (a) *The Great Gatsby* (1925)
   (b) *The Sound and the Fury* (1929)
   (c) *Tender is the Night* (1924)
   (d) *The Last Tycoon* (1914)

116. *The Sound and the Fury* is a novel by
   (a) William Faulkner
   (b) Fitzgerald
   (c) Sinclair Lewis
   (d) Richard Aldington

117. Who is a brilliant mathematician?
   (a) Joseph Belloc
   (b) Nietzsche
   (c) T.S. Eliot
   (d) Bertrand Russell

118. Which one is not a drama by Lord Dunsany
   (a) *The Gods of the Mountain* (1911)
   (b) *A Night at an Inn* (1916)
   (c) *The Shadowy Waters* (1900)
   (d) *The Laughters of the Gods* (1919)

119. *The Shadowy Waters* is a play by
   (a) W.B. Yeats
   (b) Masefield
   (c) Robert Bridges
   (d) W.H. Auden

120. "If I should die, think only this of me" is a sonnet by
   (a) Masefield
   (b) Rupert Brooke
   (c) Robert Bridges
   (d) W.H. Auden

121. W.H. Auden was not
   (a) Anti-Romantic
   (b) Clinical
   (c) Proletarian
   (d) Unrealistic

122. *The Playboy of the Western World* is an extravaganza play by
   (a) Synge
   (b) Fry
   (c) Isherwood
   (d) Thornton Wilder

123. The Abbey Theatre was founded in
   (a) 1900
   (b) 1904
   (c) 1907
   (d) 1912

124. Henrik Ibsen (1828-1906) was a ________ dramatist
   (a) Norwegian
   (b) Swedish
   (c) Russian
   (d) German

125. Who is the real advocate of Surrealism?
   (a) Pound
   (b) Eliot
   (c) Andre Breton
   (d) Grierson

126. *Johnson Over Jordan* (1939) is a modern morality play by
   (a) Noel Coward
   (b) Sean O' Casey
   (c) J.B. Priestley
   (d) G.B. Shaw

127. The elegy "In Memory of W.B. Yeats" was written by
   (a) Eliot
   (b) Christopher Fry
   (c) Stephen Spender
   (d) Auden

128. Which one of the following works of George Moore is not a novel?
   (a) *Sister Theresa* (1901)
   (b) *The United Field* (1903)
   (c) *The Lake* (1905)
   (d) *Aphrodite in Aulis* (1930)

129. Which novel of Galsworthy became the first part of his immense family novel *The Forsyte Saga*?
(a) *The Man of Property*
(b) *Indian Summer of a Forsyte*
(c) *In Chancery*
(d) *To Let*

130. *The Star Turns Red* (1940) is a play by
(a) Goldsmith
(b) Sheridan
(c) Yeats
(d) Sean O' Casey

131. Which one is not a play by Granville Barker?
(a) *Waste* (1907)
(b) *The Madras House* (1910)
(c) *Peter Pan* (1904)
(d) *The Secret Life* (1923)

132. *Peter Pan* is a play by
(a) Galsworthy
(b) Pinero
(c) Gilbert
(d) James Barrie

133. Which one is a biography of by E.C. Blunden?
(a) *Leigh Hunt*
(b) *Thomas Hardy* (1942)
(c) *Shells by a Stream* (1944)
(d) *Shelley* (1946)

134. Blunden's *Shells by a Stream* is a collection of
(a) Novels
(b) Biographies
(c) Lyrics
(d) Memories

135. Which one is not a novel by E.M. Forster?
(a) *Where Angels Fear to Tread* (1905)
(b) *A Room With a View* (1908)
(c) *Howard's End* (1910)
(d) *Jacob's Room*

136. *The Cantos* is an unfinished work by
(a) T.S. Eliot
(b) Ezra Pound
(c) Maugham
(d) W.B. Yeats

137. *Fondie* (1916) is a regional novel by
(a) Eliot
(b) May Webb
(c) E.C. Booth
(d) Bennett

138. Who is not a Marxist critic?
(a) F.O. Mathiessen
(b) Clifford Bax
(c) Harold Rosenberg
(d) Christopher Caudwell

139. Who is the producer of the *Theatre of the Absurd* (1961)
(a) Albert Camus
(b) Martin Esslin
(c) Arthur Adamov
(d) Jean Genet

140. *The Fall* (1956) is a confessional novel by
(a) Albert Camus
(b) Rousseau
(c) Sylvia
(d) Snodgrors

141. *Doll's House* is a play written by
(a) Ibsen
(b) Shaw
(c) Galsworthy
(d) Browning

142. Piscator produced his epic theatre *War and Peace* in
(a) 1948
(b) 1942
(c) 1903
(d) 1936

143. *A Confession* is the subtitle of a short novel by Joseph Conrad, the name of which is

(a) *Chance* (1914)
(b) *Victory* (1915)
(c) *The Shadow Line* (1917)
(d) *The Rescue* (1920)

144. Whose generosity founded the Abbey Theatre?
(a) Miss Horniman
(b) Yeats
(c) Synge
(d) Pinero

145. The most remarkable and popular work of George Moore is his autobiographical comedy. Identify it.
(a) *Hail and Farewell*
(b) *Evelyn Inns*
(c) *Heloise and Abelard*
(d) *Esther Waters*

146. G.M. Hopkins used a technical term which means the combination of the usual regularity of stress patterns with freely varying numbers of syllables in each line. What is that term called?
(a) Spondee
(b) Dactyl
(c) Sprung rhythm
(d) Anapest

147. Who discovered the terms 'inscape' and 'instress'?
(a) Henry James
(b) G.M. Hopkins
(c) James Joyce
(d) Virginia Woolf

148. Hopkin's "The Wreck of the Deutschland" is a
(a) Lyric
(b) Sonnet
(c) Ode
(d) Essay

149. Which one of the Victorian poets came to be recognised in The Modern Period?
(a) Tennyson
(b) G.M. Hopkins
(c) Rossetti
(d) Mrs. Browning

150. Who said, "Before we have done, we will have all life within the scope of the novel"?
(a) Kipling
(b) Conrad
(c) Wells
(d) Hardy

151. Whose models of problem plays did Galsworthy follow in writing his plays?
(a) T.W. Robertson
(b) Henry Jones
(c) Arthur Pinero
(d) Henrik Ibsen

152. In which year was John Galsworthy awarded the Nobel Prize for literature?
(a) 1930
(b) 1931
(c) 1932
(d) 1934

153. The central theme of Galsworthy's "Silver Box" is
(a) Labour and capital conflict
(b) Inhuman system of law and justice
(c) Conflict between the rich and the poor
(d) Social and economic inequalities

154. The play *Justice* is a satire on
(a) the system of paying of wages.
(b) the system of social customs.
(c) the system of economic disparity.
(d) the system of legal trial.

155. Dancy and Dr. Levis are the leading characters of one of the following by Galsworthy
(a) *The Pigeon*
(b) *Loyalties*

(c) *The Skin Game*
(d) *The Eldest Son*

156. In which play of Galsworthy does Falder appear as the central character?
(a) *Justice*
(b) *Loyalties*
(c) *The Escape*
(d) *The Strife*

157. *New Worlds for Old; Mind at the End of Its Tether*; and *The Open Conspiracy* by H.G. Wells are
(a) Social novels
(b) Fantasies
(c) Didactic Works
(d) Romances

158. *The Time Machine; The Invisible Man*; and *The War of the Worlds* by H.G. Wells are
(a) Social novels
(b) Didactic Stories
(c) Social romances
(d) Fantasies

159. A.E. Housman was basically a/an
(a) Realist
(b) Optimist
(c) Pessimist
(d) Imaginist

160. *A Shropshire Lad; Into My Heart*; and *When I was One and Twenty* are the works of
(a) William Watson
(b) A.E. Housman
(c) S.T. Dobell
(d) Francis Thompson

161. Robert Bridges was appointed the Poet Laureate in
(a) 1913
(b) 1914
(c) 1915
(d) 1916

162. Which one is not a subject of the poetry of Robert Bridges?
(a) Beauties of nature
(b) Social issues
(c) Joy of love
(d) Idyllic childhood

163. Who was not in favour of the New Traditionalism?
(a) Roy Campbell
(b) Edwin Muir
(c) Andrew Young
(d) Robert Bridges

164. *A Simple Tale* is the subtitle of a detective work by Joseph Conrad, the name of which is
(a) *Nostromo* (1904)
(b) *The Mirror of the Sea* (1906)
(c) *The Secret Agent* (1907)
(d) *The Set of Six* (1908)

165. Which one of the following works of Robert Bridges is not a collection of poems?
(a) *Demeter* (1904)
(b) *October and Other Poems* (1920)
(c) *New Verse* (1925)
(d) *The Testament of Beauty* (1929)

166. Demeter is a/an
(a) Opera
(b) Autobiography
(c) Masque
(d) Absurd play

167. A.W. Pinero and Henry Arthur Jones popularised the ________ in the eighties and nineties.
(a) romantic play
(b) psychological play
(c) problem play
(d) historical play

168. Which one of the realistic problem plays was not written by J.G. Ervine?

(a) *Mixed Marriage* (1911)
(b) *John Ferguson* (1915)
(c) *The Master of the House* (1910)
(d) *Robert's Wife* (1937)

169. Which novel of J.B. Priestley is about the adventures of a touring concert party?
(a) *The Good Companions* (1929)
(b) *Angel Pavement* (1930)
(c) *Daylight on Saturday* (1943)
(d) *Bright Day* (1946)

170. Which one is not a play by Sir Noel Coward?
(a) *The Young Idea* (1923)
(b) *The Vortex* (1924)
(c) *Fallen Angels* (1925)
(d) *An Inspector Calls* (1946)

171. Who is a movement poet
(a) Auden
(b) Owen
(c) Philip Larkin
(d) Pound

172. *Juno and Paycock* is a play by
(a) Shaw
(b) Sean O' Casey
(c) Ibsen
(d) Yeats

173. The first Labour Government in England was formed in
(a) 1924
(b) 1916
(c) 1942
(d) 1918

174. Who produced "Pilgrim's Regress" (1933)
(a) John Bunyan
(b) C.S. Lewis
(c) George Orwell
(d) Jean Genet

175. Who is of the view that "the business of the dramatist is so to pose the group as to bring that moral poignantly to the light of day"?
(a) Galsworthy
(b) Pinero
(c) Jones
(d) Synge

176. Which one is not a fiction by G.K. Chesterton?
(a) *The Napoleon of Notting Hill* (1904)
(b) *The Man Who Was Thursday* (1908)
(c) *Manalive* (1912)
(d) *Green Mansions* (1904)

177. *Green Mansions* (1904) is a very famous novel by
(a) W.H. Hudson
(b) Walter De la Mare
(c) G.K. Chesterton
(d) Rupert Brooke

178. From which novel of Compton Mackenzie, *The Sylvia Scarlett* trilogy emerged
(a) *Carnival* (1912)
(b) *Sinister Street* (1913-14)
(c) *The Altar Steps* (1922)
(d) *The Parson's Progress* (1923)

179. Which of the following is an autobiographical novel of James Joyce?
(a) *Stephen Hero* (1944)
(b) *A Portrait of the Artist as a Young Man* (1916)
(c) *The Voyage Out* (1915)
(d) *Mrs. Dalloway* (1925)

180. The character Stephen Dedalus was modelled on
(a) James Joyce
(b) Aldous Leonard Huxley
(c) Edward Morgan Forster
(d) William Somerset Maugham

181. In which novel James Joyce used 'Stream of Consciousness' technique?
   (a) *Dubliners*
   (b) *Stephen Hero* (1944)
   (c) *Ulysses* (1922)
   (d) *Finnegan's Wake* (1939)

182. Which novel of Edward Morgan Forster deals with conflict between two different cultures?
   (a) *The Longest Journey* (1907)
   (b) *Two Cheers for Democracy* (1951)
   (c) *A Passage to India* (1924)
   (d) *Where Angels Fear to Tread* (1905)

183. In which novel Forster deals with the misunderstanding between individual and races?
   (a) *Howards End*
   (b) *The Longest Journey*
   (c) *Two Cheers for Democracy*
   (d) *A Room with a View*

184. Which novel of Joseph Conrad was not written in collaboration with Ford Maddox Ford?
   (a) *The Inheritors* (1901)
   (b) *Romance* (1903)
   (c) *Suspense* (1925)
   (d) None of the above

185. *A Kiss for Cinderella* (1916) is a play by
   (a) James Barrie
   (b) Galsworthy
   (c) Jones
   (d) Pinero

186. Which one is not a play by Stephen Phillips?
   (a) *Herod* (1901)
   (b) *The Sin of David* (1904)
   (c) *Nero* (1906)
   (d) *King Lear's Wife* (1920)

187. *King Lear's Wife* was written by
   (a) Masefield
   (b) Gordon Bottomley
   (c) Lady Gregory
   (d) John Ervine

188. How many poems are there in Houseman's *A Shropshire Lad*?
   (a) 60
   (b) 63
   (c) 79
   (d) 71

189. Who wrote the novel *The Thirty-Nine Steps* (1915)?
   (a) H.G. Wells
   (b) John Buchan
   (c) J.B. Priestley
   (d) Kingsley Amis

190. To protect against the low standard of the morals of the English people was the purpose of
   (a) Neo-classicists
   (b) Methodists
   (c) Chicago Group
   (d) New Poets

191. Who is the central figure in "The Waste Land"?
   (a) Tiresias
   (b) Dolittle
   (c) King Fisher
   (d) Lily

192. Who declared that "God is dead"?
   (a) Ezra Pound
   (b) Eliot
   (c) Brooks
   (d) Nietzsche

193. Y.Y. is the pseudonym of an essayist and literary critic who real name was
   (a) Robert Lynd
   (b) W.B. Yeats
   (c) Oscar Wilde
   (d) Ezra Pound

194. Which of Kipling's poems is an English version of Indian lullaby?
   (a) "Our Lady of the Snows"
   (b) "Shiva and the Grasshopper"
   (c) "Mother O' Mine"
   (d) "Gungadin"

195. Who called Webster "a very great literary and dramatic genius directed towards chaos"?
   (a) T.S. Eliot
   (b) Arnold
   (c) W.B. Yeats
   (d) None of the above

196. Who said, "The Twentieth Century is still the nineteenth, although it may in time acquire its own character"?
   (a) W.H. Auden
   (b) T.S. Eliot
   (c) W.B. Yeats
   (d) G.B. Shaw

197. The poem "The Hollow Men" was written by
   (a) Lawrence
   (b) Hopkins
   (c) Eliot
   (d) Sinclair

## ANSWERS

| | | | | | |
|---|---|---|---|---|---|
| 1. (b) | 2. (d) | 3. (a) | 4. (b) | 5. (c) | 6. (a) |
| 7. (d) | 8. (a) | 9. (d) | 10. (b) | 11. (c) | 12. (c) |
| 13. (b) | 14. (c) | 15. (c) | 16. (b) | 17. (d) | 18. (b) |
| 19. (d) | 20. (c) | 21. (a) | 22. (c) | 23. (b) | 24. (d) |
| 25. (b) | 26. (a) | 27. (b) | 28. (d) | 29. (b) | 30. (b) |
| 31. (c) | 32. (a) | 33. (b) | 34. (d) | 35. (c) | 36. (d) |
| 37. (c) | 38. (c) | 39. (a) | 40. (c) | 41. (a) | 42. (b) |
| 43. (a) | 44. (c) | 45. (c) | 46. (c) | 47. (b) | 48. (a) |
| 49. (c) | 50. (c) | 51. (b) | 52. (a) | 53. (b) | 54. (a) |
| 55. (c) | 56. (b) | 57. (a) | 58. (d) | 59. (d) | 60. (a) |
| 61. (a) | 62. (d) | 63. (b) | 64. (d) | 65. (c) | 66. (a) |
| 67. (d) | 68. (c) | 69. (d) | 70. (d) | 71. (c) | 72. (a) |
| 73. (a) | 74. (c) | 75. (a) | 76. (b) | 77. (b) | 78. (d) |
| 79. (d) | 80. (d) | 81. (a) | 82. (b) | 83. (d) | 84. (d) |
| 85. (c) | 86. (c) | 87. (a) | 88. (d) | 89. (b) | 90. (d) |
| 91. (d) | 92. (c) | 93. (a) | 94. (c) | 95. (a) | 96. (c) |
| 97. (a) | 98. (d) | 99. (b) | 100. (c) | 101. (b) | 102. (d) |
| 103. (b) | 104. (d) | 105. (c) | 106. (c) | 107. (b) | 108. (b) |
| 109. (b) | 110. (a) | 111. (c) | 112. (d) | 113. (b) | 114. (b) |
| 115. (b) | 116. (a) | 117. (d) | 118. (c) | 119. (a) | 120. (b) |
| 121. (d) | 122. (a) | 123. (b) | 124. (a) | 125. (c) | 126. (c) |

| | | | | | |
|---|---|---|---|---|---|
| 127. (d) | 128. (b) | 129. (a) | 130. (d) | 131. (c) | 132. (d) |
| 133. (a) | 134. (c) | 135. (d) | 136. (b) | 137. (c) | 138. (b) |
| 139. (b) | 140. (a) | 141. (a) | 142. (b) | 143. (c) | 144. (a) |
| 145. (a) | 146. (c) | 147. (b) | 148. (c) | 149. (b) | 150. (c) |
| 151. (d) | 152. (c) | 153. (b) | 154. (d) | 155. (b) | 156. (a) |
| 157. (c) | 158. (d) | 159. (c) | 160. (b) | 161. (a) | 162. (b) |
| 163. (d) | 164. (c) | 165. (a) | 166. (c) | 167. (c) | 168. (c) |
| 169. (a) | 170. (d) | 171. (c) | 172. (c) | 173. (a) | 174. (b) |
| 175. (a) | 176. (d) | 177. (a) | 178. (b) | 179. (b) | 180. (a) |
| 181. (c) | 182. (c) | 183. (a) | 184. (c) | 185. (a) | 186. (d) |
| 187. (b) | 188. (b) | 189. (b) | 190. (b) | 191. (a) | 192. (d) |
| 193. (a) | 194. (b) | 195. (a) | 196. (b) | 197. (c) | |

# 7

# The Contemporary Period

1. In which of the following age has there been a tremendous increase in science fiction?
   (a) Romantic period
   (b) Victorian period
   (c) Modern period
   (d) Contemporary period
2. Which of the following is not written by Graham Greene?
   (a) *England Made Me* (1935)
   (b) *Lolita* (1955)
   (c) *The Heart of the Matter* (1948)
   (d) *The Quiet American* (1955)
3. In which book Greene satirizes contemporary spy novels?
   (a) *May We Borrow Your Husband* (1967)
   (b) *Shades of Greene* (1976)
   (c) *Our Man in Havana* (1958)
   (d) *The Quiet American*
4. Who is known to have brought Narayan to the focus of the international literary community?
   (a) Oscar Wilde
   (b) Angus Wilson
   (c) Evelyn Waugh
   (d) Graham Greene
5. Charles Percy Snow is also known as
   (a) Eliot Snow
   (b) Lord Snow
   (c) God Snow
   (d) Lord Eliot
6. Which book is not written by Snow?
   (a) *The Light and the Dark* (1947)
   (b) *The Conscience of the Rich* (1958)
   (c) *Corridors of Power* (1964)
   (d) *Travels with My Aunt* (1969)
7. Which of the following is a funeral custom-related satire on America?
   (a) *Vile Bodies*
   (b) *Black Mischief* (1932)
   (c) *The Loved One* (1948)
   (d) *The New Men* (1954)
8. Which novel shows the sign of Evelyn Waugh's growing seriousness?
   (a) *Scoop* (1938)
   (b) *Put Out More Flags* (1942)
   (c) *Men at Arms* (1952)
   (d) *The Loved One* (1948)
9. Evelyn Waugh's *Brideshead Revisited* (1945) is the result of his
   (a) hospital experience
   (b) army experience
   (c) teaching experience
   (d) political experience
10. Which of the following is not included in Evelyn Waugh's *Trilogy: Sword of Honour*?
   (a) *Time of Hope* (1949)
   (b) *Men at Arms* (1952)

(c) *Officers and Gentlemen* (1955)
(d) *Unconditional Surrender* (1961)

11. Which of the following novels of Lionel Poles Hartley is a trilogy?
(a) *The Betrayal* (1966)
(b) *Facial Justice* (1960)
(c) *Eustace and Hilda* (1944-47)
(d) *The Go-Between* (1953)

12. Which of the following is not written by Hartley?
(a) *The Harness Room* (1971)
(b) *The Hireling* (1957)
(c) *The Betrayal* (1966)
(d) *The Kindly Ones* (1962)

13. Anthony Powell owes much of his major work to the French novelist, Marcel Proust and to
(a) Christopher Fry
(b) John Aubrey
(c) C.P. Snow
(d) Elizabeth Bowen

14. What is Anthony Powell's sequence of twelve novels collectively known as?
(a) *A Dance to the Music of Time*
(b) *Hearing Secret Harmonies*
(c) *The Valley of Bones*
(d) *The Kindly Ones*

15. The most important character in Anthony Powell's *A Dance to the Music of Time*, who is a failure in life but who evokes the style of an Elizabethan courtier is
(a) Stringham
(b) Sillery
(c) Widmerpool
(d) Deacon

16. Angus Wilson was born in
(a) Argentina
(b) Ireland
(c) India
(d) South Africa

17. Wilson, in his works, reacted against the dominance of the narrative technique of
(a) Henry James
(b) James Joyce
(c) Graham Greene
(d) Aldous Huxley

18. Identify the novel of Angus Wilson which deals with issues like responsibility, guilt and problems of loneliness?
(a) *Late Call*
(b) *The Middle Age of Mrs Eliot*
(c) *As If By Magic*
(d) *Setting the World on Fire*

19. Which novel of Angus Wilson reflects the influence of Virginia Woolf on the writer?
(a) *Setting the World on Fire*
(b) *Anglo-Saxon Attitudes*
(c) *No Laughing Matter*
(d) *The Old Men at the Zoo*

20. *Emily Zola* was written by Angus Wilson in 1952. It is a
(a) Critical Work
(b) Novel
(c) Ballad
(d) Play

21. David Cohen British Literature Prize was awarded to
(a) Ted Hughes
(b) V.S. Naipaul
(c) Stephen Spender
(d) Kingsley Amis

22. Which novel of V.S. Naipaul written in 1917 is a satirical examination of the economic power structure of an imaginary island located in West Indian Islands?
(a) *The Mimic Men*
(b) *Companion*
(c) *The Mystic Masseur*
(d) *Guerillas*

23. Novels like *A Bend in the River* (1987), *The Enigma of Arrival* and *In a Free State* (1971) are written by
    (a) Christopher Isherwood
    (b) W.H. Auden
    (c) V.S. Naipaul
    (d) William Golding

24. V.S. Naipaul got the Nobel Prize for literature in
    (a) 1999
    (b) 2000
    (c) 2001
    (d) 2005

25. Who wrote *A House for Mr. Biswas* in 1967 describing therein the story of the search of identity of a Brahmin Indian residing in Trinidad?
    (a) Rudyard Kipling
    (b) Salman Rushdie
    (c) Ruskin Bond
    (d) V.S. Naipaul

26. Which of the following is not a work of V.S. Naipaul?
    (a) *Finding the Centre*
    (b) *The Return of Eva Peron*
    (c) *The Middle Passage*
    (d) *Sour Sweet*

27. *The Inheritors*, a novel written in 1955, is a science fiction about the remote human past. Who is its author?
    (a) Christopher Fry
    (b) H.G. Wells
    (c) William Golding
    (d) Thomas Dylan

28. Name the novel of William Golding which describes the Salisbury Catherdral and the conflict between faith and reason?
    (a) *Sometime Never*
    (b) *The Spire*
    (c) *The Scorpion God*
    (d) *Close Quarters*

29. Golding's *The Pyramid* (1967) was followed by what appeared to be a period of abstention from fiction, an abstention broken in 1969 by
    (a) *Free Fall*
    (b) *Darkness Visible*
    (c) *The Paper Men*
    (d) *Rites of Passage*

30. Christopher Isherwood wrote a number of plays with
    (a) Louis MacNeice
    (b) C. Day Lewis
    (c) W.H. Auden
    (d) Stephen Spender

31. Christopher Isherwood's novel which expresses an autobiographical treatment of sexual problems is
    (a) *A Single Man*
    (b) *A Meeting by the River*
    (c) *Mr. Norris Changes Trains*
    (d) *Goodbye to Berlin*

32. Which novel of Christopher Isherwood expresses the writer's interest in Hindu religious mysteries?
    (a) *A Single Man*
    (b) *Goodbye to Berlin*
    (c) *Mr. Norris Changes Trains*
    (d) *A Meeting by a River*

33. Dorris Lessing was born in
    (a) Algeria
    (b) Poland
    (c) Persia
    (d) Rhodesia

34. In which novel does Dorris Lessing give the story of a relationship between a white woman and a black man in Rhodesia?

(a) *Sentimental Agent in the Volyen Empire*
(b) *The Marriage Between Zones Three, Four and Five*
(c) *Shikasta*
(d) *The Grass is Singing*

35. *Children of Violence* by Lessing is a series of
(a) Four novels
(b) Five novels
(c) Six novels
(d) Seven novels

36. Which of the following contains essays, reviews and an interview by Dorris Lessing?
(a) *Sentimental Agents*
(b) *The Golden Notebook*
(c) *A Small Personal Voice*
(d) *The Sirian Experiments*

37. Which is the first volume of autobiography by Dorris Lessing?
(a) *African Laughter*
(b) *Under my Skin*
(c) *The Golden Notebook*
(d) *London Observed*

38. Who was awarded the Booker Prize for his book *The Siege of Krishnapur*?
(a) Dorris Lessing
(b) Muriel Spark
(c) Euelyn Waugh
(d) James Gordon Farrel

39. Which of the following is not written by James Gordon Farrel?
(a) *Troubles*
(b) *The Siege of Krishnapur*
(c) *A Man from Elsewhere*
(d) *The Lung*
(e) *The Second Coming*

40. The leader of the group nicknamed as 'The Macspaunday' was
(a) W.H. Auden
(b) Spender
(c) MacNeice
(d) C. Day-Lewis

41. "The Orators", "The Dance of Death" and "Look Stranger" are the early poems of
(a) C.P. Snow
(b) W.B. Yeast
(c) Rebecca West
(d) W.H. Auden

42. *The Dog Beneath the Skin* and *On the Frontier* are Auden's plays which he wrote with
(a) Christopher Isherwood
(b) C. Day-Lewis
(c) MacNeice
(d) P.G. Wodehouse

43. "Now he is scattered among a hundred cities/ And wholly given over to unfamiliar affections."
(a) "City Without Walls"
(b) "In Memory of W.B. Yeats"
(c) "Epistle to a Godson"
(d) "Think You Fog"

44. Auden moved from Marxist alignment in his early poetic career to the Christian existentialism of
(a) Hobbes
(b) Rousseau
(c) Kierkegaard
(d) Nietzsche

45. Whose first novel *The Comforters* is concerned with a neurotic woman, Caroline Rose, having come to terms with her new-found Catholicism, with her hallucinations and with her God-like status as a creator?
(a) Dorris Lessing
(b) Evelyn Waugh
(c) Irish Murdoch
(d) Muriel Spark

46. *The Room*, *The Dumb Waiter* and *The Birthday Party* are the first three plays of
   (a) Harold Pinter
   (b) John Arden
   (c) Arnold Wesker
   (d) Joe Orton
47. When did Harold Pinter receive the Nobel Prize for literature?
   (a) 2002
   (b) 2003
   (c) 2004
   (d) 2005
48. Irwing Wardle calls the work of Pinter as
   (a) Comedy of Words
   (b) Comedy of Humour
   (c) Comedy of Menace
   (d) Comedy of Strife and Struggle
49. Harold Pinter's later plays which leave a residual sense of negativity include
   (a) *The Home Coming*
   (b) *Betrayal*
   (c) *Old Times*
   (d) All of the above
50. Pinter's *Mountain Language* is concerned with acts of interrogation and with
   (a) Adultery
   (b) Pettiness of values
   (c) Language
   (d) All of the above
51. Which of the following is a one-act play by Harold Pinter?
   (a) *The Basement*
   (b) *Silence*
   (c) *The Handmaid's Tale*
   (d) *Night School*
52. Kingsley Amis wrote a sparkling novel about a young English lecturer in a university and his constant struggle against the academic establishment. Identify that novel
   (a) *Lucky Jim*
   (b) *One Fat Englishman*
   (c) *The Uncertain Feeling*
   (d) *I Like It Here*
53. Which of the following is a detective novel by Kingsley Amis?
   (a) *The Riverside Villa's Murder*
   (b) *The Old Devils*
   (c) *Russian Hide and Seek*
   (d) *You Can't Do Both*
54. Poems like "Bright November", "A Frame of Mind" and "A Case of Samples" were written by
   (a) Kingsley Amis
   (b) Angus Wilson
   (c) C.P. Snow
   (d) Stephen Spender
55. Kingsley Amis wrote an essay on science fiction. Identify it.
   (a) *Dear Illusion*
   (b) *The Evans Country*
   (c) *The Egyptologists*
   (d) *New Maps of Hell*
56. Samuel Beckett was a poet, dramatist and novelist, who wrote proficiently in two languages—English and
   (a) German
   (b) French
   (c) Italian
   (d) Spanish
57. The most famous of Beckett's works have been his mysterious but highly innovative drama. Name that drama.
   (a) *All That Fall*
   (b) *Embers*
   (c) *Waiting for Godot*
   (d) *Endgame*
58. Anthony Burgess wrote a fictional account of Shakespeare's love affairs in

(a) *The Wanting Seed*
(b) *The Devil's Mode*
(c) *Earthly Powers*
(d) *Nothing Like the Sun*

59. Samuel Beckett was conferred the Nobel Prize for literature in
(a) 1965
(b) 1969
(c) 1974
(d) 1981

60. In which of his plays Samuel Beckett uses blindness of Hamm as a mode of suggesting that one kind of deprivation may alert audiences to the force of alternative ways of perceiving?
(a) *Endgame*
(b) *Happy Days*
(c) *Waiting for Godot*
(d) *Embers*

61. Which of his plays Samuel Beckett was first written in French *Fin de Partie* in 1957?
(a) *Embers*
(b) *Krapp's Last Tape*
(c) *Happy Days*
(d) *Endgame*

62. Who wrote the famous novel *Borstal Boy* in 1958?
(a) Christopher Fry
(b) Samuel Beckett
(c) Brendan Behan
(d) Kingsley Amis

63. Which play did Brendan Behan write in 1956?
(a) *The Go-Between*
(b) *The Quare Fellow*
(c) *The Little Girls*
(d) *Poor Things*

64. Who wrote the famous play *A Man For All Seasons* in 1960?
(a) Samuel Beckett
(b) Kingsley Amis
(c) Malcolm Bradbury
(d) Robert Bolt

65. Robert Bolt wrote an outstanding play in 1965. Name that play.
(a) *Dr. Zhivago*
(b) *All That Fall*
(c) *A Man For All Seasons*
(d) *The Quare Fellow*

66. *Billiards at Half Past Nine* (1959) *The Lost Honour of Katharina Blum* (1964) are written by
(a) Cecil Day-Lewis
(b) Pablo Neruda
(c) Brendan Behan
(d) Heinrich Boll

67. Name the writer of *Live Like Pigs* is a play about the resettlement of Gypsies in a housing estate which explores anti-social behaviour.
(a) Arnold Wesker
(b) Joe Orton
(c) Agatha Christie
(d) John Arden

68. Who among the following could describe the scenes of crime with graphic reality?
(a) Elizabeth Bowen
(b) Agatha Christie
(c) Muriel Spark
(d) Harold Pinter

69. In which novel of Agatha Christie did her famous character, Belgian, Hercule Poirot, first appear?
(a) *Murder at Mesopotamia*
(b) *The Mysterious Affair at Styles*
(c) *Murder of the Vicarage*
(d) *Appointment with Death*

70. Agatha Christie wrote two novels by prefixing her second husband's name

Mallowan. One of them is *Come, Tell Me How You Live*. Identify the second one.
(a) *The Rose and the Yew Tree*
(b) *Death on the Nile*
(c) *A Daughter's Daughter*
(d) *Star Over Bethlehem*

71. Which of the following is not a work of criticism by David Lodge?
(a) *Nice Work*
(b) *Language of Fiction*
(c) *The Novelist at the Crossroads*
(d) *Working with Structuralism*

72. Tony Curtis edited an anthology of poetry and prose with Sian James in 1991. What is that anthology called?
(a) *Walk Down a Welsh Wind*
(b) *Love from Wales*
(c) *Letting Go*
(d) *Preparations*

73. Which of the following is not the work of Tony Curtis?
(a) *Selected Poems* (1986)
(b) *Album* (1974)
(c) *Collected Poems* (1956)
(d) *The Art of Seamus Heaney* (1982)

74. *Stone and Flower*, *The Hollow Hill* and *The Oracle in the Heart* are the famous work of
(a) Tony Curtis
(b) Kathleen Raine
(c) John Wain
(d) David Lodge

75. Stella Rodney and Robert Kelway appear as lovers in Elizabeth Bowen's
(a) *Look at Those Roses*
(b) *The Last September*
(c) *The Death of the Heart*
(d) *Heat of the Day*

76. Who said, "An archaeologist is the best husband a woman can have; the older she gets, the more interested he is in her"?
(a) Goethe
(b) Emily Zola
(c) Agatha Christie
(d) Ezra Pound

77. Works like *Flowering Rifle*, *Geogriad and the Flaming Terrapin* were produced by
(a) Roy Campbell
(b) Roy Fuller
(c) Agatha Christie
(d) William Empson

78. Which modern dramatist got a wide acclaim on account of his mysterious plays?
(a) Roy Fuller
(b) Chinua Achebe
(c) T.S. Eliot
(d) Ronald Duncan

79. The analytical prose like, "The Seven Types of Ambiguity" and "The Structure of Complex Words" are written by
(a) Ronald Duncan
(b) Peter Ackroyd
(c) William Empson
(d) Geoffrey Hill

80. "Poems" (1932) and "A Lost Season" (1942) were the first two poetry works of an excellent Freudian English poet.
(a) Samuel Beckett
(b) Ted Hughes
(c) Joe Orton
(d) Roy Fuller

81. Who is the protagonist in John Osborne's *Look Back in Anger*?
(a) Murphy
(b) Luther
(c) Jimmy Porter
(d) Martin

82. What are the poems of John Osborne known as, which were written after Celtic poetry?
    (a) Phlegmatic poems
    (b) Oceanic poems
    (c) Georgian poems
    (d) None of the above
83. Which of the following is written by Louis de Berniers?
    (a) *Senor Vivo and the Coca Lord*
    (b) *The Remains of the Day*
    (c) *Sexing the Cherry*
    (d) *The Comfort of Strangers*
84. John Osborne's pungently observant and equally spiteful autobiography is
    (a) *A Better Class of Person*
    (b) *That Time*
    (c) *A Bond Honoured*
    (d) *The Unnameable*
85. Who wrote the famous works *In Parenthesis* and *The Sleeping Lord*?
    (a) John Wain
    (b) G.M. Hopkins
    (c) David Jones
    (d) William Golding
86. Antonia Byatt wrote five fairy stories in 1994 in a collection. Name that collection.
    (a) *The Matisse Stories*
    (b) *The Djinn in the Nightingale's Eye*
    (c) *Still Life*
    (d) *Unruly Times*
87. *A Pardoner's Tale* (1978), *A Winter in the Hills* (1970) and *Hurry on Down* (1953) are the prose fictions of
    (a) Alan Sillitoe
    (b) James Barrie
    (c) John Wain
    (d) Antonia Susan Byatt
88. Which of the following is not a poetry collection of John Wain?
    (a) *Wild Track*
    (b) *Living in the Present*
    (c) *Feng*
    (d) *A Word Carved on a Sill*
89. Which of the following is not written by John Wain?
    (a) *The Life Guard*
    (b) *A Tree on Fire*
    (c) *The Smaller Sky*
    (d) *The Young Visitors*
90. Campus novels, *Changing Places: A Tale of Two Campuses*, *Small World: An Academic Romance* and *Nice Work* all loosely centred on the university of Rummidge, were written by
    (a) Alan Sillitoe
    (b) Malcolm Bradbury
    (c) David Lodge
    (d) John Wain
91. Which of the following is not a play by Alan Sillitoe?
    (a) *This Foreign Field*
    (b) *Pit Strike*
    (c) *Snow Drop*
    (d) *The Interview*
92. Which of the following is not written by Alan Sillitoe?
    (a) *Unruly Times*
    (b) *The Lost Flying Boat*
    (c) *Saturday Night and Sunday Morning*
    (d) *The Death of William Posters*
93. Antonia Susan Byatt, a great novelist and critic, was greatly influenced by Proust, and a woman writer named
    (a) Dorris Lessing
    (b) Virginia Woolf
    (c) Iris Murdoch
    (d) Margret Drabble
94. An academic detective story by Antonia Susan Byatt describing the tale of

relationship between two fictional Victorian poets is
(a) *Passions of the Mind*
(b) *The Virgin in the Garden*
(c) *Possession*
(d) None of the above

95. In which book of Byatt do you find a study of Wordsworth and Coleridge?
(a) *The Virgin in the Garden*
(b) *Still Life*
(c) *Angels and Insects*
(d) *Unruly Times*

96. Name the most witty and inventive play of Tom Stoppard which was written in 1974 and has Henry Carr as its central character
(a) *If You're Glad, I'll Be Frank*
(b) *Travesties*
(c) *Jumpers*
(d) *The Real Inspector Hound*

97. The play *Rosencrantz and Guildenstern are Dead* was written by
(a) Harold Pinter
(b) Tom Stoppard
(c) Arnold Wesker
(d) Joe Orton

98. What is the real name of George Orwell?
(a) Eric Blair
(b) Eric Ambler
(c) Eric Evans
(d) Smith

99. "All animals are equal, but some animals are more equal." Which novel has this famous line been taken from?
(a) *The Castle*
(b) *Old Man and the Sea*
(c) *Animal Farm*
(d) *The Plague*

100. About which of his novels did George Orwell say this
"This moral to be drawn...is simple. Don't let it happen! It depends on you!"?
(a) *The Road to Wigan Pier*
(b) *Burmese Days*
(c) *Nineteen Eighty Four*
(d) *Animal Farm*

101. Which of the following novels of George Orwell paints the picture of squalor and hopelessness during the great depression?
(a) *Animal Farm*
(b) *The Road to Wigan Pier*
(c) *Nineteen Eighty Four*
(d) *Keep the Aspidistra Flying*

102. George Orwell's *Keep the Aspidistra Flying* deals with his contempt for the
(a) Higher class
(b) Lower middle class
(c) Upper middle class
(d) Lower class

103. Orwell's *Animal Farm* deals with
(a) Communism
(b) Aristocracy
(c) Democracy
(d) None of the above

104. Pamela Hensford Johnson is also known as
(a) Lady Snow
(b) Mary Snow
(c) George Eliot
(d) Pamela Snow

105. Which of the following is considered the best work of Pamela Hensford Johnson?
(a) *The Humbler Creation*
(b) *Catherine Carter*
(c) *The Unspeakable Skipton*
(d) *The Last Resort*

106. Which of the following novels of Pamela Hensford Johnson contains the portrayal of a mad self-centred novelist working on an endless book?

(a) *The Good Listener*
(b) *The Honours Board*
(c) *The Unspeakable Skipton*
(d) *Cork Street, Next to the Hatter's*

107. Which famous novel of Margaret Drabble portrays the struggle of its heroine Rosamund for independence, achieving some stability through her love for her baby daughter born of a casual relation?
(a) *Gates of Ivory*
(b) *The Millstone*
(c) *A Natural Curiosity*
(d) *The Waterfall*

108. One of the novels of Margaret Drabble, written in 1977, paints a dark picture of the corrupt and sterile condition of Britain in the mid-seventies. Identify that novel.
(a) *The Waterfall*
(b) *The Radiant Way*
(c) *The Ice Age*
(d) *The Realms of Gold*

109. Which of the following is not a work of Drabble?
(a) *Jerusalem the Golden*
(b) *Staying On*
(c) *The Waterfall*
(d) *A Natural Curiosity*

110. *The Map of Love* (1939) and *Deaths and Entrances* (1946) are the literary works of
(a) V.S. Naipaul
(b) C.D. Lewis
(c) Dylan Thomas
(d) J.M. Barrie

111. Name the poetical play fantasy of Dylan Thomas which got wide acclaim posthumously.
(a) *After the Funeral*
(b) *A Refusal to Mourn*
(c) *Gates of Ivory*
(d) *Under Milk Wood*

112. Identify the Angry Young Men of the 1950s in the following.
(a) Dylan Thomas
(b) J.M. Synge
(c) John Braine
(d) Graham Greene

113. Which of the following is not a work by John Braine?
(a) *Stay with Me Till Morning*
(b) *The Area of Darkness*
(c) *Waiting for Sheila*
(d) *Life at the Top*

114. Which of the following novels was written by John Braine in 1957 and which deals with the social mobility and anxiety, characteristic of Britain since the Second World War?
(a) *The Crying Game*
(b) *Room at the Top*
(c) *The Jealous God*
(d) *The Pious Agent*

115. Who wrote a *Portrait of the Artist as a Young Dog* in 1940?
(a) *Christopher Isherwood*
(b) *C.D. Lewis*
(c) *J.M. Barrie*
(d) *Dylan Thomas*

116. The hero of a novel by Alan Sillitoe, Arther Seaton, is a type-figure of the post-1945 industrial Welfare State working man. Identify the novel.
(a) *A Tree on Fire*
(b) *Key to the Door*
(c) *Saturday Night and Sunday Morning*
(d) *A Start in Life*

117. *The Archetypal Approach* is associated with
(a) William Empson
(b) Northrop Fry
(c) Philip Larkin
(d) Elizabeth Bowen

118. Christopher Fry is a
   (a) Poet
   (b) Novelist
   (c) Critic
   (d) Playwright

119. Which work is not done by Rebecca West?
   (a) *The Return of the Soldier* (1918)
   (b) *A Train of Powder* (1955)
   (c) *The Judge* (1922)
   (d) *The Deep Blue Sea* (1952)

120. Who wrote *Harriet Hume: A London Fantasy* (1929)?
   (a) Terence Rattigan
   (b) Rebecca West
   (c) Philip Larkin
   (d) Angela Carter

121. Who wrote *French Without Tears*, *The Winslow Boy* and *The Deep Blue Sea*?
   (a) Arther Miller
   (b) Tom Stoppard
   (c) Terence Rattigan
   (d) John Fowles

122. Which play of Samuel Beckett suggests despair of a society?
   (a) *Endgame*
   (b) *Krapp's Last Tape*
   (c) *Waiting For Godot*
   (d) None of the above

123. His novels depict the role of sin and suffering in human life where divine compassion and solution are the only remedies. Who is referred to here?
   (a) Graham Greene
   (b) George Orwell
   (c) Evelyn Waugh
   (d) Anthony Powell

124. Who is the central character in Salman Rushdie's famous novel *Midnight's Children*?
   (a) Abdul Gaffur
   (b) Saleem Sinai
   (c) Meera Menon
   (d) None of the above

125. Identify the novel of Salman Rushdie which has been interpreted by many Muslims as his deliberate blasphemy.
   (a) *Sour Sweet*
   (b) *The Moor's Last Sigh*
   (c) *The Ground Beneath Her Feet*
   (d) *Satanic Verses*

126. Who said, "My face looks like a wedding cake left out in the rain"?
   (a) W.H. Auden
   (b) Stephen Spender
   (c) Ezra Pound
   (d) John Barth

127. Who did not join the group of Angry Young Men?
   (a) John Braine
   (b) Henry Greene
   (c) Kingley Amis
   (d) Alan Sillitoe

128. *My Early Life* (1930) is an autobiography by
   (a) Maugham
   (b) Winston Churchill
   (c) James G. Frazer
   (d) Virginia Woolf

129. "He was found by the Bureau of Statistics to be one against whom there was no official complaint."

   One of the poems of W.H. Auden begins with these lines. Identify the poem.
   (a) "The Unknown Citizen"
   (b) "The Shield of Achilles"
   (c) "The Age of Anxiety"
   (d) None of the above

130. Stephen Spender, W.H. Auden, C. Day Lewis and Louis MacNeice formed a very

influential group of left-wing writers in the 1930's along with a novelist and playwright named
(a) Christopher Fry
(b) William Golding
(c) Christopher Isherwood
(d) Anthony Burgess

131. In 1953, Stephen Spender was made the co-editor of a monthly review of culture and world affairs named
(a) *The Chronicle*
(b) *Encounter*
(c) *Patriot*
(d) *The Dawn*

132. The theme of *The Temple* by Stephen Spender, a novel that was written almost fifty years before its publication is
(a) Homosexuality
(b) Polygamy
(c) Polyandry
(d) All of the above

133. An anti-communist collection of essays by Stephen Spender is
(a) *The God That Failed*
(b) *The Temple*
(c) *Love-Hate Relations*
(d) *Ruins and Visions*

134. *The Thirties and After* that Stephen Spender wrote in 1978 is a critical study of
(a) W.H. Auden
(b) T.S. Eliot
(c) C.P. Snow
(d) W.B. Yeats

135. *The Earth Compels*, *Autumn Journal* and *Holes in the Sky* are the famous poetry collections of
(a) Arthur Miller
(b) Anthony Powell
(c) Louis MacNeice
(d) Christopher Fry

136. *Letters from Iceland* by Louis MacNeice was collaborated with
(a) C. Day-Lewis
(b) W.H. Auden
(c) Stephen Spender
(d) Christopher Fry

137. Whose painting does Auden refer to in his poem "Musee de Beaux Arts"?
(a) Raphael
(b) Brughel
(c) Leonardo da Vinci
(d) None of the above

138. Name the unfinished autobiography of William Louis MacNeice.
(a) *Holes in the Sky*
(b) *Plant and Phantom*
(c) *The Last Ditch*
(d) *The Strings are False*

139. *The Three Arrows*, *The Servants and the Snow* and *Art and Eros* are the plays written by
(a) Anthony Burgess
(b) William Golding
(c) Irish Murdoch
(d) Stephen Spender

140. Iris Murdoch read Beckett's *Murphy* as an undergraduate at Oxford and paid homage to it in her first novel. Name that novel.
(a) *Burno's Dream*
(b) *The Sandcastle*
(c) *The Flight from the Enchanter*
(d) *Under the Net*

141. Identity the volumes of poetry by Muriel Spark.
(a) *Memento Mori*
(b) *The Takeover*
(c) *The House by the East River*
(d) *Going upto Sotheby's*

142. *The Driver's Seat*, *The Public Image* and, *Not to Disturb* by Muriel Spark are the

(a) Poems
(b) Plays
(c) Essays
(d) Novellas

143. Cecil Day-Lewis became The Poet Laureate in
(a) 1970
(b) 1969
(c) 1968
(d) 1971

144. Which of the following is not a work of Muriel Spark?
(a) *Territorial Rights*
(b) *The Third Man*
(c) *The Comforters*
(d) *Robinson*

145. In which novel does Muriel Spark narrate the story of the influence of a school teacher in Edinburgh over a group of school girls? Identify the novel.
(a) *The Public Image*
(b) *Loitering with Intent*
(c) *The Prime of Miss Jean Brodie*
(d) *The Girls of Slender Means*

146. *The Doctor is Sick*, *One Hand Clapping*, *The Worm and the Ring*, *The Wanting Seed* and *Inside Mr. Enderby* were all written by a novelist in a single year (1959) though they were published in different years. Identify the novelist.
(a) Stephen Spender
(b) Noel Coward
(c) Iris Murdoch
(d) Anthony Burgess

147. Which of the following is not a work of Anthony Burgess?
(a) *Emile Zola*
(b) *Mozarat and the Wolf*
(c) *Nothing Like the Sun*
(d) *One Hand Clapping*

148. Which novel of Anthony Burgess used the Nadsat, an invented teenage underworld slang, based on Russian words and British colloquialism?
(a) *Any old Iron*
(b) *The Devil's Mode*
(c) *A Clock Work Orange*
(d) *The Piano Player*

149. Who is the author of philosophical studies such as *The Sovereignty of God*, *The Fire and the Sun: Why Plato Banished the Artists*, and *Metaphysics as a Guide to Morals?*
(a) Muriel Spark
(b) William Golding
(c) Angus Wilson
(d) Iris Murdoch

150. Identify the novel of Iris Murdoch that has a religious theme.
(a) *The Sacred and Profane Love Machine*
(b) *Henry and Cato*
(c) *The Time of the Angels*
(d) *Nuns and Soldiers*

151. *The Lady's Not for Burning*, *Venus Observed* and *A Yard of Sun* are the works of
(a) Samuel Beckett
(b) Anthony Powell
(c) Christopher Fry
(d) Malcolm Bradbury

152. Which of the following is not a work of Christopher Fry?
(a) *Stepping Westward*
(b) *The Dark is Light Enough*
(c) *A Yard of Sun*
(d) *A Sleep of Prisoners*

153. William Golding got the Booker Prize for his novel
(a) *Close Quarters*
(b) *Lord of the Flies*
(c) *The Spire*
(d) *Rites of Passage*

154. Which novel of William Golding reflects the mood of the post-war and post-Hitler years and shows pessimistic vision of human nature and epitomises mid-twentieth century disillusionment with 19th century optimism?
(a) *Lord of the Flies*
(b) *The Pyramid*
(c) *Rites of Passage*
(d) *The Scorpion God*

155. When did William Golding get the Nobel Prize for literature?
(a) 1983
(b) 1984
(c) 1985
(d) 1982

156. Cecil Day-Lewis volumes of poetry do not include
(a) *Collected Poems*
(b) A Time to Dance
(c) *The Working Day*
(d) *The Magnetic Mountain*

157. Who wrote his detective novels under the pseudonym Nicholas Blake?
(a) Robert Bolt
(b) Brendan Behan
(c) Cecil Day-Lewis
(d) Noel Coward

158. *A Hope for Poetry* (1934) and *The Poetic Image* (1947) are the critical works of
(a) W.H. Auden
(b) Cecil Day-Lewis
(c) Robert Bridges
(d) T.S. Eliot

159. *Eating People is Wrong*, *Stepping Westward* and *The History Man* are the works of
(a) Christopher Fry
(b) William Golding
(c) Robert Bolt
(d) Malcolm Bradbury

160. Which book of Malcolm Bradbury deals with the structuralist theories in an eastern European setting?
(a) *Rates of Exchange*
(b) *Stepping Westward*
(c) *Eating People is Wrong*
(d) *The History Man*

161. Seamus Heaney won the Nobel Prize in
(a) 1990
(b) 1992
(c) 1995
(d) 1997

## ANSWERS

| | | | | | |
|---|---|---|---|---|---|
| 1. (d) | 2. (b) | 3. (c) | 4. (d) | 5. (b) | 6. (d) |
| 7. (c) | 8. (d) | 9. (b) | 10. (a) | 11. (c) | 12. (d) |
| 13. (b) | 14. (a) | 15. (a) | 16. (d) | 17. (a) | 18. (b) |
| 19. (c) | 20. (a) | 21. (b) | 22. (a) | 23. (c) | 24. (c) |
| 25. (d) | 26. (d) | 27. (c) | 28. (b) | 29. (b) | 30. (c) |
| 31. (a) | 32. (a) | 33. (c) | 34. (a) | 35. (b) | 36. (c) |
| 37. (b) | 38. (d) | 39. (e) | 40. (a) | 41. (d) | 42. (a) |
| 43. (b) | 44. (c) | 45. (d) | 46. (a) | 47. (d) | 48. (c) |
| 49. (d) | 50. (c) | 51. (b) | 52. (a) | 53. (a) | 54. (a) |
| 55. (d) | 56. (b) | 57. (c) | 58. (d) | 59. (b) | 60. (a) |

| | | | | | |
|---|---|---|---|---|---|
| 61. (d) | 62. (c) | 63. (b) | 64. (d) | 65. (a) | 66. (d) |
| 67. (d) | 68. (b) | 69. (b) | 70. (d) | 71. (a) | 72. (b) |
| 73. (c) | 74. (b) | 75. (d) | 76. (c) | 77. (a) | 78. (d) |
| 79. (c) | 80. (d) | 81. (c) | 82. (b) | 83. (a) | 84. (a) |
| 85. (c) | 86. (b) | 87. (c) | 88. (b) | 89. (b) | 90. (c) |
| 91. (c) | 92. (a) | 93. (c) | 94. (c) | 95. (d) | 96. (b) |
| 97. (b) | 98. (a) | 99. (c) | 100. (c) | 101. (b) | 102. (c) |
| 103. (a) | 104. (b) | 105. (c) | 106. (c) | 107. (b) | 108. (c) |
| 109. (b) | 110. (c) | 111. (d) | 112. (c) | 113. (b) | 114. (b) |
| 115. (d) | 116. (c) | 117. (b) | 118. (d) | 119. (d) | 120. (b) |
| 121. (c) | 122. (c) | 123. (a) | 124. (b) | 125. (d) | 126. (a) |
| 127. (b) | 128. (b) | 129. (a) | 130. (c) | 131. (b) | 132. (a) |
| 133. (a) | 134. (b) | 135. (c) | 136. (b) | 137. (b) | 138. (d) |
| 139. (c) | 140. (d) | 141. (d) | 142. (d) | 143. (c) | 144. (b) |
| 145. (c) | 146. (d) | 147. (a) | 148. (c) | 149. (d) | 150. (b) |
| 151. (c) | 152. (a) | 153. (d) | 154. (a) | 155. (a) | 156. (a) |
| 157. (c) | 158. (b) | 159. (d) | 160. (a) | 161. (c) | |

# 8

# American Literature and Non-British Literatures

1. America became independent in
   (a) 1772
   (b) 1775
   (c) 1774
   (d) 1776
2. Who, among the following, is considered the practitioner of "Naturalism" in America?
   (a) Frank Norris
   (b) Henry James
   (c) Edgar Allen Poe
   (d) Emerson
3. Herman Melville's famous book is spelt as
   (a) Moby-Dick
   (b) Mobydick
   (c) Mobi-Dick
   (d) Moby-Dicke
4. The above work is a ______ in epic form
   (a) verse drama
   (b) parable
   (c) beast fable
   (d) novella
5. Cetology is a branch of Zoology that deals with
   (a) Sea-monsters
   (b) Whales
   (c) Fish
   (d) Sharks
6. The subtitle of Melville's novel is
   (a) *A Sea Story*
   (b) *A Simple Story*
   (c) *The Whale*
   (d) *The White Whale*
7. Who is obsessed with the pursuit of the Whale?
   (a) Ishmael
   (b) Daggoo
   (c) Fedallah
   (d) Captain Ahab
8. Who is the narrator in Melville's *Moby-Dick*?
   (a) Alijah
   (b) Gabriel
   (c) Captain Ahab
   (d) Ishmael
9. Who is the principal character in Melville's *Moby-Dick*?
   (a) Captain Ahab
   (b) Ishmael
   (c) Gabriel
   (d) None of the above
10. Match the characters and the works in which they appear.

| | |
|---|---|
| A. Willy Loman | 1. *Moby-Dick* |
| B. Humbert Humbert | 2. *Death of a Salesman* |
| C. Amanda Wingfield | 3. *Lolita* |

D. Captain Ahab — 4. *The Glass Menagerie*

| Codes: | A | B | C | D |
|---|---|---|---|---|
| (a) | 2 | 3 | 4 | 1 |
| (b) | 1 | 2 | 3 | 4 |
| (c) | 4 | 3 | 2 | 1 |
| (d) | 3 | 1 | 4 | 2 |

11. Melville's *Moby-Dick* was published in
    (a) 1849
    (b) 1851
    (c) 1850
    (d) 1855

12. Who is the father of American poetry?
    (a) William Cullen Bryant
    (b) J.F. Cooper
    (c) Washington
    (d) None of the above

13. Who has been called the "Romancer of the Sea"?
    (a) Washington
    (b) Edgar Allan Poe
    (c) James F. Cooper
    (d) W.C. Bryant

14. Who is the "father of American Transcendentalism"?
    (a) Thoreau
    (b) Emerson
    (c) Melville
    (d) Edgar Allan Poe

15. Who wrote the essay *Nature* (1836)?
    (a) Walt Whitman
    (b) Edgar Allan Poe
    (c) Emerson
    (d) Thoreau

16. Who said, "Nature will not have us fret and fume"?
    (a) Henry David Thoreau
    (b) Robert Frost
    (c) R.W. Emerson
    (d) Margaret Fuller

17. Which of the following is not a part of *Nature*?
    (a) Beauty
    (b) Spirit
    (c) Prospects
    (d) Knowledge

18. Which work of R.W. Emerson has been called his "First Philosophy"?
    (a) *English Traits*
    (b) *Nature*
    (c) *The Conduct of Life*
    (d) *Representative Men*

19. Which work of Emerson comprises biographies of eminent men from the world of literature, history, philosophy, etc.?
    (a) *The Conduct of Life*
    (b) *Self-Reliance*
    (c) *Representative Men*
    (d) *The American Scholar*

20. Match the men of letters and the titles Emerson gave them.

| | |
|---|---|
| A. Plato | 1. Poet |
| B. Swedenborg | 2. Philosopher |
| C. Montaigne | 3. Skeptic |
| D. Shakespeare | 4. Mystic |

| Codes: | A | B | C | D |
|---|---|---|---|---|
| (a) | 2 | 4 | 3 | 1 |
| (b) | 1 | 3 | 4 | 2 |
| (c) | 3 | 2 | 1 | 4 |
| (d) | 4 | 1 | 2 | 3 |

21. *The Dial*, also called "little magazine", was founded by
    (a) Emerson and Fuller
    (b) Emerson and Thoreau
    (c) Elizabeth Palmer Peabody
    (d) James Freemen Clarke

22. "Life is a train of moods like a string of beads, and, as we pass through them they prove to be many-coloured lenses which

paint the world their own hue, and each shows only what lies in its focus." Who said it?

(a) Henry James
(b) Nathaniel Hawthorne
(c) Margaret Fuller
(d) R.W. Emerson

23. Which quarterly journal was associated with Transcendentalism?
(a) *The Germ*
(b) *The Dial*
(c) *The Heaven*
(d) *The Spirit of the Poet*

24. Who said, "Nature is a greater and more perfect art"?
(a) Emerson
(b) Thoreau
(c) Walt Whitman
(d) Wallace Stevens

25. Thoreau's masterpiece "Walden" (1854) is divided into?
(a) 10 Chapters
(b) 15 Chapters
(c) 18 Chapters
(d) 20 Chapters

26. Who wrote the essay, "Civil Disobedience"?
(a) Emerson
(b) Thoreau
(c) Walt Whitman
(d) Edgar Allan Poe

27. "Aeolian harp" was the favourite image for poetry used by
(a) Wordsworth
(b) Emerson
(c) Edgar Allan Poe
(d) Walt Whitman

28. Who among the following influenced Gandhi Ji's idea of Civil Disobedience?
(a) Emerson
(b) Melville
(c) Thoreau
(d) Ruskin

29. Who among the following is called "the Sage of Concord"?
(a) Cooper
(b) Bryant
(c) Emerson
(d) Melville

30. "The Purloined Letter" is a seminal short-story by
(a) J.F. Cooper
(b) Anton Chekhov
(c) Edgar Allan Poe
(d) Washington Irving

31. Who is the writer of such poems "The Raven", "The Haunted Palace", "The Conqueror Worm", "The Bells" and "To Helen"?
(a) Emerson
(b) Melville
(c) Edgar Allan Poe
(d) J.F. Cooper

32. Who himself classified his tales as 'grotesque', 'Arabesque' and 'ratiocinative'?
(a) Edgar Allan Poe
(b) Emerson
(c) Mark Twain
(d) Thoreau

33. In Poe's *Ms. Found in a Bottle*, Ms. is read as
(a) miss
(b) manuscript
(c) mistress
(d) mrs.

34. Who wrote the poem, "Hugh Selwyn Mauberley" (1920)?
(a) Wallace Stevens
(b) Robert Frost
(c) Ezra Pound
(d) T.E. Hulme

35. Which one is not by Ernest Hemingway?
    (a) *The Sun Also Rises* (1926)
    (b) *Men without Women* (1927)
    (c) *A Farewell to Arms* (1926)
    (d) *The Silver Cord* (1926)
36. "Paterson" (1948) is written by
    (a) William Carlos Williams
    (b) Wallace Stevens
    (c) Langston Hughes
    (d) E.E. Cummings
37. Who is the central character in Hemingway's novel "The Old Man and the Sea"?
    (a) Santiago
    (b) Manolin
    (c) Marlin
    (d) None of the above
38. Who said, "All modern American literature came from one book by Mark Twain called *Huckleberry Finn*"?
    (a) Wallace Stevens
    (b) Ernest Hemingway
    (c) Walt Whitman
    (d) Langston Hughes
39. Which work of Hemingway portrays his love of Spain and his passion for bullfighting?
    (a) *A Farewell to Arms*
    (b) *The Sun also Rises*
    (c) *Death in the Afternoon*
    (d) *For Whom the Bell Tolls*
40. Which Hemingway novel's title in England was Fiesta?
    (a) *The Sun Also Rises*
    (b) *The Old Man and the Sea*
    (c) *Death in the Afternoon*
    (d) *A Farewell to Arms*
41. Match the characters and the novels in which they appear.

| | |
|---|---|
| A. Jake Barnes | 1. *A Farewell to Arms* |
| B. Catherine Barkley | 2. *The Old Man and the Sea* |
| C. Robert Jordan | 3. *The Sun also Rises* |
| D. Santiago | 4. *For Whom the Bell Tolls* |

| **Codes:** | A | B | C | D |
|---|---|---|---|---|
| (a) | 3 | 1 | 4 | 2 |
| (b) | 1 | 2 | 3 | 4 |
| (c) | 4 | 3 | 2 | 1 |
| (d) | 2 | 4 | 1 | 3 |

42. How many days has Santiago passed with out Catching a fish?
    (a) 74
    (b) 86
    (c) 84
    (d) 75
43. Which of the following novels of Hemingway is about Africa?
    (a) *A Farewell to Arms*
    (b) *The Sun also Rises*
    (c) *True At First Light*
    (d) *For Whom the Bell Tolls*
44. Which of the following novels of Hemingway derives its title from John Donne?
    (a) *To Have and Have not*
    (b) *In Our Time*
    (c) *For Whom the Bell Tolls*
    (d) *The Garden of Eden*
45. Which American novelist is known for his Yoknapatawpha cycle?
    (a) Faulkner
    (b) Hemingway
    (c) Saul Bellow
    (d) Scott Fitzgerald

46. Which of the following was Faulkner's longest novel?
    (a) *The Sound and the Fury*
    (b) *A Fable*
    (c) *Intruder in the Dust*
    (d) *As I Lay Dying*

47. Which of the following is a three act play?
    (a) *Light in August*
    (b) *Requiem for a Nun*
    (c) *Absalom, Absalom!*
    (d) *Hamlet*

48. Which Faulkner novel is about the decay and fall of the aristocratic Compson Family?
    (a) *The Sound and the Fury*
    (b) *Sanctuary*
    (c) *Go Down, Moses*
    (d) *Intruder in the Dust*

49. Match the characters with the novels in which they appear.

| | |
|---|---|
| A. "Chick" Mallison | 1. *The Sound and the Fury* |
| B. Quentin Compson | 2. *Absalom, Absalom!* |
| C. Thomas Sutpen | 3. *As I Lay Dying* |
| D. Addie Bundren | 4. *Intruder in the Dust* |

| **Codes:** | A | B | C | D |
|---|---|---|---|---|
| (a) | 4 | 1 | 2 | 3 |
| (b) | 1 | 2 | 3 | 4 |
| (c) | 3 | 4 | 1 | 2 |
| (d) | 2 | 3 | 4 | 2 |

50. Which one is a Stream-of-Consciousness novel?
    (a) Fitzgerald's *The Great Gatsby* (1925)
    (b) Hemingway's *A Farewell to Arms* (1929)
    (c) William Faulkner's *The Sound and the Fury* (1929)
    (d) Saul Bellow's *Herzog* (1964)

51. What is the name of the first Volume of Robert Frost's poems?
    (a) "North of Boston"
    (b) "Steeple Bush"
    (c) "A Boy's Will"
    (d) "A Masque of Reason"

52. Which of the following is not a poem by Frost?
    (a) "Stopping by Woods on a Snowy Evening"
    (b) "Two Tramps in Mud Time"
    (c) "The Road Not Taken"
    (d) "Song of Myself"

53. Which Frost poem carries this famous line?
    "Good fences make good neighbours."
    (a) "Mowing"
    (b) "The Black Cottage"
    (c) "Mending Wall"
    (d) "Out, Out"

54. Which of the following is not a Sonnet?
    (a) "Two Tramps in Mud Time"
    (b) "Mowing"
    (c) "Meeting and Passing"
    (d) "The Silken Tent"

55. Who said, "But I have promises to keep, and miles to go before I sleep"?
    (a) Robert Frost
    (b) William Faulkner
    (c) Wallace Stevens
    (d) Langston Hughes

56. Who says, "Earth is the right place for love"?
    (a) Sylvia Plath
    (b) Langston Hughes
    (c) Wallace Stevens
    (d) Robert Frost

57. Which one is a great patriotic poem by Frost?
    (a) "Mending Wall"
    (b) "Birches"

(c) "The Gift Outright"
(d) "Directive"

58. Who among the following is called the New England poet?
(a) Carl Sandburg
(b) Robert Frost
(c) William Carlos Williams
(d) Wallace Stevens

59. The original name of Tennessee Williams is
(a) Tommy Pester Williams
(b) Tom Williams
(c) Thomas Lanier Williams
(d) Thomas Stuart Williams

60. "The Poker Night" was later retitled as
(a) *The Glass Menagerie*
(b) *The Rose Tattoo*
(c) *A Street Car Named Desire*
(d) *Cat on a Hot Tin Roof*

61. Blanche is the central figure in one of Tennessee William's play
(a) *The Glass Menagerie* (1945)
(b) *A Street Car Named Desire* (1947)
(c) *Cat on a Hot Tin Roof* (1953)
(d) *The Rose Tattoo* (1950)

62. In which one of the following Tennessee Williams's plays, Laura appeared?
(a) *The Glass Menagerie* (1945)
(b) *A Street Car Named Desire* (1947)
(c) *Cat on a Hot Tin Roof* (1955)
(d) *Orpheus Descending* (1957)

63. Tennessee Williams's "In the Winter of Cities" (1956) is collection of
(a) Poems
(b) Plays
(c) Short Stories
(d) None of the above

64. Who wrote "Leaves of Glass"?
(a) Robert Frost
(b) Emily Dickinson
(c) R.W. Emerson
(d) Walt Whitman

65. Which of the following is not a poem by Whitman?
(a) "Song of Myself"
(b) "Crossing Brooklyn Ferry"
(c) "O Captain! My Captain!"
(d) "Success is Counted Sweetest"

66. Match the following:

| | |
|---|---|
| A. *Desire Under the Elms* | 1. Arthur Miller |
| B. *Death of a Salesman* | 2. Charles Fuller |
| C. *A Soldier's Play* | 3. Eugene O'Neill |
| D. *A Street Car Named Desire* | 4. Tennessee Williams |

| **Codes:** | A | B | C | D |
|---|---|---|---|---|
| (a) | 3 | 1 | 2 | 4 |
| (b) | 1 | 2 | 3 | 4 |
| (c) | 4 | 3 | 2 | 1 |
| (d) | 2 | 4 | 1 | 3 |

67. Which of the following plays is set during World War II?
(a) *The Glass Menagerie*
(b) *Death of a Salesman*
(c) *Cat on a Hot Tin Roof*
(d) *A Soldier's Play*

68. Match the following:

| | |
|---|---|
| A. Henry James | 1. *Their Eyes were Watching God* |
| B. Z.N. Hurston | 2. *Cat on a Hot Tin Roof* |
| C. Tennessee Williams | 3. *The Bostonians* |
| D. Arthur Miller | 4. *All My Sons* |

| **Codes:** | A | B | C | D |
|---|---|---|---|---|
| (a) | 3 | 1 | 2 | 4 |
| (b) | 1 | 3 | 4 | 2 |
| (c) | 4 | 2 | 3 | 1 |
| (d) | 2 | 4 | 1 | 3 |

69. Which one book is now regarded as "The Bible of Democracy"?
    (a) Melville's *Moby-Dick*
    (b) Howthorne's *The Scarlet Letter*
    (c) Whitman's *Leaves of Grass*
    (d) None of the above

70. Whitman's "When Lilacs Last in the Dooryard Bloom'd" is an elegy on
    (a) Herman Melville
    (b) Hawthorne
    (c) Abraham Lincoln
    (d) None of the above

71. Who said the following?
    "I am the poet of the body
    And I am the poet of the soul....
    I am the poet of Equality"
    (a) Walt Whitman
    (b) Edgar Allen Poe
    (c) P.B. Shelley
    (d) Tennyson

72. Which one of the following novels is gothic in treatment?
    (a) *The Wings of the Dove*
    (b) *Washington Square*
    (c) *Daisy Miller*
    (d) *Turn of the Screw*

73. Match the heroines of Henry James with their respective novels.

| | |
|---|---|
| A. Catherine Sloper | 1. *The Wings of the Dove* |
| B. Milly Theale | 2. *Washington Square* |
| C. Isabel Archer | 3. *The American* |
| D. Christopher Newman | 4. *The Portrait of a Lady* |

| **Codes:** | A | B | C | D |
|---|---|---|---|---|
| (a) | 2 | 1 | 4 | 3 |
| (b) | 1 | 3 | 4 | 2 |
| (c) | 3 | 4 | 2 | 1 |
| (d) | 4 | 2 | 3 | 1 |

74. The one act drama *The American Dream* (1959) was written by
    (a) Tennessee Williams
    (b) Edward Albee
    (c) Eugene O'Neill
    (d) Edith Wharton

75. The poem "Chicago" is written by
    (a) Ezra Pound
    (b) E.E. Cummings
    (c) Carl Sandburg
    (d) William Carlos Williams

76. In "The People Yes" (1936) Sandburg emerges
    (a) a lyric poet like Poe
    (b) a satirist like Swift
    (c) an epic poet like Whitman
    (d) a narrative poet like Tennyson

77. Who is the narrator in F. Scott Fitzgerald's novel *The Great Gatsby* (1925)?
    (a) Gatsby
    (b) Nick
    (c) Buchannan
    (d) None of the above

78. Which one of the following novels of Fitzgerald is unfinished?
    (a) *The Last Tycoon*
    (b) *Tender is the Night*
    (c) *The Great Gatsby*
    (d) *The Beautiful and the Damned*

79. Who is associated with the "Jazz Age"?
    (a) Ernest Hemingway
    (b) Scott Fitzgerald
    (c) John Dos Passos
    (d) Sherwood Anderson

80. "This Side of Paradise" (1920) was written by
    (a) Henry James
    (b) Norman Mailer
    (c) Ernest Hemingway
    (d) Scott Fitzgerald

81. O'Neill uses in *The Hairy Ape* the technique of
   (a) Impressionism
   (b) Absurdism
   (c) Expressionism
   (d) Realism
82. O'Neill's first play was
   (a) *The Hairy Ape*
   (b) *The Iceman Cometh*
   (c) *Under the Elms*
   (d) *The Emperor Jones*
83. Which of the following plays of O'Neill is autobiographical?
   (a) *Long Day's Journey into Night*
   (b) *Strange Interlude*
   (c) *Emperor Jones*
   (d) *Mourning Becomes Electra*
84. Match the following:

| | |
|---|---|
| A. *Humboldt's Gift* | 1. Mark Twain |
| B. *Adventures of Huckleberry Finn* | 2. Saul Bellow |
| C. *The Scarlet Letter* | 3. F. Scott Fitzgerald |
| D. *The Great Gatsby* | 4. Nathaniel Hawthorne |

| **Codes:** | A | B | C | D |
|---|---|---|---|---|
| (a) | 2 | 1 | 4 | 3 |
| (b) | 3 | 4 | 1 | 2 |
| (c) | 1 | 2 | 3 | 4 |
| (d) | 4 | 3 | 2 | 1 |

85. "Success is counted sweetest
   By those who ne'er succeed
   To comprehend a nectar
   Requires sorest need"

   Who said the following?
   (a) Robert Frost
   (b) Walt Whitman
   (c) Emily Dickinson
   (d) Emerson
86. Which of the following is a Dickinson poem?
   (a) "I Heard a Fly Buzz When I Died"
   (b) "Out of the Cradle Endlessly Rocking"
   (c) "Choose Something Like a Star"
   (d) "The Gum Gatherer"
87. "If I read a book and it makes my whole body so cold no fire can warm me, I know that is poetry. If I feel physically as if the top of my head were taken off, I know that is poetry."

   Who defined poetry thus?
   (a) Henry James
   (b) Robert Frost
   (c) Emily Dickinson
   (d) T.S. Eliot
88. Which of the following is not a Dickinson poem?
   (a) "Because I could Not Stop for Death"
   (b) "Before I Got my Eye Put out"
   (c) "This is my Letter to the World"
   (d) "After Apple-Picking"
89. *Catch 22* is a novel by?
   (a) Philip Roth
   (b) Joseph Heller
   (c) Joyce Cary
   (d) John Russel
90. The Character Nick Carter was created by
   (a) Jone Russel Coryell
   (b) Joseph Heller
   (c) Johnston McCulley
   (d) Martin Cruz Smith
91. The name of the commander of the 256th Squadron of the U.S. Airforce in *Catch 22* is

(a) Major Major
(b) Major Major Major
(c) Captain Major
(d) Captain Captain Major

92. *Harmonium* (1923) was written by
(a) R.W. Emerson
(b) Robert Frost
(c) Wallace Stevens
(d) Edith Wharton

93. Who first used the phrase "lost generation"?
(a) Henry James
(b) T.S. Eliot
(c) Ernest Hemingway
(d) Gertrude Stein

94. Who said, "Rose is a rose is a rose is a rose"?
(a) Ernest Hemingway
(b) F.R. Leavis
(c) Gertrude Stein
(d) John Steinbeck

95. *The Autobiography of Alice B. Toklas* (1933) was actually the autobiography of
(a) Iris Murdoch
(b) Dorris Lessing
(c) Toni Morrison
(d) Gertrude Stein

96. *Q.E.D.* is the name of a/an
(a) Organisation
(b) Novel
(c) Short story
(d) Author

97. Who coined the title *Q.E.D.*?
(a) Toni Morrison
(b) Gertrude Stein
(c) J.D. Salinger
(d) Joseph Heller

98. *Of Mice and Men* was written by?
(a) Hemingway
(b) Steinbeck
(c) Faulkner
(d) Saul Bellow

99. Which novel is about the migration of a dispossessed family from Oklahoma Dust Bowl to California?
(a) *The Great Gatsby*
(b) *The Grapes of Wrath*
(c) *Catcher in the Rye*
(d) *Herzog*

100. In which novel would we find the Rostov Family?
(a) *War and Peace*
(b) *Anna Karenina*
(c) *Brother Karamazov*
(d) *Father and Sons*

101. O'Neill uses Greek mythology in which of the following Plays?
(a) *Mourning Becomes Electra*
(b) *Desire Under the Elms*
(c) *The Iceman Cometh*
(d) *The Hairy Ape*

102. Who gave the slogan to modern poets, "Make It New; Make It Hard"?
(a) T.S. Eliot
(b) Ezra Pound
(c) W.B. Yeats
(d) Robert Frost

103. Who of the following said, "Poetry should be at least as well-written as prose"?
(a) D.H. Lawrence
(b) Wallace Stevens
(c) T.S. Eliot
(d) Ezra Pound

104. John Steinbeck derived the title of his novel, *In Dubious Battle*, from

(a) Shakespeare
(b) Donne
(c) Milton
(d) Marlowe

105. The title of Steinbeck's *Of Mice and Men* is taken from
(a) Robert Burns
(b) Lord Byron
(c) John Milton
(d) John Dryden

106. The title of Steinbeck's *The Winter of Our Discontent* comes from
(a) Chaucer
(b) Langland
(c) Shakespeare
(d) Tennyson

107. Which of the following novels of Steinbeck is considered his classic?
(a) *The Grapes of Wrath*
(b) *The Pastures of Heaven*
(c) *Cup of Gold*
(d) *East of Eden*

108. Joe Christmas is the central character in which of the following novels of Faulkner?
(a) *Absalom, Absalom*
(b) *Light in August*
(c) *As I Lay Dying*
(d) *Sanctuary*

109. *Death of a Salesman* by Arthur Miller is
(a) an expressionistic play
(b) a realist drama
(c) an allegorical drama
(d) an impressionistic play

110. Which of the following plays of Arthur Miller is a critique of McCarthism of the 1950's?
(a) *All my Sons*
(b) *The Crucible*
(c) *A View from the Bridge*
(d) *After the Fall*

111. Biff and Happy are Characters in
(a) *The Sound and the Fury*
(b) *The Price*
(c) *A Memory of Two Mondays*
(d) *Death of a Salesman*

112. "Who is Afraid of Virginia Woolf?" was written by
(a) Edward Albee
(b) Thornton Wilder
(c) Eugene O'Neill
(d) Arthur Miller

113. Which of the following is an "absurdist" play?
(a) *A Memory of Two Mondays*
(b) *The Emperor Jones*
(c) *Who is Afraid of Virginia Woolf?*
(d) *A Street Car Named Desire*

114. Ralph Ellison's famous novel *Invisible Man* which tells the story of a New York immigrant black, appeared in?
(a) 1950
(b) 1951
(c) 1952
(d) 1953

115. The Famous novel *The Red Badge of Courage* (1895), a study of an inexperienced soldier (Henry Fleming), is written by
(a) Stephen Crane
(b) Edward Bellamy
(c) Sherwood Anderson
(d) Hart Crane

116. Whose belief is that "Language is a virus" and led him to employ the 'cut-up' technique?
(a) William Burroughs
(b) Alan Gingsberg
(c) J. Kerouac
(d) Nonc of the above

117. Which one is not associated with Harlem Renaissance?
   (a) Langston Hughes
   (b) Claude Mckay
   (c) Wallace Stevens
   (d) Jean Toomer

118. Which one of the following plays is not by Eugene O'Neill?
   (a) *Beyond the Horizon*
   (b) *A View from the Bridge*
   (c) *The Iceman Cometh*
   (d) *Long Day's Journey Into Night*

119. Irving Babbit, the leader of American New Humanism, is a
   (a) Poet
   (b) Essayist
   (c) Dramatist
   (d) Critic

120. Which one is a work by Irving Babbit?
   (a) *The New Laokoon* (1910)
   (b) *Rousseau and Romanticism* (1919)
   (c) *Democracy and Leadership* (1924)
   (d) All of the above

121. *American Renaissance* (1940) is written by
   (a) F.R. Leavis
   (b) Henry James
   (c) F.O. Matthiessen
   (d) Eugene O'Neill

122. Which among the following is not a work by Mark Twain?
   (a) *The Adventure of Tom Sawyer* (1876)
   (b) *Life on the Mississippi* (1883)
   (c) *The Adventures of Huckleberry Finn* (1885)
   (d) *The Old Man and the Sea*

123. Who edited *The Poems of Emily Dickinson* (1955)
   (a) T.S. Eliot
   (b) T.H. Johnson
   (c) W.H. Auden
   (d) None of the above

124. Who is the principal Character in Hawthorne's novel *The Scarlet Letter* (1850)?
   (a) Hester Prynne
   (b) Arthur Dimmesdale
   (c) Chillingworth
   (d) Pearl

125. Hart Crane's famous poem, "The Bridge" (1930) which explores the 'Myth of America' is an echo of
   (a) "Whitman's Leaves of Grass"
   (b) "Thoreau's Walden"
   (c) "Emerson's Nature"
   (d) None of the above

126. Which of the following books is written by Cleanth Brooks, an American new critic?
   (a) *Understanding Poetry* (1938)
   (b) *Modern Poetry and the Tradition* (1939)
   (c) *The Well-Wrought Urn* (1947)
   (d) All of the above

127. Which one of the following is a critical work by Lionel Trilling?
   (a) *The Liberal Imagination* (1950)
   (b) *The Opposing Self* (1955)
   (c) *Sincerity and Authenticity* (1972)
   (d) All of the above

128. Which Russian novel is a reflection of the author's belief that revolutionaries possessed the soul of Russia and that, unless exorcised, they would drive the country over the precipice?
   (a) *The Possessed*
   (b) *The House of the Dead*
   (c) *The Cossacks*
   (d) *Bend Sinister*

129. Henry James's *Art of Fiction* came out in
   (a) 1884
   (b) 1886
   (c) 1888
   (d) 1890

130. *The Tragic Muse* (1890) by Henry James is a
   (a) Drama
   (b) Prose work
   (c) Novel
   (d) Anthology of poems

131. Henry James called his novella *Turn of the Screw* a
   (a) tale of terror
   (b) fable
   (c) gothic novel
   (d) ghost story

132. "Twenty-six Men and a Girl" is a famous short story by
   (a) W.W. Jacobs
   (b) Maxim Gorky
   (c) Leo Tolstoy
   (d) Katherine Mansfield

133. The Word "Gorky" means
   (a) Clever
   (b) Pure
   (c) Sweet
   (d) Bitter

134. "Mark Twain"—the name was a take off from the field of
   (a) Navigation
   (b) Mining
   (c) Farming
   (d) Bakery

135. Who mocked Cooper's "The Deerslayer" and "The Pathfinder" in "Fennimore Cooper's Literary Offences"?
   (a) T.S. Eliot
   (b) Henry James
   (c) Mark Twain
   (d) F.R. Leavis

136. The story of which Cooper novel is set in The American War of Independence?
   (a) *Precaution*
   (b) *The Spy*
   (c) *The Red Rover*
   (d) *The Pathfinder*

137. Who founded the "Bread and Cheese" Club?
   (a) R.W. Emerson
   (b) Fenimore Cooper
   (c) Thomas Jefferson
   (d) Mark Twain

138. Billy Budd is a character from
   (a) Mark Twain
   (b) Thomas Aldrich
   (c) Herman Melville
   (d) Nathaniel Hawthorne

139. Pulitzer Prize is awarded by
   (a) Columbia University
   (b) Harward University
   (c) Massachusetts University
   (d) Albama State University

140. Match the characters and the works.

| | |
|---|---|
| A. Pyncheon | 1. *The Assistant* |
| B. Lily Bart | 2. *The House of the Seven Gables* |
| C. Frank Alpine | 3. *The House of Mirth* |
| D. Frederick Henry | 4. *A Farewell to Arms* |

| **Codes:** | A | B | C | D |
|---|---|---|---|---|
| (a) | 2 | 3 | 1 | 4 |
| (b) | 1 | 2 | 3 | 4 |
| (c) | 4 | 1 | 2 | 3 |
| (d) | 3 | 4 | 1 | 2 |

141. Match the following

| | |
|---|---|
| A. *The Assistant* | 1. Saul Bellow |
| B. *The House of Mirth* | 2. Bernard Malamud |
| C. *Herzog* | 3. William Faulkner |
| D. *As I Lady Dying* | 4. Edith Wharton |

| **Codes:** | A | B | C | D |
|---|---|---|---|---|
| (a) | 2 | 4 | 1 | 3 |
| (b) | 4 | 2 | 3 | 1 |
| (c) | 1 | 2 | 3 | 4 |
| (d) | 3 | 1 | 2 | 4 |

142. Which novel deals with two days in the life of a 16-year old Holden Caulfield after he has been expelled from prep School?
   (a) *Loneliness of the Long Distance Runner*
   (b) *Saturday Night and Sunday Morning*
   (c) *Catcher in the Rye*
   (d) *A Clockwork Orange*

143. *The Snows of Kilimanjaro* was written by
   (a) Rudyard Kipling
   (b) Wallace Stevens
   (c) Ernest Hemingway
   (d) J.D. Salinger

144. *The Education of Henry Adams* (1907) was written by
   (a) Henry James
   (b) Henry Miller
   (c) Henry Adams
   (d) William James

145. Henry James's short novels (*What Maisie Knew*, *The Turn of the Screw*, *The Awkward Age*, and *The Sacred Fount*) deal with the theme of
   (a) Bravery
   (b) Evil
   (c) Cowardice
   (d) Nationalism

146. Stephen Crane's *The Red Badge of Courage* (1895) has as protagonist
   (a) The artist-hero
   (b) The crafty-hero
   (c) The boy-hero
   (d) The aged-hero

147. Who wrote *Maggie : A Girl of the Streets*?
   (a) Frank Norris
   (b) Mark Twain
   (c) Henry James
   (d) Stephen Crane

148. Which one is not an example of the expressionistic technique?
   (a) O'Neill's *The Hairy Ape*
   (b) Elmer Rice's *Adding Machine*
   (c) Thorton Wilder's *Skin of Our Teeth*
   (d) Tennessee Williams's *In the Winter of Cities*

149. Which one of the following writers is not associated with the Genteel Tradition?
   (a) Alan Locke
   (b) W.V. Moody
   (c) Bailey Aldrich
   (d) Trumbull Stickney

150. Richard Wright is a/an
   (a) Black American Writer
   (b) Australian Poet
   (c) South African Novelist
   (d) None of the above

151. Which one is not a work by Hawthorne?
   (a) *The Scarlet Letter* (1850)
   (b) *The House of the Seven Gables* (1851)
   (c) *The Blithedale Romance* (1852)
   (d) *Billy Budd* (1891)

152. "Poetry is the rhythmic creation of beauty". This statement was made by
   (a) John Keats
   (b) Lord Byron
   (c) Edgar Allan Poe
   (d) P.B. Shelley

153. The author of "Twice-Told Tales" was
   (a) Edgar Allan Poe
   (b) Nathaniel Hawthrone
   (c) Herman Melville
   (d) Willa Cather

154. In Hawthorne's *The Scarlet Letter* (1850), the villain is
   (a) Dimmesdale
   (b) The Puritan Minister
   (c) Hester Prynne
   (d) Chillingworth

155. Which of the following novels of Hawthorne in his last?

(a) *The Marble Faun*
(b) *The Scarlet Letter*
(c) *The Blithedale Romance*
(d) *The House of the Seven Gables*

156. Who championed the cause of Realism in the American novel?
(a) Hawthorne
(b) Howells (William Dean)
(c) Melville
(d) Mark Twain

157. Which of the following novels of Howells is considered his classic?
(a) *The Rise of Silas Lapham*
(b) *A Modern Instance*
(c) *A Hazard of New Fortunes*
(d) *A Traveller From Altruria*

158. Who among the following is the villain in *The Portrait of a Lady*?
(a) Gilbert Osmond
(b) Ralph Touchett
(c) Casper Goodwood
(d) Lord Warburton

159. "Lilies that fester smell far worse than weeds" appears in which of the following novels of Willa Cather?
(a) *Death Comes for the Archbishop*
(b) *A Lost Lady*
(c) *My Antonia*
(d) *The Song of the Lark*

160. Sylvia Plath is known as a confessional poet. Who else among the following belong to the same category?
(a) Robert Browning
(b) John Berryman
(c) Robert Lowell
(d) Wallace Stevens

161. Who among the following is known as the leader of the Beats?
(a) Allen Ginsberg
(b) Robert Lowell
(c) E.E. Cummings
(d) Randall Jarrell

## ANSWERS

| | | | | | |
|---|---|---|---|---|---|
| 1. (d) | 2. (a) | 3. (a) | 4. (b) | 5. (b) | 6. (c) |
| 7. (d) | 8. (d) | 9. (a) | 10. (a) | 11. (b) | 12. (a) |
| 13. (c) | 14. (b) | 15. (c) | 16. (c) | 17. (d) | 18. (b) |
| 19. (c) | 20. (a) | 21. (a) | 22. (d) | 23. (b) | 24. (b) |
| 25. (c) | 26. (b) | 27. (b) | 28. (c) | 29. (c) | 30. (c) |
| 31. (c) | 32. (a) | 33. (b) | 34. (c) | 35. (b) | 36. (a) |
| 37. (a) | 38. (b) | 39. (c) | 40. (a) | 41. (a) | 42. (b) |
| 43. (c) | 44. (c) | 45. (a) | 46. (b) | 47. (b) | 48. (a) |
| 49. (a) | 50. (c) | 51. (c) | 52. (d) | 53. (c) | 54. (a) |
| 55. (a) | 56. (d) | 57. (c) | 58. (b) | 59. (c) | 60. (c) |
| 61. (b) | 62. (a) | 63. (a) | 64. (d) | 65. (d) | 66. (a) |
| 67. (d) | 68. (a) | 69. (c) | 70. (c) | 71. (a) | 72. (d) |
| 73. (a) | 74. (b) | 75. (c) | 76. (c) | 77. (b) | 78. (a) |
| 79. (b) | 80. (d) | 81. (c) | 82. (d) | 83. (a) | 84. (a) |
| 85. (c) | 86. (a) | 87. (c) | 88. (d) | 89. (b) | 90. (a) |

| | | | | | |
|---|---|---|---|---|---|
| 91. (b) | 92. (c) | 93. (d) | 94. (c) | 95. (d) | 96. (b) |
| 97. (b) | 98. (b) | 99. (b) | 100. (a) | 101. (a) | 102. (b) |
| 103. (d) | 104. (c) | 105. (a) | 106. (c) | 107. (a) | 108. (b) |
| 109. (a) | 110. (b) | 111. (d) | 112. (a) | 113. (c) | 114. (c) |
| 115. (a) | 116. (a) | 117. (c) | 118. (b) | 119. (d) | 120. (d) |
| 121. (c) | 122. (d) | 123. (b) | 124. (a) | 125. (a) | 126. (d) |
| 127. (d) | 128. (a) | 129. (b) | 130. (c) | 131. (c) | 132. (b) |
| 133. (d) | 134. (a) | 135. (c) | 136. (b) | 137. (b) | 138. (c) |
| 139. (a) | 140. (a) | 141. (a) | 142. (c) | 143. (c) | 144. (c) |
| 145. (b) | 146. (c) | 147. (d) | 148. (d) | 149. (d) | 150. (a) |
| 151. (d) | 152. (c) | 153. (b) | 154. (d) | 155. (a) | 156. (b) |
| 157. (a) | 158. (a) | 159. (b) | 160. (c) | 161. (a) | |

## NON-BRITISH LITERATURES

1. Elechi Amadi's first novel was
   (a) *Dancer of Johannesburg*
   (b) *Estrangement*
   (c) *The Woman of Calabar*
   (d) *The Concubine*
2. *The African Image* (1962) is written by
   (a) Ezekiel Mphahlele
   (b) Elechi Amadi
   (c) Ayi Kwei Armah
   (d) Chinua Achebe
3. Baako is a character in the novel *Fragments* (1971) by
   (a) Ayi Kwei Armah
   (b) J.M. Coetzee
   (c) Wole Soyinka
   (d) Assia Djebar
4. Jacob is the central character in the novel *The Slave* by
   (a) Isaac Bashevis Singer
   (b) Ben Okri
   (c) Ayi Kwei Armah
   (d) Toni Morrison
5. *The Palm-Wine Drinkard* (1952) is a novel by
   (a) Amos Tutuola
   (b) Wole Soyinka
   (c) Toni Morrison
   (d) Ngugi wa Thiong'o
6. *Things Fall Apart* by Chinua Achebe was published in
   (a) 1957
   (b) 1948
   (c) 1958
   (d) 1947
7. Which of the following work is not written by Ngugi wa Thiong'o
   (a) *Weep Not, Child*
   (b) *The River Between*
   (c) *A Sport of Nature*
   (d) *A Grain of Wheat*
8. *DecoLonising the Mind* (1986) is written by
   (a) Wole Soyinka
   (b) Ngugi wa Thiong'o
   (c) Joseph Conrad
   (d) Toni Morrison
9. Which of the following novels is not a post-apartheid novel

(a) *Weep Not, Child by* Ngugi wa Thiong'o
(b) *The Rights Of Desire* by Andre Brink
(c) *Disgrace* by J.M. Coetzee
(d) *Like Water In Wild Places* by Pamela Jooste

10. The novel, *The Last Harmattan of Alusine Dunbar* (1990) relates part of African-Canadian history with a magic realism twist is written by
(a) J.M. Coetzee
(b) Assia Djebar
(c) Syl Cheney-Coker
(d) Yvonne Vera

11. Mariama Ba's *So Long a Letter* is a/an
(a) Epistolary novel
(b) Drama
(c) Poetry
(d) Essay

12. *Long Walk to Freedom* is an autobiographical work written by
(a) Chinua Achebe
(b) Wole Soyinka
(c) Nelson Rolihlahla Mandela
(d) Yasmina Khadra

13. *The House Gun* by Nadine Gordimer is a/an
(a) Apartheid novel
(b) Post-apartheid novel
(c) Mau Mau rebellion novel
(d) Racial novel

14. Which was the first novel to be published by a woman writer in Nigeria
(a) Flora Nwapa's *Efuru*
(b) Ben Okri's *The Famished Road*
(c) Nadine Gordimer's *Burger's Daughter*
(d) Farida Karodia's *Daughters of Twilight*

15. *Purple Hibiscus* (2003) is written by
(a) Njabulo Ndebele
(b) Chimamanda Ngozi Adichie
(c) J.M. Coetzee
(d) Niq Mhlongo

16. *Dust* is a 1985 film directed by Marion Hänsel based on the J.M. Coetzee's novel
(a) *Dusklands*
(b) *In the Heart of the Country*
(c) *Waiting for the Barbarians*
(d) *Disgrace*

17. Which of the following is not a Nobel prize winner writer of Africa
(a) Ben Okri
(b) John Maxwell Coetzee
(c) Nadine Gordimer
(d) Wole Soyinka

18. *In the Heart of the Country* (1977) is written by
(a) Ben Okri
(b) J.M. Coetzee
(c) Nadine Gordimer
(d) Wole Soyinka

19. Which of the following is not a character in *Death and The King's Horseman*, a play by Wole Soyinka?
(a) Elesin Oba
(b) Olunde
(c) Simon Pilkings
(d) Victor

20. *July's People* is written by
(a) Toni Morrison
(b) Nadine Gordimer
(c) Ama Ata Aidoo
(d) Gabeba Baderoon

21. *Canopus in Argos: Archives* is a sequence of five science fiction novels by Nobel Prize in literature-winning author
(a) Nadine Gordimer
(b) Wole Soyinka
(c) Doris May Lessing
(d) Cameron Duodu

22. Ama Ata Aidoo won a Commonwealth Writers Prize for her novel
    (a) *The Dilemma of a Ghost*
    (b) *Changes: A Love Story* (1991)
    (c) *Anowa*
    (d) *Our Sister Killjoy*
23. *When Rain Clouds Gather* (1968) is a novel written by
    (a) Ngugi wa Thiong'o
    (b) Farida Karodia
    (c) Bessie Head
    (d) Barbara Adair
24. Sonny is the central character in *My Son's Story* written by
    (a) Alan Paton
    (b) Oliver Schreiner
    (c) Nadine Gordimer
    (d) Bloke Modisane
25. Stephen Kumalo, a black Anglican priest, is a character in Alan Paton's novel
    (a) *Lost in the Stars*
    (b) *Cry, the Beloved Country*
    (c) *Too Late the Phalarope*
    (d) *The Long View*
26. Which of the following works is considered as the first African classic analysis of racial and sexual issues?
    (a) *Story of an African Farm* (1883)
    (b) *Africa Is People*
    (c) *Blame Me on History*
    (d) *Heart of Darkness*
27. *Story of an African Farm* (1883) is written by
    (a) Bessie Head
    (b) Oliver Schreiner
    (c) Alan Paton
    (d) Moses Isegawa
28. *Blame Me on History* (1963) is the autobiography of
    (a) Doris May Lessing
    (b) Chinua Achebe
    (c) Bloke Modisane
    (d) R.R.R. Dhlomo
29. Tatamkhulu Ismail Afrika's first novel is
    (a) *The Innocents* (1994)
    (b) *Broken Earth* (1940)
    (c) *Tightrope* (1996)
    (d) *Bitter Eden* (2002)
30. The first African novel written in English in 1911 is written by
    (a) Joseph Ephraim Casely Hayford (also known as Ekra-Agiman)
    (b) Peter Abrahams
    (c) Ngugi wa Thiong'o
    (d) J.M. Coetzee
31. The first African novel written in English in 1911 is
    (a) *A Wreath for Udom*
    (b) *Ethiopia Unbound: Studies in Race Emancipation*
    (c) *Things Fall Apart*
    (d) *An African Tragedy*
32. *Cry the Beloved Country* (1948) is written by
    (a) Mia Couto
    (b) John Pepper Clark
    (c) Wole Soyinka
    (d) Alan Paton
33. *Heart of Darkness* written by Joseph Conrad centers around
    (a) Sonny
    (b) Victor
    (c) Okonkwo
    (d) Charles Marlow
34. *The Black Hermit*, a play by Ngugi wa Thiong'o, is about
    (a) Racialism
    (b) Tribalism
    (c) Sexual and racial issues
    (d) Political issues

35. In 1962, Ngugi wa Thiong'o of Kenya wrote the first East African drama.
    (a) *This Time Tomorrow*
    (b) *A Meeting in the Dark*
    (c) *A Grain of Wheat*
    (d) *The Black Hermit*

36. *The Grass is Singing* (1950) is written by
    (a) Nadine Gordimer
    (b) Doris May Lessing
    (c) Alan Paton
    (d) Chinua Achebe

37. *Things Fall Apart* by Chinua Achebe is about the character.
    (a) Kurtz
    (b) Ngotho
    (c) Mwihaki
    (d) Okonkwo

38. The title of the novel (*Things Fall Apart*) comes from William Butler Yeats's poem
    (a) "A Poet to His Beloved"
    (b) "No Second Troy"
    (c) "The Magi"
    (d) "The Second Coming"

39. Which of the following novel/s is/are written by Chinua Achebe
    (a) *Things Fall Apart*
    (b) *No Longer at Ease*
    (c) *Arrow of God*
    (d) *A Man of the People*
    (e) All of the above

40. *The Golden Notebook* is the story of writer Anna Wulf.
    (a) True
    (b) False

41. *The Golden Notebook* is divided into
    (a) Four books
    (b) Five books
    (c) Six books
    (d) Three books

42. *An African Tragedy* (1928) is a novel by
    (a) Joseph Conrad
    (b) Athol Fugard
    (c) R.R.R. Dhlomo
    (d) Ellen Kuzwayo

43. *I Will Marry When I Want* (1982) by Ngugi wa Thiong'o is
    (a) Essay
    (b) Poem
    (c) Play
    (d) Novel

44. *In Tangier We Killed the Blue Parrot* (2004) is written by
    (a) Barbara Adair
    (b) Cyprian Ekwensi
    (c) John Eppel
    (d) Athol Fugard

45. *Daughters of Twilight* (1986) a novel by Farida Karodia, is about
    (a) Racism
    (b) Mau Mau
    (c) Discriminatory acts of apartheid
    (d) Post-Apartheid

46. *Daughters of Twilight* (1986) is novel by
    (a) Bloke Modisane
    (b) Ama Ata Ai doo
    (c) Tatamkhulu Ismail Afrika
    (d) Farida Karodia

47. *The Blood Knot* (1961) is a play by
    (a) Ngugi wa Thiong'o
    (b) Flora Nwapa
    (c) Athol Fugard
    (d) Barbara Adair

48. *Call Me Woman* (1985) the autobiography of
    (a) Ellen Kuzwayo
    (b) Nadine Gordimer
    (c) R.R.R. Dhlomo
    (d) Alan Paton

49. Chinua Achebe's Presidential Fellow Lecture for the World Bank Group was
    (a) *Chike and the River* (1966)
    (b) *Africa is People* (1998)
    (c) *Morning Yet on Creation Day* (1975)
    (d) *Home and Exile* (2000)
50. *Death and the King's Horseman* (1975) is written by
    (a) Wole Soyinka
    (b) Ben Okri
    (c) Flora Nwapa
    (d) Nadine Gordimer
51. Which Australian writer develop a kind of journalistic drama?
    (a) Barry Oakley
    (b) Jack Hibberd
    (c) Scott Rankin
    (d) David Williamson
52. Who was awarded the international Hans Christian Andersen Award for lifetime achievement in children's literature?
    (a) Clive James
    (b) Patricia Wrightson
    (c) Robert Hughes
    (d) Geoffrey Robertson
53. *To the Islands* (1958) is written by
    (a) Joseph Furphy
    (b) Randolph Stow
    (c) Norman Lindsay
    (d) Germaine Greer
54. Dr Jack (John Charles) Hibberd is an Australian.
    (a) Novelist
    (b) Playwright
    (c) Poet
    (d) Critic
55. *Summer of the Seventeenth Doll*, a play by Ray Lawler revolves around
    (a) Six Characters
    (b) Five Characters
    (c) Four Characters
    (d) Seven Characters
56. *The Thorn Birds* (1977) is written by
    (a) Thomas Keneally
    (b) Nevil Shute
    (c) Colleen McCullough
    (d) Morris West
57. Australia's highest selling novel and one of the largest selling novels of all time is
    (a) *The Thorns Birds*
    (b) *For the Term of His Natural Life*
    (c) *Robbery Under Arms*
    (d) *The Harp in the South*
58. "My Country" is an iconic patriotic poem about Australia, written by
    (a) Julian Randolph Stow
    (b) Dorothea Mackellar
    (c) Kate Grenville
    (d) David Malouf
59. The first Aboriginal book of verse: *We are Going* (1964) is written by
    (a) Les Murray
    (b) Barbara Baynton
    (c) Oodgeroo Noonuccal
    (d) Murray Bail
60. The first Aboriginal author is
    (a) Geoffery Blainey
    (b) Bennelong
    (c) Murray Bail
    (d) David Unaipon
61. *Hitler's Daughter* (1999) is a children's novel by Australian children's author
    (a) Norman Lindsay
    (b) Ursula Dubosarsky
    (c) Jacqueline Anne "Jackie" French
    (d) Ruth Park
62. Who is known as Australia's "greatest writer"?
    (a) Paul Jennings
    (b) Henry Lawson

(c) Clive James
(d) Jeannie Gunn

63. *The Secret River*, (2005) is a historical fiction written by
(a) Rodney Hall
(b) Glenda Adams
(c) Kate Grenville
(d) David Malouf

64. *Rascal Series* is written by
(a) Rodney Hall
(b) David Ireland
(c) John Shaw Neilson
(d) Paul Jennings

65. Which was the first novel published on mainland Australia and the first in the continent by a woman?
(a) Adam Lindsay Gordon
(b) Goldie Alexander
(c) *The Guardian: a Tale (by an Australian)* (1838)
(d) Morris Gleitzman

66. Which of the following works is not written by Thomas Keneally
(a) *The Magic Pudding*
(b) *Schindler's Ark*
(c) *The Chant of Jimmy Blacksmith*
(d) *The Place at Whitton*

67. *Tales for the Bush* appeared in 1845 is written by
(a) Adam Lindsay Gordon
(b) Thomas Keneally
(c) Mary Vidal
(d) Lennie Lower

68. *Flaws in the Glass* (1981) is an autobiography written by
(a) Patrick Victor Martindale White
(b) David Ireland
(c) Clive James
(d) Kate Jennings

69. *My Place* (1987) is an autobiography written by
(a) Morris West
(b) Tim Winton
(c) Amy Witting
(d) Sally Morgan

70. The only Australian to have been awarded the Nobel prize is
(a) David Malouf
(b) David Marr
(c) Patrick Victor Martindale White
(d) Dorothy Porter

71. Oodgeroo Noonuccal's (Kath Walker) first volume of poetry is
(a) *The Complete Book of Australian Verse*
(b) *We are Going* (1964)
(c) *The Censor*
(d) *Copy Paper*

72. Barbara Baynton only novel is
(a) *Maestro*
(b) *Oceana Fine*
(c) *Gilgamesh*
(d) *Human Toll* (1907)

73. Catherine Helen Spence first novel is
(a) *Happy Valley*
(b) *The Twyborn Affair*
(c) *Riders in the Chariot*
(d) *Clara Morison* (1854)

74. First woman novelist in Australia
(a) Deborah Abela
(b) Anna Maria Bunn
(c) Deborah Abela
(d) Trudi Canavan

75. Dr Jack (John Charles) Hibberd, first play is
(a) *White With Wire Wheels* (1967)
(b) *Bread and Butter Woman*
(c) *The Season at Sarsaparilla*
(d) *Big Toys*

76. *Memoirs of an Old Bastard* (1989), *The Life of Riley* (1990), *Perdita* (1992) are the novels written by
   (a) Marcus Clarke
   (b) Jack (John Charles) Hibberd
   (c) Miles Franklin
   (d) Patrick White

77. Raymond Evenor Lawler's most notable play is
   (a) *The Club*
   (b) *Life after George*
   (c) *On Our Selection*
   (d) *Summer of the Seventeenth Doll* (1953)

78. Joseph Furphy is best known for his novel
   (a) *To the Burning City*
   (b) *Kindling Does for Firewood*
   (c) *Such is Life* (1903)
   (d) *The Irishman*

79. Who wrote under the pseudonym Tom Collins?
   (a) Joseph Furphy
   (b) Thomas Keneally
   (c) Henry Kendall
   (d) Christopher Koch

80. Who is widely regarded as the "Father of the Australian novel"?
   (a) Alex Miller
   (b) Frank Moorhouse
   (c) Joseph Furphy
   (d) Harry "Breaker" Morant

81. *The Female Eunuch* (1970) is written by
   (a) Anne Summers
   (b) Germaine Greer
   (c) Lucy Sussex
   (d) Charlotte Wood

82. *Fly Away Peter* (1982) by David Malouf is a novella set in Queensland just before
   (a) World War II
   (b) World War I
   (c) American Independence
   (d) Apartheid

83. *Fly Away Peter* (1982) by David Malouf is
   (a) Novel
   (b) Play
   (c) Poem
   (d) Novella

84. *Schindler's Ark* is a Booker Prize-winning novel published in 1982 by Australian novelist
   (a) Thomas Keneally
   (b) Simon Haynes
   (c) Wendy James
   (d) Paul Jennings

85. Which of the following works is not written by Patrick White?
   (a) *Happy Valley* (1939)
   (b) *The Living and the Dead* (1941)
   (c) *The Golden Dress*
   (d) *The Aunt's Story* (1948)

86. Clarke and Rolf Boldrewood were pseudonyms of
   (a) Thomas Alexander Browne
   (b) Brian Castro
   (c) Dymphna Cusack
   (d) Victor Daley

87. *Recollections of Geoffry Hamlyn* (1859) is written by
   (a) Glenda Adams
   (b) Henry Kingsley
   (c) Jessica Anderson
   (d) Thea Astley

88. The first widely known novel of Australia is
   (a) *Such is Life*
   (b) *A Fortunate Life*
   (c) *Recollections of Geoffry Hamlyn* (1859)
   (d) *Too Many Men*

89. The first Australian novel is
   (a) *Happy Valley*
   (b) *A Haunted Land*
   (c) *Visitants*
   (d) *Quintus Servinton*

90. The first Australian novel *Quintus Servinton* was written by
   (a) Charles Harpur
   (b) Nicholas Hasluck
   (c) Henry Savery
   (d) Shirley Hazzard

91. *Winter Sun*, *The Dumbfounding*, and *Sunblue* are written by
   (a) Margaret Atwood
   (b) Margaret Avison
   (c) Jean Jay Macpherson
   (d) Leonard Norman Cohen

92. What is the theme in *Surfacing* a novel by Margaret Atwood?
   (a) Nostalgia
   (b) Racial
   (c) Separation
   (d) Alienation

93. *Lullabies for Little Criminals* (2006) novel by Heather O'Neill centers around
   (a) Salim
   (b) Raja
   (c) Mohan
   (d) Baby

94. *Tales from Firozsha Baag* is a collection of 11 short stories by
   (a) Irving Abella
   (b) Hugh Abercrombie
   (c) Margaret Atwood
   (d) Rohinton Mistry

95. *Griselda* (1900) is written by
   (a) Marianne Ackerman
   (b) Basil King
   (c) Janice Acoose
   (d) Milton James Rhode Acorn

96. *Unidentified Human Remains and the True Nature of Love* is a 1989 stage play written by
   (a) Ken Adachi
   (b) Evan Tlesla Àdams
   (c) Ian Adams
   (d) Brad Fraser

97. *Mrs. Spring Fragrance* was a popular short story collection by
   (a) Edith Maude Eaton (Sui Sin Far)
   (b) Gil Adamson
   (c) Caroline Adderson
   (d) Marie-Célie Agnant

98. Grace Marks is central character in the novel *Alias Grace* by
   (a) Freda Ahenakew
   (b) Agnes Strickland
   (c) Kelley Aitken
   (d) Margaret Eleanor Atwood

99. *A Perfect Night to Go to China* (2005) is a novel by
   (a) Donald Harman Akenson
   (b) David Gilmour
   (c) Kateri Akiwenzie-Damm
   (d) Linda Aksomitis

100. *Anatomy of Criticism: Four Essays* (1957) is written by
   (a) Linda Aksomitis
   (b) Scott Albert
   (c) Robert Arthur Alexie
   (d) Northrop Frye

101. *Fearful Symmetry* (1947) is an important work of
   (a) Edna Alford
   (b) André Alexis
   (c) Robert Arthur Alexie
   (d) Northrop Frye

102. *The Wars* (1977) is written by
   (a) Edna Alford
   (b) Donna Allard

(c) Sandra Alland
(d) Timothy Findley

103. Vancouver's Chinese community is the subject in the novel *Disappearing Moon Café* (1990) by
(a) Sky lee
(b) Charlotte Vale-Allen
(c) Grant Blairfindie Allen
(d) David Gilmour

104. *Walking through the Valley* (1994) is an autobiography of
(a) Margaret Atwood
(b) Margaret Avison
(c) Jean Jay Macpherson
(d) George Woodcock

105. Margaret Avison's most reputed work is
(a) *The Man That Got Away*
(b) *Twice Tempted*
(c) *Winter Sun* (1960)
(d) *Protector With a Past*

106. *The Stone Angel* (1964) is a psychological novel written by
(a) Margaret Laurence
(b) George Woodcock
(c) Margaret Atwood
(d) Jean Jay Macpherson

107. Which Canadian writer writes about Ontario?
(a) Charlotte Vale-Allen
(b) Joanne Arnott
(c) Joanne Arnott
(d) Stephen Leacock

108. *Amigo's Blue Guitar* (1990) is a play by
(a) Ken Babstock
(b) Joan MacLeod
(c) Martha Baillie
(d) Richard Scott Bakker

109. *Autobiography of Red* (1998) is a verse novel by
(a) Shauna Singh Baldwin
(b) Winifred Estella Bambrick
(c) Himani Bannerji
(d) Anne Carson

110. *The Boatman* (1957) by Jean Jay Macpherson is dedicated to
(a) Gary William Bannerman
(b) Nick Bantock
(c) Northrop Frye
(d) Bruce Barber

111. *Welcoming Disaster* (1974) is a major work by
(a) Bruce Barber
(b) Joan Louise Barfoot
(c) Robert Laurence "Bob" Barr, Jr.
(d) Jean Jay Macpherson

112. Who has been called the Canadian "unofficial poet laureate"?
(a) Charlotte Vale-Allen
(b) Gary Barwin
(c) Alfred Wellington Purdy
(d) Rodrigo Salago Bascuñán

113. *Jacob Two-Two* series for children is written by
(a) Michel Basilières
(b) William Bauer
(c) Mordecai Richler
(d) Nancy Bauer

114. *The Edible Woman* (1969) by Margaret Atwood moves around the character
(a) Joan Foster
(b) Arthur
(c) Marian
(d) Simon Jordan

115. *People of the Deer* (1952) is the first book of
(a) Kevin Bazzana
(b) Yves Beauchemin
(c) Farley Mowat
(d) Doug Beardsley

116. *Anil's Ghost* was the winner of the 2000 Giller Prize, the Prix Médicis, the Kiriyama Pacific Rim Book Prize, the 2001 Irish Times International Fiction Prize and Canada's Governor General's Award is written by
   (a) Michael Ondaatje
   (b) Denis Yvan Béchard
   (c) Peter Behrens
   (d) Henry Eric Beissel

117. Anil Tissera is the central character in the novel.
   (a) *The Curve*
   (b) *Are You Afraid of Thieves?*
   (c) *Anil's Ghost*
   (d) *Goya*

118. *The Handmaid's Tale* received the first Arthur C. Clarke Award in 1987 is written by
   (a) Ken Belford
   (b) William E. Bell
   (c) John Bemrose
   (d) Margaret Eleanor Atwood

119. Margaret Avison is compared to
   (a) Metaphysical poets
   (b) Political poets
   (c) Racial poets
   (d) Feminist poets

120. Torture is the main theme in *Morning in the Burned House* a book of poetry by
   (a) John Bemrose
   (b) Margaret Eleanor Atwood
   (c) Nigel Bennett
   (d) David Bergen

121. Gustad Noble is the central character in the Rohinton Mistry's novel
   (a) *Tales from Firozsha Baag*
   (b) *A Fine Balance*
   (c) *Family Matters*
   (d) *Such a Long Journey*

122. *Goodnight Desdemona (Good Morning Juliet)* is a 1988 comedic play by
   (a) Earle Alfred Birney
   (b) Bill Bissett
   (c) Stephanie Bolster
   (d) Ann-Marie MacDonald

123. *Fearful Symmetry* (1947), that led to the reinterpretation of the poetry of William Blake is written by
   (a) Margaret Buffie
   (b) Bonnie Burnard
   (c) Allan Casey
   (d) Northrop Frye

124. Which one of the following is not the work of Eli Mandel?
   (a) *Black and Secret Man*
   (b) *Out of Place*
   (c) *Family Matters*
   (d) *An Idiot Joy*

125. Who has been described as a 'mythopoeic' poet?
   (a) Allan Casey
   (b) Margaret Atwood
   (c) Anne Carson
   (d) Jean Jay Macpherson

126. *No Great Mischief* (1999), a novel by Alistair MacLeod, has taken its title from James Wolfe's assertion in the
   (a) *Battle of Spain*
   (b) *Battle of the Plains of Abraham*
   (c) *Civil War*
   (d) *American War of Independence*

127. *Coming Through Slaughter* is a fictionalised version of the life of the New Orleans jazz pioneer
   (a) Jan E. Conn
   (b) Patrick deWitt
   (c) Buddy Bolden
   (d) Sandra Dempsey

128. *Coming Through Slaughter* (1976) is written by

(a) David Chariandy
(b) Michael Ondaatje
(c) Bliss Carman
(d) Gillian Chan

129. Which of the following writer got the first and only "Life-time Achievement Award" from the National Outdoor Book Award in 2005?
(a) Sandra Dempsey
(b) Bill Gaston
(c) Farley McGill Mowat
(d) Claude-Henri Grignon

130. *The Favorite Game* (1994) and *Beautiful Losers* (2003) are written by singer-songwriter, musician, poet, and novelist.
(a) Bliss Carman
(b) Leonard Norman Cohen
(c) David C. Carpenter
(d) Anne Carson

131. Dorothy Livesay's first collection of poetry, published in 1928 was
(a) *The Colour of God's Face*
(b) *Call My People Home*
(c) *Cereus Blooms at Night*
(d) *Green Pitcher*

132. The novel *The Dragon can't Dance* centers on the life of
(a) Fisheye
(b) Ms. Caroline
(c) Pariag
(d) Aldrick Prospect

133. *Raise the Lanterns High* (2004) is written by
(a) V.S. Naipaul
(b) Lakshmi Persaud
(c) Shani Mootoo
(d) Honor Ford-Smith

134. Jean Rhys' final collection of short stories was
(a) *Good Morning, Midnight,*
(b) *The Collected Short Stories*
(c) *Tales of the Wide Caribbean*
(d) *Sleep It Off Lady*

135. *A Small Place* is a memoir published in 1988 by
(a) Aurora Levins Morales
(b) M.G. Smith
(c) Jamaica Kincaid
(d) Jane King

136. Shani Mootoo's first literary publication is
(a) *Out on Main Street*
(b) *Cereus Blooms at Night*
(c) *He Drown She in the Sea*
(d) *Valmiki's Daughter*

137. *The Final Passage* is the debut novel of
(a) Caryl Phillips
(b) Giannina Braschi
(c) Wilson Harris
(d) Albert Gomes

138. "The End", "Home", "England", "The Passage", and "Winter" are the chapters in the novel *The Final Passage* by
(a) Lindsay Barrett
(b) Caryl Phillips
(c) Lorna Goodison
(d) A.L. Hendriks

139. *Henri Christophe: A Chronicle in Seven Scenes* (1949) is the first play by
(a) Derek Walcott
(b) Jamaica Kincaid
(c) Caryl Phillips
(d) Leone Ross

140. *Jonestown* is written by
(a) Wilson Harris
(b) Jean Rhys
(c) Lakshmi Persaud
(d) Caryl Phillips

141. *The Children of Sisyphus* is written by
   (a) Derek Walcott
   (b) Orlando Patterson
   (c) George Lamming
   (d) Hubert Harrison

142. Dinah is the central character in the novel
   (a) *The Children of Sisyphus*
   (b) *Slavery and Social Death*
   (c) *Rituals of Blood: Consequences of Slavery in Two American Centuries*
   (d) *Freedom: Freedom in the Modern World*

143. Methodism and spirituality are the main themes in the works of
   (a) Jean Rhys
   (b) Derek Walcott
   (c) V.S. Naipaul
   (d) Pablo Neruda

144. *All the Blood is Red* is written by
   (a) Leone Ross
   (b) Derek Walcott
   (c) Jamaica Kincaid
   (d) Wilson Harris

145. *The Dragon Can't Dance* is a novel, set in a slum of Port of Spain, is written by
   (a) Jean Rhys
   (b) Earl Lovelace
   (c) Leone Ross
   (d) Pablo Neruda

146. Whose writing was influenced by the work of the American poets, Robert Lowell and Elizabeth Bishop
   (a) Shani Mootoo
   (b) Lakshmi Persaud
   (c) Derek Walcott
   (d) Wilson Harris

147. *Jonestown* (1996), tells of the mass-suicide of followers of cult leader
   (a) Jacob
   (b) Sonny
   (c) Anna Wulf
   (d) Jim Jones

148. *The Writer and the World* (2002) is a collection of essays and reportage by,
   (a) Oonya Kempadoo
   (b) Pauline Melville
   (c) Bliss Carman
   (d) V.S. Naipaul

149. *A House for Mr Biswas* (1961) novel by V.S. Naipaul moves around
   (a) Raja
   (b) Salim
   (c) Bobby
   (d) Mohun Biswas

150. *The Mystic Masseur* is a comic novel by
   (a) Denis Williams
   (b) Beryl Gilory
   (c) Jan Shinebourne
   (d) V.S. Naipaul

151. *Freedom in the Making of Western Culture* (1991) is written by
   (a) Denis Williams
   (b) René Depestre
   (c) Dany Laferrière
   (d) Orlando Patterson

152. Who described Naipaul as "a master of modern English prose"?
   (a) Dany Laferrière
   (b) Ruel Johnson
   (c) Beryl Gilroy
   (d) J.M. Coetzee

153. *Wide Sargasso Sea* by Jean Rhys centers around
   (a) Sergeant Major Plunkett
   (b) Antoinette Cosway
   (c) Maud
   (d) Helen

154. *Wide Sargasso Sea* (1966) is written by
   (a) Wilson Harris
   (b) Orlando Patterson

(c) V.S.Naipaul
(d) Jean Rhys

155. *The World Is What It Is: The Authorized Biography of V. S. Naipaul* is written by
(a) Patrick French
(b) Colin Channer
(c) Alvin Bennett
(d) Kamau Brathwaite

156. *The Secret Ladder* is a novel by
(a) Marie-Elena John
(b) Jamaica Kincaid
(c) Roger Mais
(d) Wilson Harris

157. *The Black Jacobins* is written by
(a) C.L.R. James
(b) Shake Keane
(c) Derek Walcott
(d) Lasana M. Sekou

158. *A Morning at the Office* (1950) symbolizes 'contradiction of being white in mind and black in body' is written by
(a) Edgar Mittelholzer
(b) Anthony Kellman
(c) Julio Vega Battle
(d) Roger Mais

159. Samuel Selvon portrayed the Indians in Trinidad in his novel
(a) *A Brighter Sun*
(b) *A Morning at the Office*
(c) *A Tale of Three Places*
(d) *Latticed Echoes*

160. *Rights of Passage* (1967), considered as the starting point of West Indian literary studies, is written by
(a) John Hearne
(b) Edward Kamau Braithwaite
(c) Olive Senior
(d) Frantz Fanon

161. *Voyage in The Dark* (1934) is written by
(a) Edgar Mittelholzer
(b) V.S. Reid
(c) Jean Rhys
(d) Samuel Selvon

162. *The Intended* (1991), *The Counting House* (1996), *Our Lady of Demerara* (2004) is written by
(a) Una Marson
(b) Nalo Hopkinson
(c) David Dabydeen
(d) Mutabaruka

163. John Edgar Colwell Hearne's first published work was the novel
(a) *The Sure Salvation*
(b) *Voices under the Window*
(c) *The Faces of Love*
(d) *Stranger at the Gate*

164. *Fever Grass*, *The Candywine Development*, and *The Checkerboard Caper* were written by Morris Cargill and John Edgar Colwell Hearne under the pseudonym
(a) John Morris
(b) Frank Collymore
(c) George Lamming
(d) Morris John

165. *Guyana Boy* (1960), *Old Thom's Harvest* (1965) are written by
(a) Peter "Lauchmonen" Kempadoo
(b) Anthony Joseph
(c) Lawrence Scott
(d) Frances-Anne Solomon

166. Nancy Morejón is the writer of
(a) *Amor, ciudad atribuída, poemas*
(b) *With Eyes and Soul: Images of Cuba*
(c) *Where the Island Sleeps Like a Wing*
(d) All of the above

167. Who is often referred to as "Bob Marley with a pen,"

(a) John La Rose
(b) Patricia Powell
(c) Herbert de Lisser
(d) Colin Channer

168. *Me Dying Trial* (1993), *The Pagoda: A Novel* (1998), *A Small Gathering of Bones* (2003), *The Fullness of Everything* (2009) are written by
(a) Gloria Escoffery
(b) Herbert de Lisser
(c) John Figueroa
(d) Patricia Powell

169. Dr. Armando Lampe writes that "he's considered the 'Walcott' of the Dutch Caribbean", who is this writer
(a) O.R. Dathorne
(b) Lasana M. Sekou
(c) Beryl Gilroy
(d) Jan Shinebourne

170. *No Telephone to Heaven*, the sequel to *Abeng*, is the second novel published by
(a) Michelle Cliff
(b) Roy A.K. Heath
(c) Pauline Melville
(d) Grace Nichols

171. Clare Savage is the bi-racial protagonist in Michelle Cliff's novel
(a) *No Telephone to Heaven*
(b) *The Store of a Million Items*
(c) *Bodies of Water*
(d) *Abeng*

172. *Banjo* (1930), and *Banana Bottom* (1933) are written by
(a) V.S. Naipaul
(b) Claude McKay
(c) Jean Rhys
(d) Constance Hollar

173. Claude Mckay's, which novel centers on black seamen in Marseilles
(a) *Banana Bottom*
(b) *Banjo*
(c) *A Long Way from Home*
(d) *Gingertown*

174. *The Last English Plantation* (1988) is a novel by
(a) Kwame Dawes
(b) Honor Ford-Smith
(c) Jan Lowe Shinebourne
(d) Edward Baugh

175. *Lazy Thoughts of a Lazy Woman* (1989) is a poetry collection by
(a) Kwame Dawes
(b) Gloria Escoffery
(c) Grace Nichols
(d) Colin Channer

176. *My Brother* (1997) is a AIDS memoir by
(a) Edward Baugh
(b) Alvin Bennett
(c) George Campbell
(d) Jamaica Kincaid

177. *Wide Sargasso Sea* (1966) is written as a "prequel" to
(a) *Jane Eyre*
(b) *Pride and Prejudice*
(c) *Hard Times*
(d) *Mill on the Floss*

## ANSWERS

| | | | | | |
|---|---|---|---|---|---|
| 1. (d) | 2. (a) | 3. (a) | 4. (a) | 5. (a) | 6. (c) |
| 7. (c) | 8. (b) | 9. (a) | 10. (c) | 11. (a) | 12. (c) |
| 13. (b) | 14. (a) | 15. (b) | 16. (b) | 17. (a) | 18. (b) |
| 19. (d) | 20. (b) | 21. (c) | 22. (b) | 23. (c) | 24. (c) |
| 25. (b) | 26. (a) | 27. (b) | 28. (c) | 29. (b) | 30. (a) |
| 31. (b) | 32. (d) | 33. (d) | 34. (b) | 35. (d) | 36. (b) |
| 37. (d) | 38. (d) | 39. (e) | 40. (a) | 41. (c) | 42. (c) |
| 43. (c) | 44. (a) | 45. (c) | 46. (d) | 47. (c) | 48. (a) |
| 49. (b) | 50. (a) | 51. (d) | 52. (b) | 53. (b) | 54. (b) |
| 55. (a) | 56. (c) | 57. (a) | 58. (b) | 59. (c) | 60. (d) |
| 61. (c) | 62. (b) | 63. (c) | 64. (d) | 65. (c) | 66. (a) |
| 67. (c) | 68. (a) | 69. (d) | 70. (c) | 71. (b) | 72. (d) |
| 73. (d) | 74. (b) | 75. (a) | 76. (b) | 77. (d) | 78. (c) |
| 79. (a) | 80. (c) | 81. (b) | 82. (b) | 83. (d) | 84. (a) |
| 85. (c) | 86. (a) | 87. (b) | 88. (c) | 89. (d) | 90. (c) |
| 91. (b) | 92. (c) | 93. (d) | 94. (d) | 95. (b) | 96. (d) |
| 97. (a) | 98. (d) | 99. (b) | 100. (d) | 101. (d) | 102. (d) |
| 103. (a) | 104. (d) | 105. (c) | 106. (a) | 107. (d) | 108. (b) |
| 109. (d) | 110. (c) | 111. (d) | 112. (c) | 113. (c) | 114. (c) |
| 115. (c) | 116. (a) | 117. (c) | 118. (d) | 119. (a) | 120. (b) |
| 121. (d) | 122. (d) | 123. (d) | 124. (c) | 125. (d) | 126. (b) |
| 127. (c) | 128. (b) | 129. (c) | 130. (b) | 131. (d) | 132. (d) |
| 133. (b) | 134. (d) | 135. (c) | 136. (a) | 137. (a) | 138. (b) |
| 139. (a) | 140. (a) | 141. (b) | 142. (a) | 143. (b) | 144. (a) |
| 145. (b) | 146. (c) | 147. (d) | 148. (d) | 149. (d) | 150. (d) |
| 151. (d) | 152. (d) | 153. (b) | 154. (d) | 155. (a) | 156. (d) |
| 157. (a) | 158. (a) | 159. (a) | 160. (b) | 161. (c) | 162. (c) |
| 163. (b) | 164. (a) | 165. (a) | 166. (d) | 167. (d) | 168. (d) |
| 169. (b) | 170. (a) | 171. (a) | 172. (b) | 173. (b) | 174. (c) |
| 175. (c) | 176. (d) | 177. (a) | | | |

# 9

# Literary Theory and Criticism

## (I) ANCIENT GREEK CRITICISM

**PLATO (428-347 B.C.) : HIS DIALOGUES**

1. Early period : Apology, Charmides, Crito, Euthyphro, Gorgias, Ion, Laches, Protagoras, Lysis.
2. Middle period : Gorgias, Meno, Apology, Crito, Phaedo, Symposium, Republic.
3. Later Period : Philebus, Sophist, Parmenides.

**IMPORTANT WORKS BY ARISTOTLE (384-322 B.C.)**

(1) Dialogues (2) On Monarchy (3) Natural History (4) Organon, or The Instrument of Correct Thinking (5) Rhetroic (6) Logic (7) Educational Ethics (8) Nico-Machean Ethics (9) Physics (10) Metaphysics (11) Politics (12) Poetics.

1. Plato's comments on poetry occur in
   (a) *Apology*
   (b) *Gogias*
   (c) *Ion and Republic*
   (d) None of the above
2. The 'Cave image' in Plato's *Republic, Book VII*, explains Plato's
   (a) Conception of human nature
   (b) Theory of the nature of knowledge
   (c) Ignorance
   (d) Theory of the subconscious mind
3. What, according to Plato, should be the ideal age of the poet?
   (a) Less than thirty years
   (b) Less than forty years
   (c) Less than fifty years
   (d) More than fifty years
4. Plato's use of the allegorical imagery of the soul as the charioteer and the higher and the lower passions as his pair of horses occur in
   (a) *Republic* (b) *Ion*
   (c) *Phaedrus* (d) *Meno*
5. In which of the following has Plato treated the relation of language to reality?
   (a) *Ion* (b) *Cratylus*
   (c) *Phaedrus* (d) *Protagoras*
6. Who said, "I soon realized that poets compose their poetry not by wisdom but by a force of nature, and inspiration, just like soothsayers who also say many fine things but lack knowledge of what they mean"?
   (a) Plato (b) Horace
   (c) Aristotle (d) Longinus
7. In which of his books has Plato said, "For the poet is a light and winged and holy thing, and there is no invention in him until he has been inspired, and is out of his senses...."?
   (a) *Phaedrus* (b) *Republic*
   (c) *Apology* (d) *Ion*

8. Who said that, "poetical imitations are ruinous to the understanding of the hearers...."?
   (a) Stephen Gosson (b) Plato
   (c) Horace (d) Longinus
9. In which book of the *Republic* does Plato discuss his theory of imitation?
   (a) *II* (b) *X*
   (c) *VI* (d) *III*
10. In which book of the *Republic* do the following lines occur?

    If a person who imitates all things should come to our city and makes a proposal to exhibit himself and his poetry, we will fall down and worship him as a sweet and holy and wonderful being; but we must also inform him that in our State such as he are not permitted to exist, the law will not allow them"?

    (a) *V* (b) *VI*
    (c) *X* (d) *III*
11. According to Plato, "a state of language anterior to the word" is called _______?
    (a) Chora (b) Surrealism
    (c) Organic form (d) Semiotics
12. Give the correct chronological sequence.
    (a) Renaissance, Hellenistic, Graeco – Roman, Hellenic
    (b) Hellenic, Hellenistic, Graeco – Roman, Renaissance
    (c) Graeco – Roman, Renaissance, Hellenistic, Hellenic
    (d) Hellenistic, Hellenic, Renaissance, Graeco – Roman

(The Hellenic period (500-300 B.C.) is the "classic" period of Greek culture. It is taken to be the period between the defeat of the Persians and the conquests of Alexander, the Great. Greece enjoyed a cultural flowering and economic prosperity seldom matched in the ancient world. Drama, philosophy, and sculpture all underwent significant refinement in this period. It was the period of great philosophers like Plato (428-347 B.C.), Aristotle (384-322 B.C.) and dramatists like Aristophanes (445-380 B.C.). The Hellenistic period is the period which followed the conquests of Alexander, the Great. It was so named by the great historian J.G. Droysen. It is said to begin with Alexander's death in 323 B.C. It is regarded as a period of decadence in Greek culture. It followed Aristotle and ending with the beginning of neo-platonism, which was founded by Plotinus (AD 204-270). It was the period of 'Sophism', 'Cynicism', 'Platonism' (a philosophy developed by the followers of Plato). The 'Graeco-Roman' refers to the period when literary and cultural activity shifted from Alexandria to Rome during the Augustan era (31 B.C to 14 A.D.). During this period, such figures as Virgil, Ovid, Horace, Longinus, et al. made brilliant achievements in the field of literature. The Renaissance period began with the fall of Constantinople to the Turks in 1453. It was the period of critics like Sidney and Ben Jonson, and dramatists such as the University Wits and Shakespeare in the sixteenth century during the Elizabethan era.)

13. How many chapters does Aristotle's *Poetics* consist of?
    (a) XX (b) XXVI
    (c) XXV (d) XXIV
14. According to Aristotle, poetry originally began in two kinds:
    (a) Heroic and tragic
    (b) Comic and tragic
    (c) Heroic and Satiric
    (d) Heroic and Comic
15. In which chapter of the *Poetics* does Aristotle compare tragedy with epic?
    (a) XXIV (b) XIX
    (c) XXI (d) XXVI

16. Aristotle regards tragedy superior to epic because
    (a) all the parts of an epic are included in tragedy.
    (b) tragedy brings about catharsis.
    (c) tragedy can be staged.
    (d) tragedy has great heroes as characters.
17. In tragedy, according to Aristotle, the objects of imitation are
    (a) plot and thought.
    (b) plot and character.
    (c) character and thought.
    (d) plot, character and thought.
18. According to Aristotle, the tragic action must be according to
    (a) The law of probability
    (b) The law of necessity
    (c) Both (a) and (b)
    (d) None of the above.
19. Aristotle defines a plot as 'simple' in which there is no
    (a) Peripety
    (b) Discovery
    (c) Denouement
    (d) Peripety and Discovery
20. According to Aristotle, the soul of tragedy is
    (a) Character (b) Plot
    (c) Spectacle (d) Song
21. The peculiar pleasure of tragedy is
    (a) derived from imitation.
    (b) derived from rhythm and harmony.
    (c) derived from well-imitated action.
    (d) caused by the catharsis of the emotions of pity and fear.
22. In the *Poetics*, tragedy should imitate
    (a) men worse than they are.
    (b) men in action.
    (c) ordinary mortals.
    (d) eloquent men.
23. Aristotle prefers the plot of tragedy to be made out of stories taken from
    (a) History (b) Mythology
    (c) Legend (d) All of the above
24. A tragic plot, according to Aristotle, must depict the hero passing from
    (a) happiness to misery.
    (b) misery to happiness.
    (c) misery to prosperity.
    (d) happiness to prosperity.
25. In the *Poetics*, the change from ignorance to knowledge has been called
    (a) Peripety (b) Hamartia
    (c) Anagnorisis (d) Denouement
26. Aristotle considers 'poetic justice' to be
    (a) necessary for tragedy.
    (b) not necessary for tragedy.
    (c) the right end of tragedy.
    (d) the function of tragedy.
27. According to Aristotle, a tragic hero should be
    (a) an ordinary man.
    (b) a rich man.
    (c) a notorious man.
    (d) a man of high reputation or status or noble descent.
28. Which unity was not even mentioned by Aristotle in the *Poetics*?
    (a) Unity of Place
    (b) Unity of Action
    (c) Unity of Time
    (d) None of the above
29. The first five chapters of Aristotle's *Poetics* deal with
    (a) Tragedy
    (b) Comedy
    (c) Satire
    (d) Different imitative arts
30. According to Aristotle, it is not the function of the poet to narrate events that

have actually happened; but events such as might occur (*Poetics IX*). But toward the end of the *Poetics*, he says that the poet must imitate

(a) things that were.
(b) things that are now or things that people say and think to be.
(c) things which ought to be.
(d) All of the above.

31. If Aristotle says that the poet must imitate things that were, things that are now or things that people say and think to be, or things that ought to be, then it means that his definition of imitation also refers to
(a) Morality
(b) Realism
(c) Conventional opinions of people
(d) All of the above

32. For Aristotle, the most important feature of the plot is
(a) Character (b) Story
(c) Thought (d) Unity

33. In order that there should be unity of action in a tragedy, the plot must have a
(a) Beginning (b) Middle
(c) End (d) All of the above

34. The hero of a tragedy, according to Aristotle, besides being a man of high status or reputation or noble descent, should be
(a) Morally good
(b) Appropriate
(c) Consistent and true to life
(d) All of the above

35. Who first said that the poet is not only an imitator but also a creator?
(a) Aristotle (b) Plato
(c) Shelley (d) Pope

36. Aristotle's main focus in the *Poetics* is on
(a) Comedy (b) Tragedy
(c) Epic (d) Satire

37. In which chapter of *Poetics* Aristotle asserts that poetry is "more philosophical and more significant than history"?
(a) XI (b) XII
(c) IX (d) XIII

38. On what grounds does Aristotle defend 'mimemis' or what are his observations about mimesis?
(a) Mimesis is fundamental to our nature as human beings.
(b) Human beings are most imitative of all creatures. Besides this, the first learning experiences take place through mimesis.
(c) All human beings take pleasure in mimesis because all find "learning and inference" essentially pleasant.
(d) All of the above.

39. What, according to Aristotle, are the elements or quantitative parts of the formal structure of a tragedy?
(a) Prologue
(b) Episode and Exode
(c) Parode and Satismon
(d) All of the above

(The 'prologue' is that part of a tragedy which precedes the 'parode' of the chorus. It provides the audience with a summary of the past events that have led up to the play. They also build pace and prepare the audience for the entrance of the central character. The 'episode' is that part of a tragedy which has no choric song after it. Of the choric part, 'parode' is the first individual utterance of the chorus. The 'satismon' is the choric ode without anapaests (two unaccented syllables followed by an accented one) or trochaic tetrameters (lines of four trochaic feet. A trochee is a metrical foot with an accented syllable followed by a unaccented one.)

40. Which are the arts, according to Aristotle, which use rhythm, tune, and metre
    (a) Dithyrambic and Nomic poetry
    (b) Tragedy
    (c) Comedy
    (d) All of the above

41. According to Aristotle, pity and fear in a tragedy arise only when someone who is ____________ falls from happiness to misery.
    (a) very much like ourselves
    (b) but not very virtuous
    (c) and also not very flawed
    (d) All of the above

42. What, according to Aristotle, can be the conclusion of a tragedy?
    (a) Happy ending.
    (b) The death of the hero.
    (c) The conflict is resolved and harmony restored.
    (d) Unhappy ending.

43. In what respects is epic different from tragedy?
    (a) An epic ends happily.
    (b) An epic has many heroes.
    (c) An epic differs from tragedy in length and metre.
    (d) None of the above.

44. A well-crafted tragedy has
    (a) a great man as hero.
    (b) virtuous characters.
    (c) tragic ending.
    (d) a masterfully written complication and unravelling.

45. What, according to Aristotle, should be the goal of tragedy?
    (a) To arouse fear
    (b) To arouse pity
    (c) To arouse pity and fear
    (d) None of the above

46. What type of poetry does Aristotle say is addressed to a much more cultivated audience?
    (a) Epic (b) Comic
    (c) Lyric (d) Tragic

47. An epic differs from a tragedy, because it has
    (a) a representation form.
    (b) a narrative form.
    (c) no metre.
    (d) None of the above.

48. What type of tragedy, according to Aristotle, does not require impressive visual effects?
    (a) An episodic tragedy
    (b) A tragedy with a great hero
    (c) A tragedy with a complex plot
    (d) A tragedy with a simple plot

49. Which form of art, according to Aristotle, uses language only?
    (a) Painting (b) Dance
    (c) Music (d) Literature

50. According to Aristotle, the medium of imitation is
    (a) Narration
    (b) Dramatic representation
    (c) Dance
    (d) Both (a) and (b)

## ANSWERS

| | | | | | |
|---|---|---|---|---|---|
| 1. (c) | 2. (b) | 3. (c) | 4. (c) | 5. (b) | 6. (a) |
| 7. (d) | 8. (b) | 9. (b) | 10. (d) | 11. (a) | 12. (b) |
| 13. (b) | 14. (c) | 15. (a) | 16. (a) | 17. (d) | 18. (c) |
| 19. (d) | 20. (b) | 21. (d) | 22. (b) | 23. (d) | 24. (a) |

| | | | | | |
|---|---|---|---|---|---|
| 25. (c) | 26. (b) | 27. (d) | 28. (a) | 29. (d) | 30. (d) |
| 31. (d) | 32. (d) | 33. (d) | 34. (d) | 35. (a) | 36. (b) |
| 37. (c) | 38. (d) | 39. (d) | 40. (d) | 41. (d) | 42. (c) |
| 43. (c) | 44. (d) | 45. (c) | 46. (a) | 47. (b) | 48. (c) |
| 49. (d) | 50. (d) | | | | |

## (II) GRAECO-ROMAN CRITICISM

51. Which form of literature received the greatest attention in Horace's *Ars Poetica*?
    (a) Poetry (b) Drama
    (c) Satire (d) Comedy
52. Who is conventionally associated with the notion that 'a poem is like a painting'?
    (a) Horace (b) Longinus
    (c) Sidney (d) Rossetti
53. Who said, "When words advance in age, they pass away, and others born but lately, like the young, flourish and thrive"?
    (a) Aristotle (b) Longinus
    (c) Horace (d) Ovid
54. According to Horace, the principle of 'decorum' calls for a 'proper' relationship between
    (a) form and content; expression and thought.
    (b) style and subject matter.
    (c) diction and character.
    (d) All of the above.
55. Horace's *Ars Poetica* is in the form of an epistle to
    (a) Plato (b) Pisos
    (c) Aristotle (d) Homer
56. Scaliger called *Ars Poetica*
    (a) a great work of art.
    (b) a great treatise of poetry.
    (c) an art of poetry written without art.
    (d) None of the above.
57. Horace's *Ars Poetica* is divided into
    (a) two parts (b) three parts
    (c) four parts (d) five parts

    (The three parts are: 1. Poesis (subject) 2. Poema (form) 3. Poeta (poet)
58. Horace says the poets must
    (a) Please
    (b) Instruct
    (c) Please and instruct
    (d) None of the above
59. *Ars Poetica* opens with the assertion that a poem must have
    (a) an organic unity and propriety.
    (b) beautiful theme.
    (c) passion.
    (d) a new idea.
60. Horace advises the poet to strictly follow
    (a) the Greek models.
    (b) romantic tenets.
    (c) only Homer.
    (d) None of the above.
61. Which poet named one of his poems as "Ars Poetica"?
    (a) T.S. Eliot
    (b) Wordsworth
    (c) Archibald Macleish
    (d) Philip Larkin
62. According to Horace, a play must have at least
    (a) Seven acts (b) Five acts
    (c) Three acts (d) Four acts

63. According to Horace, the fountain source of good writing is
   (a) sound judgment (nature).
   (b) good craftsmanship (art).
   (c) Both (a) and (b).
   (d) None of the above.

64. Who said, "As the woods change their leaves at the year's decline, and first leaves fall first, so words perish with old age, and other newly born, thrive and flourish like youths"?
   (a) Aristotle (b) Plato
   (c) Sidney (d) Horace

65. According to Horace, the subject matter of poetry should be
   (a) Simple
   (b) Consistent
   (c) Ordinary
   (d) Both (a) and (b)

66. Horace says that language of poetry should be
   (a) the language of the common man.
   (b) different from the language of the common man.
   (c) the language of the scholars.
   (d) the language of the city people.

67. Who said, "Study the Greek originals of Greece/Dream of them by night and ponder them by day"?
   (a) Dryden (b) Johnson
   (c) Horace (d) Longinus

68. According to Horace, literature influences our
   (a) Emotions
   (b) Reason
   (c) Senses
   (d) None of the above

69. Horace's *Ars Poetica* is the
   (a) first book of Epistles.
   (b) second book of Epistles.
   (c) third book of Epistles.
   (d) fourth book of Epistles.

70. For Horace, the important elements of the 'structure' of a work are
   (a) Unity (b) Propriety
   (c) Arrangement (d) All of the above

71. "The humblest craftsman over near the Aemilian school will model fingernails and imitate waving hair in bronze; but the total work will be unhappy because he does not know how to represent it as a unified whole. I should no more wish to be like him, if I desired to compose something, than to be praised for my dark hair and eyes and yet go through life with my nose turned awry. You who write, take a subject equal to your powers, and consider at length how much your shoulders can bear. Neither proper words nor lucid order will be lacking to the writer who chooses a subject within his powers. The excellence and charm of the arrangement, I believe, consists in the ability to say only what needs to be said at the time, deferring or omitting many points for the moment. The author of the long-promised poem must accept and reject as he proceeds."

   Horace here
   (a) Gives advice (b) Criticizes
   (c) Evaluates (d) Inspires

72. Who called Longinus "the first romantic critic"?
   (a) David Daiches
   (b) Abercrombie
   (c) R.A. Scott-James
   (d) T.S. Eliot

73. Longinus believed that the decay of eloquence and decline of literature is due to
   (a) the rise of democracy.
   (b) the end of democracy.

(c) the end of monarchy.
(d) degradation and corruption of the human soul.

74. Longinus makes use of
(a) historical method.
(b) comparative method.
(c) analytical method.
(d) All of the above.

75. Which factor has Longinus emphasized in the treatise *On the Sublime*?
(a) Simplicity
(b) Clear expression
(c) Figures of speech
(d) Nobility of thought

76. What, according to Longinus, is the power of suitable words?
(a) Emotional effect
(b) They can breathe voice into dead things
(c) Spiritual effect
(d) None of the above

77. Longinus as a critic is a
(a) Classicist
(b) Romanticist
(c) Both (a) and (b)
(d) Neither (a) nor (b)

78. What, according to Longinus, are the elements of the sources of the sublime?
(a) Great ideas; strong and inspired person.
(b) The appropriate use of figures and the right diction.
(c) A skilful composition.
(d) All of the above.

(Longinus identifies the above five elements as the sources of the sublime)

79. *On the Sublime* is addressed to
(a) Terentianus (b) Plato
(c) Aristotle (d) Homer

80. What, according to Longinus, are the faults of style that tend to spoil the loftiness of language?
(a) Timidity or bombast
(b) Puerility and grandiloquence
(c) Frigidity
(d) All of the above

81. Who has said, "Great literature springs from great and lofty souls, and not from those with whom the world is too much"?
(a) Plato (b) Aristotle
(c) Longinus (d) Horace

82. According to Longinus, which are the sources of sublimity that cannot be cultivated?
(a) Dignity of composition.
(b) Appropriate use of figures.
(c) Nobility of diction.
(d) Capacity for strong emotion and grandeur of thought.

83. Choose the correct chronological sequence:
(a) Plat, Aristotle, Horace, Longinus
(b) Longin us, Aristotle, Horace, Plato
(c) Horace, Plato, Longinus, Aristotle

(1. Plato {428-347 B.C.} 2. Aristotle {384-322 B.C.} 3. Horace {65-8 B.C.} 4. Longinus {first century A.D.})

**INDIAN LITERARY THEORY**

**1.** *Natyasastra* (Bharata) **2.** *Kavyadarsan* (Dandin) **3.** *Kavyalamkar* (Bhambaha) **4.** *Agnipurana* (related to Poetics) (one of the 18 Mahapuranas) **5.** *Kavyalankarasutra* (Vamana) **6.** *Dhvanyaloka* (Anandauardhana) **7.** *Kavyamimansa* (Rajasekhra) **8.** *Dasharupaka* (Dhananjya) **9.** *Vakrokijivita* (Kuntaka) **10.** *Vaktiviveka* (Mahimambhatta) **11.** *Abhinavabharati* (Abhinavgupta) **12.** *Ancitya Vichara – charcha* (Ksemandra) **13.** *Kavya Prakasa* (Mammata) **14.** *Alambkarasarvasva* (Ruyyaka) **15.** *Candraloka* (Jayadeva) **16.** *Rasamanjari* (Bhanudatta) **17.** *Rasatarangini* (Bhanudatta) **18.** *Sahityadarpana* (Viswanatha) **19.** *Ujjvalanilamani* (Rupagoswami) **20.** *Kavyalayananda* (Appaya Diksita) **21.** *Citramimamsa* (Appaya Diksita) **22.** *Rasagandhara* (Pt. Jagannatha)

## ANSWERS

| | | | | | |
|---|---|---|---|---|---|
| 51. (b) | 52. (a) | 53. (c) | 54. (d) | 55. (b) | 56. (c) |
| 57. (b) | 58. (c) | 59. (a) | 60. (a) | 61. (c) | 62. (b) |
| 63. (c) | 64. (d) | 65. (d) | 66. (b) | 67. (c) | 68. (a) |
| 69. (c) | 70. (d) | 71. (a) | 72. (c) | 73. (d) | 74. (d) |
| 75. (c) | 76. (b) | 77. (c) | 78. (d) | 79. (a) | 80. (d) |
| 81. (c) | 82. (d) | 83. (a) | | | |

## (III) RENAISSANCE CRITICISM

84. To which period of criticism does Philip Sidney "An Apology for Poetry" belong?
    (a) Renaissance criticism
    (b) Classical criticism
    (c) Modern criticism
    (d) Neo-classical criticism

85. Who is regarded both as a classicist and a romanticist?
    (a) Aristotle (b) Plato
    (c) Sidney (d) Ben Jonson

86. Dramatic criticism in England began with
    (a) Ben Jonson
    (b) John Dryden
    (c) Dr. Samuel Johnson
    (d) Philip Sidney

87. What, according to Sidney, is the function of poetry?
    (a) To teach people the substance of poetry.
    (b) To move people to virtuous action.
    (c) To impress upon the people the transitory and worthless nature of worldly affairs.
    (d) All of the above.

88. Who said, "Poetry is a speaking picture"?
    (a) Horace (b) Longinus
    (c) Sidney (d) Shelley

89. Sidney broadly divides poetry into
    (a) religious and philosophic.
    (b) religious and right or true.
    (c) philosophic and right or true.
    (d) religious, philosophic and true.

    (The purpose of 'religious' poetry is to sing the praise of God, while 'philosophic' poetry contains knowledge of subjects and the purpose of 'true' poetry is to delight as well as instruct)

90. The 'true' kind of poetry, according to Sidney, is of the following kinds:
    (a) heroic, lyric, tragic.
    (b) comic, satiric.
    (c) iambic, pastoral.
    (d) All of the above.
91. While Aristotle said that poetry is superior to history, Sidney says that
    (a) poetry is inferior to philosophy.
    (b) poetry is superior to history.
    (c) poetry is superior to philosophy.
    (d) poetry is superior to both history and philosophy.

    (This is because the end of all learning is virtuous action, and poetry best serves this end)
92. To Stephen Gosson's observation that poetry is "the mother of lies", Sidney's reply is that
    (a) the poet never lies.
    (b) poetry deals with truth.
    (c) the poet "nothing affirms and, therefore, he never lieth".
    (d) he agrees with him.
93. What, according to Sidney, is the function of tragedy?
    (a) Admiration and commiseration
    (b) Admiration
    (c) Commiseration
    (d) Giving pleasure
94. Sidney's *Apology for Poetry* was published in
    (a) 1579 (b) 1580-81
    (c) 1583 (d) 1585
95. Stephen Gosson's *The School of Abuse* was published in
    (a) 1575 (b) 1577
    (c) 1579 (d) 1580
96. *The Art of English Poetry* by George Puttenham was published in
    (a) 1568 (b) 1589
    (c) 1591 (d) 1592
97. According to Sir Philip Sidney, which is the "best, and most accomplished kind of poetry"?
    (a) Religious (b) Lyric
    (c) Satiric (d) Heroic
98. Who, among the following, said that "it is not poetry which abuses man's wit but man's wit that abuses poetry"?
    (a) Sidney (b) Shelley
    (c) Wordsworth (d) Peacock
99. Who said, "For a man to write well there are required three necessaries: to read the best authors; observe best speakers, and much exercise of his own style"?
    (a) Sidney (b) Horace
    (c) Ben Jonson (d) Longinus
100. Ben Jonson lays particular stress on
    (a) the unity of place.
    (b) the unity of time.
    (c) the unity of action.
    (d) All of the above.
101. Who said about whom: "My answer hath been would he have blotted a thousand"?
    (a) Shelley about Wordsworth
    (b) Sidney about Homer
    (c) Dr. Johnson about Donne
    (d) Ben Jonson about Shakespeare
102. Who said, "Spenser writ no language"?
    (a) Ben Jonson (b) Sidney
    (c) Dr. Johnson (d) Joseph Addison
103. Who said, "Ben Jonson was the first, complete and consistent English Classicist"?
    (a) Dr. Samuel Johnson
    (b) Joseph Addison
    (c) Spingarn
    (d) John Dryden

104. Who said that the ancients must be followed "as Guides and not Commanders. Truth lies open to all, it is no man's servant"?
(a) Philip Sidney
(b) Ben Jonson
(c) Alexander Pope
(d) Joseph Addison

105. Ben Jonson's *Timber or Discoveries* was published in
(a) 1637 (b) 1639
(c) 1640 (d) 1643

106. Who said that Aristotle, "not only found out the way to err, but the short way we should take not to err"?
(a) Dr. Johnson (b) Alexander Pope
(c) Joseph Addison (d) Ben Jonson

107. Thomas Campion attacked rhyme in *The Art of English Poesie.* Who answered Campion's attack?
(a) Philip Sidney
(b) John Puttenham
(c) Samuel Daniel
(d) John Dryden

(Samuel Daniel (1562-1619) defended the use of rhyme in poetry in his book *A Defence of Rhyme* (1603))

108. George Granville's *Essay Upon Unnatural Flights in Poetry* was published in
(a) 1702 (b) 1709
(c) 1703 (d) 1705

109. *The Art of Rhetoric* (1553) was written by
(a) Sidney (b) Ben Jonson
(c) Thomas Wilson (d) Hocace

## ANSWERS

| | | | | | |
|---|---|---|---|---|---|
| 84. (a) | 85. (c) | 86. (d) | 87. (d) | 88. (c) | 89. (d) |
| 90. (d) | 91. (d) | 92. (c) | 93. (a) | 94. (b) | 95. (b) |
| 96. (b) | 97. (d) | 98. (a) | 99. (c) | 100. (c) | 101. (d) |
| 102. (a) | 103. (c) | 104. (b) | 105. (c) | 106. (d) | 107. (c) |
| 108. (a) | 109. (c) | | | | |

## (IV) NEO-CLASSICAL CRITICISM

110. In which book John Dryden says that "With Ovid ended the golden age of the Roman tongue; from Chaucer the purity of the English language began"?
(a) *Essay of Dramatic Poesy*
(b) *Essay on Satire*
(c) *Fables : Ancient and Modern*
(d) *Essay on Heroic plays*

111. John Dryden's *Essay of Dramatic Poesy* was published in
(a) 1668 (b) 1671
(c) 1669 (d) 1672

112. John Dryden's *Essay of Dramatic Poesy* is a work of
(a) Comparative criticism
(b) Descriptive criticism
(c) Biographical criticism
(d) None of the above

113. Who said, "Shakespeare was the man who of all modern and perhaps ancient poets had the largest and most comprehensive soul"?
(a) Dr. Samuel Johnson
(b) John Dryden

(c) Ben Jonson
(d) Alexander Pope

114. The *Essay of Dramatic Poesy* was occasioned by Dryden's dispute with
(a) Lord Buckhurst
(b) Charles Sackville
(c) Sir Charles Sedley
(d) Sir Robert Howard

115. The chief purpose of Dryden's *Essay of Dramatic Poesy* was
(a) to defend drama.
(b) to criticize.
(c) to defend the ancients.
(d) "To vindicate the honour of our English writers, from the censure of those who unjustly prefer the French."

116. The issues taken up in the *Essay of Dramatic Poesy* are
(a) the classical unities of time, place and action.
(b) the rigid classical distinction between various genres such as tragedy and comedy.
(c) classical decorum ad propriety as well as use of rhyme in drama.
(d) All of the above.

117. In which book is the definition of a play offered as "A just and lively image of human nature, representing its passions and humours, and changes of fortune to which it is subject, for the delight and instruction of mankind"?
(a) *Ars Poetica*
(b) *Essay of Dramatic Poesy*
(c) *Poetics*
(d) *Timber or Discoveries*

118. Whom does Dryden regard as the "most learned and judicious writer which any theatre ever had"?
(a) William Shakespeare
(b) Sophocles
(c) Ben Jonson
(d) Marlowe

119. Who says, "Shakespeare was the Homer, or father of our dramatic poets; Johnson was the Virgil, the pattern of elaborate writing"?
(a) Dryden (b) Pope
(c) Addison (d) Steele

120. What elements, according to Dryden, are essential for the composition of poems?
(a) Wit (b) Fancy
(c) Elocution (d) All of the above

(In his 1666 preface to "Annus Mirabilis", Dryden regards wit not other than the faculty of imagination in the writer which contributes to invention or finding of the thought. 'Fancy' moulds the writer's thought and 'elocution' is the clothing or adorning that thought in apt and significant words)

121. Who said that the poet's task is to 'imitate well', to 'affect the soul', 'excite the passions' and cause 'admiration' or 'wonder'?
(a) Horace (b) Sidney
(c) Dryden (d) Pope

122. The genre of 'tragicomedy' is uniquely the invention of
(a) the French
(b) the English
(c) the Greeks
(d) the Romans

123. According to Dryden, comedy begets
(a) malicious pleasure.
(b) sensuous pleasure.
(c) spiritual pleasure.
(d) divine pleasure.

124. Who, among the following, was the first to use the term 'poetic diction'?
(a) John Dryden (b) John Dennis
(c) Alexander Pope (d) Dr. Johnson

125. Who, among the following, said that John Donne "affected metaphysics"?
  (a) Dr. Johnson
  (b) Pope
  (c) Dryden
  (d) H.J.C. Grierson

126. Who said, "It is sufficient to say, according to the proverb, that here's God's plenty"?
  (a) Joseph Addison
  (b) John Dryden
  (c) Alexander Pope
  (d) Dr. Johnson

  (This famous quotation occurs in *Fables: Ancient and Modern*. This statement refers to Chaucer's "Canterbury Tales")

127. Dryden's *Essay of Dramatic Poesy* is written in the manner of
  (a) Horace's *On the Sublime*
  (b) Aristotle's *Poetics*
  (c) Philip Sidney's *An Apology for Poetry*
  (d) Plato's *Republic*

128. In the *Essay of Dramatic Poesy*, the number of interlocutors is
  (a) Two (b) Three
  (c) Four (d) Five

129. Who, among the following, has said, "Delight is the chief, if not the only end of poetry; instruction can be admitted but in the second place, for poesy instructs as it delights"?
  (a) John Dryden (b) Dr. Johnson
  (c) Horace (d) Alexander Pope

130. Who among the following said, "Aristotle drew his models of tragedy from Sophocles and Euripides; and, if he had seen ours, might have changed his mind"?
  (a) Dr. Johnson (b) Alexander Pope
  (c) John Dryden (d) Bernard Shaw

131. Who represents Dryden in the *Essay of Dramatic Poesy*?
  (a) Lisideius (b) Eugenius
  (c) Crites (d) Neander

  (In *Essay of Dramatic Poesy*, Crites defends the Greek dramatists, Lisideius defends the French, while Eugenius is the spokesman of the last age. He defends the English and the French drama from Shakespeare's to Dryden's times. The fourth interlocutor, Neander, defends the English dramatists and the so-called liberties they had taken with regard to the canons of the art of writing and producing plays as laid down by Aristotle. He represents Dryden.)

**Important works by Thomas Rymer (1641-1714), John Dennis (1657-1734), Jeremy Collier (1650-1726)**

1. Thomas Rhymer: (i) *Reflections on Aristotle's Poetics* (1677) (ii) *The Tragedies of the Last Age* (1678) (iii) *A Short View of Tragedy*
2. John Dennis: (i) *The Advancement and Reformation of Modern Poetry* (1701) (ii) *The Impartial Critic* (1693)
3. *The Grounds of criticism in Poetry* (1704)
4. Jeremy Collier: (i) *Short View of the Immorality and Profaneness of the English Stage* (1698)

132. Which of his works did Addison write about the concept of the aesthetic theory of the period?
  (a) *The Spectator Papers*
  (b) *Account of the Great English Poets*
  (c) *Papers on the Pleasures of Imagination*
  (d) None of the above

133. In Addison's *Account of the Greatest English Poets* (1694), which author was not even mentioned?

(a) Cowley (b) Shakespeare
(c) Dryden (d) Chaucer

134. Who has defined taste as "that faculty of the soul, which discerns the Beauties of an Author with pleasure, and the imperfections with dislike"?
(a) Alexander Pope
(b) John Dryden
(c) Joseph Addison
(d) Dr. Johnson

135. How many essays did Addison write on the 'tragedy'?
(a) Five (b) Three
(c) Four (d) Six

136. Alexander Pope's *Essay on Criticism* is divided into
(a) Five parts (b) Three parts
(c) Two parts (d) Four parts

137. Pope's philosophic poem "An Essay on Man" (1733-32) was a bitter attack on human arrogance or pride in
(a) failing to observe the due limits of human reason.
(b) questioning divine authority.
(c) seeking to be self–reliant on the basis of rationality and science.
(d) All of the above

138. Who said, "True wit is Nature to Advantage drest/ What often was thought, but ne'er so well expressed"?
(a) John Dryden
(b) Alexander Pope
(c) Dr. Johnson
(d) Horace

(These oft-quoted lines occur in Pope's *Essay on Criticism*. According to Pope, expression is the dress of thought and that "true expression" throws light on objects without altering them. If wit is the dress of nature, it will express nature without altering it. "Wit", for Pope, is a mode of knowing or apprehension unique to literature. In general, in Pope's time, it referred to intelligence or intelligent acuity, i.e. ability to think or perceive clearly.)

139. In which of the following books written by Alexander Pope does the following line appear: "The sound must seem an Echo to the sense".
(a) *Essay on Man*
(b) *Essay on Criticism*
(c) *Imitation of Horace*
(d) *An Epistle to Dr. Arbuthnot*

(Pope means to say that the expression or style must be suited to the subject matter and meaning)

140. Who, among the following, said that "those who cou'dnot win the Mistress, Woo'd the Maid"?
(a) Alexander Pope
(b) Ben Jonson
(c) John Dryden
(d) Dr. Johnson

(It is Pope's comment in *Essay on Criticism* on the decline of criticism from its earlier higher status)

141. *Essay on Criticism* is written in the manner of
(a) Plato's *Republic*
(b) Horace's *Ars Poetica*
(c) Longinus's *On the Sublime*
(d) Aristotle's *Poetics*

142. Who among the following said, "To judge Shakespeare by Aristotle's rules is like trying a man by the laws of one country, who acted under those of another"?
(a) John Dryden
(b) Dr. Johnson
(c) Alexander Pope
(d) Joseph Addison

143. Who wrote *Preface to the Works of Shakespeare* (1725)?

(a) Dr. Johnson
(b) John Dryden
(c) Ben Jonson
(d) Alexander Pope

144. Pope's *Essay on Criticism* sums up art of poetry as first taught by
(a) Aristotle (b) Horace
(c) Longinus (d) Homer

145. Who, among the following, said that language is the external "dress of thought"?
(a) Alexander Pope
(b) Dr. Johnson
(c) John Dryden
(d) Joseph Addison

146. Pope's *Essay on Man* is based on the ideas of
(a) Lord Petric (b) Theobald
(c) Lord Bolingbroke (d) Lord Harvey

147. Two of the concepts central to neo-classical theory and practice were
(a) Imitation (b) Nature
(c) Imagination (d) Both (a) and (b)

(The Neo-classicists imitated the classical models, especially Homer and Virgil. Nature, for them, meant human nature, i.e. what was central, timeless, universal in human experience. It also referred to harmonious and hierarichal order to the universe, including the various social and political hierarchies of the world.)

148. Who was the first to write *A Dictionary of the English Language*?
(a) John Dryden
(b) Alexander Pope
(c) Dr. Johnson
(d) Joseph Addison

149. How many years did Dr. Samuel Johnson take to compile his *Dictionary*?
(a) Nine years (b) Seven years
(c) Six years (d) Ten years

150. Name the book about which Dr. Johnson said that "modern English prose begins here"?
(a) *On the Sublime*
(b) *Essay of Dramatic Poesy*
(c) *An Apology for Poetry*
(d) *Aeropagitica*

151. James Boswell's biography of Dr. Johnson *Life of Samuel Johnson LL.D* was published in
(a) 1795 (b) 1785
(c) 1791 (d) 1793

152. Dr. Samuel Johnson's *Preface to Shakespeare* was published in
(a) 1785 (b) 1765
(c) 1755 (d) 1761

153. Dr. Johnson's edition of *Shakespeare* had
(a) Six volumes (b) Five volumes
(c) Eight volumes (d) Seven volumes

154. Dr. Johnson's *Preface to Shakespeare* deals broadly with
(a) the question how a poet's reputation is established.
(b) the poet's relation to nature.
(c) the relative virtues of nature and experience of life as against a reliance on principles established by criticism and convention.
(d) All of the above.

155. Who among the following said that "nothing can please many, and please long, but just representations of nature"?
(a) John Dryden
(b) Dr. Samuel Johnson
(c) Joseph Addison

(This line occurs in *Preface to Shakespeare*)

156. Who, according to Dr. Johnson, is "the poet of nature: that poet that holds up to his readers a faithful mirror of manners and life"?

(a) Chaucer (b) John Dryden
(c) Shakespeare (d) John Milton

157. Dr. Johnson in *Preface to Shakespeare* defends Shakespeare for not observing
(a) Unity of action (b) Unity of time
(c) Unity of place (d) Both (b) and (c)

158. In which of the following books has it been said that "the stage is only a stage and the players are only players"?
(a) *Essay of Dramatic Poesy*
(b) *Theatre of the Absurd*
(c) *Preface to Shakespeare*
(d) None of the above

159. What, according to Dr. Johnson, are the great virtues of a play?
(a) To delight
(b) To instruct
(c) To delight and instruct
(d) To copy nature and instruct life

160. About which poet did Dr. Johnson say: "He found if (poetry) brick, and he left it marble"?
(a) John Milton
(b) John Dryden
(c) William Shakespeare
(d) Alexander Pope

161. Who, among the following, said, "If Pope be not a poet, where is poetry to be found"?
(a) Dr. Johnson
(b) Matthew Arnold
(c) T.S. Eliot
(d) S.T. Coleridge

162. Dr. Johnson's criticism was based on the classical foundation of adherence to
(a) Nature
(b) Reason and truth
(c) Moral instruction
(d) All of the above

163. Choose the correct chronological sequence:
(a) John Dryden, Alexander Pope, Dr. Samuel Johnson, Joseph Addison
(b) Alexander Pope, Joseph Addison, Dr. Samuel Johnson, John Dryden
(c) John Dryden, Joseph Addison, Alexander Pope, Dr. Samuel Johnson
(d) Dr. Samuel Johnson, Joseph Addison, Alexander Pope, John Dryden

(John Dryden (1631-1700); Joseph Addison (1672-1719); Alexander Pope (1688-1744); Dr. Samuel Johnson (1709-84)

164. Choose the correct pair:
(a) *Apology for Poetry* : (a) Philip Sidney
(b) *Lives of the Poets* : (b) Alexander Pope
(c) *Essay on Criticism* : (c) John Dryden
(d) *Essay of Dramatic Poesy* : (d) Dr. Samuel Johnson

165. Who, among the following, said, "The task of an author is, either to teach what is not known, or to recommend known truths by his manner of adorning them,...."
(a) Joseph Addison
(b) Dr. Johnson
(c) Alexander Pope
(d) John Dryden

(Dr. Johnson in "Rambler", March 27, 1750)

166. Dr. Samuel Johnson is a pioneer in the field of
(a) Historical criticism
(b) Biographical criticism
(c) Formalist criticism
(d) Psychoanalytical criticism

(Dr. Johnson is also an advocate of 'comparative criticism')

167. The *Lives of the English Poets* (1779-81) was written by
   (a) Dr. Samuel Johnson
   (b) John Dryden
   (c) Alexander Pope
   (d) Shelley

   (The full title of *Lives of the Poets* is *Lives of the Most Eminent English Poets*)

168. *Lives of the English Poets* deals with the lives of
   (a) 50 poets (b) 48 poets
   (c) 52 poets (d) 54 poets

169. According to several critics, in *Lives of the English Poets*, Dr. Johnson was unjust in his criticism of
   (a) John Dryden
   (b) John Milton
   (c) Alexander Pope
   (d) Cowley

170. Who among the following said: Poetry is "the art of uniting pleasure with truth, by calling imagination to the help of reason"?
   (a) Alexander Pope
   (b) Horace
   (c) John Dryden
   (d) Dr. Johnson

   (Dr. Johnson made this comment in *Life of Milton*)

171. Which kind of poetry did Dr. Johnson regard as the highest?
   (a) Epic (b) Lyric
   (c) Ode (d) Satire

172. Who, among the following, said that "the essence of poetry is invention; such invention as, by producing something unexpected, surprises, and delights"?
   (a) John Dryden (b) Horace
   (c) Dr. Johnson (d) Alexander Pope

   (Dr. Johnson made this observation in *Life of Waller*)

173. About whom has it been said that "in his appreciation of Shakespeare's mingling of the tragic and the comic, and his violation of the unities, he ceases to be a classic and goes over to the other camp"?
   (a) Dr. Johnson (b) Alexander Pope
   (c) John Dryden (d) Ben Jonson

174. "In his tragic scenes there is always something wanting, but his comedy often surprises expectation or desire", says Dr. Johnson. About whom has it been said?
   (a) Marlowe (b) Shakespeare
   (c) Ben Jonson (d) Robert Greene

175. Who among the following said that "Shakespeare has no heroes, his scenes are occupied only by men, who act and speak as the reader thinks he should himself have spoken or acted on the same occasion"?
   (a) Dr. Johnson (b) Alexander Pope
   (c) Thomas Rymer (d) Arnold

176. Who, among the following, has made the observation about Dr. Johnson that "He tries Shakespeare by the tests of time, of nature, of universality, and finds him supreme in all"?
   (a) R.A. Scott-James
   (b) David Daiches
   (c) John Bailey
   (d) T.S. Eliot

177. Who among the following made the comment that "Before the greatness displayed in Milton's poem ("Paradise Lost"), all other greatness melts away"?
   (a) John Dryden (b) Alexander Pope
   (c) David Daiches (d) Dr. Johnson

178. In which context did Dr. Johnson say: "The business of him that republishes an ancient book is, to correct what is corrupt, and to explain what is obscure"?
   (a) Spenser's "The Fairie Queene"
   (b) Milton's "Paradise Lost"

(c) Shakespeare's plays
(d) Gorboduc

179. About whom has Dr. Johnson made the observation, "A quibble was to him the fatal Cleopatra for which he lost the world, and was content to lose it"?
(a) Shakespeare (b) Milton
(c) John Dryden (d) Thomas Gray

180. In *Lives of the Poets* (1779-81), in whose poet's life has Dr. Johnson made the following observation:

"The most heterogeneous ideas are yoked by violence together, nature and art are ransacked for illustrations, comparisons, and allusions; their learning instructs, and their subtlety surprises; ________"?
(a) Life of Milton
(b) Life of Gray
(c) Life of William King
(d) Life of Cowley

(These observations by Dr. Johnson are about the Metaphysical poets)

181. About which poem has Dr. Johnson said that it "abounds with images which find a mirror in every mind, and with sentiments to which every bosom returns an echo"?
(a) Gray's "Bard"
(b) Milton's "Lycidas"
(c) Thomas Gray's "Elegy Written in a Country Churchyard"
(d) Milton's "Paradise Lost"

182. While discussing the plays of Shakespeare, why does Dr. Johnson defend "mingled drama", i.e. tragic-comedy?
(a) "Mingled drama", conforms to what Johnson calls the "laws of nature"
(b) It is according to the rules of classicism
(c) It suits the genius of Shakespeare
(d) None of the above

183. It has been said about Milton's "Samson Agonistes" that it possesses
(a) a beginning, middle and end.
(b) a beginning and end but no "middle".
(c) a beginning and middle but no end.
(d) a middle and end but no "beginning".

## Dr. Johnson's *Lives of the Poets*

The poets included were:

| | | |
|---|---|---|
| Abraham Cowley | Charles Montague, Earl of Halifax | Richard Savage |
| Sir John Denham | Thomas Parnell | Jonathan Swift |
| John Milton | Samuel Garth | William Broome |
| Samuel Butler (Hudibras) | Nicholas Rowe | Alexander Pope |
| John Wilmot, Earl of Rochester | Joseph Addison | Christopher Pitt |
| Wentworth Dillon, | John Hughes | James Thomson |
| Earl of Roscommon | John Sheffield, | Isaac Watts |
| Thomas Otway | Duke of Buckingham | Ambrose Philips |
| Edmund Waller | Matthew Prior | Gilbert West |
| John Pomfret | William Congreve | William Collins |
| Charles Sackville, Earl of Dorset | Sir Richard Blackmore | John Dyer |
| George Stepney | Elijah Fenton | William Shenstone |
| John Philips | John Gay | Edward Young |

| William Walsh | George Granville, Lord Lansdown | David Mallet |
|---|---|---|
| John Dryden | Thomas Yalden | Mark Akenside |
| Edmund Smith | Thomas Tickell | Thomas Gray |
| Richard Duke | James Hammond | George Lord Lyttelton |
| William King | William Somervile | Thomas Sprat |

184. Who has been called the "Last Augustan"?
   (a) John Dryden
   (b) Alexander Pope
   (c) Addison
   (d) Johnson

185. The most obvious feature of Johnson's *The Lives of the Poets* is the equipoise between
   (a) language and form.
   (b) style and content.
   (c) biography and criticism.
   (d) myth and psychoanalytical criticism.

186. With whom was Dr. Johnson intimately associated in his personal life?
   (a) Boswell (b) Dryden
   (c) Pope (d) Bolingbroke

187. Dr. Johnson's *The Lives of the Poets* is
   (a) Biographical commentary
   (b) Generic criticism
   (c) Textual and practical criticism
   (d) All of the above

188. Dr. Johnson's *The Lives of the Poets* (1779 to 1781) was originally called
   (a) Biographical sketches
   (b) Prefaces to the Poetic Works
   (c) Prefaces, Biographical and Critical to the works of the English Poets
   (d) Works of the English Poets

189. Who wrote the following and in which work?

   "That praises are lavished on the dead and that honours due only to excellence are paid to antiquity, is a complaint likely to be always continued those, who being able to add nothing to truth, hope for eminence from the heresies of paradox; or those, who, being forced by disappointment upon consolatory expedients, are willing to hope from posterity what the present age refuses and flatter thousands that the regard which is yet denied by envy, will be at last bestowed by time."
   (a) Longinus – *On the Sublime*
   (b) Sir Philip Sidney – *An Apology for Poetry*
   (c) Samuel Johnson – *Preface to Shakespeare*
   (d) John Dryden – *An Essay on Dramatic Poesy*

190. The following extract is from:

   "To begin, then, with Shakespeare. He was the man who of all modern, and perhaps ancient poets, had the largest and most comprehensive soul. All the images of nature were still present to him, and he drew them, not laboriously, but luckily; when he describes anything, you more than see it, you feel it too. Those who accuse him to have wanted learning, give him the greater commendation : he was naturally learned, he needed not the spectacles of books to read nature; he looked inwards, and found her there."
   (a) *An Essay on Dramatic Poesy*
   (b) *An Essay on Criticism*
   (c) *On the Pleasures of the Imagination*
   (d) *Preface to Shakespeare*

191. The following extract is from:

"Our sight is most perfect and most delightful of all our senses. It fills the mind with the largest variety of ideas, converses with the largest variety of ideas, converses with its objects being tired or satiated with its proper enjoyments. The sense of feeling can indeed give us a notion of extension, shape, and all other ideas that enter at the eye except colors; but at the same time it is very much straitened and confined in its operations, to the number, bulk, and distance of its particular objects."

(a) *The Study of Poetry*
(b) *The Salon of 1859*
(c) *Studies in the History of the Renaissance*
(d) *On the Pleasures of the Imagination* (Addison)

**Find out the Authors of the Following Extracts:**

192. "Our next subject will be the style of expression. For it is not enough to know, what we ought to say; we must also say it as we ought; much help is thus afforded towards producing the right impression of a speech. The first question 'to receive attention was naturally the one that comes first naturally—how persuasion can be produced from the facts themselves. The second is how to set these out in language. A third would be the proper method of delivery; this is a thing that affects the success of a speech greatly; but hitherto the subject has been neglected."

193. He shows, however, in the Odyssey (and this further observation deserves attention on many grounds) that, when genius is declining, the special token of old age is the love of marvelous tales. It is clear from many indications the Odyssey was his second subject. A special proof is the fact that he introduces in that poem remnants of the adventures before Ilium as episodes, so to say, of the Trojan War. And indeed, he there renders a tribute of mourning and lamentation to his heroes as though he was carrying out long-cherished purpose. In fact the Odyssey is simply an epilogue to the Iliad."

194. "Because, if I am not mistaken, we shall have to say that about man, poets and story-tellers are guilty of making the gravest misstatements when they tell us that wicked men are often happy, and the good miserable, and that injustice is profitable when undetected, but that justice is a man's own loss and another's gain—these things we shall forbid them to utter, and command them to sing and say the opposite."

195. "And first, truly, to all them, professing learning inveigh against poetry may justly be objected, that they go very near to ungratefulness, to seek to deface that which, in the noblest nations and languages that are known, hath been the first high-giver to ignorance, and first nurse whose milk by little and little enabled them to feed afterwards of tougher knowledges."

196. "For the second unity which is that of place, the ancients meant by it, that the scene ought to be continued through the play, in the same place where it was laid in the beginning : for the stage on which it is represented being but one and the same place, it is unnatural to conceive it many; and those far distant from each other."

197. In what context does Dr. Johnson say: "There is always an appeal open from criticism to nature."?

(a) Unity of place
(b) Unity of action
(c) Unity of time
(d) the mingling of tragic and comic elements in Shakespeare's play

198. *A Philosophical Inquiry into the Origin of Our Ideas of the Sublime* (1757) was written by?
(a) Kennteth Burke
(b) Edmund Burke
(c) Wayne Booth
(d) Locke

**ANSWERS**

| | | | | | |
|---|---|---|---|---|---|
| 110. (c) | 111. (a) | 112. (a) | 113. (b) | 114. (d) | 115. (d) |
| 116. (d) | 117. (b) | 118. (c) | 119. (a) | 120. (d) | 121. (c) |
| 122. (b) | 123. (a) | 124. (b) | 125. (c) | 126. (b) | 127. (d) |
| 128. (c) | 129. (a) | 130. (c) | 131. (d) | 132. (c) | 133. (b) |
| 134. (c) | 135. (c) | 136. (b) | 137. (d) | 138. (b) | 139. (b) |
| 140. (a) | 141. (b) | 142. (c) | 143. (d) | 144. (d) | 145. (a) |
| 146. (c) | 147. (d) | 148. (c) | 149. (a) | 150. (b) | 151. (c) |
| 152. (b) | 153. (c) | 154. (d) | 155. (b) | 156. (c) | 157. (d) |
| 158. (c) | 159. (d) | 160. (b) | 161. (a) | 162. (d) | 163. (c) |
| 164. (a) | 165. (b) | 166. (b) | 167. (a) | 168. (c) | 169. (b) |
| 170. (d) | 171. (a) | 172. (c) | 173. (a) | 174. (b) | 175. (a) |
| 176. (c) | 177. (d) | 178. (c) | 179. (a) | 180. (d) | 181. (c) |
| 182. (a) | 183. (b) | 184. (d) | 185. (c) | 186. (a) | 187. (d) |
| 188. (c) | 189. (c) | 190. (a) | 191. (d) | | |
| 192. Aristotle | | 193. Longinus | | 194. Plato | |
| 195. Sidney | | 196. Dryden | | 197. (d) | 198. (b) |

## (V) ROMANTIC CRITICISM

199. Wordsworth's *Lyrical Ballads* was published in
(a) 1800 (b) 1798
(c) 1802 (d) 1805

200. Wordsworth's *Preface to the Lyrical Ballads* was written in
(a) 1800 (b) 1798
(c) 1802 (d) 1797

201. The *Preface to the Lyrical Ballads* was revised and enlarged in...
(a) 1798 (b) 1800
(c) 1802 (d) 1797

202. Which edition of *Lyrical Ballads* contained an "Appendix on Poetic Diction"?
(a) First edition
(b) Second edition
(c) Third edition
(d) None of the above

203. Wordsworth's "Preface" is regarded as the manifesto of
(a) Classicism (b) Romanticism
(c) Neo-classicism (d) Aestheticism

204. Who, among the following said, that the poet "sings a song in which all human

beings join with him...he looks before and after"?

(a) Shelley (b) Keats
(c) Wordsworth (d) Coleridge

205. In which of the following do these lines occur?

"Poets do not write for poets alone, but for men,...the poet must descend from this supposed height; and in order to excite rational sympathy, he must express himself as other men express themselves."

(a) *Biographia Literaria*
(b) *Preface to the Lyrical Ballads*
(c) *Apology for Poetry*
(d) *Defense of Poetry*

206. Who, among the following, said, "Classicism is health, Romanticism is disease"?

(a) Walter Pater (b) Goethe
(c) Tomas Carlyle (d) T.S. Eliot

207. Who defined Romanticism as 'the Renaissance of wonder'?

(a) Goethe
(b) Walter Pater
(c) Theodore Watts Dunton
(d) Ruskin

208 Who coined the phrase "egotistical sublime"?

(a) Keats (b) Coleridge
(c) Wordsworth (d) Arnold

('Egotistical Sublime' is a phrase by which Keats criticised what he felt to be the excessive self-centred quality of Wordsworth's poetry, in contrast with his own ideal of 'negative capability', which he found in Shakespeare.)

209. Who called the Romantic Movement as 'Liberalism in literature'?

(a) T.S. Eliot (b) I.A. Richards
(c) Victor Hugo (d) F.R. Leavis

210. Who among the following said, *Preface to the Lyrical Ballads* explains the poetic process of the type of poetry only Wordsworth wrote"?

(a) I.A. Richards (b) T.S. Eliot
(c) F.R. Leavis (d) Cleanth Brooks

211. Who, among the following said, "The essence of romantic art is that in it the spirit counts far more than the form" ?

(a) T.S. Eliot
(b) Grierson
(c) F.R. Leavis
(d) Matthew Arnold

212. Who said, "Mr. Wordswoth, on the other hand, was to propose to himself as his object to give the charm of novelty to the things of everyday"?

(a) Matthew Arnold
(b) Shelley
(c) Keats
(d) S.T. Coleridge

213. Who, among the following, has given 11,396 definitions of Romanticism?

(a) F.L. Lucas (b) Victor Hugo
(c) Immanuel Kant (d) Goethe

214. Who, among the following has said, "Poetry sheds no tears, such as angels weep, but nature and human tears..."?

(a) William Wordsworth
(b) Shelly
(c) Keats
(d) Arnold

215. Who made the remark that "men who do not wear fine clothes can feel deeply"?

(a) Shelley (b) Keats
(c) Wordsworth (d) Coleridge

216. About which of the following books has this remark been made: "It cannot be read too often; every time it seems to

contain something new and unexpected. It marks the beginning of the new age"?

(a) *Apology for Poetry*
(b) *Preface to the Lyrical Ballads*
(c) *Defence of Poetry*
(d) *Biographia Literaria*

217. Wordsworth did not like the language used by neo-classical poets because

(a) it was Latinised.
(b) it was very difficult to understand.
(c) it was pedantic.
(d) it had "gaudiness and inane phraseology".

218. Who made the following observation about Wordsworth?

"Wordsworth himself was a great critic, and it is to be sincerely regretted that he has not left us more criticism."

(a) S.T. Coleridge (b) T.S. Eliot
(c) Matthew Arnold (d) F.R. Leavis

219. Wordsworth's contribution to literary theory mainly depends on

(a) *Preface to the Lyrical Ballads* (1800)
(b) *Preface to Poems* (1815)
(c) *Essays upon Epitaphs* (1810)
(d) All of the above

220. Wordsworth, in his *Preface to Lyrical Ballads*, defines a poet is a

(a) man speaking to man.
(b) divinely-inspired being.
(c) man living next door.
(d) man specially gifted by God.

221. How, according to Wordsworth, is a poet different from an ordinary man?

(a) A poet has superior sensibility and greater knowledge of human nature.
(b) A poet has more immediate sympathy.
(c) A poet has more spontaneous expressiveness.
(d) All of the above.

222. Who, among the following, condemns Alexander Pope's epitaphs as "little better than a tissue of false thoughts, languid and vague expression unmeaning antithesis and laborious attempt at discrimination"?

(a) S.T. Coleridge
(b) Matthew Arnold
(c) William Wordsworth
(d) I.A. Richards

223. Who, among the following, has said, "Words are too awful an instrument for good and evil to be trifled with: they hold above all external powers a dominion over thoughts. If words be not...an incarnation of the thought but only a clothing for it, then surely will they prove an ill gift"?

(a) T.S. Eliot
(b) William Wordsworth
(c) F.R. Leavis
(d) S.T. Coleridge

(This statement has been made by Wordsworth in *Essays upon Epitaphs* while discussing the power of language.)

224. Wordsworth considers poetry to be superior to

(a) Philosophy (b) History
(c) Science (d) All of the above

225. According to Wordsworth, the primary purpose of poetry is to give

(a) Pleasure
(b) Moral courage
(c) Knowledge
(d) None of the above

226. *Lyrical Ballads* was a cooperative volume of poems by

(a) Wordsworth and Keats
(b) Coleridge and Shelley
(c) Wordsworth and Coleridge
(d) Shelley and Keats

227. The preface added to the second edition of *Lyrical Ballads* in 1800 provides justification for
   (a) the critical principles of Romantic Movement.
   (b) classicism.
   (c) aestheticism.
   (d) None of the above.

228. After Wordsworth's 'Preface', the central function of the poetic process became the
   (a) Mimetic function
   (b) Expressive function
   (c) Affective function
   (d) None of the above

229. William Wordsworth was born in
   (a) 1770 (b) 1772
   (c) 1773 (d) 1775

230. What was Wordsworth's preferred aim in the *Lyrical Ballads*?
   (a) Free poetry of all conceit
   (b) Simplicity of diction
   (c) Make it intelligible to common people
   (d) All of the above

231. The *Lyrical Ballads* opens with
   (a) Kubla Khan
   (b) Ode to Duty
   (c) Rime of the Ancient Mariner
   (d) Immortality Ode

232. The *Lyrical Ballads* closes with
   (a) Kubla Khan
   (b) Immortality Ode
   (c) Christabel
   (d) Tintern Abbey

233. Who was the third person with Coleridge and Wordsworth at Quantico Hills when the *Lyrical Ballads* was composed?
   (a) Dorothy Wordsworth
   (b) Robert Southey
   (c) Walter Scott
   (d) William Hazlitt

**WORDSWORTH'S PRINCIPAL OBJECT OF THE POEMS IN *LYRICAL BALLADS***

Wordsworth wanted to choose incidents and situations from common life, and to relate or describe them, throughout, as far as was possible in a selection of language really used by men, and, at the same time, to throw over them a certain colouring of imagination, whereby ordinary things should be presented to the mind in an unusual aspect; and, further, and above all, to make these incidents and situations interesting by tracing in them, the primary laws of our nature: chiefly, as far as regards the manner in which we associate ideas in a state of excitement. Humble and rustic life was generally chosen, because, in that condition, the essential passions of the heart find a better soil in which they can attain their maturity, are less under restraint, and speak a plainer and more emphatic language; because in that condition of life our elementary feelings coexist in a state of greater simplicity, and, consequently, may be more accurately contemplated, and more forcibly communicated; because the manners of rural life germinate from those elementary feelings, and, from the necessary character of rural occupations, are more easily comprehended, and are more durable; and, lastly, because in that condition the passions of men are incorporated with the beautiful and permanent forms of nature. The language, too, of these men has been adopted because such men hourly communicate with the best objects from which the best part of language is originally derived; and because, from their rank in society and the sameness and narrow circle of their intercourse, being less under the influence of social vanity, they convey their feelings and notions in simple and unelaborated expressions. Accordingly, such a language, arising out of repeated experience and regular feelings, is a more permanent, and a far more philosophical language, than that which is frequently substituted for it by Poets, who think that they are conferring honour upon themselves and their art, in proportion as they separate themselves from the sympathies of men, and indulge in arbitrary and capricious habits of expression, in order to furnish food for fickle tastes, and fickle appetites, of their own creation."

**Important Quotable lines from Preface to Lyrical Ballads**

1. For all good poetry is the spontaneous overflow of powerful feelings.
2. My purpose was to imitate and, as far as possible, to adopt the very language of man.
3. He (the poet) is a man speaking to man.
4. Poetry is the most philosophical of all writing.
5. Poetry is the breath and finer spirit of all knowledge, it is the impassioned expression which is in the countenance of all science.
6. There neither is, nor can be, any essential difference between the language of prose and metrical composition.
7. Every great poet has to create the taste by which he is enjoyed and appreciated.
8. Every great poet is a teacher or nothing.
9. The poet sings "a song in which all human beings join with him...he looks before and after".

234. When was Coleridge born?
(a) 1770 (b) 1772
(c) 1774 (d) 1776

235. When was *Biographia Literaria* written?
(a) 1817 (b) 1820
(c) 1823 (d) 1825

236. Who called Coleridge the 'Mediator' between England and Germany?
(a) I.A. Richards (b) T.S. Eliot
(c) Rene Wellek (d) F.R. Leavis

237. Coleridge's criticism is
(a) Legislative (b) Comparative
(c) Historical (d) Descriptive

238. 'Imagination' in Coleridge's theory corresponds to
(a) Understanding
(b) Reason
(c) Intuition
(d) None of the above

239. 'Esemplastic' for Coleridge means
(a) Flexible (b) Plasticity
(c) Fancy (d) Shaping power

240. Coleridge's "primary imagination" expresses itself in
(a) Hyperbole (b) Simile
(c) Metaphor (d) Personification

241. Who referred to nature as the "language of God"?
(a) Wordsworth (b) Coleridge
(c) Rousseau (d) Keats

242. The *Biographia Literaria* is a work combining
(a) Intellectual biography
(b) Philosophy
(c) Imagination
(d) All of the above

243. According to Coleridge, 'reason' includes
(a) Sense (b) Understanding
(c) Imagination (d) All of the above

244. Who said that the poetry of the neo-classical poets is "characterised not so much by poetic thoughts as thoughts translated into the language of poerty"?
   (a) Wordsworth (b) Keats
   (c) Coleridge (d) Byron

245. Coleridge defines 'poetic faith' as
   (a) faith in the poem.
   (b) faith in the poet.
   (c) poet's faith in the people.
   (d) 'willing suspension of disbelief'.

246. Who among the following said that "the person of poetry must be clothed with generic attributes, with the common attributes of the class; not with such as one gifted individual might possibly possess...".
   (a) Coleridge (b) Dryden
   (c) Dr. Johnson (d) Pope

247. Which of the following was defined by Coleridge as "a mode of Memory emancipated from the order of time and space"?
   (a) Primary imagination
   (b) Secondary imagination
   (c) Fancy
   (d) None of the above

248. Who, among the following, said, "No man was ever yet a great poet without being at the same time a profound philosopher"?
   (a) Dr. Johnson
   (b) Sidney
   (c) Matthew Arnold
   (d) S.T. Coleridge

(This opinion was expressed by Coleridge in Chapter XV of *Biographia Literaria*)

249. In which chapter of *Biographia Literaria* does Coleridge criticise Wordsworth's theory of poetry?
   (a) IV
   (b) XIV-XV
   (c) XVI-XVIII
   (d) All of the above

250. According to Coleridge, primary imagination is
   (a) superior to secondary imagination.
   (b) inferior to primary imagination.
   (c) God's revelation.
   (d) demands no active response from the poet.
   (e) Options (b), (c) and (d)

251. In which chapter of *Biographia Literaria* has Coleridge used the expression 'willing suspension of disbelief'?
   (a) XI (b) XIV
   (c) XIII (d) XV

**FROM CHAPTER XIV OF *BIOGRAPHIA LITERARIA***

**(This is a statement of the objects originally proposed for William Wordsworth and S.T. Coleridge)**

"...it was agreed, that my endeavours should be directed to persons and characters supernatural, or at least romantic, yet so as to transfer from our inward nature a human interest and a semblance of truth sufficient to procure for these shadows of imagination that willing suspension of disbelief for the moment, which constitutes poetic faith. Mr. Wordsworth, on the other hand, was to propose to himself as his object, to give the charm of novelty to things of every day, and to excite a feeling analogous to the supernatural, by awakening the mind's attention from the lethargy of custom, and directing it to the loveliness and the wonders of the world before us; an inexhaustible treasure, but for which in consequence of the film of familiarity and selfish solicitude we have eyes, yet see not, ears that hear not, and hearts that neither feel nor understand."

252. Who, among the following, said, "Milton had a highly imaginative, Cowley a very fanciful mind"?
(a) Dr. Johnson (b) T.S. Eliot
(c) Wordsworth (d) Coleridge

253. How many chapters does Coleridge's *Biographia Literaria* have?
(a) X (b) XII
(c) XXII (d) XXIII

254. In which chapter does Coleridge make a distinction between 'fancy' and 'imagination'?
(a) IV (b) V
(c) XI (d) XII

255. In which chapter does Coleridge make a distinction between 'primary' and 'secondary' imagination?
(a) XI (b) X
(c) XIII (d) XIV

(Coleridge makes a distinction between 'fancy' and 'imagination' in chapter IV and between 'primary' and 'secondary' imagination in chapter XIII. Fancy, to be brief, is mechanical. It operates through memory and deals with things which are 'fixed ' and 'dead'. On the other hand, imagination is synthesizing, unifying and creative power. Imagination 'dissolves', 'diffuses' , 'dissipates' in order to recreate. It is an esemplastic power. Fancy is not creative, it only combines what it perceives. Fancy is the mechanical mixture in which the ingredients are mixed up, but do not lose their individual properties. Imagination, on the other hand, is like a chemical compound in which different ingradients combine to form something new.

Primary imagination, to put it simply, is merely the power of receiving impressions of the external world through the senses. The secondary imagination is the same faculty "in a heightened power as creative in a poetic sense." The primary imagination is the consciousness shared by all men. The secondary imagination is limited to poets.)

256. In which chapter of *Biographia Literaria* does Coleridge make the statement: "A poem is that species of composition which is opposed to works of science by proposing for its immediate object pleasure, not truth"?
(a) X (b) XI
(c) XII (d) XIV

257. In which chapter does Coleridge draw a distinction between a poem and poetry?
(a) XII (b) XIV
(c) XV (d) XXI

(In chapter XIV of *Bioagraphia Literaria* Coleridge expresses his views about 'poet', 'poem' and 'poetry'. According to Coleridge, "The poet, described in ideal perfection, brings the whole soul of man into activity...." In chapter XV, he says, "No man was ever yet a great poet, without being at the same time a profound philosopher." For Coleridge, "poetry is the blossom and the fragrancy of all human knowledge, human thoughts, human passions, emotions, language."

Imagination is the soul of poetry of the highest kind may be written in prose and without metre. On the other hand, a poem is a metrical composition which has for its immediate object pleasure, not truth. According to David Daiches, poetry for Coleridge is a wider "category than the category to which poem belongs. Poetry is a kind of activity which can be pursued by painters, philosophers, scientists.")

258. In which chapter does Coleridge talk about those qualities which are the marks of genius?
(a) X (b) IV
(c) V (d) XII

(These qualities are: 1. Sweetness of perfection, 2. The choice of words remote from the personal interests and circumstances of the poet, 3. Images modified by predominant passion or when they create the effect of reducing multitude to unity, or succession to an instant, or lastly "When the poet is able to transfer to them, from his own spirit, a human and intellectual life." 4. The depth of thought.

259. In which chapter of *Biographia Literaria* does Coleridge criticize Wordsworth's theory of poetic diction?
(a) XII (b) XIV
(c) XVII (d) XXI

260. According to S.T. Coleridge,
1. Primary imagination has the "esemplastic" power.
2. On the way to the supernatural from natural if the poet fails to carry on, he ends up as a "materialist".
3. Allegory is superior to symbol.
4. Being an organic whole is the quality of good poetry.
(a) 2, 3 and 4 (b) 1, 2 and 3
(c) 2 and 4 (d) 1, 2, 3 and 4

261. According to Coleridge, the purpose of his literary life was
(a) to inspire hope and love.
(b) to stimulate young minds.
(c) to inspire religion.
(d) to stimulate educators.

262. What, according to Coleridge, did Descartes develop?
(a) Feudalism (b) Dualism
(c) Psychology (d) Humanism

263. How does Coleridge describe man's spirit?
(a) Free (b) Sinful
(c) Innocent (d) Wholesome

264. Coleridge says that God will never reject a soul who
(a) loves Him.
(b) ignores Him.
(c) sees Him.
(d) writes about Him.

265. In Chapter XI of *Biographia Literaria* Coleridge advises young men
(a) to worship God.
(b) never pursue literature as a profession.
(c) to respect their elders.
(d) to be excellent poets.

266. "...went on refining,/ And thought of convincing, while they thought of dining."
The above lines are from which chapter?
(a) X (b) XI
(c) XII (d) XIII

267. In order to render philosophy intelligible, how many thesis does Coleridge propose?
(a) Eight (b) Twelve
(c) Ten (d) Nine

268. Coleridge claims that sensation may exist for
(a) a very short time.
(b) years.
(c) an indefinite time in a latent state.
(d) None of the above.

269. The quotation "a repetition in the finite mind of the eternal act of creation in the infinite I am" appear in
(a) Preface to the Lyrical Ballads
(b) *Biographia Literaria*
(c) *Defence of Poetry*
(d) *Letters to Keats*

(This occurs in Chapter XIII of *Biographia Literaria* in the context of primary imagination)

270. To Descartes, according to Coleridge, what was intelligence?
(a) The body (b) The brain
(c) The soul (d) The heart

271. Which kind of poets, according to Coleridge, use natural language, but which is dignified, attractive and interesting?

(a) Neo-classical poets
(b) Modern poets
(c) Older poets
(d) Movement poets

272. Who, among the following, has said, "The communication of pleasure is the introductory means by which alone the poet must expect to moralize the readers"?
(a) Wordsworth (b) Sidney
(c) Shelley (d) Coleridge

(Coleridge has said it in Chapter XXII of *Biographia Literaria*)

273. In his 1817 review of *Biographia Literaria*, Francis Bacon Jeffrey grouped the following poets together as the *Lake School of Poets*
(a) Keats, Wordsworth and Coleridge
(b) Wordsworth, Coleridge and Byron
(c) Blake, Wordsworth and Coleridge
(d) Wordsworth, Coleridge and Southey

274. Wordsworth's contribution to literary theory mainly depends on
(a) *Preface to the Lyrical Ballads* (1800)
(b) *Preface to Poems* (1815)
(c) *Essays upon Epitaphs* (1810)
(d) Lectures and Notes on Shakespeare and Other English Poets

275. In which of the following does the following definition of poetry occur?

"It is essential to poetry that it should be simple, and appeal to the elements and primary laws of our nature; that it should be sensuous, and by its imagery elicit truth at a flash; that it be impassioned, and be able to move our feelings and awaken our affections."
(a) *Biographia Literaria*
(b) *Aids to Reflections*
(c) *Essays Upon Epitaphs*
(d) All of the above

276. Who, among the following, has said that Coleridge "succeeds for the first and for the last time in English Criticism in marrying the twin studies of Philosophy and Literature"?
(a) George Watson (b) T.S. Eliot
(c) I.A. Richards (d) F.R. Leavis

277. Who among the following, called *Biographia Literaria* a 'romantic bildungsgeschichte'?
(a) George Watson
(b) William K. Wimsatt and Cleanth Brooks
(c) M.H. Abrams
(d) George Watson

('Bildungsgeschichte' is the name of a genre developed in Germany. The term applies to those works which deal with the development of an individual from infancy into maturity through psychological stresses. The genre came to include such major achievements as Elizabeth Barrett Browning's *Aurora Leigh* and James Joyce's *Portrait of the Artist as a Young Man*.

278. Who, among the following, explained the distinction between organic form and mechanical form?
(a) Coleridge (b) Cleanth Brooks
(c) T.S. Eliot (d) Dryden

279. Which thesis is described as an act of self-consciousness as a source of knowledge?
(a) Thesis I (b) Thesis V
(c) Thesis VIII (d) Thesis X

280. Coleridge says that the elements of metre owe their existence to a state of increased
(a) Happiness (b) Excitement
(c) Fear (d) Anger

281. Who, according to Coleridge, is so unique that he cannot be imitated?
(a) Southey (b) Shakespeare
(c) Wordsworth (d) Bowles

282. Coleridge says that the ultimate end of poetry is

(a) Truth, moral or intellectual
(b) Pleasure
(c) Happiness
(d) None of the above

283. Who, among the following, wrote *Defence of Poetry*?
(a) Philip Sidney (b) Horace
(c) Shelley (d) Dryden

284. When was *Defence of Poetry* written?
(a) 1821 (b) 1823
(c) 1825 (d) 1827

(It was a posthumously published in 1840)

285. Who, among the following, said, "poetry is the record of the best and happiest moments of the happiest and best minds"?
(a) Wordsworth (b) John Keats
(c) Sidney (d) Shelley

286. Who, among the following said, "Poetry is indeed something divine : It is at once the centre and circumference of knowledge; it is that which comprehends all science, and to which all science must be referred"?
(a) Sidney (b) Wordsworth
(c) Shelley (d) Coleridge

287. Shelley's *Defense of Poetry* is in the tradition of
(a) Plato (b) Sidney
(c) Dryden (d) Horace

288. The immediate occasion for writing *Defence of Poetry* was in reply to
(a) Thomas Peacock's attack on poetry
(b) Plato's attack on poets
(c) Gossan's attack on poetry
(d) None of the above

289. Who, among the following, wrote, *The Four Ages of Poetry*?
(a) Ben Jonson
(b) Sidney
(c) Keats
(d) Thomas Love Peacock

290. When was *The Four Ages of Poetry* published?
(a) 1820 (b) 1821
(c) 1822 (d) 1823

291. What, according to Peacock, are the four ages of poetry?
(a) Iron Age and Golden Age
(b) Silver Age and Brass Age
(c) Iron Age and Copper Age
(d) Both (a) and (b)

292. Who, among the following, said, "A poet in our times is a semi-barbarian in a civilised community"?
(a) Plato (b) Ben Jonson
(c) Peacock (d) Gosson

293. "Hence all original religions are allegorical, or susceptible of allegory, and, like Janus, have a double face of false and true. Poets, according to the circumstances of the age and nation in which they appeared, were called in earlier epochs of the world, legislators, or prophets : a poet essentially comprises and unites both these characters."

This is from:
(a) *Art of Poetry*
(b) *An Apology for Peotry*
(c) *Defence of Poetry*
(d) *The Four Ages of Poetry*

294. Who, among the following, said, "Poetry is the record of the best and the happiest moments of the happiest minds"?
(a) Sidney (b) Shelley
(c) Wordsworth (d) Coleridge

295. Who, among the following, said, "A man to be greatly good must imagine intensely and comprehensively.... Poetry strengthens the faculty which is the organ of the moral nature"?
(a) Sydney (b) Wordsworth
(c) Shelley (d) Coleridge

296. "Poetry turns all things to loveliness; it exalts the beauty of that which is most beautiful, and it adds beauty to that which is most deformed; it marries exultation and horror, grief and pleasure, eternity and change; it subdues to union under its light yoke all irreconcilable things."

This is from:

(a) *Apology for Poetry*
(b) *Art of Poetry*
(c) *Preface to Lyrical Ballads*
(d) *Defence of Poetry*

297. According to Shelley, the functions of poetic faculty are

(a) Two-fold
(b) Three-fold
(c) Four-fold
(d) Five-fold

(According to Shelley, the functions of poetic faculty are two-fold: by one it creates new materials of knowledge, and power, and pleasure; by the other it engenders in the mind a desire to reproduce and arrange them according to a certain rhythm and order which may be called the beautiful and the good.)

298. "Poets are the unacknowledged legislators of the world", says Shelley. This seems to be a claim which is

(a) True (b) Grandiose
(c) Unjustified (d) Pointless

299. Who, among the following said, that the "Defence of Poetry" is more a visionary poem about poetry than it is a reasoned argument"?

(a) T.S. Eliot
(b) Cleanth Brooks
(c) Harold Bloom
(d) I.A. Richards

300. According to Shelley, there are two classes of mental action

(a) Reason (b) Imagination
(c) Intuition (d) Both (a) and (b)

301. Who, among the following said, that "didactic poetry is my abhorrence"?

(a) John Keats (b) P.B. Shelley
(c) Coleridge (d) T.S. Eliot

(This occurs in the preface to *Prometheus Unbound*)

302. "Until the mind can love, and admire, and trust, and hope, and endure, reasoned principles of moral conduct are seeds cast upon the highway of life which the unconscious passenger tramples into dust, although they would bear the harvest of his happiness."

This is from

(a) Shelley's *Defence of Poetry*
(b) Peacock's *The Four Ages of Poetry*
(c) Horrace's *Ars Poetica*
(d) Shelley's Preface to *Prometheus Unbound*

303. Who, among the following, defined poetry as "a sword of lightening ever, unsheathed, which consumes the scabbard that would contain it"?

(a) Sydney (b) Shelley
(c) Keats (d) Coleridge

304. Who wrote *The Spirit of the Age* (1825)?

(a) Robert Graves
(b) Matthew Arnold
(c) William Hazlitt
(d) Helen Gardner

305. Who has said, the poet "proposes Beauty as his main end" whereas the philosopher proposes Truth?

(a) Emerson
(b) Keats
(c) Shelley
(d) Hazlitt

306. Who, among the following said, "We hate poetry that has a palpable design upon us"?
(a) John Keats
(b) Shelley
(c) T.S. Eliot
(d) I.A. Richards

(Expressed this opinion in his letter to John Hamilton Reynolds (Feb. 3, 1818). The phrase 'palpable design' means that we hate the poem when we feel that a poet is trying to do something to us.)

307. The quotation "When a man is capable of being in uncertainties, mysteries, doubts, without any irritable reaching after fact and reasons" refers to
(a) Dissociation of sensibility
(b) Objective correlative
(c) Negative capability
(d) Affective fallacy

(The term 'Negative Capability' was coined by Keats to describe the quality he regarded as essential to the poet. The above lines occur in a letter to George and Tom Keats, December 21- 27, 1817. The same letter goes on to cite Shakespeare as the supreme example of negative capability, and to note its absence in Coleridge. 'Negative Capability', as Keats understood it, enables the poet to avoid doctrinal utterances about the nature of life, about life's goodness or badness, or perfectability. Keats understands a poet to be a detached being who to comprehend experience and attain freedom from its bondage, dissolves his identity.)

308. Who, among the following, said that "the true philosopher and the true poet are one, and a beauty, which is truth, and a truth which is beauty, is the aim of both"?
(a) John Keats
(b) Emerson
(c) Rousseau
(d) Wordsworth

309. *On Knocking at the Gate in 'Macbeth'* was written by
(a) De Quincey
(b) T.S. Eliot
(c) Coleridge
(d) Arnold

310. Who, among the following, said, "All that is literature seeks to communicate power, all that is not literature to communicate knowledge"?
(a) Kenneth Burke
(b) De Quincey
(c) Richard Johnson
(d) Richard Hoggart

**ANSWERS**

| | | | | | |
|---|---|---|---|---|---|
| 199. (b) | 200. (a) | 201. (c) | 202. (c) | 203. (b) | 204. (c) |
| 205. (b) | 206. (b) | 207. (c) | 208. (a) | 209. (c) | 210. (a) |
| 211. (b) | 212. (d) | 213. (a) | 214. (a) | 215. (c) | 216. (b) |
| 217. (d) | 218. (c) | 219. (a) | 220. (a) | 221. (d) | 222. (c) |
| 223. (b) | 224. (d) | 225. (a) | 226. (c) | 227. (a) | 228. (b) |
| 229. (a) | 230. (d) | 231. (c) | 232. (d) | 233. (a) | 234. (b) |

| | | | | | |
|---|---|---|---|---|---|
| 235. (a) | 236. (d) | 237. (d) | 238. (c) | 239. (d) | 240. (c) |
| 241. (b) | 242. (d) | 243. (d) | 244. (c) | 245. (d) | 246. (a) |
| 247. (c) | 248. (d) | 249. (d) | 250. (e) | 251. (b) | 252. (d) |
| 253. (c) | 254. (a) | 255. (c) | 256. (d) | 257. (b) | 258. (b) |
| 259. (c) | 260. (d) | 261. (b) | 262. (b) | 263. (d) | 264. (a) |
| 265. (b) | 266. (a) | 267. (c) | 268. (c) | 269. (b) | 270. (c) |
| 271. (c) | 272. (d) | 273. (d) | 274. (d) | 275. (d) | 276. (a) |
| 277. (c) | 278. (a) | 279. (d) | 280. (b) | 281. (c) | 282. (a) |
| 283. (c) | 284. (a) | 285. (d) | 286. (c) | 287. (b) | 288. (a) |
| 289. (d) | 290. (a) | 291. (d) | 292. (c) | 293. (c) | 294. (b) |
| 295. (c) | 296. (d) | 297. (a) | 298. (d) | 299. (c) | 300. (d) |
| 301. (b) | 302. (d) | 303. (b) | 304. (c) | 305. (a) | 306. (a) |
| 307. (c) | 308. (b) | 309. (a) | 310. (b) | | |

## (VI) VICTORIAN CRITICISM

311. In which of the following does Arnold say that poetry is superior to history?
   (a) The Study of Poetry
   (b) Milton
   (c) Wordswoth
   (d) Keats

312. An important aspect of Arnold's classicism was his concept of
   (a) sensuousness
   (b) grand style
   (c) emphasis on diction
   (d) None of the above

313. Arnold sought to bring about a harmony between
   (a) Hebraism and Romanticism
   (b) Classicism and Romanticism
   (c) Hebraism and Hellenism
   (d) Medievalism and Romanticism

314. About whom did Arnold make the remark that they "did not know enough"?
   (a) The English Romantics
   (b) Metaphysical Poets
   (c) Neo-classical Poets
   (d) None of the above

315. Who, among the following, said that criticism should embrace "the Indian virtue of detachment"?
   (a) Coleridge
   (b) T.S. Eliot
   (c) Matthew Arnold
   (d) Cleanth Brooks

316. Criticism, according to Arnold, can be disinterested by
   (a) keeping aloof from the practical view of things.
   (b) following the law of its own nature, which is to be a free play of the mind on all subjects which it touches.
   (c) steadily refusing to lend itself to any of those ulterior, political, practical considerations.
   (d) All of the above

317. Who, according to Arnold, are the two great "Classics of our prose"?
   (a) Bacon and Milton
   (b) Johnson and Dryden
   (c) Dryden and Pope
   (d) Steele and Addison

318. Arnold deals with the subject of Education in
   (a) *Culture and Anarchy*
   (b) *The Study of Poetry*
   (c) *The Function of Criticism at the Present Time*
   (d) *Literature and Dogma*

319. Who defined poetry as "Criticism of Life"?
   (a) T.S. Eliot
   (b) Matthew Arnold
   (c) Shelley
   (d) Sidney

320. Who said, "the greatness of a poet lies in his powerful and beautiful application of ideas to life"?
   (a) T.S. Eliot
   (b) Wordsworth
   (c) Arnold
   (d) Shelley

321. Shakespeare incurred the biggest censure by mixing comic and tragic scenes in all his works. And this very faculty of Shakespeare made him, even "nobler than both the Greek and the Roman dramatists" was the view of
   (a) Dr. Johnson
   (b) John Dryden
   (c) Matthew Arnold
   (d) Ben Jonson

**Some Important Works by Matthew Arnold**

1. *The Preface to the Poems* (1853)
2. *On Translating Homer* (1856)
3. *Essays in Criticism, First Series* (1866)
4. *On the Study of Celtic Literature* (1866)
5. *Culture and Anarchy* (1869)
6. *St. Paul and Protestanism* (1870)
7. *Literature and Dogma* (1873)
8. *God and The Bible* (1875)
9. *Essays in Criticism, Second Series* (1888)

322. What kind of judgments does Arnold call 'fallacious'?
   (a) Historical estimate, Personal estimate
   (b) Biographical and Historical
   (c) Psychoanalytical and Formalist
   (d) Historical and Social

323. Who, among the following, said, "More and more mankind will discover that we have to turn to poetry to interpret life for us, to console us, to sustain us"?
   (a) Sidney
   (b) Shelley
   (c) Matthew Arnold
   (d) Wordsworth

   (This is from the essay *The Study of Poetry*)

324. The duty of a critic is to know "the best that is known and thought in the world ...and to establish a current of true and fresh ideas" is the view of
   (a) Matthew Arnold
   (b) Coleridge
   (c) T.S. Eliot
   (d) I.A. Richards

(This is from the essay *The Function of Criticism at the Present Time*)

325. In what, according to Arnold, consists the high quality of poetry?
(a) Matter and substance
(b) Manner and style
(c) Thought and diction
(d) Both (a) and (b)

326. Matthew Arnold, as a critic, was a
(a) Formalist
(b) Classicist
(c) Romantic
(d) Feminist

327. In which of his essays, Arnold said, "Poetry at bottom is a criticism of life" ?
(a) Shelley
(b) Byron
(c) Wordsworth
(d) Gray

(The essay on Wordsworth was written in 1879)

328. Who regards Arnold more a propagandist than a critic?
(a) F.R. Leavis
(b) Tillotson
(c) T.S. Eliot
(d) Scott-James

329. Which approach, according to Arnold, should be used in evaluating literature?
(a) Comparative
(b) Historical
(c) Formalist
(d) Marxist

330. In order to attain an impartial and disinterested evaluation of literature, Arnold prescribed the
(a) Personal estimate
(b) Historical estimate
(c) Touchstone (Comparative) method
(d) Formalist approach

331. Who, among the following, said that "Tennyson has the finest ear, perhaps of any English poet"?
(a) W.H. Auden
(b) T.S. Eliot
(c) I.A. RIchards
(d) William Empson

332. Who has made the observation that "The function of poetry is immense, our race, as time goes on, will find an ever surer and surer stay"?
(a) William Wordsworth
(b) Coleridge
(c) Arnold
(d) Sidney

333. Who, among the following, has said, "Mr. Arnold did not merely criticise books himself. He taught others how to criticise them. He laid down principles, if he did not always keep the principles he laid down"?
(a) T.S. Eliot
(b) Herbert Paul
(c) Cazamian
(d) Compton-Rickett

334. Whose comment is this: "Aristotle dissects a work of art. Arnold dissects a critic. The one gives us the principles which govern the making of a poem; the other, the principles by which the best poems should be selected and made known"?
(a) Compton-Rickett
(b) Cazamian
(c) Scott-James
(d) Herbert Paul

335. The function of the critic, according to Arnold, in the broadest sense of term is to promote

(a) Learning
(b) Culture
(c) Science
(d) Philosophy

336. Who, among the following, has said, "For half-a-century, Arnold's position in this country was comparable with that of the venerable Greek in respect of the wide influence he exercised, the mark he impressed upon criticism, and the blind faith with which he was trusted by his votaries"?
(a) R.A. Scott-James
(b) J.A. Symonds
(c) Walter Pater
(d) T.S. Eliot

337. Who, among the following, said, "Keats is with Shakespeare"?
(a) T.S. Eliot
(b) I.A. Richards
(c) Matthew Arnold
(d) John Ruskin

338. Arnold said that he heard at Oxford in the early 1840's 'four voices'. Whose 'voices' they were?
(a) Aristotle, Sainte-Beuve, Senancour, Goethe
(b) Goethe, Emerson, Newman, Carlyle
(c) Goethe, Sainte-Beuve, Emerson, Senancour
(d) Senancour, Aristotle, Emerson, Carlyle

339. "Without poetry our science will appear incomplete and most of what now passes with us for religion and philosophy will be replaced by poetry." Whose view is this?
(a) Matthew Arnold
(b) Wordsworth
(c) Coleridge
(d) Cazamian

340. "He is the greatest gainsayer of English criticism, the most insistent and professional of non-conformists." Who made this comment about Arnold?
(a) Scott-James
(b) Compton-Rickett
(c) George Watson
(d) Cazamian

341. Critics allege that Arnold's definition of the function of criticism, 'a disinterested endeavor to learn and propagate the best that is known and thought in the world' was borrowed from
(a) Sainte-Beuve
(b) Dr. Johnson
(c) Alexander Pope
(d) Joseph Addison

342. Who, among the following, made the observation that, "For a literary masterpiece, two powers must concur, the power of the man, and the power of the moment, and the man is not enough without the moment"?
(a) Dr. Johnson
(b) T.S. Eliot
(c) Matthew Arnold
(d) I.A. Richards

343. Arnold is "a propagandist for criticism rather than a critic, a popularizer rather than a creator of ideas." Who made this observation?
(a) I.A. Richards
(b) T.S. Eliot
(c) Compton-Rickett
(d) Tillotson

344. In his essay *On Style*, Pater gives importance to
(a) use of archaic words
(b) diction
(c) figure of speech
(d) beauty of expression

345. Who, among the following, said, "Great art has something of the soul of humanity"?

(a) Walter Pater
(b) John Ruskin
(c) Matthew Arnold
(d) Shelley

346. Who said that "it is the function of literature to create, from the rough material of actual existence, a new world that will be more marvelous and more enduring, and more true than the world that common eyes look upon"?
(a) Walter Pater
(b) Emerson
(c) Oscar Wilde
(d) Baudelaire

(This occurs in Oscar Wilde's essay *The Critic as Artist* included in his critical work *Intentions* (1891).)

347. Oscar Wilde was of the opinion that criticism in its essence is
(a) Purely subjective
(b) Absolutely objective
(c) Biased
(d) None of the above

348. Who said, "Language may be defined as the expression of thought by means of speech sounds"?
(a) I.A. Richards
(b) F.R. Leavis
(c) Keats
(d) Henry Sweet

349. Who, among the following, said, "Literature always anticipates life. It does not copy it but moulds it to its purpose"?
(a) Oscar Wilde
(b) Arnold
(c) Ezra Pound
(d) Coleridge

350. Oscar Wilde advocated one of the following theories:
(a) Art for humanity's sake
(b) Art for art's sake
(c) Art for morality's sake
(d) Art for culture's sake

351. According to Pater, three factors determine the style of the author. Which are they?
(a) Grammar, diction, design
(b) Personality of the author, expression, diction
(c) Design, grammar, grandeur of thought
(d) Diction, design, personality of the author

352. For John Ruskin, the concept of 'beauty' is linked to
(a) Proportion
(b) Morality
(c) Design
(d) Utility

353. In this theory of art, Ruskin may be compared with
(a) Plato
(b) Aristotle
(c) Walter Pater
(d) None of the above

354. For Ruskin, the beautiful was simply described as
(a) worthless.
(b) a blessing for mankind.
(c) a gift of God.
(d) indescribable.

355. For Ruskin, the feeling of the beautiful does not depend upon
(a) The sense
(b) The intellect
(c) Heart
(d) None of the above

356. "Art properly so called, is no recreation, it cannot be learnt at spare moments, nor pursued when we have nothing better to do. It is no handiwork for drawing-room tables, no relief for the ennui of boudoirs; it must be understood and taken seriously, or not at all."

This is from
(a) John Ruskin's *Modern Painters*
(b) Walter Pater's *Appreciations*
(c) Oscar Wilde's *The Picture of Dorian Gray*
(d) Arnold's *Culture and Anarchy*

357. Those who were associated with the Aesthetic Movement brought out a journal called
(a) *Black Book*
(b) *Red Book*
(c) *Yellow Book*
(d) *Blue Book*

358. Walter Pater's *Appreciations* was published in
(a) 1889
(b) 1891
(c) 1892
(d) 1894

359. Walter Pater's *Studies in the History of the Renaissance* was published in
(a) 1873
(b) 1875
(c) 1880
(d) 1889

360. Walter Pater was a votary of
(a) Art for morality's sake
(b) Art for art's sake
(c) Art for culture's sake
(d) Art for society's sake

361. Who, among the following, were for the theory of art for morality's sake?
(a) Arnold
(b) Ruskin
(c) Carlyle
(d) All of the above

362. About whom did A.C. Benson make the observation that "he moves like a bee from flower to flower gathering drops of sweet honey"?
(a) Matthew Arnold
(b) John Ruskin
(c) Walter Pater
(d) Oscar Wilde

363. Who is known as the greatest letter writer of English language?
(a) William Godwin
(b) George Eliot
(c) William Anderson
(d) Jane Welsh Caryle

364. Who has defined poetry as "The Rhythmical Creation of Beauty"?
(a) Keats
(b) Shelley
(c) Sydney
(d) Edgar Allan Poe

365. Who, among the following, has said, "We must be simple, precise, terse. We must be cool, calm, and unimpassioned"?
(a) Bacon
(b) Steele
(c) Addison
(d) Edgar Allan Poe

366. Who coined the term "the heresy of the Didactic"?
(a) Rossetti
(b) Swinburne
(c) Edgar Allan Poe
(d) Walter Pater

(In his essay *The Poetic Principle* (1850), Poe refers to the view that "The ultimate object of all poetry is Truth" and that every poem "should inculcate a moral". As against this, Poe insists that the most dignified work is the "poem per se—this poem which is a poem is nothing more—this poem written solely for the poem's sake.")

367. *Criticism and Fiction* (1891) was written by

(a) William Dean Howells
(b) Wayne Booth
(c) David Lodge
(d) E.M. Forster

368. Who among the following, has said, "Realism is nothing more and nothing less than the truthful treatment of the material"?
(a) George Eliot
(b) W.D. Howells
(c) Henry James
(d) David Lodge

(Howells's book is a closely argued manifesto for realism)

369. *The Art of Fiction* is the title of
(a) A book
(b) A lecture and pamphlet
(c) An essay
(d) All of the above

(*The Art of Fiction* was written by David Lodge in 1992. The essay *Art of Fiction* was written by Henry James in 1884 in response to a lecture and pamphlet of same title by the novelist and critic Walter Basant in 1884.)

370. Who, among the following, has said, "The only reason for the existence of a novel is that it does attempt to represent life...as the picture is reality, so the novel is history"?
(a) Henry James
(b) Walter Besant
(c) David Loge
(d) Margret Macdonald

371. "The province of art is all life, all feeling, all observation, all vision...it is all experience" is the view of
(a) E.M. Forster
(b) Henry James
(c) David Lodge
(d) Walter Pater

**Some of the Distinctive phrases/ expressions associated with Arnold**

1. Grand style
2. Disinterestedness
3. Sweetness and light
4. The Touchstone Method
5. Poetic Truth and Poetic Beauty
6. Historic estimate and personal estimate
7. High seriousness
8. The best that is known and thought and in the world
9. Current of true and fresh ideas
10. Criticism of life

372. In his evaluation of poets, Matthew Arnold observes; "their poetry is conceived and composed in wits, genuine poetry is conceived and composed in the soul." 'Their' here refers to
(a) Metaphysical Poets
(b) Romantic Poets
(c) Neo-classical poets
(d) Renaissance poets

373. Two of the ingredients of the grand style according to Arnold are
(a) Simplicity
(b) Severity
(c) Grandeur
(d) Both (a) and (b)

374. Who, among the following, said, "Seeing the thing as it really is"?
(a) Matthew Arnold
(b) Dr. Johnson
(c) T.S. Eliot
(d) Cleanth Brooks

375. About which poet did Arnold make the remark, "as incoherent as the dark itself"?
(a) Milton
(b) Gray
(c) Shelley
(d) Byron

376. Who, among the following, said, "The critic of poetry should have the finest tact, the nicest moderation, the most free, flexible, and elastic spirit imaginable"?
    (a) Dr. Johnson
    (b) Coleridge
    (c) T.S. Eliot
    (d) Arnold

377. Arnold's masters, according to Herbert W. Paul, were
    (a) The ancient Greeks
    (b) Goethe
    (c) Sainte-Beuve
    (d) All of the above

378. Who has called Arnold "a spirit of contradiction incarnate"?
    (a) T.S. Eliot
    (b) George Watson
    (c) George Saintsbury
    (d) All of the above

379. About which poet Arnold made the remark that he was "a beautiful and ineffectual angel, beating in the void his luminous wings in vain"?
    (a) Byron
    (b) Coleridge
    (c) Shelley
    (d) Keats

380. He was a "poet and philosopher wrecked in a mist of opium," said Arnold. To which poet does he refer to?
    (a) Byron
    (b) Coleridge
    (c) Gray
    (d) Keats

381. He was a poet who carried across Europe "the pageant of his bleeding heart." Which poet does Arnold refer to?
    (a) Coleridge
    (b) Gray
    (c) Byron
    (d) Shelley

382. According to Arnold, Chaucer had
    (a) divine liquidness of diction.
    (b) divine fluidity of movement.
    (c) superior substance.
    (d) All of the above.

383. According to Arnold, Chaucer lacked
    (a) high seriousness
    (b) beautiful expression
    (c) fine style
    (d) All of the above

384. Who, among the following, said that Arnold's essays were "High pamphleteering"?
    (a) T.S. Eliot
    (b) F.R. Leavis
    (c) I.A. Richards
    (d) Cleanth Brooks

385. Who said, "Not the fruit of expression, but experience itself, is the end.... To burn always with this hard, gem –like flame, to maintain this ecstasy, is success in life"?
    (a) Arnold
    (b) Carlyle
    (c) Walter Pater
    (d) John Ruskin

386. Who, among the following, said, "Beauty has many meanings as man has moods"?
    (a) John Ruskin
    (b) Walter Pater
    (c) Oscar Wilde
    (d) Arnold

387. The major influences on Oscar Wilde were
    (a) John Ruskin
    (b) Swinburne
    (c) Walter Pater
    (d) All of the above

**Epigrammatic Statements of Oscar Wilde**

1. I have nothing to declare except my genius.
2. I make up for being over-dressed by being over-educated.
3. Punctuality is the thief of time.
4. There is no sin except stupidity.
5. The public is wonderfully tolerant. It forgives everything except genius.
6. There is no such thing as a moral or immoral book.
7. No artist has ethical sympathies.
8. Books are well-written or badly written. That is all.
9. All art is quite useless.
10. It is the spectator, and not life, that art really mirrors.

388. Choose the correct chronological sequence:
   (a) *Appreciations, Modern Painters, The Picture of Dorian Gray, Culture and Anarchy*
   (b) *Modern Painters, Culture and Anarchy, Appreciations, The Picture of Dorian Gray*
   (c) *Culture and Anarchy, The Picture of Dorian Gray, Modern Painters, Appreciations*
   (d) *The Picture of Dorian Gray, Modern Painters, Culture and Anarchy, Appreciations*

389. Choose the correct chronological sequence:
   (a) Oscar Wilde, Walter Pater, Matthew Arnold, John Ruskin
   (b) Walter Pater, Matthew Arnold, Oscar Wilde, John Ruskin
   (c) John Ruskin, Matthew Arnold, Walter Pater, Oscar Wilde
   (d) Matthew Arnold, Oscar Wilde, John Ruskin, Walter Pater

   (John Ruskin (1819-1900), Matthew Arnold (1822-88), Walter Pater (1839-94), Oscar Wilde (1854-1900)

390. "Of this wisdom, the poetic passion, the desire of beauty, the love of art for art's sake has most; for art comes to you professing frankly to give nothing but the highest quality to your moments as they pass, and simply for those moment's sake"

   This is from:
   (a) *Modern Painters*
   (b) *Studies in the History of the Renaissance*
   (c) *The Picture of Dorian Gray*
   (d) *Appreciations*

391. G. Wilson Knight's *The Wheel of Fire* was published in
   (a) 1925
   (b) 1929
   (c) 1930
   (d) 1931

392. Who said that "the province of art is all life, all feeling, all observation, all vision...it is all experience"?
   (a) Henry James
   (b) Henry Fielding
   (c) Walter Pater
   (d) Walter Besant

393. Who, among the following, has said that "criticism should be biased, impassioned, partisan"?
   (a) Charles Baudelaire
   (b) Fichte
   (c) Ezra Pound
   (d) Mallarme

394. "Imagination is the queen of truth" is a statement made by
   (a) Edgar Allan Poe
   (b) C. Baudelaire
   (c) Paul Verlaine
   (d) Mallarme

395. The challenge, "who would dare to assign to art the sterile function of imitating nature" was issued by
   (a) Paul Veraine
   (b) Paul Velary
   (c) Baudelaire
   (d) Rossetti

**Baudelaire's Important Quotable Statements**

1. A frenzied passion for art is a canker that devours everything else.
2. Always be a poet, even in prose.
3. Any healthy man can go without food for two days, but not without poetry.
4. Beauty is the sole ambition, the exclusive goal of taste.
5. The study of beauty is a duel in which the artist cries with terror before being defeated.
6. Two fundamental literary qualities: supernaturalism and irony.

396. The statement, "An artist is an artist only because of his exquisite sense of beauty, a sense which implies and contains an equally exquisite sense of all deformities and all disproportion" was made by?
   (a) Baudelaire
   (b) I.A. Richards
   (c) Henry James
   (d) John Ruskin

397. Who said that a novel in its broadest definition, a personal, direct impression of life"?
   (a) Cleanth Brooks
   (b) Henry James
   (c) E.M. Forster
   (d) F.R. Leavis

   (This observation was made by Henry James in *The Art of Fiction*)

**ANSWERS**

| | | | | | |
|---|---|---|---|---|---|
| 311. (a) | 312. (b) | 313. (c) | 314. (a) | 315. (c) | 316. (d) |
| 317. (c) | 318. (a) | 319. (b) | 320. (c) | 321. (c) | 322. (a) |
| 323. (c) | 324. (a) | 325. (d) | 326. (b) | 327. (c) | 328. (c) |
| 329. (a) | 330. (c) | 331. (a) | 332. (c) | 333. (b) | 334. (c) |
| 335. (b) | 336. (a) | 337. (c) | 338. (b) | 339. (a) | 340. (c) |
| 341. (a) | 342. (c) | 343. (b) | 344. (d) | 345. (a) | 346. (c) |
| 347. (a) | 348. (d) | 349. (a) | 350. (b) | 351. (d) | 352. (b) |
| 353. (a) | 354. (c) | 355. (c) | 356. (a) | 357. (c) | 358. (a) |
| 359. (a) | 360. (b) | 361. (d) | 362. (c) | 363. (d) | 364. (d) |
| 365. (d) | 366. (c) | 367. (a) | 368. (b) | 369. (d) | 370. (a) |
| 371. (b) | 372. (c) | 373. (d) | 374. (a) | 375. (c) | 376. (d) |
| 377. (d) | 378. (b) | 379. (c) | 380. (b) | 381. (a) | 382. (d) |
| 383. (a) | 384. (b) | 385. (c) | 386. (c) | 387. (d) | 388. (b) |
| 389. (c) | 390. (b) | 391. (c) | 392. (b) | 393. (a) | 394. (b) |
| 395. (c) | 396. (a) | 397. (b) | | | |

## (VII) MODERN CRITICISM AND NEW CRITICISM

### 1. IMPORTANT CRITICAL WORKS OF T.S. ELIOT

1. *The Use of Poetry and the Use of Criticism* (1933).
2. *The Idea of a Christian Society* (1939)
3. *Notes Towards the Definition of Culture* (1948)
4. *Selected Essays, Third Edition* (1951)
5. *On Poetry and Poets* (1957)
6. *To Critise the Critic* (1965)
7. *The Sacred Wood* (1921)

### 2. IMPORTANT ESSAYS

(1) *Traditional and Individual Talent* (1919) (2) *Poetry and Drama* (1951) (3) *The Function of Criticism* (1923) (4) *The Metaphysical Poets* (1921) (5) *The Frontiers of Criticism* (1956) (6) *Hamlet and His Problems* (1919)

398. Which one of the following essays is regarded as an unofficial manifesto of Eliot's criticism?
   (a) *Tradition and Individual Talent*
   (b) *The Function of Criticism*
   (c) *The Frontiers of Criticism*
   (d) *The Metaphysical Poets*

399. Who coined the phrase "Objective Correlative"?
   (a) C.S. Lewis
   (b) T.S. Eliot
   (c) Virginia Woolf
   (d) Matthew Arnold

   (The term was used by Eliot in his essay *Hamlet and his Problems*. Eliot defines it as "a set of objects, a situation, a chain of events, which shall be the formula" for the poet's emotion so that when the external facts are given, the emotion is at once evoked.

400. Who coined the term "Disassociation of Sensibility"?
   (a) Matthew Arnold (b) I.A. Richards
   (c) T.S. Eliot (d) F.R. Leavis

   (Eliot used this term in his essay *The Metaphysical Poets* (1921). In this essay, Eliot expressed the view that there was a "fusion of thought and feeling" ('unification of sensibility') in the Metaphysical poets, especially John Donne. Eliot was of the view that "a recreation of thought into feeling", "a direct sensuous apprehension of thought"—qualities possessed by the Metaphysical poets were essential for good poetry. The influence of Milton and Dryden led to a separation of thought from feeling, which Eliot calls 'dissociation of sensibility'.)

401. It is "exactly as wasteful for a poet to do what has been done already as for a biologist to rediscover Mendel's discoveries". Whose opinion is this?
   (a) I.A. Richards
   (b) T.S. Eliot
   (c) F.R. Leavis
   (d) John Crowe Ransom

402. Who, among the following, said, "The rudiment of criticism is the ability to choose a good poem and reject a bad poem; and its most severe test is of its ability to select a good new poem, to respond properly to a new situation"?

(a) T.S. Eliot
(b) Allen Tate
(c) John Crowe Ransom
(d) Cleanth Brooks

403. In which of the following did T.S. Eliot argue that the literature of Western Europe could be viewed as a "simultaneous order" of works where the value of any new work depended on its relation to the order of the tradition?
(a) *The Function of Criticism*
(b) *Tradition and Individual Talent*
(c) *The Frontiers of Criticism*
(d) None of the above

404. In which of his essays has Eliot talked about "the historical sense"?
(a) *The Function of Criticism*
(b) *The Frontiers of Criticism*
(c) *Tradition and Individual Talent*
(d) *The Metaphysical Poets*

(According to T.S. Eliot, *The historical sense* involves a perception, not only of the pastness of the past, but of its presence; the historical sense compels a man to write not merely with his own generation in his bones, but with a feeling that the whole of the literature of Europe from Homer within it the whole of the literature of his own country has a simultaneous existence and composes a simultaneous order".)

405. "Yet if the only form of tradition, of handling down, consisted in the way of the immediate generation before us in a blind or timid adherence to its successes, 'tradition' should positively be discouraged. We have seen many such simple currents soon lost in the sand; and novelty is better than repetition. Tradition is a matter of much wider significance." Who said this?
(a) Alexander Pope
(b) T.S. Eliot
(c) P.B. Shelley
(d) Matthew Arnold

406. In one of his essays, T.S. Eliot makes the observation, "It cannot be inherited and if your want it you must obtain it by great labour". What does 'It' refer to?
(a) Property (b) Wealth
(c) Tradition (d) Talent

407. *Notes Towards a Definition of Culture* (1948) was written by
(a) F.R. Leavis
(b) I.A. Richards
(c) Matthew Arnold
(d) T.S. Eliot

408. Whose theory claimed that the major works of art, both past and present, formed an "ideal order" which is continually modified by subsequent works of art?
(a) Matthew Arnold (b) T.S. Eliot
(c) Ezra Pound (d) Marcel Proust

409. Who has used the expression 'the lemon-squeezer school of criticism'?
(a) I.A. Richards
(b) F.R. Leavis
(c) T.S. Eliot
(d) William Empson

(The expression was used by Eliot in The Frontiers of Criticism in a lecture given by him at the University of Minnesota in 1956. It was reprinted in *On Poetry and Poets*, a collection of Eliot's essays published in 1957. The essay is significant because he criticizes those critical methods that relied on 'close reading' and 'practical criticism'.)

410. About which poets does Eliot make the observation that "they think, but they do

not feel their thought as the odour of a rose"?

(a) Tennyson and Browning
(b) Wordsworth and Coleridge
(c) Shelley and Keats
(d) Dryden and Pope

411. "A thought to _______ was an experience; it modified his sensibility. When a poet's mind is perfectly equipped for its work, it is constantly amalgamating, disparate experiences...."

Fill in the blank with one of the following:

(a) Tennyson
(b) Browning
(c) John Donne
(d) Wordsworth

(The line has been taken from Eliot's essay *The Metaphysical Poets*)

412. Who, among the following, has said, "the more perfect the artist, the more completely separate in him will be the man who suffers and the mind which creates".

(a) S.T. Coleridge
(b) I.A. Richards
(c) William Empson
(d) T.S. Eliot

413. "Poetry is not a turning loose of emotion, but an escape from emotion; it is not the expression of personality, but an escape from personality".

This is from:

(a) Arnold's *Function of Criticism at the Present Time*
(b) Arnold's *Study of Poetry*
(c) T.S. Eliot's *Tradition and Individual Talent*
(d) Wordsworth's *Preface to Lyrical Ballads*

414. Who, among the following, has said, "Honest criticism and sensitive appreciation is directed not upon the poet but upon the poetry"?

(a) T.S. Eliot
(b) Cleanth Books
(c) John Crowe Ransom
(d) Allen Tate

415. T.S. Eliot's emphasis has been on the importance of intimate relationship between literature and

(a) Philosophy (b) Art
(c) Religion (d) Science

416. Eliot's essay *The Function of Criticism* was written in response to

(a) Arnold's essay *The Function of Criticism at the Present Time*
(b) Pater's essay *Criticism and Romanticism*
(c) Middleton Murry's essay *Romanticism and the Tradition*
(d) None of the above

417. Which of the following are definitions/ aims of criticism given by T.S. Eliot?

(a) Criticism as "the commentation and exposition of works by means of written words".
(b) The end of criticism is "elucidation of works of art and the correction of taste".
(c) The aim of criticism is "the promotion of understanding and enjoyment of literature".
(d) All of the above

418. Who, among the following, pointed out that the difference between classicism and romanticism is "the difference between the complete and the fragmentary, the adult and the immature, the orderly and the chaotic"?

(a) Walter Pater
(b) John Ruskin
(c) T.S. Eliot
(d) Matthew Arnold

419. Who propounded the "inner voice" theory in criticism?
(a) Middleton Murry
(b) S.T. Coleridge
(c) Wordsworth
(d) T.S. Eliot

420. What did T.S. Eliot call the "inner voice" theory?
(a) Irritating (b) Stupid
(c) Valuable (d) Whiggery

("Whiggery" connotes non-conformism. To Eliot, the concept of 'inner voice' is doing 'what one likes'. T.S. Eliot is against the critical impressionism of critics like Middleton Murry. Eliot says that those who believe in the "inner voice" do not want any principles. Such a criticism can never be objective, for it is coloured and mixed up with the critic's own emotions. He contemptuously calls such criticism 'Whiggery'.)

421. Who, among the following, claimed that he was a "Classicist in literature, royalist in politics and Anglo-Catholic in religion"?
(a) Arnold (b) Dr. Johnson
(c) T.S. Eliot (d) Dryden

422. According to T.S. Eliot, "the longer part of the labour of an author in composing his work is critical labour..." What does this critical labor consist of?
(a) Shifting, combining
(b) Constructing, expunging
(c) Correcting, testing
(d) All of the above

423. Who, among the following, said, "Eliot behaves towards the dead poets of Europe with all the casual skill of a shoplifter in a department store"?
(a) George Watson
(b) F.R. Leavis
(c) John Hayward
(d) R.P. Blackmur

424. What, according to T.S. Eliot, are the chief tools of a critic?
(a) Comparison
(b) Analysis
(c) Giving personal opinions and impressions
(d) Both (a) and (b)

425. "But on giving the matter a little attention, we perceive that criticism, far from being a simple and orderly field of beneficient activity, from which impostors can be readily ejected, is no better than a Sunday Park of contending and contentious orators, who have not even arrived at the articulation of their differences."

This is from
(a) Arnold's *Function of Criticism at the Present Time*
(b) Eliot's *The Function of Criticism*
(c) Eliot's *The Frontiers of Criticism*
(d) None of the above

426. What, according to Eliot, is the foremost quality of a critic?
(a) He should have a highly developed sense of fact
(b) He should be liberal in his views
(c) He should not be biased
(d) He should judge a work according to his ideology

427. Eliot is critical of
(a) Impressionistic criticism
(b) Interpretive criticism
(c) Both impressionist and interpretive criticisms
(d) None of the above

428. Complete the following:

"The possessors of the inner voice ride ten in a compartment to a football match at Swansea, listening to the inner voice, which breathes the eternal message of...."

(a) Vanity (b) Fear
(c) Lust (d) All of the above

429. T.S. Eliot's *A Dialogue on Dramatic Poetry* was written in

(a) 1928 (b) 1929
(c) 1931 (d) 1933

430. The form of *A Dialogue on Dramatic Poetry* is according to

(a) Sidney's *Apology for Poetry*
(b) Shelley's *Defence of Poetry*
(c) Dryden's *Essay of Dramatic Poetry*
(d) Arnold's *The Study of Poetry*

431. Who, among the following, said, "All poetry tends towards drama and all drama towards poetry"?

(a) Arnold (b) T.S. Eliot
(c) Dr. Johnson (d) Dryden

432. Who, among the following, is the author of 'Rhetoric and Drama' (1919)

(a) T.S. Eliot (b) I.A. Richards
(c) F.R. Leavis (d) Cleanth Brooks

433. According to T.S. Eliot, the great weakness of Elizabethan drama "is not its lack of realism, but its attempt at realism; not its conventions, but its lack of conventions". This is from:

(a) *A Dialogue on Dramatic Poetry*
(b) *Rhetoric and Poetic Drama*
(c) *Four Elizabethan Dramatists*
(d) *The Possibility of Poetic Drama*

434. For a work of art "actual life is the material, and, on the other hand, an abstraction from actual life is a necessary condition" whose view is this?

(a) T.S. Eliot
(b) I.A. Richards
(c) John Hayward
(d) William Empson

435. Who, among the following, said, "Eliot's theory of the impersonality of poetry is the greatest theory on the nature of the poetic process after Wordsworth's romantic conception of poetry"?

(a) George Watson
(b) William Empson
(c) John Hayward
(d) A.G. George

436. Who said, "No critic, indeed, since Coleridge, has shown more clearly the use of poetry and the use of criticism"?

(a) John Hayward
(b) A.G. George
(c) John Crowe Ransom

437. About whom has John Hayward said, "I cannot think of a critic who has been more widely read and discussed in his own life time, and not only in English but almost in every language, except Russian, throughout the civilized world"?

(a) Dr. Johnson
(b) Matthew Arnold
(c) Coleridge
(d) T.S. Eliot

438. According to T.S. Eliot, poetry is not inspiration, it is

(a) Organization (b) A divine gift
(c) Natural (d) Spontaneous

439. Who, among the following, said, "The business of the poet is not to find new emotions but to use ordinary ones."

(a) Cleanth Brooks (b) T.S. Eliot
(c) Wordsworth (d) Coleridge

440. For Eliot, the essence of poetry is
(a) Metaphor (b) Metonymy
(c) Personification (d) Simile

441. Who found Eliot's acknowledgement that the poem has 'in some sense its own life', "a doctrine of poetic automatism"?
(a) I.A. Richards
(b) Yvor Winters
(c) John Crowe Ransom
(d) F.R. Leavis

442. "Criticism as a distinct form of creation and enjoyment consists of asking and answering rational questions about literature". Who said it?
(a) L. Abercrombie
(b) T.S. Eliot
(c) Arnold
(d) I.A. Richards

**SOME QUOTABLE STATEMENTS OF T.S. ELIOT**

1. Anxiety is the hand-maiden of creativity.
2. Any poet, if he is to survive beyond 25th year, must alter; he must seek new literary influences; he will have different emotions to express.
3. Art never improves...the material of art never remains the same.
4. Immature poets imitate; mature poets steal.
5. Poetry may make us from time to time a little more aware of the deeper, unnamed feelings which form the substratum of our being, to which we rarely penetrate; for our lives are mostly a constant evasion of ourselves.
6. The bad poet is usually unconscious where he ought to be conscious, and conscious where he ought to be unconscious.
7. The business of the poet is not to find new emotions, but to use the ordinary ones and, in working them up into poetry, to express feelings which are not in actual emotions at all.
8. The most important thing for poets to do is to write as little as possible.
9. There is not a most repulsive spectacle than an old man who will not forsake the world, which has already forsaken him.
10. This is the way the world ends, not with a bang, but a whimper.

443. Who, among the following said, "The sole task of criticism is to ask three questions. What has the author tried to express? How has he succeeded in expressing it? What is worth expressing"?
(a) J.E. Spingarn (b) T.S. Eliot
(c) I.A. Richards (d) F.R. Leavis

444. *Language of Fiction* by Margaret McDonald was published in
(a) 1952 (b) 1954
(c) 1956 (d) 1958

445. Who regarded life as a 'luminous halo, a semi-transparent envelope surrounding us from the beginning of conscious to the end"?
(a) T.S. Eliot
(b) I.A. Richards
(c) Virginia Woolf
(d) F.R. Leavis

(This is from Woolf's essay *Modern Novel*)

446. Who, among the following, said that "interpretation is intellect's revenge upon art"?
(a) T.S. Eliot (b) Susan Sontag
(c) I.A. Richards (d) Cleanth Brooks

447. The essay *The Tragic Fallacy* was written by
   (a) Joseph Krutch
   (b) W.K. Wimsatt
   (c) Monroe Beardsley
   (d) Allen Tate

448. Who wrote the preface to "Gitanjali"?
   (a) T.S. Eliot (b) E.M. Forster
   (c) W.B. Yeats (d) G.B. Shaw

449. *The Cost of Strangeness* (1982) was written by
   (a) Wayne C. Booth
   (b) M.H. Abrams
   (c) Anthony Conran
   (d) Henry James

450. To whom among the following critics, comparison, analysis and elucidation were of supreme importance?
   (a) T.S. Eliot
   (b) I.A. Richards
   (c) F.R. Leavis
   (d) Cleanth Brooks

451. I.A. Richards' *Principles of Literary Criticism* was published in
   (a) 1921 (b) 1924
   (c) 1926 (d) 1928

452. How many essays does *Principles of Criticism* have
   (a) XXV (b) XXIII
   (c) XXXV (d) XXX

453. I.A. Richards *Practical Criticism* was published in
   (a) 1924 (b) 1929
   (c) 1931 (d) 1935

454. I.A. Richards wrote *Meaning of Meaning* (1923) in collaboration with
   (a) James Woods (b) T.S. Eliot
   (c) William Empson (d) C.K. Ogden

455. Who is the author of *Coleridge on Imagination* (1935)?
   (a) F.R. Leavis
   (b) William Wordsworth
   (c) I.A. Richards
   (d) T.S. Eliot

456. Who, among the following, said that the "*Preface to Lyrical Ballads* explains the poetic process of the type of poetry only Wordsworth wrote"?
   (a) T.S. Eliot (b) Helen Gardner
   (c) F.R. Leavis (d) I.A. Richards

457. I.A. Richards's approach to poetry is
   (a) Psychological
   (b) Cognitive
   (c) Formalist
   (d) None of the above

   (Richard's Criticism is called 'Affective Criticism')

458. The concept of 'Emotive' and 'Scientific' use of language is given by
   (a) Coleridge (b) I.A. Richards
   (c) Cleanth Brooks (d) T.S. Eliot

   ("A statement may be used for the sake of *reference*, true and false, which it causes. This is the *scientific* use of language. But it may also be used for the sake of the effect in emotion and attitude.... This is the emotive use of language"—Essay No. 34 "The Two Uses of Language" from *Principles of Literary Criticism*)

459. Who, among the following, said, "Richard's claim to have pioneered Anglo-American New Criticism of the thirties and forties is unassailable"?
   (a) T.S. Eliot (b) F.R. Leavis
   (c) George Watson (d) Yvor Winters

460. What, according to I.A. Richards, are the four kinds of meaning?

(a) Sense and Feeling
(b) Tone and Intention
(c) Denotative and Connotative
(d) Both (a) and (b)

('Sense', according to I.A. Richards, is something that is communicated by the plain literal meanings of the words. We have an attitude towards certain items and state of affairs. We use language to express these feelings. Feeling refers to emotions, emotional attitudes or desires. 'Tone' is the speaker's attitude to the listener. 'Intention' is the effect the speaker is trying to produce. He speaks for a purpose and his purpose modifies his speech.)

461. What are the objectivese that Richards proposes in *Practical Criticism*?
(a) To document 'the contemporary state of culture'.
(b) To create a new kind of reading-habit for poetry.
(c) To reform the teaching of literature.
(d) All of the above.

462. I.A. Richards dismisses all European criticism before him with the following remarks:

"A few conjectures, a supply of admonitions, many acute isolated observations, some brilliant guesses, much oratary and applied poetry, inexhaustible confusion, a sufficiency of dogma, no small stock of prejudices, whimsies and crotchets, a profusion of mysticism, a little genuine speculation, sundry stray inspirations...."

In which of the following essays (*Principles of Literary Criticism*) have these remarks been made?
(a) The Chaos of Critical Theory
(b) The Critics' Concern with Value
(c) Actual and Possible Misapprehensions
(d) Judgment and Divergent Readings

463. I.A. Richards divides impulses into
(a) Two (b) Three
(c) Four (d) Five

(These two kinds of impulses are "appetencies and aversions", i.e. desires and dislikes.)

464. Richards' *Principles of Literary Criticism* (1924) advanced critical notions such as
(a) Irony (b) Tension
(c) Balance (d) All of the above

465. Who said, "Nobody who read I.A. Richards' *Practical Criticism* when it appeared in 1929 could read any poem as he had ready it before"?
(a) Allen Tate
(b) John Crowe Ransom
(c) Cleanth Brooks
(d) T.S. Eliot

(Allen Tate made this remark in *Essays of Four Decades* (1968))

466. I.A. Richards is a votary of
(a) Art for Art's sake
(b) Art for Morality's sake
(c) Art for Culture's sake
(d) Art for Society's sake

467. "It will be convenient at this point to introduce two definitions. In a full critical statement which states not only that an experience is valuable in certain ways, but also that it is caused by certain features in a contemplated object, the part which describes the value of the experience we shall call the critical part. That which describes the object we shall call the technical part".

This is taken from
(a) *Seven Types of Ambiguity*
(b) *The Heresy of the Paraphrase*

(c) *The Principles of Literary Criticism*
(d) *The New Criticism*

468. Who, among the following, has said, "Stable meanings derive from stable contexts"?
(a) F.R. Leavis
(b) I.A. Richards
(c) John Crowe Ransom
(d) Cleanth Brooks

469. How many kinds of metaphors, according to I.A. Richards, there are?
(a) Two (b) Three
(c) Four (d) Five

(These two kinds of metaphor are 'sense' metaphors and 'emotive' metaphors). In 'sense' metaphor, the shift is due to a similarity between the original object and the new one. In the 'emotive' metaphor, the shift is due to a "similarity between the feelings the new situation and the normal situation arouse". According I.A. Richards, "Metaphor is a semi-surreptitious method by which a greater variety of elements can be brought into the fabric of the experience".

470. According to I.A. Richards, poetry makes
(a) Statements
(b) Comments
(c) Pseudo-statements
(d) None of the above

(According to I.A. Richards, the referential value of a pseudo-statement is nil. What it apparently says has the larger purpose of evoking an emotion or attitude of mind which the poet considers valuable but for which there are no verbal equivalents)

471. What is valuable, according to Richards' theory of value?
(a) That which gives pleasure
(b) That which gives moral instruction
(c) That which removes mental tension
(d) That which satisfies our impulses

472. What, according to I.A. Richards, is the function of art?
(a) To delight
(b) To instruct
(c) To organize impulse
(d) None of the above

473. How many definitions of 'beauty' have I.A. Richards and his colleagues have given?
(a) 8 (b) 10
(c) 12 (d) 13

474. What, according to I.A. Richards, are the two ways in which impulses can be organized?
(a) By exclusion and by inclusion
(b) By synthesis and by elimination
(c) By training and by experience
(d) Both (a) and (b)

475. *The Foundation of Aesthetics* (1922) was written by
(a) George Santayana
(b) I.A. Richards
(c) T.S. Eliot
(d) Allen Tate

476. I.A. Richards *Philosophy of Rhetoric* was published in
(a) 1932 (b) 1935
(c) 1936 (d) 1939

477. Who is associated in criticism with the "context" theory of meaning?
(a) I.A. Richards
(b) William Empson
(c) George Santayana
(d) None of the above

478. Which of his books did I.A. Richards call "a machine for thinking with"?
(a) *Philosophy of Rhetoric*
(b) *Principles of Literary Criticism*

(c) *Practical Criticism*
(d) *The Foundation of Aesthetics*

479. When was I.A. Richards' *Science and Poetry* published?
(a) 1921 (b) 1923
(c) 1926 (d) 1931

480. Who said, "Beauty is pleasure objectified—pleasure regarded as the quality of an object"?
(a) T.S. Eliot
(b) I.A. Richards
(c) John Keats
(d) George Santayana

(This is the most typical and concrete assertion of the stand-point that beauty is subjective. This assertion is made by Santayana in his book *The Sense of Beauty* (1896). It means that 'beauty is the objectification of pleasure'. When we are in a pleasurable state of mind, the objects look beautiful.)

**SOME IMPORTANT WORKS BY F.R. LEAVIS**

1. *New Bearings in English Poetry* (1932) 2. *Revaluation* (1936) 3. *The Great Tradition* (1948) 4. *The Common Pursuit* (1952)

481. F.R. Leavis's *The Great Tradition* (1948) gives his critical views on
(a) Novel (b) Drama
(c) Epic (d) Poetry

482. In *Revaluation* (1936), F.R. Leavis expresses his critical views on
(a) Novel
(b) Drama
(c) Post-Shakespearean Poetry
(d) Modern Poetry

483. Which of the following books has F.R. Leavis's critical views on 'modern poetry'?
(a) *The Common Pursuit*
(b) *New Bearings in English Poetry*
(c) *The Great Tradition*
(d) *Revaluation*

484. Which of the following novelists are not mentioned in Leavis's *The Great Tradition*?
(a) Jane Austen
(b) Thomas Hardy
(c) Charles Dickens
(d) Both (b) and (c)

(The novelists which are mentioned are Jane Austen, George Eliot, Joseph Conrad, Henry James, and D.H. Lawrence.)

485. In which of the following categories can F.R. Leavis's criticism be placed?
(a) Biographical Criticism
(b) Comparative Criticism
(c) Historical Criticism
(d) Analytical Criticism

486. *Culture and Environment* (1933), *Education and University* (1943) were written by
(a) I.A. Richards
(b) F.R. Leavis
(c) William Empson
(d) Q.D. Leavis

487. F.R. Leavis's *English Literature in Our Time and the University* was published in
(a) 1961 (b) 1966
(c) 1969 (d) 1971

488. Who said that literature is "the storehouse of recorded values. It is the writer's exploration of the cultural traditions of his age"?
(a) F.R. Leavis (b) I.A. Richards
(c) Matthew Arnold (d) T.S. Eliot

489. F.R. Leavis was the editor of the journal *Scrutiny* from
(a) 1930-50 (b) 1932-51
(c) 1932-53 (d) 1929-49

490. The statement that a poet must have "the power of making words express what he feels" was made by
   (a) I.A. Richards
   (b) F.R. Leavis
   (c) T.S. Eliot
   (d) William Empson

491. About which book did F.R. Leavis say that for "the next few years I read it through several times a year, pencil in hand"?
   (a) Aristotle's *Poetics*
   (b) Wordsworth's *Preface to Lyrical Ballads*
   (c) Coleridge's *Biographia Literaria*
   (d) T.S. Eliot's *The Sacred Wood*

492. Who, among the following, said that literature is "the storehouse of recorded values"?
   (a) F.R. Leavis
   (b) Ezra Pound
   (c) T.S. Eliot
   (d) Matthew Arnold

493. According to F.R. Leavis, a critic "endeavours to see the poetry of the present as a continuation and development, the most significant life of literary tradition". Whose critic's influence on F.R. Leavis is reflected here?
   (a) Ezra Pound's
   (b) I.A. Richard's
   (c) T.S. Eliot's
   (d) Matthew Arnold's

494. Which of the following are the two important words used by Leavis?
   (a) Enactment
   (b) Realisation
   (c) Both (a) and (b)
   (d) None of the above

   (By 'enactment', Leavis means that great literary works embody or enact moral and cultural values. Leavis explains 'realisation' as "the signs of something grasped and held, something presented in the ordering of words....")

495. "Literature matters vitally to civilization". Whose view is this?
   (a) Matthew Arnold's
   (b) T.S. Eliot's
   (c) I.A. Richards'
   (d) F.R. Leavis's

496. Who, among the following, are adjudged the most 'significant' modern poets in Leavis's *New Bearings in English poetry*?
   (a) G.M. Hopkins, W.B. Yeats, Ezra Pound, T.S. Eliot
   (b) W.H. Auden, W.B. Yeasts, Ezra Pound, T.S. Eliot
   (c) E.E. Cummings, W.H. Auden, Ezra Pound, T.S. Eliot
   (d) G.M. Hopkins, W.B. Yeats, Robert Frost, Wallace Stevens

497. Leavis's criticism belongs to the school of
   (a) Neo-classicism
   (b) Romanticism
   (c) Verbal analysis
   (d) Historical criticism

498. In his verbal analysis of literary works, F.R. Leavis was influenced by
   (a) I.A. Richards
   (b) T.S. Eliot
   (c) Ezra Pound
   (d) John Crowe Ransom

499. In which one of the following essays of T.S. Eliot, is F.R. Leavis most admired?
   (a) The Frontiers of Criticism
   (b) The Function of Criticism
   (c) Metaphysical Poets
   (d) Hamlet and His Problems

500. In *The Great Tradition* Dickens is excluded from a title to greatness, but

Leavis regards one of the following novels as a masterpiece. Name the novel.

(a) *David Copperfield*
(b) *Bleak House*
(c) *Hard Times*
(d) *Great Expectations*

501. One of the charges against F.R. Leavis is that his criticism is

(a) too abstruse.
(b) too abstract.
(c) subjective.
(d) it does not discuss the standards by which it proceeds, i.e. he does not follow any theory or system.

502. F.R. Leavis's *Mass Civilization and Mass Culture* was published in

(a) 1929 (b) 1930
(c) 1932 (d) 1935

503. In his essay *Sociology and Literature* (*The Common Pursuit*) F.R. Leavis says that "a real literary interest is an interest in"

(a) Man (b) Society
(c) Civilization (d) All of the above

(For F.R. Leavis, the study of literature is "an intimate study of the complexities, potentialities, and essential conditions of human nature". He was for a broad study of literature which went beyond looking at "the words on the page". This is what separated him from the New Critics.)

504. Yvor Winter's *Anatomy of Nonsense* was published in

(a) 1941 (b) 1943
(c) 1945 (d) 1947

505. Choose the correct pair:

(a) I.A. Richards (i) *Principles of Literary Criticism*
(b) F.R. Leavis (ii) *Meaning of Meaning*
(c) T.S. Eliot (iii) *Practical Criticism*
(d) Oscar Wilde (iv) *Modern Painters*

506. *The Mind in Chains* by C.D. Leavis was published in

(a) 1935 (b) 1937
(c) 1939 (d) 1941

507. The author of *Seven Types of Ambiguity* is

(a) William Empson
(b) Monroe Beardsley
(c) William K. Wimsatt
(d) I.A. Richards

508. William K. Empson's *Seven Types of Ambiguity* was published in

(a) 1929 (b) 1930
(c) 1932 (d) 1933

509. Who suggested that the name of *Seven Types of Ambituity* should have been *Seven Types of Plurisignation*?

(a) Monroe Beardsley
(b) William K. Wimsatt
(c) Philip Wheelwright
(d) John Crowe Ransom

510. "An ambiguity, in ordinary speech, means something very pronounced, and as a rule witty or deceitful. I propose to use the word in an extended sense, and shall think relevant to my subject any verbal nuance, however slight, which gives room for alternative reactions to the same piece of language".

This is from a book by

(a) I.A. Richards
(b) William Empson
(c) John Crowe Ransom
(d) Cleanth Brooks

511. *Seven Types of Ambiguity* points to the fact of the

(a) slipperiness of meaning.
(b) meaninglessness of a text.

(c) many–sidedness of language.
(d) None of the above.

512. William Empson's *The Structure of Complex Words* was published in
(a) 1951 (b) 1953
(c) 1954 (d) 1956

513. William Empson's *Milton's God* was published in
(a) 1959 (b) 1960
(c) 1961 (d) 1963

**SEVEN TYPES OF AMBIGUITY**

1. The first type of ambiguity is the metaphor, that is, when two things are said to be alike which have different properties. This concept is similar to that of metaphysical conceit.
2. Two or more meanings are resolved into one. Empson characterizes this as using two different metaphors at once.
3. Two ideas that are connected through context can be given in one word simultaneously.
4. Two or more meanings that do not agree but combine to make clear a complicated state of mind in the author.
5. When the author discovers his idea in the act of writing. Empson describes a simile that lies halfway between two statements made by the author.
6. When a statement says nothing and the readers are forced to invent a statement of their own, most likely in conflict with that of the author.
7. Two words that within context are opposites that expose a fundamental division in the author's mind.

514. *Counter–Statement* (1931) was written by
(a) Kenneth Burke
(b) Edmund Burke
(c) Wayne Booth
(d) I.A. Richards

515. *A Grammar of Motives* by Kenneth Burke was published in
(a) 1940 (b) 1942
(c) 1943 (d) 1945

516. Who, among the following, wrote *A Rhetoric of Motives* (1950)?
(a) I.A. Richards
(b) Allen Tate
(c) Kenneth Burke
(d) Cleanth Brooks

517. Kenneth Burke's *Language as Symbolic Action* was published in
(a) 1960 (b) 1966
(c) 1969 (d) 1970

518. William Empson's *Seven Types of Ambiguity* is
(a) a structuralist study of a narrative.
(b) a piece of psycho-analytical criticism.
(c) a study of media.
(d) an analysis of poetic ambivalence.

**TENETS OF NEW CRITICISM**

1. That the primary concern of criticism is with the problem of unity–the kind of whole which the literary work forms or fails to form, and the relation of the various parts to each other in building up this whole.
2. That, in a successful work, form and content cannot be separated.
3. That form is meaning.
4. That literature is ultimately metaphorical and symbolic.
5. That the general and the universal are not seized upon by abstraction, but got at through the concrete and the particular.

6. That literature is not a surrogate for religion.
7. That, as Allen Tate says, "specific moral problems" are the subject matter of literature, but that the purpose of literature is not to point a moral.
8. That the principles of criticism define the area relevant to literary criticism; they do not constitute a method for carrying out the criticism.

519. Who is known as the theoretician of the New Criticism?
 (a) Cleanth Brooks
 (b) John Crowe Ransom
 (c) Allen Tate
 (d) R.P. Blackmur

520. Who coined the term 'New Criticism'?
 (a) J.E. Spingarn
 (b) Kenneth Burke
 (c) John Crowe Ransom
 (d) Cleanth Brooks

521. Who among the following wrote *The New Criticism* (1941)?
 (a) J.E. Spingarn
 (b) John Crowe Ransom
 (c) Cleanth Brooks
 (d) Allen Tate

522. John Crowe Ransom's *God Without Thunder* was published in
 (a) 1929 (b) 1931
 (c) 1930 (d) 1935

523. According to John Crowe Ransom, poetry can be
 (a) Physical (b) Platonic
 (c) Metaphysical (d) All of the above

524. What, according to Ransom, are the two types of discourses?
 (a) Philosophical and Scientific
 (b) Philosophical and Religious
 (c) Poetic and Scientific
 (d) Religious and Scientific

(In a 'poetic' discourse, there is free interpretation because of irony and ambiguities. The 'scientific' discourse has an authoritative and absolute meaning.)

525. With which critic would you identify the terms 'Spreaders', 'Rufflers', and 'Imposters'?
 (a) I.A. Richards
 (b) John Crowe Ransom
 (c) Cleanth Brooks
 (d) T.S. Eliot

(In "William Wordsworth : Notes Toward an Understanding of Poetry" (an essay published in *The Kenyan Review* (1950), John Crowe Ransom praised Wordsworth's theory of poetic diction. He finds in Wordsworth's theory a passion for a concrete object. In support of this, Ransom introduced novel terms for three of the four devices which he noted in poetic language. These are first, Singular Terms or Spreaders to illuminate the vivid concreteness of objects and events; secondly, Dystactical terms or Rufflers, which deliberately cultivate logical confusion: inversions, ambiguities, ellipses, etc.; thirdly, Metaphysical terms or Imposters, which introduce foreign objects by analogy or association; and finally of these devices, Wordsworth composed poems whose purity of style has finally won Ransom's admiration.)

526. By whom the terms 'Structure' and 'Texture' are used?
 (a) John Crowe Ransom
 (b) Allen Tate
 (c) T.S. Eliot
 (d) D.A. Richards

('Texture' stands for the surface details or elements of a work, especially of a poem, apart from its structure, content, etc. Details include imagery, metre, rhyme, the sensuous aspects, etc. 'Structure' is the internal framework of a poem, i.e. the arrangements of the parts to form a unified whole; the planned framework or 'architecture' of a literary work, just as we have an octave and a sestet in a Petrarchan sonnet or a beginning, middle and end in a drama.)

527. *Criticism Inc* is an influential essay written by
   (a) Cleanth Brooks
   (b) T.S. Eliot
   (c) I.A. Richards
   (d) John Crowe Ransom

528. According to John Crowe Ransom, Romantic and Victorian poets are
   (a) Platonic
   (b) Metaphysical
   (c) Neo-classical
   (d) None of the above

529. Who coined the term 'tension'?
   (a) John Crowe Ransom
   (b) William Empson
   (c) I.A. Richards
   (d) Allen Tate

(The term 'tension' was used by Allen Tate in his book *Tension in Poetry* (1938). According to Ross Murfin, the term means "the totality of, or interrelation between, what he defines as the two types of meaning in a poem : "extension" (concrete, denotative meaning) and 'intension' (abstract, metaphorical meaning). In a distinct but related usage, other New Critics drew on Tate's use of tension to refer to "conflict structures", that is, the binary oppositions of various ideas and qualities..."). According to Tate, the tension sustains the whole structure of meaning, and he derives the term by lopping the prefixes 'off' the logical terms 'extension' and 'intension' (which defines the abstract and denotative aspects of poetic language and respectively the concrete and connotative one). The meaning of the poem is "the full organized body of all the extension and intension that we find in it".)

530. In which of his essays has Ransom mentioned the term "New Criticism"?
   (a) *Criticism Inc*
   (b) *The Ontological Critic*
   (c) *Wanted: An Ontological Critic*
   (d) None of the above

('New criticism' started in the Vanderbilt University, Nashville, Tennessee, U.S.A.) Ransom announced in the essay *Wanted: An Ontological Critic* that it was time to identify a powerful intellectual movement which deserved to be called "New Criticism".)

531. Cleanth Brooks was born in
   (a) 1889 (b) 1892
   (c) 1902 (d) 1906

532. Cleanth Brooks wrote *Understanding Poetry* and *Understanding Fiction* in collaboration with
   (a) Robert B. Heilman
   (b) I.A. Richards
   (c) Robert Pen Warren
   (d) John Crowe Ransom

533. Cleanth Brooks wrote *Understanding Drama* in collaboration with
   (a) Robert B. Heilman
   (b) Robert Pen Warren
   (c) C.K. Ogden
   (d) Allen Tate

534. Cleanth Brooks wrote *Literary Criticism: A Short History* in collaboration with

(a) Robern Pen Warren
(b) W.K. Wimsatt
(c) Robert B. Heilman
(d) John Crowe Ransom

535. The "Well-Wrought Urn: Studies in the Structure of Poetry" by Cleanth Brooks was published in
(a) 1943 (b) 1945
(c) 1947 (d) 1949

536. Cleanth Brooks' *Modern Poetry and the Tradition* was published in
(a) 1936 (b) 1939
(c) 1941 (d) 1943

537. *Understanding Poetry* was published in
(a) 1933 (b) 1936
(c) 1938 (d) 1941

538. *Understanding Fiction* was published in
(a) 1939 (b) 1943
(c) 1945 (d) 1947

539. *Literary Criticism: A Short History* was published in
(a) 1957 (b) 1959
(c) 1961 (d) 1963

540. Cleanth Brooks has mainly focused his critical attention on
(a) Fiction (b) Poetry
(c) Drama (d) Prose

541. According to Cleanth Brooks, a poem lends its meaning through
(a) Irony
(b) Ambiguity
(c) Paradox
(d) All of the above

542. The New Critics laid main emphasis on
(a) Form (b) Theme
(c) Style (d) Content

543. Who coined the term "The Intentional Fallacy" (1946)?
(a) I.A. Richards
(b) F.R. Leavis
(c) William Empson
(d) W. K. Wimsatt and Monroe Beardsley

544. Who coined the term "The Affective Fallacy" (1949)?
(a) T.S. Eliot
(b) William Empson
(c) Wimsatt and Beardsley
(d) Paul Valery

("The Intentional Fallacy" and "The Affective Fallacy" are two essays included in the *Verbal Icon*—a collection of essays published between 1941 and 1952. Wimsatt revised some of original versions and *Verbal Icon* was finally published in 1954. The affective fallacy is the belief that the meaning or value of a work may be determined by its effect on the reader. The intentional fallacy is the belief that the meaning or value of a work can be determined by the author's intention.)

545. Who authored the following paragraph:

"Judging a poem is like judging a pudding or a machine. One demands that it works. It is only because an artifact works that we infer the intention of an artificer. "A poem should not mean but be". A poem can be only through its meaning–since its medium is words–yet it is, simply is, in the sense that we have no excuse for inquiring what part is intended or meant."
(a) John Crowe Ransom
(b) W.K. Wimsatt
(c) Monroe Beardsley
(d) Both (b) and (c)

546. What, according to Wimsatt and Beardsley, are the 'evidences' for the meaning of a poem?
(a) Internal (b) External
(c) Intermediate (d) All of the above

(The 'Internal' is what is public: "it is discovered through the semantics and syntax of a poem, through our habitual knowledge of the language, through grammar, dictionaries, and all the literature which is the source of dictionaries, in general through all that makes a language and cultures". The 'External' is private or 'idiosyncratic'; not part of the work as a linguistic fact; it consists of revelations...about how or why the poet wrote the poem. The 'Intermediate' is "private or semi-private meanings attached to words or topics by an author".

547. In which of the following meanings do New Critics believe?
(a) Single
(b) Symbolic
(c) Single and Symbolic
(d) Multiple

548. Who has written "The Heresy of Paraphrase"?
(a) T.S. Eliot
(b) Cleanth Brooks
(c) John Crowe Ransom
(d) Allen Tate

(It is the title of a chapter in Cleanth Brooks' *The Well-Wrought Urn*. The New Critics believed that poems cannot be paraphrased. The idea of non-paraphrasability of poetry was one of the central tenets of the New Criticism.)

549. New critics want to know how the work speaks itself through
(a) Harmony, Order
(b) Tension, Paradox
(c) Ambivalence, Ambiguity
(d) All of the above

550. New critics are primarily concerned with
(a) the language, i.e. the verbal meaning of a text.
(b) the organization (overall structure) of a text.
(c) Both (a) and (b).
(d) None of the above.

551. New Critics are concerned with the
(a) biography of the author.
(b) historical and social context.
(c) effects on the reader.
(d) None of the above.

552. Who is the author of *The New Criticism: A Lecture Delivered at Columbia University* (1910)?
(a) J.E. Spingarn
(b) John Crowe Ransom
(c) Allen Tate
(d) William Empson

553. Who said that the "language of poetry is a language of paradox"?
(a) Allen Tate
(b) John Crowe Ransom
(c) Cleanth Brooks
(d) W.K. Wimsatt

(This occurs in Cleanth Brooks, *The Language of Paradox* (1947). Here he argues that the language of poetry at its core is the language of paradox.)

554. Choose the correct chronological sequence:
(a) *The Well-Wrought Urn, Principles of Criticism, Tradition and Individual Talent, The Great Tradition*
(b) *Tradition and Individual Talent, Principles of Literary Criticism, The Great Tradition, The Well-Wrought Urn*
(c) *Principles of Literary Criticism, The Well-Wrought Urn, The Great Tradition, Tradition and Individual Talent*
(d) *Principles of Literary Criticism, Tradition and Individual Talent, The Well-Wrought Urn, The Great Tradition*

555. William K. Wimsatt and Monroe C. Beardsley propounded two central positions of New Criticism. Which are they?
(a) Objective Correlative and Intentional Fallacy
(b) Dissociation of Sensibility and Affective Fallacy
(c) Affective Fallacy an Intentional Fallacy
(d) Affective Fallacy and Pathetic Fallacy

556. R.S. Crane's *Critics and Criticism: Ancient and Modern* was published in
(a) 1950 (b) 1952
(c) 1954 (d) 1955

557. Wayne C. Booth's *The Rhetoric of Fiction* was written in
(a) 1961 (b) 1962
(c) 1964 (d) 1966

558. *Theory of Literature* written by Rene Wellek and Austin Warren was published in
(a) 1945 (b) 1947
(c) 1949 (d) 1950

(In *Theory of Literature*, they distinguished between the "intrinsic" and "extrinsic" study of literature. The former concentrates on the work as a "stratified system of norms", whereas the latter relegates literary biography, history, psychology and sociology to the "extrinsic" domain.)

559. Who is the author of *The Double Agent* (1935)
(a) Rene Wellek
(b) Austin Warren
(c) R.P. Blackmur
(d) None of the above

560. R.P. Blackmur's *Language as Gesture* was published in
(a) 1949 (b) 1950
(c) 1951 (d) 1952

561. *The Art of the Novel* (1934) was written by
(a) E.M. Forster
(b) R.P. Blackmur
(c) David Lodge
(d) Henry James

562. R.P. Blackmur's *The Lion and the Honeycomb : Essays in Solicitude and Critique* was published in
(a) 1951 (b) 1953
(c) 1955 (d) 1956

563. Ronald Crane's book *The Languages of Criticism and the Structure of Poetry* was published in
(a) 1951 (b) 1953
(c) 1955 (d) 1957

(In this polemic book, Crane criticized New Criticism and called for a radical pluralism: Ronald Crane was the leader of what is known as the "Chicago School of Critics" or "Neo-Aristotelians".)

564. 'New Criticism' considers text as a
(a) Cultural construct
(b) Historical construct
(c) Linguistic construct
(d) Autotelic

565. 'Chicago Criticism' is said to begin in
(a) 1930s (b) 1940s
(c) 1950s (d) 1960s

566. Ronald Crane's essay *History versus Criticism in the Study of Literature* was published in
(a) 1935 (b) 1937
(c) 1938 (d) 1940

(In this essay, he defined literary criticism as "simply the disciplined consideration, at once analytical and evaluative of literary works as works of art.")

567. Give the correct chronological sequence :
(a) Elder Olson, Norman Maclean, Ronald C. Crane, Bernard Weinberg
(b) Norman Maclean, Bernard Weinberg, Elder Olson, Ronald C. Crane
(c) Ronald C. Crane, Norman Maclean, Bernard Weinberg, Elder Olson
(d) Bernard Weinberg, Norman Maclean, Ronald C. Crane, Elder Olson

(Ronald C. Crane (1886-1967); Norman Maclean (1902-90); Bernard Weinberg (1907-73); Elder Olson (1909-92)—all of them belong to the Chicago School of Critics.)

568. Ronald C. Crane's argument, "The moral is surely that we ought to have at our command, collectively at least, as many different critical methods as there are distinguishable major aspects in the construction, appreciation, and use of literary works" suggests
(a) Judicial Criticism
(b) Comparative Criticism
(c) Critical Pluralism
(d) Disinterested Criticism

569. Who, among the Chicago School of Critics, made the observation that "Criticism in our time is a sort of Tower of Babel"?
(a) Ronald Crane
(b) Elder Olson
(c) Bernard Weinberg
(d) Norman Maclean

('Tower of Babel' was built in Shinar (Babilonia). There is a reference to it in the *Book of Genesis*. It stands for confusion of voices, sounds, languages, etc. Olson used this term in an article entitled "An Outline of Poetic Theory" (1949). He means to say there is a lot of confusion in criticism because of different principles, different methods, and then reaching different conclusions.)

570. David Ritcher's *The Critical Tradition: Classic Texts and Contemporary Trends* was first published in
(a) 1989 (b) 1990
(c) 1991 (d) 1992

571. Who made the observation about the Chicago critics that they are "group of disappointed priests seeking in literature a new world to replace the one the world had lost"?
(a) John Crowe Ransom
(b) Cleanth Brooks
(c) David H. Ritcher
(d) Allen Tate

572. One of the following does not belong to the Chicago School of Criticism
(a) Ronald Crane
(b) Elder Olson
(c) Norman Maclean
(d) William Empson

573. Rene Wellek's *Concept of Criticism* was published in
(a) 1963 (b) 1965
(c) 1960 (d) 1962

574. Who said, "creating a poem is itself a poem"?
(a) Stephan Mallarme
(b) Paul Valery
(c) Baudelaire
(d) None of the above

575. The New Critics were also known as
(a) Fugitives
(b) Southern Agrarians
(c) Impressionistic
(d) Both (a) and (b)

576. Which of the following journals/ magazines are associated with New Criticism?

(a) *Fugitive*
(b) *Southern Review*
(c) *Kenyan Review*
(d) *Sewanee Review*
(e) All of the above

(John Crowe Ransom edited *Fugitive* from 1922-25 with a group of writers including Allen Tate, Robert Penn Warren, and Donal Davidson. *Southern Review* was edited by Pen Warren and Cleanth Brooks (1935-41). The *Kenyan Review* was run by Ransom (1938-59) and is still existent. *Sewanee Review* was edited by Allen Tate and others published since 1892 by the University of South Sewanee, Tennessee.)

577. Which of the following did the New Critics want to exclude from criticism?
(a) Personal impressions and moral content.
(b) Synopsis and paraphrase.
(c) Historical, linguistic studies and studies dealing with abstract content taken out of work.
(d) All of the above.

578. Choose the Chronological sequence of the following:
(a) T.S. Eliot, John Crowe Ransom, William K. Wimsatt, Monroe C. Beardsley
(b) Monroe C. Beardsley, T.S. Eliot, John Crowe Ransom, William K. Wimsatt
(c) John Crowe Ransom, Monroe C. Beardsley, T.S. Eliot, William K. Wimsatt
(d) William K. Wimsatt, Monroe C. Beardsley, T.S. Eliot, John Crowe Ransom

(T.S. Eliot (1888-1965); John Crowe Ransom (1888-1974); William K. Wimsatt (1907-75); Monroe C. Beardsley (1915-85).)

579. *The New Apologies for Poetry* was written by
(a) E.D. Hirsch
(b) Monroe Beardsley
(c) Murray Kriergar
(d) Austin Warren

580. Murray Kriergar's *The New Apologies for Poetry* was published in
(a) 1951 (b) 1953
(c) 1954 (d) 1956

581. Give the correct chronological sequence of the following:
(a) Validity in Interpretation, The Affective Fallacy, Verbal Icon, The Intentional Fallacy
(b) The Intentional Fallacy, The Affective Fallacy, Verbal Icon, Validity in Interpretation
(c) The Affective Fallacy, Validity in Interpretation, The Intentional Fallacy, Verbal icon
(d) Verbal Icon, Validity in Interpretation, The Affective Fallacy, The Intentional Fallacy

(The Intentional Fallacy (1946). The Affective Fallacy (1949), Verbal Icon (1954), Validity in Interpretation (1967).)

582. Who, among the following, has said, "Like Walking, criticism is a pretty nearly universal art...and few perform either very well"?
(a) R.P. Blackmur
(b) I.A. Richards
(c) John Crowe Ransom
(d) AllenTate

(This is from the concluding essay "A Critic's Job of Work" published in *The Double Agent*.)

## ANSWERS

| | | | | | |
|---|---|---|---|---|---|
| 398. (a) | 399. (b) | 400. (c) | 401. (b) | 402. (a) | 403. (b) |
| 404. (c) | 405. (b) | 406. (c) | 407. (d) | 408. (b) | 409. (c) |
| 410. (a) | 411. (c) | 412. (d) | 413. (c) | 414. (a) | 415. (c) |
| 416. (c) | 417. (d) | 418. (c) | 419. (a) | 420. (d) | 421. (c) |
| 422. (d) | 423. (a) | 424. (d) | 425. (b) | 426. (a) | 427. (c) |
| 428. (d) | 429. (a) | 430. (c) | 431. (b) | 432. (a) | 433. (c) |
| 434. (a) | 435. (d) | 436. (a) | 437. (d) | 438. (a) | 439. (b) |
| 440. (a) | 441. (c) | 442. (a) | 443. (a) | 444. (b) | 445. (c) |
| 446. (b) | 447. (a) | 448. (c) | 449. (c) | 450. (a) | 451. (b) |
| 452. (c) | 453. (b) | 454. (d) | 455. (c) | 456. (d) | 457. (a) |
| 458. (b) | 459. (c) | 460. (d) | 461. (d) | 462. (a) | 463. (a) |
| 464. (d) | 465. (a) | 466. (b) | 467. (c) | 468. (b) | 469. (a) |
| 470. (c) | 471. (d) | 472. (c) | 473. (d) | 474. (d) | 475. (b) |
| 476. (c) | 477. (a) | 478. (b) | 479. (d) | 480. (c) | 481. (a) |
| 482. (c) | 483. (b) | 484. (d) | 485. (d) | 486. (b) | 487. (c) |
| 488. (a) | 489. (c) | 490. (b) | 491. (d) | 492. (a) | 493. (c) |
| 494. (c) | 495. (d) | 496. (a) | 497. (c) | 498. (a) | 499. (b) |
| 500. (c) | 501. (d) | 502. (b) | 503. (d) | 504. (b) | 505. (a) |
| 506. (b) | 507. (a) | 508. (b) | 509. (c) | 510. (b) | 511. (c) |
| 512. (a) | 513. (c) | 514. (a) | 515. (d) | 516. (c) | 517. (b) |
| 518. (d) | 519. (b) | 520. (a) | 521. (b) | 522. (c) | 523. (d) |
| 524. (c) | 525. (b) | 526. (a) | 527. (d) | 528. (a) | 529. (d) |
| 530. (c) | 531. (d) | 532. (c) | 533. (a) | 534. (b) | 535. (c) |
| 536. (b) | 537. (c) | 538. (b) | 539. (a) | 540. (b) | 541. (d) |
| 542. (a) | 543. (d) | 544. (c) | 545. (d) | 546. (d) | 547. (d) |
| 548. (b) | 549. (d) | 550. (c) | 551. (d) | 552. (a) | 553. (c) |
| 554. (b) | 555. (c) | 556. (b) | 557. (a) | 558. (c) | 559. (c) |
| 560. (d) | 561. (b) | 562. (c) | 563. (a) | 564. (d) | 565. (a) |
| 566. (a) | 567. (c) | 568. (c) | 569. (b) | 570. (a) | 571. (c) |
| 572. (d) | 573. (a) | 574. (b) | 575. (d) | 576. (e) | 577. (d) |
| 578. (a) | 579. (c) | 580. (d) | 581. (b) | 582. (a) | |

## (VIII) (RUSSIAN) FORMALISM, STRUCTURALISM AND SEMIOTICS

583. Who, among the following, said, "The object of study in literary science is not literature but literariness, that is, what makes a given work a literary work"?
   (a) Roman Jakobson
   (b) Vladimir Propp
   (c) Victor Shklovsky
   (d) Rene Wellek

   (According to Baldick, "Literariness is the organization of language which through special linguistic and formal properties distinguishes literary texts from non-literary texts.")

584. Who said that the literariness of a work consists in "the maximum foregrounding of the utterance"?
   (a) Roman Jakobson
   (b) Jan Mukravosky
   (c) Kenneth Burke
   (d) R.S. Crane

585. Who made the distinction between story (fabula) and plot syuzhet (sjuzhet)-pronounced (soojay)?
   (a) Vladimir Propp
   (b) Roman Jakobson
   (c) Eichenbaum
   (d) Boris Tomashevsky

   ('Fabula' is the raw material of the story while 'syuzhet' is the way a story is organized.)

586. Who did a formalist analysis of the basic plot components of Russian folk-tales to identify the simplest irreducible narrative elements?
   (a) Roman Jakobson
   (b) Victor Shklovsky
   (c) Vladimir Propp
   (d) Eichenbaum

587. Who coined the term 'defamiliariasation'?
   (a) Roman Jakobson
   (b) Mikhail Bakhtin
   (c) Vladimir Propp
   (d) Victor Shklovsky

   (To 'defamiliarize' is to make fresh, new, strange, different what is familiar and known. Shklovsky used this term in his essay *Art as Technique* (1917).)

588. This essay *Two Aspects of Language and Two Aspects of Aphasic Disturbances* (1956) was written by
   (a) Vladimir Propp
   (b) Ronald Barthes
   (c) Roman Jacobson
   (d) V. Propp

589. What, according to Roman Jakobson, are the two poles of language?
   (a) Metaphor and symbol
   (b) Sign and metonymy
   (c) Metaphor and sign
   (d) Metaphor and metonymy

590. The Formalists regard a literary work as
   (a) an object in its own right
   (b) autonomous
   (c) autotelic
   (d) All of the above

591. The Formalist approach focusses on
   (a) the paraphrase of a work
   (b) the formal structure of a work
   (c) the historical approach
   (d) the biographal approach

592. The Formalist approach to literature isolates the literary work from
   (a) social forces
   (b) political forces
   (c) personal circumstances of the author
   (d) All of the above

593. The essay *Art as Technique* (1917) was written by
(a) V. Propp
(b) R. Jakobson
(c) V. Shklovsky
(d) Coleridge

594. Who wrote *Discourse in the Novel* (1934-35)?
(a) V. Propp
(b) M. Bakhtin
(c) R. Jakobson
(d) Eichenbaum

595. According to Roman Jakobson, the poetic function of language is concerned with
(a) society
(b) culture
(c) transmission of ideas
(d) message for its own sake

596. A critic examining John Milton's *Paradise Lost* focuses on the physical description of the Garden of Eden, on the symbol of hands, seed, flower, and on the characters of God, Satan, Eve, Adam. He pays special attention to the epic similes and metaphors and the point of view from which the tale is being told. He looks for meaning in the text itself, and does not refer to any biography of Milton. He is most likely a ______ critic.
(a) formalist
(b) mimetic
(c) reader Response
(d) mimetic

597. The Russian Formalists were more interested in
(a) the theme of a text
(b) style of a text
(c) literariness of a text
(d) language of a text

598. The Russian Formalists undermined the
(a) the form of a text
(b) the structure of a text
(c) the mimetic nature of literature
(d) None of the above

599. The Russian Formalists argued that the primary task of literary criticism is to analyze the constructional devices whereby daily objects are transformed into 'new'. For this they used the term
(a) Novelty
(b) Defamiliarisation
(c) Literariness
(d) Artfulness

600. Who defined literature as "the sum total of all stylistic devices employed in it"?
(a) Roman Jakobson
(b) M. Bakhtin
(c) V. Propp
(d) V. Shklovsy

601. According to Formalists, the function of literary language is to
(a) offer the reader a special mode of experience by drawing attention to its own 'formal' features
(b) convey the intentions of the author
(c) give a message
(d) delight the reader

602. Which of the following, according to Roman Jakobson, constitute the metaphoric pole?
(a) Selection
(b) Substitution
(c) Combination
(d) Both (a) and (b)

603. According to Roman Jakobson, which of the following constitute the metonymic pole?
(a) Selection
(b) Combination
(c) Contextualization
(d) Both (b) and (c)

604. According to Jakobson, language seen from the addressee's point of view is
(a) emotive (addresser's point of view)
(b) conative (seeking an effect)
(c) referential
(d) None of the above

605. Which critic is known for 'dialogic criticism'?
(a) R. Jakobson
(b) V. Propp
(c) M. Bakhtin
(d) Eichenbaum

606. What term has Mikhail Bakhtin coined for his view that the novel has many divergent and contending social views that achieve their full significance only in the process of their dialogic interaction both with each other and with the voice of the narrator?
(a) Carnivalesque
(b) Monologic
(c) Dialogic or Polyphonic
(d) None of the above

(The terms 'monologic', 'dialogic' or 'polyhonic' are used by Bakhtin in his discussion of language and literature. He believes a text has different 'voices' and the their use disrupts the authority of a single voice. In his book *Problems of Dostoevesky's Poetics* (1929) he makes a contrast between the novels of Tolstoy and those of Dostoevesky. In his view, Dostoevesky's novels are dialogic or polyphonic while those of Tolstoy monologic ('single voice'). In Dostoevsky's novels, characters are allowed to speak 'in their own voices'. According to Bakhtin, the characters speak a "plurality of independent and unmerged voices and consciousness, a genuine polyphony of fully valid voices....")

607. Who coined the term 'carnivalesque'?
(a) R. Jakobson
(b) M. Bakhtin
(c) V. Propp
(d) None of the above

608. In which work did M. Bakhtin propose the concept of 'Carnivalesque'?
(a) *Problems of Dostoevsky's Poetics*
(b) *Rabelais and His World*
(c) *Discourse in the Novel*
(d) *The Dialogic Imagination*

(In popular use, the word 'carnival' means a festival or a travelling amusement show. According to Ross Murfin and Supriya M. Ray, "Bakhtin used the term *carnival* to refer not only to such festivities at Mardi Gras—celebrations during which commoners (and the more privileged classes) were temporarily free to transgress all kinds of written or unwritten social, ecclesiastical laws—but also to "low" or popular culture, such as fair and spontaneous folk drama (including puppet shows.) Thus, people were free to flout all social norms by coarse joking and indulging in profanity.)

609. When was M. Bakhtin's *Rabelais and His World* published?
(a) 1940
(b) 1941
(c) 1942
(d) 1944

610. Whose novels, according to Bakhtin, are 'dialogic'?
(a) Leo Tolstoy's
(b) F. Dostoevsky's
(c) Maxim Gorky's
(d) Dickens'

611. Bakhtin's *Problems of Dostoevsky's Poetics* was published in

(a) 1979
(b) 1980
(c) 1982
(d) 1984

612. Bakhtin's *The Dialogic Imagination* was published in
(a) 1989
(b) 1993
(c) 1995
(d) 1997

613. Bakhtin's *Towards a Philosophy of the Act* was published in
(a) 1989
(b) 1993
(c) 1995
(d) 1997

614. *Questions of Literature and Aesthetic* (1973) was written by
(a) M. Bakhtin
(b) V. Propp
(c) Roman Jakobson
(d) V. Shklovsky

615. 'The Moscow Linguistic Circle' was formed in
(a) 1910
(b) 1912
(c) 1915
(d) 1917

616. 'The Prague Linguistic Circle' was formed in
(a) 1916
(b) 1920
(c) 1923
(d) 1926

617. *Morphology of the Folktale* (1928, trans 1968) was written by
(a) V. Propp
(b) R. Jakobson
(c) Felex Vodicka
(d) B. Eichenbaum

618. For Roman Jakobson, the verbal linguistic facts of a literary work are
(a) of no use
(b) primary
(c) secondary
(d) None of the above

619. According to Russian Formalists, practical language, as against poetic language, is
(a) scientific
(b) pragmatic
(c) used in day-to-day communication to convey information
(d) None of the above

(According to Lev Jakubinsky, "the practical goal retreats into the background and linguistic combinations acquire a *value in themselves*. When this happens language becomes defamiliarized, utterances poetic".)

620. Russian Formalists were the first to study the function of sound patterns in poetry
(a) Systematically
(b) Objectively
(c) Subjectively
(d) Both (a) and (b)

621. Mikhail Bakhtin defined 'carnivalesque' literature as
(a) medieval poetry with its eclectic choice of subject matter
(b) literature which can engage in a "dialogue" with readers from various social backgrounds"
(c) literature which mixes various languages and styles so as to undermine the one voice of a privileged language
(d) literature which espouses anti-authoritian views

622. Which would be considered an example of intratextual criticism?

(a) Formalist criticism
(b) Mimetic criticism
(c) Historicist criticism
(d) Bakhtinian criticism

623. 'Formalist Criticism' relates to the structure of
(a) Literary devices
(b) Myths
(c) Content
(d) Form

624. In Formalistic School of Criticism, art is
(a) Entertainment
(b) Preaching
(c) Style
(d) None of the above

625. *Narrative Discourse* (1972) is written by
(a) V. Propp
(b) R. Jakobson
(c) Gerard Genette
(d) Ronald Barthes

626. Who wrote *Theses on Language* in collaboration with Jakobson?
(a) B. Eichenbaum
(b) Mikhail Bakhtin
(c) V. Propp
(d) Yuri Tynyanov

627. R. Jakobson's *Fundamentals of Language* was published in
(a) 1956
(b) 1957
(c) 1958
(d) 1959

628. Roman Jakobson's *The Sound Shape of Language* was published in
(a) 1976
(b) 1975
(c) 1972
(d) 1979

629. *The Framework of Language* (1980) was written by
(a) V. Propp
(b) R. Jakobson
(c) V. Shklovsky
(d) Mkihail Bakhtin

630. R. Jakobson's *Verbal Art, Verbal Sign, Verbal Time* was published in
(a) 1980
(b) 1982
(c) 1983
(d) 1985

631. Theory of the "Formal Method" (1925) was written by
(a) Roman Jakobson
(b) V. Propp
(c) Boris Eichenbaum
(d) M. Bakhtin

632. Russian Formalism flourished during the
(a) 1910s
(b) 1920s
(c) 1940s
(d) 1950s

633. In Russian Formalism, genre is understood as a particular selection and combination of which of the following elements?
(a) Stylistic
(b) Thematic
(c) Compositional
(d) All of the above

634. According to Victor Shklovsky, the literary work at any given point of time consists of the following co-existing oppositional generations
(a) The old-timers
(b) The central trend
(c) The avant-garde
(d) All of the above

635. Who coined the term 'structuralism'?
   (a) Roman Jakobson
   (b) Ferdinand de Saussure
   (c) J.L. Austin
   (d) V. Propp

   (Roman Jakobson coined it in 1929)

636. Who is regarded as the founder of 'structuralism'?
   (a) Roman Jakobson
   (b) Ferdinand de Saussure
   (c) V. Propp
   (d) M. Bakhtin

637. Saussure's *Course in General Linguistics* was published in
   (a) 1913
   (b) 1915
   (c) 1916
   (d) 1917

638. "One remark in passing : when semiology becomes organized as a science, the question will arise whether or not it properly includes modes of expression based on completely natural signs, such as pantomime. Supposing that the new science welcomes them, its main concern will still be the whole group of systems grounded on the arbitrariness of the sign".

   This is from:
   (a) *Practical Criticism*
   (b) *Course in General Linguistics*
   (c) *Biographia Literaria*
   (d) *Semiotics and Philosophy of Language*

639. Michel Foucault was a major practitioner of this school of criticism
   (a) Structuralism
   (b) Mimetic Criticism
   (c) Deconstruction
   (d) Formalist Criticism

640. The essay *Introduction to the Structural Analysis of Narrative* (1966 trans 1977) was written by
   (a) V. Propp
   (b) M. Bakhtin
   (c) Roland Barthes
   (d) R. Jakobson

641. *Structural Semantics* (1966, trans 1983) was written by
   (a) Geoffery Leech
   (b) V. Propp
   (c) V. Shklovsky
   (d) Gremais

642. Structuralism is mainly concerned with the descriptions of
   (a) Signs
   (b) Signifiers
   (c) Signifieds
   (d) Structures

643. Structuralism claims that a linguistic element in any given situation has
   (a) nothing to do with the rest of the context
   (b) no significance by itself
   (c) significance by itself
   (d) None of the above

644. Semiotics is the study of
   (a) Structures
   (b) Signifiers
   (c) Signs
   (d) Signifieds

645. In Structuralism, a text is seen as
   (a) a system in itself; its own constitutive elements and laws (grammar)
   (b) as one element within a literary system as a whole (generic)
   (c) it relates to the culture as a whole
   (d) All of the above

646. According to Saussure, the connection between words and things was ________.
   (a) natural
   (b) conventional
   (c) logical
   (d) None of the above

647. According to structuralists, reality was
(a) independent of language
(b) existing outside language
(c) a language construct
(d) None of the above

648. The structuralists replaced 'defamiliarization' by
(a) Foregrounding
(b) Form
(c) Style
(d) Content

649. Who, among the following, is not a structuralist?
(a) Claude Levi-Strauss
(b) Roland Barthes
(c) Roman Jakobson
(d) Jacques Derrida

650. Who, among the following, argued that the savage mind has the same structures as the 'civilized mind' and that the human characters are the same everywhere
(a) Freud
(b) Claude Levi-Strauss
(c) C.L. Jung
(d) Northrop Frye

651. Both 'Structuralism' and 'Formalism' devoted their attention to
(a) Social content
(b) Historical content
(c) Literary form
(d) None of the above

(Russian Formalists made the focus of their study the artistic strategies of the author.)

652. Structuralists sought to bring to literary analysis
(a) a subjective assessment
(b) an objective criterion
(c) historical approach
(d) humanistic approach

653. Russian Formalists laid emphasis on
(a) the psycho-analytic approach
(b) the historical approach
(c) the cultural approach
(d) the functional role of literary devices

654. Which two of the concepts are associated with Victor Shklovsky?
(a) Defamiliarisation
(b) Literariness
(c) Plot/story distinction
(d) Both (a) and (c)

('Defamiliarisation' is making familiar things look 'new', 'strange', etc. 'Story' ('fabula') is the chronological sequence of events while plot (syuzhet) is the artistic arrangement of events by means of such devices as repetition, parallelism, gradation, and retardation.)

655. Who, among the following critics, defined literature as 'thinking in images'?
(a) V. Shklovsky
(b) Belinsky
(c) V. Propp
(d) I.A. Richards

656. Give the correct chronological sequence of the following:
(a) *Problems of Dostoevsky's Poetics, Art as Technique, Morphology of the Folktale, Fundamentals of Language*
(b) *Fundamentals of Language, Art as Technique, Morphology of the Folktale, Problems of Dostoevsky's Poetics*
(c) *Art as Technique, Morphology of the Folktale, Problems of Dostoevsky's Poetics, Fundamentals of Language*
(d) *Morphology of the Folktale, Fundamentals of Language, Art as Techniques, Problems of Dostoevsky's Poetics*

(*Art as Technique* (1917); *Morphology of the Folktale* (1928); *Problems of Dostoevsky's Poetics* (1929; trans 1973); *Fundamentals of Language* (1956).)

657. According to Terry Eagleton, structuralism is a ________ of inquiry whereas semiotics is a ________ of study.
(a) method, field
(b) manner, field
(c) type, manner
(d) field, type

658. Structuralism has proved that there is nothing ________ about codes.
(a) natural
(b) innocent
(c) factual
(d) arbitrary

659. In structuralism, the relationship between the sign and the referent (i.e. what it refers to) is
(a) Natural
(b) Logical
(c) Arbitrary
(d) Identical

660. Which literary movement, according to Terry Eagleton, brought structuralist and post-structuralist criticism to birth in the first place?
(a) Surrealism
(b) Romanticism
(c) Classicism
(d) Modernism

661. Which of the following term is about "lexical items" (words) which cross the boundaries between sentences binding them into a single continuous utterance, even though they are grammatically separate sentences?
(a) Cohesion
(b) Coherence
(c) Trace
(d) Syntax

(The concept of 'cohesion' has been discussed in *Cohension in English* (1976) written by M.A.K. Halliday and Ruqaiya Hasan. In 'Linguistics', cohension is the grammatical and lexical relationship within a text or sentence. It can be defined as those links that hold a text together and give it meaning. For example, A says "Peter came" and B replies "But he was very late". In this interchange, the role of conjunction 'but' and the link between the pronoun 'he' and the noun Peter, are both aspects of cohesion. Halliday and Hasan have identified five general categories of cohesive devices that create coherence in texts : a ellipsis, substitution, lexical cohesion, and conjunction and such connectives as *then*, *however*, *therefore*, *consequently*, etc.)

662. The stop-start quality can be removed and cohesion achieved by what linguists call 'pronomilization' using ________.
(a) nouns
(b) pronouns
(c) adverbs
(d) adjectives

663. *Structuralism and Semiotics* (1977) was written by
(a) Saussure
(b) Roman Jakobson
(c) Roland Barthes
(d) Terence Hawkes

664. Who, among the following, makes a distinction between the semiotic and the symbolic?
(a) Ferdinand de Saussure
(b) Jacques Lacan
(c) Roland Barthes
(d) Julia Kristeva

665. *Semiotics of Poetry* (1978) was written by
   (a) I.A. Richards
   (b) Cleanth Brooks
   (c) John Crowe Ransom
   (d) Michael Riffaterre

666. M. Bakhtin's model of human psyche is
   (a) I-for-myself
   (b) I-for-the-other
   (c) the other-for-me
   (d) All of the above

   (A: How I feel from inside to my own consciousness

   B: How I look from outside to someone else

   C: For me and for other people, images, impressions, etc. must cross the boundary between one consciousness and another before identity as such is registered.)

667. Who, among the following, was not a member of "Society for the Study of Poetic Language"?
   (a) Victor Shklovsky
   (b) Boris Eichenbaum
   (c) Yuri Tynyanov
   (d) Osip Brik

668. Which school of criticism rejected the notion that viewed the form as an envelope or vessel into which a liquid (content) is poured?
   (a) New Criticism
   (b) Modernism
   (c) Postmodernism
   (d) Russian Formalism

669. Who viewed form as "a complete thing, something concrete, dynamic, self-contained"?
   (a) Russian Formalists
   (b) New critics
   (c) Post-structuralists
   (d) None of the above

670. According to Formalism, the techniques of plot construction included
   (a) Parallelism
   (b) Framing
   (c) The weaving of motifs
   (d) All of the above

671. Who said that the most significant influence in the history of literature is the influence of "work on work"?
   (a) Roman Jakobson
   (b) Ferdinand Brunetiere
   (c) Victor Shklovsky
   (d) Boris Eichenbaum

672. *Verbal Melody* (1922) was written by
   (a) V. Propp
   (b) R. Jakobson
   (c) B. Eichenbaum
   (d) V. Shklovsky

673. How many styles of poetry did B. Eichenbaum distinguish?
   (a) Two
   (b) Three
   (c) Four
   (d) Five

   (The three styles that Eichenbaum distinguish in *Verbal Melody* are : declamatory (oratorial); melodic, and conversational.)

674. Who, among the following, was not a structuralist?
   (a) Roman Jakobson
   (b) Claude Levi-Strauss
   (c) I.A. Richards
   (d) Michael Riffaterre

675. *Structuralism in Literature: An Introduction* (1974) was written by
   (a) Robert Scholes
   (b) R. Jakobson

(c) V. Propp
(d) Mikhail Bakhtin

676. Who has said, "One can neither divide sound from thought nor thought from sound"?
(a) Noam Chomsky
(b) Jonathan Culler
(c) C.S. Peirce
(d) Saussure

677. According to Ronald Barthes, the "elements" of semiology are contained in the following sets of terms:
(a) language and speech
(b) signifier and signified
(c) syntagm and system
(d) All of the above

678. Who defines language as "a collective contract which one most accept in its entirety if one wishes to communicate"?
(a) R. Jakobson
(b) Roland Barthes
(c) Saussure
(d) C.S. Peirce

679. Who made the statement that "private property in the sphere of language does not exist"?
(a) Roman Jakobson
(b) Roland Barthes
(c) C.S. Peirce
(d) None of the above

680. Who rejects Saussure's claim that the connection between the signifier and the signified is arbitrary?
(a) Jacques Lacan
(b) Roland Barthes
(c) Roman Jakobson
(d) Charles Morris

(Ronald Barthes is of the view that the connection between the signifier and the signified is the result of a collective contract and training, and so, becomes *naturalized* over a period of time. He seems to agree with Benveniste's view that which is arbitrary is the connection between the signifier and *the thing*.)

681. Which are the categories, according to C.S. Peirce, into which all signs fit?
(a) Icon
(b) Index
(c) Symbol
(d) All the above

(1. Icon: The sign bears a direct resemblance to something else (e.g. picture of London. A Map 2. Index: There is link between the sign and the object it represents (e.g. A baby is crying = Needs milk) 3. Symbol : It bears no resemblance to the object (e.g. Cross for Christianity).)

682. *Revolution in Poetic Language* (1974) is written by
(a) Terry Eagleton
(b) David Lodge
(c) Julia Kristeva
(d) M.H. Abrams

(It is in this book that she draws the distinction between the 'semiotic' and the 'symbolic'. According to Kristeva, the semiotic process includes "drives, their disposition, and their division of the body, plus the ecological and social system surrounding the body, such as objects and pre-Oedipal relations with parents". The symbolic marks the emergence of subject and object as well as the constitution of meaning structured according to categories tied to the social order.)

683. *How to Do Things With Words* (1962) was written by
(a) C.S. Peirce
(b) Saussure
(c) J.L. Austin
(d) H.P. Grice

684. *Speech Acts: An Essay in the Philosophy of Language* (1970) was written by
   (a) H.P. Grice
   (b) John Searle
   (c) J.G. Herder
   (d) J.L. Austin

685. *Logic and Conversation* (1975) was written by
   (a) J.G. Herder
   (b) J.L. Austin
   (c) C.S. Peirce
   (d) H.P. Grice

686. According to Formalists, literature aims at representing
   (a) Reality
   (b) Character
   (c) Society
   (d) None of the above

687. The Formalists were associated with the journal
   (a) *Fugitive*
   (b) *LEF*
   (c) *Southern Review*
   (d) *Kenyan Review*

   (*LEF* stands for the *Left Front of Art*)

688. "The technique of art is to make objects 'unfamiliar', to make forms difficult, to increase the difficulty and length of perception because the process of perception is an aesthetic end in itself and must be prolonged. Art is a way of experiencing the artfulness of an object, the object is not important".

   This is from:
   (a) *Revolution in Poetic Language*
   (b) *Art as Technique*
   (c) *Art of Fiction*
   (d) *Theory of the* 'formal method'

689. Ferdinand de Saussure called for the
   (a) synchronic study of language
   (b) diachronic study of language
   (c) philological study of language
   (d) None of the above

   (In *Course in General Linguistics*, Saussure emphasized the need for the scientific, i.e. 'synchronic' study of language as as opposed to historical, i.e. 'diachronic' study of language done in the nineteenth century. Synchronic linguistics sees language as existing as a 'state' at a particular point in time. On the other hand, diachronic linguistics deals with the development of language through time.)

690. Which are the assumptions on which Saussure's systematic re-examination of language is based?
   (a) The systematic nature of language.
   (b) The relational conception of elements of language and the arbitrary nature of the linguistic elements.
   (c) The social nature of language.
   (d) All of the above.

691. Who, among the following, emphasized the relationship between structuralism and cultural institutions?
   (a) Roman Jakobson
   (b) H.P. Grice
   (c) Claude Levi-Strauss
   (d) M. Bakhtin

692. Who wrote the *The Structural Study of Myth* (1955)?
   (a) Levi-Strauss
   (b) Roland Barthes
   (c) V. Propp
   (d) V. Shklovsky

693. *Structural Poetics* (1975) was written by
   (a) Roman Jakobson
   (b) V. Propp
   (c) Jonathan Culler
   (d) M. Bakhtin

694. *The Poetics of Prose* (1971) was written by
   (a) Roland Barthes
   (b) Jonathan Culler
   (c) Tzvetan Todorov
   (d) Greimas

   (It was translated into English in 1977)

695. *Poetry of Grammar and Grammar of Poetry* was written by
   (a) T. Todorov
   (b) Greimas
   (c) R. Jakobson
   (d) Jonathan Culler

696. Who, among the following, wrote *History of Structuralism : The Rising Sign*?
   (a) Gremais
   (b) F. Dosse
   (c) Jonathan Culler
   (d) Roland Barthes

697. When was Francois Dosse's *History of Structuralism : The Rising Sign* was published?
   (a) 1991
   (b) 1992
   (c) 1993
   (d) 1994

698. *On Style* was written by
   (a) F. Dosse
   (b) Demetrius
   (c) A.J. Gremais
   (d) Charles Bally

699. *Style and Structure in Literature : Essays in the New Stylistics* (1975) was written by
   (a) Donald Freeman
   (b) Leo Spitzer
   (c) Roger Fowler
   (d) M.A.K. Halliday

700. *Essays on Style and Language* (1981) was written by
   (a) Roger Fowler
   (b) Donald Freeman
   (c) L. Spitzer
   (d) Jonathan Culler

701. *Language as Social Discourse* (1978) was written by
   (a) M.A.K. Halliday
   (b) Roger Fowler
   (c) L. Spitzer
   (d) Gremais

702. Structuralism as an intellectual movement started in
   (a) Italy
   (b) England
   (c) France
   (d) Germany

703. Structuralism began in Britain and the U.S.A. in the
   (a) 1950s
   (b) 1960s
   (c) 1970s
   (d) 1980s

704. The basis of stylistic analysis is
   (a) Objective
   (b) Scientific
   (c) Subjective
   (d) Both (a) and (b)

705. According to Stuart Hall, there are some general approaches to the question of the work done by representation. Which are they?
   (a) The reflective approach
   (b) The intentional approach
   (c) The constructionist approach
   (d) All of the above

   (Paul Cobley comments that according to Stuart Hall, the world is not given to us in pure form. It is always mediated or 're-presented'. The 'reflective' approach sees as residing in the person or thing in the real world; a representation such as narrative 'reflects' that meaning. The 'intentional' approach sees meaning in the control exercised by the producer of a representational form such as narrative, he or she uses representation to make the world 'mean'. The 'constructionist' approach sees meaning neither in the control of the producer nor in the thing represented. Instead, it identifies the thoroughly social nature of the construction of meaning, the fact that representation systems, rather than their users and objects, allow meaning to occur.)

706. *Morphology of the French Folk Tale* was written by
   (a) Claude Bremod
   (b) Roland Barthes
   (c) Michael Foucault
   (d) Paul Cobley

707. *Morphology of the French Folk Tale* by Claude Bremod was published in
   (a) 1970
   (b) 1973
   (c) 1975
   (d) 1977

708. Choose the correct chronological sequence:
   (a) *Course in General Linguistics, The Dialogic Imagination, Rabelais and His World, Art as Technique*
   (b) *The Dialogic Imagination, Art as Technique, Rabelais and His World, Course in General Linguistics*
   (c) *Course in General Linguistics, Art as Technique, Rabelais and His World, The Dialogic Imagination*
   (d) *Art as Technique, The Dialogic Imagination, Course in General Linguistics, Rabelias and His World*

709. Who coined the term 'heteroglossia'?
   (a) Roman Jakobson
   (b) M. Bakhtin
   (c) V. Propp
   (d) V. Shklovsky

710. Choose the correct chronological sequence:
   (a) *Fundamentals of Language, Narrative Discourse, Sound Shape of Language, Towards a Philosophy of the Act*
   (b) *Philosophy of the Act, Narrative Discourse, Sound Shape of Language*
   (c) *Narrative Discourse, Fundamentals of Language, Philosophy of the Act, Sound Shape of Language*
   (d) *Sound Shape of Language, Philosophy of the Act, Narrative Discourse, Fundamental of Language.*

   (*Fundamentals of Language* (1956), *Narrative Discourse* (1972), *Sound Shape of Language* (1979), *Towards a Philosophy of the Act* (1993))

711. *Language of Fiction* (1966) was written by
   (a) Henry James
   (b) David Lodge
   (c) E.M. Forster
   (d) V. Propp

712. *Elements of Semiology* (1964) was written by?
   (a) C.S. Peirce
   (b) Roland Barthes
   (c) Jacques Derrida
   (d) Charles Morris

713. *Mythologies* (1957) was written by
   (a) Paul de Man
   (b) Levi-Strauss
   (c) C.L. Jung
   (d) Roland Barthes

714. *Writing Zero Degree* (1953) is written by

(a) Roland Barthes
(b) Jacques Derrida
(c) Hillis Miller
(d) Michael Foucault

715. Who, among the following, said, "The Man is the Style himself"?
(a) Fancis Bacon
(b) Joseph Addison
(c) John Dryden
(d) Buffon

716. Roland Barthe's *S/Z* is a reading of Balzac's short novella *Sarrasine*. Into how many reading units or segments does he divide it?
(a) 559
(b) 561
(c) 563
(d) 565

717. According to Roland Barthes, each segment in "Sarrasine"—contains never more than
(a) Three meanings
(b) Four meanings
(c) Five meanings
(d) Six meanings

718. Into how many codes has Roland Barthes divided "Sarrasine"?
(a) Two
(b) Three
(c) Four
(d) Five

(Roland Barthes uses five codes. These are 1. Hermeunic 2. Semic 3. Symbolic 4. Proairetic 5. Cultural. The *proairetic* corresponds to the sequences of actions or behavioural patterns; the *hermeneutic*, to the disclosure of truth, the *semic* to descriptions of significant features, the *cultural*, to the quotations from scientific or cultural models, the *symbolic*, to the symbolic architecture of language.)

719. Levi-Strauss argued that the "savage" had the same structure as the civilized mind and human characteristics are the same everywhere.

Which literary theory does the sentence suggest?
(a) Structuralism
(b) Formalism
(c) Poststructuralism
(d) Archetypal

720. *The Savage Mind* (1962) was written by
(a) Claude Levi-Strauss
(b) Northrop Frye
(c) Roland Barthes
(d) Julia Kristeva

**ANSWERS**

| | | | | | |
|---|---|---|---|---|---|
| 583. (a) | 584. (b) | 585. (d) | 586. (c) | 587. (d) | 588. (c) |
| 589. (d) | 590. (d) | 591. (b) | 592. (d) | 593. (c) | 594. (b) |
| 595. (d) | 596. (a) | 597. (c) | 598. (c) | 599. (b) | 600. (d) |
| 601. (a) | 602. (d) | 603. (d) | 604. (b) | 605. (c) | 606. (c) |
| 607. (b) | 608. (b) | 609. (a) | 610. (b) | 611. (d) | 612. (c) |
| 613. (b) | 614. (a) | 615. (c) | 616. (d) | 617. (a) | 618. (b) |
| 619. (b) | 620. (d) | 621. (c) | 622. (a) | 623. (d) | 624. (c) |

| | | | | | |
|---|---|---|---|---|---|
| 625. (c) | 626. (d) | 627. (a) | 628. (d) | 629. (b) | 630. (b) |
| 631. (c) | 632. (b) | 633. (d) | 634. (d) | 635. (a) | 636. (b) |
| 637. (c) | 638. (b) | 639. (a) | 640. (c) | 641. (d) | 642. (d) |
| 643. (b) | 644. (c) | 645. (d) | 646. (b) | 647. (c) | 648. (a) |
| 649. (d) | 650. (b) | 651. (c) | 652. (b) | 653. (d) | 654. (d) |
| 655. (b) | 656. (c) | 657. (a) | 658. (b) | 659. (c) | 660. (d) |
| 661. (a) | 662. (b) | 663. (d) | 664. (d) | 665. (d) | 666. (d) |
| 667. (d) | 668. (d) | 669. (a) | 670. (d) | 671. (b) | 672. (c) |
| 673. (b) | 674. (c) | 675. (a) | 676. (d) | 677. (d) | 678. (b) |
| 679. (a) | 680. (b) | 681. (d) | 682. (c) | 683. (c) | 684. (b) |
| 685. (d) | 686. (d) | 687. (b) | 688. (b) | 689. (a) | 690. (d) |
| 691. (c) | 692. (a) | 693. (c) | 694. (c) | 695. (c) | 696. (b) |
| 697. (a) | 698. (b) | 699. (a) | 700. (a) | 701. (a) | 702. (c) |
| 703. (c) | 704. (d) | 705. (d) | 706. (a) | 707. (b) | 708. (c) |
| 709. (b) | 710. (a) | 711. (b) | 712. (b) | 713. (d) | 714. (a) |
| 715. (d) | 716. (b) | 717. (b) | 718. (d) | 719. (a) | 720. (a) |

## (IX) POSTSTRUCTURALISM

721. Poststructuralists see all knowledge as
    (a) Illogical
    (b) Textual
    (c) Arbitrary
    (d) Unrealistic

722. Poststructuralists rejected Saussure's concepts of
    (a) Signifiers and signified
    (b) The centrality of structure
    (c) Binary oppositions
    (d) Both (b) and (c)

723. In the construction of human subjectivity, poststructuralists laid emphasis on
    (a) Operations of power
    (b) Ideology
    (c) Knowledge
    (d) Both (a) and (b)

724. Who said, "There are no facts, but interpretations"?
    (a) Roland Barthes
    (b) Michel Foucault
    (c) Nietzsche
    (d) Derrida

725. While structuralism derives from linguistics, poststructuralism derives from
    (a) Philosophy
    (b) Science
    (c) Geography
    (d) History

726. For poststructuralists meanings are
    (a) Stale
    (b) Fluid
    (c) Unchangeable
    (d) fixed

727. *The Death of the Author* was written by
    (a) Jacques Derrida
    (b) Michael Foucault

(c) Ronald Barthes
(d) Felix Guattari

728. Roland Barthes' essay *The Death of the Author* was published in
(a) 1957
(b) 1960
(c) 1965
(d) 1968

729. The essay *From Work to Text* was written by
(a) Paul de Man
(b) Hillis Miller
(c) Michel Foucault
(d) Roland Barthes

(Roland Barthes has made the distinction between 'work' and 'text' in his essay *From Work to Text* (1971). According to M.A.R. Habib, "The object of linguistic and literary studies used to be stable, fixed object, enclosed within one discipline. But now that is fluid, has many levels of meaning, and ranges across disciplinary boundaries. The former is the 'work' and the latter is the 'text'". "Work" and "Text" are two ways in which the literary object might be viewed. Traditionally, a "work" is associated with certain material qualities, occupying a bookshelf, having certain dimension and tangibility. A text, on the other hand, resists easy classification according to traditional categories. A "work" has two levels of meaning : literal and concealed. A "text", on the other hand, is "engaged in a deferral of meaning, a play of signification and intertextuality without origin or destination. The "work" is a commodity—an object of consumption whereas a 'text' is an object of production". ("Readerly/Writerly Texts").)

730. Roland Barthes' essay *From Work to Text* was published in
(a) 1969
(b) 1970
(c) 1971
(d) 1973

731. Who said, "It is language that speaks, not the author"?
(a) Mallarme
(b) Lacan
(c) Foucault
(d) Kristeva

732. Who says that a text's unity "lies not in its origin, but in its destination"?
(a) Lacan
(b) Roland Barthes
(c) Derrida
(d) Flaubert

733. Who said, "Linguistically, the author is never more than the instance writing, just as I nothing other than the instance saying I : language knows a 'subject', not a person..."?
(a) Roland Barthes
(b) Michel Foucault
(c) Julia Kristeva
(d) Derrida

(This is from Roland Barthes' essay *Death of the Author*.)

734. *The Pleasure of the Text* (1973) was written by
(a) Roland Barthes
(b) Michel Foucault
(c) Jacques Derrida
(d) Julia Kristeva

735. Who, among the following, wrote *S/Z*?
(a) Gilles Deleuze
(b) Julia Kristeva
(c) Roland Barthes
(d) Michel Foucault

(Roland Barthes' *S/Z* marks the transition between Barthes' earlier structuralism and his later poststructuralism)

736. Roland Barthes *S/Z* was published in
   (a) 1971
   (b) 1970
   (c) 1975
   (d) 1977

737. In his story Balzac, describing a Castrato disguised as a woman, writes the following: "Who is speaking thus? Is it the hero of the story bent on remaining ignorant of the Castrato hidden beneath the woman? Is it Balzac the individual, furnished by his personal experience with a philosophy of woman? It is Balzac the author professing 'literary' ideas on feminity? Is it universal wisdom? Romantic psychology? We shall never know, for the good reason that writing is the destruction of every voice, of every point of origin. Identity is lost, starting with the very identity of the body writing".

   The paragraph points to
   (a) Structuralism
   (b) Poststructuralism
   (c) Formalism
   (d) Expressionism

738. *Image : Music : Text* was written by
   (a) Julia Kristeva
   (b) Michel Foucault
   (c) Roland Barthes
   (d) None of the above

739. English translation of Roland Barthes *Image : Music : Text* appeared in
   (a) 1975
   (b) 1977
   (c) 1979
   (d) 1981

740. *Roland Barthes by Roland Barthes* was published in
   (a) 1973
   (b) 1975
   (c) 1977
   (d) 1978

741. Who wrote *A Lover's Discourse* (1977)?
   (a) Julia Kristeva
   (b) Charles Baudelaire
   (c) Roland Barthes
   (d) Bataille

742. Poststructuralists call into question the coherence of discourse or the capacity for language to communicate.

   True/False

743. In *S/Z* Barthes advocates a productive reading of the text and says "Writerly is our value" because the goal of a literary work is to make the reader no longer a consumer, but a producer of the text.

   These lines point to
   (a) Surrealism
   (b) Formalism
   (c) Structuralism
   (d) Poststructuralism

744. According to Ronald Barthes, the text never conveys a single meaning but is subject to multiple interpretations, not only because the readers are different, but primarily because of the instability of the linguistic sign.

   Which of the following theories do these lines suggest?
   (a) Historicism
   (b) Formalism
   (c) Poststructuralism
   (d) Formalism

745. Barthes distinguishes the 'text' from the 'work' as fluid, with any levels of meaning, ranging across disciplinary boundaries,

something that is held in "intertextuality" in the network of signifiers.

These lines suggest

(a) Structuralism
(b) Formalism
(c) Psychoanalytical criticism
(d) Poststructuralism

746. It is difficult to know what a sign 'originally' means because its context is always different. I can never be fully present to you through what I say or write because the meaning of the signs is always in a flux. I can also never have a pure meaning or intention as I am made up of language.

These lines suggest one of the following theories

(a) Historicism
(b) Structuralism
(c) Poststructuralism
(d) Formalism

747. Poststructuralism divides the

(a) sign from the signifier.
(b) signifier from the signified.
(c) signified from the referent.
(d) None of the above.

748. Arrange the following in chronological order:

(a) *Course in General Linguistics, The Death of the Author, S/Z, Literary Theory: A Very Short Introduction*
(b) *The Death of the Author, Literary Theory: A Very Short Introduction, S/Z, Course in General Linguistics*
(c) *Literary Theory: A Very Short Introduction, Course in General Linguistics, S/Z, The Death of the Author*
(d) *S/Z, Literary Theory: A Very Short Introduction, The Death of the Author, Course in General Linguistics*

(*Course in General Linguistics* (1916); *The Death of the Author* (1968); *S/Z* (1970); *Literary Theory : A Very Short Introduction* (1991).)

749. Who, among the following, said, "we are forced to accept the notion of the incessant sliding of the signified under the signifier"?

(a) Roland Barthes
(b) Jacques Lacan
(c) Michel Foucault
(d) Saussure

750. Poststructuralism holds that language can no longer guarantee any empirically certifiable reality.

True/False

751. For Lacan, the self is constituted by

(a) Society
(b) Culture
(c) Language
(d) Ideology

752. Why is the term post-structuralism preferred by most scholars to postmodernism with which it was often used interchangeably?

(a) The term underlines that post-structuralism is not confined to a particular postmodern period and is a position which shares more with structuralism than with its opponents, as scholar Waever argues.
(b) Postmodernism connotes 'anti-modernism' and poststructural theory is concerned with modern events.
(c) International scholars were too overtly critical of 'postmodernism' theories.
(d) None of the above.

753. Who said that writing creates "an opening where the writing subject endlessly disappears"?

(a) Roland Barthes
(b) Jacques Derrida

(c) Michel Foucault
(d) Paul de Man

754. Who says that the subject is "the slave of the language"?
(a) Jacques Derrida
(b) Jacques Lacan
(c) Saussure
(d) Roland Barthes

(In Lacan's view, it is language which governs and constitutes the subject.)

755. Who wrote *Revolution in Language* (1974)?
(a) Roman Jakobson
(b) Todorov
(c) Julia Kristeva
(d) Jacques Lacan

756. Who coined the term 'intertexuality'?
(a) Helen Cixous
(b) Roland Barthes
(c) Michel Foucault
(d) Julia Kristeva

('Intertextuality' is the condition of interconnectedness among texts, or the concept that any text is an amalgam of others, either because it exhibits signs of influence or because its language inevitably contains common points of reference with other texts through such things as illusion, quotation, genre, style, and even revisions. T.S. Eliot's *The Waste Land* is a good example of intertextuality)

757. *Desire in Language: A Semiotic Approach to Literature and Art* was written by
(a) Roland Barthes
(b) C.S. Peirce
(c) Julia Kristeva
(d) Michel Foucault

758. Kristeva's *Desire in Language : A Semiotic Approach to Literature and Art* was published in
(a) 1969
(b) 1970
(c) 1971
(d) 1973

(It was translated into English in 1980)

759. Who coined the term 'semanalysis'?
(a) Roland Barthes
(b) Julia Kristeva
(c) Michel Foucault
(d) Hillis Miller

(Julia Kristeva describes semanalysis as a combination of 'semiology' from Saussure and 'psychoanalysis' from Freud).

760. According to poststructuralists, language is a stable system.

True/False

761. Poststructuralists believe that signified is altered by the various chains of signifiers in which it is entangled.

True/False

762. *Madness and Civilization* (1965) was written by
(a) Roland Barthes
(b) Julia Kristeva
(c) Michel Foucault
(d) Hillis Miller

763. The full title of *Madness and civilization* is
(a) *A History of Insanity*
(b) *Madness without Reason*
(c) *A History of Insanity in the Age of Reason*
(d) *Madness in the Age of Reason*

764. *The Birth of the Clinic : An Archeology of Medical Perception* was written by
(a) Freud
(b) C.L. Jung
(c) Michel Foucault
(d) Roland Barthes

765. *The Birth of Clinic* was written in
(a) 1963
(b) 1965
(c) 1967
(d) 1968

766. Foucault's *The Order of Things : An Archeology of the Human Sciences* was published in
(a) 1960
(b) 1966
(c) 1968
(d) 1969

767. *The Archeology of Knowledge* was written by
(a) Michel Foucault
(b) Jacques Derrida
(c) Julia Kristeva
(d) Roland Barthes

768. *The Archeology of Knowledge* was published in
(a) 1963
(b) 1965
(c) 1969
(d) 1971

(The English version was published in 1972)

769. *Discipline and Punish : The Birth of the Prison* was written by
(a) Jean Baudillard
(b) Michel Foucault
(c) Gilles Deleuze
(d) Roland Barthes

770. *Discipline and Punish* was published in
(a) 1970
(b) 1972
(c) 1975
(d) 1978

(The English version was published in 1977)

771. *The History of Sexuality, Vol I : An Introduction* was written by
(a) Freud
(b) C.L. Jung
(c) Adler
(d) Michel Foucault

772. *The History of Sexuality* was published in
(a) 1976
(b) 1978
(c) 1979
(d) 1980

(The English version was published in 1977)

**Some Other Books by Michel Foucault**

1. *Mental Illness and Psychology* (1954 trans 1976) 2. *Death and the Labyninth : The World of Raymond Roussel* (1963, trans 1986) 3. *This is not a Pipe* (1973, trans. 1981) 4. *Language, Counter Memory, Practice : Selected Essays and Interviews* (trans 1977) 5. *The Use of Pleasure, Vol. 2 of the History of Sexuality* (1984, trans 1985) 6. *The Care of the Self, Vol. 3 of the History of Sexuality* (1984, trans 1986)

773. In whose view 'knowledge is power'?
(a) Antonio Gramsci
(b) Michel Foucault
(c) Roland Barthes
(d) Althousser

774. *Difference and Repetition* (1968) was written by
(a) Michel Foucault
(b) Felix Guattari
(c) Gilles Deleuze
(d) Jacques Derrida

775. *Logic of Sense* was written by
(a) Paul de Man
(b) Gilles Deleuze

(c) Michel Foucault
(d) Julia Kristeva

776. *Logic of Sense* was published in
(a) 1962
(b) 1968
(c) 1969
(d) 1971

777. The essay *What is an Author* (1969) is written by
(a) Michel Foucault
(b) Ronald Barthes
(c) Guattari
(d) Derrida

778. Who, among the following, said that "god and man died a common death"?
(a) Roland Barthes
(b) Michel Foucault
(c) Derrida
(d) Nietzsche

779. Who said that new methods of power operate not "by right but technique, not by law but by normalization, not by punishment but by control"?
(a) Roland Barthes
(b) Jacques Derrida
(c) Michel Foucault
(d) Hillis Miller

780. Who said that a text is "a multi-dimensional space in which as variety of writings, none of them original, blend and clash. The text is a tissue of quotations drawn from immeasurable centres of culture"?
(a) Jacques Derrida
(b) Roland Barthes
(c) Jacques Lacan
(d) Michel Foucault

781. Who said, "Poststructuralism was a product of that blend of euphoria and disillusionment, liberation and dissipation, carnival and catastrophe, which was 1968"?
(a) Roland Barthes
(b) Jonathan Culler
(c) Antonio Gramsci
(d) Terry Eagleton

782. *Does 'Text' Exist* (1985) was written by
(a) Jean Bellemin-Noel
(b) Louis Hay
(c) Michael Gordon
(d) Mary Visick

(The view of the Genetic critics is that many texts exist within any text. Its search for an open-ended aesthetic, or logic, of the possibilities of writing clearly have much in common with the poststructuralists version of texts as fields of free-playing signifiers)

783. Gerard Genette's *Narrative Discourse : An Essay in Method* was published in
(a) 1978
(b) 1981
(c) 1985
(d) 1972

784. *The Architect : An Introduction* (1979, trans 1992) was written by
(a) Louis Hay
(b) Gerard Genette
(c) Roland Barthes
(d) David Ferrer

785. *Paratexts: Thresholders of Interpretation*" (1987, trans 1997), *Fiction and Diction* (1990, trans 1993) and *The Work of Art* (1994-97) were written by
(a) Gerard Genette
(b) R.D. Genette
(c) Louis Hay
(d) D. Ferrer

(Genette defines paratexts as those things in a published work that accompany the text, things such as the author's name, the title, preface or introduction, or illustrations. Paratextuality is the study of the way each literary work is enveloped by smaller texts, subtitles, etc. The concept of paratext is closely related to the concept of hypotext, which is the earlier text that serves as a source for the current text.)

786. Who said, "True criticism is creation, a recasting of the work of art, more conscious than the original and more transparent"?
   (a) Louis Hay
   (b) Marcel Raymond
   (c) Roland Barthes
   (d) G. Genette

787. According to Michael Foucault,
   (a) discourses constitute authority and knowledge.
   (b) discourses are irrelevant.
   (c) poststructuralists use the term to mean that the link between knowledge and power is mutually constitutive.
   (d) 'The State' is the most important element in international politics.

788. 'Anti-Foundationalism' holds that
   (a) all truth claims can be judged true or false, usually against empirical facts.
   (b) every theory poses different questions and, therefore, what counts as 'fact' or ' truth' differs in every case.
   (c) casual statements about the relationship between dependent facts and independent variables can be made.
   (d) None of the above.

## ANSWERS

| | | | | | |
|---|---|---|---|---|---|
| 721. (b) | 722. (d) | 723. (d) | 724. (c) | 725. (a) | 726. (b) |
| 727. (c) | 728. (d) | 729. (d) | 730. (c) | 731. (a) | 732. (b) |
| 733. (a) | 734. (a) | 735. (c) | 736. (b) | 737. (b) | 738. (c) |
| 739. (a) | 740. (b) | 741. (c) | 742. (T) | 743. (d) | 744. (c) |
| 745. (d) | 746. (c) | 747. (b) | 748. (a) | 749. (b) | 750. (T) |
| 751. (c) | 752. (a) | 753. (c) | 754. (b) | 755. (c) | 756. (d) |
| 757. (c) | 758. (a) | 759. (b) | 760. (F) | 761. (T) | 762. (c) |
| 763. (c) | 764. (c) | 765. (a) | 766. (b) | 767. (a) | 768. (c) |
| 769. (b) | 770. (c) | 771. (d) | 772. (a) | 773. (b) | 774. (c) |
| 775. (b) | 776. (c) | 777. (a) | 778. (b) | 779. (c) | 780. (b) |
| 781. (d) | 782. (b) | 783. (d) | 784. (a) | 785. (a) | 786. (b) |
| 787. (a) | 788. (b) | | | | |

## (X) DECONSTRUCTION

'Differance' is an important concept in Derrida. According to Derrida, there is no fixed meaning in a text. The text is described as always in a state of change providing only provisional meanings. Meaning can point to an indefinite number of other meanings. For example, 'bed' signifies *a place of sleeping, a garden plot, a layer of oysters, channel of a river, a stratum.* This process continues endlessly, as the signifiers lead a chameleon—like existence, changing their colours with each new context. The result is that the meaning is always deferred. Derrida coined the word 'differance' thereby both the constant 'deferral' (to defer) to signifiers and the 'difference' (to differ) that distinguishes the various signifiers in the system from each other. So there is no stable, fixed or final meaning, because it remains suspended between 'defer' and 'differ' without settling into one or the other.

789. Who coined the term 'deconstruction'?
   (a) Paul de Man
   (b) Derrida
   (c) Hillis Miller
   (d) Harold Bloom

790. "Structure, Sign and Play in the Discourse of the Human Sciences" was written by
   (a) Jacques Derrida
   (b) Roland Barthes
   (c) Hillis Miller
   (d) Paul de Man

   ("Structure, Sign and Play in the Discourse of the Human Sciences" was a lecture delivered at John Hopkins University, U.S.A. in 1966 by Jacques Derrida. This gave birth to what is known as 'Deconstruction'.)

791. One of the following critical approaches assumes that language does not refer to any external reality. It can assert several, contradictory interpretations of one text
   (a) Formalist Criticism
   (b) Structuralism
   (c) Deconstruction
   (d) Mimetic Criticism

792. What is known as the "Yale School of Critics" is associated with
   (a) Structuralism
   (b) Deconstruction
   (c) Formalism
   (d) Historicism

793. One of the following does not belong to the "Yale School of Critics" :
   (a) J. Hillis Miller
   (b) Paul de Man
   (c) Geoffery Hartman
   (d) Ronald Crane

794. The term 'alterity' means
   (a) Alternative
   (b) Otherness
   (c) Uniqueness
   (d) Loneliness

795. In American Deconstruction (Yale School of Critics), why does literary criticism becomes "ironic, uneasy business"? This is because
   (a) it lays bare the permanence of meaning.
   (b) the physicality of meaning.
   (c) the temporality of meaning.
   (d) the illusioriness of meaning.

796. This literary theory of criticism shows how texts come to embarrass their own ruling systems of logic.
   (a) Deconstruction
   (b) Formalism

(c) Structuralism
(d) Psychoanalytical

797. What, according to Terry Eagleton, is the oldest form of criticism?
(a) Deconstruction
(b) Rhetoric
(c) Historicism
(d) Formalism

798. The rejection of 'universalism' is a mark of
(a) Structuralism
(b) New Historicism
(c) Deconstruction/Poststructuralism
(d) Formalism

799. *The Allegories of Reading* (1973) was written by
(a) Paul de Man
(b) Hillis Miller
(c) Harold Bloom
(d) Hartman

800. *Blindness and Insight* (1971) was written by
(a) Hillis Miller
(b) Paul de Man
(c) Hartman
(d) Harold Bloom

801. Who, among the following, wrote *A Map of Misreading* (1975)?
(a) Jacques Derrida
(b) Julia Kristeva
(c) Harold Bloom
(d) Paul de Man

802. *The Ethics of Reading* (1987) was written by
(a) Hillis Miller
(b) G. Hartman
(c) Paul de Man
(d) Derrida

803. Who, among the following, wrote *The Fate of Reading*?
(a) G. Hartman
(b) Paul de Man
(c) Harold Bloom
(d) H. Miller

804. Hartman's *The Fate of Reading* was published in
(a) 1971
(b) 1973
(c) 1975
(d) 1977

805. Who wrote *Criticism in the Wilderness* (1980)?
(a) Elaine Showalter
(b) G. Hartman
(c) Hillis Miller
(d) H. Bloom

806. *The Anxiety of Influence* (1973) was written by
(a) Harold Bloom
(b) Paul de Man
(c) J. Hillis Miller
(d) G. Hartman

**Some other works by Harold Bloom**

1. *Ruin and the Sacred Truths* (1989) 2. *The Book of J* (1991) 3. *The American Religion : The Emergence of Post-Christian Nation* (1992) 4. *The Western Canon : The Books and Schools of the Ages* (1994) 5. *Shakespeare : The Invention of the Human* (1999) 6. *How to Read and Why* (2000) 7. *Genius : A Mosaic of One Hundred Exemplary Creative Minds* (2002) 8. *Hamlet : Poem Unlimited* (2003)

807. *Of Grammatology* was written by
(a) Jacques Derrida
(b) Hartman
(c) Paul de Man
(d) Harold Bloom

808. Jacques Derrida's *Of Grammatology* was published in

(a) 1965
(b) 1967
(c) 1968
(d) 1969

(The English version appeared in 1998. It was translated by Gyatari Spivak.)

809. Who, among the following, wrote *Margins of Philosophy*?
(a) Paul de Man
(b) Hartman
(c) Derrida
(d) Harold Bloom

810. *Margins of Philosophy* was published in
(a) 1972
(b) 1973
(c) 1975
(d) 1977

(The English version appeared in 1982)

811. Who, among the following, wrote *Writing and Difference*?
(a) Hartman
(b) Derrida
(c) Bloom
(d) Paul de Man

812. Derrida's *Writing and Difference* was published in
(a) 1963
(b) 1965
(c) 1967
(d) 1968

(It was translated into English in 1978)

813. Who wrote *Resistances of Psychoanalysis*?
(a) Hartman
(b) Bloom
(c) Jacques Lacan
(d) Jacques Derrida

814. *Ristances of Psychoanalysis* was published in
(a) 1994
(b) 1996
(c) 1998
(d) 1999

(The English version appeared in 1998)

815. *Dissemination* was written by
(a) Jacques Derrida
(b) Julia Kristeva
(c) Harold Bloom
(d) Hillis Miller

816. *Dissemination* was published in
(a) 1970
(b) 1972
(c) 1973
(d) 1975

(The English version appeared in 1981)

817. Who wrote *Speech and Phenomena* (1967)
(a) Jacques Derrida
(b) Roman Jakobson
(c) C.S. Peirce
(d) J.L. Austin

(The English version appeared in 1973)

818. Who coined the term 'Phallogocentrism'?
(a) Julia Kristeva
(b) Nietzsche
(c) Jacques Derrida
(d) Paul de Man

('Phallogocentrism' is a combination of 'phallocentrism' and 'logocentrism')

819. According to Derrida, Western philosophy is founded on the theory of
(a) Absence
(b) Presence
(c) Arbitrariness
(d) Difference

820. Derrida calls Western Philosophy
(a) Logocentric
(b) Phonocentric
(c) Egocentric
(d) Both (a) and (b)

821. Which of the following books written by Derrida were published in 1967?
   (a) *Writing and Difference*; *Speech and Phonemen.*
   (b) *Of Grammatology*, *Dissemination*
   (c) *Dissemination*, *Speech and Phenomenon*, *Writing and Difference*
   (d) *Dissemination*, *Speech and Phenomena*

822. In which book of Derrida has relation between speech and writing been discussed?
   (a) *Speech and Phenomena*
   (b) *Of Grammatology*
   (c) *Margins of Philosophy*
   (d) *Writing and Difference*

823. Deconstruction always reveals difference within unity.
   True/False

824. Harold Bloom's theory of literary influence as mediated through 'anxiety' drew upon:
   (a) Carl Jung's 'collective unconscious'
   (b) Freud's 'unconscious'
   (c) Freud's 'Oedipus Complex'
   (d) Lacan 'symbolic order'

825. Who, among the following, said that "the centre in a text is not fixed but functional"?
   (a) Roland Barthes
   (b) Jacques Derrida
   (c) Julia Kristeva
   (d) Paul de Man

826. What is the name given by Derrida to, what he calls, an endless substitution of one signifier for another?
   (a) Signified
   (b) Signifier
   (c) Metaphor
   (d) Metonymy

827. What phrase does Derrida use for what we call "binary oppositions"?
   (a) Transcendental signified
   (b) Metaphysics of presence
   (c) Logo-centrism
   (d) Violent hierarchy

828. The most significant opposition treated by Derrida is between
   (a) Nature and culture
   (b) Intellect and sense
   (c) Speech and writing
   (d) Centre and margin

829. The essay *Plato's Pharmacy* is written by
   (a) Aristotle
   (b) Foucault
   (c) Lacan
   (d) Derrida

830. J. Hillis Miller's *The Disappearance of God* was published in
   (a) 1961
   (b) 1963
   (c) 1965
   (d) 1959

**Some Other Works by J. Hillis Miller**

1. *Charles Dickens : The World of His Novels* (1958) 2. *Poets of Reality* (1965) 3. *Fiction and Repetition* (1982) 4. *The Linguistic Moment* (1985) 5. *Versions of Pygmalion* (1990)

831. Who coined the term "School of Resentment"?
   (a) Harold Bloom
   (b) Paul de Man
   (c) Julia Kristeva
   (d) Foucault

   (Harold Bloom coined this term to describe related schools of literary criticism which have gained prominence in academia since the 1970s and which Bloom contends are preoccupied with politics and social activism at the expense of aesthetic values.

The 'School of Resentment' is usually defined as scholars who wish to enlarge the Western Canon by adding more minority, political and/ or female authors regardless of aesthetic merit of their writings and/or who argue that the canon promotes sexist, racist or otherwise biased values. Bloom contends that the 'School of Resentment' threatens the nature of the canon and may lead to its eventual demise. The term occurs in Bloom's book *The Western Canon : The Books and School of the Ages.*)

832. Who coined the term 'logocentrism'?
 (a) Jacques Derrida
 (b) Jacques Lacan
 (c) Ludwig Klages
 (d) Roland Barthes

 (Ludwig Klages was a German philosopher and he coined this term in the 1920s.)

833. Who popularized the term 'logocentricism'?
 (a) Jacques Derrida
 (b) Julia Kristeva
 (c) Micheal Foucault
 (d) Paul de Man

 (According Derrida, the entire Western tradition of thought right from Plato favours *speech* over *writing*. He calls this logocentrism. The term comes from *logos*, the Greek word that means *word*, *truth*, *reason* and *law*. The scholar C.H. Dodd observes that the root of the Hebrew equivalent for *logos* means 'to speak', and that this word is used for God's self-revelation. A further sense of 'logos' in the fourth Gospel is the "word of God", his self-revelation to man. It denotes the central truth revealed to man by God. For example, in the New Testament, the Gospel of St. John declares : "In the beginning was the Word/And the Word was with God/And the Word was God".)

834. According to Derrida, 'logocentricism' represents Western Culture's desire for a language whose authority is guaranteed by
 (a) Scholars
 (b) Philosophers
 (c) Linguists
 (d) A divine, transcendental signified

 (In Western philosophy, other names have stood for the *transcendental signified*—names such as the Ideal, the World Spirit, Mind, the Divine Will, Consciousness, etc. These inner principles and the words which express them are central in Western thought and involve a *metaphysics of presence*. It is the notion that there is a transcendental signified, the God-Word that underlies all philosophic talk and guarantees its meaning. Its like when, I am talking with somebody now, it seems as if my talking with you is a present, direct expression of my thoughts, my emotions, even my spirit. My talk is how I *present* my thoughts and feelings to him. My words come directly from myself. I am always *present* to him when I am speaking and my *presence* helps him understand me. This is not so with writing.)

835. Who has defined deconstruction as "a process which is often referred to 'as reading against the grain' or 'reading the text against itself', with the purpose of 'knowing the text as it cannot know itself"?
 (a) Barbara Johnson
 (b) Terry Eagleton
 (c) Jonathan Culler
 (d) Paul de Man

836. A text "can be read as saying something quite different from what it appears to be saying, and that it may be read as carrying a plurality of significance or as saying many different things which are fundamentally at variance with,

contradictory to and subversive of what may be (or may have been) seen by criticism as a single, stable 'meaning'. Thus, a text may 'betray' itself".

Which literary theory do these lines suggest?
(a) Poststructuralism
(b) Psychoanalytical Criticism
(c) Marxist Criticism
(d) Deconstruction

837. Who coined the term 'differance'?
(a) Jacques Derrida
(b) Julia Kristeva
(c) Micheal Foucault
(d) Paul de Man

838. Who said, "There is nothing outside the text"?
(a) Jacques Derrida
(b) Roland Barthes
(c) Julia Kristeva
(d) Jacques Lacan

(The most–often quoted statement of Derrida occurs in *Of Grammatology*. It means that "there is no such a thing as out-of-the-text". In other words, the context is an integral part of the text. There is no "truth" or "reality" which stands outside language. Reality is constructed by language. So languge is all embracing. According to M.A.R. Habib, "textuality governs all interpretive operations. For example, there is no history outside of language or textuality: history itself is a linguistic and textual construct.")

839. The term 'aporia' is associated with
(a) Psychoanalytical criticism
(b) Deconstruction
(c) Marxist Criticism
(d) Russian Formalism

(According to Ross Murfin and Supriya M. Ray, 'Aporia' is a "term borrowed from logic for use in literary criticism, most frequently in *deconstruction*, to indicate an interpretative dilemma or impasse involving some *textual* contradiction that readers—or seems to render—meaning *undecidable.* Deconstructors often speak of the aporic 'juncture' or 'moment' as the point at which the reader lacks the justification to choose or cannot choose between two meanings.

*Aporia* can also be used more generally to refer to any indecision or doubt expressed by the speaker of a work, whether actual or voiced with *ironic* intent.")

## ANSWERS

| | | | | | |
|---|---|---|---|---|---|
| 789. (b) | 790. (a) | 791. (c) | 792. (b) | 793. (d) | 794. (b) |
| 795. (d) | 796. (a) | 797. (b) | 798. (c) | 799. (a) | 800. (b) |
| 801. (c) | 802. (a) | 803. (a) | 804. (c) | 805. (b) | 806. (a) |
| 807. (a) | 808. (b) | 809. (c) | 810. (a) | 811. (b) | 812. (c) |
| 813. (d) | 814. (b) | 815. (a) | 816. (b) | 817. (a) | 818. (c) |
| 819. (b) | 820. (d) | 821. (c) | 822. (b) | 823. (T) | 824. (c) |
| 825. (b) | 826. (c) | 827. (d) | 828. (c) | 829. (d) | 830. (b) |
| 831. (a) | 832. (c) | 833. (a) | 834. (d) | 835. (b) | 836. (d) |
| 837. (a) | 838. (a) | 839. (b) | | | |

## (XI) MARXIST CRITICISM

840. Marxist Criticism is concerned with
 (a) Social meanings of literature
 (b) Political meanings of literature
 (c) Aesthetic meanings of literature
 (d) Both (a) and (b)

841. Language, according to, Marxists is
 (a) a self-sufficient system
 (b) a social practice
 (c) a political practice
 (d) a commodity

842. *Literature and Revolution* (1923) was written by
 (a) Marx
 (b) Engels
 (c) Leon Trotsky
 (d) Bukhanin

843. *Ideology and Ideological State Apparatuses* was written by
 (a) Louis Althusser
 (b) Terry Eagleton
 (c) George Lukacs
 (d) Engels

844. *Culture and Society* 1780-1950 was written by
 (a) Georg Lukacs
 (b) Louis Althusser
 (c) Raymond Williams
 (d) Leon Trostsky

845. Frederic Jameson's *The Political Unconscious* was published in
 (a) 1975
 (b) 1981
 (c) 1982
 (d) 1983

**Some Important Works by Frederic Jameson**

1. *Sartre: The Origins of Style* (1961) 2. *Marxism and Form* (1971) 3. *The Prison House of Language* (1972) 4. *The Political Unconscious : Narrative as a Socially Symbolic Act* (1981) 5. *Postmodernism, or The Cultural Logic of Late Capitalism* (1991) 6. *Signatures of the Visible* (1990) 8. *The Geopolitical Aesthetic* (1992) 9. *The Cultural Turn* (1998)

846. In Marxism, 'base' means
 (a) Lower class
 (b) Middle class
 (c) Foundation
 (d) Primary economic activities

847. In Marxism, 'superstructure' means
 (a) structure built on a structure.
 (b) a skyscraper.
 (c) the cultural aspects of a society (life style, culture, arts, literature, religion, etc.).
 (d) None of the above.

848. Louis Althusser and later Marxists were of the opinion that the cultural realm enjoys a certain degree of autonomy from the economic base.

 True/False

849. Marxism rejects the notion of identity.

 True/False

850. Marxists hold that art should express what is typical about a class.

 True/False

851. Louis Althusser rejected the economic determinism of Classical Marxist thought.

 True/False

852. Who coined the term 'hegemony'?
 (a) Louis Althusser
 (b) Antonio Gramsci
 (c) Terry Eagleton
 (d) Michael Foucault

853. The term 'hegemony' means
(a) the dominant cultural group that determines that culture's ideology.
(b) the cultural background of a society.
(c) rule by aristocracy.
(d) None of the above.

(The term has been made popular by Antonio Gramsci, an Italian Marxist. Gramsci used this term in *Prison Notebooks* (1929-35) to denote the predominance of one social class over others. In 1957, the first English translations of the book appeared in print. According to M.H. Abrams, "a social class achieves a predominant influence and power not by direct and covert means, but by succeeding in making its ideological view of society so persuasive that the subordinate classes unwittingly accept and participate in their oppression".)

854. According to Marxists, the economic base influences the
(a) common people.
(b) middle class.
(c) upper class.
(d) superstructure.

855. According to Gramsci, the dominant classes maintain their power through
(a) Coercion
(b) Consent
(c) Both (a) and (b)
(d) None of the above

856. Louis Althusser's 'overdetermination' means
(a) very much determined.
(b) determined more than others.
(c) unnecessarily determined.
(d) a range of different social forces that could result in a single overdetermined (having multiple causes) such as a political revolution.

857. What, according to Louis Althusser, are two kinds of state apparatuses?
(a) Repressive
(b) Ideological
(c) Religious
(d) Both (a) and (b)

(Louis Althusser makes a distinction between two kinds of state apparatuses in his essay *Ideology and Ideological State Apparatuses (Notes Towards an Investigation)*. The repressive State apparatuses (RSAs) constitute administrative, political, repressive (army, police, etc.) and the ideological state apparatuses (ISAs) are family, education, religion, culture, etc.)

858. Into how many classes does Antonio Gramsci divide intellectuals?
(a) Two
(b) Three
(c) Four
(d) Five

859. The two classes in which Gramsci divides intellectuals are
(a) organic and materialistic
(b) organic and traditional
(c) traditional and religious
(d) organic and religious

(According to Gramsci, organic intellectuals are those who emerge with new class in history and to which they are, therefore, organically tied (e.g. capital entrepreneur needs a technician, overseer, accountant, etc.). Traditional intellectuals are not concerned with production and distribution as they explain matters in the private domain of ideology—morality, religion, ethics, and also contribute to contemporary politics.)

860. In 'Marxist Criticism' what was the name of the group that had flourished in the 1920s until disbanded by the communist

party, even though their work was not strictly Marxist in spirit?

(a) Bourgeoisie Critics
(b) New Critics
(c) Russian Formalists
(d) Historicists

861. What is the relationship between 'base' and 'superstructure'?

(a) The change in the economic base of society leads to a change in the superstructure.
(b) The change in the superstructure leads to a change in the economic base of society.
(c) Both (a) and (b)
(d) Neither (a) nor (b)

862. What is Antonio Gramsci's view of power?

(a) It comes out of the barrel of a gun.
(b) It is combination of coercion and consent.
(c) It is purely economic.
(d) All of the above.

863. Gramsci shifted the focus of Marxist analyses through which of the following ideas?

(a) Hegemony is a product of the lack of class conflict.
(b) That consent for a particular social and political system was produced and reproduced through the operation of hegemony.
(c) Both (a) and (b).
(d) Neither (a) nor (b).

(Gramsci's notion of 'hegemony' explains how the moral, political, and cultural values of the economically dominant group become dispersed and accepted throughout society.)

864. One of the following does not belong to the Frankfurt School of Criticism?

(a) Theodor Adorno
(b) Max Horkheimer
(c) Herbert Marcuse
(d) Terry Eagleton

865. What are the main concerns of the members of the Frankfurt School?

(a) The social basis and the nature of authoritarianism.
(b) The structure of the family.
(c) The concepts of reason and rationality.
(d) All of the above.

866. Marxists see globalization as

(a) an anomaly in the history of the development of capitalism.
(b) part of long term trends in the development of capitalism.
(c) something to be prevented.
(d) All of the above.

867. Which of the following statements are correct?

Marxists critics

(a) apply the economical/social principles and ideas of Karl Marx to the interpretation of literature.
(b) believe that society is based on a dialectic (or conflict) between employers (capitalists) and employers (workers). The ruling class and workers struggle for economic power.
(c) see the individual as a product of society's value system (the individual is constructed by class and society).
(d) All of the above

868. Which of the following statements are correct?

Marxist critics

(a) believe that the values of capitalism, such as the primacy of the profit and consumerism, infuse all aspects of our society.

(b) think that the beliefs and attitudes, and values of a society form an ideological base, which influences the superstructure of a society, its laws, politics, religion, education, art, literature, film urban development, etc.
(c) believe that the ideological base influences the economic base of society, the way the society produces materials, the economic organization of a group : capitalism, socialism, barter, trade.
(d) All of the above.

869. Marxism has been described as
(a) an economic theory.
(b) a revolutionary theory.
(c) a theory of philosophy, history, society and capitalism.
(d) All of the above.

870. The first collaborative work between Marx and Engels was
(a) *The German Ideology*
(b) *The Holy Family*
(c) *Das Capital*
(d) *Marx and Engels on Literature and Art*

871. Who was the father of Russian Marxism?
(a) Lenin
(b) Stalin
(c) Georgi Plekhanov
(d) Leo Trotsky

872. By whom *Historical Materialism* (1921, trans 1925) was written?
(a) Marx
(b) N.I. Bukharin
(c) Lenin
(d) Trotsky

873. Who has coined the term 'interpellation'?
(a) Louis Althusser
(b) Antonio Gramsci
(c) Georg Lukacs
(d) Roland Barthes

(According to French Marxist critic Louis Althousser, all 'ideology' "hails or interpellates concrete individuals as concrete subjects, by the functioning of the category of the subject". In simple words, it calls upon the individual to take up a position as a person with certain views and values which serve the ultimate interests of the ruling class.)

874. *Jargon of Authenticity* (1973) was written by
(a) Sartre
(b) Marcel Proust
(c) Theodor Adorno
(d) Roland Barthes

875. John Starchey's *Literature and Dialectical Materialism* was published in
(a) 1934
(b) 1936
(c) 1938
(d) 1940

876. Who, among the following, said, "Life is not determined by consciousness, but consciousness by life"?
(a) Engels
(b) Karl Marx
(c) Trotsky
(d) Gramsci

877. *Art and Social Life* written by Georgi Plekhanov was published in
(a) 1910
(b) 1911
(c) 1912
(d) 1914

878. Who said, "Although one can speak of intellectuals, one cannot speak of non-intellectuals, because non-intellectuals do not exist. There is no human activity from which every form of intellectual participation can be excluded"?
(a) Georg Lukacs
(b) Louis Althusser

(c) Lucien Goldman
(d) Antonio Gramci

879. Who, among the following, is the author of *A Note on Literary Criticism* (1936)?
(a) Edmund Wilson
(b) James T. Farrel
(c) Wayne C. Booth
(d) Rene Wellek

(Farrel's book *A Note on Literary Criticism* has a compelling defence of Marxist principles of literary criticism. It liberated a section of the Great Depression's radical intelligentsia from vulgar, over-politicised approaches to cultural criticism. Farrel challenges the leading radical literary critics of the 1930s such as Michael Cold and Graneville Hicks, reconsidering issues including the relative autonomy of literature from society and economics; the role of tradition in literary creation; the role of literature in propaganda; and the nature of aesthetic value. This is a broadside against literary critics aligned with the orthodox communist party.)

880. *History and Class Consciousness* (1923, trans 1971) was written by
(a) Antonio Gramsci
(b) Louis Althussar
(c) Georg Lukacs
(d) Terry Eagleton

881. Who, among the following, wrote *The Making of the English Working Class* (1963)?
(a) E.M. Thompson
(b) Raymond Williams
(c) Richard Haggart
(d) Antonio Gramsci

**Works by Georg Lukacs**

1. *History and Class Consciousness* (1923, trans 1971) 2. *Studies in European Realism* (1950) 3. *The Historical Novel* (1937, trans 1962) 4. *Essays on Realism* (1948) 5. *Realism in Our Time* (1958 trans 1964) 6. *Slozhenitysn* (1964, trans 1970) 7. *The Young Hegel* (1948, trans 1976) 8. *The Destruction of Reason* (1954, trans 1981) 9. *The Process of Democratisation* (1991) 10. *German Realists in Nineteenth Century* (1992) 11. *A Defence of the History and Class Consciousness* (2000)

## ANSWERS

| | | | | | |
|---|---|---|---|---|---|
| 840. (d) | 841. (b) | 842. (b) | 843. (a) | 844. (c) | 845. (b) |
| 846. (d) | 847. (c) | 848. (T) | 849. (T) | 850. (T) | 851. (T) |
| 852. (b) | 853. (a) | 854. (d) | 855. (c) | 856. (d) | 857. (d) |
| 858. (a) | 859. (b) | 860. (c) | 861. (c) | 862. (b) | 863. (b) |
| 864. (d) | 865. (d) | 866. (b) | 867. (d) | 868. (d) | 869. (d) |
| 870. (c) | 871. (c) | 872. (b) | 873. (a) | 874. (c) | 875. (a) |
| 876. (b) | 877. (c) | 878. (d) | 879. (b) | 880. (c) | 881. (a) |

## (XII) PSYCHOANALYTICAL CRITICISM

882. Who coined the term 'psychoanalysis'?
   (a) Sigmund Freud
   (b) Adler
   (c) Carl Jung
   (d) Ernest Jones

883. Who, for the first time, postulated that we bear a form of 'otherness' within ourselves?
   (a) Carl Jung
   (b) Freud
   (c) Marx
   (d) Alfred Adler

884. *Hamlet and Oedipus* (1948) was written by
   (a) Sigmund Freud
   (b) Carl Jung
   (c) Ernest Jones
   (d) Otto Rank

885. Who, among the following, modified Freudian theory of sexuality, rejecting the primacy of the Oedipus Complex?
   (a) Elda Freedom Sharpe
   (b) Ernest Jones
   (c) Marie Bonaparte
   (d) Melaine Kalein

886. In psychoanalytical criticism, the focus is primarily on
   (a) social conditions.
   (b) political conditions.
   (c) religious conditions.
   (d) the individual consciousness of the author or character.

887. A critic argues that in John Milton's *Samson Agonistes*, "the shearing of Samson's locks is symbolic of his castration at the hands of Delilah". What kind of critical approach is this critic using?
   (a) Psychoanalytical approach
   (b) Mimetic approach
   (c) Historical approach
   (d) Formalist approach

888. The term "psychoanalysis" was coined by Freud in
   (a) 1886
   (b) 1888
   (c) 1896
   (d) 1898

889. According to Freud, how many levels of personality are there in man's 'psychological apparatus'?
   (a) Two
   (b) Three
   (c) Four
   (d) Five

   (They are, *id*, *ego*, and *superego*)

890. According to psychoanalytical critics, all texts have
   (a) an explicit account.
   (b) hidden account.
   (c) Both (a) and (b).
   (d) Neither (a) nor (b).

891. According to Freud, the three stages of the libido are
   (a) oral, anal, phallic.
   (b) oral, ego, id.
   (c) anal, phallic, superego.
   (d) oral, superego, anal.

892. The concept of 'collective unconsciousness' is associated with
   (a) Sigmund Freud
   (b) Carl Jung
   (c) James Frazer
   (d) Lacan

893. Carl Jung was a
   (a) British psychiatrist
   (b) French psychiatrist

(c) Canadian psychiatrist
(d) Swiss psychiatrist

894. What is 'id'?
(a) Part of the psyche that controls the impulses.
(b) Part of the psyche that reduces anxiety.
(c) A descripton of innate instinctual needs.
(d) Part of the psyche that controls our morals.

895. According to the psychoanalytical approach, an attempt to integrate values from society and parents is called
(a) Id
(b) The sublimation
(c) The oral stage
(d) The superego

896. Sigmund Freud was the pioneer of which of the following models of psychopathology?
(a) Behaviorist
(b) Cognitive
(c) Psychodynamic
(d) Humanistic

897. Which one of the following is an example of repression?
(a) Stopping yourself from behaving the way you want to.
(b) Suppressing the current thoughts that cause anxiety.
(c) Suppressing natural instincts.
(d) All of the above.

898. Carl Jung believed that the 'collective unconsciousness' was
(a) Primordial
(b) Universal
(c) Both (a) and (b)
(d) Neither (a) nor (b)

899. According to critics, many of Sigmund Freud's ideas concern aspects of
(a) Death
(b) Sexuality
(c) Conservation
(d) Madness

900. Which one is essentially a Freudian Concept?
(a) Archetype
(b) The uncanny
(c) The absurd
(d) The imaginary

901. At what age, according to Freud, does the Oedipus Complex develop?
(a) Three
(b) Four
(c) Five
(d) Six

902. When a girl is drawn to her father, in Freudianism, it is
(a) Oedipus Complex
(b) Electra Complex
(c) Narcissism
(d) Thanatos

("Electra Complex" is a term coined by Carl Jung in 1913. It occurs in the phallic stage when a girl has a psychological Competition with the mother for the possession of father. As a psychoanalytical metaphor for daughter-mother psychosexual conflict. The Electra Complex derives from 5th century B.C. Greek mythological Character Electra (on which Sophocles' tragedy "Electra" is based) who plotted matricidal revenge with Orestes, her brother, against Clytemnestra, their mother and Aegisthus, their step-father, for their murder of Agamemnon, their father)

903. Who, among the following, wrote the *Psychology of the Unconscious* (1916)?
(a) Freud
(b) Jung

(c) Adler
(d) Ernest Jones

904. What, according to Freud, are the sources of our suffering?
(a) Our bodies
(b) The external world
(c) Our relationship with others
(d) All of the above

905. Freud's psychoanalytic literary criticism takes into account the author's
(a) Historical period
(b) Psychology
(c) Biography
(d) Both (b) and (c)

906. In the light of Freud's psychoanalytical criticism, T.S. Eliot's poem "The Love Song of J. Alfred Prufrock" might be analysed in terms of
(a) the history of Eliot's own attitudes towards women.
(b) his childhood relationship with his mother and father.
(c) Baudelaire's and Laforgue's sustained tortuous relationships with the feminine.
(d) All of the above.

907. Jacques Lacan's *Ecrits* was published in
(a) 1961
(b) 1962
(c) 1966
(d) 1968

908. The orders or states/phases of human mental disposition that Lacan posits are
(a) The Imaginary Order
(b) The Mirror Phase
(c) The Symbolic Order and Real
(d) All of the above

(The imaginary order is a pre-Oedipal phasc when an infant is yet able to distinguish itself from its mother's body. It is unable to recognize the lines of demarcation between itself and the objects in the world. During this stage, the child has a feeling of unity between itself and the objects in the world, i.e. its surroundings. It is a world of images (imaginary). The mirror phase is the origin of a fundamental alienation in the child's sense of the self. This development occurs between the ages of six and eighteen months. The child sees in its mirror stage a self which it would like to be, an ideal self. But this is a misconception, an illusion. The passing of the mirror stage marks the child's entry into the social world, what Lacan calls, the *symbolic order*, the world of language. According to Ross Murfin and Supriya M. Ray, "The Real is the intractable and substantial world that resists and exceeds interpretation. The Real cannot be imagined, symbolized or known directly; it constantly eludes our efforts to name it." It is something 'impossible to say', 'impossible to imagine', 'an aspect where words fail.')

909. Who has referred to woman as a "dark continent"?
(a) Elaine Showalter
(b) Freud
(c) Carl Jung
(d) Alfred Adler

910. Who is known as the 'French Freud'?
(a) Michel Foucault
(b) Jacques Derrida
(c) Jacques Lacan
(d) Helene Cixous

911. Who is the author of *On The Nightmare* (1910)?
(a) Ernest Jones
(b) Alfred Adler
(c) Freud
(d) Jung

912. Who said: "The unconscious is structured like a language"?
(a) Jacques Lacan
(b) Ferdinand de Saussure
(c) Sigmund Freud
(d) Ernest Jones

(Psychoanalysis "discovers in the unconscious...the structure of a language". It is not formed of instincts or fantasies. Language and its structure exist prior to the moment at which the speaking subject makes his entry into it. The unconscious is subject to, and constituted by, the same linguistic processes as is the conscious mind. "It is thinking with words, with thoughts that escape your vigilance, your state of watchfulness". Both Freud and Lacan believe that the unconscious is the place where hidden desires live. According to Freud, there were 'four formations of the unconscious': 1. Symptoms 2. Errors of everyday life 3. Jokes 4. Dreams. So Lacan understands these four categories as linguistic functions, as a kind of reading and writing. All these categories function as signifiers. According to M.A.R. Habib, "The unconscious is as much a product of signifying systems, and indeed is itself as much a signifying system, as the consciousness mind: both are like language in their openness, their constant deferral of meaning, their susceptibility to changing definition, and their constitution as a system of relations (rather than existing as entities in their own right)".)

913. The major criticism of Freud's theory is:
(a) the Oedipus conflict is considered too extreme.
(b) most of Freud's theories are about sex.
(c) most of Freud's theories defy scientific testing.
(d) None of the above.

914. The unconscious system of the personality which contains the life and death instincts and operates on the pleasure principle is
(a) Ego
(b) Superego
(c) Preconscious
(d) Id

915. Who defines bourgeoisie "as the class which does not want to be named"?
(a) Marx
(b) Roland Barthes
(c) Louis Althussar
(d) Gramsci

916. Which of the following books can give a sense of Freud's "Literary critical procedure"?
(a) *Totem and Taboo*
(b) *Civilization and Its Dicontents*
(c) *Creative Writers and Day Dreaming*
(d) *Beyond the Pleasure Principle*

917. Which of the following terms best fit the definition: "a form of literary criticism which uses some of the teachings of psychoanalysis in the interpretation of literature"?
(a) Pschoanalytical criticism
(b) Practical criticism
(c) Applied criticism
(d) Impressionistic criticism

**Important Works by Sigmund Freud (1856-1939)**

1. *The Interpretatation of Dreams* (1900) 2. *The Psychopathy of Everdya Life* (1901) 3. *Three Essays on the Theory of Sexuality* (1905) 4. *Jokes and their Relation to the Unconscious* (1905) 5. *Totem and Taboo* (1913) 6. *On Narcissim* (1914) 7. *Introduction to Psychoanalysis* (1917)

**Important Works by Jacques Lacan**

1. *The Four Fundamental Concepts of Psychoanalysis* (1964, trans 1973)
2. *The Language of the Self, Other Side of Psychoanalysis* (1968)
3. *The Ethics of Psychoanalysis* (1959–60)
4. *Ecrits* (1966, trans 1977)
5. *The Seminars of Jacques Lacan*

**ANSWERS**

| | | | | | |
|---|---|---|---|---|---|
| 882. (a) | 883. (b) | 884. (c) | 885. (d) | 886. (d) | 887. (a) |
| 888. (c) | 889. (b) | 890. (b) | 891. (a) | 892. (b) | 893. (d) |
| 894. (c) | 895. (d) | 896. (c) | 897. (b) | 898. (c) | 899. (b) |
| 900. (b) | 901. (c) | 902. (b) | 903. (b) | 904. (d) | 905. (d) |
| 906. (d) | 907. (a) | 908. (d) | 909. (b) | 910. (c) | 911. (a) |
| 912. (a) | 913. (c) | 914. (d) | 915. (b) | 916. (c) | 917. (a) |

**(XIII) ASSERTION AND REASONING**

918. **Assertion (A):** Thomas Gradgrind, in *Hard Times*, is a wealthy, retired merchant in the industrial city of Coketown. He raises his oldest children, Louisa and Tom, according to utilitarian philosophy and never allows them to engage in fanciful or imaginative pursuits. He founds a school and charitably takes in one of the students.

**Reason (R):** Because he devotes his life to a philosophy of rationalism, self-interest, and fact.

(a) Both (A) and (R) are true; (R) is the correct explanation.
(b) Both (A) and (R) are true, but (R) is not the correct explanation.
(c) (A) is true, but (R) is false.
(d) (A) is false, but (R) is true.

919. **Assertion (A):** *The Second Sex* deals with the treatment of women throughout history. This work is not often regarded as a major work of feminist philosophy and the starting point of second wave feminism.

**Reason (R):** Because Simone de Beauvoir considers patriarchal dominance responsible for women's oppression and a foundational basis of contemporary feminism.

(a) Both (A) and (R) are true; (R) is the correct explanation.
(b) Both (A) and (R) are true, but (R) is not the correct explanation.
(c) (A) is true, but (R) is false.
(d) (A) is false, but (R) is true.

920. **Assertion (A):** In the Elizabethan age in Christopher Marlow's *Dr. Faustus* there is a reference to Helena, and Helena in the end alludes to Helen of Troy.

**Reason (R):** As allusion is a passing reference, without explicit identification, to a literary or historical person, place, or event, or to another literary work or passage.

(a) Both (A) and (R) are true; (R) is the correct explanation.
(b) Both (A) and (R) are true, but (R) is not the correct explanation.
(c) (A) is true, but (R) is false.
(d) (A) is false, but (R) is true.

921. **Assertion (A):** The use of antiheroic protagonists occurs as early as the picaresque novel of the sixteenth century, and the heroine of Defoe's *Moll Flanders* is a thief and a prostitute.

**Reason (R):** Instead of manifesting largeness, dignity the antihero is petty, ignominious, passive, clownish, or dishonest.

(a) Both (A) and (R) are true; (R) is the correct explanation.
(b) Both (A) and (R) are true, but (R) is not the correct explanation.
(c) (A) is true, but (R) is false.
(d) (A) is false, but (R) is true.

922. **Assertion (A):** The chief representative of the Black Art movement in 1960s, were Allen Ginsberg and other beat writers.

**Reason (R):** Social injustice always demands equal rights for all men and women, black and whites.

(a) Both (A) and (R) are true; (R) is the correct explanation.
(b) Both (A) and (R) are true, but (R) is not the correct explanation.
(c) (A) is true, but (R) is false.
(d) (A) is false, but (R) is true.

923. **Assertion (A):** Chaucer describes "Madama Elgentyne thus: She was so charitable and so pious,/ She wolde wepe, if that she saw a mous caught in a trappe".

**Reason (R):** On her 'broche of gold full shene' was written *Amor Vincit Omnia*.

In the context of the two statements, which one of the following is correct?

(a) Both (A) and (R) are true and (R) is the correct explantation of (A).
(b) Both (A) and (R) are true but (R) is not the correct explanation of (A).
(c) (A) is true but (R) is false.
(d) (A) is the false but (R) is true.

924. **Assertion (A):** In *The Duchess of Malfi* Ferdinard sets a whole group of mad men on the Duchess and they dance and sing in a crazy manner.

**Reason (R):** His desire was to provide a strange entertainment to drive the duchess mad.

In the context of the two statements, which one of the following is correct?

(a) (A) is correct, but (R) is wrong.
(b) Both (A) and (R) are correct.
(c) (A) is wrong, but (R) is correct.
(d) Both (A) and (R) are wrong.

925. **Assertion (A):** At the end of *Heart of Darkness*, Marlow tells a lie to the Intended about Kurtz when he tells her: "The last word he pronounced was your name".

**Reason (R):** Marlow tells this lie because he is secretly in love with the Intended and tells her what she wants to hear.

(a) Both (A) and (R) are true, (R) is the correct explantation.
(b) Both (A) and (R) are true, but (R) is not the correct explanation.
(c) (A) is true but (R) is false.
(d) (A) is false, but (R) is true.

926. **Assertion (A):** "Tam O' Shanter" by John Clare is about the experience of an ordinary human being and became quite popular during that time.

**Reason (R):** John Clare, having suffered bouts of madness, could really feel for the misery of common man.

In the context of the two statements, which of the following is correct?

(a) Both (A) and (R) are true and (R) explains (A).
(b) Both (A) and (R) are true, but (R) does not explain (A).
(c) (A) is true, but (R) is false.
(d) (A) is false but (R) is true.

927. **Assertion (A):** In *The Power and the Glory*, Greene shows how the whisky priest transcends his weakness for drink and his human fears, moving towards martyrdom.

**Reason (R):** Transcedence in Greene's novels is generally an outcome of love for humanity, but pride is also an essential ingredient in the Priest's character.

(a) (A) is true, but (R) is false.
(b) (A) is false, but (R) is true.
(c) Both (A) and (R) are true, but (R) is not the correct explanation for (A).
(d) Both (A) and (R) are true and (R) is the correct explanation for (A).

928. **Assertion (A):** In Charlotte Bronte's novel *Jane Eyre*, Rochester confines his wife, Bartha Mason, to an attic room.

**Reason (R):** Rochester does so because Bartha is deranged.

(a) Both (A) and (B) are true and (R) is the correct explanation.
(b) Both (A) and (R) are true that (R) is not the correct explanation.
(c) (A) is true but (R) is false.
(d) (A) is false but (R) is true.

929. **Assertion (A):** In Balzac's novel *Old Goriot* Rastignac extracts money from his already poor family.

**Reason (R):** His desire was to move into high society.

(a) Both (A) and (R) are true; (R) is the correct explanation.
(b) (A) is true but (R) is false.
(c) (A) is false but (R) is true.
(d) Both (A) and (R) are true; but (R) is not the correct explanation.

930. **Assertion (A):** In Nadine Gordimer's novel *July's People* the Smales, a liberal South African family, does not leave Johannesburg.

**Reason (R):** The black South Africans have violently overturned the system of Apartheid.

(a) (A) is true but (R) is false.
(b) Both (A) and (R) are true.
(c) (A) is false and (R) is the correct explanation.
(d) (A) is true and (R) is the not the collect explanation.

931. **Assertion (A):** In the novel *One Hundred Years of Solitude*, the isolated and peaceful town of Macondo, loses its innocent and solitary state.

**Reason (R):** The town establishes contact with other towns in the region.

(a) Both (A) and (R) are correct.
(b) (A) is false but (R) is true.
(c) (A) is true but (R) is false.
(d) (A) is true but (R) is not the correct explanation.

932. **Assertion (A):** In Virginia Woolf's novel *Mrs. Dalloway*, Clarissa goes to market to buy flowers.

**Reason (R):** She wanted to celebrate her birthday with a show of flowers.

(a) (A) is true and (R) is true.
(b) (A) is false and (R) is true.
(c) (A) is true but (R) is not the correct explanation.
(d) (A) is true and (R) is the correct explanation.

933. **Assertion (A):** In *King Lear*, Lear does not give Cordelia her share of kingdom and he divided the kingdom between Goneril and Regan.

**Reason (R):** Cordelia refuses to join her sisters in exaggerated public declarations of love for her father and so she is deprived of her share of kingdom.

(a) (A) is false (R) is true.
(b) (A) is true but (R) is false.
(c) (A) is true but (R) is not the correct explanation.
(d) (A) is true and (R) is the correct explanation.

934. **Assertion (A):** In Voltaire's novel *Candide*, the scholar Pangloss expels his tutee, Candide, from his home.

**Reason (R):** Pangloss found him stealing money.

(a) (A) is false (R) is true.
(b) Both (A) and (R) are false.
(c) (A) is true but (R) is not the correct explanation.
(d) (A) is true and (R) is the correct explanation.

935. **Assertion (A):** In Flaubert's novel *Madam Bovary*, Emma Bovary, wife of Dr. Charles Bovary, has adulterous affairs and lives beyond her means.

**Reason (R):** Emma wanted to escape the banalities and emptiness of her provincial life.

(a) (A) is true but (R) is false.
(b) (A) is false but (R) is true.
(c) (A) is true but (R) is not the correct explanation.
(d) (A) is true and (R) is the correct explanation.

936. **Assertion (A):** In Victor Hugo's novel *Les Miserables*, Jean Valjean is released from a French prison after serving nineteen years.

**Reason (R):** He stole a loaf of bread and also made attempts to escape from prison.

(a) (A) is false but (R) is true.
(b) (A) is true but (R) is false.
(c) (A) is true and (R) is the correct explanation.
(d) (A) is true but (R) is not the correct explanation.

937. The assertion, 'we had a very restful holiday' implies

(a) We didn't exert ourselves
(b) We did nothing
(c) We were very lazy
(d) We had a very dull time

938. "The progress of an artist is a continual self-sacrifice, a continual extinction of personality". This assertion implies

(a) Merely by a continual extinction of personality an artist is sure to make progress.
(b) An artist is likely to make progress through continual self-sacrifice and extinction of personality.
(c) Continual self-sacrifice and extinction of personality will undermine the progress of the artist.
(d) An artist must have a personality to create art.

939. "The best poetry will be found to have the power of forming, sustaining and delighting us". This assertion implies that

(a) Poetry has multiple functions to perform
(b) Poetry is more useful than other arts
(c) All other arts including poetry have their limitations
(d) Poetry has no role to play

940. **Assertion (A):** In Shakespeare's play *Macbeth*, Duncan, the king of Scotland proclaimed Macbeth Thane of Cawdor.

**Reason (R):** Macbeth and Banquo, the gallant generals, rescued Duncan's threatened army in rebellion-torn Scotland.

(a) (A) is true and (R) is false.
(b) (A) is false but (R) is true.

(c) (A) is true and (R) is the correct explanation.
(d) (A) is true but (R) is not the correct explanation.

941. **Assertion (A):** In Ben Jonson's play *The Alchemist* Subtle is able to cheat several gullible persons.

**Reason (R):** He claims to be an Alchemist with possession of the philosopher's stone which can restore youth, increase wealth, etc.

(a) (A) is true but (R) is false.
(b) (A) is false but (R) is true.
(c) (A) is true but (R) is not the correct explanation.
(d) (A) is true and (R) is the correct explanation.

942. "Human beings, and especially human beings as an integral part of a social organization, are regarded as primary subject matter of literature". The assertion implies

(a) Human beings also can be the subject matter of literature.
(b) All living beings—animal and human—contribute towards the creation of literature.
(c) Humans as social beings are the nucleus of all literary exercise.
(d) Literature transcends the human and the non-human.

943. "We must learn to see more, to hear more, to feel more". The assertion implies

(a) Human beings have only three faculties at their command to comprehend all knowledge.
(b) A sharpening of three faculties mentioned would help human beings to become better.
(c) Only with the combination of all the senses, we may become better.
(d) Seeing, hearing and feeling are not enough to become better human beings.

944. In the assertion "four out of five people suffer from dreaded pyorrhea", the writer wants to arouse the feeling of

(a) Sympathy
(b) Fear
(c) Hatred
(d) Ill-will

945. "John is six feet tall and 240 lb" is an assertion of

(a) a fact
(b) a judgment
(c) an opinion
(d) None of the above

946. **Assertion (A):** In John Steinbeck's novel *The Grapes of Wrath*, the Joad family and other farm families leave Oklahoma for California.

**Reason (R):** They were deprived of land by the banks whose loans they could not pay because of drought and leave for California with prospects of livelihood.

(a) (A) is true but (R) is false.
(b) (A) is false but (R) is true.
(c) (A) is true and (R) is the correct explanation.
(d) (A) is true but (R) is not the correct explanation.

947. **Assertion (A):** In Ernest Hemingway's novel *A Farewell to Arms*, Catherine, the heroine, dies at the end of the novel.

**Reason (R):** She suffered bullet injuries during the war.

(a) (A) is true and (R) is also true.
(b) (A) is false but (R) is true.
(c) (A) is false but (R) is the correct explanation.
(d) (A) is true and (R) is not the correct explanation.

948. X: He's mean and stingy.

Y: "Oh, I wont say that, He is just thirfty".

(a) Is too careful with his money.
(b) Never spends money.
(c) Is so careful with his money that everyone admires him for good management.
(d) Is careful with his money.

949. 'I wandered lonely as a cloud' makes an assertion that

(a) The poet travelled with the cloud.
(b) The poet moved aimlessly with the cloud.
(c) Both the poet and the cloud were lonely.
(d) The poet moved so aimlessly as the cloud.

950. **Assertion (A):** Dr. Johnson's *The Lives of the Poets* carries critical and biographical studies of poets he admired. It does not, however, carry life of William Wordsworth.

**Reason (R):** Dr. Johnson singled out poets whom he not only admired but also adored. This explains his omission of Wordsworth.

(a) (A) is wrong but (R) is correct.
(b) (A) is true but (R) is false.
(c) (A) and (R) are true.
(d) Neither (A) nor (R) is true.

951. **Assertion (A):** In Henry Melville's novel *Moby Dick*, captain Ahab expresses his desire to pursue and kill Moby Dick, the legendary great White Whale.

**Reason (R):** His desire was to take revenge because the White Whale had taken Captain Ahab's leg during his last voyage.

(a) (A) is correct but (R) is wrong.
(b) (A) is wrong but (R) is correct.
(c) (A) is correct and (R) is the correct explanation.
(d) (A) is wrong but (R) is the correct explanation.

952. **Assertion (A):** In Nathaniel Hawthorne's novel *The Scarlet Letter*, Hester Prynne, the heroine of the novel, is sent to prison along with her daughter, Pearl.

**Reason (R):** She was punished for stealing money from a shop.

(a) Both (A) and (R) are true.
(b) Neither (A) nor (R) is true.
(c) (A) is not true but (R) is the correct explanation.
(d) (A) is true but (R) is not the correct explanation.

953. **Assertion (A):** In F. Scott Fitzerald's novel *The Great Gatsby*, George Wilson, the owner of garage, killed Jay Gatsby, the hero of the novel.

**Reason (R):** George wanted to take revenge on Gatsby because his car had struck and killed his wife, Myrtle.

(a) (A) is correct and (R) is the correct explanation.
(b) (A) is wrong and (R) is the correct explanation.
(c) (A) is correct and (R) is not the correct explanation.
(d) (A) is wrong and (R) is also not the correct explanation.

954. **Assertion (A):** In William Faulkner's novel *The Sound and the Fury*, Jason, the second youngest of the Compson children, is spurned by other compson children.

**Reason (R):** Jason is mean spirited, petty and cynical.

(a) (A) is not correct but (R) is correct.
(b) (A) is correct but (R) is not correct.
(c) (A) is correct and (R) is not the correct explanation.
(d) (A) is correct and (R) is the correct explanation.

955. **Assertion (A):** In Arthur Miller's play *Death of a Salesman*, Willy Loman, the hero of the play, an insecure, self-deuded travelling salesman, commits suicide at the end of the play.

**Reason (R):** He feels depressed as his illusions begin to fail under the pressing realities of his life.

(a) (A) is not correct but (R) is the correct explanation.
(b) (A) is correct and (R) is the correct explanation.
(c) Both (A) and (R) are wrong.
(d) (A) is correct but (R) is wrong.

956. **Assertion (A):** In Charles Dickens's novel *Hard Times* Thomas Gradgrind allows his children to engage in fanciful pursuits.

**Reason (R):** He does not allow his philosophy of rationalism and self-interest to interfere in their development.

(a) (A) is wrong but (R) is true.
(b) (A) is true but (R) is wrong.
(c) (A) is not true (B) but (R) is the correct explanation.
(d) (A) is not true and (R) is not the correct explanation.

957. **Assertion (A):** In Fyodor Dostoevsky's novel *Crime and Punishment*, Raskolnikov, the hero of the novel, kills Alyona Ivanovna, the pawnbroker.

**Reason (R):** He did not kill her for exploiting people.

(a) (A) is wrong and (R) is not the correct explanation.
(b) (A) is correct and (R) is the correct explanation.
(c) (A) is correct but (R) is wrong.
(d) (A) is wrong but (R) correct.

958. **Assertion (A):** In Henry Fielding's novel *Tom Jones*, Squire Allworthy sends Jenny Jones away from the country and her tutor leaves of his own accord.

**Reason (R):** Allworthy thinks that the baby found in his bed was the illegitimate child of the two.

(a) (A) is true but (R) is false.
(b) (A) is false but (R) is true.
(c) (A) is true and (R) is the correct explanation.
(d) Both (A) and (R) are false.

959. **Assertion (A):** In Daniel Defoe's novel *Moll Flanders,* Moll Flander's mother was transported to America soon after her birth.

**Reason (R):** She had been convicted of felony.

(a) (A) is true and (R) is the correct explanation.
(b) (A) is true but (R) is not the correct explanation.
(c) (A) is false but (R) is true.
(d) Both (A) and (R) are false.

960. **Assertion (A):** In Samuel Beckett's play *Waiting for Godot*, Vladimir and Estragon stand near a tree and talk about various topics.

**Reason (R):** They are waiting there for Pozzo and Lucky.

(a) (A) is true and (R) is the correct explanation.
(b) (A) is true and (R) is not the correct explanation.
(c) (A) is false but (R) is true.
(d) Both (A) and (R) are false.

961. **Assertion (A):** Henry David Thoreau's *Walden* details Thoreau's experiences over the course of two years, two months and two days in a cabin he built near Walden Pond to live in the lap of nature.

**Reason (R):** Thoreau hoped to gain a more objective understanding of society through personal introspection, simple living and self-sufficiency.

(a) (A) is true and (R) is the correct explanation.
(b) (A) is true and (R) is not the correct explanation.
(c) (A) is false but (R) is true.
(d) Both (A) and (R) are false.

962. **Assertion (A):** In Saul Bellow's novel *Herzog*, the hero Herzog's career as a writer as an academic has floundered.

**Reason (R):** He is mentally disturbed because he has a large amount of money that he has to pay to his lenders which he fails to manage.

(a) (A) is true and (R) is the correct explanation.
(b) (A) is true and (R) is not the correct explanation.
(c) Both (A) and (R) are false.
(d) (A) is false but (R) is true.

963. **Assertion (A):** In Luigi Pirandello's play *Six Characters in Search of an Author*, the Father insists on the staging of the characters' drama.

**Reason (R):** The author unjustly denied the characters stage-life and its immortality, so they have brought their drama to the Manager of the Company.

(a) (A) is true and (R) is the correct explanation.
(b) (A) is true but (R) is not the correct explanation.
(c) Both (A) and (R) are false.
(d) (A) is false but (R) is true.

964. **Assertion (A):** In William Golding's novel *Lord of the Flies*, one of the youngest boys disappears, presumably dead.

**Reason (R):** The boy might have been the victim of some ferocious animal like the lion.

(a) (A) is true but (R) is the correct interpretation.
(b) (A) is true but (R) is not the correct interpretation.
(c) Both (A) and (R) are false.
(d) (A) is false but (R) is true.

965. **Assertion (A):** In Emily Bronte's novel *Wuthering Heights*, Healthcliff, who grew up in his adopted family, suddenly disappears and goes to an unknown place.

**Reason (R):** He runs away from Wuthering Heights because Catherine whom he loves decides to marry another young man, Edgar.

(a) (A) is true and (R) is the correct explanation.
(b) (A) is true but (R) is not correct explanation.
(c) Both (A) and (R) are false.
(d) (A) is false but (R) is true.

966. **Assertion (A):** Muriel Spark described her novel *Driver's Seat* as a 'Whydunnit'.

**Reason (R):** This is because in the novel's third chapter it is revealed that Lisa, the heroine, will be murdered.

(a) (A) is true but (R) is not the correct explanation.
(b) (A) is true and (R) is the correct explanation.
(c) Both (A) and (R) are false.
(d) (A) is false but (R) is true.

967. **Assertion (A):** In Emile Zole'a novel *Germinal* the novel's central character had to come to the coal mining town of Montson to earn living as a minor.

**Reason (R):** He had been sacked from his previous job on the railways for assaulting a superior.

(a) (A) is correct but (R) is wrong.
(b) (A) is wrong but (R) is correct.
(c) Both (A) and (R) are wrong.
(d) Both (A) and (R) are correct.

**ANSWERS**

| | | | | | |
|---|---|---|---|---|---|
| 918. (a) | 919. (d) | 920. (a) | 921. (a) | 922. (b) | 923. (b) |
| 924. (b) | 925. (b) | 926. (b) | 927. (c) | 928. (a) | 929. (a) |
| 930. (c) | 931. (a) | 932. (c) | 933. (d) | 934. (c) | 935. (d) |
| 936. (c) | 937. (a) | 938. (b) | 939. (a) | 940. (c) | 941. (d) |
| 942. (c) | 943. (c) | 944. (b) | 945. (a) | 946. (c) | 947. (d) |
| 948. (a) | 949. (c) | 950. (d) | 951. (c) | 952. (d) | 953. (a) |
| 954. (d) | 955. (b) | 956. (d) | 957. (c) | 958. (c) | 959. (a) |
| 960. (b) | 961. (a) | 962. (b) | 963. (a) | 964. (b) | 965. (a) |
| 966. (b) | 967. (d) | | | | |

## (XIV) ARCHETYPAL/MYTH CRITICISM

968. Who developed the 'archetypal criticism', i.e. the theory that interprets a text by focusing on myths and archetypes?
   (a) Maud Baudkin
   (b) C.L. Jung
   (c) Northrop Frye
   (d) James Frazer

969. Into how many categories do archetypes fall?
   (a) Three
   (b) Two
   (c) Four
   (d) Five

   (The two categories are : 1. Characters 2. Situations/Symbols/Images. In the category of 'Characters' are the *hero*, the *outcaste*, the *scapegoat*, etc. In the second category, we have the *task*, the *Quest*, the *Loss of Innocence*, etc.)

970. In a Freudian approach to literature, concave images are usually seen as
   (a) Male symbols
   (b) Female symbols
   (c) Phallic symbols
   (d) Evidence of Oedipus Complex

971. Who was an influential force in Archetypal Criticism?
   (a) Tate
   (b) Freud
   (c) Jung
   (d) Richards

972. Seven is an archetype associated with
   (a) Evil
   (b) Death
   (c) Birth
   (d) Perfection

973. Derrida deconstructs the binary opposition between nature and culture as discussed in one of Levi-Strauss's books. What is the name of the book?
   (a) *Tristes and Tropiques* (Sad Topics' (1955)
   (b) *Mythologies*
   (c) *The Elementary Structures of Kingship*
   (d) *The Savage Mind*

974. *The Golden Bough* (1890-1915) was written by
   (a) James Frazer
   (b) Levi Strauss
   (c) Roland Barthes
   (d) Foucault

975. *Archetypal Patterns in Poetry* (1934) was written by
   (a) C.L. Jung

(b) Maud Baudkin
(c) Freud
(d) Frazer

976. Archetypal Criticism is a criticism that focusses on
(a) Myths
(b) Archetypes
(c) Characters
(d) All of the above

977. Northrop Frye's *Anatomy of Criticism* was published in
(a) 1967
(b) 1957
(c) 1968
(d) 1958

978. Northrop Frye aligns tragedy with
(a) Summer
(b) Winter
(c) Spring
(d) Autumn

(Northrop Frye indicates the correspondent genres for the seasons as follows:
1. Spring: comedy, 2. Summer : romance, 3. Autumn/Fall: tragedy, 4. Winter: irony.)

979. The *journey* archetypal in classical Western literature is
(a) Tom Jones
(b) Odyssey
(c) Iliad
(d) Divine Comedy

980. 'Femme Fatale' is a female character that is associated with
(a) Good fortune
(b) Fate
(c) Catastrophic events
(d) Death

981. Who, among the following, is a Canadian critic?
(a) F.R. Leavis
(b) Roman Jacobson
(c) Jacques Lacan
(d) Northrop Frye

982. Which literary critic described value judgments as "the donkey's carrot of literary criticism"?
(a) T.S. Eliot
(b) Northrop Frye
(c) William Empson
(d) I.A. Richards

983. Myth criticism focusses on
(a) a study of myths and mythology.
(b) archetypes of spiritual experience.
(c) recurrence of archetypal patterns.
(d) the confluence of different traditions.

984. Which criticism is also known as 'Totemic Mythological or Ritualistic Criticism'?
(a) Ontological criticism
(b) Orientalism
(c) Phenomenological Criticism
(d) Archetypal Criticism

985. To which school of criticism do Richard Chase, Leslie Fedler, Daniel Hoffman and Philip Wheelwright belong?
(a) Psychoanalytical criticism
(b) Myth criticism
(c) Biographical criticism
(d) Historical criticism

986. Who regards language as born "in one fell sweep"?
(a) Saussure
(b) Peirce
(c) Levi-Strauss
(d) Derrida

**Important Works by Claude Levi-Strauss**

1. *The Elementary Structures of Kingship* (1949)
2. *Tristes and Tropiques* (Sad Tropics) (1955)
3. *The Savage Mind* (1962)
4. *Mythologies I–IV* (1969-1981)
5. *The Raw and the Cooked–Part I* (1969)

987. One archetype in literature is the *scapegoat*, which of these literary characters serves the purpose?
   (a) Captain Ahab
   (b) Billy Bud
   (c) Hamlet
   (d) Ophelia

   (Billy Bud is a character in Henry Melville's novel of the same title . He is foretopman in the British Fleet. Claggart, the master-of-arms, who was at fault, is exonerated and in his place Billy Bud is executed for no fault of his own.)

988. With which of the following is "The Good Mother" not associated?
   (a) Life Principles
   (b) Nourishment
   (c) Protection
   (d) Destruction

989. The Trickster does not stand for
   (a) Wisdom
   (b) Fraud
   (c) Conman
   (d) Picaro

990. Outoboros symbolises
   (a) the eternal cycle of life.
   (b) primordial consciousness.
   (c) the unity of opposing forces.
   (d) All of the above.

991. Myths are by nature
   (a) Individual
   (b) Collective
   (c) Communal
   (d) Both (b) and (c)

992. In 'Yang-Yin', a Chinese symbol, representing the masculine and female principles, Yin symbolises
   (a) Darkness
   (b) Passivity
   (c) The unconscious
   (d) All of the above

993. C.L. Jung's *Symbols of Transformations*, a revised version of *Psychology of the Unconscious* (1912), was published in
   (a) 1956
   (b) 1958
   (c) 1959
   (d) 1961

**C.L. JUNG'S MAIN ARCHETYPES**

(According to C.L. Jung, "archetypes" are patterns of psychic energy that originate in the collective unconscious and finding their most common and normal manifestations in dreams. But for Frye, according to William K. Wimsatt and Cleanth Brooks, "archetype, borrowed from Jung, means a primordial image, a part of the collective unconscious, the psychic residue of numberless experiences of some kind, and thus part of the inherited response-pattern of the race"). Jung's main forms of archetypes are generally regarded as:

1. **Shadow** reflects deeper elements of our psyche. It consists of the sex and life instincts.
2. **Anima/Animus** Anima is the male image of a woman and animus is the female image of a man. The anima/animus represents our true self.
3. **Self** represents the unification of the consciousness and the unconsciousness. It is the centre and totality of the entire psyche.
4. **Ego** is the centre of consciousness. It is identity.
5. **Persona** is the image we present to the world.

**Some Common Literary Situational/ Symbolic Archetypes of Colours and Numbers**

| S.N. | Colour | Positive (Negative) |
|---|---|---|
| 1. | Black | power (death, mourning) |
| 2. | Blue | nobility, tranquility (depression) |
| 3. | Brown | earth, nature (confusion) |
| 4. | Green | fertility, renewal, wealth (greed, envy) |
| 5. | Orange | adventure, change (disruptiveness) |
| 6. | Purple | royalty, positive personal growth (injury) |
| 7. | Red | sex, love (sacrifice, taboo, rebirth, humiliation, danger) |
| 8. | White | purity, wholesomeness, rebirth (emptiness) |

| S.N. | Numbers | |
|---|---|---|
| 1. | Three | light, spiritual awareness and unity (cf. the Holy Trinity) |
| 2. | Four | circle, life circle, four seasons, four elements (earth, air, fire, water) |
| 3. | Five | integration, the four limbs together with the head, the four cardinal points plus the centre |
| 4. | Seven | the union of three and four, the completion of a circle, perfect order |

994. Who is generally known as the "second father" of archetypal psychology?
   (a) James Hillman
   (b) Henry Coblin
   (c) David L. Miller
   (d) Paul Kugler

995. Who said, "Literary products of highly dubious merit are often of the greatest interest to the psychologist"?
   (a) Freud
   (b) Levi-Strauss
   (c) Carl Jung
   (d) Henry Coblin

996. What was Northrop Frye's three recurring patterns of symbolism in literature?
   (a) Tragic, comic, romantic
   (b) analogical, demonic, tragic
   (c) apocalyptic, analogical, demonic
   (d) comic, analogical, romantic

   ('Apocalyptic' typifies the revelation of heaven and ultimate fulfilment of all desire. In this state, literary structure points towards unification of all things in a single analogical symbol. 'Analogical' depicts the states that are similar to paradise or hell, but not identical. The 'demonic' typifies the unfulfilment, perversion or opposition of human nature. In this state, things tend toward anarchy or tyranny.)

**ANSWERS**

| | | | | | |
|---|---|---|---|---|---|
| 968. (a) | 969. (b) | 970. (b) | 971. (c) | 972. (d) | 973. (a) |
| 974. (a) | 975. (b) | 976. (d) | 977. (b) | 978. (d) | 979. (b) |
| 980. (c) | 981. (d) | 982. (b) | 983. (c) | 984. (d) | 985. (b) |
| 986. (c) | 987. (b) | 988. (d) | 989. (a) | 990. (d) | 991. (d) |
| 992. (d) | 993. (a) | 994. (b) | 995. (c) | 996. (c) | |

## (XV) POSTMODERNISM

997. The term 'postmodern' was first used in the context of
   (a) Literature
   (b) Architecture
   (c) Sculpture
   (d) Painting

   (The Architect Charles Jencks used the term 'Postmodernism' in his book *The Language of Postmodern Architecture* (1977). It was originally used by the Spanish writer Frederico De Onis in 1934 to describe a poetic reaction to modernist poetry. The term was used in 1975 by historian Arnold Toynbee to describe pluralism in literature and art after World War II and the rise of non-Western cultures.)

998. Who are regarded as the high priests of postmodernism?
   (a) Jean Baudrillard
   (b) Jean Francois Lyotard
   (c) Jurgen Habermas
   (d) Both (a) and (b)

999. Which two terms are used interchangeably?
   (a) Modernism and Postmodernism
   (b) Poststructuralism and Postmodernism
   (c) Modernism and Structurlism
   (d) Structuralism and Postmodernism

1000. The postmodernism, in part, emerges from the dissatisfaction of some on the left with an emphasis on
   (a) Social class
   (b) Gender
   (c) Bourgeoisie
   (d) The proletariat

1001. Postmodernism would criticize Marxism as
   (a) a fallacious theory.
   (b) a meta-narrative.
   (c) irrelevant.
   (d) impractical.

1002. Who, among the following, has not been a direct influence on postmodern thought?
   (a) Derrida
   (b) Heidegger
   (c) Morgenthau
   (d) Ronald Barthes

1003. With which of the following pairs is Michel Foucault particularly associated?
   (a) Men/women
   (b) Theory/practice
   (c) Politics/economics
   (d) Knowledge/power

1004. Postmodernists say there are no 'facts' about the world. What do they say we have instead?
   (a) Guesses
   (b) Evaluations
   (c) Interpretations
   (d) Suppositions

1005. Which method did Foucault use to 'trace the discontinuities and ruptures in history to emphasize the singularity of events rather than seeking historical trends'?
   (a) Quantification
   (b) Genealogy
   (c) Geology
   (d) Physics

1006. *The Postmodern Condion: A Report on Knowledge* (1979) was written by
   (a) Julia Kristeva
   (b) Michel Foucault
   (c) Lyotard
   (d) Derrida

1007. Jean Baudrillard's *Simulacra and Simulation* was published in
   (a) 1975
   (b) 1981

(c) 1985
(d) 1987

1008. *Postmodernism: The Cultural Logic of Late Capitalism* (1981) was written by
(a) Lyotard
(b) Baudrillard
(c) Frederic Jameson
(d) Jurgen Habermas

1009. Who has said that postmodernism is characterised by "incredulity towards metanarratives"?
(a) Baudrillard
(b) Foucault
(c) Julia Kristeva
(d) Lyotard

(Metanarratives or 'grand narratives' are those abstract ideas in terms of which thinkers since the time of the Enlightenment have attempted to construct comprehensive expressions of historical experience such as 'reason', 'truth', 'progress', etc. Marxism is also a metanarrative. A grand narrative in American culture, for example, might be the story that democracy will lead to most enlightened or rational form of government, and that democracy will lead to universal human progress.)

1010. *The Political Unconsciousness* (1981) was written by
(a) Lyotard
(b) Baudrillard
(c) Fraderic Jameson
(d) Habermas

1011. *The Structural Transformation of the Public Sphere* by Jurgen Habermas was published in
(a) 1958
(b) 1962
(c) 1963
(d) 1965

1012. Baudrillard argues that in the postmodern stage, reality has been replaced by
(a) artificiality
(b) fictitiousness
(c) simulacara
(d) none of the above

**Some Important Works by Baudrillard**
1. *The Consumer Society: Myths and Structures* (1970)
2. *The Mirror of Production* (1973)
3. *Seduction* (1979)
4. *Simulacra and Simulation* (1981)
5. *Simulations* (1983)
6. *The Ecstasy of Communication* (1987)
7. *The Illusion of the End* (1994)
8. *The Vital Illusion* (2000)

1013. Many postmodernists believe that reality is a
(a) language construct.
(b) social construct.
(c) cultural construct.
(d) None of the above.

1014. Who was the major theorist of postmodernism?
(a) Lyotard
(b) Habermas
(c) Baudrillard
(d) Andre Gide

1015. Lyotard's essay *Answering the Question: What is Postmodernism*, was first published in
(a) 1982
(b) 1983
(c) 1985
(d) 1987

1016. Who coined the term "hypertext"?
(a) Michel Foucault
(b) Ted Nelson
(c) Jacques Lacan
(d) Roland Barthes

(A *hypertext* is a text displayed on a computer or other electronic device with references (hyperlinks) to other texts that the reader can easily access, usually by a mouse click or key press sequence. Apart from the running text, hypertext may contain images, tables and other presentation devices.)

1017. Who coined the term 'avant-texte'?
(a) Paul Valery
(b) John Peterson
(c) Jean Bellemin-Noel
(d) G.E. Bentley

(This term occurs in Bellemin-Noel's book *The Text and the Avante-texte*: *The Rough Drafts of a Poem by Milosz* published in 1972. The term designated all the documents that precede a work when it is considered as text and both documents and text are regarded as part of a system.)

1018. Who is associated with the term 'hyperreality'?
(a) Frederic Jameson
(b) Lyotard
(c) Baudrillard
(d) Roland Barthes

(Hyperreality is used in semiotics and postmodern philosophy to describe the inability of the consciousness to distinguish reality from fantasy, especially in technologically advanced postmodern cultures. For example, Disneyland, with its settings such as Main Street and full-sized houses, has been created to look 'absolutely realistic'.)

1019. Who, among the following, has written *The Postmodern Turn* (1987)?
(a) Ihab Hassan
(b) Lyotard
(c) Baudrillard
(d) Habermas

1020. According to Peter Barry, Jean Baudrillard was associated with what is known as
(a) the forfeit of the real.
(b) the gain of the real.
(c) the knowledge of the real.
(d) the loss of the real.

(Ihab Hassan has made the following schematic differences between modernism and postmodernism in *The Postmodern Turn*)

| **Modernism** | **Postmodernism** |
|---|---|
| Romanticism/Symbolism | Pataphysics/Dadaism |
| Form (conjunctive, closed) | Antiform (disjunctive, open) |
| Purpose | Play |
| Design | Chance |
| Hierarchy | Anarchy |
| Mastery/Logos | Exhaustion/Silence |
| Distance | Participation |
| Creation/Totalization | Decreation/ Deconstruction |
| Synthesis | Antithesis |
| Presence | Absence |
| Centering | Dispersal |
| Semantics | Rhetoric |
| Paradigm | Syntagm |
| Hypotaxis | Parataxis |
| Metaphor | Metonymy |
| Selection | Combination |
| Root/Depth | Rhizome/Surface |
| Interpretation/Reading | Against Interpretation/ Misreading |
| Signified | Signifier |
| Lisible (Readerly) | Scriptible (Writerly) |
| Master Code | Idiolect |
| Genital/Phallic | Polymorphous/ Androgynous |
| Paranoia | Schizophrenia |
| Origin/Cause | Difference-Differance/ Trace |
| Metaphysics | Irony |
| Determinancy | Indeterminancy |
| Transcendence | Immanence |

The preceding table draws on ideas in many fields—rhetoric, linguistics, literary theory, philosophy, anthropology, psychoanalysis, political science, even theology—and draws on many authors.)

1021. Who is associated with the term 'Heterology'?
   (a) Martin Heidegger
   (b) Georges Bataille
   (c) Marquis de Sade
   (d) Paul Berman

(Bataille defines 'heterology' as "the science of what is completely other." Known as an 'excremental pshilosopher', Bataille wanted to produce writings which were often designed to shock and appall, all that had been excreted and rejected as waste matter or undesirable by conventional thought: sacrifice, excrement, violence, blood, incest, etc.)

1022. Who is associated with "Epic Theatre"?
   (a) Bertolt Brecht
   (b) Martin Esslin
   (c) A. Artaud
   (d) None of the above

("Epic Theatre" was a theatrical movement arising in the early to mid-20th century from the theories and practice of a number of theatre practitioners, including Erwin Piscator, V. Mayakovsky, V. Meyerhold, and Bertolt Brecht. Many argue that Brecht did not coin the term "Epic Theatre". It was Erwin Piscator who claimed that he was the inventor of this term.)

1023. Who coined the term "alienation effect"?
   (a) Irwin Piscator
   (b) Bertolt Brecht
   (c) Kafka
   (d) Martin Esslin

(One of the dramatic techniques employed by Brecht in his plays is what he calls "distancing "or "alienation effect". It means that Brecht does not want the audience to be emotionally involved with his characters. Instead, the audience should be consciously critical observer.)

1024. "Theatre of the Absurd" was a term coined by
   (a) Derrida
   (b) Kafka
   (c) Martin Esslin
   (d) Michel Foucault

(The term was coined in his 1960 essay *Theatre of the Absurd*. It designates particular plays of absurdist fiction written by a number of primarily European playwrights in the late 1960s (e.g. *Waiting for Godot* by Samuel Beckett).)

1025. The term 'The Theatre of Cruelty' was coined by
   (a) Albert Camus
   (b) Kafka
   (c) Antonin Artaud
   (d) None of the above

("Theatre of the Cruelty" is a surrealist form of theatre theorised by Atraud in his book *The Theatre and Its Double* (1958). Atraud spoke of cruelty not in the sense of violent behaviour but rather the cruelty it takes to show an audience a truth that they do not wish to see.)

1026. Who is associated with "Theatre of Silence" (1920)?
   (a) Jean Jacques Bernard
   (b) Georg Lukacs
   (c) Martin Esslin
   (d) Atonin Artaud

(Bernard's "Theatre of Silence" presents sensitive studies of shy or reticent characters whose silences betray more than their speech. Plays include *Martine* (1922), *Imitation to Voyage* (1924).)

1027. Who has coined the terms 'genotext' and 'phenotext'?
   (a) Helene Cixous
   (b) Kate Millet
   (c) Julia Kristeva
   (d) Toril Moi

(The term 'genotext' refers to 'underlying foundation' of language, the underlying play of energies and drives which give rise to a text and which can be discerned through various linguistic devices (such as rhyme, melody, intonation and rhythm), but which is itself not linguistic. The term 'phenotext', on the other hand, denotes communicative language, it is structure which obeys the rules of communication and 'presupposes a subject of enunciation and addressee'.)

1028. Jean Baudrillard's *The Illusion of the End* was published in
   (a) 1991
   (b) 1994
   (c) 1996
   (d) 1998

**ANSWERS**

| | | | | | |
|---|---|---|---|---|---|
| 997. (b) | 998. (b) | 999. (b) | 1000. (a) | 1001. (b) | 1002. (c) |
| 1003. (d) | 1004. (c) | 1005. (b) | 1006. (c) | 1007. (b) | 1008. (c) |
| 1009. (d) | 1010. (c) | 1011. (b) | 1012. (c) | 1013. (b) | 1014. (c) |
| 1015. (a) | 1016. (b) | 1017. (c) | 1018. (c) | 1019. (a) | 1020. (d) |
| 1021. (b) | 1022. (a) | 1023. (b) | 1024. (c) | 1025. (c) | 1026. (a) |
| 1027. (c) | 1028. (b) | | | | |

## (XVI) FEMINIST CRITICISM, LESBIAN AND GAY STUDIES/QUEER THEORY

1029. Who said, "One is not born a woman, but becomes one"?
    (a) Kate Millet
    (b) Elaine Showalter
    (c) Simone de Beauvoir
    (d) Virginia Woolf

1030. The word 'feminism' was coined by
    (a) Elaine Showalter
    (b) Charles Fourier
    (c) Gayatri Spivak
    (d) Simone de Beauvoir

(It originated from the French word 'feminisme')

1031. How many waves of feminism have the historians of feminism identified?
    (a) Three
    (b) Four
    (c) Five
    (d) Six

(1. The First Wave (19th and early 20th Century: (1830-1920). The focus is on legal rights, political power, and for woman suffrage.
2. The Second Wave (1960 and 1980s): It is concerned with issues of equality, i.e. end to discrimination in society, work and education.
3. The Third Wave (1980s): Women and former European colonies and the Third World have proposed post-colonial and "Third World" feminisms.)

1032. The article "Third Wave" was written by
    (a) Virginia Woolf
    (b) Kate Millet
    (c) Judith Butler
    (d) Rebecca Walker

1033. Which slogan became synonymous with second wave feminism and women's liberation movement?
    (a) Equality to Women
    (b) The Personal is Political
    (c) Freedom to women
    (d) Hell with Man

(This is the title of an essay by Carol Hanisch)

1034. The right to vote was granted to women in Britain for the first time in
    (a) 1928
    (b) 1938
    (c) 1921
    (d) 1931

(The right to vote was granted in 1918, but only to those women who were over the age of 30 and owned property. However, in 1928, all women over the age of 21 were given voting rights. In the U.S.A. it was granted in 1919)

1035. The term 'Women's Liberation' was first used in the U.S.A. in
    (a) 1961
    (b) 1962
    (c) 1964
    (d) 1968

1036. Mary Wollstonecraft's *A Vindication of the Rights of Women* was published in
    (a) 1792
    (b) 1789
    (c) 1791
    (d) 1795

1037. Who coined the term 'Other' in feminism?
    (a) Julia Kristeva
    (b) Helene Cixous
    (c) Toril Moi
    (d) Simone de Beauvoir

1038. Who coined the term 'gynocriticism'?
    (a) Helene Cixous
    (b) Luce Irigaray

(c) Elaine Showalter
(d) Kate Millet

1039. The term 'gynocriticism' is broadly concerned with
(a) examining the works written by men.
(b) developing a female framework for dealing with works by women.
(c) writing according to male model and theories.
(d) None of the above.

(It deals with "the history, styles, themes, genres, and structures of writing by women".)

1040. In how many phases has Elaine Showalter divided literature by women?
(a) Two
(b) Three
(c) Four
(d) Five

(The three phases are:

1. Feminine phase (1840-80) : Women writers, imitated male writers.
2. Feminist phase (1880-1920) : Women maintained a separate position and protested against male domination in literature.
3. Female phase (1920 onwards) : Women have a distinct female identity, style, etc.)

1041. *The Second Sex* (1949) was written by
(a) Simone de Beauvoir
(b) Elaine Showalter
(c) Kate Millet
(d) Luce Irigaray

1042. *The Feminine Mystique* (1963) was written by
(a) Julia Kristeva
(b) Betty Friedman
(c) Judith Butler
(d) Virginia Woolf

1043. *The Laugh of Medusa* (1975) is written by
(a) Toril Moi
(b) Kate Millet
(c) Helene Cixous
(d) Luce Irigaray

(*Medusa* : In Greek mythology, Medusa was a monster, generally having the face of a hideous human female with living venomous snakes in place of hair. Gazing directly upon her would term onlookers to stone. The myth has been adopted as a symbol of female rage in feminism.

*The Laugh of the Medusa*, Cixous says that "women must write herself, must write about women, and bring women to writing from which they have been driven away as violently as their bodies". Cixous and Irigaray, associated with feminist writing, refuse to accept traditional Western separation of mind and body. The mind has been linked with the male and body with the female. But these authors refuse the subordination of body to mind. These feminists see female sexuality as something that is apparent in a woman's written text. Language should emerge from the body of 'woman' and women should write about their bodily experience. Such a writing would help to overturn the grandnarratives of Western culture and enable them to attain what Cixous calls Jouissance, a pleasure that combines the erotic, the mystical and the political.)

1044. *The Mad Woman in the Attic* by Sandra Gilbert and Susan Guber was published in
(a) 1971
(b) 1972
(c) 1975
(d) 1979

1045. *A Room of One's Own* (1929) was written by
(a) Virginia Woolf

(b) Simone de Beauvoir
(c) Kate Millet
(d) Toril Moi

1046. Who argued that traditional writing and philosophy are 'phallocentric'?
(a) Toril Moi
(b) Helene Cixous
(c) Julia Kristeva
(d) Showalter

1047. Who wrote *A Literature of Their Own* (1977)?
(a) Virginia Woolf
(b) Luce Irigaray
(c) Elaine Showalter
(d) Kate Millet

1048. *Gender Trouble* (1990) is written by
(a) Kate Millet
(b) Helene Cixous
(c) Toril Moi
(d) Judith Butler

1049. What, according to Showalter, is the reason for the current impasse in feminist criticism?
(a) Women are not bold.
(b) Women are not laborious.
(c) Women are not as intelligent as men.
(d) Women have divided consciousness.

(Women live in the male tradition, but their participation in women movement creates another kind of awareness and commitments.)

1050. *Sexual Politics* (1970) was written by
(a) Virginia Woolf
(b) Kate Millet
(c) Elaine Showalter
(d) Helene Cixous

1051. *Women's Estate* (1971) was written by
(a) Virginia Woolf
(b) Juliet Mitchell
(c) Elaine Showalter
(d) Kate Millet

1052. *This Sex Which is Not One* (1981) was written by
(a) Luce Irigaray
(b) Carde Pateman
(c) Ellen Mores
(d) Kate Millet

1053. *The New Feminist Criticism* by Elaine Showalter was published in
(a) 1981
(b) 1983
(c) 1985
(d) 1987

1054. "The openness of feminist criticism appealed particularly to Americans who perceived the structuralist, post-structuralist, and deconstructionist debates of the 1970s as arid and falsely objective, the epitome of a pernicious masculine discourse from which many feminists wanted to escape. Recalling in *A Room of One's Own* how she had been prohibited from entering the University Library, the symbolic sanctuary of the male logos, Virginia Woolf wisely observed that while it is 'unpleasant to be locked out...it is, perhaps worse, to be locked in'."

Which critical theory does the passage point to?
(a) Structuralist
(b) Poststructuralism
(c) Deconstruction
(d) Feminist

(The passage is from Elaine Showalter's essay *Feminist Criticism in Wilderness* (1981).)

1055. Who is the author of *Thinking About Women* (1968)?

(a) Elaine Showalter
(b) Marry Elman
(c) Helene Cixous
(d) Kate Millet

(Mary Elman's *Thinking About Women* (1968) and Kate Millet's *Sexual Politics* (1970) are pioneering works of feminist criticism)

1056. *The Female Eunuch* (1970) was written by
(a) Germane Greer
(b) Virginia Woolf
(c) Toril Moi
(d) Helene Cixous

1057. Who has been called the "Mao Tse-Tung of Women's Liberation"?
(a) Toril Moi
(b) Kate Millet
(c) Judith Butler
(d) Showalter

1058. Why do feminists embrace the work of Jaques Lacan despite the fact that he was contemptuous of the women's movement?
(a) Because he rejected Freudianism.
(b) Because Lacan criticised Freud.
(c) Because he rewrote Freudianism.
(d) None of the above.

1059. According to Peter Barry, which theory is best understood by seeing it initially in the context of its own origins within feminism in the 1980s?
(a) Radical Feminism
(b) Endangered Feminism
(c) Beginning Feminism
(d) Lesbian Feminism

1060. Barbara Smith's *Towards a Black Feminist Criticism* (1977) made a lesbian reading of
(a) Sula
(b) The Bluest Eye
(c) The Colour Purple
(d) The Beloved

1061. Who coined the term 'queer'?
(a) Dorothy Allisson
(b) Teressa de Lauretis
(c) Barbara Smith
(d) Audre Lorde

(Teresa coined this term in a special issue she edited in 1991 for the feminist Journal *Differences*.)

1062. Who said, "We are all chimeras, theorised and fabricated hybrids of machine and organism; in short, we are cyborgs. The cyborg is our Ontology; it gives us our politics"?
(a) Donna Haraway
(b) Patricia Ducker
(c) Jonathan Dollimore
(d) Douglas Crimp

(The reference here is to 'lesbianism')

1063. Who, among the following, broke away from feminism and made new allegiances in particular with gay men rather than with other women?
(a) Muriel Spark
(b) Paulina Palmer
(c) Anne Koedt
(d) Bonnie Zimmerman

1064. The concept of "mad woman in the attic" can be traced to
(a) *The Tenant of Wildlife Hall*
(b) *Villete*
(c) *Jane Eyre*
(d) *Wuthering Heights*

(The reference here is to *The Mad Woman in the Attic* (1979) written by Gilbert and Guber. The title is derived from Charlotte Bronte's novel *Jane Eyre* (Chapter 26) in which Rochester's wife Bartha Mason is kept locked in the attic by Rochester himself.)

1065. The earliest tract on feminism is:
- (a) Simone de Beauvoir's *The Second Sex.*
- (b) Virginia Woolf's *A Room of One's Own.*
- (c) Mary Wollstonecraft's *A Vindication of the Rights of Women.*
- (d) Mary Astell's *A Serious Proposal to the Ladies.*

[(a): 1949; (b): 1929; (c): 1792; (d): 1694]

1066. *Sea Changes: Culture and Feminism* by Cora Kaplan was published in
- (a) 1985
- (b) 1986
- (c) 1987
- (d) 1988

1067. The thesis that language is 'masculine' is developed in the book *Man Made Language* (1981) written by
- (a) Julia Kristeva
- (b) Helene Cixous
- (c) Dale Spender
- (d) Luce Irigaray

1068. E. K. Sedgwick's *Epistemology of the Closet* (1992) is about
- (a) Cultural Materialism
- (b) New Historicism
- (c) Psychoanalytical Criticism
- (d) Lesbian/Gay Criticism

1069. *The Critical Difference* 1980 was written by
- (a) Barbara Johnson
- (b) Roland Barthes
- (c) Julia Kristeva
- (d) Gayatri Spivak

1070. Gayatri Spivak's *In Other Worlds : Essays in Cultural Politics* was published in
- (a) 1985
- (b) 1987
- (c) 1988
- (d) 1989

(In this classic work, Spivak analyzes the relationship between language, women and culture in both Western and non-Western contexts. Developing an original integration of deconstruction, Marxism and feminism, Spivak turns this model on major debates in the study of literature and culture.)

1071. Jill Johnston's *Lesbian Nation* was published in
- (a) 1971
- (b) 1972
- (c) 1973
- (d) 1975

(In *Lesbian Nation: The Feminist Solution*, Jill outlines her vision of radical lesbian feminism. She argues in favour of lesbian separatism, writing that women should make a total break from men and male-dominated capitalist institutions.)

1072. *Unbearable Weight: Feminism, Western Culture and the Body* (1993) was written by
- (a) Susan Bordo
- (b) Judith Butler
- (c) Helene Cixous
- (d) Toril Moi

1073. The author of *Bodies that Matter* (1993) is
- (a) Toril Moi
- (b) Judith Butler
- (c) Gayatri Spivak
- (d) Virginia Woolf

(*Bodies That Matter: On the Discursive Limits of 'Sex'* seeks to clear up readings and supposed misreadings of performativity that view the enactment of sex/gender as a daily choice. To do this, Butler emphasizes the role of repetition in performativity, making use of Derrida's use of iterability.)

1074. E.K. Sedgwick's *A Dialogue on Love* was published in
   (a) 1993
   (b) 1995
   (c) 1999
   (d) 2001

(As a founder of the academic discipline of 'queer studies', Sedgwick's special domain is postmodern discourse on sexuality. While undergoing therapy for depression while recovering from breast cancer, she finally confronts the question between her own sexual nature and her life's work, while also facing her feelings about death and family. In a narrative structured around her sessions with a male therapist, she spends a good deal of her time questioning whether he can appreciate her intellect or ever understand her world view, particularly her deep infatuations with gay men.)

1075. *Psychoanalysis and Feminism* (1974) was written by
   (a) Helene Cixous
   (b) Juliet Mitchell
   (c) Michele Burret
   (d) Rosalind Coward

(In this book, Mitchell tried to reconcile psychoanalysis and feminism at a time when many considered them incompatible. It was regarded as great contribution to the feminist debate on Freud, rising above Freud's male chauvinism in its analysis.)

1076. Juliet Mitchell's *Women: The Longest Revolution* was published in
   (a) 1966
   (b) 1981
   (c) 1983
   (d) 1985

1077. Jacqueline Rose's *Sexuality in the Field of Vision* was published in
   (a) 1982
   (b) 1984
   (c) 1986
   (d) 1988

(In this book, Rose argues for the importance of sexual difference and fantasy as key concepts through which an interrogation of contemporary theory should be sustained. She explores the interface between feminism, psychoanalysis and film theory.)

1078. The author of *The Daughter's Seduction: Feminism and Psychoanalysis* (1982) is
   (a) Rosalind Coward
   (b) Juliet Mitchell
   (c) Judith Butler
   (d) Jane Gallop

(The book studies the relation between contemporary feminist theory and the psychoanalysis of Jacques Lacan, and also dedicates three full chapters to a critical discussion of the work of Luce Irigaray.)

1079. Donna Haraway's *Simians, Cyborgs and Women: The Reinvention of Nature* was published in
   (a) 1991
   (b) 1993
   (c) 1995
   (d) 1997

(The book is a collection of ten powerful essays written between 1978 and 1989. Although on the surface, simians, cyborgs and women may seem an odd threesome, Haraway describes their profound link as 'creatures' which have had a great destabilizing place in Western evolutionary technology and biology. She analyses accounts, narratives, and stories of the creation of nature, living organisms, and cyborgs.)

1080. Anne Balsanco's *Technologies of the Gendered Bodies: Reading Cyborg Women* was published in
   (a) 1992
   (b) 1996
   (c) 1994
   (d) 1997

1081. Who is the author of *Talk on the Wilde Side: Toward a Genealogy of a Discourse on Male Sexualities* (1993)?
   (a) Dollimore
   (b) Robert K. Martin
   (c) Ed Cohen
   (d) Alan Bray

1082. Alan Bray's *Homosexuality in the Renaissance England* was published in
   (a) 1980
   (b) 1982
   (c) 1985
   (d) 1987

1083. The theoretical position of lesbian feminism was shaped by
   (a) The 'homophile movement'
   (b) The Furies
   (c) Radicalesbians
   (d) Both (b) and (c)

1084. The Radicalesbian's manifesto known as *The Woman Identified Woman* was published in
   (a) 1970
   (b) 1972
   (c) 1973
   (d) 1975

   (*The Women Identified Woman* was a ten-paragraph manifesto written by Radicalesbians in 1970. It was distributed during the 'Lavender Menace' protest at the *Second Congress to Unite Women*, on May 1070 in New York City. It is now considered a turning point in the history of radical feminism, and one of the founding documents of lesbian feminism.)

1085. Who, among the following, said, "Feminism at heart is a massive complaint, lesbianism is the solution"?
   (a) Jill Johnston
   (b) Ed Cohen
   (c) Dollimore
   (d) Alan Bray

1086. The journal associated with lesbian theory is
   (a) *The Pleasures of Lesbianism*
   (b) *Woman and Woman*
   (c) *Sinister Wisdom*
   (d) None of the above

1087. Adrienne Rich's essay *Compulsory Hetrosexuality and Lesbian Existence* was published in
   (a) 1980
   (b) 1982
   (c) 1983
   (d) 1985

1088. *Surpassing the Love of Men* (1981) was written by
   (a) Adrienne Rich
   (b) Lillian Faderman
   (c) Alan Bray
   (d) Dollimore

   (A classic of its kind, the fascinating cultural history draws on everything from private correspondence to pornography to explore five hundred years of friendship and love between women. *Surpassing the Love of Men*, throws new light on shifting theories of female sexuality and the changing status of women over the centuries.)

1089. The essay "The Beast in the Closet" was written by
   (a) Dollimore
   (b) Alan Bray
   (c) Eve Kosofsky Sedgwick
   (d) Judith Butler

(The essay first appeared in *Sex, Politics, and Science in the Nineteenth Century Novel* (1986).)

1090. Audre Lorde's *Zami : A New Spelling of My Name* was published in
   (a) 1981
   (b) 1983
   (c) 1985
   (d) 1986

1091. Gloria Anzaldua's *Borderlands/La Frontera* was published in
   (a) 1987
   (b) 1988
   (c) 1989
   (d) 1990

1092. The author of *Skin: Talking about Sex, Class, and Literature* (1994) was written by
   (a) Jill Johnston
   (b) Alan Bray
   (c) Ed Cohen
   (d) Dorothy Elison

1093. *One Hundred Years of Homosexuality* (1989) was written by
   (a) David Halperin
   (b) Douglas Crimp
   (c) Lee Edelman
   (d) Jonathan Dollimore

1094. What is fundamental to the gender criticism is the premise that ________ is distinct
   (a) sex (Male/Female)
   (b) gender (Masculine/Feminine)
   (c) sexuality (Homosexuality/ Hetrosexuality)
   (d) All of the above

1095. *The Last Nude* (2012) is written by
   (a) Debra Anderson
   (b) Bert Archer
   (c) Ellis Avery
   (d) Etel Adnan

(A stunning story of love, sexual obsession, treachery and her most famous muse in Paris between the World Wars.)

1096. *Troublesome Helpmate* (1966) was written by
   (a) Katherine M. Roger
   (b) Julia Kristeva
   (c) Judith Butler
   (d) Kate Millet

1097. Judith Butler's *The Psychic Life of Power* was written in
   (a) 1995
   (b) 1997
   (c) 1999
   (d) 2001

(*The Psychic Life of Power—Theories in Subjection* draws upon Hegel, Nietzsche, Freud, Foucault and Althusser. This lucid work offers a theory of subject formation that illuminates as ambivalent the psychic effects of social power.)

1098. Pater Schwenger's *Phallic Critiques: Masculinity and Twentieth Century Literature* was published in
   (a) 1980
   (b) 1983
   (c) 1984
   (d) 1987

(Extending feminist literary criticism beyond the study of masculine bias on women, *Phallic Critiques* examines literature by the School of Virility in order to study the effects of masculine biases on men who possess them.)

1099. The author of *Between Men: English Literature and Homosexual Desire* (1985) is
   (a) E.K. Sedgwick
   (b) Helene Cixous
   (c) Kate Millet
   (d) Toril Moi

1100. David Halperin's *Saint Foucault: Towards a Gay Hagiography* was published in
(a) 1990
(b) 1995
(c) 1993
(d) 1996

(David Halperin's book is an uncompromising and impassioned defense of the late French philosopher and historian whose career, as a theorist and activist will continue to serve as a model for other gay intellectuals, activists and scholars.)

1101. Richard Dellamora's *Masculine Desire: The Sexual Politics of Victorian Aestheticism* was published in
(a) 1987
(b) 1989
(c) 1998
(d) 1990

(Beginning with Tennyson's *In Memoriam* and continuing by way of Hopkins and Swinburne to the novels of Oscar Wilde and Thomas Hardy, Delamore draws on journals, letters, concerned texts, and pornography to examine the cultural construction of masculity in Victorian literature.)

1102. *The Companion Species Manifesto : Dogs, People, and the Significant Otherness* by Donna Haraway was published in
(a) 1998
(b) 2001
(c) 2003
(d) 2005

(The book is about the implosion of nature and culture in the joint lives of dogs and people, who are bonded in 'significant otherness'. In all their historical complexity, Haraway tells us, dogs matter. They are not here just to think with. Neither are they just an alibi for other themes, dogs are fleshly material—semiotic presence in the body of technoscience. They are here to live with.)

1103. The author of *Private Visions: Gender, Race and Nature in the World of Modern Science* (1989) was written by
(a) Donna Haraway
(b) Judith Butler
(c) Helene Cixous
(d) Kate Millet

1104. Who is the author of *Simians, Cyborgs, and Women: The Reinvention of Nature* (1991)
(a) Helene Cixous
(b) Donna Haraway
(c) Kate Millet
(d) Toril Moi

1105. "Black Feminism" arose in the
(a) 1960s
(b) 1970s
(c) 1980s
(d) 1990s

(Black feminism argues that sexism, class oppression, and racism are inextricably bound together. The way they are related to each other is called intersectionality. Forms of feminism that strive to overcome sexism and class oppression but ignore race can discrimate against many people, since it would require the end of racism, sexism and class oppression. One of the theories that evolved out of Black feminist movement was Alice Walker's 'womanism'. Alice pointed out black women experienced a different and more intense kind of oppression from that of white woman.)

1106. *The First Sex* (1971) was written by
(a) Toril Moi
(b) Kate Millet
(c) Elizabeth Gould Davis
(d) Helene Cixous

(*The First Sex* is considered part of the Second Wave of Feminism. In this book, Gould Davis aimed to show that early human society consisted of matriarchal 'queendoms' based around the worship of the 'Great Goddess' and characterized by pacifism and democracy. Davis argued that the early matriarchal societies attained a high level of civilization, which was largely wiped out as a result of the 'patriarchal revolution'.)

1107. Kate Millet described sexual politics as
(a) politics against women.
(b) considering women as sex objects.
(c) role of women in politics.
(d) the "arrangements whereby one group of persons is controlled by other".

1108. The "arrangements" to which Kate Millet refers may be
(a) physical and economic.
(b) social and psychological.
(c) ideological.
(d) All of the above.

1109. The concept 'anxiety of authorship' is associated with
(a) Gilbert and Gubar
(b) Nancy Chodorow
(c) Harold Bloom
(d) Judith Butler

(As against Harold Bloom's *Anxiety of Influence*, here Gilbert and Guber question the ability of the anxious woman writer even to contemplate her status as an author in a culture whose literary tradition is in vast majority a patriarchal one, with a distinct death of female writers and an overabundance of flighty female characters appearing in texts authored by members of both sexes. In such a situation, how a woman can arrive at the confident self-conception necessary to write successfully.)

1110. Marry Ellman's *Thinking about Women* was published in
(a) 1961
(b) 1968
(c) 1964
(d) 1966

(The essay *Thinking about Women* discusses the evolution of feminity representation in British and American literature, namely by exhibiting sexual analogies and women stereotypes from the text and contrasting criticism from male and female authors.)

1111. The term 'Chora' was introduced by
(a) Toril Moi
(b) Kate Millet
(c) Julia Kristeva
(d) Gayatri Spivak

(The term is introduced in Kristeva's *Revolution in Poetic Language* (1974). It is a philosophical term described by Plato in *Timaes* as a receptable, a space, or an interval between in which "forms" were originally held. It is symbolic of "womb". Kristeva uses the term as part of her analysis of the difference between the semiotic and the symbolic realms.)

1112. Which of the following critics made great contribution to the French feminist movement?
(a) Luce Irigarey
(b) Helene Cixous
(c) Simone de Beauvoir
(d) None of the above

1113. *The Bounded Text* (1980) was written by
(a) Julia Kristeva
(b) Roland Barthes
(c) Michel Foucault
(d) Derrida

1114. *The Prisoner of Sex* (1971) was written by
(a) Luce Irigaray
(b) Norman Mailer
(c) Helene Cixous
(d) Toril Moi

1115. "The Gay Liberation Movement" started in
(a) 1989
(b) 1979
(c) 1969
(d) 1975

(The Gay Liberation Movement had its origin in the Stonewall Riots of 1969. The riots broke out when the police raided the Stonewall Tavern in New York-the meeting point of Gays and Lesbians.)

1116. Adrienne Rich's essay *Compulsory Hetrosexuality and Lesbian Existence* was published in
(a) 1973
(b) 1980
(c) 1975
(d) 1979

(Adrienne Rich argues that heterosexuality is a violent political institution making way for the "male right of physical, economical, and emotional access" to women. She urges women to direct their energies towards other women rather than men, and portrays lesbianism as an extension of feminism.)

1117. Who said, "There is nothing outside or before nature, no nature that is not always and already enculturated"?
(a) Levi-Strauss
(b) Derrida
(c) Teressa de Lauretis
(d) Northrop Frye

(The reference is to 'Queer Theory')

1118. 'The Queer Theory' emerged in the
(a) 1970s
(b) 1980s
(c) 1960s
(d) 1990s

1119. *Yaraana: Gay Writing from India* (1999) was edited by
(a) Chetan Bhagat
(b) Hoshang Merchant
(c) E.K. Sedgwick
(d) Audre Lorde

1120. *The Lesbian and Gay Studies Reader* was published in
(a) 1993
(b) 1995
(c) 1997
(d) 1981

1121. *Coming Out* (1977) and *Sexualities and its Discontents* (1985) are written by
(a) Judith Butler
(b) Jeffrey Weeks
(c) Sedgwick
(d) D.A. Miller

1122. *Queer Theory/Sociology* edited by Steven Saidman was published in
(a) 1921
(b) 1994
(c) 1996
(d) 1998

1123. *The Newly Born Woman* (1975 trans 1986) was written by Helene Cixous in collaboration with
(a) Catherine Clement
(b) Toril Moi
(c) Julia Kristeva
(d) Luce Irigaray

1124. The metaphorical significance of 'Room' in Virginia Woolf's *A Room of One's Own* is that
(a) a woman should remain within limits.
(b) a woman should live separately from her family.
(c) a woman should never leave her room.
(d) a "woman must have money and a room of her own if she is to write fiction".

(Woman needs financial and psychological independence in order to exercise their creative potentiality. They need a "tradition, language, economic and intellectual independence".)

1125. *The Ethics of Ambiguity* (1947) was written by
(a) William Empson
(b) Cleanth Brooks
(c) Simone de Beauvoir
(d) Luce Irigaray

1126. Who said, "Legislators, priests, philosophers, writers, and scientists have striven to show that the subordinate position of woman is willed in heaven and advantageous on earth"?
(a) Elaine Showalter
(b) Simone de Beauvoir
(c) Stuart Mill
(d) Luce Irigaray

1127. Who were the women writers that were pioneers in gaining access to the literary profession in the 17th century?
(a) Aphra Behn
(b) Christine de Pisan
(c) Anne Bradstreet
(d) Both (a) and (c)

1128. *The Dialectic of Sex* (1970) was written by
(a) Betty Friedman
(b) Shulamith Firestone
(c) Marry Ellman
(d) Michele Barret

1129. *Women's Oppression Today* (1980) was written by
(a) Michele Barret
(b) Virginia Woolf
(c) Judith Fetterley
(d) Betty Friedman

(In this book, she outlines some of the problems facing any attempt to forge a coalition of Marxist and Feminist perspectives.)

1130. Who was the first female writer who earned her living by writing?
(a) Emile Bronte
(b) George Eliot
(c) Aphra Behn
(d) Mary Shelley

1131. Who has said, "Movement and change are the essence of our being; rigidity is death; conformity is death"?
(a) Sartre
(b) Virginia Woolf
(c) Camus
(d) Kierkgaard

1132. Who has said, "Poetry ought to have a mother as well as a father"?
(a) Virginia Woolf
(b) Kate Millet
(c) Toril Moi
(d) Julia Kristeva

1133. Virginia Woolf made the following observation about a woman writer in her book *A Room of One's Own*: she 'mastered the first great lesson; she wrote as a woman, but as a woman who has forgotten that she is a woman, so that her pages were full of that curious sexual quality which comes only when sex is unconscious of itself." Who is this woman writer?

(a) George Eliot
(b) Dorothy Richardson
(c) Mary Charmichael (a fictional woman writer)
(d) Emile Bronte

1134. Who said, "Among all savage beasts none is found so harmful as a woman"?
(a) St. Ambrose
(b) St. John Chrysostom
(c) St. Thomas
(d) Tertullian

(Quoted in *The Second Sex* by Simone de Beauvoir)

1135. Who, among the following, said, that the body is not a thing but a situation?
(a) Helene Cixous
(b) Simone de Beauvoir
(c) Elaine Showalter
(d) Toril Moi

1136. Who is 'feminist' for Virginia Woolf?
(a) One who writes for women.
(b) One who defends women.
(c) One who shares the problems of women.
(d) One who champions the rights of women.

1137. *The Subjection of Women* (1869) was written by
(a) John Stuart Mill
(b) Virginia Woolf
(c) Julia Kristeva
(d) Elaine Showalter

(Stuart Mill has observed that it would be very difficult for women to free themselves from the constraints and influences of the male literary tradition.)

1138. Who expressed the view that gender is not what one is, but what one does?
(a) Helene Cixous
(b) Judith Butler
(c) Simone de Beavoir
(d) Kate Millet

1139. Luce Irigaray's *Speculum of Other Woman* was published in
(a) 1970
(b) 1973
(c) 1977
(d) 1979

(The book is one of the most important works in feminist theory. Irigaray believes that female sexuality has remained a 'dark continent' for the profession of psychoanalysis. Its nature can only be misunderstood by those who continue to regard women in masculine terms.)

1140. Whose view is that women have "sex organs more or less everywhere" and that "she is indefinitely in herself"?
(a) Helene Cixous
(b) Luce Irigaray
(c) Julia Kristeva
(d) Toril Moi

(Luce Irigaray expressed this view in her book *This Sex is Not One* (1985).)

1141. Luce Irigaray's *Towards a Culture of Difference* was published in
(a) 1990
(b) 1992
(c) 1994
(d) 1996

(This series of short essays on language, power, women, gender, and patriarchal mythologies lays out what for Irigaray has become the central problem in the modern world. Irigaray believes that 'social change' depends upon 'linguistic change'. Only then can mothers educate their daughters and need to find out their own subjectivity.)

1142. Who coined the term "Homosocial desire"?

(a) Julia Kristeva
(b) E.K. Sedgwick
(c) Helene Cixous
(d) Kate Millet

(In sociology, 'homosociality' describes same sex relationships that are not of a romantic or sexual nature such as friendship, mentorship, etc. 'Homosocial' was popularised by Sedgwick in her discussion of male homosocial desire. She identifies a continuum between homosociality and homosexuality. She defines male homosociality as a form of male bonding with a characteristic triangular structure. In this triangle men have intense but non-sexual bonds with either men and women serve as the conduits through which these bonds are expressed. In this love triangle, two men appear to be competing for a woman's love.)

1143. *An Ethics of Sexual Difference* (1984, trans 1993) was written by
(a) Helene Cixous
(b) Luce Irigaray
(c) Showalter
(d) Simone de Beauvoir

**ANSWERS**

| | | | | | |
|---|---|---|---|---|---|
| 1029. (c) | 1030. (b) | 1031. (a) | 1032. (d) | 1033. (b) | 1034. (a) |
| 1035. (c) | 1036. (a) | 1037. (d) | 1038. (c) | 1039. (b) | 1040. (b) |
| 1041. (a) | 1042. (b) | 1043. (c) | 1044. (d) | 1045. (a) | 1046. (b) |
| 1047. (c) | 1048. (d) | 1049. (d) | 1050. (b) | 1051. (b) | 1052. (a) |
| 1053. (c) | 1054. (d) | 1055. (b) | 1056. (a) | 1057. (b) | 1058. (c) |
| 1059. (d) | 1060. (a) | 1061. (b) | 1062. (a) | 1063. (b) | 1064. (c) |
| 1065. (d) | 1066. (b) | 1067. (c) | 1068. (d) | 1069. (a) | 1070. (b) |
| 1071. (c) | 1072. (a) | 1073. (b) | 1074. (c) | 1075. (b) | 1076. (a) |
| 1077. (c) | 1078. (d) | 1079. (a) | 1080. (b) | 1081. (c) | 1082. (b) |
| 1083. (d) | 1084. (a) | 1085. (a) | 1086. (c) | 1087. (a) | 1088. (b) |
| 1089. (c) | 1090. (a) | 1091. (a) | 1092. (d) | 1093. (a) | 1094. (d) |
| 1095. (c) | 1096. (a) | 1097. (b) | 1098. (c) | 1099. (a) | 1100. (b) |
| 1101. (d) | 1102. (c) | 1103. (a) | 1104. (b) | 1105. (b) | 1106. (c) |
| 1107. (d) | 1108. (d) | 1109. (a) | 1110. (b) | 1111. (c) | 1112. (b) |
| 1113. (a) | 1114. (b) | 1115. (c) | 1116. (b) | 1117. (c) | 1118. (d) |
| 1119. (b) | 1120. (a) | 1121. (b) | 1122. (c) | 1123. (a) | 1124. (d) |
| 1125. (c) | 1126. (b) | 1127. (d) | 1128. (b) | 1129. (a) | 1130. (c) |
| 1131. (b) | 1132. (a) | 1133. (c) | 1134. (b) | 1135. (b) | 1136. (d) |
| 1137. (a) | 1138. (b) | 1139. (c) | 1140. (b) | 1141. (a) | 1142. (a) |
| 1143. (a) | | | | | |

## (XVII) HERMENEUTICS, PHENOMENOLOGY AND RECEPTION THEORY

1144. Who is regarded as the pioneer of phenomenology?
(a) Edmund Husserl
(b) Homi K. Bhabha
(c) C.L. Jung
(d) Freud

1145. One of the following does not belong to the Geneva School of Phenomenological Criticism:
(a) Georges Poulet
(b) Jean Rousset
(c) Hillis Miller
(d) Terry Eagleton

1146. *The Range of Interpretation* (2000) was written by
(a) Stanley Fish
(b) Wolfgang Iser
(c) Steven Mailloux
(d) Norman

1147. *Aesthetic Experience and Literary Hermeneutics* by Hans Robert Jauss was published in English in
(a) 1980
(b) 1981
(c) 1982
(d) 1984

1148. "Interpretation Theory" (1976) was written by
(a) Hans Robert Jauss
(b) Stanley Fish
(c) Hans-Georg Gadamer
(d) Paul Ricoeur

1149. Who coined the term "hermeneutic circle"?
(a) Hans-Georg Gadamer
(b) Julia Kristeva
(c) Wilhelm Dilthey
(d) Martin Heidegger

(In 1819, German Theologian, Friedrich Schleiemacher first developed a theory of hermeneutics in the general sense of textual interpretation. Wilhelm Dilthey, a German philosopher, coined the term 'hermeneutic circle' to refer to a procedure originally described by Schleiermacher, who was referring to the idea that to understand the parts of a whole, one must begin with some general conception of what the whole is and vice versa. While this may seem to a circular task, Dilthey argued that our perception and, therefore, our interpretation of both the whole and its component parts are modified as we move through the work.)

1150. Who, among the following, wrote, *The Phenomenology of Spirit (Or of Mind)*
(a) G.W. Hegel
(b) Nietzsche
(c) Kant
(d) Husserl

1151. *Being and Time* (1927) was written by
(a) Edmund Husserl
(b) Martin Heidegger
(c) Roman Ingarden
(d) Georges Poulet

1152. Edmund Husserl's *Ideas Pertaining to a Pure Phenomenology and Phenomenological Philosophy* was published in
(a) 1916
(b) 1914
(c) 1913
(d) 1919

1153. Who coined the term "implied reader"?
(a) Edmund Husserl
(b) Hans Robert Jauss
(c) D.W. Harding
(d) Wolfgang Iser

(The term was coined by the German critic Wolfgang Iser. In Iser's view, the literary text in part controls the readers' responses, but always contains a number of 'gaps' or 'indeterminate elements'. These the reader must fill in by a creative participation in what is given in the text before him.)

1154. Umberto Eco's *The Role of the Reader* was published in
(a) 1979
(b) 1980
(c) 1982
(d) 1985

1155. By whom was hermeneutic phenomenology developed?
(a) Hans-Georg Gadamer
(b) Paul Ricoeur
(c) Edmund Husserl
(d) Both (a) and (b)

1156. *Lectures and Phenomenology of Inner Time Consciousness* (1928) was written by
(a) Edmund Husserl
(b) Georges Poulet
(c) Martin Heidegger
(d) Paul Ricoeur

1157. *Time and Modes of Being* (trans 1964) was written by
(a) Martin Heidegger
(b) Roman Ingarden
(c) Georges Poulet
(d) Edmund Husserl

1158. The essay "Reading Ourselves: Towards a Feminist Theory of Reading" is written by
(a) Edmund Husserl
(b) Stanley Fish
(c) Patrocinio P. Schweickart
(d) E.D. Hirsch

1159. Who is known as the founding father of phenomenological aesthetics?
(a) Martin Heidgger
(b) Edmund Husserl
(c) E.D. Hirsch
(d) Roman Ingarden

1160. One of the disadvantages of this school of criticism is that it tends to make readings too subjective:
(a) Historical Criticism
(b) Reader Response Criticism
(c) Formalist Criticism
(d) None of the above

1161. "As the reader uses the various perspectives offered him by the text in order to relate the patterns and the 'schematized views' to one another, he sets the work in motion, and this very process results ultimately in the awakening of responses within himself. Thus, the reading process causes the literary work to unfold its inherently dynamic character".

Which critical theory do these lines suggest?
(a) Psychoanalytical Criticism
(b) Formalist Criticism
(c) Reception Theory
(d) New Criticism

(The lines occur in Wolfgang Iser's essay "The Reading Process: A Phenomenological Approach".)

1162. Who, among the following, was a Polish phenomenologist?
(a) Martin Heideggar
(b) Edmund Husserl
(c) Georges Poulet
(d) Marcuse

1163. *Cartesian Meditations* (1931) was written by

(a) Edmund Husserl
(b) Georges Poulet
(c) Heidegger
(d) Ingarden

1164. The "Constance School" at the University of Constance in Germany is associated with
(a) Phenomenological Criticism
(b) Reader-Response and Reception Theory
(c) Archetyptal Criticism
(d) Marxist Criticism

1165. Much of the Reader-response theory had its origins in
(a) Psychoanalysis
(b) Phenomenology
(c) Marxism
(d) None of the above

1166. Who is associated with the concept "phenomenological reduction"?
(a) Wolfgang Isser
(b) Hans Robert Jauss
(c) Marcuse
(d) Husserl

(According to Edmund Husserl, phenomenology shifts our emphasis away from the study of "external" world of objects toward examining the ways in which these objects *appear* to the human subject. This "bracketing" of the external world is referred to by Husserl as "phenomenological reduction". According to Husserl, "phenomenological reduction" is the method for effecting "radical purification of the phenomenological field of consciousness from all obtrusions from objective actualities".)

1167. What, according to Martin Heidegger, characteristics a human being (*dasein*)?
(a) Facticity
(b) Existentiality or Transcendence
(c) Fallenness
(d) All of the above

("Facticity" is 'Thrownness' into the world, i.e. the fact of a human being already cast into a series of relationships and surroundings and constitute his or her 'world'. "Existentiality" or "Transcendence" means that a human being appropriates, impressing upon it the unique image of his own existence and potential. "Falleness", happens when a man tries to create himself in this world through appropriation, he falls from true being. This is because he becomes immersed in the distractions of day-to-day living, being entangled in particular beings.)

1168. Heidegger's *The Origin of the Work of Art* was published in
(a) 1950
(b) 1953
(c) 1955
(d) 1958

1169. *Language* (1950) was written by
(a) Martin Heidegger
(b) Jakobson
(c) Shklovsky
(d) Saussure

1170. While defining art, who has said, "Art then is the becoming and happening of truth"?
(a) Walter Pater
(b) A.C. Swinburne
(c) Martin Heidegger
(d) Rossetti

(Heidegger means to say that art creates as well as preserves truth.)

1171. *Literary History as a Challenge to Literary Theory* (1969) was written by
(a) Edmund Husserl
(b) Hans Robert Jauss

(c) Heidegger
(d) William Empson

1172. Who is associated with the concept "horizon of expectations"?
(a) Heidegger
(b) Husserl
(c) Hirsch
(d) Hans Robert Jauss

(For Jauss, readers have a mind set, a limit of their *experience*, *interest*, *knowledge* from which perspective they, at any given time in history, read a text. The response of a reader to a text is the "joint product of the reader's own horizon of expectations", and the confirmations, disappointments, refutations, and reformulations of these expectations when they are "challenged by the features of the text itself" (M.H. Abrams).)

1173. Who is associated with the concept "intentional sentence correlatives"?
(a) Heidegger
(b) Ingarden
(c) Wolfgang Iser
(d) Hans Robert Jauss

(According to this concept, a series of sentences in a work of literature does not refer to any objective reality outside itself. Rather, the complex of these sentences gives rise to a "particular world", the world presented in the literary work, i.e. the 'connections' between various sentences are established by the work itself, but are determined by the reader). (Reader-response Theory)

1174. In which of the following does Stanley Fish's concept 'Interpretive Communities' occur?
(a) Surprised by Sin: The Reader in Paradise Lost (1967)
(b) Self-consuming Artifacts: The Experience of Seventeenth Century Literature (1976)
(c) Interpreting the *Varionum* (1976)
(d) None of the above

(This concept has been explored more fully in his book Is There a Text in This Class? The Authority of Interpretive Communities (1980) Fish used this term to acknowledge the existence of multiple and diverse reading groups within any large reading population.)

1175. Marcel Raymond's book *From Baudelaire to Surrealism* to which the Geneva School of critics, acknowledge their indebtedness, was published in
(a) 1933
(b) 1935
(c) 1937
(d) 1939

(The English version of the book appeared in 1949)

1176. Who said, "Man...is not merely a living creature possessing among other faculties that of language. Language is rather the house of being and man exists dwelling therein as he guards the truth of Being to which he belongs"?
(a) J.L. Austin
(b) John Searle
(c) Martin Heidegger
(d) Peirce

(Martin Heidegger expressed this view in *On the Way to Language* (1959).)

1177. *The Origin of Art* (1933-34) was written by
(a) Martin Heidegger
(b) Neitzsche
(c) Pater
(d) Sartre

1178. Heidegger's *The End of Philosophy and the Task of Thinking* was published in
(a) 1969
(b) 1972
(c) 1973
(d) 1974

1179. Wolfgang Iser's *The Fictitive and the Imaginary* was published in
(a) 1990
(b) 1991
(c) 1993
(d) 1995

1180. When did the phenomenological movement begin?
(a) 1905
(b) 1907
(c) 1909
(d) 1911

1181. Reader-response Criticism focuses on the
(a) Content
(b) Reader
(c) Author
(d) Style

1182. *A Phenomenology of Reading* (1969) was written by
(a) Georges Poulet
(b) Edmund Husserl
(c) Wolfgang Iser
(d) Hans Robert Jauss

1183. Who is an 'implied reader'?
(a) An ideal audience envisioned by the author and to whom the work of literature is implicitly addressed.
(b) A reader who embodies all those predispositions necessary for a literary work to exercise its effect.
(c) The ideal average reader who can approach the work of literature with no preconceived ideas.
(d) The reader of a work of literature which is approximated overtime by the successive responses of generations of actual readers.

1184. Critics have long disagreed over how to interpret Milton's portrayal of Satan in "Paradise Lost". Which of the following theses would be considered an example of Reader-response criticism?
(a) The fact that readers can so easily sympathise with Milton's Satan suggests that the meaning of "Paradise Lost" lies in the poem's capacity to read us.
(b) Milton intended Satan to be read as a Promethean figure who would appeal to all readers at all times.
(c) Milton wrote for an audience that would have shared his idiosyncratic theological beliefs.
(d) Satan is only one character among many in "Paradise Lost", and he should be read in the context of a didactic poem whose overall message is more important than the vividness of any of its parts.

1185. Which of the following has not been offered by Reader–response critics as constraint upon interpretation?
(a) Agreement with an 'interpretive community'.
(b) Resonance with respect to given archetypes.
(c) The rhetorical constraints upon the author at the time of composition.
(d) The textuality established predispositions of an 'implied reader'.

1186. The German philosopher Edmund Husserl argued that objects can be regarded as things ____________ by consciousness.

Fill in the blanks with one of the following which you think to be the appropriate answer.

(a) intended
(b) evaluated
(c) understood
(d) realized

1187. According to Terry Eagleton, Stanley Fishe's model (Reception Theory) excludes the possibility that there is a _______ of interpretations.

Fill in the blanks with one of the following:

(a) dominance
(b) acception
(c) rejection
(d) struggle

1188. Eagleton argues that for Stanley Fish, what a text 'does' to us is a matter of what we do to the __________.

(a) reader
(b) author
(c) critic
(d) text

1189. What is the name of the American hermeneutics E.D. Hirsch's famous 1967 book?

(a) *Being and Time*
(b) *Validity in Interpretation*
(c) *Meaning or Method*
(d) *Truth and Fact*

1190. The Reader-response theory implies that

(a) there is no meaning in the text.
(b) the readers of an age construct the meaning.
(c) beliefs determine meaning.
(d) style is the hallmark of the text.

## ANSWERS

| | | | | | |
|---|---|---|---|---|---|
| 1144. (a) | 1145. (d) | 1146. (b) | 1147. (c) | 1148. (d) | 1149. (c) |
| 1150. (a) | 1151. (b) | 1152. (c) | 1153. (d) | 1154. (a) | 1155. (d) |
| 1156. (a) | 1157. (b) | 1158. (c) | 1159. (d) | 1160. (b) | 1161. (c) |
| 1162. (d) | 1163. (a) | 1164. (b) | 1165. (b) | 1166. (d) | 1167. (d) |
| 1168. (b) | 1169. (a) | 1170. (c) | 1171. (b) | 1172. (d) | 1173. (b) |
| 1174. (c) | 1175. (a) | 1176. (c) | 1177. (a) | 1178. (b) | 1179. (c) |
| 1180. (a) | 1181. (b) | 1182. (b) | 1183. (b) | 1184. (a) | 1185. (c) |
| 1186. (a) | 1187. (c) | 1188. (d) | 1189. (b) | 1190. (b) | |

## (XVIII) EXISTENTIALISM

1191. Who is known as the father of Existentialism?

(a) Sartre
(b) Camus
(c) Soren Kierkgaard
(d) Kafka

1192. What all existentialists, according to Sartre, are of the view is that

(a) God does not exist, and so everything is permitted.
(b) all humans have a common nature.
(c) essence precedes existence.
(d) existence precedes essence.

(This view of existentialists is just the opposite of Cartesian philosophy of dualism. Rene Descartes, the French philosopher, held the view that essence precedes existence. His famous sentence is: "I think, therefore I am".)

1193. According to Sartre, existentialism is a doctrine intended strictly for
(a) all people.
(b) all specialists and philosophers.
(c) Europeans.
(d) atheists.

1194. In Sartre's view, when one chooses how to live one is choosing to live
(a) For all people
(b) Only for oneself
(c) For one's family
(d) One's friends

1195. Sartre claims that when he speaks of forlornness, he means that
(a) we can never truly know another human being.
(b) God does not exist and we must face all the consequences of this, i.e. for our actions.
(c) we are not responsible for our passions.
(d) All of the above.

1196. According to Sartre, the existentialist finds that the fact that God does not exist
(a) Liberating
(b) Clarifying
(c) Very distressing
(d) Unimportant

1197. In Sartre's view, humans are responsible for
(a) Their actions
(b) Their passions
(c) Both (a) and (b)
(d) Neither (a) nor (b)

1198. Sartre claims that the view of one's affection is determined by
(a) the way one acts.
(b) the way one feels.
(c) the way one thinks.
(d) All of the above.

1199. Sartre claims that according to existentialism, there is no reality, except in
(a) Passion
(b) Action
(c) Contemplation
(d) Living

1200. According to Camus, the only truly philosophical problem is
(a) Free will
(b) God's existence
(c) Skepticism
(d) Suicide

1201. Camus describes the feeling of absurdity as the feeling
(a) of divorce between man and his life.
(b) that logic itself is inconsistent.
(c) that one who has undermined one's own basic projects that one cannot achieve anything.
(d) that one cannot achieve anything.

1202. Camus claims that we should respond to the recognition that life is absurd by
(a) ignoring it.
(b) refusing to hope.
(c) committing suicide.
(d) taking steps so that one's life may not longer be absurd.

1203. Camus says that knowing whether man is free is
(a) the most important problem of metaphysics.
(b) crucial to determining whether life is absurd.

(c) easy for the common man but difficult for the philosopher.
(d) of no interest to him.

1204. Camus thinks that what truly matters in life is
(a) living as well as possible.
(b) living as kindly as possible.
(c) living as much as possible.
(d) living as selfishly as possible.

1205. According to a Greek myth, Sisyphus was condemned to
(a) spend eternity in Hades.
(b) roll a rock to the top of mountain everyday.
(c) serve humans forever.
(d) to fly on wings of wax.

(According to a Greek myth, Sisyphus was the king of Corinth. The reasons for his punishment vary. Some say he revealed to Aegina's father, the river-god Asophus, that she had been abducted by Zeus. Another reason suggested was that Zeus sent Thanatos (Death) to kill Sisyphus, who imprisoned him so that no mortals can die. Zeus forced him to release Thanatos, whose first victim was Sisyphus, but he had asked his wife, Merope, to make sure that no funerary were paid so that when he reached the underworld, he persuaded the gods to return to earth to punish his wife. He was allowed to return to earth and lived to a great age. When he died, the gods decided that he should not escape again and set him the unending task of rolling a rock to the top of mountain everyday. Hence, a ceaseless and fruitless task that must be repeated is called a burden or labour of Sisyphus or a Sisyphean task.)

1206. According to Camus, the myth of Sisyphus is tragic only because he is
(a) treated unfairly.
(b) morally admirable.
(c) conscious.
(d) defeated.

1207. Camus says that we must imagine Sisyphus to be
(a) Exhausted
(b) Bored
(c) Angry
(d) Happy

1208. In her theory of existentialism, Simone de Beauvoir was influenced by
(a) Camus
(b) Kierkegaard
(c) Sartre
(d) Kafka

1209. Who coined the term 'existentialism'?
(a) Satre
(b) Gabriel Proust
(c) Kierkegaard
(d) Camus

1210. When did Sartre discuss his own existential position?
(a) 1940
(b) 1941
(c) 1943
(d) 1945

(Sartre made his existential position clear in a lecture to the "Club Maintenant" in Paris, on October 29, 1945.)

1211. Who is the author of *Being and Nothingness* (1943)?
(a) Pascal
(b) Kafka
(c) Sartre
(d) Camus

1212. Sartre's book *Existentialism is a Humanism* was published in
(a) 1946
(b) 1948

(c) 1949
(d) 1950

1213. Who is the author of *The Tragic Sense of Life in Men and Nations* (1912)?
(a) Sartre
(b) Kafka
(c) Unamunoy Jugo
(d) Kierkegaard

1214. *Existence and Objectivity* (1925) was written by
(a) Kierkegaard
(b) Simone de Beauvoir
(c) Sartre
(d) Gabriel Marcel

1215. Name Sartre's works which are based on existenial themes.
(a) *Nausea*
(b) *The Flies*
(c) *In Camera*
(d) All of the above

(*Nausea* (1938) is a novel, while *The Flies* (1943) and *In Camera* (1946) are plays. Sartre's collection of short stories *The Wall* (1939) is also based on existential themes.)

1216. Who is the author of *The Plague* (1947)?
(a) Sartre
(b) Kafka
(c) Camus
(d) None of the above

1217. Who is the author of the *The Blood of Others* (1945)?
(a) Simone de Beauvoir
(b) Sartre
(c) Kafka
(d) Camus

1218. *What is Literature* (1947) was written by
(a) Kafka
(b) Gabriel Marcel
(c) Camus
(d) Sartre

1219. The author of *Caligula* (1944) is
(a) Sartre
(b) Camus
(c) Kafka
(d) Simone de Beauvoir

1220. The works *The Rebel*, *The Stranger*, *The Myth of Sisyphus* and *Summer in Algiers* are written by
(a) Camus
(b) Kafka
(c) Kierkegaard
(d) Sartre

**ANSWERS**

| | | | | | |
|---|---|---|---|---|---|
| 1191. (c) | 1192. (d) | 1193. (b) | 1194. (a) | 1195. (b) | 1196. (c) |
| 1197. (c) | 1198. (a) | 1199. (b) | 1200. (d) | 1201. (a) | 1202. (b) |
| 1203. (d) | 1204. (c) | 1205. (b) | 1206. (c) | 1207. (d) | 1208. (c) |
| 1209. (b) | 1210. (d) | 1211. (c) | 1212. (a) | 1213. (c) | 1214. (d) |
| 1215. (d) | 1216. (c) | 1217. (a) | 1218. (d) | 1219. (b) | 1220. (a) |

## (XIX) HISTORICISM, NEW HISTORICISM AND CULTURAL MATERIALISM

1221. Which approach to literary criticism requires the critic to know about the author's life and times?
   (a) Mimetic
   (b) Formalist
   (c) Historical
   (d) Comparative

1222. One of the potential disadvantages of this approach to literature is that it can reduce meaning to a certain time frame, rather than making it universal throughout the ages.
   (a) Formalist
   (b) Mimetic
   (c) Feminist
   (d) Historical

1223. A critic of Thomas Otway's *Venice Preserv'd* wishes to know why the play's conspirators, despite the horrible, bloody details of their obviously brutish plan, are portrayed in a sympathetic light. She examines the author's life and times and discovers that there are obvious similarities between the conspiracy in the play and the Popish plot. She is most likely a _______ critic.
   (a) feminist
   (b) historical
   (c) marxist
   (d) psychological

1224. Who used the term 'New Historicism'?
   (a) Stephen Greenblatt
   (b) Raymond Williams
   (c) Louis Montrose
   (d) None of the above

   (Greenblatt used the term in introduction to the issue of journal *Genre.*)

1225. 'New Historicism' rejects the notion that "history is a series of events that have a linear, causal relationship : event A caused even B and so on."
   True/False

1226. New historicists believe that we interpret historical events as products of our time and culture.
   True/False

1227. New Historicism as a critical theory developed in the
   (a) 1980s
   (b) 1990s
   (c) 1970s
   (d) 1960s

1228. Who phrased New Historicism's motto as "The text is historical, and history is textual"?
   (a) Stephen Greenblatt
   (b) Raymond Williams
   (c) Graham Holderness
   (d) Michael Warner

1229. In *New Historicism and Cultural Materialism*, what does the word 'panoptic' mean: Michel Foucault's pervasive image of the state is that of 'panoptic'?
   (a) All-seeing
   (b) All-knowing
   (c) Almighty
   (d) All-hearing

1230. The New Historicists include
   (a) Greenblatt, Showalter, Montrose
   (b) Greenblatt, Sinfield, Butler
   (c) Greenblatt, Montrose, Goldberg
   (d) Showalter, Belsey, Montrose

1231. The term 'Cultural Materialism" is associated with
   (a) Stephen Greenblatt
   (b) Raymond Williams
   (c) Matthew Arnold
   (d) Richard Hoggart

1232. The terms 'resonance' and 'wonder' are associated with
   (a) Stephen Greenblatt
   (b) Terence Hawkes
   (c) Terry Eagleton
   (d) Roland Barthes

   (By 'resonance' is meant the power of the displayed object to reach out of its final boundaries to a larger world; they evoke in the viewer the complex dynamic cultural forces from which it has emerged and for which it may be taken by a viewer to stand. By 'wonder', according to Greenblatt, is meant the power of displayed object to stop the viewer in his or her tracks, to convey an arresting sense of uniqueness to evoke an exalted attention.)

1233. *Renaissance Fashioning : From More to Shakespeare* (1980) was written by
   (a) Terry Eagleton
   (b) Frederic Jameson
   (c) Stephen Greenblatt
   (d) Michel Foucault

1234. Graham Holderness *The Shakespeare Myth* was published in
   (a) 1983
   (b) 1985
   (c) 1986
   (d) 1988

1235. Jonathan Dollimore and Alan Sinfield *Political Shakespeare : New Essays in Cultural Materialism* was published in
   (a) 1983
   (b) 1985
   (c) 1987
   (d) 1989

1236. Who is the author of *Practising New Historicism* (2001)?
   (a) E.M.W. Tillyard
   (b) Arnold Toynbee
   (c) Stephen Greenblatt
   (d) Jonathan Dollimore

1237. Jonathan Dollimore's *Radical Tragedy* was published in
   (a) 1979
   (b) 1984
   (c) 1985
   (d) 1986

1238. *The Power of Forms in the English Renaissance* (1982) was written by
   (a) Stephen Greenblatt
   (b) Montrose
   (c) Raymond Williams
   (d) Terence Hawkes

1239. The essay "Towards a Poetic of Culture" by Stephen Greenblatt was published in
   (a) 1981
   (b) 1987
   (c) 1990
   (d) 1991

1240. *Alternative Shakespeares* edited by John Drakakis was published in
   (a) 1981
   (b) 1983
   (c) 1984
   (d) 1985

1241. New Historicism saw the literary text as a complex network of
   (a) religious discourses.
   (b) political discourses.
   (c) cultural discourses.
   (d) historical discourses.

1242. Who, among the following, has defined New Historicism as "a combined interest in the textuality of history, the historicity of texts"?
   (a) Stephen Greenblatt
   (b) Louis Montrose

(c) Dollimore
(d) None of the above

1243. Who, among the following, is of the view that New Historicism involves "an intensified willingness to read all of the textual traces of the past with the intention traditionally conferred on literary texts"?
(a) Jonathan Dollimore
(b) Raymond Williams
(c) Stephen Greenblatt
(d) Louis Montrose

1244. Who has described Cultural Materialism as "a politicized form of historiography"?
(a) Graham Holderness
(b) Hyden White
(c) Richard Rorty
(d) Jonathan Goldberg

1245. Cultural Materialism, according to Jonathan Dollimore and Alan Sinfield, has the following characteristics:
(a) Historical context and Textual analysis
(b) Theoretical Method and Political commitment
(c) Author's biography and social background
(d) Both (a) and (b)

1246. Jonathan Goldberg's *James I and the Politics of Literature* was published in
(a) 1980
(b) 1981
(c) 1983
(d) 1985

1247. *The Field of Cultural Production* (1993) was written by
(a) Pierre Bourdieu
(b) Louis Montrose
(c) Douglas Bruster
(d) Stephen Greenblatt

1248. Doughlas Bruster's *Drama and the Market in the Age of Shakespeare* was published in
(a) 1991
(b) 1992
(c) 1994
(d) 1996

1249. *Desire and Anxiety* written by Valerie Traub was published in
(a) 1989
(b) 1990
(c) 1992
(d) 1994

## ANSWERS

| | | | | | |
|---|---|---|---|---|---|
| 1221. (c) | 1222. (d) | 1223. (b) | 1224. (a) | 1225. (T) | 1226. (T) |
| 1227. (a) | 1228. (d) | 1229. (a) | 1230. (c) | 1231. (b) | 1232. (a) |
| 1233. (c) | 1234. (d) | 1235. (b) | 1236. (c) | 1237. (b) | 1238. (a) |
| 1239. (b) | 1240. (d) | 1241. (c) | 1242. (b) | 1243. (c) | 1244. (a) |
| 1245. (d) | 1246. (c) | 1247. (a) | 1248. (b) | 1249. (c) | |

## (XX) CULTURE STUDIES, DIASPORIC STUDIES AND CAMPUS NOVELS

1250. *Culture and Study* written by Raymond Williams was published in
(a) 1953
(b) 1955
(c) 1957
(d) 1959

1251. *Understanding Popular Culture* (1989) was written by
(a) Raymond Williams
(b) John Fiske
(c) Richard Johnson
(d) Richard Hoggart

1252. Who, among the following, wrote *Visual Pleasure and Narrative Cinema* (1975)?
(a) John Fiske
(b) Janice Radway
(c) Laura Mulvey
(d) Dick Hebdiya

1253. When was the journal *Cultural Studies* launched?
(a) 1982
(b) 1984
(c) 1985
(d) 1987

(The goal of the journal was to foster "developments in the area world-wide, putting academics, researchers, students and practioners in different countries" and to keep them in touch with each other's work.)

1254. *Strange Weather; Culture, Science and Technology in the Age of Limits* (1991) was written by
(a) Andrew Ross
(b) Jonathan Dollimore
(c) Donna Haraway
(d) John Fiske

1255. Who coined the term 'auteur theory'?
(a) Christian Metz
(b) Andrew Sarris
(c) Kristin Thompson
(d) Susan Sontag

(Andrew Sarris is an American film critic. According to Sarris, there are three basic premises of this theory: 1. "technical competence of a director as a criterion of value" 2. "distinguishable personality of the director as a criterion of value" 3. "the ultimate glory of the cinema as an art".)

1256. *The Birth of the Seventh Art* by Riccioto Canudo was published in
(a) 1910
(b) 1912
(c) 1915
(d) 1917

1257. *The Photoplay: A Psychological Study* (1916) by Hugo Munsterberg relates to
(a) Psychoanalytical Criticism
(b) Postmodernism
(c) Deconstruction
(d) Film Theory

1258. *The Dialectic of Enlightenment* (1944) by Adorno and Horkeheimer relates to
(a) Culture Studies
(b) The Philosophy of Enlightenment
(c) New Historicism
(d) Phenomenological Criticism

1259. Who formed the "centre for contemporary cultural studies" at the University of Birmigham in 1964?
(a) Raymond Williams
(b) Stuart Hall
(c) Richard Hoggart
(d) Hazel Carky

1260. Dick Hebdige's *Subculture: The Meaning of Style* about culture studies was published in
(a) 1969
(b) 1972
(c) 1975
(d) 1979

1261. *Television Culture* (1987) was written by
(a) Dick Hebdige
(b) John Fiske
(c) Raymond Williams
(d) Richard Hoggart

1262. Who, among the following, is not associated with British Culture Studies?
(a) Richard Hoggart
(b) Raymond Williams
(c) E.P. Thompson
(d) F.R. Leavis

1263. With whom is the concept 'Structure of feeling' associated?
(a) Raymond Williams
(b) Fredric Jameson
(c) Terry Eagleton
(d) Jonathan Culler

('Structure of feeling' are meanings and values as they are actively lived and felt. The concept alludes to the complex array and disarray of the feelings and desires and commitments towards social life that we already hold because of the lives we live. Raymond Williams first used the concept to characterize the lived experience of the quality of life at a particular time and place. It suggests a common set of perceptions and values shared by a particular generation and is most clearly articulated in artistic forms and conventions. The industrial novel of the 1840s would be one example of the structures of feeling which emerged in middle-class consciousness out of the development of Industrial Capitalism. Each generation produces it own 'structures of feeling'. Raymond adopted this concept in *Marxism and Literature* (1977) as a methodological tool for understanding culture and cultural change. Much of culture consists of collective or shared feelings.)

1264. Culture Studies is broadly conceived as the study of
(a) dominant culture.
(b) working class culture.
(c) popular, marginal and subaltern cultures.
(d) Both (b) and (c).

1265. *Making of the English Working Class* (1963) was written by
(a) Stuart Hall
(b) E.P. Thompson
(c) Raymond Williams
(d) Richard Hoggart

1266. *Policing the Crisis: Mugging, the State, and Law and Order* (1978) was written by
(a) Stuart Hall and Chas Critcher
(b) Tonny Jefferson and John N. Clarke
(c) Brian Roberts
(d) All of the above

1267. A campus novel is a novel whose main action is set in and around a
(a) School
(b) City
(c) Garden
(d) University

1268. A campus novel is also known as
(a) an academic novel
(b) a modern novel
(c) a realistic novel
(d) a romantic novel

1269. The campus novel dates back to the
   (a) 1840s
   (b) 1950s
   (c) 1960s
   (d) 1970s

1270. One of the earliest examples of campus novel is
   (a) *The Groves of Academe*
   (b) *The Masters*
   (c) *The Professor's House*
   (d) None of the above

1271. *Lucky Jim* is written by
   (a) Kingley Amis
   (b) Disgrace
   (c) Philip Roth
   (d) C.P. Snow

1272. One of the following novels does not belong to David Lodge's 'trilogy' of campus novels
   (a) *Changing Places : A Tale of Two Campsuses*
   (b) *Small World : An Academic Romance*
   (c) *Nice Work*
   (d) *The Picture-goers*

1273. The first Indian Campus novel was written by
   (a) P.M. Nityanandan
   (b) Chetan Bhagat
   (c) M.V. Rama Sarma
   (d) Saros Cowasjee

1274. *Five Point Someone* (2004) was written by
   (a) Vikram Seth
   (b) Chetan Bhagat
   (c) Anita Desai
   (d) Jhumpa Lahiri

**TOP TEN CAMPUS NOVELS**

| |  | |  |
|---|---|---|---|
| 1. | Kingley Amis | – | *Lucky Jim* (1954) |
| 2. | Vladimir Nabokov | – | *Pale Fire* (1962) |
| 3. | J.M. Coetzee | – | *Disgrace* (1999) |
| 4. | David Lodge | – | *Nice Work* (1988) |
| 5. | Muriel Spark | – | *The Prime of Miss Jean Brodie* (1969) |
| 6. | Philip Roth | – | *The Human Stain* (2000) |
| 7. | Willa Cather | – | *The Professor's House* (1925) |
| 8. | Malcolm Bradbury | – | *The History Man* (1975) |
| 9. | Dietrich Schwantiz | – | *Der Campus* (1995) |
| 10. | Michael Chabon | – | *Wonder Boys* (1995) |

1275. *The Namesake* was written by
   (a) Amitav Ghosh
   (b) Jhumpa Lahiri
   (c) Shashi Tharoor
   (d) Bharati Mukherjee

1276. *The American Brat* is written by
   (a) Shaila Abdullah
   (b) Yasmine Gooneratne
   (c) Manju Kapur
   (d) Bapsi Sidhwa

1277. Which one of the following novels has been written by Monica Ali?
   (a) *The God of Small Things*
   (b) *The Hungry Tide*
   (c) *Brick Lane*
   (d) *A Suitable Boy*

1278. In which award-winning novel has Yasmine Gooneratne captured the Sri Lankan diaspora?

(a) *A Change of Skies*
(b) *Relative Merits*
(c) *Pleasures of Conquest*
(d) *New Ceylon Writing*

1279. Which one of the following novels was not been written by Nadeem Aslam?
(a) *Season of Rainbirds* (1993)
(b) *Map for Lost Lovers* (2004)
(c) *The Wasted Vigil*
(d) *The Immigrant* (2008)

1280. Who developed the science of translation?
(a) Eugene Nida
(b) I.C. Catford
(c) James Homes
(d) Jose Lambert

(Eugene Nida, the American Bible translator, developed the 'science of translation' in the 1960s.)

1281. The discipline known as the translation studies emerged in the
(a) 1960s
(b) 1970s
(c) 1980s
(d) 1990s

1282. Who is associated with the term of "Third Space"?
(a) Homi K. Bhabha
(b) Gayatri Spivak
(c) Michel Foucault
(d) Ray Oldenburg

(The 'third space' or the 'third place' is a term used in the concept of community building to refer to social surroundings separate from the two usual social environments of home and the work place. In his influential book *The Great Good Place*, Ray Oldenburg argues that the third places are important for civil society, democracy, civic engagement, and establishing feelings of a sense of place. Oldenburg calls one's "first place" the home and those that one lives with. The "second place" is the workplace—where people may actually spend most of their time. Third places are, then, are "anchors" of community life and facilitate and foster broader more creative interaction. They are informal meeting places.)

1283. The 'True Cinema Movement' (Expressive Cinema) was founded by
(a) Mahesh Bhatt
(b) Subhash Ghai
(c) Rajan Sarma
(d) None of the above

(True Cinema movement is a film movement founded by Rajan Sarma, a Tamil film director of the 1980s. The movement mainly focuses on imitiating necessary steps on developing 'expressive cinema' in contrast to the so-called 'dramatic cinema' prevalent commonly in India.

The main principles of the *True Cinema Movement* are:

1. Cinema is not only a medium of entertainment, but also a medium of expression 2. Cinema should not be called as a visual medium, but instead as a 'medium of expression' 3. The cinema should not be restricted to as a mere story-telling medium. It should be used as a 'language' 4. Cinema should depend only on its own 'audio and visuals'. The music should necessarily be avoided as it reduces the trueness of the cinema.)

1284. Who is associated with the term "Contact Zone"?
(a) Mary Pratt
(b) Gayatri Spivak
(c) Raymond Williams
(d) Stuart Hall

(Mary Louise Pratt discusses the concept of 'contact zone' in her essay *Arts of the Contact Zone* (1991), Pratt defined the contact zone as "social spaces where cultures meet, clash and grapple with each other, often in contexts of highly asymmetrical relations of power; such as colonialism, slavery, or their aftermaths as they are lived out in many parts of the world today". The idea of the contact zone is intended in part to contrast with ideas of community that trigger much of the thinking about, language, communication, and culture.)

**ANSWERS**

| | | | | | |
|---|---|---|---|---|---|
| 1250. (a) | 1251. (b) | 1252. (c) | 1253. (d) | 1254. (a) | 1255. (b) |
| 1256. (c) | 1257. (d) | 1258. (a) | 1259. (c) | 1260. (d) | 1261. (b) |
| 1262. (d) | 1263. (a) | 1264. (a) | 1265. (b) | 1266. (d) | 1267. (d) |
| 1268. (a) | 1269. (b) | 1270. (a) | 1271. (a) | 1272. (d) | 1273. (a) |
| 1274. (b) | 1275. (b) | 1276. (d) | 1277. (c) | 1278. (a) | 1279. (d) |
| 1280. (a) | 1281. (b) | 1282. (d) | 1283. (c) | 1284. (a) | |

## (XXI) POSTCOLONIALISM

1285. Postcolonial is also referred to as
   (a) Third World Literature Studies
   (b) Commonwealth Literature
   (c) Dalit Literature
   (d) Both (a) and (b)

1286. Postcolonial literature refers to writings
   (a) before and after domination of colonized countries.
   (b) after decolonization of colonized countries.
   (c) during colonization of African countries.
   (d) during British rule over India.

1287. The term "Third World Studies" was coined by
   (a) Afred Sauvy
   (b) Gayatri Spivak
   (c) Homi Bhabha
   (d) Edward Said

1288. Who said, "To be colonized is to be removed from history"?
   (a) Frantz Fanon
   (b) Walter Rodney
   (c) Albert Memmi
   (d) Edward Said

1289. Defining the situation of the colonized, who claimed that "the most serious blow suffered by the colonized is being removed from history"?
   (a) Ngugi Wa Thiong'o
   (b) Edward Said
   (c) Frantz Fanon
   (d) Albert Memmi

1290. Who, among the following, comprises the "Holy Trinity" in the context of postcoloniasm?
   (a) Gayatri Spivak
   (b) Homi Bhabha
   (c) Edward Said
   (d) All of the above

1291. Edward Said's *Orientalism* was published in
   (a) 1975

(b) 1978
(c) 1980
(d) 1982

1292. Ngugi Wa Thiong'o was a
(a) Psychoanalytic Critic
(b) Formalist Critic
(c) Marxist Cultural Critic
(d) Structuralist Critic

1293. Frantz Fanon wrote two of the following books
(a) *Black Skin, White Masks*
(b) *Things Fall Apart*
(c) *The Wretched of the Earth*
(d) Both (a) and (c)

(*Black Skin*, *White Masks* was published in 1952 and *The Wretched of the Earth* in 1961.)

1294. *The Empire Writes Back* (1989) was written by
(a) Bill Ashcroft
(b) Gareth Griffiths
(c) Helen Tiffin
(d) All of the above

1295. One of the following is not strictly a postcolonial critic
(a) Edward Said
(b) Frantz Fanon
(c) Homi K. Bhabha
(d) Gayatri Spivak

1296. *Culture and Imperialim* (1993) was written by
(a) Frantz Fanon
(b) Edward Said
(c) Gayatri Spivak
(d) Homi Bhabha

1297. *The Location of Culture* by Homi K. Bhabha was published in
(a) 1941
(b) 1944
(c) 1945
(d) 1946

1298. The concept 'unhomeliness' ('double consciousness' by some critics) means
(a) not feeling at home.
(b) neither the culture of the colonizer nor that of the colonized feels like home.
(c) without a home.
(d) living abroad.

(The term is coined by Homi K. Bhabha)

1299. Who coined the term 'hybridity'?
(a) Homi K. Bhabha
(b) Edward Said
(c) Gayatri Spivak
(d) Fanon

(When two cultures commingle, the nature and characteristic of the newly-created culture changes, each of the cultures causing ambivalence. This process is called hybridity.)

1300. Frantz's concept of 'white masks' means that
(a) masks are made of white cloth.
(b) masks are painted white.
(c) the blacks try to look like the whites.
(d) None of the above.

1301. What, according to Frantz Fanon, is neo-colonialism?
(a) Rule by the Americans
(b) Rule by native elites
(c) Rule by proletariat
(d) None of the above

1302. The essay "Of Mimicry and Man—The Ambivalence of the Colonial Discourse" is written by
(a) Gayatri Spivak
(b) Edward Said
(c) Homi K. Bhabha
(d) Fanon

1303. Who originated the term 'subaltern'?
(a) Antonio Gramsci

(b) Althusser
(c) Lyotard
(d) Gayatri Spivak

1304. Who founded the 'Subaltern Studies Group'?
(a) Gayatri Spivak
(b) Ranajit Guha
(c) Edward Said
(d) Homi Bhabha

1305. Who, among the following, is not a member of the Subaltern Studies Group?
(a) Partha Chatterjee
(b) Gayatri Spivak
(c) Dipesh Chakrabarty
(d) Homi K. Bhabha

1306. The concept of 'Negritude' is associated with
(a) Aime Cesaire
(b) Homi Bhabha
(c) Frantz Fanon
(d) Edward Said

('Negritude' means, in Cesaire's words, "the simple recognition of the fact that one is black, the acceptance of this fact and of our destiny as black, of out history and culture".)

1307. Graema Turner argues that novels are of specific value to postcolonial studies. What is the rationale he offers for this argument?
(a) That there have been too many political science theories based purely on the works of academics.
(b) That because stories and novels are generated by culture, they therefore produce meanings and significances that are indicative of the culture.
(c) Novels and stories are more enjoyable to read than works of theory so postcolonial studies will garner more followers using this method.
(d) Turner didn't have access to academic works when he was writing.

1308. World-travelling is a postcolonial methodology associated with which group?
(a) African male scholars who were educated in the U.S.A.
(b) Indian scholars who had spent years abroad studying the cultures of those in other countries.
(c) Feminist scholars with Latin American backgrounds.
(d) Academics who had been to many countries.

1309. Why does post-colonial scholar Homi Bhabha argue that colonial discourse was ambivalent about the colonized?
(a) Portrayal of the colonized errs towards either a passive and conquerable subject or an irrational, untamed barbarian. This means that the colonized subject becomes constantly stereotyped.
(b) Scholars did not travel to colonies and therefore could not establish an accurate picture of colonized peoples.
(c) Postcolonial scholars were too focused on the colonizing power rather than colonized peoples.
(d) The colonized did not make enough effort to have their voices heard.

1310. The socio-cultural anthropologist Arjun Appadurai writes about five types of global cultural flows. What are they?
(a) Ethnoscapes, econoscapes, culturescapes, finanscapes, ideoscapes.

(b) Ethnoscapes, mediascapes, technoscapes, financscapes, ideoscapes.
(c) Geographical flows, cultural flows, idea-flows, technological flows, ethnicity flows.
(d) Liberal flows, realistic flows, postcolonial flows, poststructuralist flows, financial flows.

1311. Postcolonial spelt without a hyphen is used to suggest
(a) that the entire world is now in the post-colonial era. It functions as a historical category.
(b) that the global south alone is now in the post-colonial era.
(c) that post-colonialism, spelled with a hyphen, is a concept only applicable to those countries that experienced colonialism.
(d) that there was a grammatical mistake in the earlier spelling.

1312. Criticisms levelled against post-colonial studies include which of the following?
(a) That the theory entered international relations too recently to be considered an academic theory.
(b) That it is too similar to realism and serves no function.
(c) That it is not sophisticated enough to be an academic theory.
(d) That the field focuses so heavily on identity and language that it ignores the urgent question of whether those in the global south can eat, leaving this problem to Western agencies to sort out.

1313. In his renowned work *Orientalism* Edward Said argues that the 'Orient' is portrayed in Western novels, media and art work as
(a) a place prone to liberal democracy and revolutionary feminism.
(b) an accurate depiction of the modern day Middle East and Asia.
(c) lost in the past, prone to despotic rule and plagued by "odd" cultural traditions.
(d) too focused on historical facts and accurately portraying the experience of life in the region.

1314. When does dissemination occur?
(a) When people with hybrid identities and cultures become diasporic, travelling physically from South to North to live.
(b) When people from different nations come together in a new country.
(c) When people from one nation emigrate *en masse* to another country.
(d) When people of many communities leave their country to settle in another.

1315. "Imagined communities" is a concept propounded by
(a) Benedict Anderson
(b) Homi Bhabha
(c) Aijaz Ahmed
(d) Partha Chatterjee

(It means that a nation is a community, socially constructed, imagined by people who perceive themselves as part of a group. It was propounded by Anderson in 1983.)

1316. Who has written *Signs Taken for Wonders: Questions of Ambivalence and Authority Under a Tree Outside Delhi 1817* (1985)?
(a) Edward Said
(b) Homi Bhabha
(c) Aijaz Ahmed
(d) Spivak

1317. The concept of "White Man's Burden" is associated with
   (a) Macaulay
   (b) Robert Young
   (c) Rudyard Kipling
   (d) Henry Louis Gates

1318. When was the journal *Tricontinental* launched, which, according to Robert Young, is the founding moment of the postcolonial theory?
   (a) 1966
   (b) 1968
   (c) 1970
   (d) 1972

1319. *A Critique of Postcolonial Reason* (1999) was written by
   (a) Edward Said
   (b) Robert Young
   (c) Homi Bhabha
   (d) Gayatri Spivak

1320. The book *Figures in Black: Words, Signs and the Racial Self* was written by
   (a) Robert Young
   (b) Henry Louis Gates
   (c) Edward Said
   (d) Frantz Fanon

1321. Henry Louis Gates's *The Signifying Monkey : A Theory of African American Literary Criticism* was published in
   (a) 1980
   (b) 1983
   (c) 1988
   (d) 1989

1322. *The Postcolonial Critic* (1990) was written by
   (a) Gayatri Spivak
   (b) Edward Said
   (c) Benita Parry
   (d) Homi Bhabha

1323. Who, among the following, wrote *Decolonising the Mind* (1986)?
   (a) Chinua Achebe
   (b) Ngugi Wa Thiong'o
   (c) Homi Bhabha
   (d) Spivak

1324. "The Literature of Combat" is associated with
   (a) Homi Bhabha
   (b) Edward Said
   (c) Frantz Fanon
   (d) Spivak

   (Frantz Fanon has used this term in his book. *The Wretched of the Earth* (1963) in which he speaks of a national literature, a literature which takes up and explore themes that are nationalist. This is called the 'literature of combat' because "it calls on the whole people to fight for the existence as a nation".)

1325. Edward Said's *Beginnings* was published in
   (a) 1970
   (b) 1972
   (c) 1975
   (d) 1977

1326. The term 'mimicry' is associated with
   (a) Edward Said
   (b) Homi Bhabha
   (c) Spivak
   (d) Fanon

1327. *The World, the Text, and the Critic* (1983) was written by
   (a) Rene Wellek
   (b) Gayatri Spivak
   (c) Homi Bhabha
   (d) Edward Said

1328. *Black Literature and Literary Theory* (1984) was written by
   (a) Chinua Achebe
   (b) Homi Bhabha
   (c) Edward Said
   (d) Henry Louis Gates

1329. *Home Coming* (1972) was written by
   (a) Ngugi Wa Thiong'o
   (b) Fanon
   (c) Spivak
   (d) Edward Said

1330. Who argued that African literature can only be written in African languages?
   (a) Chinue Achebe
   (b) Ngugi Wa Thiong'o
   (c) Frantz Fanon
   (d) Edward Said

1331. Which African writer bade "farewell to the English language as a vehicle for any of my writings"?
   (a) Chinna Achebe
   (b) Julius Nyerere
   (c) Nguigi Wa Thiong'o
   (d) Frantz Fanon

1332. *Past the Last Post : Theorizing Post-Colonialism and Postmodernism* by Ian Adam and Helen Tiffin was published in
   (a) 1990
   (b) 1991
   (c) 1992
   (d) 1993

1333. Who said that "texts are worldly, to some degree they are events, and, even when they appear to deny it, they have nevertheless a part of the social world, human life, and of course of historical moments in which they are located and interpreted"?
   (a) Terry Eagleton
   (b) Jonathan Culler
   (c) Edward Said
   (d) None of the above

1334. Edward Said's approach to 'Orientalism' is
   (a) as an academic discipline.
   (b) as a Eurocentric style based on binary notions of Orient/Occident.
   (c) as a discourse that confirms the need for colonial power, domination and hegemony.
   (d) None of the above.

1335. Wole Soyinka's *Myth, Literature and the African World* was published in
   (a) 1973
   (b) 1975
   (c) 1976
   (d) 1977

   (Wole Soyinka, a Nigerian, was the first African writer to receive the Nobel Prize in literature.)

1336. Which of the following books is regarded as the corner-stone of postcolonial canon?
   (a) *Orientalism*
   (b) *The Wretched of the Earth*
   (c) *Location of Culture*
   (d) *Home Coming*

1337. Who, among the following, said that Edward Said's *Orientalism* "inaugurated the postcolonial field"?
   (a) Gayatri Spivak
   (b) Homi K. Bhabha
   (c) Robert Young
   (d) Louis Gates

**Main figures and Key Terms associated with Post-Colonial Discourse**

1. Edward Said—"Orientalism" 2. Gayatri Spivak and Ranajit Guha—"Subaltern Studies" 3. Jan Mohmed—"Minority Discourse" 4. Barabara Harlow—"Resistance Literature" 5. Tiffin, Ashcroft and Griffiths—"The Empire Writes Back" 6. Peter Nazareth, Fredric Jameson and Georg M. Gugel Berger—"Third World Literature" 7. Homi K. Bhabha—"hybridity", "mimicry", "ambivalence", "civility".

**ANSWERS**

| | | | | | |
|---|---|---|---|---|---|
| 1285. (d) | 1286. (a) | 1287. (a) | 1288. (b) | 1289. (d) | 1290. (d) |
| 1291. (b) | 1292. (c) | 1293. (d) | 1294. (d) | 1295. (b) | 1296. (b) |
| 1297. (b) | 1298. (b) | 1299. (a) | 1300. (c) | 1301. (b) | 1302. (c) |
| 1303. (a) | 1304. (b) | 1305. (d) | 1306. (a) | 1307. (b) | 1308. (c) |
| 1309. (a) | 1310. (b) | 1311. (a) | 1312. (a) | 1313. (c) | 1314. (a) |
| 1315. (a) | 1316. (b) | 1317. (c) | 1318. (a) | 1319. (d) | 1320. (b) |
| 1321. (c) | 1322. (a) | 1323. (b) | 1324. (c) | 1325. (c) | 1326. (b) |
| 1327. (c) | 1328. (d) | 1329. (a) | 1330. (b) | 1331. (c) | 1332. (a) |
| 1333. (c) | 1334. (b) | 1335. (c) | 1336. (a) | 1337. (b) | |

## (XXII) ECOCRITICISM OR GREEN OR ENVIRONMENTAL STUDIES

1338. ‘Ecocriticism’ developed in the U.S.A. in the early
    (a) 1960s
    (b) 1970s
    (c) 1980s
    (d) 1990s

1339. ______ is a co-founder of Ecocriticism with Harold Fromm.
    (a) Robert Henlein
    (b) Cheryll Glotfelty
    (c) Frank Herbert
    (d) George Orwell

1340. What is another term for ecocriticism?
    (a) Earth Studies
    (b) Wind Studies
    (c) Green Studies
    (d) Water Studies

1341. Ecocritics emphasize writers who highlight ______ as their subject matter.
    (a) nature
    (b) children
    (c) animals
    (d) women

1342. *The Comedy of Survival: Studies in Literary Ecology* by Joseph Meeker was published in
    (a) 1969
    (b) 1972
    (c) 1974
    (d) 1975

(The book tells us how we can learn a lot about human survival in life and how literature shows the way. It shows how contingency means so much in life. Mecker finds the paradigm of modern situation in Dante's ‘Comedia’, in which Hell is described in imagery strikingly similar to the modern ‘industrial, technological, overpopulated, polluted world’, while Purgatory's peak is a ‘divine forest dense and green’. Paradise is a ‘state of mind’ an adaption of man to nature rather than change nature to suit man.)

1343. *Environmentalism : A Global History* (2000) was written by
    (a) Donna Haraway
    (b) Greta Gaard
    (c) Ramchandra Guha
    (d) Donald Worster

1344. Donald Worster's *Nature's Economy: A History of Ecological Ideas* was published in

(a) 1991
(b) 1993
(c) 1994
(d) 1996

(*Nature's Economy* is a wide-ranging investigation of ecology's past. It traces the origins of the concepts, discusses the thinkers who have shaped it, shows how it in turn has shaped the modern perception of our place in nature.)

1345. *Mankind and Mother Earth* (1976) was written by
(a) Richard Grove
(b) Arnold Toynbee
(c) Madhav Gadgil
(d) Vandana Shiva

1346. The Association for the Study of Literature and Environment (ASLE) committed to the study of literature and environment was formed in
(a) 1992
(b) 1994
(c) 1996
(d) 1998

1347. The journal *Interdisciplinary Studies in Literature and Environment* (ISLE) was first published in
(a) 1990
(b) 1993
(c) 1995
(d) 1997

1348. *The Ecocriticism Reader: Landmarks in Literary Ecology* edited by Cheryll Glotfelty and Harold Fromm was published in
(a) 1990
(b) 1992
(c) 1996
(d) 1998

(*The Ecocriticism Reader* is the first collection of its kind, an enthology of classic writings in the field of ecology. Exploring the relationship between literature and physical environment, literary ecology is the study of the ways that writing both reflects and influences our interactions with the natural world.)

1349. ______ read major works from an ecocentric point of view and extend the application of concepts to areas other than the natural world.
(a) Ecocritics
(b) Ecologists
(c) Ecocentrists
(d) Ecofeminists

1350. The word "Ecocriticism" can be traced back to
(a) *The Ecocriticism Reader : Landmarks in Literary Ecology*
(b) *Literature and Ecology : An Experiment in Ecocriticism*
(c) *Mankind and Mother Earth*
(d) *The Comedy of Survival*

1351. William Rueckett's essay "Literature and Ecology: An Experiment in Ecocriticism" was published in
(a) 1972
(b) 1974
(c) 1978
(d) 1979

1352. *The Green Studies Reader : From Romanticism to Ecocriticism* was written by
(a) Harold Fromm
(b) Edward Abbey
(c) Lawrence Buell
(d) Lawrence Coupe

(*The Green Studies Reader* is a comprehensive selection of critical texts which address the connection between ecology, culture, and literature. It offers a complete guide to the growing area of 'ecocriticism' and a wealth of material on green issues from the romantic period to the present.)

1353. *Desert Solitaire* by Edward Abbey was published in
   (a) 2000
   (b) 2004
   (c) 2006
   (d) 2008

(*Desert Solitaire : A Season in the Wilderness* is an autobiographical work by Edward Abbey. It depicts Abbey's preoccupation with the deserts of the American Southwest. He describes how the desert affects society and more specifically the individual on a multifaceted sensor level. Abbey introduces the desert as 'the flaming globe, blazing on the prinnacles and minarets and balanced rocks'.)

1354. The major nineteenth century American writers who can be said to draw attention to nature and environment are
   (a) R.W. Emerson
   (b) Margaret Fuller
   (c) Henry David Thoreau
   (d) All of the above

1355. Emerson's book *Nature* was published in
   (a) 1830
   (b) 1836
   (c) 1839
   (d) 1841

(*Nature* is an essay written by Emerson. It is in this essay that the foundation of transcendentalism is put forth, a belief system that expouses a non-traditional appreciation of nature.)

1356. Jonathan Bate's *Romantic Ecology: Wordsworth and the Environmental Tradition* was published in
   (a) 1970
   (b) 1971
   (c) 1991
   (d) 1975

(First published in 1991, *Romantic Ecology* reassesses the poetry of Wordsworth in the context of the abiding pastoral tradition in English Literature. Bate explores the politics of poetry and argues that contrary to critics who suggest that Wordsworth was a reactionary who failed to represent the harsh economic reality of his native Lake District, the poet's politics were fundamentally green. As our first truly ecological poet, Wordsworth articulated a powerful and enduring vision of human integration with nature which exercised a formative influence on future conservation movements and is of great relevance to the great environmental issues today.)

1357. Who has defined ecocriticism as "the study of the relationship between literature and the physical environment"?
   (a) Cheryll Glotfelty
   (b) Harold Fromm
   (c) W. Rueckett
   (d) Lawrence Buell

## ANSWERS

| | | | | | |
|---|---|---|---|---|---|
| 1338. (d) | 1339. (b) | 1340. (c) | 1341. (a) | 1342. (b) | 1343. (c) |
| 1344. (d) | 1345. (b) | 1346. (a) | 1347. (b) | 1348. (c) | 1349. (a) |
| 1350. (b) | 1351. (c) | 1352. (d) | 1353. (b) | 1354. (d) | 1355. (b) |
| 1356. (c) | 1357. (a) | | | | |

## (XXIII) MATCH THE PAIRS AND CHOOSE THE CORRECT CHRONOLOGICAL SEQUENCE

1358. Match each type of criticism associated with each statement:

**List I**

(i) Historical Criticism
(ii) Feminist Criticism
(iii) Archetypal/Myth Criticism
(iv) Marxist Criticism
(v) Cultural Criticism
(vi) Reader-response Criticism

**List II**

A. An Examination or explanation of the relationship between the dominant cultures and the dominated is essential.
B. Certain characters recur—the hero, the trickster, the wise old man. Certain motifs recur—the quest, the journey, and certain symbols recur—olive branch.
C. A text cannot be separated from its historical context which is a web of social, cultural, personal and political factors.
D. The basic struggle in human and society between the haves and the have-nots—those with power and wealth, and those without power and wealth.
E. Fictional portrayals of female characters often reflect and create stereotypical social and political attitudes towards women.
F. An interpretation of text will differ, according to the personal experiences that reader is projecting into the text.

1359. Match the correct pairs:

| List I | List II |
|---|---|
| (i) Chandralok | : a. Bhanudatta |
| (ii) Rasamanjri | : b. Jayadeva |
| (iii) Vaktiviveka | : c. Rajasekhra |
| (iv) Kavyamimansa | : d. Mahimambhatta |

1360. Which of the following thinker-concept pairs is rightly matched?

| List I | List II |
|---|---|
| (i) Stanley Fish | : a. Reader-response |
| (ii) Jacques Derrida | : b. New Historicism |
| (iii) Northrope Fry | : c. Practical Criticism |
| (iv) I.A. Richards | : d. Archetypical Criticism |

1361.

| List I | List II |
|---|---|
| (i) Vamana | : a. Dhwanyloka |
| (ii) Bharata | : b. Natya Shastra |
| (iii) Mammata | : c. Vakrokti |
| (iv) Abhinva Gupta | : d. Kavya Alankar |

1362. Which of following thinker-concept pairs is correctly matched?

(i) Northrop Frye : a. Mysticism
(ii) Jacques Derrida : b. Deconstruction
(iii) I.A. Richards : c. Archetypal Criticism
(iv) Terry Eagleton : d. Psychological Criticism

1363.

| List I | List II |
|---|---|
| (i) Abhinava Gupta | : a. Dhwanyaloka |
| (ii) Vaman | : b. Kavya Alankar |
| (iii) Mammata | : c. Kavya Prakash |
| (iv) Bharata | : d. Vakrokti |

1364. Match the pairs:

(i) Sartre : a. Practical Criticism
(ii) I.A. Richards : b. Existentialism
(iii) Roman Jakobson : c. Ecocriticism

(iv) Cheryll Glotfelty :d. Russian Formalism

1365. **List I** **List II**

(i) Lyotard : a. Phenomenological Criticism

(ii) Louis Althusser : b. New Criticism

(iii) John Crowe Ransom : c. Postmodernism

(iv) Edmund Husserl : d. Marxist Criticism

1366. **List I** **List II**

(i) Hillis Miller : a. Postmodernism

(ii) Baudrillard : b. Psychoanalytical Criticism

(iii) Carl Jung : c. Deconstruction

(iv) Antonio Gramsci : d. Marxist Criticism

1367. Choose the correct chronological sequence:

(a) Sign Structure and Play, Signs Taken for Wonder, The Death of the Author, Two Uses of Language

(b) Two Uses of Language, Sign, Structure and Play, The Death of the Author, Signs Taken for Wonder

(c) The Death of the Author, Two Uses of Language, Signs Taken for Wonder, Sign, Structure and Play

(d) Two Uses of language, The Death of the Author, Sign, Structure and Play, Signs Taken for Wonder

1368. Choose the correct sequence of the following Schools of Criticism:

(a) Structuralism, New Criticism, Deconstruction, Reader-response

(b) Reader-response, Deconstruction, Structuralism, New Criticism

(c) New Criticism, Structuralism, Deconstruction, Reader-response

(d) Deconstruction, New Criticism, Structuralism, Reader-response

1369. Give the correct chronological sequence:

(a) D.H. Lawrence, E.M. Tillyard, G. Wilson Knight, C.S. Lewis

(b) E.M. Tillyard, D.H. Lawrence, C.S. Lewis, G. Wilson Knight

(c) G. Wilson Knight, D.H. Lawrence, E.M. Tillyard, C.S. Lewis

(d) C.S. Lewis, D.H. Lawrence, G. Wilson Knight, E.M. Tillyard

1370. (a) Walter Benjamin, Max Horkheimer, Herbert Marcuse, Theodor Adorno

(b) Theodor Adorno, Walter Benjamin, Herbert Marcuse, Max Horkheimer

(c) Herbert Marcuse, Max Horkheimer, Theodor Adorno, Walter Benjamin

(d) Max Horkheimer, Herbert Marcuse, Walter Banjamin, Theodor Adorno

1371. (a) Marxism and Literarcy Criticism, Anatomy of Criticism, Structural Poetics, The Pleasures of the Text

(b) Anatomy of Criticism, The Pleasures of the Text, Structural Poetics, Marxism and Literary Criticism

(c) Structural Poetics, Anatomy of Criticism, The Pleasures of the Text, Marxism and Literary Criticism

(d) The Pleasures of the Text, Marxism and Literary Criticism, Anatomy of Criticism, Structural Poetics

1372. (a) Creative Writers and Day-dreaming, The Interpretation of Dreams, Civilization and its Discontents, Totem and Taboo

(b) Totem and Taboo, Civilization and its Doscontents, Creative Writers and Day-dreaming, The Interpretation of Dreams

(c) Civilization and its Discontents, Totem and Taboo, The

Interpretation of Dreams, Creative Writers and Day-Dreaming
(d) The Interpretation of Dreams, Creative Writers and Day-Dreaming, Totem and Taboo, Civilization and its Discontents

1373. (a) Jacques Lacan, Carl Jung, Alfred Adler, Sigmund Freud
(b) Carl Jung, Jacques Lacan, Sigmund Freud, Alfred Adler
(c) Sigmund Freud, Alfred Adler, Carl Jung, Jacques Lacan
(d) Alfred Adler, Jacques Lacan, Sigmund Freud, Carl Jung

1374. (a) The Intentional Fallacy, The Affective Fallacy, The Verbal Icon, Validity in Interpretation
(b) The Affective Fallacy, Validity in Interpretation, The Verbal Icon, Intentional Fallacy
(c) Validity in Interpretation, The Verbal Icon, Intentional Fallacy, The Affective Fallacy
(d) The Intentional Fallacy, The Affective Fallacy, Validity in Interpretation, The Verbal Icon

1375. (a) William K. Wimsatt, T.S. Eliot, Monroe C. Beardsley, John Crowe Ransom
(b) T.S. Eliot, John Crowe Ransom, William K. Wimsatt, Monroe C. Beardsley
(c) John Crowe Ransom, Monroe C. Beardsley, T.S. Eliot, William K. Wimsatt
(d) Monroe C. Beardsley, T.S. Eliot, John Crowe Ransom, William K. Wimsatt

1376. (a) *The Pleasures of the Text, From Work to Text, Writing Zero Degree, Mythologies*
(b) *Mythologies, The Pleasures of the Text, Writing Zero Degree, From Work to Text*
(c) *Writing Zero Degree, Mythologies, From Work to Text, The Pleasures of the Text*
(d) *From Work to Text, Writing Zero Degree, Mythologies, The Pleasures of the Text*

1377. (a) *Orientalism, The Wretched of the Earth, The Location of Culture, A Critique of Postcolonial Reason*
(b) *The Location of Culture, The Wretched of the Earth, Orientalism, A Critique of Postcolonial Reason*
(c) *A Critique of Postcolonial Reason, The Location of Culture, Orientalism, The Wretched of the Earth*
(d) *The Wretch of the Earth, Orientalism, A Critique of Postcolonial Reason, The Location of Culture*

1378. (a) *The Range of Interpretation, Interpretation Theory, Being and Time, The Role of Reader*
(b) *Interpretation Theory, The Role of Reader, The Range of Interpretation, Being and Time*
(c) *Being and Time, Interpretation Theory, The Role of Reader, The Range of Interpretation*
(d) *The Role of Reader, The Range of Interpretation, Being and Time, Interpretation Theory*

1379. (a) *Being and Nothingness, Existence and Objectivity, What is Literature, Caligula*
(b) *Caligula, What is Literature, Being and Nothingness, Existence and Objectivity*
(c) *What is Literature, Caligula, Existence and Objectivity, Being and Nothingness*

(d) *Existence and Objectivity, Being and Nothingness, Caligula, What is Literature*

1380. (a) *The Power of Forms in the English Renaissance, Desire and Anxiety, Political Shakespeare, Radical Tragedy*
(b) *The Power of Forms in the English Renaissance, Radical Tragedy, Political Shakespeare, Desire and Anxiety*
(c) *Desire and Anxiety, Political Shakespeare, The Power of Forms in the English Renaissance, Radical Tragedy*
(d) *Political Shakespeare, The Power of Forms in the English Renaissance, Desire and Anxiety, Radical Tragedy*

1381. (a) S.T. Coleridge, R.W. Emerson, William Wordsworth, Walter Pater
(b) William Wordsworth, S.T. Coleridge, R.W. Emerson, Walter Pater
(c) Walter Pater, S.T. Coleridge, R.W. Emerson, William Wordsworth
(d) R.W. Emerson, Walter Pater, William Wordsworth, S.T. Coleridge

1382. (a) *Literature and Revolution, The Political Unconscious, Jargon of Authenticity, Art and Social life*
(b) *Jargon of Authencity, Literature and Revolution, Jargon of Authencity, The Political Unconscious*
(c) *Art and Social Life, Literature and Revolution, Jargon of Authencity, The Political Unconscious*
(d) *The Political Unconscious, Jargon of Authencity, Literature and Revolution, Art and Social Life.*

1383. (a) Martin Heidegger, Ferdinand de Saussure, Roland Barthes, Sigmund Freud
(b) Ferdinand de Saussure, Roland Barthes, Sigmund Freud, Martin Heidegger
(c) Roland Barthes, Sigmund Freud, Ferdinand de Saussure, Martin Heidegger
(d) Sigmund Freud, Martin Heidegger, Ferdinand de Saussure, Roland Barthes

1384. (a) Stuart Hall, Laura Mulvey, Raymond Williams, Susan Bordo
(b) Raymond Williams, Stuart Hall, Laura Mulvey, Susan Bordo
(c) Susan Bordo, Laura Mulvey, Raymond Williams, Stuart Hall
(d) Laura Mulvey, Susan Bordo, Stuart Hall, Raymond Williams

1385. (a) *A Literature of Their Own, The Madwoman in the Attic, The Dialectic of Sex, Women's Estate*
(b) *The Madwoman in the Attic, A Literature of Their Own, The Dialectic of Sex, Women's Estate*
(c) *The Dialectic of Sex, Women's Estate, A Literature of Their Own, The Madwoman in the Attic.*
(d) *The Women's Estate, A Literature of Their Own, The Madwoman in the Attic, The Dialectic of Sex.*

## ANSWERS

1358. (i) c, (ii) e, (iii) b, (iv) d, (v) a, (vi) f
1359. (i) b, (ii) a, (iii) d, (iv) c
1360. (a) 1361. (b) 1362. (b) 1363. (c)
1364. (i) b, (ii) a, (iii) d, (iv) c
1365. (i) c, (ii) d, (iii) b, (iv) a
1366. (i) c, (ii) a, (iii) b, (iv) d
1367. (b) 1368. (c) 1369. (a)
1370. (a) 1371. (b) 1372. (d) 1373. (c) 1374. (a) 1375. (b)
1376. (c) 1377. (b) 1378. (c) 1379. (d) 1380. (b) 1381. (b)
1382. (c) 1383. (a) 1384. (b) 1385. (c)

# 10

# Rhetoric and Prosody

Choose the correct option to which the given statement belongs. (Q1-15)

1. "At one fell swoop, he lost his wife, his house, his dog."
   (a) Climax
   (b) Paradox
   (c) Anti-climax
   (d) Epigram
2. "Man proposes, God disposes."
   (a) Anti-climax
   (b) Epigram
   (c) Oxymoron
   (d) Antithesis
3. "To take arms against a sea of troubles."
   (a) Simile
   (b) Mixed metaphor
   (c) Metaphor
   (d) Epigram
4. "There is no one so poor as a wealthy miser."
   (a) Epigram
   (b) Anti-climax
   (c) Paradox
   (d) Metaphor
5. "An ambassador is one who *lies* abroad for the good of his country."
   (a) Pun
   (b) Zeugma
   (c) Oxymoron
   (d) Synecdoche
6. "Fear knocked on the door. Faith answered. There was no one there."
   (a) Paradox
   (b) Personification
   (c) Metonymy
   (d) Metaphor
7. "I don't believe it ever entered his wise head."
   (a) Irony
   (b) Anti-climax
   (c) Epigram
   (d) Oxymoron
8. "The man is *no fool*."
   (a) Euphemism
   (b) Synecdoche
   (c) Litotes
   (d) Epigram
9. "As many farewells as there are stars in heaven."
   (a) Hyperbole
   (b) Metaphor
   (c) Apostrophe
   (d) Oxymoron
10. "Oh ! Tiber ! father Tiber

    To Whom the Romans pray."
   (a) Personification
   (b) Apostrophe

(c) Hyperbole
(d) None of the above

11. "Man is a Wolf."
(a) Metaphor
(b) Mixed metaphor
(c) Simile
(d) Oxymoron

12. "A little *noiseless noise* among the leaves
Born of the very *sigh that silence heaves.*"
(a) Simile
(b) Metaphor
(c) Personification
(d) Oxymoron

13. "God made him, and therefore, let him pass for a man."
(a) Metaphor
(b) Sarcasm
(c) Irony
(d) Oxymoron

14. "A full purse never lacks friends."
(a) Synecdoche
(b) Metaphor
(c) Metonymy
(d) Climax

15. "He is a young man of *twenty summers.*"
(a) Metonymy
(b) Metaphor
(c) Paradox
(d) Synecdoche

(There is invariably some confusion in distinguishing between 'metonymy' and 'synecdoche'. According to M.H. Abrams, in *metonymy* "a change of name" "the literal term for one thing is applied to another with which it has become closely associated because of a recurrent relationship in common experience. Thus "the crown" or "the scepter" can be used to stand for a "king" and "Hollywood" for the film industry; "Milton" can signify the writings of Milton...". In *synecdoche* (taking together), "a part of something is used to signify the whole, or (more rarely) the whole is used to signify a part. We use the term "ten hands" for ten workmen, or "a hundred sails" for ships....")

Choose the correct option to which the given statement belongs. (Q16-22)

16. "Thy soul was like a *star*, and dwelt apart."
(a) Simile
(b) Metaphor
(c) Hyperbole
(d) Metonymy

17. "O Wind / If winter comes, can spring be far behind."
(a) Personification
(b) Rhetorical question
(c) Metonymy
(d) Synecdoche

18. "The years to come seemed a *waste of breath*, A *Waste of breath* the years behind."
(a) Understatement
(b) Hyperbole
(c) Chiasmus
(d) Oxymoron

19. "Or stain her honour, or her new brocade."
(a) Metaphor
(b) Metonymy
(c) Zeugma
(d) None of the above

20. "More is thy due than more than all can pay."
(a) Weak-ending
(b) Inversion
(c) Alexandrine
(d) Extra syllable

(It is also called 'anastrophe'—a rhetorical term for the inversion of the normal order of the parts of a sentence. The other term is 'hyperbaton')

21. "He is a citizen of no mean city."
    (a) Periphrasis
    (b) Tautology
    (c) Prolepsis
    (d) Litotes
22. 'Aposiopesis' is a rhetorical device in which
    (a) a speech is completed but half-heartedly.
    (b) a speech is completed on a sad note.
    (c) a speech is concluded on a happy note.
    (d) a speech is broken off abruptly and the sentence is left unfinished.
23. 'Asyndenton' is a rhetorical device where
    (a) conjunctions, articles, even pronouns are not used for the sake of economy and speed.
    (b) conjunctions are over-used.
    (c) verbs are omitted.
    (d) None of the above.

    (Example: "I slip, I slide, I gloom, I glance")
24. 'Hendiadys' is a figure of speech in which
    (a) one idea is expressed by two pronouns joined by a conjunction
    (b) one idea is expressed by two nouns joined by a conjunction
    (c) an idea is left unexpressed
    (d) an idea is fully expressed without using a verb.

    (Example: Her looks drew *audience* and *attention.*)
25. "The plowman homeward plods his weary way" is an example of
    (a) Oxymoron
    (b) Litotes
    (c) antithesis
    (d) Hypallage

    (It is also known as *transferred* epithet. This figure consists in transferring an adjective or adverb from the word with which it is used to another with which it is associated.)
26. "And here and there a lusty trout / And here and there a grayling" is an example of
    (a) Tautology
    (b) Polysyndeton
    (c) Hendiadys
    (d) Asyndenton

    (This is a figure of speech in which there is excessive use of conjunctions)
27. "I am myself personally responsible for this" is an example of
    (a) Hyperbole
    (b) Tautology
    (c) Apostrophe
    (d) Anaphora

    ("An unmarried bachelor" is a good example of taulology, which means 'saying the same thing')
28. "He gave the beggars a few coppers"
    (a) Synedoche
    (b) Metonymy
    (c) Simile
    (d) Metaphor
29. Sprung rhythm is an example of
    (a) Verse
    (b) Syllable
    (c) Stress
    (d) Meter
30. Unrhymed metrical composition consisting of five iambic measures in each line is
    (a) Rhyme royal
    (b) Run-on-lines
    (c) Blank verse
    (d) Spenserian stanza
31. "United we stand, divided we fall" is an example of
    (a) Antithesis
    (b) Bathos

(c) Tautology
(d) Litotes

32. A metre in which an unaccented syllable precedes the accented is called
(a) Anapaestic
(b) Dactylic
(c) Cataletic
(d) Iambic

33. A figure of speech in which two terms opposite in meaning are placed side by side in one phrase is known as
(a) Paradox
(b) Oxymoron
(c) Sarcasm
(d) Antithesis

(For example : open secret, alone together, living dead)

34. A stanza of eight iambic pentameters on the pattern of ab, ab, cc, is known as
(a) Rhyme Royal
(b) Ottava rima
(c) Tennysonian stanza
(d) Spenserian stanza

35. "Careless she is with artful care / Affecting to seem unaffected" is an example of
(a) Irony
(b) Paradox
(c) Simile
(d) Metaphor

36. A metrical foot containing a stressed, followed by an unstressed syllable is
(a) Anapaest
(b) Iamb
(c) Trochee
(d) Dactyl

37. The rhyme scheme of a Spenserian stanza is
(a) abba, cbcb, cdcd, ee
(b) abab, bccb, ccdd, ee
(c) aabb, bcbc, ccdd, ee
(d) abab, bcbc, cdcd, ee

38. Using the expression "Crown" for the monarchy" is an example of
(a) Metonymy
(b) Synecdoche
(c) Irony
(d) Metaphor

39. Using "the Bench" for the judiciary is an example of
(a) Metaphor
(b) Irony
(c) Synecdoche
(d) Metonymy

40. Four feet, comprising a monosyllable, trochee, dactyl and first paeon is often called
(a) Running rhythm
(b) Sprung rhythm
(c) Blank verse
(d) Rhymed verse

("Trochee" is a metrical foot containing a stressed syllable followed by an unstressed syllable (the reverse of 'iamb'). 'Dactyl' is a metrical foot consisting of one stressed syllable followed by two unstressed ones. "Paeon" is a foot of one stressed and three unstressed syllables. 'Sprung rhythm' is a metre in which the number of accents in a line are counted but the number of syllables doesn't matter.)

41. In the "Windhover" Hopkins uses
(a) Alternative rhyme
(b) Disyllabic rhyme
(c) Cross rhyme
(d) Split rhyme

('Split rhyme' is also known as 'broken rhyme'. The rhyme scheme in the poem is: a, bb, aa, bbb, cd, cd, cd (octave and sestet).)

42. Feminine ending refers to
    (a) a stressed final syllable in a line of verse.
    (b) the ending of a poem in a stressed syllable.
    (c) the ending of a poem in an unstressed syllable.
    (d) an unstressed final syllable in a line of verse.

43. Which are the figures of speech used in the following lines by Blake?
    "Tyger, tyger, burning bright
    In the forest of the might
    What immortal hand or eye
    Could frame thy fearful symmetry?"
    (a) Simile and personification
    (b) Irony and synecdoche
    (c) Apostrophe and synecodoche
    (d) Metonymy and apostrophe

44. Heroic couplet is a pair of
    (a) rhyming iambic pentameter lines.
    (b) unrhyming iambic pentameter lines.
    (c) rhyming iambic hexameter.
    (d) unrhyming iambic hexameter.

45. Heroic quatrain is
    (a) a stanza in blank verse.
    (b) eight line stanza in iambic pentameter.
    (c) four line stanza in iambic pentameter.
    (d) six line stanza in iambic pentameter.

46. Internal rhyme is
    (a) the basic rhythmic structure of a poem.
    (b) rhyming of two words in alternative lines.
    (c) rhyming of two or more words in the same line of poetry.
    (d) all the lines of a poem ending with the same line pattern.

    (It is also called *middle rhyme* or *leonine rhyme.*)

47. A "Foot" is in prosody is a basic unit of
    (a) Rhyme
    (b) Length
    (c) Rhythmic measurement
    (d) Height

48. Heptameter consists of
    (a) five metrical feet
    (b) six metrical feet
    (c) seven metrical feet
    (d) eight metrical feet

49. "Iambus" is a metrical foot consisting of
    (a) Two syllables
    (b) Three syllables
    (c) Four syllables
    (d) One syllable

50. The rhyme scheme of Shakespeare's sonnet is
    (a) abab, cdcd, efef, gg
    (b) abba, cddc, effe, gg
    (c) abab, cdcd, efef, gg
    (d) aabb, ccdd, eeff, gg

51. Hyperbole is

    1. an extravagant exaggeration 2. a racist slur 3. a metrical skill 4. a figure of speech
    (a) 1 is correct
    (b) 1 and 4 are correct
    (c) 1 and 3 are correct
    (d) 3 is correct

52. 'Inversion' is the change in the word order for creating rhetorical effect, e.g. *this book I like*. Another term for inversion is
    (a) Hypallage
    (b) Hubris
    (c) Haiku
    (d) Hyperbaton

    (The other term for inversion is 'anastrophe')

53. Verse that has no set theme—no regular meter, rhyme or stanzaic pattern is

1. open form 2. flexible form 3. free verse 4. blank verse

(a) 1, 2, 3 are correct
(b) 3 and 4 are correct
(c) 2, 3 and 4 are correct
(d) 1 and 3 are correct

54. A sequence of repeated consonantal sounds in a stretch of language is

(a) Alliteration
(b) Acrostic
(c) Assent
(d) Syllable

(e.g. "Five miles meandering with a mazy motion")

55. A sequence of repeated vowel sounds in a stretch of language is

(a) Alliteration
(b) Acrostic
(c) Assonance
(d) Assent

(e.g. "Hear the mellow wedding bells")

56. "Out of this house"—said rider to the reader
"Yours never will"—said farer to the fearer
"They're looking for you" said hearer to horror

These lines are an example of

(a) Alliteration
(b) Consonance
(c) Assonance
(d) Assent

(Consonance ("to harmonise") is the close repetition of identical sound before and after differing vowel sounds, e.g. leave/love, short/shirt.)

57. The rhetorical pattern used by Chaucer in "The Prologue to Canterbury Tales" is

(a) Tcn-syllable line
(b) Eight-syllable line
(c) Rhyme royal
(d) Ottava rima

("Rhyme royal" has seven lines of iambic pentameter rhyming *ababbcc*. "Ottava rima" is a 8-line stanza of iambic pentameter rhyming *abababcc*.)

58. A pause marking a rhythmic point of division in a line of poetry is a/an

(a) Iamb
(b) Foot
(c) Caesura
(d) Kenning

59. A "metaphor" is

(a) the rhyming of words within a line of poetry.
(b) the use of a word to imitate the sound its describes.
(c) the comparison of two unlike things using "like" or "as".
(d) the direct comparison of two unlike things.

60. "Onomatopoeia" is

(a) the rhyming of words within a line of poetry.
(b) the comparison of two unlike things using "like" or "as".
(c) the use of a word to imitate the sound it describes .
(d) the direct comparison of two unlike things.

(e.g. "The moan of doves in immemorial elms/ And murmuring of innumberable bees.")

61. A 'simile' is

(a) the comparison of two unlike things using "like" or "as".
(b) the direct comparison of two unlike things.
(c) thc rhyming of words at the end of cach line in a stanza.
(d) the use of a word to imitate the sound it describes.

62. A metre is a
    (a) fixed pattern of accented syllables.
    (b) fixed pattern of unaccented syllables.
    (c) fixed pattern of accented and unaccented syllables in the lines of a poem.
    (d) None of the above.

63. The basic unit of rhythm is
    (a) Foot
    (b) Syllable
    (c) Consonants
    (d) Vowels

64. A 'foot' has
    (a) one accented syllable.
    (b) one unaccented syllable.
    (c) at least one accented and one or more unaccented syllables.
    (d) two accented syllables.

65. 'Metre' is determined by
    (a) type of feet in a line.
    (b) number of feet in a line.
    (c) type and number of feet in a line.
    (d) None of the above.

    (The most common types of metre in English poetry are iambic, anapestic, trochaic and dactylic. Two other feet are 'spondaic' and 'pyrrhic'.)

66. An 'iambic' (the noun is *iamb*) consists of
    (a) two unaccented syllables.
    (b) two accented syllables.
    (c) two syllables, one accented followed by one unaccented syllable.
    (d) an unstressed syllable followed by a stressed syllable.

67. An 'anapestic' (the noun is *anapest*) consists of
    (a) two unstressed syllables followed by a stressed syllable.
    (b) one unstressed syllable followed by one stressed syllable.
    (c) one stressed syllable followed by two unstressed syllables.
    (d) three unstressed syllables followed by one stressed syllable.

68. A trochaic (the noun is *trochee*) consists of
    (a) an unstressed syllable followed by one stressed syllable.
    (b) a stressed syllable followed by an unstressed syllable.
    (c) two stressed syllables followed by an unstressed syllable.
    (d) two stressed syllables followed by two unstressed syllables.

69. A *dactylic* (the noun is *dactyl*) consists of
    (a) a stressed syllable followed by an unstressed syllable.
    (b) an unstressed syllable followed by a stressed syllable.
    (c) a stressed syllable followed by two unstressed syllables.
    (d) two stressed syllables followed by two unstressed syllables.

70. Analysis of the metre of a poem is called
    (a) Scansion
    (b) Mansion
    (c) Tension
    (d) Comprehension

71. Which, among the following, is called "rising meter"?
    (a) Iambs
    (b) Anapests
    (c) Trochees
    (d) Both (a) and (b)

72. Which, among the following, is called "falling meter"?
    (a) Anapests
    (b) Trochees
    (c) Dactyls
    (d) Both (b) and (c)

73. 'Iambs' and anapests are called "rising meter" because
    (a) they have the strong stress at the end.
    (b) they have strong stress at the beginning.
    (c) they have no stress at the end.
    (d) they have no stress at the beginning.

74. 'Trochees' and 'dactyls' are called "falling meter" because
    (a) they have no stress at the beginning.
    (b) they have the strong stress at the beginning.
    (c) they have a strong stress at the end.
    (d) they have no stress at the end.

75. How many syllables do "Iambs" and "trochees" have?
    (a) One
    (b) Two
    (c) Three
    (d) Four

76. 'Iambs' and 'trochees' are called "duple meter" because they have
    (a) One syllable
    (b) Three syllables
    (c) Two syllables
    (d) Four syllables

77. How many syllables do "anapests" and "dactyles" have?
    (a) One
    (b) Two
    (c) Three
    (d) Four

78. 'Anapests' and 'dactyls' are called "triple meter" because they have
    (a) One syllable
    (b) Two syllables
    (c) Four syllables
    (d) Three syllables

(There are two other meters in English: *Spondaic* (the noun form is "spondee") and the "Pyrrhic". "Spondee" has two successive syllables with approximately equal strong stresses. While "pyrrhic" is a foot composed of two successive syllables with approximately equal light stresses.

**A metric line is named according to the number of feet composing it**

1. *Monometer* : one foot 2. *Dimeter*: two feet 3. *Trimeter*: three feet 4. *Tetrameter*: four feet 5. *Pentameter*: five feet 6. *Hexameter*: six feet 7. *Heptameter*: Seven feet 8. *Octameter*: eight feet

**Note :** An 'Alexandrine' (see no. 6) is a line of six iambic feet. A 'Fourteener' (see no. 7) is another term for a line of seven iambic feet. It tends to break into a unit of four feet followed by a unit of three feet.

79. The metre of a line of poetry having five iambic feet is called
    (a) Iambic pentametre
    (b) Trachaic tetrametre
    (c) Anapestic trimetre
    (d) Dactylic hexametre

80. The metre of a line having four trochaic feet is called
    (a) Iambic pentametre
    (b) Trochaic tetrametre
    (c) Anapestic trimetre
    (d) Dactylic hexametre

81. The metre of a line having three anapestic feet is called
    (a) Iambic pentametre
    (b) Trochaic tetrametre
    (c) Anapestic trimetre
    (d) Dactylic hexametre

82. The metre of a line having six dactylic feet is called
    (a) Iambic pentametre
    (b) Trochaic tetrametre

(c) Anapestic trimetre
(d) Dactylic hexametre

83. "I wandered lonely as a cloud" is an example of
(a) Metaphor
(b) Hyperbole
(c) Simile
(d) Personification

84. A Shakespearean sonnet has
(a) Three quartrains and a couplet.
(b) An octave and a sestet.
(c) Two sestets and a couplet.
(d) None of the above.

85. A Petrarchan sonnet has
(a) three quatrains and a couplet .
(b) an octave and a sestet.
(c) two sestes and a couplet.
(d) a sestet and two quatrains.

86. Chaucer's "Canterbury Tales" is written in
(a) Trochaic tetrametre
(b) Heroic couplet
(c) Dactylic hexametre
(d) Iambic hexametre

87. How many lines does a ballad stanza have?
(a) Two
(b) Three
(c) Four
(d) Six

88. The rhyme scheme of a ballad stanza generally is
(a) abcb
(b) abbc
(c) aabb
(d) abca

89. 'Blank Verse' poetry is written in
(a) Heroic couplet
(b) Ottava rima
(c) Rhyme royal
(d) Unrhymed iambic pentameter

90. A 'rhyme royal' has
(a) Six lines
(b) Seven lines
(c) Eight lines
(d) Four lines

91. An 'Ottava Rima" has
(a) Four lines
(b) Six lines
(c) Seven lines
(d) Eight lines

92. John Milton in "Paradise Lost" used
(a) Ottava rima
(b) Blank verse
(c) Heroic couplet
(d) Rhyme royal

93. How many cantos does Alexander Pope's "Rape of the Lock" have?
(a) Three
(b) Two
(c) Five
(d) Four

94. Into how many cantos is Spenser's "Faerie Queene" (Book I) divided
(a) Eight
(b) Six
(c) Ten
(d) Twelve

95. The rhyme scheme of Milton's sonnet "On His Blindness" is
(a) abba, abba, cde, cde
(b) abc, abc, cd, cd, cd
(c) abbc, abbc, de, de, de
(d) abc, abc, abc, abc, de

96. The form of Coleridge's "The Rime of the Ancient Mariner" is
(a) Rhyme royal
(b) Ballad form
(c) Ottava rima
(d) None of the above.

97. The rhyme scheme in "The Rime of the Ancient Mariner" is
    (a) aabb
    (b) abba
    (c) abcb
    (d) abcd
98. A 'dimeter' is a line of poetry consisting of
    (a) one metrical foot.
    (b) two metrical feet.
    (c) three metrical feet.
    (d) four metrical feet.
99. A 'double rhyme' is a rhyme consisting of
    (a) an accented syllable followed by an unaccented (unstressed) syllable.
    (b) an unaccented syllable followed by an accented syllable.
    (c) a stressed syllable followed by two unstressed syllables.
    (d) None of the above.

    (It is also called '*feminine rhyme*')
100. An elagiac stanza has
    (a) three lines.
    (b) four lines in iambic pentameter.
    (c) six lines.
    (d) eight lines.

    (It is also called *heroic stanza or quatrain or elegiac stanza.*)
101. The rhyme scheme of an elegiac stanza is
    (a) aabb
    (b) abba
    (c) abab
    (d) abca
102. 'Enjambent' means
    (a) carrying of sense and grammatical structure in a poem beyond the end of one line, couplet, or stanza into the next.
    (b) carrying the sense into the middle of a line.
    (c) completing the sense at the end of a line.
    (d) None of the above.
103. 'End-stopped lines' are those in which
    (a) the sense is carried over beyond the line.
    (b) the grammatical structure, the sense, and the metre are completed at the end of the line.
    (c) in which the sense is completed at the end of the stanza.
    (d) in which the sense is completed in the middle of the line.
104. 'Exact or true rhyme' is a rhyme in which
    (a) the stressed syllables and all succeeding sounds are identical between two words.
    (b) the one unstressed followed by another unstressed syllable.
    (c) one stressed syllable followed by another stressed syllable.
    (d) there are two unstressed syllables and two stressed syllables.

    (for example : *feature / creature*)
105. Blank verse in English was introduced by
    (a) Shakespeare
    (b) Spenser
    (c) Eliot
    (d) Surrey
106. English iambic pentameter was brought to its first maturity in
    (a) Sonnet
    (b) Dramatic verse
    (c) Lyric
    (d) Elegy
107. 'Villanelle' is a poem of
    (a) Eight lines
    (b) Twelve lines
    (c) Nineteen lines
    (d) Sixteen lines

(It is lyric made up of five stanzas of three lines (tercets) followed by a final stanza of four lines (quatrain).)

108. A 'free verse'
   (a) has irregular beat of metre.
   (b) lacks rhyme.
   (c) often has irregular line lengths and fragmented syntax.
   (d) All of the above.

109. 'Masculine rhyme' is
   (a) the rhyming of single stressed syllables.
   (b) the rhyming of two stressed syllables.
   (c) the rhyming of two unstressed syllables.
   (d) the rhyming of one stressed and one unstressed syllabl.

   (For example : *bark / dark*)

110. 'Near rhyme' is a rhyme in which
   (a) the last stressed vowels are identical.
   (b) the last stressed vowels differ, but the following sounds are identical.
   (c) the last syllables differ.
   (d) None of the above.

   (It is also called *imperfect rhyme*, *partial rhyme*, *slant rhyme*, or *para rhyme*. Example : *fish / dash*, *smiling / falling*)

111. 'Terza rima' is a form of verse composed of
   (a) Eight lines
   (b) Ten lines
   (c) Twelve lines
   (d) Fourteen lines

   (It is composed of three-line stanzas, or *tercets*, linked by rhyme : *abc*, *bcb*, *cdc*, *ded*, and so on. The word at the end of the middle line of each stanza rhymes with the words at the end of the first and third lines of each succeeding stanza. A poem in *terza rima* concludes with a *couplet* rhyming with the middle line of the previous stanza.)

112. The first known use of 'terza rima' was made in
   (a) Dante's *Divine Comedy*
   (b) Homer's *Iliad*
   (c) Spenser's *Faerie Queene*
   (d) Milton's *Paradise Lost*

113. T.S. Eliot's "The Waste Land" is written in
   (a) Heroic couplet
   (b) Free verse
   (c) Terza rima
   (d) Blank verse

114. The most usual rhyme scheme of a 'rondel' is
   (a) abba, abab, abba
   (b) abcb, abbc, abcd
   (c) aabb, acca, abab
   (d) abca, abba, acbc, acbc

115. Robert Browning's "The Ring and the Book" is written in
   (a) Ottava rima
   (b) Free verse
   (c) Blank verse
   (d) Heroic couplet

## ANSWERS

| | | | | | |
|---|---|---|---|---|---|
| 1. (c) | 2. (d) | 3. (b) | 4. (c) | 5. (a) | 6. (b) |
| 7. (a) | 8. (c) | 9. (a) | 10. (b) | 11. (a) | 12. (d) |
| 13. (b) | 14. (c) | 15. (d) | 16. (a) | 17. (b) | 18. (c) |
| 19. (c) | 20. (b) | 21. (d) | 22. (d) | 23. (a) | 24. (b) |
| 25. (d) | 26. (b) | 27. (b) | 28. (a) | 29. (d) | 30. (c) |
| 31. (a) | 32. (d) | 33. (b) | 34. (b) | 35. (b) | 36. (c) |
| 37. (d) | 38. (a) | 39. (d) | 40. (b) | 41. (d) | 42. (c) |
| 43. (d) | 44. (a) | 45. (c) | 46. (c) | 47. (c) | 48. (c) |
| 49. (a) | 50. (a) | 51. (b) | 52. (d) | 53. (d) | 54. (a) |
| 55. (c) | 56. (b) | 57. (c) | 58. (c) | 59. (d) | 60. (c) |
| 61. (a) | 62. (c) | 63. (a) | 64. (c) | 65. (c) | 66. (d) |
| 67. (a) | 68. (b) | 69. (c) | 70. (a) | 71. (d) | 72. (d) |
| 73. (a) | 74. (b) | 75. (b) | 76. (c) | 77. (c) | 78. (d) |
| 79. (a) | 80. (b) | 81. (c) | 82. (d) | 83. (c) | 84. (a) |
| 85. (b) | 86. (b) | 87. (c) | 88. (a) | 89. (d) | 90. (b) |
| 91. (d) | 92. (b) | 93. (c) | 94. (d) | 95. (a) | 96. (b) |
| 97. (c) | 98. (b) | 99. (a) | 100. (b) | 101. (c) | 102. (a) |
| 103. (b) | 104. (a) | 105. (d) | 106. (a) | 107. (c) | 108. (d) |
| 109. (a) | 110. (b) | 111. (c) | 112. (a) | 113. (d) | 114. (a) |
| 115. (c) | | | | | |

# Paper III

# 1

# The History of the English Language and English Language Teaching

### The History of English Language

1. Into how many main periods is the history of the English language traditionally divided?
   (a) Two
   (b) Three
   (c) Four
   (d) Five
2. The names of the main periods into which the history of the English language is divided are
   (a) Old English
   (b) Middle English
   (c) Modern English
   (d) All of the above
3. What is broadly the period-wise division of the three main periods of the history of the English language?
   (a) Old English : 450-1100 A.D.
   (b) Middle English : 1100-1500 A.D.
   (c) Modern English : Since 1500 A.D.
   (d) All the above are correct
4. Which is regarded as the 'great grand-mother' of the Indo-European languages?
   (a) Ancient Greek
   (b) Ancient Latin
   (c) Gaelic
   (d) Proto-Indo-European
5. What was broadly the number of the languages that were derived from the Proto-Indo-European?
   (a) Four
   (b) Five
   (c) Six
   (d) Eight

   (These are: Germanic, Celtic, Italic, Hellenic, Balto-Salvic, Indo-Iranian)
6. To which branch of languages does the English language belong?
   (a) Germanic
   (b) Celtic
   (c) Hellenic
   (d) Balto-Slavic
7. To which branch of languages does the French language belong?
   (a) Germanic
   (b) Italic
   (c) Celtic
   (d) Hellenic
8. To which branch of languages does the Greek language belong?
   (a) Balto-Slavic
   (b) Italic
   (c) Hellenic
   (d) Celtic

9. To which branch of languages does Latin belong?
   (a) German
   (b) Hellenic
   (c) Celtic
   (d) Italic
10. Match the following cognates:

| | | | |
|---|---|---|---|
| A. | Pita | 1. | Greek |
| B. | Pater | 2. | English |
| C. | Father | 3. | Gothic |
| D. | Fadar | 4. | Sanskrit |

   (a) A-4, B-1, C-2, D-3
   (b) A-3, B-2, C-4, D-1
11. English was initially the language of one of the following tribes:
   (a) The Jutes
   (b) The Angles
   (c) The Saxons
   (d) None of the above
12. After A.D. 1000 'England' was used to denote the Germanic peoples in Britain, and their language was known as
   (a) English
   (b) Englis
   (c) Englise
   (d) Englic
13. Which period in the history of the English language is known as the 'period of' levelled inflections?
   (a) Old English period
   (b) Middle Period
   (c) Modern Period
   (d) Early Modern Period
14. Which period in the history of the English language is known as the period of 'lost inflections'?
   (a) Early Middle Period
   (b) Later Middle Period
   (c) Modern Period
   (d) Old Period
15. How many dialects did old English have?
   (a) Two
   (b) Four
   (c) Three
   (d) Five

   (These four dialects are : Northunibrairi, Mercian, West Saxon and Kentish)
16. Linguists say that old English is a 'Synthetic language'. What does it mean? It means that words typically have
   (a) more than one morphemes.
   (b) no morphemes.
   (c) only two morpheme.
   (d) only three morphemes.
17. For how man cases are the noun and the adjective inflected in the singular and the plural?
   (a) Three
   (b) Four
   (c) Two
   (d) Five
18. How many principal dialects were there in Middle English?
   (a) Two
   (b) Three
   (c) Four
   (d) Five

   (These dialects were : Northern, West Midland, East Midland, Southern)
19. The English language developed into a very "borrowing" language with a highly disparate vocabulary.
   True/False
20. Which dialect became the most popular and standard dialect by the end of the 14th century?
   (a) Northern
   (b) West Midland
   (c) Southern
   (d) East Midland

21. Modern English is called an 'analytic language'. What does it mean. It means that it has
    (a) one morpheme.
    (b) two morphemes.
    (c) three morphemes.
    (d) four morphemes.
22. The history of the English language really started with arrival of ________ Germanic tribes.
    (a) two
    (b) four
    (c) three
    (d) five

    (These three tribes were the Angles, the Saxons, and the Jutes)
23. Linguists talk of ________ great changes in the history of English language.
    (a) three
    (b) four
    (c) five
    (d) six

    (Renaissance was the first great change which brought about the birth of Modern English. The second was the Industrial Revolution. The third was the migration to and settlement in the new lands, the U.S.A., Australia, Canada and New Zealand, The fourth was the colonization of Asia and Africa.)
24. Old English period is described as "a period of full inflections". This is because
    (a) it had an elaborate system.
    (b) it had two inflectional endings.
    (c) it had three inflectional endings.
    (d) None of the above.
25. In Old English, nouns had different forms for different cases.

    True/False
26. Old English nouns were classified into strong and weak declensions according to the ending.

    True/False

    ('Declension' is the way in which some sets of nouns, adjectives, and pronouns change their form or endings to show case, number or gender.)
27. In how many vowels did 'Strong' declension end?
    (a) Three
    (b) Two
    (c) Four
    (d) Five

    (These vowels were : a, o, i or u)

    (The inflections for the strong and weak nouns have been classified as the '-s' and '-n' declensions respectively.)
28. What was the number of gender in old English?
    (a) Two
    (b) Three
    (c) Four
    (d) None of the above

    (Masculine, feminine, neuter)
29. How many forms did adjectives have in Old English?
    (a) Two
    (b) Three
    (c) Four
    (d) Five

    (These forms were 'strong' and 'weak')
30. Into how many groups were the verbs divided in old English?
    (a) Three
    (b) Two
    (c) Four
    (d) Five

(These were 'strong' and 'weak' verbs like the adjectives.)

31. Which is "the oldest historical prose in any Germanic language"?
   (a) The Ecclesiastical History of the English people
   (b) A Table Alphabetical
   (c) The Parker Chronicle
   (d) None of the above
32. Robert Cowdrey's *A Table Alphabetical, the First All-English Dictionary* appeared in
   (a) 1600
   (b) 1601
   (c) 1602
   (d) 1604
33. *The Oxford English Dictionary* appeared in
   (a) 1933
   (b) 1935
   (c) 1936
   (d) 1937
34. John Walker's *A Critical Pronouncing Dictionary* appeared in
   (a) 1790
   (b) 1791
   (c) 1792
   (d) 1793
35. *The English Pronouncing Dictionary* (1917) was written by
   (a) John Walker
   (b) Robert Cawdrey
   (c) David Jones
   (d) Bede
36. Henry Bradley's *The Making of English* appeared in
   (a) 1900
   (b) 1901
   (c) 1903
   (d) 1904
37. *Growth and Structure of the English Language* (1905) was written by
   (a) Spir
   (b) Whorf
   (c) Bradley
   (d) Otto Jesperson
38. To which family does Sanskrit, Hindi, Bengali, Punjabi, Gujrati, Marathi belong?
   (a) Indo-Iranian (or Aryan)
   (b) Dravidian
   (c) Italic
   (d) Germanic
39. To which family do Tamil, Telugu, Malayalam and Kannada belong?
   (a) Indo-Aryan
   (b) Dravidian
   (c) Germanic
   (d) None of the above
40. Which becomes the first recognizable language of the English people?
   (a) Angli
   (b) Saxonee
   (c) Anglo-Saxon
   (d) None of the above
41. The maximum change that took place in language during the course of time is in
   (a) Grammar
   (b) Words
   (c) Speech
   (d) Vocabulary
42. What can possibly be the reasons for change in the language system?
   (a) Millions of people speak a language under varying conditions.
   (b) Language changes when it comes into contact with other languages.
   (c) The geographical division may also lead to change.
   (d) All of the above.

43. The Dravidian languages—Tamil, Telugu, Kannada, Malayalam are not Indo-European languages.

    True/False

44. All Indo-European languages have two features. Which are they?
    (a) They are all inflectional.
    (b) They have a common word-stock.
    (c) They have common grammar.
    (d) Both (a) and (b).

45. Old English was influenced by
    (a) Celtic
    (b) Latin
    (c) Scandinavian
    (d) All of the above

46. How many sets of correspondences were shown in which the Germanic sound system diverged from that of Indo-European?
    (a) Five
    (b) Seven
    (c) Nine
    (d) Ten

    (This sound shift from Indo-European to Germanic is known Grimm's Law in linguistics. Jakob Grimm (1785-1863) worked out this SOUND LAW first in 1822.)

47. Certain important sound changes characterizing the Old English were
    (a) Gradation
    (b) i-Mutation
    (c) Fracture
    (d) All of the above

    (Jakob Grimm made use of the term 'Abault' to describe this process. Gradation may be defined as the patterned variation of vowel sounds for grammatical purposes, e.g. sing, sang, sung. i-Mulation was a development peculiar to Primitive Old English. It is also called 'Umlaut'. It was a gradual and slow process and was complete about 700 A. D. i-Mutation is the name given to the modification of a vowel or diphthong. Under the influence of an 'i' or 'j' in the next syllable. It is a kind of 'assimilation' 'Fracture' (or Breaking) is a major sound change in Old English. It refers to the formation of diphthongs from vowels.)

48. How many tense forms did Old English verbs have?
    (a) Two
    (b) Three
    (c) Four
    (d) Five

    (The two tense forms were the 'present' and the 'past'. There was no separate form for the future tense just as it is in Modern English.)

49. Which language influenced Middle English?
    (a) Latin
    (b) French
    (c) Danish
    (d) Celtic

50. During the Middle English Period, French became the language of
    (a) law courts and learned professions.
    (b) nobility.
    (c) King's court.
    (d) All of the above.

    (The upper classes used French and the lower classes used English. It gave rise to what is known as Middle English (Anglo-French). However, the resultant language was predominantly Saxon.)

51. In which of the fields was the French influence predominant?
    (a) Religion and law
    (b) Government and military affairs
    (c) Clothes and words associated with the Feudal system
    (d) All of the above
52. In how many phases was the Latin influence felt an Old English?
    (a) Two
    (b) Three
    (c) Four
    (d) Five

    ("The First or continental Phase refers to the influence of Latin on the Angles, Saxons and Jutes before they settled in Britain. The 'Second Phase' of Latin influence reached when English was under the control of the Romans (45 B.C. to 410 A.D.) The 'Third Phase' is associated with the visit of St. Augustine and his missionary monks to England and converting the natives to Christianity around 596 A.D.)
53. Benedictine Reform aimed at the general improvement of
    (a) Law
    (b) Politics
    (c) Education
    (d) Cultural and religious life
54. French was finally abolished by an Act of Parliament passed in
    (a) 1729
    (b) 1731
    (c) 1733
    (d) 1735
55. The change of places by two sounds in a word involving consonants is known as
    (a) Metonymy
    (b) Metathesis
    (c) Meterule
    (d) Micronesia

    (It generally occurred with 'r' or 's'. In 'ask' for example, the 's' and 'k' have changed places.)
56. English came to be generally adopted in writing in
    (a) 1420
    (b) 1422
    (c) 1425
    (d) 1427
57. Which of the following were the important works of the 14th century?
    (a) Canterbury Tales
    (b) Piers Plowman
    (c) Sir Gawaine and the Green Knight
    (d) All of the above
58. The major change in English grammar during the Middle English period was a general reduction of inflection endings on
    (a) Nouns
    (b) Adjectives
    (c) Verbs
    (d) All of the above
59. The principal change in verbs in the Middle English period was a
    (a) steady decrease in the number of strong verbs.
    (b) increase in the number of weak verbs.
    (c) increase in the number of strong as well as weak verbs.
    (d) Both (a) and (b).
60. In Middle English, the greatest loss among pronouns was in the
    (a) Demonstratives
    (b) Personal pronouns
    (c) Possessive pronouns
    (d) Interrogative pronouns

61. In Middle English, the decay of inflections resulted in the
    (a) change of the grammatical gender.
    (b) loss of the grammatical gender
    (c) increase in the grammatic gender categories
    (d) None of the above.

    (The idea of sex became the only determining factor. One could refer to the female as 'she', the male as 'he' and inanimate object as 'it')

62. The Runic alphabet used by the Anglo-Saxons before their conversion to Christianity had
    (a) Twenty letters
    (b) Twenty-two letters
    (c) Twenty-four letters
    (d) Twenty-three letters

63. There was a greater correlation between sound and letter in Old English than there is in Modern English today.

    True/False

64. One of the most noticeable features of the transition from Old to Middle English was the change in
    (a) Nouns
    (b) Spellings
    (c) Sounds
    (d) Adjectives

65. The problem of bringing about great uniformity in English spellings was widely recognized in the
    (a) 14th century
    (b) 15th century
    (c) 16th century
    (d) 17th century

66. Swedish philologist R.E. Zachrisson proposed a respelled English called 'Anglie' in
    (a) 1927
    (b) 1928
    (c) 1929
    (d) 1930

67. Some of the major processes through which language change proceeds are:
    (a) assimilation and rejection
    (b) invention and derivation
    (c) adaptation/modification
    (d) all the above

68. Choose the correct sequence:
    (a) Angle, Angli, Engle, Anglcynn, England.
    (b) Angli, Angle, Anglcynn, Engle, England.
    (c) England, Engle, Angle, Anglcynn, Angli.
    (d) Engle, Anglcynn, Angli, Angle, England.

69. There are today ________ sounds in the Queens English.
    (a) forty
    (b) forty-two
    (c) forty-four
    (d) forty-eight

70. How many consonants are there in English?
    (a) Twenty
    (b) Twenty-two
    (c) Twenty-three
    (d) Twenty-four

71. How many diphthongs are there in English?
    (a) Six
    (b) Eight
    (c) Twelve
    (d) Ten

72. How many vowel sounds are there in English?
    (a) Ten
    (b) Eight
    (c) Twelve
    (d) Fourteen

73. Old English had _______ consonants.
    (a) Two
    (b) Three
    (c) Four
    (d) Five

    (There two consonants were (x) and (r) The consonant (x) by the early modern period changed to 'gh' as in light and bought or 'f' as in 'rough' and 'tough'. The (r) changed to (g).)

74. People who study the history of language are called
    (a) Etymologists
    (b) Philologists
    (c) Psephologists
    (d) None of the above

75. Who coined the term "the great vowel shift"?
    (a) Sapir
    (b) Whorf
    (c) Otto Jesperson
    (d) None of the above

    (English vowels underwent a great change after the fourteenth century and this change has been called the "great vowel shift".)

76. The consonantal alphabet originated from the
    (a) The Phoenicians
    (b) The Greeks
    (c) The Romans
    (d) The French

77. Who, among the following, tried to bring about greater uniformity in English spelling on the phonetic lines in the sixteenth century?
    (a) John Hart
    (b) William Bullokar
    (c) Richard Mulcaster
    (d) All of the above

78. Besides Greek, which of the following languages made great contribution to the English vocabulary?
    (a) Latin
    (b) French
    (c) Scandinavian
    (d) All of the above

79. Which preposition becomes quite common in Old English after the Scandinavian influence?
    (a) Through
    (b) Till
    (c) Wherever
    (d) Along

80. Many places in English with place names ending -'by', 'thirp', 'waite' and 'loft' show a clear evidence of
    (a) French influence
    (b) Latin influence
    (c) Scandinavian Influence
    (d) Greek influence

81. William Caxton brought the printing press to England in
    (a) 1476
    (b) 1478
    (c) 1479
    (d) 1480

82. Which year marks the beginning of the Modern English period
    (a) 1480
    (b) 1485
    (c) 1490
    (d) 1500

83. Which major events left their impact on Modern English in the sixteenth century
    (a) Renaissance and Reformation
    (b) The invention of printing Press
    (c) The discovery of America
    (d) All of the above

84. Sir Thomas North's translation of Plutarch's *Lives of the Noble Grecians and Romans* appeared in
    (a) 1579
    (b) 1598
    (c) 1582
    (d) 1584

85. George Chapman's translation of *Homer* appeared in
    (a) 1596
    (b) 1598
    (c) 1599
    (d) 1601

86. Some scholars of the sixteenth century were against borrowings from foreign languages. Who were they?
    (a) George Pettie
    (b) Richard Mulcaster
    (c) Sir John Cheke
    (d) All of the above

87. When did the word 'puritan' appear in English?
    (a) 15th century
    (b) 14th century
    (c) Middle of the 16th century
    (d) End of the 16th century

88. One of the important outcomes of the Reformation was John Tyndale's translation of the Bible which appeared in
    (a) 1520
    (b) 1525
    (c) 1530
    (d) 1535

89. Which of the following made English language more uniform?
    (a) Renaissance
    (b) Reformation
    (c) The printing press
    (d) The Bible

    (This was because of the printing of books, which became available to all)

90. "King James Version" of the Bible appeared in
    (a) 1611
    (b) 1613
    (c) 1613
    (d) 1618

91. Which was the decisive factor in fixing English spelling?
    (a) *Tyndale's translation of the Bible*
    (b) *King James Version*
    (c) *Dr. Johnson's Dictionary*
    (d) None of the above

92. Who, among the following, introduced new words in English to make it beautiful and expressive?
    (a) Dr. Johnson
    (b) Caxton
    (c) George Chapman
    (d) Tyndale

93. When was great literature produced in the English language?
    (a) In the early Middle English period
    (b) In the later Middle English period
    (c) In the early sixteenth century
    (d) Towards the end of the sixteenth century

94. Which of the following are the most important features of early Modern English?
    (a) Great vowel shift
    (b) Emergence of standard English
    (c) Modernization of spellings
    (d) Both (a) and (b)

95. The characteristics of the Modern English are
    (a) a fixed word-order.
    (b) use of function words.

(c) an elaborate auxiliary system.
(d) All of the above.

96. A series of changes called the 'Great Vowel Shift' by Jesperson brought about the most characteristic differences between the
   (a) Old English and early Middle English pronunciation.
   (b) early Middle English Pronunciation and later Middle English pronunciation.
   (c) Chaucerian pronunciation and that of early Modern English.
   (d) early Modern English pronunciation and later Modern English pronunciation.

97. How many vowels underwent changes according to Jesperson?
   (a) Six
   (b) Seven
   (c) Eight
   (d) Nine

98. Which was regarded as the most eminent work in the field of lexicography?
   (a) *Dr. Johnson's Dictionary*
   (b) *Webster's Dictionary*
   (c) *Oxford English Dictionary*
   (d) *The English Pronouncing Dictionary*

99. The most important American lexicographers were
   (a) Noah Webster
   (b) J.E. Worcester
   (c) H.W. Fowler
   (d) Both (a) and (b)

100. *The English Pronunciation Dictionary* was prepared by
   (a) Daniel Jones
   (b) Henry Bradley
   (c) C.T. Onions
   (d) James Murray

(James Murray, Henry Bradley, Sir William Craig and C.T. Onions were the editors of the great *Oxford English Dictionary* which appeared in instalments from 1883 to 1928.)

### English Language Teaching

101. In the fifteenth century, the dominant language of education was
   (a) Latin
   (b) Greek
   (c) French
   (d) English

102. In the sixteenth, seventeenth and in the eighteenth centuries, students were taught Latin through
   (a) the learning of grammar rules.
   (b) the study of declensions and conjugations.
   (c) the study of translation and practice in writing sample sentences.
   (d) All of the above.

103. During the Renaissance, who, among the following, were against the teaching of formal grammars?
   (a) Luther
   (b) Roger Ascham
   (c) Montaigne
   (d) All of the above

104. Who, among the following, made specific proposals for curriculum reform in the seventeenth century?
   (a) Comenius
   (b) John Locke
   (c) Ratich
   (d) Both (a) and (b)

105. In the last quarter of the eighteenth century, the usual practice in schools was for the teacher to
   (a) teach grammar.
   (b) to translate from the second language to the first language.

(c) to teach vocabulary.
(d) make the students writing the second language.

106. Textbooks consisted of
(a) statements of abstract grammar rules.
(b) lists of vocabulary.
(c) the sentences for translation.
(d) All of the above.

107. At the beginning of the nineteenth century, Karl Plotz, the German textbook writer, wrote textbooks consisting of
(a) a series of grammatical rules illustrated by examples, etc.
(b) a large number of exercises in which sentences in the mother-tongue were to be translated into foreign language.
(c) a list of vocabulary.
(d) Both (a) and (b).

(This approach to foreign language teaching became known as the Grammar-Translation Method.)

108. One of the most important British language teaching approaches was
(a) The Oral Approach or Situational Language Teaching
(b) Grammar-Translation Method
(c) The Communicative Approach
(d) The Lexical Approach

109. One of the important American teaching methods is
(a) The Grammar-Translation Method
(b) Audiolingual Method
(c) Total Physical Response
(d) Competency-Based Language Teaching

110. Grammar-Translational Method was the adopted by the
(a) German Scholars
(b) British Scholars
(c) American Scholars
(d) None of the above

111. Who made the remark that the object of Grammar-Translation Method was "to know everything about something rather than the thing itself"?
(a) Johann Meidinger
(b) H.S. Ollendorf
(c) W.H.D. Rouse
(d) Kelly

112. The Grammar-Translation Method was first known in the United States as the
(a) Russian Method
(b) Prussian Method
(c) British Method
(d) German Method

113. According to the Grammar-Translation Method, the goal of foreign English language study is to
(a) learn a language in order to read its literature.
(b) to benefit from the mental discipline and intellectual development resulting from foreign language study.
(c) speak the foreign language properly.
(d) Both (a) and (b).

114. The Grammar-Translation Method is a way of studying a language
(a) through a detailed analysis of its grammar rules.
(b) by applying the knowledge of grammar to translate sentences and texts into the target language.
(c) translating sentences and texts into the mother tongue.
(d) All of the above.

115. The major focus in the Grammar-Translation Method is on
(a) Reading
(b) Writing
(c) Listening
(d) Both (a) and (b)

116. The method of teaching words in the Grammar-Translation Method is
   (a) through bilingual word lists.
   (b) dictionary study.
   (c) memorization.
   (d) All of the above.

117. The distinctive feature of the G.T. Method is the focus on
   (a) The sentence
   (b) The word
   (c) The grammar
   (d) The text

118. The medium of instruction in G.T. Method is the
   (a) Target language
   (b) Mother tongue
   (c) Both (a) and (b)
   (d) None of the above

119. G.T. Method dominated foreign language teaching from
   (a) 1810-40
   (b) 1840-60
   (c) 1840-1940
   (d) 1860-1930

120. Who, among the following, wrote *The Practical Study of Languages* (1899)?
   (a) Henry Sweet
   (b) Paul Passy
   (c) W. Victor
   (d) F. Gouin

121. Which, among the following principles, did Henry Sweet set forth in his book *The Practical Study of Languages* (1899)?
   (a) Careful selection of what is to be taught and limits on what is to be taught.
   (b) Arranging the matter according to the four skills of listening, speaking, reading and writing.
   (c) Grading materials from simple to complex.
   (d) All of the above.

122. The reformers in the late nineteenth century were of the view that
   (a) the spoken language is primary.
   (b) words should be presented in sentences, and sentences should be practised in meaningful contexts.
   (c) translation should be avoided.
   (d) All of the above.

123. Some of the features of the Direct Method of teaching language were
   (a) emphasis on the oral language.
   (b) intensive speech practice.
   (c) the exclusive use of the target language.
   (d) All of the above.

124. The most active period in the history of approaches and methods was from
   (a) 1940 to 1950
   (b) 1950 to 1960
   (c) 1950 to 1980
   (d) 1960 to 1980

125. Who identified three levels of conceptualization and organization of language teaching?
   (a) Henry Sweet
   (b) Edward Anthony
   (c) Otto Jesperson
   (d) Harold Palmer

126. What are the levels of conceptualization and organization of language teaching according to Edward Anthony?
   (a) Approach
   (b) Method
   (c) Technique
   (d) All of the above

(This scheme was proposed by Edward Anthony, an American Applied Linguist, in 1963. According to *Longman Dictionary of Applied Linguistics*, "different themes about the nature of language and how languages are learned (approach) imply different ways of teaching language (the method) and different methods make use of different kinds of classroom activity (techniques).")

127. What does the 'S-O-S' approach stand for?
(a) Save our Souls
(b) Structural-Oral-Situational
(c) Structure of Syllabus
(d) None of the above

128. The Structural Approach is an outcome of the experiments carried out in language teaching in the U.S.A. in
(a) Schools
(b) Colleges
(c) Army camps
(d) Universities

129. The "Army Specialized Training Program" (ASTP) was established in
(a) 1940
(b) 1942
(c) 1944
(d) 1945

130. The "S-O-S" approach emerged during the
(a) 1940s
(b) 1950s
(c) 1960s
(d) 1970s

131. Which linguist applied the principles of structural linguistics to language teaching?
(a) Charles Fries
(b) Harold Palmer
(c) A.S. Hornby
(d) Hubbard

132. In the structural approach, language was taught by
(a) oral drilling of basic sentence patterns.
(b) systematic attention was paid to pronunciation.
(c) teachers used mother tongue in teaching English.
(d) Both (a) and (b).

133. "Oral approach or Situational Language Teaching" was developed by British applied linguists from
(a) 1930s to 1960s
(b) 1930s to 1960s
(c) 1940s to 1950s
(d) 1950s to 1960s

134. Two of the most prominent figures in British twentieth century language teaching were
(a) Harold Palmer
(b) A.S. Hornby
(c) Charles Fries
(d) Both (a) and (b)

135. Who used the term 'Situational approach'?
(a) Harold Palmer
(b) Charles Fries
(c) A.S. Hornby
(d) None of the above

136. There was a general consensus among language teaching specialists, during the 1930s, that one of the most important aspects of foreign language learning was
(a) Vocabulary
(b) Grammar
(c) Pronunciation
(d) None of the above

137. Who was the British language specialist who had examined the role of English in India in the 1920s?
(a) Harold Palmer
(b) Michael West
(c) A.S. Hornby
(d) Coleman

138. *A General Service List of English Words* (1953) was written by
(a) A.S. Hornby
(b) Harold Palmer

(c) Michael West
(d) Coleman

139. The "S-O-S" approach made its advent in India in
(a) 1940
(b) 1945
(c) 1950
(d) 1952

140. The First state in India to use the "S-O-S" approach was
(a) Tamil Nadu
(b) W. Bengal
(c) Kerala
(d) Karnataka

141. The Regional Institute of English at Banglore was started in
(a) 1960
(b) 1962
(c) 1963
(d) 1965

142. Which of the following principles are involved in the methodology of the Structural-situational approach?
(a) Selection, i.e. choosing lexical and grammatical items.
(b) Gradation, i.e. organizing and sequencing content.
(c) Presentation, i.e. techniques for presenting and practising items in the course.
(d) All of the above.

(Structural-situational approach is an oral approach like the Direct Method. But the former attempted to develop a more scientific foundation. In this method new words or structures are taught through classroom situations or through demonstration of a particular object. It did not mean the use of language in real-life situations but to the structural drills in which concrete objects, pictures, actions, gestures, etc. were used to teach language.)

143. In the "S-O-S" approach, which order was advocated for the learning of the language skills?
(a) Listening, speaking, reading, writing
(b) Listening, writing, speaking, reading
(c) Speaking, listening, speaking, listening
(d) Writing, reading, speaking, l istening

(For short, it is called LSRW)

144. What are the main principles on which the "S-O-S" approach is based?
(a) Language is primarily speech.
(b) A language is a set of habits.
(c) The use of mother tongue can be avoided in teaching language by using situations.
(d) All of the above.

145. Which of the following factors led to the development of 'Audio-Lingual' method?
(a) The new technology of language laboratory.
(b) Behaviorist psychology.
(c) The development of constrastive Linguistics.
(d) All of the above.

(Contrastive linguistics is an investigation in which the structures of the two languages are compared and contrasted, thereby helping teachers to remedy errors made by learners of one in learning another.)

146. Who coined the term 'Audio-Lingual'?
(a) Nelson Brooks
(b) Harold Palmer
(c) Charles Fries
(d) Hornby

147. The 'Audio-Lingual' method was based on

(a) Linguistics
(b) Psychology
(c) Sociology
(d) Both (a) and (b)

148. The focus in this method was on the learner's gaining skills of
(a) Listening
(b) Speaking
(c) Reading
(d) Only (a) and (b)

**William Moulton enumerated five slogans which formed the basis of the 'Audio-Lingual Method'**

1. Language is speech, not writing
2. A language is a set of habits
3. Teach the language, not about the language
4. A language is what native speakers say, not what someone thinks they say
5. Languages are different

149. Which of the following are some of the features of 'Audio-Lingual' method?
(a) Using dialogues
(b) The introduction of language as an important teaching aid
(c) Avoiding the use of mother tongue
(d) All of the above

150. Which of the following are the main strengths of the 'Audio-Lingual' method?
(a) The teaching materials are very scientifically designed.
(b) Student motivation is very high.
(c) Structural patterns are systematically introduced and practised in the classroom.
(d) All of the above.

151. The 'Bilingual Method' was developed by
(a) C.J. Dodson
(b) Michael West
(c) Colemn
(d) Harold Palmer

152. The 'Bilingual Method' tried to incorporate different aspects of the
(a) Direct Method
(b) Grammar-Translation Method
(c) Audio-Lingual Method
(d) Both (a) and (b)

153. The aim of the bilingual method is to
(a) help learners to speak fluently and accurately in the English language.
(b) help learners to write fluently and accurately in English.
(c) prepare learners so that they can achieve true bilingualism.
(d) All of the above.

154. Put the traditional 'P-P-P' structure in language teaching in proper order
(a) production, practice, presentation
(b) presentation, practice production
(c) practice, presentation, production

155. According to William Mackey, which are the cardinal principles of language teaching methodology?
(a) Selection, Gradation
(b) Presentation, Repetition
(c) Both (a) and (b)
(d) Neither (a) nor (b)

156. Which of the following are the principles of the 'Bilingual Method'?
(a) Controlled systematic use of the mother tongue by the teacher.
(b) The introduction of writing/reading early in the course of language leaning.
(c) Integration of 'writing' and 'speaking' skills.
(d) All of the above.

157. Which of the following steps of presentation are involved in the 'Bilingual Method'?

(a) Imitation and Interpretation
(b) Substitution and Extension
(c) Independent production of sentences
(d) All of the above

(**Imitation:** Students learn how to speak small number of basic sentences. **Interpretation:** Helping the student to overcome the difficulty putting together sound and meaning and to switch over rapidly from one language to the other. **Substitution and Extension:** The learner is able to speak independently about limited situations without an oral or printed stimulus. **Independent production of Sentences:** Learners begin to speak related sentences without a spoken stimulus either in the mother tongue or English.)

158. Which of the following dements should a sound 'method' have?
(a) A set of objectives.
(b) A detailed analysis of the means whereby these objectives can be achieved.
(c) An operational plan for achieving the objectives through selected means.
(d) All of the above.

159. Who, among the following, were the advocates of 'The Communicative Approach' or 'Communicative Language Teaching'?
(a) Christopher Candlin
(b) Henry Widdowson
(c) M.A.K. Halliday
(d) Both (a) and (b)

160. "The Communicative Approach" drew on
(a) Functional linguistics
(b) Sociologists
(c) Philosophers
(d) All of the above

161. Who among the following, is the author of *National Syllabuses*?
(a) D.A. Wilkins
(b) Christopher Brumfit
(c) Keith Johnson
(d) Henry Widdowson

162. "The Communicative Approach" aims to develop
(a) grammatical competence.
(b) communicative competence.
(c) to develop procedures for the teaching of four language skills.
(d) Both (b) and (c).

163. Who coined the term 'Communicative Competence'?
(a) Christopher Brumfit
(b) Henry Widdowson
(c) Dell Hymes
(d) Chomsky

164. Which of the following terms are used for "The Communicative Approach"?
(a) Functional Approach
(b) National-Functional Approach
(c) Both (a) and (b)
(d) Neither (a) nor (b)

165. Who, among the following, said, "One of the most characteristic features of communicative language teaching is that it pays systematic attention to functional as well as structural aspects of language"?
(a) W. Littlewood
(b) Henry Widdowson
(c) Christopher Brumfit
(d) Dell Hymes

166. How many functions, according to Halliday, does language perform for the children?
(a) Five
(b) Three
(c) Six
(d) Seven

(These functions are:

**1. The instrumental function:** Using language to get things done. **2. The regulatory function:** Using language to control the behaviour of others. **3. The interactional function:** Using language to create interaction with others. **4. The personal function:** Using language to express personal feelings and meanings. **5. The heuristic function:** Using language to learn and to discover. **6. The imaginative function:** Using language to create a world of the imagination. **7. The representational function:** Using language to communicate information.)

167. How many dimensions of communicative competence are identified by M. Canale and M. Swain?
   (a) Two
   (b) Three
   (c) Four
   (d) Five

   (These are: grammatical competence, socio-linguistic competence, discourse competence and strategic competence.)

168. Which of the following are some of the characteristic features of the communicative approach?
   (a) They all aim to make the learner use language accurately and appropriately.
   (b) The main focus is on the learner.
   (c) The syllabuses are functional.
   (d) All of the above.

169. Which of the following are some of the techniques used in the communicative approach?
   (a) Language games
   (b) Role play and group or pair work
   (c) Mind engaging tasks
   (d) All of the above

170. Which of the following, according to Richards and Rogers, are some of the characteristics of communicative view of language?
   (a) Language is a system for the expression of meaning and the primary function of language is to allow interaction and communication.
   (b) The structure of language reflects its functional and communicative uses.
   (c) The primary units of language are not merely its grammatical and structural features, but categories of functional and communicative meaning as exemplified in discourse
   (d) All of the above.

171. Who devised the 'Silent Way' of teaching language?
   (a) C. Brumfit
   (b) H. Widdowson
   (c) Caleb Gattegno
   (d) Dell Hymes

172. The 'Silent Way' belongs to a tradition that views learning as
   (a) problem solving
   (b) creative
   (c) discovering
   (d) All of the above

173. Which of the following, according to Bruner, are the benefits derived from 'discovering learning'?
   (a) An increase in intellectual potency and the shift from extrinsic to intrinsic rewards.
   (b) The learning of heuristics (a method of solving problems by finding practical ways of dealing with them, learning from past experience) by discovering.
   (c) The aid to conserving memory.
   (d) All of the above.

174. The 'Silent Way' belongs to what is called the 'Humanistic approach'. According to

Earl Stevic, which are the things that are specifics to the humanistic course?

(a) It is a course which does not belong to any specific tradition.
(b) It is a course in which the feeder is not 'incharge'.
(c) It is a course in which getting a good grade is not the aim.
(d) All of the above.

175. How has Benjamin Franklin phrased the problem solving approaches?

(a) Tell me and I forget
(b) Teach me and I remember
(c) Involve me and I learn
(d) All of the above

176. Which of the following teaching aids are used in the 'Silent Way'?

(a) Fidel Chart
(b) Cusiniere Rods
(c) Both (a) and (b)
(d) Neither (a) nor (b)

(The fidel chart consists of blocks of different colours on a black background. Each block of colour represents a different sound in the target language. Cusiniere rods are coloured wooden rods of different lengths, each of which stands for different words or sounds. They are used to build up words and sentences.)

177. Who, among the following, advocated the "Suggestopaedia" method of language teaching?

(a) Dr. Georgi Lozanov
(b) Charles A. Curran
(c) Caleb Gattegno
(d) James Asher

178. On which of the following principles is the "Suggestopaedia" method based?

(a) Joy
(b) Easiness
(c) Harmonious collaboration of the conscious and the unconscious
(d) All of the above

179. "Suggestopaedia" is a

(a) Scientific theory
(b) Philosophic theory
(c) Psychological theory
(d) A sociological theory

(Suggestopaedia is the pedagogic application of suggestion. Its aim is to help learners overcome the feeling that they cannot learn. It helps them reach hidden reserves of the mind.)

180. Which of the following are the aids of the 'Suggestopaedia' method?

(a) Posters
(b) Charts
(c) Music
(d) All of the above

181. Who, among the following, developed the 'Total Physical Response' approach?

(a) C.A. Curran
(b) James Asher
(c) G. Lozanor
(d) C.A. Curran

182. Which of the following are some of the pedagogic principles of the 'Total Physical Response' approach?

(a) Learners learn best by doing things.
(b) Listening should precede other skills.
(c) Learners should be given time to absorb the target language before they are asked to speak.
(d) All of the above.

183. Which of the following are some of the characteristics of the 'Total Physical Response' approach?

(a) The teacher plays an active and direct role.
(b) Learners have the primary roles of listener and performer.

(c) Pictures, realia, slides and word charts play an important role.
(d) All of the above.

184. Who, among the following, developed the 'Community Language Learning' (CLL) approach?
(a) G. Lozanor
(b) James Isher
(c) Charles Curran
(d) Gattegno

185. Which of the following, according to La Forge, are the tasks of the foreign learners in the 'Community Language Learning' approach?
(a) To apprehend the sound system
(b) To assign fundamental meanings
(c) To construct a basic grammar of the foreign language
(d) All of the above

186. What is the teacher generally referred to in the 'CLL' approach?
(a) Scholar
(b) Knower
(c) Guide
(d) All of the above

187. What is the interactional view of language underlying the 'CLL' approach?
(a) Language is people
(b) Language is persons in contact
(c) Language is persons in response
(d) All of the above

188. What is the most important aid in learning in 'CLL' approach?
(a) A tape recorder
(b) A camera
(c) A blackboard
(d) A computer

189. What, according to Curran, are the elements of what he terms the 'Whole-process learning'?
(a) Cognitive
(b) Affective
(c) Both (a) and (b)
(d) Neither (a) nor (b)

(It is called the 'Whole-process learning' because learning takes place in a communicative situation where teachers and learners are involved in "an interaction...in which both experience a sense of their own wholeness.")

190. Into how many stages is the process of relationship between the learner and the teacher in the 'CLL' approach?
(a) Two
(b) Five
(c) Four
(d) Three

(The first is called the "birth stage" in which feelings of security and belonging are established. In the second, the learner begins to achieve some independence from the parents. In the third stage, the learner speaks independently. In the fourth stage, the learner feels secure enough to take criticism. In the last stage, the child has become an adult.)

191. Who coined the acronym 'SARD' in the 'CLL' approach
(a) Curran
(b) Widdowson
(c) H. Palmer
(d) Brumfit

('SARD': 'S' Stands for 'security', 'A' stands for 'attention and aggression'; 'R' stands for 'retention and reflection'; 'D' stands for 'discrimination'.)

192. Who developed 'The Reading Method' in second language learning?
(a) Brumfit
(b) Curran
(c) Michael West
(d) Palmer

193. What, according to West, was the best order among the following in second language learning?
   (a) Reading, writing, speech
   (b) Speech, writing, reading
   (c) Writing, reading, speech
   (d) All of the above

194. Michael West had in mind specially the second language learners in
   (a) Africa
   (b) India
   (c) Afghanistan
   (d) China

195. Which, among the following, was the objective of the 'Reading Method'?
   (a) To develop writing skills.
   (b) To teach the learner how to speak fluently.
   (c) To make learners fluent readers.
   (d) To develop listening skill.

196. Into how many kinds were the texts divided in the 'Reading Method'?
   (a) Two
   (b) Three
   (c) Four
   (d) Five

   (There were 'intensive' and 'extensive' reading texts. In the former, the texts were taught using such strategies as inferring meaning from the context, etc. and grammatical points were discussed. Comprehension was checked mainly through questions and answers. In the later, speed and overall comprehension was the aim.)

197. Which of the following were the main features of what came to be known as 'The Army Method'?
   (a) Small groups of trainees
   (b) Highly motivated students
   (c) Long hours of drilling with specially prepared graded materials
   (d) All of the above

198. Which of the following are of primary importance in "The Lexical Approach"?
   (a) words
   (b) word combinations
   (c) meanings of words
   (d) Both (a) and (b)

199. When was the term 'Whole Language' in language teaching created?
   (a) 1960s
   (b) 1970s
   (c) 1980s
   (d) 1990s

200. Who has advocated the 'Student-activated, Multi-Skill Approach' in language Teaching?
   (a) The Madras Language Teaching (MELT) Campaign
   (b) The Regional Institute of English at Bangalore
   (c) The Central Institute of English and Foreign Languages, Hyderabad
   (d) None of the above

## ANSWERS

| | | | | | |
|---|---|---|---|---|---|
| 1. (b) | 2. (d) | 3. (d) | 4. (d) | 5. (c) | 6. (a) |
| 7. (b) | 8. (c) | 9. (d) | 10. (a) | 11. (b) | 12. (c) |
| 13. (b) | 14. (c) | 15. (b) | 16. (a) | 17. (b) | 18. (c) |
| 19. (T) | 20. (d) | 21. (a) | 22. (c) | 23. (b) | 24. (a) |
| 25. (T) | 26. (T) | 27. (c) | 28. (b) | 29. (a) | 30. (b) |
| 31. (c) | 32. (d) | 33. (a) | 34. (b) | 35. (c) | 36. (c) |
| 37. (d) | 38. (a) | 39. (b) | 40. (c) | 41. (c) | 42. (d) |
| 43. (T) | 44. (d) | 45. (d) | 46. (c) | 47. (d) | 48. (a) |
| 49. (b) | 50. (d) | 51. (d) | 52. (b) | 53. (d) | 54. (b) |
| 55. (b) | 56. (c) | 57. (d) | 58. (d) | 59. (d) | 60. (a) |
| 61. (b) | 62. (c) | 63. (T) | 64. (b) | 65. (c) | 66. (d) |
| 67. (d) | 68. (a) | 69. (c) | 70. (d) | 71. (b) | 72. (c) |
| 73. (a) | 74. (b) | 75. (c) | 76. (a) | 77. (d) | 78. (d) |
| 79. (b) | 80. (c) | 81. (a) | 82. (d) | 83. (d) | 84. (a) |
| 85. (b) | 86. (d) | 87. (c) | 88. (b) | 89. (c) | 90. (a) |
| 91. (c) | 92. (b) | 93. (d) | 94. (d) | 95. (d) | 96. (c) |
| 97. (b) | 98. (c) | 99. (d) | 100. (a) | 101. (a) | 102. (d) |
| 103. (d) | 104. (d) | 105. (b) | 106. (d) | 107. (d) | 108. (a) |
| 109. (b) | 110. (a) | 111. (c) | 112. (b) | 113. (d) | 114. (d) |
| 115. (d) | 116. (d) | 117. (a) | 118. (b) | 119. (c) | 120. (a) |
| 121. (d) | 122. (d) | 123. (d) | 124. (c) | 125. (b) | 126. (d) |
| 127. (b) | 128. (c) | 129. (b) | 130. (b) | 131. (a) | 132. (d) |
| 133. (b) | 134. (d) | 135. (c) | 136. (a) | 137. (b) | 138. (c) |
| 139. (d) | 140. (a) | 141. (c) | 142. (d) | 143. (a) | 144. (d) |
| 145. (d) | 146. (a) | 147. (d) | 148. (d) | 149. (d) | 150. (d) |
| 151. (a) | 152. (d) | 153. (d) | 154. (b) | 155. (c) | 156. (d) |
| 157. (d) | 158. (d) | 159. (d) | 160. (d) | 161. (a) | 162. (d) |
| 163. (c) | 164. (c) | 165. (a) | 166. (d) | 167. (c) | 168. (d) |
| 169. (d) | 170. (d) | 171. (c) | 172. (d) | 173. (d) | 174. (d) |
| 175. (d) | 176. (c) | 177. (a) | 178. (d) | 179. (c) | 180. (d) |
| 181. (b) | 182. (d) | 183. (d) | 184. (c) | 185. (d) | 186. (b) |
| 187. (d) | 188. (a) | 189. (c) | 190. (b) | 191. (a) | 192. (c) |
| 193. (a) | 194. (b) | 195. (c) | 196. (a) | 197. (d) | 198. (d) |
| 199. (c) | 200. (c) | | | | |

2

# European Literature from Classical Age to the 20th Century

1. Homer was a
   (a) Greek poet
   (b) Latin poet
   (c) French poet
   (d) German poet
2. Which of the following two epics did he write?
   (a) *The Iliad*
   (b) *The Odyssey*
   (c) *The Aeneid*
   (d) Both (a) and (b)
3. How many books does the *The Iliad* consist of?
   (a) XX
   (b) XXIV
   (c) XXV
   (d) XXVI
4. *The Iliad* is about the war between the
   (a) Trojans and the Greeks
   (b) Trojans and Romans
   (c) Greeks and Romans
   (d) Trojans and Prussians
5. What was the cause of war between the Trojans and the Greeks?
   (a) Dispute over territory
   (b) Abduction of Helen by Trojan prince, Paris
   (c) The Greeks killed the Trojan king
   (d) None of the above
6. Who was the husband of Helen?
   (a) Agamemnon
   (b) Hector
   (c) Menelaus
   (d) Achilles
7. The war actually originated from a quarrel between the goddesses
   (a) Athena
   (b) Hera
   (c) Aphrodite
   (d) All of the above
8. Who, among the following, was the commander-in-chief of the Greek army?
   (a) Menelaus
   (b) Agamemnon
   (c) Achilles
   (d) Ulysses
9. Who sends the plague to the Achean (Greek) camp near the beginning of the Iliad?
   (a) Apollo
   (b) Zeus
   (c) Aphrodite
   (d) Hera
10. Name the great Greek warrior who does not die in *The Iliad* but was fatally injured?
   (a) Ulysses
   (b) Agamemnon
   (c) Menelaus
   (d) Achilles

11. Who killed the Trojan prince Hector?
    (a) Agamemnon
    (b) Menelaus
    (c) Achilles
    (d) Ulysses
12. For how many years did the Trojan war was fought?
    (a) Ten years
    (b) Eight years
    (c) Twelve years
    (d) Five years
13. The Greeks won the war. Who made the plan for their victory?
    (a) Achilles
    (b) Agamemnon
    (c) Ulysses
    (d) Menelaus
14. How many books does the *The Odyssey* consist of?
    (a) XX
    (b) XXV
    (c) XXIV
    (d) XXVI
15. Who is the hero of *The Odyssey*?
    (a) Odysseus
    (b) Agamemnon
    (c) Achilles
    (d) Hector

    (Odysseus was also known as 'Ulysses')
16. What is *The Odyssey* about?
    (a) The Trojan War
    (b) The quarrel between Achilles and Agamemnon
    (c) Odysseus and his journey back after the fall of Troy
    (d) None of the above
17. How many years does it take Odysseus to reach Ithaca?
    (a) Eight years
    (b) Ten years
    (c) Twelve years
    (d) Fourteen years
18. What was the name of Odysseus's wife?
    (a) Hera
    (b) Aphrodite
    (c) Venus
    (d) Penelope
19. What was the name of Odysseus's son?
    (a) Achilles
    (b) Agamemnon
    (c) Telemachus
    (d) Proci
20. Which plant makes the sailors forget their desire to go home?
    (a) Lotus
    (b) Poppy
    (c) Lethe-root
    (d) Hemlock
21. Who is Argos?
    (a) The master of the winds
    (b) Penelope's chief suitor
    (c) The cyclops
    (d) Odysseus's old dog
22. Menelaus is the king of which city?
    (a) Pylos
    (b) Sparta
    (c) Athens
    (d) Argos
23. Who begs Odysseus to bury him?
    (a) Leartes
    (b) Polyphemus
    (c) Elpenor
    (d) Achilles
24. Who transforms Odysseus's sailor into pigs?
    (a) Circe
    (b) Calypso
    (c) Athene
    (d) Aphrodite

25. Which goddess often assists Odysseus and Telemachus?
    (a) Calypso
    (b) Athene
    (c) Circe
    (d) Aphrodite
26. How old is Telemachus at the start of *The Odyssey*?
    (a) About 30 years
    (b) About 20 years
    (c) About 10 years
    (d) About 40 years
27. Why does Poseidon despise 'Odysseus'?
    (a) Odysseus does not respect the sea
    (b) Odysseus attacked Poseidon
    (c) Odysseus blinded his son
    (d) Odysseus tricked him with his disguise
28. Odysseus was the king of
    (a) Athens
    (b) Sparta
    (c) Ithaca
    (d) Mycenae
29. How long does Odysseus spend on Calypso's island?
    (a) 7 years
    (b) 5 years
    (c) 10 years
    (d) 15 years
30. Who does Zeus send to rescue Odysseus from Clypso?
    (a) Athena
    (b) Hermes
    (c) Poseidon
    (d) Venus
31. *The Odyssey* opens in
    (a) Sparta
    (b) Ithaca
    (c) Ogygia
    (d) Athens
32. Sophocles was one of the Greek writers of
    (a) Tragic plays
    (b) Comic plays
    (c) Lyrics
    (d) Epics
33. How many tragic plays did sophocles write?
    (a) Four
    (b) Five
    (c) Six
    (d) Seven
34. Which of his plays bears three titles?
    (a) *Ajax*
    (b) *Oedipus*
    (c) *Electra*
    (d) *Antigone*

    (It is called *Oedipus Tyrannus* or *Oedipus Rex* or *Oedipus, The King*.)
35. *Oedipus at Colonus* was written by
    (a) Sophocles
    (b) Aeschylus
    (c) Euripides
    (d) Aristophanes
36. Oedipus killed his father, Laius, and became the king of
    (a) Athens
    (b) Sparta
    (c) Thebes
    (d) Ithaca
37. What sin did he commit after killing his father?
    (a) He got the priests killed
    (b) He married his mother
    (c) He seduced his sister
    (d) None of the above
38. Freud named a *Complex*, based on the story of *Oedipus, The King*, which is known as
    (a) Superiority complex
    (b) Inferiority complex

(c) Oedipus complex
(d) Electra complex

39. Which of D.H. Lawrence's novels, according to critics, is based on the theme of *Oedipus Complex*?
(a) *Sons and Lovers*
(b) *Women in Love*
(c) *The Plumed Serpent*
(d) *Lady Chatterly's Lover*

40. Which of the following are the Theban plays written by Sophocles?
(a) *Oedipus, The King*
(b) *Antigone*
(c) *Oedipus at Colonus*
(d) All of the above

41. What was the end of Antigone, the heroine of Sophocles' tragedy *Antigone*?
(a) She was murdered
(b) She was killed accidentally
(c) She hanged herself
(d) She died of a deadly disease

**Seven Tragic Plays of Sophocles**

1. *Ajax* 2. *Antigone* 3. *Oedipus Rex* 4. *Electra* 5. *The Trachiniae* 6. *Philoctetes* 7. *Oedipus at Colonus*

42. Besides Sophocles who, among the following, are the other Greek writers of tragedies?
(a) Euripides
(b) Aeschylus
(c) Aristophanes
(d) Both (a) and (b)

43. In which of Euripides' tragedies, does a woman take revenge on her husband?
(a) *Medea*
(b) *Andromache*
(c) *The Trojan Women*
(d) *Hecuba*

44. In which tragic play of Euripides is there a reference to Helen, who caused the Trojan war?
(a) *The Trojan Women*
(b) *Hecuba*
(c) *Orestes*
(d) *Andromache*

45. In which tragic play of Euripides does a father sacrifice his daughter?
(a) *Hippolytus*
(b) *Electra*
(c) *Becchae*
(d) *Iphigenia at Aulis*

(Agamemnon sacrifices his daughter Iphigenia to goddess Artemis to get a favourable wind so that the Greek forces sail for Troy to secure the release of Helen.)

**Some Tragic Plays of Euripides**

1. *Alcestis* 2. *Medea* 3. *Hippolytus* 4. *Andromache* 5. *The Trojan Women* 6. *Hecuba* 7. *Heracles* 8. *Phoenician* 9. *Orestes* 10. *Bacchae* 11. *Ipheginia at Aulis* 12. *Rhesus*

46. Besides tragic plays, Euripides also wrote
(a) Romantic dramas
(b) Political dramas
(c) Satyr plays
(d) All of the above

47. Aeschylus was a
(a) Latin dramatist
(b) Greek dramatist
(c) Italian dramatist
(d) French dramatist

48. Who is described as the father of tragedy?
(a) Sophocles
(b) Euripides
(c) Aeschylus
(d) Shakespeare

49. Who was the first dramatist to present plays as a trilogy?
    (a) Aeschylus
    (b) Sophocles
    (c) Euripides
    (d) None of the above
50. Which of Aeschylus's plays constitute the trilogy 'Oresteia'?
    (a) *Agamemnon*
    (b) *Libation Bearers*
    (c) *The Eumenides*
    (d) All of the above
51. In which tragedy of Aeschylus does a wife kill her husband?
    (a) *The Eumenides*
    (b) *Agamemnon*
    (c) *Prometheus Bound*
    (d) *The Libation Bearers*

    (Aeschylus's tragedy *Agamemnon* describes Agamemnon's death at the hands of his wife, Clytemnestra.)
52. In which tragedy of Aeschylus is the mother killed by her son?
    (a) *The Libation Bearers*
    (b) *Prometheus Bound*
    (c) *The Eumenides*
    (d) *The Suppliants*

    (It is in *The Libation Bearers* that Orestes kills his mother Clytemnestra and her lover Aegisthus and takes revenge on them for the murder of his father, Agamemnon.)
53. Whose tragedies are referred to as "Oedipodea"?
    (a) Sophocles's
    (b) Euripides's
    (c) Aeschylus's
    (d) None of the above

**Some Important Aeschylus' Tragedies**

1. *The Persians* 2. *Seven Against Thebes* 3. *The Suppliants* 4. *Agamemnon* 5. *Oresteia* 6. *Prometheus Bound*

54. Who, among the following, is a famous Greek Comic playwright?
    (a) Aeschylus
    (b) Sophocles
    (c) Euripides
    (d) Aristophanes
55. Who, among the following, is known as the father of comedy?
    (a) Shakespeare
    (b) Aristophanes
    (c) Phrynichus
    (d) Ben Jonson
56. The ancient Greek comedies are full of
    (a) Obscenity
    (b) Abuse
    (c) Insult
    (d) All of the above
57. In Aristotle's view, comic drama developed from
    (a) Song
    (b) Festivities
    (c) Marriage ceremonies
    (d) None of the above
58. In Aristophanes' comedies, known as Old comedy, the emphasis was on
    (a) Real personalities
    (b) Local issues
    (c) Both (a) and (b)
    (d) Neither (a) nor (b)
59. Aristophanes' comic dramas satirized
    (a) opportunists.
    (b) the exponents of new religious practices.
    (c) war-profiteers and political fanatics
    (d) All of the above.

60. While Aristophanes was known as the master of Old comedy, who, among the following, was known as the master of New Comedy?
   (a) William Congreve
   (b) Menander
   (c) Ben Jonson
   (d) Robert Greene

61. In which of his plays did Aristophanes ridicule democracy?
   (a) *The Achamians*
   (b) *The Knights*
   (c) *The Birds*
   (d) *The Frogs*

62. In which of his plays did Aristophanes attack Socrates?
   (a) *The Clouds*
   (b) *The Frogs*
   (c) *The Wasps*
   (d) *The Knights*

63. Aristophanes denounced war in which of his plays?
   (a) *The Wasps*
   (b) *Lysistrata*
   (c) *The Frogs*
   (d) *The Knights*

64. *The Knights* is a satire on
   (a) Political life
   (b) Social life
   (c) Both (a) and (b)
   (d) Neither (a) nor (b)

65. In which of his plays does Aristophanes ridicule the law-courts?
   (a) *The Wasps*
   (b) *The Frogs*
   (c) *The Birds*
   (d) *The Knights*

66. In which play does Aristophanes deal with the contest between Euripides and Aeschylus for the throne of tragedy?
   (a) *The Wasps*
   (b) *The Frogs*
   (c) *The Knights*
   (d) *The Clouds*

**Important Plays of Aristophanes**

1. *The Achamians* 2. *The Knights* 3. *The Clouds* 4. *The Wasps* 5. *Peace* 6. *The Birds* 7. *Lysistrata* 8. *The Frogs* 9. *The Assembly Women* 10. *Wealth*

67. Virgil was a
   (a) Latin poet
   (b) Greek poet
   (c) French poet
   (d) British poet

68. Virgil is famous for his epic
   (a) *The Odyssey*
   (b) *The Aeneid*
   (c) *The Iliad*
   (d) *The Divine Comedy*

69. *The Aeneid* is divided into
   (a) Eight books
   (b) Ten books
   (c) Twelve books
   (d) Fourteen books

70. The hero of *The Aeneid* is
   (a) Ulysses
   (b) Achilles
   (c) Hector
   (d) Aeneas

71. Who was Aeneas?
   (a) A Greek Prince
   (b) A Trojan Prince
   (c) A Latin Prince
   (d) None of the above

72. *The Aeneid* opens with
   (a) an invocation to the gods.
   (b) Aeneas' prayer for success in his journey.

(c) a storm caused by Juno against Aeneas' fleet.
(d) None of the above.

73. In which book of *The Aeneid* does Aeneas slip away from Carthage?
(a) II
(b) IV
(c) VI
(d) VIII

74. What was the name of the Queen of Carthage who died of grief at the departure of Aeneas from Carthage?
(a) Dido
(b) Fido
(c) Anne
(d) Lido

75. On which of the following poets did Virgil have the greatest influence?
(a) Goethe
(b) Dante
(c) Milton
(d) Spenser

76. Who, among the following, is a famous ancient Greek poetess?
(a) Paros
(b) Alcaeus
(c) Sappho
(d) Pindarus (Pindar)

77. Who, among the following, was the first Greek poet to reflect on the nature of poetry and on the poet's role?
(a) Pindar
(b) Sappho
(c) Paros
(d) Alcaeus

78. Pindar was famous for one of the following genres
(a) Odes
(b) Tragedies
(c) Comedies
(d) Satires

79. A classical ode was divided into
(a) Two parts
(b) Three parts
(c) Four parts
(d) Five parts

(The three parts are: strophe, antistrophe, epode)

80. Which of the following Gray's Odes were in imitation of Pindaric Odes?
(a) The Progress
(b) The Bard
(c) Both (a) and (b)
(d) Neither (a) nor (b)

81. Horace was a leading lyric poet of
(a) Rome
(b) Greece
(c) Germany
(d) France

82. Which century's English poets imitated Horation Odes?
(a) 16th
(b) 17th
(c) 15th
(d) 18th

83. Ovid, the Roman poet, wrote which of the following?
(a) *The Art of Love*
(b) *The Cure of Love*
(c) *Metamorphoses*
(d) All of the above

84. Ovid's *Metamorphoses* is divided into
(a) Ten books
(b) Twelve books
(c) Fifteen books
(d) Twenty books

85. Ovid's *Metamorphoses* is about the transformations in
(a) Greek mythology
(b) Roman mythology

(c) Both (a) and (b)
(d) Neither (a) nor (b)

86. Which of the following English poets were influenced by Ovid's writings?
(a) Chaucer
(b) Shakespeare
(c) Milton
(d) All of the above

87. Plautus was a Roman writer of
(a) Comedies
(b) Tragedies
(c) Satires
(d) Epics

88. In his plays, Plautus ridiculed
(a) The politicians
(b) The gods
(c) The wealthy people
(d) The courtiers

89. Plautus is well known for his
(a) Metaphors
(b) Style
(c) Puns
(d) None of the above

90. By which of the following names is a play of Plautus known?
(a) *Mostellaria*
(b) *The Little Ghost*
(c) *The Haunted House*
(d) All of the above

91. One of the stock characters in Plautus's plays who plays a major role is a
(a) Slave
(b) Ghost
(c) Miser
(d) Soldier

92. Which of the following plays is generally regarded as Plautus's greatest play?
(a) *The Little Ghost*
(b) *Menaechmi*
(c) *Perse*
(d) *Casina*

93. Plautus's play *Menaechmi* is a comedy about
(a) A love-affair
(b) Fraud
(c) Mistaken identity
(d) Trickery

94. Which of Plautus plays has the quote: "Things we don't hope happen more frequently than things which you do hope"?
(a) *Mostellaria* (*The Little Ghost*)
(b) *Amphitryon*
(c) *Bacchides*
(d) *Epidicus*

95. The theme of *The Haunted House* (*The Little Ghost*) is
(a) Fraud
(b) Revenge
(c) Love
(d) Trickery

96. Terence was a playwright of
(a) Rome
(b) France
(c) Greece
(d) German

97. In which of Terence's plays appeared the line, "I am a human being. I consider nothing that is human alien to me"?
(a) *Heauton*
(b) *The Brothers*
(c) *Eunuchs*
(d) *Phormio*

98. Terence's play *Adephoe/Adephoi/Adephi* (*The Brothers*) explores the theme of
(a) Love
(b) Child-rearing
(c) Greed
(d) Jealousy

99. How many plays did Terence write?
    (a) Seven
    (b) Eight
    (c) Six
    (d) Nine

**Terence's Plays**

1. *Andria* (*The Girls from Andros*, 166 B.C.)
2. *Hecyra* (*The Mother-in-Law*, 166 B.C.)
3. *Heauton* (*The Self-Tormentor*, 163 B.C.)
4. *Phormio*, (161 B.C.)
5. *Eunuchs*, (161 B.C.)
6. *Adephoe* (*The Brothers*, 160 B.C.)

100. Seneca was a
    (a) Roman playwright
    (b) Greek lyric poet
    (c) French dramatist
    (d) German epic poet

101. "The Silver Age" of the Latin literature began with
    (a) Plautus
    (b) Seneca
    (c) Virgil
    (d) Horace

102. Seneca's plays were written keeping in mind his
    (a) Mother
    (b) Wife
    (c) Pupil, Nero
    (d) Father

103. In his plays, Seneca reflects on the
    (a) certainty of death and the fickleness of fate.
    (b) the instability of power and happiness.
    (c) the virtue of Stoic moderation and obscurity.
    (c) All of the above

104. Which Seneca's play in particular is said to have influenced Shakespeare, Webster and Tourneur?
    (a) *Thyestes*
    (b) *The Trojan Women*
    (c) *Medea*
    (d) *Phaedra*

105. Seneca is known as the father of
    (a) Romantic tragedy
    (b) Revenge Tragedy
    (c) Tragicomedy
    (d) Romantic comedy

106. Seneca's tragedies are divided into
    (a) Three acts
    (b) Two acts
    (c) Five acts
    (d) Seven acts

107. One of the university wits who was influenced by Seneca was
    (a) Marlowe
    (b) Peele
    (c) Greene
    (d) Thomas Kyd

    (Thomas Kyd's *The Spanish Tragedy* clearly shows Seneca's influence.)

108. Which University Wit was influenced by Seneca's fascination with magic, death and the supernatural?
    (a) Marlowe
    (b) Greene
    (c) Peele
    (d) Kyd

109. In which Seneca's play, the bodies of children are served at a banquet?
    (a) *Medea*
    (b) *Thyestes*
    (c) *Oedipus*
    (d) *Phaedra*

110. The theme of *Medea* is
    (a) Jealousy
    (b) Greed
    (c) Revenge
    (d) None of the above

**Seneca's Tragedies**

1. *The Madness of Hercules* 2. *The Trojan Women* 3. *The Phoenician Women* 4. *Phaedra* 5. *Thyestes* 6. *Agamemnon* 7. *Oedipus* 8. *Mead*

111. Dante's *The Divine Comedy* is divided into:
(a) Two parts
(b) Three parts
(c) Four parts
(d) Five parts

112. What is the correct sequence of the three parts of *The Divine Comedy*?
(a) Inferno, Purgatorio, Paradiso
(b) Paradiso, Inferno, Purgtorio
(c) Purgatorio, Paradiso, Inferno

113. Dante's *The Divine Comedy* describes
(a) Dante's meeting with Adam
(b) Dante's fight with Satan
(c) Dante's journey towards redemption
(d) None of the above

114. Who is known as the muse of Dante about whom there is a reference in *The Divine Comedy*?
(a) Aphrodite
(b) Beatrice
(c) Venus
(d) Athena

115. Which poet guides Dante through hell and purgatory?
(a) Chaucer
(b) Homer
(c) Hesiod
(d) Virgil

116. Each part of *The Divine Comedy* consists of
(a) 30 cantos
(b) 33 cantos
(c) 35 cantos
(d) 25 cantos

117. The verse scheme of *The Divine Comedy* is
(a) Terza rima
(b) blank verse
(c) ottava rima
(d) rhyme royal

118. Who guides Dante through Heaven?
(a) Virgil
(b) Dante's brother
(c) Beatrice
(d) An angel

119. *The Divine Comedy* begins on the night before
(a) Good Friday
(b) Easter
(c) Christmas
(d) None of the above

120. On which day do Virgil and Dante arrive in purgatory?
(a) Christmas
(b) Easter Sunday
(c) Good Friday
(d) St. Patrick's Day

121. The first seven spheres of Heaven deal solely with the cardinal virtues of
(a) Prudence and Fortitude
(b) Justice and Temperance
(c) Both (a) and (b)
(d) Neither (a) nor (b)

122. Who, among the following, is the author of *The Decameron*?
(a) Boccaccio
(b) Dante
(c) Balzac
(d) Flaubert

123. *The Decameron* is also called
(a) *A Decade*
(b) *Meron*

(c) *Prince Galehaut*
(d) *Cameron*

124. *The Decameron* consists of
(a) 80 tales
(b) 100 tales
(c) 120 tales
(d) 150 tales

125. The tales in *The Decameron* are
(a) Tales of wit
(b) Bawdy tales of love
(c) Practical jokes
(d) All of the above

126. The tales in *The Decameron* are told by
(a) Ten young people
(b) Eight young people
(c) Seven young people
(d) Nine young people

127. Who is the author of *The Prince*?
(a) Boccaccio
(b) R. Tasso
(c) Machiavelli
(d) Ariosto

128. *The Prince* is a
(a) Philosophic work
(b) Political treatise
(c) Economic guide
(d) Historical document

(*The Prince* is the quintessence of Machiavelli's political thought and statecraft. Some critics regard him as an advocate of "Splendid wickedness".)

129. "The Oration on the Dignity of Man", called the "Manifesto of the Renaissance" was written by
(a) Tasso
(b) Moravia
(c) Giovanni Mirandola
(d) Buzzati

130. Who, among the following, is the author of the romance epic *Orlando Furioso*?
(a) Ludovico Ariosto
(b) Tasso
(c) Boccaccio
(d) Dante

131. Into how many cantos is *Orlando Furioso* divided?
(a) 40
(b) 46
(c) 48
(d) 42

132. The verse form of *Orlando Furioso* is
(a) Rhyme royal
(b) Heroic couplet
(c) Ottava rima
(d) Blank verse

133. *Orlando Furioso* was a major influence on
(a) The Paradise Lost
(b) The Aeneid
(c) The Faerie Queene
(d) None of the above

134. B. Castiglione's *The Book of the Courtier* (1528) is a
(a) Philosophical conversation
(b) Political treatise
(c) Text about court life
(d) Book about courtly love

(The book deals with the question of what constitutes an ideal Renaissance gentleman.)

135. Giorgio Vasari's *The Lives of the Artists*
(a) is a collection of biographical accounts.
(b) presents a highly influential theory of the development of Renaissance art.
(c) Both (a) and (b)
(d) Neither (a) and (b)

136. Baptista Guarini's *The Faithful Shepherd* is a

(a) Tragedy
(b) Pastoral tragicomedy
(c) Comedy
(d) Romance

137. Torquato Tasso was an
(a) Italian poet
(b) Greek dramatist
(c) French writer
(d) German artist

138. Torquato Tasso's *Jerusalem Delivered* (1580) depicts
(a) court life.
(b) life of the country side.
(c) the life of priests.
(d) a highly imaginative version of the combats between the Christians and the Muslims.

139. The climax of the epic *Jerusalem Delivered* was
(a) the death of its hero, Godfrey of Bouillon.
(b) the defeat of the Christians.
(c) the capture of the holy city by the Christians.
(d) the destruction of Jerusalem.

140. Luigi Pirandello is often seen as belonging to what is called
(a) Theatre of the Absurd
(b) Theatre of Cruelty
(c) Theatre of Silence
(d) None of the above

141. Luigi Pirandello's play *Six Characters in Search of an Author* was published in
(a) 1919
(b) 1921
(c) 1923
(d) 1924

142. *Six Characters in Search of an Author* is a play about the relationship between
(a) Authors
(b) Their characters
(c) Theatre practitioners
(d) All of the above

143. Pirandello's first widely acclaimed novel *The Late Mattia Pascal* was written in
(a) 1900
(b) 1902
(c) 1904
(d) 1906

**Luigi Pirandello's Important Plays**

1. *Six Characters in Search of an Author* 2. *Enrico IV* 3. *The Man With The Flower in His Mouth* 4. *As You Desire Me*

144. Giuseppe Ungaretti, the Italian modernist poet, is a leading representative of the experimental trend known as
(a) Surrealism
(b) Hermeticism
(c) Impressionism
(d) Expressionism

('Hermeticism' represents a set a philosophical and religious beliefs. These beliefs have heavily influenced the Western esoteric tradition.)

145. The classic novel *Confessions of Zeno or Zeno's Conscience* was written by
(a) Italo Svevo
(b) Italo Calvino
(c) Alberto Moravia
(d) Primo Levi

146. The novel *The Tartar Steppe* was written by
(a) Italo Svevo
(b) Primo Levi
(c) Dino Buzzati
(d) Italo Calvino

147. Alberto Moravio's novels deal with matters of
(a) Modern sexuality
(b) Social alienation

(c) Existentialism
(d) All of the above

148. Which, among the following, is regarded as the first modern European Existential novel by Alberto Moravia?
(a) *Time of Indifference*
(b) *The Conformist*
(c) *The Woman of Rome*
(d) *The Voyeur*

149. Which of the following is Alberto Moravia's an anti-fascist novel?
(a) *Time of Indifference*
(b) *The Conformist*
(c) *Roman Tales*
(d) *Agostino*

150. Cesare Pavese is an Italian
(a) Poet
(b) Novelist
(c) Literary critic and translator
(d) All of the above

151. Which of the following are the themes in the works of Cesare Pavese?
(a) The protagonist is loner.
(b) His relationship with others is temporary or superficial.
(c) He ends up betraying his ideals.
(d) All of the above.

152. Which of the following novels are written by Cesare Pavese?
(a) *Your Villages*
(b) *The Beach*
(c) *The Comrade*
(d) All of the above

153. Primo Levi's novel *If This is a Man* (1947) is an account of
(a) his year spent as a prisoner in a concentration camp.
(b) World War II.
(c) Nazi atrocities.
(d) his humiliation by the Nazis.

154. Which of the following books was named the best science book ever by the Royal Institution of Great Britain?
(a) *If This is a Man*
(b) *The Periodic Table*
(c) *Boredom*
(d) *The Beach*

(*The Periodic Table* is a collection of short stories by Primo Levi.)

155. Which of the following prominently features the subject of Pier Paolo Pasolini's homosexuality?
(a) Arabian Nights
(b) Days of Sodom
(c) Teorema
(d) A Violent Life

(Pasolini, an Italian, distinguished himself as a poet, journalist, philosopher, linguist, novelist, playwright, filmmaker, newspaper and magazine columnist, actor, painter, and political figure.)

156. The novel *Invisible Cities* (1972) is written by
(a) Pasolini
(b) Italo Calvino
(c) Alberto Moravia
(d) Primo Levi

157. Which novels comprise Italo Calvino's 'heraldic trilogy'?
(a) *The Cloven Viscount*
(b) *Baron in the Trees*
(c) *The Nonexistent Knight*
(d) All of the above

158. Who, among the following, is the author of *Accidental Death of an Anarchist* (1970)?
(a) Umberto Eco
(b) Dario Fo
(c) Italo Calvino
(d) Pasolini

159. Umberto Eco is best known for his novel
   (a) *The Prague Cemetery*
   (b) *The Island of the Day Before*
   (c) *The Name of the Rose*
   (d) *Foucault's Pendulum*

160. Miguel de Cervantes is a/an
   (a) Spanish novelist
   (b) Canadian playwright
   (c) French poet
   (d) Italian critic

161. *Don Quixote* was written by
   (a) Garcia Lorca
   (b) De Cervantes
   (c) Chekhov
   (d) Zola

162. *Don Quixote* is about the adventures of
   (a) Fernandes
   (b) Ilesco
   (c) Alonso Quijano
   (d) Patrick

163. What is the name of Quijano's Squire?
   (a) Racco
   (b) Fenko
   (c) Bodo
   (d) Sancho Panza

164. *Don Quixote* is a
   (a) Picarseque novel
   (b) Historical novel
   (c) Romantic novel
   (d) Realistic novel

165. The play *The Surgeon of His Honour* (1637) was written by
   (a) de Cervantes
   (b) Pedro Caledron Barca
   (c) Pablo Neruda
   (d) Kafka

166. Which of the following Barca's plays is a philosophical allegory regarding the human situation and the mystery of life?
   (a) *The Surgeon of His Honour*
   (b) *Devotion to the Cross*
   (c) *Life is a Dream*
   (d) *Eco and Narcissus*

167. Garcia Lorca was a twentieth century's Spanish
   (a) Poet
   (b) Dramatist
   (c) Theatre director
   (d) All of the above

168. *Sonnets of Dark Love*, *Book of Poems*, and *Gypsy Ballads* were written by
   (a) Garcia Lorca
   (b) Calderon Barca
   (c) Pablo Neruda
   (d) Italo Calvino

169. Lorca's *The Gypsy Ballads* comprises
   (a) Sixteen poems
   (b) Eighteen poems
   (c) Ten poems
   (d) Fifteen poems

170. Which of the following Lorca Garcia's plays deals with the theme of rebellion against the norms of bourgeois Spanish tragedy?
   (a) *Blood Wedding*
   (b) *Yerma*
   (c) *The House of Bernarda Alba*
   (d) All of the above

171. Neftali Ricardo Reyes Basoalto was known by the famous pen name of
   (a) Jan Neruda
   (b) Rielke
   (c) Pablo Neruda
   (d) John Neruda

172. Pablo Neruda, the Czech poet, won the Nobel Prize in Literature in
   (a) 1971
   (b) 1972
   (c) 1973
   (d) 1974

173. *Twenty Love Poems and a Song of Depair* was written by
   (a) Jan Neruda
   (b) Lorca
   (c) Calvino
   (d) Pablo Neruda

174. *In Praise of Folly* was written by
   (a) Bacon
   (b) D. Erasmus
   (c) More
   (d) Sartre

175. *In Praise of Folly* was used as one of the
   (a) catalysts of the Reformation.
   (b) books making a strong case against monarchy.
   (c) poems ridiculing ignorance.
   (d) plays praising foolishness.

176. To which country did Henry Ibsen (1828-1906) belong?
   (a) Chile
   (b) Ireland
   (c) Norway
   (d) Switzerland

177. Henry Isben's play *A Doll's House* (1879) is
   (a) Four-act play
   (b) Three-act play
   (c) Five-act play
   (d) Two-act play

178. *A Doll's House* was sharply critical of
   (a) Corruption
   (b) Red-tapism
   (c) Bigotry
   (d) Marriage norms

**Henry Ibsen's Major Works**

1. *Brand* 2. *Peer Gynt* 3. *An Enemy of The People* 4. *Emperor and Galileau* 5. *A Doll's House* 6. *Hedda Gabler* 7. *Ghosts* 8. *The Wild Duck* 9. *The Master Builder*

179. In his play *Ghosts*, Henry Ibsen was against
   (a) the hyporcrisy of Victorian morality.
   (b) superstitions.
   (c) faith in god and goddesses.
   (d) religious practices.

180. Ibsen's Play *An Enemy of the People* (1882) deals with
   (a) irrational tendencies of the masses.
   (b) the hypocritical and corrupt nature of the political system.
   (c) Both (a) and (b)
   (d) Neither (a) nor (b)

181. *The Son of a Servant* is the title of the autobiography of
   (a) Jean Genet
   (b) J.A. Strindberg
   (c) Pablo Neruda
   (d) Dario Fo

182. J.A. Strindberg is a playwright of
   (a) Norway
   (b) Ireland
   (c) Sweden
   (d) Germany

183. J.A. Strindberg's play *Master Olof* (1872) is a
   (a) Historical drama
   (b) Tragedy
   (c) Comedy
   (d) Tragic-comedy

184. Strindberg's play *Master Oof* is based on the theme of
   (a) Swedish Reformation
   (b) Corruption
   (c) Hypocrisy
   (d) None of the above

185. Who said, "I dream, therefore I exist"?
   (a) Rene Descartes
   (b) J.A. Strindberg

(c) Henry Ibsen
(d) Pablo Neruda

186. Strindberg's play *Lucky Peter's Travels* is a biting criticism of
(a) Politics
(b) Religion
(c) Legal system
(d) Society

187. *The Aeneid* deals with
(a) the war between the Greeks and the Trojans.
(b) the war between The Greeks and the Romans.
(c) the victory of the Greeks over the Trojans.
(d) Aeneas's journey to reach the shores of Italy to found Rome.

188. *Faust: The Second Part of the Tragedy* was published in
(a) 1812
(b) 1821
(c) 1832
(d) 1824

189. Strindberg's play *The New Kingdom* is a satire on
(a) Democracy
(b) Immorality
(c) Contemporary Sweden
(d) Church

190. *The Dance of Death* is written by
(a) Goethe
(b) Strindberg
(c) Neruda
(d) Kafka

191. *The Insect Play* is written by
(a) Karel Capek
(b) Josef Capek
(c) Both (a) and (b)
(d) Neither (a) nor (b)

192. Karel and Josef Capek's play *The Insect Play* is also known as
(a) *The Insect Comedy*
(b) *The World We Live In*
(c) *From Insect Life*
(d) All of the above

193. Almost all the characters in *The Insect Play* are insects through whom the Chapek brothers commented on
(a) government functioning.
(b) religious practices.
(c) legal flaws.
(d) human society during their period.

("The human society" refers to the Czechoslovakian Society in the post-World War I era.)

194. Robert Musil was a/an
(a) An Austrian writer
(b) A Russian writer
(c) A French writer
(d) A German writer

195. *The Man Without Qualities*, considered to be one of the most modernist novels, was written by
(a) James Joyce
(b) Camus
(c) Sartre
(d) Robert Musil

(*The Man Without Qualities* is called a "novel of ideas". It was written during the last year of the Austro-Hungarian Empire.)

196. *Gargantua and Pantagruel* is written by
(a) Francois Rabelais
(b) Moliere
(c) Racine
(d) Voltaire

197. *The Life of Gargantua and Pantagruel* is a connected series of
(a) Four novels
(b) Five novels
(c) Three novels
(d) Six novels

198. *The Life of Gargantua and Pantagruel* relates the story of
   (a) a quarrel between Gargantua and Pantagruel.
   (b) a property dispute.
   (c) religious fanaticism.
   (d) two giants and their adventures.

   (These two giants are Gargantua, the father, and his son, Pantagruel.)

199. Which of the following are some of the features of *Gargantua and Pantagruel*?
   (a) Crudity
   (b) Obscene humour
   (c) Violence
   (d) All of the above

200. Who, among the following, are the greatest seventeenth century French dramatists?
   (a) Pierre Corneille
   (b) Moliere
   (c) Racine
   (d) All of the above

201. Who has been called 'the founder of French tragedy'?
   (a) Moliere
   (b) Pierre Corneille
   (c) Racine
   (d) None of the above

202. Which is regarded as Corneille's finest play?
   (a) *Horace*
   (b) *Cinna*
   (c) *The Lord*
   (d) *Polyeucte*

203. Which one of the following is Corneille's farcical play?
   (a) *Heraclius*
   (b) *The Liar*
   (c) *Pertharite*
   (d) None of the above

204. Which of the following is Corneille's final tragedy?
   (a) *The Golden Fleece*
   (b) *Sertorius*
   (c) *Surena*
   (d) *Attila*

205. Who is the author of *Misanthrope*?
   (a) Moliere
   (b) Corneille
   (c) Rebelais
   (d) Racine

   (Moliere is one of the greatest writers of comedies in western literature)

206. *The School for Wives*, *The Hyprocite*, *The Miser*, *Gentleman*, *The Imaginary Invalid* are written by
   (a) Corneille
   (b) Stendhel
   (c) Racine
   (d) Moliere

207. In which of his plays Moliere attacks religious hypocrisy?
   (a) *The Affected Ladies*
   (b) *The School for Husbands*
   (c) *The Hypocrite*
   (d) *The King's Troupe*

208. In which of the following play does Moliere deal with the theme of marital relationships?
   (a) *The School for Wives*
   (b) *The Imaginary Cuckold*
   (c) *The Affected Ladies*
   (d) *The School of Husbands*

209. Which of the following play is considered to be Moliere's masterpiece?
   (a) *The Learned Ladies*
   (b) *The Imaginary Invalid*
   (c) *The Affected Ladies*
   (d) *Scapin's Schemings*

210. Jean Racine, the French playwright, was primarily a

(a) Tragedian
(b) Comedian
(c) Poet
(d) Novelist

211. Which one of the following plays is a comedy by Racine?
(a) *Phedre*
(b) *The Litigants*
(c) *Athalie*
(d) *Andromache*

212. Who, among the following, holds the power of life and death over other characters in Jean Racine's plays?
(a) God
(b) Demon
(c) The King
(d) The Queen

213. Which one of the following statements is correct about Racine's tragedies?
(a) His tragic characters are unaware of their flaw.
(b) His tragic characters know that they are fated to die.
(c) His tragic characters are aware of their flaw which leads them to catastrophe but do nothing to overcome it.
(d) None of the above.

214. What's Racine's concept of love as reflected in his tragedies?
(a) It closely resembles a psychological disorder.
(b) It has a pleasing effect on the psyche.
(c) It is painful and destructive.
(d) It leads to disappointment.

215. In Racine's tragedy *Phedre*, Phedre's tragic flaw is
(a) Jealousy
(b) Ambition
(c) Illicit and overpowering passion
(d) None of the above

216. Who, among the following, was known by the pen name of the French writer 'Voltaire'?
(a) Francois Coppee
(b) Francois-Mari Arouet
(c) Francois Maynard
(d) Jean-Jacques Chatelet

(It is an anagram of his surname 'AROVET LI')

217. Voltaire was a famous Enlightenment
(a) Writer
(b) Historian
(c) Philosopher
(d) All of the above

218. Two epic poems "Henriade" and "The Maid of Orleans" were written by
(a) Voltaire
(b) Balzac
(c) Racine
(d) Moliere

("Henriade" is the first epic written in French)

219. The "Henriade" was written in imitation of
(a) Homer
(b) Virgil
(c) Hesiod
(d) None of the above

220. Voltaire's best-known work *Candide* (1792) is
(a) A romantic poem
(b) A religious poem
(c) A tragic play
(d) A satire on philosophical optimism

**Some Important Plays of Voltaire**

1. *Oedipe* (1718) 2. *Mariamne* (1724) 3. *Zaire* (1732) 4. *Eriphile* (1732) 5. *Irene* 6. *Socrates* 7. *Mohomet* 8. *Merope* 9. *Nanine* 10. *The Orphan of China*

221. Dr. Pangloss, a philosopher and tutor of Candide, the hero of Voltaire's novel *Candide*, claimed that
(a) God is merciless.
(b) God created the worst world.
(c) All is for the best in this best of all possible worlds.
(d) Man should remain happy in spite of sufferings.

222. Which of the following characters in *Candide* believed that nothing is right in the world?
(a) Martin
(b) Candide
(c) The Abbe
(d) Dr. Pangloss

223. Who, among the following, is known by the pen name of Stendhal?
(a) Balzac
(b) Marie-Henri Beyle
(c) Victor Hugo
(d) Alexander Dumas

224. Stendhal was a
(a) French writer
(b) German playwright
(c) French poet
(d) Russian novelist

225. *The Red and The Black* (1830) and *The Charter-House of Parma* (1839) were written by
(a) Flaubert
(b) Balzac
(c) Stendhal
(d) Voltaire

226. Stendhal's *The Red and The Black* (in two volumes) is
(a) Romantic novel
(b) Realistic novel
(c) Picaresque novel
(d) Historical psychological novel

(The full title of the novel is *The Red and the Black: A Chronicle of the 19th Century*. It is a Bildungroman of Julien Sorel, the intelligent, ambitious protagonist from a poor family.)

227. Who, among the following, is the hero of Stendhal's novel *The Charter-House of Parma*?
(a) Fabrice del Dongo
(b) Frederick Pongo
(c) Jean-Jacques
(d) Jean Bennette

228. *The Charter-House of Parma*, besides being a "romantic thriller", is also an exploration of
(a) Human nature
(b) Human psychology
(c) Court politics
(d) All of the above

229. Who is the author of *The Human Comedy*?
(a) Voltaire
(b) Stendhal
(c) Balzac
(d) Moliere

230. Who, among the following, is regarded as one of the founders of realism in European literature?
(a) Moliere
(b) Balzac
(c) Racine
(d) Voltaire

231. Honore de Balzac's *The Human Comedy* paints a panaromic portrait of
(a) French society in all its aspects in the years after 1815 fall of Napolean.
(b) French political life.
(c) French religious life.
(d) French upper class.

232. Who, among the following, proclaimed "I am about to become a genius"?

(a) Voltaire
(b) Moliere
(c) Balzac
(d) Racine

233. Who has said, "Common sense is not so common"?
(a) Moliere
(b) Balzac
(c) Racine
(d) Voltaire

234. Who has said, "I do not agree with what you have to say, but I'll defend to the death your right to say it"?
(a) Victor Hugo
(b) Voltaire
(c) Emile Zola
(d) Balzac

235. Who has said, "If God did not exist, it would be necessary to invent him"?
(a) Voltaire
(b) Balzac
(c) Victor Hugo
(d) Moliere

236. Who is the author of *The Hunchback of Notre Dame* (1831)?
(a) Victor Hugo
(b) Alexander Dumas
(c) Voltaire
(d) Balzac

237. Victor Hugo was a
(a) Surrealist
(b) Romanticist
(c) Classicist
(d) None of the above

238. *The Miserable* (1862) is written by
(a) Balzac
(b) Voltaire
(c) Victor Hugo
(d) Racine

239. Victor Hugo was a French
(a) Poet
(b) Dramatist
(c) Novelist
(d) All of the above

240. Victor Hugo is regarded as the great French
(a) Poet
(b) Novelist
(c) Dramatist
(d) Satirist

241. Victor Hugo's intense grief at the death of his daughter and her husband is expressed in
(a) Autumn Leaves
(b) Twilight Songs
(c) Inner Voices
(d) The Contemplations

242. Victor Hugo's "The Punishments" is a collection of
(a) Short-stories
(b) Love poems
(c) Satirical poems
(d) Humorous poems

243. Victor Hugo's short epic *The Legend of the Centuries* was published in
(a) 1852
(b) 1859
(c) 1857
(d) 1855

244. Victor Hugo's novel *The Hunchback of Notre Dame* (1831) deals with
(a) the medieval life under the reign of Louis XI.
(b) poverty.
(c) the miserable life of people in France during that period.
(d) None of the above.

245. The title of the novel *The Hunchback of Notre Dame* refers to

(a) A hunchback
(b) Notre Dame Cathedral
(c) A priest
(d) A poor bagger

246. *The Hunchback of Notre Dame* explores the theme of
(a) Determinism (fate and destiny)
(b) Revolution
(c) Social strife
(d) All of the above

247. In which of his novels Victor Hugo introduced the concept of novel as Epic Theatre?
(a) *The Miserable*
(b) *The Hunchback of Notre Dame*
(c) *The Last Day of the Condemned Man*
(d) *Toilers of the Sea*

248. Victor Hugo's novel *Les Miserables* (1862) is usually translated into English as
(a) *The Miserable*
(b) *The Wretched Poor or The Poor Ones*
(c) *The Victims*
(d) All of the above

249. Which character in Hugo's novels is known by the following names?

1. Monsieur Madeleine 2. Ultime Fauchelevent 3. Monsieur Leblanc 4. Urbain Fabre 5. 24601 6. 9430
(a) Jean Valjean
(b) Javert
(c) Fantine
(d) Cosette

(Jean Valjean is the hero of *The Miserable*.)

250. In which of Hugo's novels is the protagonist convicted and sent to prison for five years for stealing a loaf of bread?
(a) *The Hunchback of Notre Dame*
(b) *The Last Day of the Condemned Man*
(c) *The Miserable*
(d) *Ninety-Three*

251. Who is the author of the novel *The Three Musketeers* (1844)?
(a) Alexander Dumas
(b) Stendhal
(c) Balzac
(d) Hictor Hugo

252. Which of the following novels by Alexander Dumas recounts the adventures of a young man named d' Artagnan?
(a) *Twenty Years After*
(b) *The Three Musketeers*
(c) *Ten Years Later*
(d) *The Victomte of Bragelonne*

(d' Artagnan is the hero of *The Three Musketeers*. He leaves home to travel to Paris to join the "Musketeers of The Guard".)

253. Which of the following novels by Dumas are together known as the 'd' Artagnan Romances'?
(a) *Twenty Years After*
(b) *The Vicomte of Bragelonne*
(c) *Ten Years Later*
(d) All of the above

254. Who is the author of the novel *The Count of Monte Cristo* (1844)?
(a) Victor Hugo
(b) Balzac
(c) Alexander Dumas
(d) Voltaire

255. "The Count of Monte Cristo" is an adventure story primarily concerned with the themes of
(a) Hope
(b) Justice, vengeance

(c) Mercy and forgiveness
(d) All of the above

256. *The Flowers of Evil* was written by
(a) Charles Baudelaire
(b) Paul Verlaine
(c) Arthur Rimbaud
(d) Stephan Mallarme

257. Among others, which of the following poets did Baudelaire influence?
(a) Paul Verlaine
(b) Arthur Rimbaud
(c) Stephan Mallarme
(d) All of the above

258. Who coined the term "modernity"?
(a) Paul Verlaine
(b) Charles Baudelaire
(c) Stephen Mallarme
(d) Arthur Rimbaud

259. Baudelaire's *Flowers of Evil* is about
(a) evil people.
(b) consequences of evil-doing.
(c) the changing nature of beauty in modern industrializing Paris.
(d) None of the above.

260. *Madame Bovary* (1857) was written by
(a) Gustave Flaubert
(b) Alexander Dumas
(c) Balzac
(d) Stendhal

261. *Madame Bovary* is a work of
(a) Surrealism
(b) Realism
(c) Impressionism
(d) Expressionism

262. What happens to Madame Bovary in the end?
(a) She becomes rich
(b) She finds happiness in the end
(c) She deserts her husband
(d) She commits suicide

263. Which of the following are written by Charles Baudelaire?
(a) *Memoirs of a Madam*
(b) *November*
(c) *Sentimental Education*
(d) All of the above

264. Who, among the following, wrote *Twenty Thousand Leagues Under the Sea* (1870), *A Journey to the Centre of the Earth* (1864), and *Around the World in Eighty Days* (1873)?
(a) Balzac
(b) Flaubert
(c) Jules Verne
(d) Voltaire

265. Emile Zola is a perfect representative of the literary school of
(a) Expressionism
(b) Naturalism
(c) Surrealism
(d) Realism

266. More than half of Zola's novels were part of a set of 20 collectively known as
(a) *Les Rougon-Macquart*
(b) *Comedie Humaine*
(c) *L' Assommoir*
(d) *Germinal*

267. Zola's novel *Germinal* (1885) deals with
(a) the life of a cancer patient.
(b) the adventurous life of a girl.
(c) the harsh and realistic story of coalminer's strike.
(d) the life of a beggar.

268. Emile Zola's novel *Drunkard* is a study of
(a) Prostitution
(b) Alcoholism
(c) Insanity
(d) None of the above

269. Who is the author of *Nana* (1880)?
(a) Voltaire
(b) Balzac
(c) Emile Zola
(d) Victor Hugo

270. Anatole France was a French
(a) Poet
(b) Journalist
(c) Novelist
(d) All of the above

271. The novel *The Crime of Sylvester Bernard* (1881) was written by
(a) Balzac
(b) Anatole France
(c) Victor Hugo
(d) Jules Verne

272. Anatole France was awarded the Nobel Prize for literature in
(a) 1921
(b) 1924
(c) 1926
(d) 1928

273. In which of the following novels appears France's characteristic scepticism?
(a) *The Aspirations of Jean Servein*
(b) *The Opinions of Jerome Coignard*
(c) *The Crime of Sylvester Bernard*
(d) *Balthasar*

(*The Crime of Sylvester Bernard* (1881) is a novel about a philologist in love with his books and bewildered by everyday life.)

274. Stephane Mallarme was a major French
(a) Playwright
(b) Novelist
(c) Short-story writer
(d) Symbolist poet

275. Which of the following artistic schools of the early 20th century were inspired by Stephane Mallarme?
(a) Dadaism
(b) Surrealism
(c) Futurism
(d) All of the above

276. Which movement was the French poet, Paul Verlaine, associated with?
(a) Symbolism
(b) Dadaism
(c) Naturalism
(d) Surrealism

277. Which of the following poets is considered one of the greatest poets of the "end of the century" in international and French poetry?
(a) Mallarme
(b) Paul Verlaine
(c) Baudelaire
(d) Mallarme

(The phrase "end of the century" (*Fin de Siecle* in French) is similar in meaning to the English idiom "turn of the century". But, besides that, it connotes a period of degeneration, and also of hope for a new beginning. The spirit of 'Fin de Siecle' often refers to the cultural hallmarks that were recognized as prominent in the 1880s and 1890s, including boredom, pessimism, and a wide-spread belief that civilization leads to decadence.)

278. Who is the author is *Songs without Words* (1874)?
(a) Mallarme
(b) Baudelaire
(c) Verlaine
(d) Rimbaud

279. Who, among the following, was described as "an infant Shakespeare" by Victor Hugo?
(a) Baudelaire
(b) Verlaine
(c) Mallarme
(d) Arthur Rimbaud

280. What is commonly called the "Letter of The Seer" expresses Rimbaud's
   (a) poetic philosophy.
   (b) political philosophy.
   (c) religious beliefs.
   (d) his changing attitude to life.

   (It was Rimbaud's second letter in which he expressed his poetic philosophy. The title was based on his belief that the poet must become a "Seer" who can penetrate infinity and who, by breaking down the restraints and controls that make up the conventional conception of individual personality, must become the instrument for the voice of the eternal.)

281. Who, among the following, wrote the poem "The Drunken Boat"?
   (a) Baudelaire
   (b) Rimbaud
   (c) Verlaine
   (d) Mallarme

282. Romain Rolland was a French
   (a) Dramatist
   (b) Novelist
   (c) Essayist
   (d) All of the above

283. Romain Rolland was awarded the Nobel Prize for literature in
   (a) 1910
   (b) 1912
   (c) 1915
   (d) 1917

284. Which, among the following, is the title of Rolland's plays collected in two cycles?
   (a) *The Wolves*
   (b) *Danton*
   (c) *Aert*
   (d) *The Tragedies of Faith*

285. Romain Rolland's most significant contribution to the theatre was his advocacy for a popular theatre in his essay "The People's Theatre" (1902). In which of the following plays did he put his theory into practice?
   (a) *Danton*
   (b) *The Fourteenth of July*
   (c) Both (a) and (b)
   (d) Neither (a) nor (b)

286. What is the title of the novel in ten volumes written by Romain Rolland?
   (a) *Jean-Christophe*
   (b) *Dawn*
   (c) *Morning*
   (d) *The Revolt*

   (These ten novels are: *Dawn*, *Morning*, *Youth*, *The Revolt*, *The Market Place*, *Antoinette*, *The House*, *Love and Friendship*, *The Burning Bush*, *The New Dawn*.)

287. Who, among the following, wrote the play *Dr. Knock, on the Triumph of Medicine*?
   (a) Rimbaud
   (b) Romain Rolland
   (c) Baudelaire
   (d) Mallarme

288. The novel *The Death of a Nobody* (1911) was written by
   (a) Victor Hugo
   (b) Flaubert
   (c) Romain Rolland
   (d) Balzac

289. Who is the author of *Remembrance of Things Past*?
   (a) Romain Rolland
   (b) Flaubert
   (c) Balzac
   (d) Marcel Proust

   (*Remembrance of Things Past* is a novel based on Proust's life, told psychologically and allegorically and often in a stream-of-consciousness style.)

(*Remembrance of Things Past* is an earlier translation of *In Search of Lost Time*. It was published in seven parts between 1913 and 1927.)

290. *In Search of Lost Time* features more than
   (a) 1,000 characters
   (b) more than 2,000 characters
   (c) 1,800 characters
   (d) 1,500 characters

291. Who called Marcel Proust the "greatest novelist of the 20th century"?
   (a) Somerset Maugham
   (b) E.M. Forster
   (c) Graham Greene
   (d) Virginia Wolf

292. Who is the author of *L' Affaire Lemoine*?
   (a) Balzac
   (b) Marcel Proust
   (c) Victor Hugo
   (d) Stendhal

293. Jean-Paul Sartre was awarded the Nobel Prize in literature in
   (a) 1964
   (b) 1961
   (c) 1958
   (d) 1955

   (Sartre refused to take this award)

294. Sartre was one of the key figures in
   (a) Structuralism
   (b) Surrealism
   (c) Existentialism
   (d) Symbolism

295. Jean-Paul Sartre was a/an
   (a) Novelist
   (b) Playwright
   (c) Existentialist
   (d) All the above

296. *The Age of Reason* (1945) was written by
   (a) Flaubert
   (b) Sartre
   (c) Victor Hugo
   (d) Marcel Proust

297. Which of the following is Sartre's first novel?
   (a) *Nausea*
   (b) *The Roads to Freedom*
   (c) *Reprieve*
   (d) *Troubled Sleep*

298. Which one of the following is Sartre's 'epistolary novel'?
   (a) *The Age of Reason*
   (b) *Nausea*
   (c) *The Flies*
   (d) *Troubled Sleep*

   (The novel concerns a dejected historian, who becomes convinced that inanimate objects and situations encroach upon his ability to define himself, on his intellectual and spiritual freedom, evoking in the protagonist a sense of nausea.)

299. Which of the following is an adaptation of the Electra myth?
   (a) *Nausea*
   (b) *Troubled Sleep*
   (c) *The Flies*
   (d) *Nausea*

   (*The Flies*, Sartre's play, recounts the story of Orestes and his sister Electra in their quest to avenge the death of their father Agamemnon, king of Argos, by killing their mother Clytemnestra and her husband Aegithus, who had deposed and killed him. Sartre incorporates an existential theme in the play.)

**Sartre's Important Plays**

1. *The Flies* (1943) 2. *In Camera* (U.S. title, *No Exit*) 3. *Crime Passionel* (U.S. title, *Dirty Hands* (1945) 4. *Lucifer and Lord* (1951) 5. *Loser Wins* (U.S. title, *The Condemned of Altona*: 1959) 6. *The Respectful Prostitute* (1946)

300. Who, among the following, is a key writer in what Martin Esslin called the "Theatre of the Absurd"?
   (a) Sartre
   (b) Samuel Beckett
   (c) Proust
   (d) Victor Hugo

   (Samuel Beckett was an Irish avant-garde novelist, playwright, theatre director and poet)

301. Who is the author of the play *Waiting for Godot*?
   (a) Marcel Proust
   (b) Balzac
   (c) Samuel Beckett
   (d) Rimbaud

**Samuel Beckett's Important Plays**

1. *Waiting for Godot* (1952) 2. *Endgame* (1951) 3. *Krapp's Last Tape* (1958) 4. *Happy Days* (1961) 5. *Not I* (1972)

302. The play *Antigone* (1943) is written by
   (a) Samuel Beckett
   (b) Jean Anouilh
   (c) Sartre
   (d) None of the above

   (Much of Anouilh's work deals with themes of maintaining integrity in a world of moral compromise.)

303. Albert Camus was a French
   (a) *Author*
   (b) *Journist*
   (c) *Philosopher*
   (d) All of the above

   (Albert Camus's views contributed to the rise of the philosophy known as *absurdism*. He wrote in his essay "The Rebel" that his life was devoted to the philosophy of nihilism.)

304. Camus was awarded the Nobel Prize for literature in
   (a) 1951
   (b) 1953
   (c) 1957
   (d) 1959

305. The novels *The Plague* (1947), *The Stranger* (1942) and *The Fall* (1956) were written by
   (a) Kafka
   (b) Camus
   (c) Sartre
   (d) Anouilh

306. The play *Caligula* (1945) was written by
   (a) Camus
   (b) Sartre
   (c) Eliot
   (d) Beckett

**Albert Camus's Plays**

1. *Caligula* (1945) 2. *Requiem for a Nun* (1956) 3. *The Misunderstanding* (1944) 4. *The State of Siege* (1946) 5. *The Just Assassins* (1949) 6. *The Possessed* (1959)

307. *Betwixt and Between* was written by
   (a) Sartre
   (b) Anouilh
   (c) Beckett
   (d) Camus

308. The play *Cross Purpose* (1944) was written by
   (a) Camus
   (b) Alexander Dumas
   (c) Marcel Proust
   (d) Anatole France

(Camus addressed the isolation of the individual in an alien universe, the enstrangement of the individual from himself, the problem of evil, and the inescapable finality of death, reflecting the anomie (rootlessness, purposelessness, of the post-war intellectual).)

309. *The Bald Soprano* (1950) was written by
   (a) Sartre
   (b) Ionesco
   (c) Beckett
   (d) Camus

   (Eugene Ionesco was a Romanian and French playwright of the 20th century. He is one of the foremost playwrights of the 'Theatre of the Absurd'.)

310. The plays *The Killer* (1959) and *Rhinoceros* (1959) were written by
   (a) Eugene Ionesco
   (b) Sartre
   (c) Camus
   (d) Kafka

   (Ionesco explored dramatic situations featuring humanized characters. One such character is Berenger, a semi-auto biographical figure. In *The Killer*, he encounters death in the figure of a serial killer. In *Rhinoceros* he watched his friends turning into rhinoceros one by one until he alone stands unchanged against this mass movement.)

**Eugene Ionesco's Plays**

1. *Amede or How to Get Rid of It* 2. *The Bald Soprano* 3. *The Chairs* 4. *Exit The King* 5. *Hunger and Thirst* 6. *Jack or the Submission* 7. *The Killer* 8. *The Lesson* 9. *Macbett* 10. *The Picture* 11. *Rhinoceros*

311. Jean Genet was a French
   (a) Novelist
   (b) Playwright
   (c) Poet and essayist
   (d) All of the above

**Jean Genet's Major Works**

**Novels:** 1. *Quarrel of Breast* 2. *The Thief's Journal* 3. *Our Lady of the Flowers* **Plays:** 1. *The Balcony* 2. *The Blacks* 3. *The Maids* 4. *The Screens*

312. Who is the author of *Our Lady of the Flowers* (1943)?
   (a) Sartre
   (b) Ionesco
   (c) Jean Genet
   (d) Proust

   (The novel is a journey through the prison underworld, featuring a fictionalized alter-ego by the name of Divine.)

313. Which of the following is Jean Genet's autobiographical novel?
   (a) *The Thief's Journal*
   (b) *Our Lady of the Flowers*
   (c) *Prisoner of Love*
   (d) *The Miracle of the Rose*

   (*The Thief's Journal* gives a complete and uninhibited account of his life as a tramp, pickpocket, and male prostitute during the 1930s. It also reveals him as an aesthete and an existentialist. Throughout his five early novels, Genet works to subvert traditional moral values. He celebrates a beauty in evil, emphasizes his singularity, raises violent criminals to icons and enjoys depictions of scenes of betrayal.)

314. Jean Genet's play *The Maids* was published in
   (a) 1943
   (b) 1945
   (c) 1947
   (d) 1949

   (Genet's plays present highly-stylized depictions of ritualistic struggles between outcasts of various kinds and their oppressors. His plays *The Balcony* (1956), *The Blacks* (1958) and *The Screens* (1961) are large-scale stylized dramas in the Expressionist manner, designed to shock and implicate an audience by revealing his hypocrisy and complicity.)

315. Who, among the following, wrote *Faust*?
   (a) Goethe
   (b) Homer
   (c) Virgil
   (d) Marlowe

   (*Faust* is a play written by the famous German poet Goethe)

316. Where does the *Faust* begin?
   (a) On earth
   (b) In Hell
   (c) In Heaven
   (d) In the underworld

317. What is the name of the devil referred to in *Faust*?
   (a) Iago
   (b) Mephistopheles
   (c) Satan
   (d) None of the above

318. What was the name of Goethe's first novel?
   (a) *The Sorrows of the Young Werther*
   (b) *From My Life: Poetry and Truth*
   (c) *Elective Affinities*
   (d) *Wilhelm Meister's Travels*

319. *Faust: The First Part of the Tragedy* was published in
   (a) 1800
   (b) 1802
   (c) 1805
   (d) 1808

320. Goethe's novel *The Sorrows of Young Werther* (1774) deals with
   (a) the life of a simple farmer
   (b) life and adventures of Young Werther
   (c) the miserable life of a prostitute
   (d) an unhappy romantic infatuation that ends in suicide.

   (*The Sorrows of Young Werther* is an epistolatory novel.)

321. Who said, "Against criticism a man can neither protest nor defend himself, he must act in a spite of it, and then it will gradually yield to him"?
   (a) Friedrich Schiller
   (b) Goethe
   (c) Rielke
   (d) Schopenhauer

322. Goethe's poetic work served as a model for a movement called
   (a) Surrealism
   (b) Dadaism
   (c) Introversion
   (d) Naturalism

323. What bet does Mephistopheles, the devil, make with God?
   (a) He can lure God's favourite human being, Faust.
   (b) He can destroy humanity in one day.
   (c) He can defeat God in a contest.
   (d) He can turn day into night.

324. What did the devil ask Faust to do if he (the devil) did everything that Faust wanted him to do?
   (a) Faust will be grateful to him.
   (b) Faust will pay him a lot of money.
   (c) Faust will serve the devil in Hell.
   (d) None of the above.

325. Faust signs the contract with the devil
   (a) on a piece of paper.
   (b) with a drop of his own blood.
   (c) on a stone.
   (d) on a piece of cloth.

326. Which British play is based on the story of Goethe's *Faust* story?
   (a) *Dr. Faustus* by Marlowe
   (b) *Macbeth*
   (c) *The Jew of Malta*
   (d) *Tamburlaine*

327. Faust sells his soul to the devil in exchange for
   (a) a lot of wealth.
   (b) unlimited property.
   (c) ruling the earth.
   (d) unlimited knowledge and worldly pleasures.

328. Who speaks the following lines at the end of Act 5 in *Faust*?

   "He who strives on and lives to strive/ Can earn redemption still."
   (a) Faust
   (b) Mephistopheles
   (c) Gretchen
   (d) The Angels

329. What happens to Faust in the end?
   (a) He is saved by God's grace and pleadings from Gretchen.
   (b) He is sent to hell to suffer eternally.
   (c) He dies a miserable death.
   (d) the devil keeps him as a servant.

330. Friedrich Schiller was a
   (a) Poet and playwright
   (b) Historian and philosopher
   (c) Both (a) and (b)
   (d) Neither (a) nor (b)

331. The first play written by Schiller was
   (a) *Fiesco*
   (b) *The Robbers*
   (c) *Intrigue and Love*
   (d) *Don Carlos*

332. Which play by Schiller is considered to be representative of Germany's Romantic 'Storm and Stress' movement?
   (a) *The Robbers*
   (b) *Don Carlos*
   (c) *The Maid of Orleans*
   (d) *The Bride of Messina*

333. Which play marks Schiller's entry into the historical drama?
   (a) *The Maid of Orleans*
   (b) *Wilhelm Tell*
   (c) *Don Carlos*
   (d) *Mary Stuart*

334. What inspired Schiller's pivotal work *On, Aesthetic Education of Man in a Series of Letters* (1794)?
   (a) Schiller's Wife
   (b) Goethe
   (c) Immanuel Kant
   (d) His disenchantment about the French Revolution

335. Who, among the following, wrote the *Duino Elegies*?
   (a) Schiller
   (b) Rainer Maria Rilke
   (c) Goethe
   (d) Herman Hesse

336. *Duino Elegies* is a set of
   (a) Eight elegies
   (b) Nine elegies
   (c) Ten elegies
   (d) Twelve elegies

337. Which of the following are Rilke's most famous prose works?
   (a) *Letters to a Young Poet*
   (b) *Notebooks of Malte Laurids*
   (c) Both (a) and (b)
   (d) Neither (a) nor (b)

   (*The Notebooks* was Rilke's only novel. It is semi-autobiographical and is written in an expressionistic style.)

**Rilke's Volumes of Poetry**

1. *Life and Songs* (1894) 2. *The Book of Hours* 3. *The Book of Images* (in four parts 1902-1906) 4. *New Poems* (1907) 5. *Sonnets to Orpheus* (1922) 6. *Dream-Crowned* (1897) 7. *Advent* (1898)

338. Thomas Mann, the German novelist, was awarded the Nobel Prize for literature in
   (a) 1929
   (b) 1931
   (c) 1933
   (d) 1935

339. Thomas Mann's first novel *Buddenbrooks* was published in
   (a) 1900
   (b) 1901
   (c) 1903
   (d) 1905

340. The novel *Buddenbrooks* relates
   (a) the tragic death of the head of an aristocratic family.
   (b) the sufferings of a middle-class family.
   (c) the decline of a merchant family. during the course of three generations
   (d) None of the above.

341. Thomas Mann's *Death in Venice* was published in
   (a) 1910
   (b) 1912
   (c) 1914
   (d) 1915

   (*Death in Venice* deals with the tragic dilemma of an artist)

342. What is the title of Thomas Mann's tetralogy (a four-part novel)?
   (a) *Magic Mountain*
   (b) *The Will to Happiness*
   (c) *Disillusionment*
   (d) *Joseph and His Brothers*

343. In which of the following does Thomas Mann deal with the theme of incest?
   (a) *The Blood of the Walsungs*
   (b) *The Holy Sinner*
   (c) Both (a) and (b)
   (d) Neither (a) nor (b)

344. *The Black Swan*, a novella by Thomas Mann, was published in
   (a) 1954
   (b) 1956
   (c) 1957
   (d) 1958

345. Herman Hesse was a German-Swiss
   (a) Poet
   (b) Novelist
   (c) Painter
   (d) All of the above

346. Herman Hesse won the Nobel Prize for literature in
   (a) 1942
   (b) 1946
   (c) 1947
   (d) 1949

347. Herman Hesse's disgust with conventional schooling is expressed in
   (a) Beneath the Wheel
   (b) Peter Camenzind
   (c) Gertude
   (d) Demian

348. Who, among the following, wrote *Siddharta* (1922)?
   (a) Friedrich Schiller
   (b) Herman Hesse
   (c) Nobokov
   (d) Flaubert

   (The novel deals with the spiritual journey of an Indian man named Siddhartha during the time of the Buddha.)

349. Herman Hesse's novel *The Glass Bead Game* was published in
    (a) 1940
    (b) 1943
    (c) 1945
    (d) 1947

    (Both *Siddhartha* and *The Glass Bead Game* explore an individual search for authenticity, self-knowledge and spirituality.)

350. Which of the following shows the influence of psycho-analysis on Herman Hesse?
    (a) Demian
    (b) Steppenwolf
    (c) Narcissus and Goldmund
    (d) The Black Swan

351. Franz Kafka's novels express
    (a) man's dissatisfaction with what he has.
    (b) man's contentment.
    (c) the anxieties and alienation of the 20th century man.
    (d) None of the above.

352. Who, among the following, is the author of the novella *The Metamorphosis*?
    (a) Goethe
    (b) Kafka
    (c) Camus
    (d) Zola

353. *The Trial*, *The Castle*, *Amerika* were written by
    (a) Kafka
    (b) Camus
    (c) Flaubert
    (d) Thomas Mann

354. Which of the following are the sub-themes of Franz Kafka's short-story "The Great Wall of China (1931)?
    (a) Why was the wall built piecemeal
    (b) The relationship of the Chinese past and the present
    (c) The emperor's imperceptible presence
    (d) All of the above

355. Peter Ulrich Weiss was a German
    (a) Writer
    (b) Artist
    (c) Painter
    (d) All of the above

356. Who, among the following, wrote "One Thousand and One Nights", a collection of West and South Asian Stories?
    (a) Kafka
    (b) Hesse
    (c) Peter Weiss
    (d) Gorky

357. Who, among the following, is the author of the plays *Marat/Sade* and *The Investigation*?
    (a) Herman Hesse
    (b) Peter Weiss
    (c) Kafka
    (d) Camus

    (The play *Marat/Sade* pits the ideals of individualism and of revolution against each other in a setting in which madness and reason seem inseparable. The play *Investigation* recreates the Frankfurt trials of the men who carried out mass murders at Auschwitz. At the same time, it attacks later German hypocrisy over the existence of concentration camps and investigates the root causes of aggression.)

358. Which of the following are Weiss's semi-autobiographical novels?
    (a) *The Shadow of Coachman's Body* (1960)
    (b) *The Leave Taking* (1961)
    (c) *Exile* (1962)
    (d) All of the above

359. Who, among the following, wrote *The Aesthetics of Resistance*?

(a) Peter Weiss
(b) Schiller
(c) Rilke
(d) Thomas Mann

(*The Aesthetics of Resistance* is a historical novel. It dramatizes antifascist resistance and the rise and fall of proletarian political parties in Europe.)

360. Bertolt Brecht was a German
(a) Poet
(b) Playwright
(c) Theatre director
(d) All of the above

361. Which of the following was Brecht's first play?
(a) *Baal*
(b) *Drums in the Night*
(c) *The Beggar*
(d) *A Respectable Wedding*

362. Who, among the following, is associated with the theory of the 'Epic Theatre'?
(a) Peter Weiss
(b) Kafka
(c) Brecht
(d) Herman Hesse

363. Brecht's play *Mother Courage and Her Children* was produced in
(a) 1939
(b) 1941
(c) 1943
(d) 1945

364. Brecht's *The Good Woman of Szechwan* (also translated as *The Good Person of Szechwan*) (1943) was written in collaboration with
(a) Margarete Steffin
(b) Ruth Berlau
(c) Both (a) and (b)
(d) Neither (a) nor (b)

(Both *The Mother courage and Her Children* and *The Good Woman of Szechwan* are examples of Brecht's non-Aristotelian drama, a dramatic form intended to be staged with the methods of epic theatre.)

365. Brecht's "The Caucasian Chalk Circle" was first produced in English in
(a) 1948
(b) 1945
(c) 1943
(d) 1941

366. Which of the following is Brecht's most important theoretical work regarding theatre?
(a) *The Life of Galileo*
(b) *A Little Organum for the Theatre*
(c) *The Resistible Rise of Arthurolli*
(d) *The Decision*

367. Brecht's *A Manual of Piety* (1927) is a collection of
(a) Poems
(b) Songs
(c) Both (a) and (b)
(d) Neither (a) nor (b)

368. Who, among the following, wrote the play *He Said Yes/He Said No* (1929/1930)?
(a) Brecht
(b) Kafka
(c) Camus
(d) Weiss

369. In which of the following plays by Brecht does each character represent a European nation in the build-up to World War II?
(a) *In the Jungle*
(b) *How Much is Your Iron?*
(c) *Round Heads and Pointed Heads*
(d) *The Flight Across The Ocean*

370. Which of the following plays of Brecht is an adaptation of *The Recruiting Officer*, an English Restoration Comedy by Farquhar?

(a) *Trumpets and Drums*
(b) *Happy End*
(c) *Man Equals Man*
(d) *The Catch*

371. Who is the author of the novel *Eugene Onegin*?
(a) Alexander Dumas
(b) Alexander Pushkin
(c) Maxim Gorky
(d) Anton Chekhov

(Pushkin has often been considered Russia's greatest poet and the founder of Modern Russian Literature.)

372. The poem "The Bronze Horseman" was written by
(a) Marcel Proust
(b) Mallarme
(c) Pushkin
(d) Baudelaire

373. The romantic poem "Russian and Lyudmila" was written by
(a) Alexander Pushkin
(b) Valery
(c) Gorky
(d) Calvino

374. The romantic narrative poems "The Prisoner of Caucasus", "The Robber Brothers", and "The Fountain of Bakhchisaraysky" were written by
(a) Edmund Spenser
(b) Pablo Neruda
(c) Alexander Pushkin
(d) Jean Genet

375. Alexander Pushkin's *Boris Godunov* is a
(a) Comedy
(b) Satire
(c) Narrative poem
(d) Historical tragedy

376. The short-story "The Queen of Spades" by Alexander Pushkin was published in
(a) 1835
(b) 1837
(c) 1839
(d) 1841

377. Alexander Pushkin's *The Captain's Daughter* was published in
(a) 1835
(b) 1836
(c) 1834
(d) 1839

378. Alexander Pushkin's poetic drama *The Stone Guest* is based on
(a) The Pugachov Rebellion
(b) A popular peasant uprising
(c) The Spanish legend of Don Juan
(d) None of the above

379. Fyodor Dostoevsky (or Dostoyevsky) was a Russian
(a) Novelist
(b) Journalist
(c) Short-story writer
(d) All of the above

(Dostoevsky's literary works explore human psychology in the troubled political, social and spiritual context of 19th century Russian society.)

380. *Crime and Punishment* was written by
(a) Pushkin
(b) Dostoevsky
(c) Tolstoy
(d) Gorky

(*Crime and Punishment* focuses on the mental anguish and moral dilemmas of Rodion Romanovich Raskolnikov.)

381. The novels *The Idiot* and *The Brothers Karamzov* were written by
(a) Dostoevsky
(b) Tolstoy
(c) Pushkin
(d) Henry Fielding

(*The Idiot* is based on prince Myshkin's struggle between a beautiful kept woman and a virtuous and pretty young girl, both of whom win his affection. *The Brothers Karamazov* is a passionate philosophical novel that enters deeply into the ethical debates of God, the free will, and morality.)

382. In which of his novels did Dostoevsky introduce the concept of the split personality or divided self that would become a common psychological feature of the characters of his later novels?
   (a) *Poor Folk*
   (b) *The Double*
   (c) *Notes from the Underground*
   (d) *The Possessed*

383. Dostoevsky's novel *The Possessed* was published in
   (a) 1870
   (b) 1872
   (c) 1874
   (d) 1875

   (It is also known as *The Devils* or *Demons*. The novel is a testimonial of life in imperial Russia in the late 19th century.)

384. *Notes from the Underground or Letters from the Underworld*, a novella by Dostoevsky, was published in
   (a) 1860
   (b) 1862
   (c) 1864
   (d) 1865

   (*Notes from the Underground* is considered by many to be the first existentialist novel. It presents itself as an excerpt from the rambling memoirs of a bitter, isolated, untamed narrator, who is a retired civil servant living in St. Petersburg.)

**Dostoevsky's Novels and Novellas**

1. *Poor Folk* (1846) 2. *The Double* (1846) 3. *Uncle's Dream* (1859) 4. *The Village of Stepanchikovo* (1859) 5. *Humiliated and Insulted* (1861) 6. *The House of the Dead* (1862) 7. *Notes From Underground* (1864) 8. *Crime and Punishment* (1866) 9. *The Gambler* (1867) 10. *The Idiot* (1869) 11. *Demons or The Possessed* (1872) 12. *The External Husband* (1870) 13. *The Adolescent* 14. *The Brothers Karamzhov*

385. Who, among the following, wrote *War and Peace* (1865-69)?
   (a) Dostoevsky
   (b) Leo Tolstoy
   (c) Pushkin
   (d) Gorky

   (Set during the Napoleonic Wars, *War and Peace* examiners the lives of a large cast of characters with the utmost objectivity. The structure of the novel, with its flawless placement of complex characters in a turbulent historical setting, is regarded as one of the great technical achievements in the history of the Western novel.)

386. The novel *Anna Karenina* (1875-77) was written by
   (a) Vladimir Nabokov
   (b) Maxim Gorky
   (c) Tolstoy
   (d) Dostoevsky

   (The novel centres on a married woman whose life ends in tragedy and early death after she deserts her husband out of love for a younger man who had seduced her. It dwells upon the ultimate meaning and purpose of life.)

387. Tolstoy's novel *A Confession* was published in

(a) 1880
(b) 1884
(c) 1885
(d) 1887

(In this novel, Tolstoy presents an account of the spiritual crisis he endured in search for an answer to the meaning of life. He eventually turned to a form of Christian anarchism and devoted himself to social reform.)

388. The novel *Resurrection* (1899) was written by
(a) Flaubert
(b) Zamyatin
(c) Tolstoy
(d) Dostoevsky

(Tolstoy intended the novel as an exposition of injustice of man-made laws and the hypocrisy of institutionalized church.)

389. *The Power of Darkness*, a five-act drama, by Leo Tolstoy was written in
(a) 1886
(b) 1888
(c) 1889
(d) 1883

(The central character in the drama is a peasant, Nikita. He seduces and abandons a young girl, Marinka, then the lovely Anisija murders her own husband and marries Nikita. He impregnates his new stepdaughter. Then, under the influence of his wife, murders the baby. On the day of his stepdaughter's marriage, he surrenders himself and confesses to the police.)

390. Who, among the following, wrote *A Dreary Story* (1889)?
(a) Dostoevsky
(b) Anton Chekhov
(c) Maxim Gorky
(d) Kafka

(*A Dreary Story* is a penetrating study of the mind of an elderly and dying professor of medicine.)

(Anton Chekhov was a Russian physician, dramatist and author. He is considered to be among the greatest writers of short-stories in history.)

391. Who, among the following, wrote under the pseudonym "Man without a Spleen" during his early career as a writer?
(a) Anton Chekhov
(b) Nobokov
(c) Koestler
(d) Dostoevsky

392. Which of the following works by Anton Chekhov remains a classic of Russian penology?
(a) *The Cherry Orchard*
(b) *Three Sisters*
(c) *The Island of Sakhalin*
(d) *The Lady with the Dog*

393. *Uncle Vanya*, one of Chekhov's greatest stage masterpieces, was published in
(a) 1890
(b) 1892
(c) 1895
(d) 1897

394. *The Proposal*, a one-act farce, was written by
(a) Chekhov
(b) Gorky
(c) Pushkin
(d) Dostoevsky

395. Some one-act farces by Chekhov are known as
(a) Varieties
(b) Vaudvilles
(c) Farcicals
(d) None of the above

(These plays are: *The Bear* (1888); *The Proposal* (1889); *The Wedding* (1889); *The Anniversary* (1891).)

396. Which of the following Chekhov's short sequence of brilliant sketches created a stir in Russia more than any other single work of Chekhov's, partly owing to his unsentimental view of the Russian peasantry?
   (a) The Neighbours
   (b) The Murder
   (c) Peasants
   (d) Ariadna

397. Which of the following are Chekhov's last plays?
   (a) *Ward Number Six*
   (b) *Three Sisters*
   (c) *The Cherry Orchard*
   (d) Both (b) and (c)
   (e) Both (a) and (b)

398. Chekhov's play *The Seagull* was written in
   (a) 1893
   (b) 1895
   (c) 1896
   (d) 1897

399. Which of the following writers is known for his naturalistic and sympathetic portraits of tramps and social outcasts?
   (a) Anton Chekhov
   (b) Nikolai Gogol
   (c) Maxim Gorky
   (d) Dostoevsky

400. Nikolai Gogol was a Russian
   (a) Humanist
   (b) Dramatist
   (c) Novelist
   (d) All of the above

401. Who, among the following, wrote the novel *Dead Souls* (1842) and the story "The Overcoat" (1842)?
   (a) Nikolai Gogol
   (b) Anton Chekhov
   (c) Maxim Gorky
   (d) Nabokov

402. In which of the following novels is there a reference to Gogol's story "The Overcoat"?
   (a) *The Namesake*
   (b) *The Immigrant*
   (c) *Cry, The Peacock*
   (d) *The God of Small Things*

403. Gogol's novel *The Government Inspector* was published in
   (a) 1834
   (b) 1836
   (c) 1838
   (d) 1839

404. In which of the following stories by Nikolai Gogol, the hero is a frustrated office drudge who ends up in a lunafic asylum?
   (a) "The Overcoat"
   (b) "Taras Bulba"
   (c) "Diary of a Madman"
   (d) None of the above

405. Which of his novels was considered by Nikolai Gogol "an epic poem in prose"?
   (a) *Dead Souls*
   (b) *The Government Inspector*
   (c) *A Bewitched Place*
   (d) *Taras Bulba*

406. Maxim Gorky's short-story "Chelkash" was published in
   (a) 1891
   (b) 1895
   (c) 1897
   (d) 1899

407. Who, among the following, wrote the short-story "Twenty-Six Men and a Girl" (1899)

(a) Anton Chekhov
(b) Gogol
(c) Nobokov
(d) Gorky

(The story realistically portrays the dismal life of twenty-six men working in a bakery in Russia in the late 19th century. It is regarded as Gorky's best short story.)

408. Who, among the following, wrote the novel *Mother* (1906)?
(a) Nabokov
(b) Chekhov
(c) Gorky
(d) Koestler

(The novel *Mother* is devoted to the Russian revolutionary movement. It is about the youths who worked in a factory and took part in the revolution.)

409. Which of the following was Gorky's first novel?
(a) *Foma Gordeyev*
(b) *The Mother*
(c) *Goremyka Pavel*
(d) *Three of Them*

(The novel *Foma Gordeyev* illustrates Gorky's admiration for strength of body and will in the barge owner and rising capitalist Gordeyev, who is contrasted with his feeble and intellectual son, Foma, a "seeker after the meaning of life".)

410. Who, among the following, is regarded a founder of the Socialist Realism in Russia?
(a) Dostoevsky
(b) Tolstoy
(c) Gorky
(d) Gogol

411. The play *Children of the Sun* (1905) was written by
(a) Gogol
(b) Gorky
(c) Nabokov
(d) Sholokhov

412. The poem "Song of the Stormy Petrel" (1901) was written by
(a) Gorky
(b) Gogol
(c) Nabokov
(d) Chekhov

(The poem is a short piece of revolutionary literature.)

413. Gorky's autobiographical trilogy, regarded as his greatest masterpiece, includes the following:
(a) *My Childhood*
(b) *In the World* (1915-16)
(c) *My Universities*
(d) All of the above

414. Which of the following are included in Gorky's reminiscences of Russian writers?
(a) Leo Tolstoy
(b) Reminiscences of Leo Nikolavich Tolstoy
(c) About Writers
(d) All of the above

415. Yevgeny Zamyatin was a Russian
(a) Novelist
(b) Playwright
(c) Satirist
(d) All of the above

(Zamyatin was one of the most brilliant and cultured minds of the post revolutionary period, and creator of anti-utopian novel.)

416. Who, among the following, is the author of *We*?
(a) Chekhov
(b) Gorky
(c) Zamyatin
(d) Gogol

(*We* is a dystopian novel. It portrays the life of workers who live in glass houses.

They have numbers rather than names, wear identical uniforms, eat chemical foods, and enjoy rationed sex.)

417. *Provincial Tale* (1913) and *At the World's End* (1914) were written by
   (a) Chekhov
   (b) Zamyatin
   (c) Gogol
   (d) Gorky

   (*Provincial Tale* is a satire on provincial life. While *At the World's End* is an attack on military life.)

418. Zamyatin's *The Islanders* was published in
   (a) 1918
   (b) 1920
   (c) 1921
   (d) 1922

   (*The Islanders* satirizes the meanness and emotional repression of English life.)

419. Boris's Pasternak was a Russian
   (a) Poet
   (b) Novelist
   (c) Literary translator
   (d) All of the above

420. Boris's Pasternak was awarded the Nobel Prize for literature in
   (a) 1956
   (b) 1958
   (c) 1959
   (d) 1960

421. Which of the following works helped Pasternak to win the Nobel Prize for literature?
   (a) *Safe Conduct* (1931)
   (b) *Second Birth* (1932)
   (c) *Doctor Zhivago* (1957)
   (d) *Goethe's Faust* (1952)

   (*Dr Zhivago* is an epic of wandering, spiritual isolation and love amid the harshness of the Russian Revolution and its aftermath. The novel became an international bestseller but circulated only in secrecy and translation in his own land.)

422. Which of the following collection of poems brought Pasternak great recognition as a major new lyrical voice?
   (a) *My Sister, Life*
   (b) *In the Interlude*
   (c) *On Early Trains*
   (d) *Over the Barriers*

423. *Lolita* (1955) was written by
   (a) Pasternak
   (b) Valadimir Nabokov
   (c) Mikhail Sholokhov
   (d) Zamyatin

   (*Lolita* was ranked at No. 4 in the list of the Modern Library 100 best Novels. The novel is notable for its controversial subject: the protagonist and unreliable narrator, a middle-age professor of literature, Humbert, is obsessed with the 12-year old Dolores Haze, with whom he becomes sexually involved after he becomes his stepfather. His private nickname for Dolores is Lolita.)

424. Nabokov's novel *Pale Fire* was published in
   (a) 1962
   (b) 1961
   (c) 1963
   (d) 1965

   (The novel is presented as a 999-line poem in four cantos, written by the fictional John Shade, with a foreward and lengthy commentary by a neighbour and academic colleague of the poet, Charles Kinbote. These elements form a narrative in which both authors are central characters. The title is from Shakespeare's *Timon of Athens*.)

425. Who, among the following, wrote the novel *Invitation to a Beheading* (1935-36, trans. 1959)?

(a) Nabokov
(b) Koestler
(c) Gorky
(d) Chekhov

(The novel is often described as *Kafkaesque*. The novel takes place in a prison and relates the final twenty days of Cincinnatus C, a citizen of a fictitious country who is imprisoned and sentenced to death for "gnostical turpitude".)

**Nabokov's Novels Written in English**

1. *The Real Life of Sebastian Knight* (1941) 2. *Bend Sinister* (1947) 3. *Lolita* (1955) 4. *Pnin* (1957) 5. *Pale Fire* (1962) 6. *Ada or Ardor : A Family Chronicle* (1969) 7. *Transparent Things* (1972) 8. *Look at the Harlequins* (1974) 9. *The Original of Laura* (2009).

426. Who, among the following, is the author of *Darkness at Noon* (1940)?
(a) Nabokov
(b) Arthur Koestler
(c) Sholokhov
(d) Zamyatin

(Arthur Koestler is a Hungarian-British author and journalist. His novel *Darkness at Noon* is an antitotalitarian work, which brought him international fame.)

**Arthur Koestler's Novels**

1. *The Gladiators* (1939) 2. *Darkness at Noon* (1940) 3. *Arrival and Departure* (1943) 4. *Thieves in the Night* (1946) 5. *The Age of Longing* (1951) 6. *The Call-Girls* (1972).

427. Which of the following novels by Koestler is about scholars making a living on the international seminar-conference circuit?
(a) *Thieves in the Night*
(b) *Arrival and Departure*
(c) *The Call Girls*
(d) *The Gladiators*

(*The Call Girls* are a group of international conference attendees who will go anywhere to discuss or promote their ideas provided that expenses are paid and the location is sufficiently exotic. It is the story of a group of academic scientists struggling to understand the human tendency towards self-destruction. In this novel, Koestler introduces the term coca-colonization to refer to the expansion of a typical modern diet, consisting of such fare as hamburgers, French fries, fat-rich snacks, soft drinks high in sugars.)

428. Mikhail Sholokhov, the Russian writer, won the Nobel Prize for literature in?
(a) 1965
(b) 1966
(c) 1967
(d) 1969

429. Mikhail Sholokhov's *Fierce and Gentle Warriors* was published in
(a) 1925
(b) 1967
(c) 1975
(d) 1980

430. Sholokhove's novel *Quiet Flows the Don*, the fist part was published in English in
(a) 1931
(b) 1932
(c) 1934
(d) 1936

(*Quiet Flows the Don* is a Great Don epic in two parts. It originally appeared in serialised form between 1928 and 1940. The novel deals with the life of the Cossacks living in the Don River Valley during the early 20th century, probably around 1912, just before World War I. The plot revolves around the Melekhov family of a Tatarsk. The novel is a panoramic view of the ten years Cossack life in the Don region of Russia. Set in the turbulent years of World War I, the Revolution and the Civil War, it deals with the main questions of the war's communist regime: how much ruthlessness can be practised in order to establish Soviet power? The Bolshevik's harsh repression of the Cossacks leads to a mass rebellion, which succeeds in driving the Reds out of the Don territory but not before the Don loses half of its population in a bloody and merciless battle.)

431. Which of the following novels have been written by Sholokhov?
   (a) *The Don Flows Home to Sea*
   (b) *Virgil Soil Upturned*
   (c) Both (a) and (b)
   (d) Neither (a) nor (b)

432. Who, among the following, was the French philosopher and writer whose treatises and novels inspired the leaders of the leaders of the French Revolution and the Romantic generation?
   (a) Voltaire
   (b) Rousseau
   (c) Montesquieu
   (d) Moliere

433. Who, among the following, wrote the novel *Julie* (1761)?
   (a) Rousseau
   (b) Voltaire
   (c) Balzac
   (d) Stendhal

   (This novel played an important role in the development of romanticism in fiction.)

434. Rousseau's novel *Emile* (1762) is a treatise on
   (a) Religion
   (b) Politics
   (c) Legal system
   (d) Education

435. Which of the following books by Rousseau are regarded as the corner stones in modern political and social thought?
   (a) *Discourse on the Origin of Inequality*
   (b) *On the Social Contract*
   (c) Both (a) and (b)
   (d) Neither (a) nor (b)

436. Jean-Jacques Rousseau's autobiographical book *Confessions* was published in
   (a) 1780
   (b) 1782
   (c) 1783
   (d) 1784

   (The book covers the first fifty-three years of Rousseau's life, upto 1765. It was completed in 1769 but published only in 1782.)

## ANSWERS

| | | | | | |
|---|---|---|---|---|---|
| 1. (a) | 2. (d) | 3. (b) | 4. (a) | 5. (b) | 6. (c) |
| 7. (d) | 8. (b) | 9. (a) | 10. (d) | 11. (c) | 12. (a) |
| 13. (c) | 14. (b) | 15. (a) | 16. (c) | 17. (b) | 18. (d) |
| 19. (c) | 20. (a) | 21. (d) | 22. (b) | 23. (c) | 24. (a) |
| 25. (b) | 26. (b) | 27. (c) | 28. (c) | 29. (a) | 30. (b) |
| 31. (c) | 32. (a) | 33. (d) | 34. (b) | 35. (a) | 36. (c) |
| 37. (b) | 38. (c) | 39. (a) | 40. (d) | 41. (c) | 42. (d) |
| 43. (a) | 44. (c) | 45. (d) | 46. (d) | 47. (b) | 48. (c) |
| 49. (a) | 50. (d) | 51. (b) | 52. (a) | 53. (c) | 54. (d) |
| 55. (b) | 56. (d) | 57. (a) | 58. (c) | 59. (d) | 60. (b) |
| 61. (c) | 62. (a) | 63. (b) | 64. (c) | 65. (a) | 66. (b) |
| 67. (a) | 68. (b) | 69. (c) | 70. (d) | 71. (b) | 72. (c) |
| 73. (b) | 74. (a) | 75. (b) | 76. (c) | 77. (a) | 78. (a) |
| 79. (b) | 80. (c) | 81. (a) | 82. (b) | 83. (d) | 84. (c) |
| 85. (c) | 86. (d) | 87. (a) | 88. (b) | 89. (c) | 90. (d) |
| 91. (a) | 92. (b) | 93. (c) | 94. (a) | 95. (d) | 96. (a) |
| 97. (a) | 98. (b) | 99. (c) | 100. (a) | 101. (b) | 102. (c) |
| 103. (d) | 104. (a) | 105. (b) | 106. (c) | 107. (d) | 108. (a) |
| 109. (b) | 110. (c) | 111. (b) | 112. (a) | 113. (c) | 114. (b) |
| 115. (d) | 116. (b) | 117. (a) | 118. (c) | 119. (a) | 120. (b) |
| 121. (c) | 122. (a) | 123. (c) | 124. (b) | 125. (d) | 126. (a) |
| 127. (c) | 128. (b) | 129. (c) | 130. (a) | 131. (b) | 132. (c) |
| 133. (c) | 134. (a) | 135. (c) | 136. (b) | 137. (a) | 138. (d) |
| 139. (c) | 140. (a) | 141. (b) | 142. (d) | 143. (c) | 144. (b) |
| 145. (a) | 146. (c) | 147. (d) | 148. (a) | 149. (b) | 150. (d) |
| 151. (d) | 152. (d) | 153. (a) | 154. (b) | 155. (c) | 156. (b) |
| 157. (d) | 158. (b) | 159. (c) | 160. (a) | 161. (b) | 162. (c) |
| 163. (d) | 164. (a) | 165. (b) | 166. (c) | 167. (d) | 168. (a) |
| 169. (b) | 170. (d) | 171. (c) | 172. (a) | 173. (d) | 174. (b) |
| 175. (a) | 176. (c) | 177. (b) | 178. (b) | 179. (a) | 180. (c) |
| 181. (b) | 182. (c) | 183. (a) | 184. (a) | 185. (b) | 186. (d) |
| 187. (d) | 188. (c) | 189. (c) | 190. (b) | 191. (c) | 192. (d) |

| | | | | | |
|---|---|---|---|---|---|
| 193. (d) | 194. (a) | 195. (d) | 196. (a) | 197. (b) | 198. (d) |
| 199. (d) | 200. (d) | 201. (b) | 202. (c) | 203. (b) | 204. (c) |
| 205. (a) | 206. (d) | 207. (c) | 208. (b) | 209. (a) | 210. (a) |
| 211. (b) | 212. (c) | 213. (c) | 214. (a) | 215. (c) | 216. (b) |
| 217. (d) | 218. (a) | 219. (b) | 220. (d) | 221. (c) | 222. (a) |
| 223. (b) | 224. (a) | 225. (c) | 226. (d) | 227. (a) | 228. (d) |
| 229. (c) | 230. (b) | 231. (a) | 232. (c) | 233. (d) | 234. (b) |
| 235. (a) | 236. (a) | 237. (b) | 238. (c) | 239. (d) | 240. (a) |
| 241. (d) | 242. (c) | 243. (b) | 244. (a) | 245. (b) | 246. (d) |
| 247. (b) | 248. (d) | 249. (a) | 250. (c) | 251. (a) | 252. (b) |
| 253. (d) | 254. (c) | 255. (d) | 256. (a) | 257. (d) | 258. (b) |
| 259. (c) | 260. (a) | 261. (b) | 262. (d) | 263. (d) | 264. (c) |
| 265. (b) | 266. (a) | 267. (c) | 268. (b) | 269. (c) | 270. (d) |
| 271. (b) | 272. (a) | 273. (c) | 274. (d) | 275. (d) | 276. (a) |
| 277. (b) | 278. (c) | 279. (d) | 280. (a) | 281. (b) | 282. (d) |
| 283. (c) | 284. (d) | 285. (c) | 286. (a) | 287. (b) | 288. (c) |
| 289. (d) | 290. (b) | 291. (c) | 292. (b) | 293. (a) | 294. (c) |
| 295. (d) | 296. (b) | 297. (a) | 298. (b) | 299. (c) | 300. (b) |
| 301. (c) | 302. (b) | 303. (d) | 304. (c) | 305. (b) | 306. (a) |
| 307. (d) | 308. (a) | 309. (b) | 310. (a) | 311. (d) | 312. (c) |
| 313. (a) | 314. (c) | 315. (a) | 316. (c) | 317. (b) | 318. (a) |
| 319. (d) | 320. (d) | 321. (b) | 322. (c) | 323. (a) | 324. (c) |
| 325. (b) | 326. (a) | 327. (d) | 328. (d) | 329. (a) | 330. (c) |
| 331. (b) | 332. (a) | 333. (c) | 334. (d) | 335. (b) | 336. (c) |
| 337. (c) | 338. (a) | 339. (b) | 340. (c) | 341. (b) | 342. (d) |
| 343. (c) | 344. (a) | 345. (d) | 346. (b) | 347. (a) | 348. (b) |
| 349. (b) | 350. (a) | 351. (c) | 352. (b) | 353. (a) | 354. (d) |
| 355. (d) | 356. (c) | 357. (b) | 358. (d) | 359. (a) | 360. (d) |
| 361. (a) | 362. (c) | 363. (b) | 364. (c) | 365. (a) | 366. (b) |
| 367. (c) | 368. (a) | 369. (b) | 370. (a) | 371. (b) | 372. (c) |
| 373. (a) | 374. (c) | 375. (d) | 376. (a) | 377. (b) | 378. (c) |
| 379. (d) | 380. (b) | 381. (a) | 382. (a) | 383. (b) | 384. (c) |
| 385. (b) | 386. (c) | 387. (b) | 388. (c) | 389. (a) | 390. (b) |

| | | | | | |
|---|---|---|---|---|---|
| 391. (a) | 392. (c) | 393. (d) | 394. (a) | 395. (b) | 396. (c) |
| 397. (d) | 398. (b) | 399. (c) | 400. (d) | 401. (a) | 402. (a) |
| 403. (b) | 404. (c) | 405. (a) | 406. (b) | 407. (d) | 408. (c) |
| 409. (a) | 410. (c) | 411. (b) | 412. (a) | 413. (d) | 414. (d) |
| 415. (d) | 416. (c) | 417. (b) | 418. (a) | 419. (d) | 420. (b) |
| 421. (c) | 422. (a) | 423. (b) | 424. (a) | 425. (a) | 426. (b) |
| 427. (c) | 428. (a) | 429. (b) | 430. (c) | 431. (c) | 432. (b) |
| 433. (a) | 434. (d) | 435. (c) | 436. (b) | | |

# 3

# Indian Writing in English

1. Who was the first great writer in Indian English Literature?
   (a) Romesh Chunder Dutt
   (b) Mulk Raj Anand
   (c) Toru Dutt
   (d) Raja Rao
2. Toru Dutt's book "A Sheaf Gleaned in French Fields" appeared in
   (a) 1871
   (b) 1875
   (c) 1881
   (d) 1885
3. *The Young Spanish Maiden*, a well-known novel, has been written by
   (a) Sri Aurobindo
   (b) Lotika Ghose
   (c) Toru Dutt
   (d) K.P. Ghose
4. In which poem Toru Dutt has tried to recapture the past and to immortalize the moments of time so recaptured?
   (a) "Our Casuarina Tree"
   (b) "Baugmaree"
   (c) "The Lotus"
   (d) "Sita"
5. "Love came to Flora asking for a flower/ That would of flowers be undisputed queen". These lines have been written by
   (a) Manmohan Ghose
   (b) Toru Dutt
   (c) Sri Aurobindo
   (d) H.L.V. Derozio
6. "In memory till the hot tears blind mine eyes!/ What is that dirge-like murmur that I hear/ Like the sea breaking on a shingle beach?"

   Who is the writer of these lines?
   (a) Sarojini Naidu
   (b) Toru Dutt
   (c) Subramania Bharati
   (d) None of the above
7. The French novel *Le Journal de Mademoiselle d'arvers* has been written by
   (a) Sarojini Naidu
   (b) Sri Aurobindo
   (c) Toru Dutt
   (d) Rabindranath Tagore
8. "Drunken with beauty then/ gaze and gaze/ On a primeval Eden, in amaze." These lines appear in which poem of Toru Dutt?
   (a) "Our Casuarina Tree"
   (b) "Baugmaree"
   (c) "The Lotus"
   (d) "The Tree of Life"
9. "In those far-off primeval days/ Fair India's daughters were not pent/ In closed zenanas."

(a) Toru Dutt
(b) Sri Aurobindo
(c) H.L.V. Derozio
(d) Manmohan Ghose

10. Whose father was Govin Chunder, a good linguist and a cultured man, with literary leanings and generous impulses?
(a) Sarojini Naidu
(b) Tagore
(c) Sri Aurobindo
(d) Toru Dutt

11. Which of the following poems is not by Toru Dutt?
(a) "The Tree of Life"
(b) "Sita"
(c) "Our Casuarina Tree"
(d) None of the above

12. Who has written the famous book, *The Economic History of British India*?
(a) Madhusudan Dutt
(b) K.P. Ghose
(c) Romesh Chunder
(d) Toru Dutt

13. "Didst thou, mother, bear the hero fathomless like ocean dread,/ whose unfailing glistening arrows like its countless billows sped." These lines have been taken from which poem of Romesh Chunder Dutt?
(a) "Lays of Ancient India"
(b) "The Ramayana"
(c) "The Mahabharata"
(d) None of the above

14. Which book of Romesh Chunder Dutt gives a picture of Bengali life in the 19th Century?
(a) *A Brief History of Ancient and Modern Bengal*
(b) *The Lake of Palms*
(c) *The Slave girl*
(d) *Lays of Ancient India*

15. Which poet adopted Locksley Hall metre?
(a) Romesh Chunder Dutt
(b) Toru Dutt
(c) Manmohan Ghose
(d) K.P. Ghose

16. Which was the only collection of poems published during the life time of Manmohan Ghose?
(a) *Love Songs and Elegies*
(b) *Songs of Life and Death*
(c) *Nala and Damayanti*
(d) *Perseus, the Gorgon Slayer*

17. Who said this? "I shall bury myself in poetry, simply and solely."
(a) Rabindranath Tagore
(b) Manmohan Ghose
(c) Aurobindo Ghose
(d) Toru Dutt

18. "O what a heaven, what land unknown/ To Julian's happy sight is shown!/ To all his agonies, all his sights/ What opening, sudden Paradise!" These lines have been written by
(a) Manmohan Ghose
(b) Sarojini Naidu
(c) Madhusudan Dutt
(d) Toru Dutt

19. Which work of Manmohan Ghose was published posthumously?
(a) *Primavera*
(b) *Songs of Life and Death*
(c) *Immortal Love*
(d) *Love Songs and Elegies*

20. "Love Poem for a Wife I", "Breaded Fish", "Still Life" and "Snakes" are all poems by
(a) A.K. Ramanujan
(b) Jayant Mahapatra
(c) R. Parthasarthy
(d) Keki Daruwalla

21. A.K. Ramanujan's "Relations" appeared in the year
    (a) 1970
    (b) 1971
    (c) 1972
    (d) 1973
22. Which of these has not been composed by A.K. Ramanujan?
    (a) *The Striders*
    (b) *Selected Poems*
    (c) *Relations*
    (d) *Draupadi and Jayadratha*
23. "Not, not only prophets/Walk on water...." These lines have been taken from which of Ramanujan's poem?
    (a) "Breaded Fish"
    (b) "The Striders"
    (c) "Obituary"
    (d) "A Plant"
24. Which poem of Ramanujan is associated with the Hindu Myth of Lord Vishnu?
    (a) "Still View of Another Grace"
    (b) "Obituary"
    (c) "The Striders"
    (d) "Breaded Fish"
25. Rabindranath Tagore got the Nobel Prize for literature in the year
    (a) 1910
    (b) 1913
    (c) 1912
    (d) 1917
26. Which of the following works of Tagore was written originally in English?
    (a) *Heaven of Freedom*
    (b) *Gora*
    (c) *The Home and the World*
    (d) *The Child*
27. It is to Indian fiction what Tolstoy's "War and Peace is to the Russian". Which of Tagore's novels has been referred to here?
    (a) *The Wreck*
    (b) *The Home and the World*
    (c) *Binodini*
    (d) *Gora*
28. Poems like "Urvashi". "The Child" and "Lover's Gift", were written by
    (a) Toru Dutt
    (b) Raja Ram Mohan Roy
    (c) Tagore
    (d) Sri Aurobindo
29. Which one of the following Tagore's novels is set in the revolutionary Bengal of 1905?
    (a) *Gora*
    (b) *The Home and the World*
    (c) *The Wreck*
    (d) *Char Adhyay*
30. Tagore's *The Crescent Moon*, a book for children, was published in
    (a) 1910
    (b) 1911
    (c) 1912
    (d) 1913
31. Who wrote *The Fugitive and Other Poems* (1921)
    (a) Tagore
    (b) Sri Aurobindo
    (c) Sarojini Naidu
    (d) Nissim Ezekiel
32. In which of the following plays Tagore articulated "An eloquent protest against the onslaught of machinery on the ancient ramparts of man's individual freedom"?
    (a) *Chandalika*
    (b) *Malini*
    (c) *Mukta Dhara*
    (d) *Natir Puja*
33. Match the Characters with their plays

| | |
|---|---|
| A. Srimati | 1. *Chandalika* |
| B. Prakriti | 2. *Natir Puja* |
| C. Dhananjaya | 3. *Chitra* |
| D. Arjuna | 4. *Mukta-Dhara* |

| | A | B | C | D |
|---|---|---|---|---|
| (a) | 2 | 1 | 4 | 3 |
| (b) | 4 | 2 | 3 | 1 |
| (c) | 1 | 2 | 3 | 4 |
| (d) | 3 | 4 | 1 | 2 |

34. "Not a man only but an age had made its way at last into history.... He has summed up in himself a whole age in which India had moved into the modern world." In the above sentence, 'a man' refers to
   (a) Aurobindo
   (b) Tagore
   (c) Raja Rao
   (d) A.K. Ramanujan

35. Tagore wrote primarily in
   (a) English
   (b) Hindi
   (c) Bengali
   (d) French

36. "The current of daily life moves slowly between the village near the hill and the one by the river bank."

   These lines appear in which poem of Tagore?
   (a) "Heaven of Freedom"
   (b) "The Gardener"
   (c) "Breezy April"
   (d) "The Child"

37. Whose lines are these? "Into that heaven of Freedom my father let my country awake."
   (a) Rabindranath Tagore
   (b) Sarojini Naidu
   (c) Anita Desai
   (d) Raja Rao

38. Name the first Indian poet who received the Nobel Prize for Literature?
   (a) Bankim Chandra Chatterjee
   (b) Sri Aurobindo
   (c) Rabindranath Tagore
   (d) Sarojini Naidu

39. Who said that no one can write about my life because it has not been on the surface for men to see?
   (a) Mulk Raj Anand
   (b) Sri Aurobindo
   (c) Tagore
   (d) Toru Dutt

40. Who said after reading "The Life Divine": Has there ever existed a more synthetic consciousness than that of Sri Aurobindo?
   (a) Dorothy Richardson
   (b) S.K. Maitra
   (c) Charles A. Moore
   (d) Wilson Knight

41. Who described "The Life Divine" as "a vast philosophical prose epic...a philosophical Divina Commedia"?
   (a) K.R. Iyengar
   (b) D.S. Sarma
   (c) Otto Wolff
   (d) Francis Younghusband

42. Which work of Sri Aurobindo is a translation of Kalidasa's Vikramorvasiya?
   (a) *The Hero and the Nymph*
   (b) *Urvasie*
   (c) *The Life Divine*
   (d) *Gitanjali*

43. In Sri Aurobindo's poetry which symbol is the supreme symbol of the essence and efflorescence of God?
   (a) Love
   (b) Light
   (c) Rose
   (d) Nature

44. Which work is considered to be the most powerful artistic work in the world for expanding man's mind towards the Absolute?
   (a) *Gitanjali*
   (b) *Savitri*
   (c) *The Life Divine*
   (d) None of the above

45. Which monthly philosophical journal devoted to the exposition of an integral view of life and existence was launched by Madame Mirra Richard (Known as the Mother) and Sri Aurobindo on 15 August 1914?
    (a) *The Bandemataram*
    (b) *The Karmayogin*
    (c) *The Arya*
    (d) None of the above
46. Aurobindo's magnum opus, the philosophical epic "Savitri", started appearing in instalments from
    (a) 1945 onwards
    (b) 1948 onwards
    (c) 1947 onwards
    (d) 1946 onwards
47. In Aurobindo's poem "The Bird of Fire" the bird symbolizes
    (a) Death
    (b) Soul's aspiration
    (c) Life
    (d) God
48. Who became editor of *The Bandemataram*, a new English daily started by Bipin Chandra Pal, in 1906?
    (a) Romesh Chunder Dutt
    (b) Monmohan Ghose
    (c) Sri Aurobindo
    (d) Tagore
49. "The natural miracle was wrought once more/ In the immutable ideal world/ One human moment was eternal made."

    These lines appear in
    (a) *Revelation*
    (b) *Satyavan and Savitri*
    (c) *Transformation*
    (d) *The Tiger and the Deer*
50. Aurobindo's masterpiece *Savitri* has been divided into ________ books.
    (a) 11
    (b) 12
    (c) 13
    (d) 14
51. Which poet had a vision of Lord Krishna in the Alipore Jail?
    (a) Sri Aurobindo
    (b) Tagore
    (c) Toru Dutt
    (d) Sarojini Naidu
52. In which poem Aurobindo observes, "An unseen Hand controls my rudder"?
    (a) "Rose of God"
    (b) "Savitri"
    (c) "The Infinite Adventure"
    (d) "The Bird of Fire"
53. Which of the following was Sarojini Naidu's first volume of poems?
    (a) *The Golden Threshold*
    (b) *The Bird of Time*
    (c) *The Broken Wing*
    (d) *The Features of the Dawn*
54. The above volume was written in
    (a) 1904
    (b) 1905
    (c) 1907
    (d) 1909
55. Which of the following poems is not by Sarojini Naidu?
    (a) Cradlesong
    (b) Child Fancies
    (c) Marriage
    (d) Leili
56. *The Temple* is a trilogy of lyric sequences by
    (a) A.K. Ramanujan
    (b) Sorojini Naidu
    (c) Rabindranath Tagore
    (d) Nissim Ezekiel

57. What is the subtitle of *The Temple*?
    (a) *A True Pilgrimage*
    (b) *A Pilgrim's Pilgrimage*
    (c) *A Pilgrimage to Heaven*
    (d) *A Pilgrimage of Love*
58. How many poems are there in *The Temple*?
    (a) Twelve
    (b) Eighteen
    (c) Twenty four
    (d) Thirty
59. "O Mystic lotus, sacred and sublime,/ In myriad-petalled grace inviolate."
    These lines are by
    (a) Rabindranath Tagore
    (b) Sarojini Naidu
    (c) Jayanta Mahapatra
    (d) Kamala Das
60. Sarojini Naidu composed an English poem at the age of
    (a) 12
    (b) 13
    (c) 14
    (d) 15
61. "Life is a prism of My light/ And Death the Shadow of My face."
    These lines have been uttered by
    (a) Toru Dutt
    (b) Sri Aurobindo
    (c) Sarojini Naidu
    (d) Rabindranath Tagore
62. "Give me to drink each joy and pain/ Which thine eternal hand can mete...."
    These lines appear in
    (a) *The Soul's Prayer*
    (b) *Indian Weavers*
    (c) *Village Song*
    (d) *Caprice*
63. Which is Sarojini Naidu's last collection of poems?
    (a) *The Broken Wing*
    (b) *The Bird of Time*
    (c) *The Golden Threshold*
    (d) *The Lotus*
64. Which poem of Sarojini Naidu is addressed to Gandhi?
    (a) "Village Song"
    (b) "The Lotus"
    (c) "Caprice"
    (d) "The Soul's Prayer"
65. In 1906, at the Calcutta Session of the Indian Social conference which poet/ poetess linked up the suppression of women's rights in India with the loss of the country's freedom?
    (a) Toru Dutt
    (b) Sri Aurobindo
    (c) Sarojini Naidu
    (d) Rabindranath Tagore
66. "Sarojini Naidu's work has a real beauty." Who said this?
    (a) Tagore
    (b) Vivekananda
    (c) Sri Aurobindo
    (d) Mahatma Gandhi
67. Which of the following poems is not by Nissim Ezekiel?
    (a) "Night of the Scorpion"
    (b) "Marriage"
    (c) "Goodbye Party for Miss Pushpa T.S."
    (d) "The Striders"
68. Which of the following plays is not by Nissim Ezekiel?
    (a) *Nalini*
    (b) *Marriage Poem*
    (c) *The Sleepwalkers*
    (d) *The Doldrummers*

69. Which one of the following is not a collection of poems by Ezekiel?
   (a) *Sixty Poems*
   (b) *The Third*
   (c) *The Interior Landscape*
   (d) *The Unfinished Man*
70. Which one is not a collection of poems by Nissim Ezekiel?
   (a) *A Time to Change*
   (b) *The Unfinished Man*
   (c) *The Parrot's Death*
   (d) *The Exact Name*
71. Nissim Ezekiel's play *Nalini* is a
   (a) Tragedy
   (b) Comedy
   (c) Romance
   (d) None of the above
72. Which one of the following Nissim Ezekiel's plays is built on the theme "Give us this day our daily American"?
   (a) *Nalini*
   (b) *The Sleepwalkers*
   (c) *Marriage Poem*
   (d) None of the above
73. Which poem of Nissim Ezekiel is a critique of the man-woman relationship in modern society?
   (a) *Island*
   (b) *Woman and Child*
   (c) *Philosophy*
   (d) *Poet, Lover, Birdwatcher*
74. Who said,

   "My Mother only said
   Thank God the scorpion picked on me
   And spared my Children"?

   (a) P. Lal
   (b) Nissim Ezekiel
   (c) Girish Karnad
   (d) A.K. Ramanujan
75. Which is Ezekiel's first book of poems?
   (a) *A Time to Change*
   (b) *The Unfinished Man*
   (c) *Woman and Child*
   (d) *Island*
76. Which poem of Ezekiel is an autobiographical poem?
   (a) *Background Casually*
   (b) *Island*
   (c) *A Time to Change*
   (d) *Woman and Child*
77. "To force the pace and never to be still/Is not the way of those who study birds or woman."

   These lines have been taken from Ezekiel's poem
   (a) *Woman and Child*
   (b) *Background Casually*
   (c) *Poet, Lover, Birdwatcher*
   (d) *Philosophy*
78. Who has uttered this? "I like to make controlled meaningful statements avoiding extremes of thought and expression."
   (a) Keki N. Daruwalla
   (b) Nissim Ezekiel
   (c) Jayanta Mahapatra
   (d) Kamala Das
79. Who wrote the poem "The Dance of Eunuchs"?
   (a) Kamala Das
   (b) Nissim Ezekiel
   (c) A.K. Ramanujan
   (d) Jayanta Mahapatra
80. In which poem Kamala Das ironically provides a panacea for a happy married life? "Husbands and Wives, here is my advice to you/ Obey each other's crazy commands."
   (a) "An Introduction"
   (b) "In Love"
   (c) "The Descendants"
   (d) "Composition"

81. Who is the writer of *A Doll for the Child Prostitute and Other Stories*?
   (a) Kamala Das
   (b) Sarojini Naidu
   (c) Anita Desai
   (d) Amrita Pritam

82. In which story of Kamala Das lesbian relationship has been described?
   (a) *Iqbal*
   (b) *The Guest*
   (c) *A Doll for the Child Prostitute*
   (d) None of the above

83. "It was not to gather knowledge/ Of yet another man that I came to you but to learn/ What I was, and by learning, to learn to grow, but every/ Lesson you gave was about yourself."

   Who has written this?
   (a) Shiv K. Kumar
   (b) A.K. Ramanujan
   (c) J. Mahapatra
   (d) Kamala Das

84. "Summer in Calcutta" is a poetical collection of
   (a) Jai Nimbkar
   (b) Kamala Das
   (c) Anita Desai
   (d) Nissim Ezekiel

85. Who has said this? "I am an Indian, very brown, born in Malabar."
   (a) K.N. Daruwalla
   (b) Adil Jussawalla
   (c) Kamala Das
   (d) Anita Desai

86. Which one of the following is a confessional poet?
   (a) Nissim Ezekiel
   (b) Kamala Das
   (c) P. Lal
   (d) Shiv K. Kumar

87. *My Story* is the autobiography of
   (a) Nissim Ezekiel
   (b) A.K. Ramanujan
   (c) Kamala Das
   (d) None of the above

88. Which is Shiv K. Kumar's latest book of verse?
   (a) *Articulate Silences*
   (b) *Cobwebs in the Sun*
   (c) *Woolgathering*
   (d) *Woodpeckers*

89. "I know where my wife's secrets lie sealed. Each night I hear the same tattoo in my skull's chamber." These lines appear in
   (a) *Insomnia*
   (b) *Sleep Walking*
   (c) *Subterfuges*
   (d) *Blackout*

90. "In this triple-baked continent/ Women don't etch angry eyebrows/ On mud walls." These lines have been written by
   (a) Jayanta Mahapatra
   (b) Anita Desai
   (c) A.K. Ramanujan
   (d) Shiv K. Kumar

91. In which year Daruwalla won the Sahitya Akademi Award?
   (a) 1981
   (b) 1983
   (c) 1985
   (d) 1984

92. Which poet has described his poetry as a "totally impressionistic recording of subjective responses"?
   (a) Keki N. Daruwalla
   (b) A.K. Ramanujan
   (c) Kamala Das
   (d) Adil Jussawalla

93. Which poem of Daruwalla revolves around the experiences of hatred, violence and death?
    (a) "Rumination"
    (b) "Death of a Bird"
    (c) "The Ghaghra in Spate"
    (d) "The Professor Condoles"

94. R. Parthasarathy is a
    (a) Poet
    (b) Critic
    (c) Editor
    (d) All of the above

95. Who wrote the poem "Towards an Understanding of India"?
    (a) Kamala Das
    (b) R. Parthasarathy
    (c) P. Lal
    (d) Nissim Ezekiel

96. Parthasarathy's *Rough Passage*, a collection of 37 poems, appeared in
    (a) 1975
    (b) 1976
    (c) 1977
    (d) 1978

97. "Cultivating an extreme austerity in style...his poems are so few but they are marble images of integrity...."

    Here 'his' refers to
    (a) G.V. Desani
    (b) R. Parthasarathy
    (c) Kamala Das
    (d) Anita Desai

98. "To live in Tamil Nadu is to be conscious everyday of an importance."

    This line appears in the poem
    (a) "Homecoming"
    (b) "Delhi"
    (c) "Dawn at Puri"
    (d) "The Mountain"

99. Which is the volume written by R. Parthasarathy?
    (a) *Rough Passage*
    (b) *Subterfuges*
    (c) *Articulate Silences*
    (d) *Woodpeckers*

100. Who, among the following poets, was a Parsi educated at Anglian School in Bombay?
    (a) Adil Jussawalla
    (b) R. Parthasarathy
    (c) Anita Desai
    (d) Gieve Patel

101. The poem "The Waiters" has been taken from Jussawalla's volume
    (a) *Missing Person*
    (b) *Land's End*
    (c) *New Writing in India*
    (d) None of the above

102. "Behind our pasted smiles; their darkness grew/ To insight in their day; they stand aloof."

    These lines appear in the poem
    (a) "Sea Breeze, Bombay"
    (b) "The Waiters"
    (c) "The Boat ride"
    (d) None of the above

103. The poems titled "Cord-Cutting", "Post-Mortem Report", "The Difference in the Morgue" and "Old Man's Death" are by
    (a) Adil Jussawalla
    (b) Keki Daruwalla
    (c) Gieve Patel
    (d) Nissim Ezekiel

104. Which of the following poets is a physician by profession?
    (a) Gieve Patel
    (b) Nissim Ezekiel
    (c) R. Parthasarathy
    (d) Jayanta Mahapatra

105. The poem titled "On Killing a Tree" is by
   (a) Gieve Patel
   (b) A.K. Ramanujan
   (c) Adil Jussawalla
   (d) Kamala Das

106. "Then the matter/ Of Scorching and choking/ In sun and air,/ Browning, hardening/ Twisting, withering." These lines appear in
   (a) "Forensic Medicine"
   (b) "Hunger"
   (c) "On Killing a Tree"
   (d) "The Mountain"

107. Jayanta Mahapatra is obsessed with the past and the present of
   (a) Assam
   (b) West Bengal
   (c) Orissa
   (d) Karnataka

108. "Thinking to escape his beliefs/ I go to meet the spectre of belief"

   These lines have been written by
   (a) Jayanta Mahapatra
   (b) Gieve Patel
   (c) Anita Desai
   (d) Arun Kolatkar

109. "Late in the evening of life/ An embarrassment prevents the world from speaking"

   These lines have been taken from
   (a) "Again One Day Walking by the River"
   (b) "Hunger"
   (c) "Dawn at Puri"
   (d) "The Mountain"

110. Which work of Mahapatra won him the Sahitya Akademi Award in 1981?
   (a) *The False Start*
   (b) *Relationship*
   (c) *Close the Sky*
   (d) *Waiting*

111. Arun Kolatkar is a bilingual poet who writes both in
   (a) Marathi and English
   (b) Bengali and English
   (c) Punjabi and English
   (d) Bengali and Marathi

112. Which poem of Kolatkar has been considered as the poet's Odyssey to the temple of Khandoba at Jejuri, a small town in western Maharashtra?
   (a) "The Boatride"
   (b) "The Bus"
   (c) "Jejuri"
   (d) None of the above

113. In the poem "The Bus" each stanza is of how many lines?
   (a) 1
   (b) 2
   (c) 3
   (d) 4

114. Who wrote *Phoenix Fled* (1953) a collection of short stories?
   (a) Miss Attia Hosain
   (b) Ruth Prawer Jhabvala
   (c) Kamala Markandaya
   (d) Anita Desai

115. *Hind Swaraj* was written by
   (a) Jawahar Lal Nehru
   (b) Mahatma Gandhi
   (c) Dr. Radhakrishnan
   (d) Bankim Chandra

116. Who is the writer of *The Mahatma and the Ism* (1958)?
   (a) D.G. Tendulkar
   (b) P.A. Wadia
   (c) E.M.S. Namboodripad
   (d) D.F. Karaka

117. Which is not written by J.L. Nehru?
   (a) *Glimpses of World History*
   (b) *Letters from a Father to a Daughter*

(c) *My Experiments with Truth*
(d) *Discovery of India*

118. Nehru dedicated his autobiography to
(a) Mahatma Gandhi
(b) Kamala Nehru
(c) People of India
(d) Indira Gandhi

119. The story of *My Experiments with Truth*, the autobiography of Mahatma Gandhi, was published in the year
(a) 1924
(b) 1925
(c) 1926
(d) 1927

120. "Quit India": Leave India to God and if that be too much, leave her to anarchy". Who has said this?
(a) Gandhi
(b) Nehru
(c) Vivekananda
(d) Radhakrishnan

121. Who gave the slogan 'Do and Learn'?
(a) Jawahar Lal Nehru
(b) Mahatma Gandhi
(c) Rabindranath Tagore
(d) K.M. Munshi

122. "Non-Violence is the first article of my faith. It is also the last article of my creed...."

Who has said this?
(a) Jawaharlal Nehru
(b) S. Radhakrishnan
(c) Mahatma Gandhi
(d) Vivekananda

123. "Kundan, the Patriot", which was written after the appearance of Gandhi on the Indian horizon, was composed by
(a) K.M. Munshi
(b) Mahatma Gandhi
(c) Vivekananda
(d) K.S. Venkataramani

124. Who gave the slogan 'Swaraj is my birthright'?
(a) Tilak
(b) Nehru
(c) Gokhale
(d) M.A. Jinnah

125. Who was the editor of *The National Herald*?
(a) Kuldip Nayar
(b) K. Rangaswami
(c) V.K. Narasimhan
(d) M. Chalapathi Rau

126. Who, among the following personalities, has been the Vice Chancellor of Benaras Hindu University?
(a) M.G. Ranade
(b) Nirad C. Chaudhuri
(c) S. Radhakrishnan
(d) Jawahar Lal Nehru

127. "Mother in one form thou art in the street, and in another form thou art the Universe.

I salute Thee Mother, I salute Thee."
(a) Vivekananda
(b) Tagore
(c) Aurobindo
(d) Gandhi

128. In which work Radhakrishnan subjected the thought of Western thinkers-Bergson, William James and Bertrand Russell, to a searching examination in the light of the absolute thought of the Upanishads?
(a) *The Reign of Religion in Contemporary Philosophy*
(b) *The Hindu View of Life*
(c) *The Philosophy of Rabindranath Tagore*
(d) *An Idealist View of Life*

129. Who has written *Reason and Intuition in Indian Culture*?

(a) Mahatma Gandhi
(b) N. Raghunathan
(c) S. Radhakrishnan
(d) Vivekananda

130. Who is the author of *A Passage to England*?
(a) Mahatma Gandhi
(b) Nirad C. Chaudhuri
(c) R.K. Narayan
(d) Khushwant Singh

131. Which was the first book of N.C. Chaudhuri?
(a) *The Autobiography of an Unknown Indian*
(b) *The Continent of Circle*
(c) *A Passage to England*
(d) None of the above

132. "I know I am extreme. It is like a tug-of-war: I cannot stand up straight, or the other side will pull me down. But know my exaggerations."

Who has said this?
(a) Mulk Raj Anand
(b) Khushwant Singh
(c) Jawaharlal Nehru
(d) N.C. Chaudhuri

133. Which play was written earlier by Asif Currimbhoy?
(a) *The Miracle Seed*
(b) *The Dissident MLA*
(c) *Sonar Bangla*
(d) *Inquilab*

134. *To Live or Not to Live* was written by
(a) Ved Mehta
(b) Khushwant Singh
(c) Nirad C. Chaudhuri
(d) R.K. Narayan

135. *Bhagwan Parashurama* was written by
(a) Dilip Kumar
(b) K.M. Munshi
(c) G.V. Desani
(d) Gita Mehta

136. *Miracles Do Still Happen* and *The Upward Spiral* are works of
(a) Gita Mehta
(b) K.M. Munshi
(c) Dilip Kumar Roy
(d) Sudhin N. Ghose

137. Who is the writer of the novel *Ambapali* (1962) an ambitious historical novel set in ancient India of the Buddha's time?
(a) Mrs. Anita Chaudhary
(b) Anita Desai
(c) Mrs. Muriel Wasi
(d) Vimala Raina

138. In which of the novel Humayun Kabir has vividly pictured the life of the children of the Padma in Bengal
(a) *Men and Rivers*
(b) *Love of Dust*
(c) *Britain and India*
(d) None of the above

139. Who, among the following writers, is the *Laureate of the Body*?
(a) Keki N. Daruwalla
(b) Shiv K. Kumar
(c) A.K. Ramanujan
(d) K.D. Katrak

140. Sisir Kumar Ghose's *Modern and Otherwise* (1975) is a collection of
(a) Essays
(b) Poems
(c) Novels
(d) Stories

141. Chandran is the central character of the novel
(a) *Swami and Friends*
(b) *The Bachelor of Arts*
(c) *The English Teacher*
(d) *Mr. Sampath*

142. "I have never opposed my husband or argued with him at any time. What he does is right. It is a wife's duty to feel so."

These lines appear in the novel *The Dark Room*.

Who is the speaker?

(a) Gangu
(b) Savitri
(c) Janamma
(d) Ponni

143. Which is the only novel of Narayan in which he has depicted a co-wife?

(a) *Grandmother's Tale*
(b) *The Dark Room*
(c) *The World of Nagraj*
(d) *The Guide*

144. Name the first recipient of the Sahitya Akademi Award for the best writing in English.

(a) R.K. Narayan
(b) Raja Rao
(c) Mulk Raj Anand
(d) Khushwant Singh

145. On which novel of R.K. Narayan a very popular film was made?

(a) *Waiting for the Mahatma*
(b) *Malgudi Days*
(c) *The Guide*
(d) *Mr. Sampath*

146. Identify the work of Narayan on which a very popular T.V. serial was made

(a) *Malgudi Days*
(b) *Mr. Sampath*
(c) *The Bachelor of Arts*
(d) *The Man-Eater of Malgudi*

147. Which is the first novel of R.K. Narayan?

(a) *The Bachelor of Arts*
(b) *Swami and Friends*
(c) *The Dark Room*
(d) *The English Teacher*

148. Which novel of Narayan won the Sahitya Akademi Award in 1960?

(a) *The English Teacher*
(b) *The Vendor of Sweets*
(c) *Waiting for the Mahatma*
(d) *The Guide*

149. "A dose of prison life is not a bad thing.

It may be just what he needs now",

Who is the speaker?

(a) Jagan in *The Vendor of Sweets*
(b) Raju in *The Guide*
(c) Margayya in *The Financial Expert*
(d) Chandran in *The Bachelor of Arts*

150. Who wrote an introduction to R.K. Narayan's novel *The Financial Expert* (1955)?

(a) Mulk Raj Anand
(b) Raja Rao
(c) Graham Greene
(d) E.M. Forster

151. In which of the novels of R.K. Narayan, Malgudi first appeared?

(a) *Swami and Friends* (1935)
(b) *Bachelor of Arts* (1936)
(c) *The Dark Room* (1933)
(d) *The Man-Eater of Malgudi* (1961)

152. Who is the *The Man-Eater of Malgudi* in R.K. Narayan's novel *The Man-Eater of Malgudi*?

(a) Natraj
(b) Muthu
(c) Vasu
(d) Kumar

153. R.K. Narayan's *A Horse with Two Goats* and *Malgudi Days* are collections of

(a) Short Stories
(b) Novellas
(c) Poems
(d) None of the above

154. Which of the following contains R.K. Narayan's US travel memoirs?
   (a) *Lawley Road*
   (b) *My Dateless Diary*
   (c) *An Astrologer's Day and Other Short Stories*
   (d) *A Horse and Two Goats*

155. Name the writer of *The Painter of Signs*.
   (a) Raja Rao
   (b) R.K. Narayan
   (c) Khushwant Singh
   (d) Ruth P. Jhabvalla

156. Narayan created the fictitious town of Malgudi which is similar to
   (a) T.S. Eliot's *Waste Land*
   (b) Hardy's *Wessex*
   (c) Pope's *London*
   (d) Chaucer's *Canterbury*

157. Which is Anand's only novel in which a woman has been chosen as the central character?
   (a) *The Village*
   (b) *Untouchable*
   (c) *Coolie*
   (d) *The Old Woman and the Cow*

158. Which novel of Anand discusses the theme of exploitation of coolies working in a tea garden at the hands of British officials?
   (a) *The Village*
   (b) *Across the Black Waters*
   (c) *The Sword and the Sickle*
   (d) *Two Leaves and a Bud*

159. Lalu is the central character in the novel
   (a) *The Big Heart*
   (b) *Untouchable*
   (c) *The Village*
   (d) *The Death of a Hero*

160. Which is the earliest book of Mulk Raj Anand?
   (a) *Curries and other Indian Dishes*
   (b) *The Golden Breath*
   (c) *Persian Painting*
   (d) *The Hindu View of Art*

161. "I regard untouchability as the greatest blot on Hinduism."

   This sentence occurs in the novel
   (a) *Coolie*
   (b) *Untouchable*
   (c) *The Village*
   (d) *Two Leaves and a Bud*

162. Which novelist sees life sometimes as a comedy sometimes as a tragedy and sometimes the two modes fuse distractingly?
   (a) Raja Rao
   (b) R.K. Narayan
   (c) Mulk Raj Anand
   (d) Bhabani Bhattacharya

163. In which one of the following novels of Mulk Raj Anand, Munoo is the chief Character?
   (a) *Untouchable* (1935)
   (b) *Coolie* (1936)
   (c) *Two Leaves and a Bud* (1937)
   (d) *The Village* (1939)

164. Name the first novel of Mulk Raj Anand which carried a preface by E.M. Forster that won him world-wide recognition?
   (a) *Coolie*
   (b) *Two Leaves and a Bud*
   (c) *Untouchable*
   (d) *The Village*

165. Which is known as a total novel of human experience written by Mulk Raj Anand?
   (a) *The Big Heart*
   (b) *Morning Face*
   (c) *Across the Black Waters*
   (d) *Coolie*

166. The first novel in the *Seven Ages of Man* series by Mulk Raj Anand is
   (a) *The Sword and the Sickle*
   (b) *The Road*
   (c) *Seven Summers*
   (d) *Two Leaves and a Bud*

167. In which novel the action is spread over some years and moves from village to town, from town to city and from city to Bombay and from Bombay to Shimla?
   (a) *The Village*
   (b) *Untouchable*
   (c) *Across the Black Waters*
   (d) *Coolie*

168. Which novel has been called 'a character novel' by Edwin Muir?
   (a) *Coolie*
   (b) *Untouchable*
   (c) *Two Leaves and a Bud*
   (d) *The Village*

169. "It actually proves to be a sort of madhouse and people are cruel because they can't be happy."

   The line appears in the novel
   (a) *Untouchable*
   (b) *Coolie*
   (c) *The Village*
   (d) None of the above

170. In which novel is there a conflict between the thathiars (the hereditary coppersmith) and the capitalists?
   (a) *Two Leaves and a Bud*
   (b) *The Big Heart*
   (c) *The Village*
   (d) *Private Life of an Indian Prince*

171. ...by Mulk Raj Anand is about adolescent, poetry and love.
   (a) *The Road*
   (b) *The Confession of a Lover*
   (c) *Lament on the Death of a Master of Arts*
   (d) *The Death of a Hero*

172. Identify the story that is not written by Mulk Raj Anand.
   (a) *The Cobbler and the Machine*
   (b) *The Astrologer*
   (c) *The Parrot in the Cage*
   (d) *Barber's Trade Union*

173. Which of the following books has not been written by Raja Rao?
   (a) *The Serpent and the Rope*
   (b) *On the Ganga Ghat*
   (c) *Swami and Friends*
   (d) *Kanthapura*

174. One of the following collections of short-stories is not of Raja Rao. Identify it.
   (a) *The Cat and Shakespeare*
   (b) *The Cow of the Barricades*
   (c) *The Policeman and the Rose*
   (d) *On the Ganga Ghat*

175. Which is the first novel of Raja Rao?
   (a) *Kanthapura*
   (b) *The Serpent and the Rope*
   (c) *The Cat and Shakespeare*
   (d) None of the above

176. What is a policeman before a Gandhi's man?

   Tell me, does a boar stand before a lion or a jackal before an elephant?

   These lines appear in the novel
   (a) *The Serpent and the Rope*
   (b) *Kanthapura*
   (c) *The Financial Expert*
   (d) *The Man-Eater of Malgudi*

177. In which novel of Raja Rao, the story has been narrated by a Brahmin widow?
   (a) *Kanthapura*
   (b) *The Cat and Shakespeare*
   (c) *The Serpent and the Rope*
   (d) None of the above

178. "...woman is the microcosm of the mind, the articulations of space, the knowing in

knowledge; the woman is fire...the woman is that which seeks against that which is sought."

Who has said this?

(a) Mulk Raj Anand
(b) Raja Rao
(c) R.K. Narayan
(d) N.C. Chaudhari

179. Ramakrishna Pai, a clerk, is the narrator in the novel
(a) *Kanthapura*
(b) *The Serpent and the Rope*
(c) *The Cat and Shakespeare*
(d) None of the above

180. Which work of Raja Rao has been called 'a Metaphysical Comedy'?
(a) *The Serpent and the Rope*
(b) *The Cat and Shakespeare*
(c) *Kanthapura*
(d) *The Cow of the Barricades*

181. Which one of the following novels by Raja Ram Mohan Rao may be summed up as 'Gandhi and Our Village?
(a) *Kanthapura* (1938)
(b) *The Serpent and the Rope* (1960)
(c) *The Cat and Shakespeare* (1965)
(d) None of the above

182. Who is the hero in Raja Rao's novel *Comrade Kirillov* (1976)?
(a) Padmanabhan Iyer
(b) Irene
(c) Kamal
(d) None of the above

183. Bhabani Bhattacharya's first published book was
(a) *So Many Hungers*
(b) *Music for Mohini*
(c) *He Who Rides a Tiger*
(d) *Shadow from Ladakh*

184. In which novel Bhattacharya tells the story of a Calcutta born Brahmin girl?
(a) *He Who Rides a Tiger*
(b) *Music for Mohini*
(c) *So Many Hungers*
(d) None of the above

185. "You are city-bred, village-wed. I am village bred, city-wed, We share one common lot: we've been pulled up by the roots."

These lines have been uttered by...in *Music for Mohini.*
(a) Mohini
(b) Jayadev
(c) Rooplekha
(d) Sudha

186. Which novel is described as "a modern fable of India at the time of Independence"?
(a) *Music for Mohini*
(b) *So Many Hungers*
(c) *A Goddess Named Gold*
(d) None of the above

187. "The dark spaces between a man and woman have to be lit with sympathy and comprehension...."

This line appears in the novel
(a) *Shadow from Ladakh*
(b) *Music for Mohini*
(c) *He who Rides a Tiger*
(d) None of the above

188. Which one of the following Bhabani Bhattacharya's novels is about the Bengal famine?
(a) *He Who Rides a Tiger*
(b) *Shadow from Ladakh*
(c) *So Many Hungers*
(d) *Music for Mohini*

189. Who is the writer of the novel *A Dream in Hawaii* (1978)?

(a) Manohar Malgonkar
(b) R.K. Narayan
(c) Bhabani Bhattacharya
(d) Khushwant Singh

190. P.P. Mehta quotes, "His novels are conceived on a large scale, they are full of action, they are exciting stories. They are also valuable documents."

Who is being referred to here?
(a) Khushwant Singh
(b) Manohar Malgonkar
(c) R.K. Narayan
(d) Raja Rao

191. Which novel of Manohar Malgonkar deals with the inter-related themes of violence and non-violence, and with the pre-independence phase of Indian history?
(a) *A Bend in the Ganges*
(b) *The Devil's Wing*
(c) *A Toast of Warm Wine*
(d) *Distant Drums*

192. Identify the novel of Malgonkar which narrates the story of the so-called Indian mutiny and Nana Sahib told from the Indian point of View?
(a) *Dead and Living Cities*
(b) *Shalimar*
(c) *The Devil's Wind*
(d) *The Princes*

193. Which of the following is not a work of Manohar Malgonkar?
(a) *The Rose World*
(b) *Spy in Amber*
(c) *Combat of Shadows*
(d) *Dead and Living Cities*

194. What is the central theme of Manohar Malgonkar's novel *A Bend in the Ganges*?
(a) The communal riots following the partition of India
(b) The Jallianwala massacre
(c) The Martyrdom of Bhagat Singh
(d) The Sepoy Rebellion of 1857

195. Which is the first novel of Manohar Malgonkar?
(a) *Distant Drums*
(b) *A Bend in the Ganges*
(c) *Combat of Shadows*
(d) *The Princes*

196. Which is the first novel of Anita Desai?
(a) *Voices in the City*
(b) *Cry, The Peacock*
(c) *Bye-Bye Blackbird*
(d) *Fire on the Mountain*

197. Which novel of Anita Desai depicts Maya, the central character, who kills her husband Gautama and then herself commits suicide?
(a) *Voices in the City*
(b) *Cry, The Peacock*
(c) *Where Shall we Go This Summer*
(d) *Clear Light of Day*

198. Which novel of Anita Desai is considered to be 'an epic on Calcutta'?
(a) *Bye-Bye Blackbird*
(b) *Voices in the City*
(c) *The Village by the Sea*
(d) *Fire on the Mountain*

199. Which novel is divided into three parts Arrival, Discovery and Recognition?
(a) *Fire on the Mountain*
(b) *Cry, The Peacock*
(c) *Baumgartner's Bombay*
(d) *Bye-Bye Blackbird*

200. Anita Desai was given Sahitya Akademi Award for which novel?
(a) *Clear Light of Day*
(b) *The Village by the Sea*
(c) *Fire on the Mountain*
(d) *Cry, The Peacock*

201. Which novel of Anita Desai has been considered more individual less generalized and conventional than her earliest fiction?
(a) *In Custody*
(b) *Cry, The Peacock*
(c) *Voices in the City*
(d) *Clear Light of Day*

202. Who is the heroine in Anita Desai's recent novel *Clear Light of Day* (1980)?
(a) Maya
(b) Bhim
(c) Tara
(d) None of the above

203. For which novel Shashi Deshpande was awarded Sahitya Akademi Award?
(a) *That Long Silence*
(b) *Roots and Shadows*
(c) *The Dark Holds No Terrors*
(d) *The Legacy*

204. Which work of Shashi Deshpande has been translated into German and Russian?
(a) *The Dark Holds No Terrors*
(b) *The Legacy*
(c) *Come up and Be Dead*
(d) *That Long Silence*

205. Deshpande's stories mainly deal with
(a) Woman's struggle
(b) Social struggle
(c) Political struggle
(d) Economic struggle

206. "Every thing in a girl's life was shaped to that single purpose of pleasing a male."
This line appears in the novel
(a) *Come up and Be Dead*
(b) *The Legacy*
(c) *The Dark Holds No Terrors*
(d) *That Long Silence*

207. Which is the first novel written by Shashi Deshpande?
(a) *The Dark Holds No Terrors*
(b) *Roots and Shadows*
(c) *Come up and Be Dead*
(d) *That Long Silence*

208. Which is the last and most satisfying novel of Shashi Deshpande?
(a) *That Long Silence*
(b) *Come up and Be Dead*
(c) *Small Remedies*
(d) None of the above

209. *Selective Memory* is the autobiography of
(a) Shobha De
(b) Anita Desai
(c) Manju Kapoor
(d) Nayantara Sahgal

210. Which is the first novel of Shobha De?
(a) *Socialite Evenings*
(b) *Sisters*
(c) *Snapshots*
(d) *Strange Obsession*

211. Which novel of Shobha De deals with a story of six women—Aparna, Rashmi, Swati, Rima, Surekha and Noor?
(a) *Sisters*
(b) *Snapshots*
(c) *Sultry Days*
(d) None of the above

212. Kamla Markanday's first novel is
(a) *Nectar in a Sieve*
(b) *Some Inner Fury*
(c) *Possession*
(d) *Two Virgins*

213. Rukmani is the central character in
(a) *Some Inner Fury*
(b) *Nectar in a Sieve*
(c) *A Silence of Desire*
(d) *A Handful of Rice*

214. Ravi and Nalini are the main characters in Markandaya's novel.
(a) *A Handful of Rice*

(b) *Nectar in a Sieve*
(c) *Some Inner Fury*
(d) None of the above

215. Which novel of Kamala Markandaya has been compared with Pearl S. Buck's *The Good Earth* and K.S. Venkataramani's *Murugan, the Tiller?*
(a) *Some Inner Fury*
(b) *A Silence of Desire*
(c) *Nectar in a Sieve*
(d) *A Handful of Rice*

216. Kamala Markandaya's novel *Two Virgins* is about two village girls
(a) Lalitha and Manju
(b) Saroja and Rewati
(c) Asha and Manju
(d) Lalitha and Saroja

217. Which novel of Kamala Markandaya is considered to be a historical novel?
(a) *The Golen Honeycomb*
(b) *No Whereman*
(c) *Nectar in a Sieve*
(d) *Some Inner Fury*

218. Which novel of Kamala Markandaya explores the evil and ugly nature of racial prejudice?
(a) *The Nowhere Man*
(b) *Possession*
(c) *Some Inner Fury*
(d) *Nectar in a Sieve*

219. In which novel, the scene shifts from India to England and America and again back to India?
(a) *A Silence of Desire*
(b) *Possession*
(c) *A Handful of Rice*
(d) *Nectar in a Sieve*

220. Which character of Ruth Prawer Jhabvala is a passionate woman longing for romantic adventures at forty?
(a) *Asha in A New Dominion*
(b) *Kusum in Get Ready for Battle*
(c) *Shakuntala in Esmond in India*
(d) *Nimmi in The Nature of Passion*

221. Jhabvala won the Booker Prize for the novel
(a) *Heat and Dust*
(b) *Esmond in India*
(c) *The Nature of Passion*
(d) *A New Dominion*

222. In which story, Ruth Prawer Jhabvala using the stream-of-consciousness technique, depicts the mind of an incompetent unemployed young graduate?
(a) *A Loss of Faith*
(b) *The Interview*
(c) *A Star and Two Girls*
(d) *Suffering Women*

223. Which is the first novel of Ruth Prawer Jhabvala?
(a) *To Whom She Will*
(b) *The Householder*
(c) *The Nature of Passion*
(d) *Esmond in India*

224. East-West encounter is the dominant theme in the stories in the collection.
(a) *A Stronger Climate*
(b) *An Experience of India*
(c) *Like Birds, like Fishes and Other Stories*
(d) *How I Became A Holy Mother and Other Stories*

225. Who is the central character in Anita Nair's novel *Ladies Coupe?*
(a) Janaki
(b) Akhilendeswari
(c) Margret
(d) Prabha

226. *The Better Man* is the first novel of
(a) Anita Nair
(b) Shobha De

(c) Bharati Mukherjee
(d) Shashi Deshpande

227. Which is the first novel written by Nayantara Sahgal?
(a) *This Time of Morning*
(b) *A Time to be Happy*
(c) *Storm in Chandigarh*
(d) *The Day in Shadow*

228. Which is the last novel of Nayantara Sahgal?
(a) *Storm in Chandigarh*
(b) *A Time to be Happy*
(c) *This Time of Morning*
(d) None of the above

229. *Rich Like Us* is a well-known novel of
(a) Shobha De
(b) Ruth Prawer Jhabvala
(c) Nayantara Sahgal
(d) Manju Kapoor

230. Which novel of Nayantara Sahgal has been written against the background of politics?
(a) *A Situation in New Delhi*
(b) *Storm in Chandigarh*
(c) *The Day in Shadow*
(d) None of the above

231. Who is the winner of the 1999 Commonwealth Writer's Prize for the best first book *Difficult Daughters*?
(a) Githa Hariharan
(b) Arundhati Roy
(c) Manju Kapoor
(d) Shashi Deshpande

232. Which novel deals with the theme of lesbianism?
(a) *Difficult Daughters*
(b) *A Married Woman*
(c) *Storm in Chandigarh*
(d) *Roots and Shadows*

233. "Communal riot is a terrible disease that kills God in man." Who has observed this?
(a) Shobha De
(b) Arundhati Roy
(c) Nayantara Sahgal
(d) Manju Kapoor

234. In which novel, the issue of Babri Masjid and Ram Janambhoomi, has been referred to?
(a) *A Married Woman*
(b) *Socialite Evenings*
(c) *That Long Silence*
(d) *Storm in Chandigarh*

235. The setting of *The God of Small Things* is in India's southern state of
(a) Kerala
(b) Karnataka
(c) Tamil Nadu
(d) Andhra Pradesh

236. Who is the untouchable in *The God of Small Things*?
(a) Esthappen
(b) Velutha
(c) Father Mulligan
(d) Pappachi

237. Which novel has won the English-speaking world's most prestigious award, the Booker Prize?
(a) *Train to Pakistan*
(b) *So Many Hungers*
(c) *The God of Small Things*
(d) *Interpreter of Maladies*

238. The title of Bharti Mukherjee's novel *The Holder of the World* is after the name of a Mughal Emperor. Who is he?
(a) Aurangzeb
(b) Humayun
(c) Shahjahan
(d) Akbar

239. Which book of Mukherjee bagged the 1988 National Book Critics Award in America?

(a) *The Tiger's Daughter*
(b) *Jasmine*
(c) *The Middleman and Other Stories*
(d) None of the above

240. Who is the first Asian writer to win an individual Pulitzer Prize, America's ultimate literary accolade?
(a) Saul Bellow
(b) Earnest Hemingway
(c) Jhumpa Lahiri
(d) Pearl S. Buck

241. According to Khushwant Singh, which story of Jhumpa Lahiri is perhaps the best in the collections?
(a) *The Third and Final Continent*
(b) *Interpreter of Maladies*
(c) *A Real Durwan*
(d) *The Blessed House*

242. Jhumpa Lahiri's *Interpreter of Maladies* has how many stories?
(a) 8
(b) 9
(c) 10
(d) 11

243. Which is the opening story in *Interpreter of Maladies*?
(a) "A Temporary Matter"
(b) "Interpreter of Maladies"
(c) "The Treatment of Bibi Halder"
(d) "A Real Durwan"

244. Which story of Lahiri has Indo-Pak war of 1971 and the birth of Bangladesh as its backdrop?
(a) "The Third and Final Continent"
(b) "A Real Durwan"
(c) "When Mr. Pirzada Came to Dine
(d) "The Temporary Matter"

245. The novel *The Namesake* is written by
(a) Jhumpa Lahiri
(b) Shashi Deshpande
(c) Anita Desai
(d) Manju Kapoor

246. *Sunlight on a Broken Column* is the first novel written by
(a) Attia Hosain
(b) Ruth Prawer Jhabvala
(c) Salman Rushdie
(d) Jhumpa Lahiri

247. *Phoenix Fled* is a collection of short stories written by
(a) Shashi Deshpande
(b) Anita Desai
(c) Attia Hosain
(d) Ruth Prawer Jhabvala

248. *Lajja* is a well known work of
(a) Shobha De
(b) Taslima Nasreen
(c) Manju Kapoor
(d) Bharti Mukherjee

249. Which novel is a recollection of Nasreen's real life incidents of her childhood days?
(a) *Mere Bachpan Ke Din*
(b) *Fera*
(c) *Aurat Ke Haque Main*
(d) *Lajja*

250. Salman Rushdie's fascination with "Aesop's Fables" and "Panchtantra" is evident from his novel
(a) *Midnight's Children*
(b) *Grimus*
(c) *The Satanic Verses*
(d) *Shame*

251. Rushdie's first novel is
(a) *Grimus*
(b) *Midnight's Children*
(c) *Shame*
(d) *The Satanic Verses*

252. For which of the following works was Salman Rushdie declared a Kafir by the Muslim world?

(a) *Midnight's Children*
(b) *Shame*
(c) *The Satanic Verses*
(d) *Grimus*

253. Which novel of the Salman Rushdie has won the Booker Prize as well as the James Tait Black Memorial Prize?
(a) *The Satanic Verses*
(b) *The Moor's Last Sigh*
(c) *Shame*
(d) *Midnight's Children*

254. The title of the novel *Midnight's Children* refers to the children born in the midnight hour of
(a) 15 August 1947
(b) 26 January 1950
(c) 15 August 1950
(d) 22 June 1942

255. Name the author of *Train to Pakistan.*
(a) Raja Rao
(b) R.K. Narayan
(c) Khushwant Singh
(d) Mulk Raj Anand

256. Who has translated Rajender Singh Bedi's Urdu novel *Ek Chadar Maili Si* into English as *I Take This Woman*?
(a) Arun Joshi
(b) Khushwant Singh
(c) Ruskin Bond
(d) Shashi Tharoor

257. In the novel *I Shall Not Hear, the Nightingale*, 'I' stands for which character?
(a) Buta Singh
(b) Champak
(c) Sher Singh
(d) Sabhrai

258. The novel *I Shall Not Hear the Nightingale* concentrates on the inner tensions and external movements of a Sikh family in the Punjab during?
(a) April 1942 - April 1943
(b) May 1942 - May 1943
(c) June 1943 - June 1944
(d) June 1942 - June 1943

259. Mohan Kumar is the central character in which of Khushwant Singh's novels?
(a) *Train to Pakistan*
(b) *Delhi*
(c) *I Shall Not Hear the Nightingale*
(d) *The Company of Women*

260. *The Shirt of Flame* is a novel in verse written by
(a) Rajender Singh
(b) Khushwant Singh
(c) Vikram Seth
(d) Mahip Singh

261. The title of which novel has been taken from T.S. Eliot's *Four Quartets?*
(a) *Train to Pakistan*
(b) *The Riot*
(c) *The Shirt of Flame*
(d) *The Golden Gate*

262. Which novel won Chaman Nahal Sahitya Akademi Award?
(a) *The English Queens*
(b) *Azadi*
(c) *Into Another Dawn*
(d) *My True Faces*

263. Which is the first novel of Chaman Nahal?
(a) *The Crown and the Loincloth*
(b) *My True Faces*
(c) *The English Queens*
(d) *Azadi*

264. Which is the first novel of Vikram Seth?
(a) *An Equal Music*
(b) *A Golden Gate*
(c) *A Suitable Boy*
(d) None of the above

265. Which two authors have been described as 'Terrible Twins' of Indo-English fiction?

(a) Salman Rushdie and Vikram Seth
(b) Vikram Seth and Shashi Tharoor
(c) Shashi Tharoor and Salman Rushdie
(d) Arun Joshi and Vikram Seth

266. Vikram Seth has written a novel in verse under the title
(a) *The Golden Breath*
(b) *The Golden Threshold*
(c) *The Golden Gate*
(d) *The Golden Bough*

267. "Once you have lived with mountains, there is no escape. You belong to them" Who has said this?
(a) Arun Joshi
(b) Rushkin Bond
(c) Shiv K. Kumar
(d) Vikram Seth

268. In Bond's work we get a glimpse of
(a) Rural life
(b) Town life
(c) City life
(d) Urban life

269. *Our Trees Still Grow at Dehradun* is a work of
(a) Ruskin Bond
(b) Manohar Malgonkar
(c) Chaman Nahal
(d) Shashi Tharoor

270. *The Last Tiger* is a well-known novel written by
(a) Ruskin Bond
(b) Ved Mehta
(c) K.M. Munshi
(d) Vikram Chandra

271. Which is the last novel of Arun Joshi?
(a) *The City and the River*
(b) *The Strange case of Billy Biswas*
(c) *The Apprentice*
(d) *The Foreigner*

272. Which novel of Arun Joshi is distantly inspired by Albert Camus's *The Outsider*?
(a) *The Foreigner*
(b) *The Apprentice*
(c) *The Strange Case of Billy Biswas*
(d) *The Last Labyrinth*

273. Which is the first novel of Arun Joshi?
(a) *The Apprentice*
(b) *The Foreigner*
(c) *The Strange Case of Billy Biswas*
(d) *The Last labyrinth*

274. Which work of Ved Mehta is autobiographical?
(a) *Face to Face*
(b) *Delinquent Chacha*
(c) *Fly and the Fly Bottle*
(d) *The New Theologian*

275. "Here, ladies and gentlemen, is a building of milk-white marble...think not that the Taj belongs only to India. It belongs to you." These lines have been spoken by
(a) Khushwant Singh
(b) Rajinder Singh Bedi
(c) Chaman Nahal
(d) Ved Mehta

276. Which novel has been written by Anand Lal?
(a) *The House at Adampur*
(b) *Seasons of Jupiter*
(c) Both (a) and (b)
(d) None of the above

277. The protagonist of Anand Lal's second novel *Seasons of Jupiter*, Rai Gyan Chand belongs to which town?
(a) Amritsar
(b) Hyderabad
(c) Udaipur
(d) Bangalore

278. *The Dark Dancer* is the first novel of
(a) Khushwant Singh

(b) Vikram Seth
(c) Salman Rushdie
(d) Balchandra Rajan

279. Tridib is the central character in Amitav Ghosh's novel
(a) *The Shadow Lines*
(b) *The Circle of Reason*
(c) *The Calcutta Chromosome*
(d) *The Countdown*

280. Which is the first novel of Amitav Ghosh?
(a) *The Glass Palace*
(b) *The Shadow Lines*
(c) *The Circle of Reason*
(d) *The Calcutta Chromosome*

281. Which novel of Amitav Ghosh takes up the issue of Malaria?
(a) *The Calcutta Chromosome*
(b) *The Countdown*
(c) *The Circle of Reason*
(d) None of the above

282. *The Shadow Lines* tells the story of three generations of the narrator's family spread over
(a) Calcutta, Dhaka and London
(b) Calcutta, Dhaka and New York
(c) Delhi, Dhaka and London
(d) Bombay, Dhaka and London

283. The partition of India and the consequent trauma of the East Bengal psyche is focussed in Amitav Ghosh's
(a) *The Countdown*
(b) *The Shadow Lines*
(c) *The Calcutta Chromosome*
(d) *In an Antique Land*

284. *The Great Indian Novel* has been written by
(a) Amitav Ghosh
(b) Shashi Tharoor
(c) Upamanyu Chatterjee
(d) Arun Joshi

285. Which novel focuses on collisions of various sorts between individuals, between cultures between ideologies and between religions?
(a) *Train to Pakistan*
(b) *The Riot*
(c) *A Bend in the Ganges*
(d) *So Many Hungers*

286. Who is the chief male character in *The Riot*?
(a) Lakshaman
(b) Rama
(c) Iqbal
(d) Bharat

287. The novel *The Riot* is divided into how many sections?
(a) 77
(b) 78
(c) 79
(d) 80

288. "From dharma comes success, from dharma comes happiness, everything emerges from dharma, dharma is the essence of the world." Which character in Tharoor's book *Show Business* speaks it?
(a) Pranay
(b) Ashok
(c) Guruji
(d) Maya

289. The first novel published in English of Indian Writing was
(a) *The Hindu Wife*
(b) *Roshinara*
(c) *Bianca*
(d) *Raj Mohan's Wife*

290. The river 'Padma' is in the background of which of the following novels?
(a) *The Cat and Shakespeare*
(b) *Men and Rivers*
(c) *Kanthapura*
(d) *The Serpent and the Rope*

291. Which novel of Bankim Chandra Chatterjee gave the Indians their national anthem 'Vande Matram'?
(a) *Raj Mohan's Wife*
(b) *Durgesh Nandini*
(c) *Anand Math*
(d) None of the above

292. Which novel of Tagore is considered to be the first modern novel in the history of Indian literature?
(a) *Gora*
(b) *The Home and the World*
(c) *The Wreck*
(d) *Choker Bali*

293. Chaman Nahal's *Azadi* (1975), which has the theme of partition is concerned about
(a) Lala Kanshi Ram
(b) Rahotullah Khan
(c) Prabhas Rani
(d) Bhavani Bharti

294. The plays *Tughlaq*, *Yayeti* and *Hayavandana* have been written by
(a) Tagore
(b) Girish Karnad
(c) Gieve Patel
(d) Vijay Tendulkar

295. The plays *Goa* and *The Dumb Dancer* have been written by
(a) Vijay Tendulkar
(b) Tagore
(c) Santha Ram Rau
(d) Asif Currimbhoy

296. The plays *Silence! The Court is in Session*, *Ghashiram Kotwal* and *Sakharam Binder* have been written by
(a) Vijay Tendulkar
(b) Santha Ram Rau
(c) Girish Karnad
(d) Asif Currimbhoy

(Some other plays are: *Kamala*, *The Vultures*, and *Encounter in Umbugland*)

297. In which of his plays has Mahesh Dattani addressed the issue of communalism?
(a) *Dance Like a Man*
(b) *Final Solutions*
(c) *Tara*
(d) *Bravely Fought The Queen*

298. G.V. Desani's novel *All About H. Hatter* was published in
(a) 1943
(b) 1945
(c) 1948
(d) 1950

299. Kiran Desai's novel *The Inheritance of Loss* won the Booker Prize in
(a) 2001
(b) 2003
(c) 2004
(d) 2006

300. Which of the following novels deals with a four-family saga set in post-independence and post-partition India?
(a) *A Suitable Boy*
(b) *A Bend in the Ganges*
(c) *Such a Long Journey*
(d) Voices in the City

(*A Suitable Boy* is a 1474-page novel by Vikram Seth, published in 1993.)

## ANSWERS

| | | | | | |
|---|---|---|---|---|---|
| 1. (c) | 2. (b) | 3. (c) | 4. (a) | 5. (b) | 6. (b) |
| 7. (c) | 8. (b) | 9. (a) | 10. (d) | 11. (d) | 12. (c) |
| 13. (c) | 14. (b) | 15. (a) | 16. (a) | 17. (b) | 18. (a) |
| 19. (b) | 20. (a) | 21. (c) | 22. (d) | 23. (b) | 24. (c) |
| 25. (b) | 26. (d) | 27. (d) | 28. (c) | 29. (b) | 30. (d) |
| 31. (a) | 32. (c) | 33. (a) | 34. (b) | 35. (c) | 36. (d) |
| 37. (a) | 38. (c) | 39. (b) | 40. (a) | 41. (b) | 42. (a) |
| 43. (c) | 44. (b) | 45. (c) | 46. (d) | 47. (b) | 48. (c) |
| 49. (b) | 50. (b) | 51. (a) | 52. (c) | 53. (a) | 54. (b) |
| 55. (c) | 56. (b) | 57. (d) | 58. (c) | 59. (b) | 60. (b) |
| 61. (c) | 62. (a) | 63. (a) | 64. (b) | 65. (c) | 66. (c) |
| 67. (d) | 68. (d) | 69. (c) | 70. (c) | 71. (b) | 72. (b) |
| 73. (b) | 74. (b) | 75. (a) | 76. (a) | 77. (c) | 78. (b) |
| 79. (a) | 80. (c) | 81. (a) | 82. (a) | 83. (d) | 84. (b) |
| 85. (c) | 86. (b) | 87. (c) | 88. (c) | 89. (a) | 90. (d) |
| 91. (d) | 92. (a) | 93. (a) | 94. (d) | 95. (b) | 96. (c) |
| 97. (b) | 98. (a) | 99. (a) | 100. (a) | 101. (b) | 102. (b) |
| 103. (c) | 104. (a) | 105. (a) | 106. (c) | 107. (c) | 108. (a) |
| 109. (d) | 110. (b) | 111. (a) | 112. (b) | 113. (c) | 114. (a) |
| 115. (b) | 116. (c) | 117. (c) | 118. (b) | 119. (b) | 120. (a) |
| 121. (b) | 122. (c) | 123. (d) | 124. (a) | 125. (d) | 126. (c) |
| 127. (a) | 128. (a) | 129. (b) | 130. (b) | 131. (a) | 132. (d) |
| 133. (d) | 134. (c) | 135. (b) | 136. (c) | 137. (d) | 138. (a) |
| 139. (b) | 140. (a) | 141. (b) | 142. (c) | 143. (a) | 144. (a) |
| 145. (c) | 146. (a) | 147. (b) | 148. (d) | 149. (b) | 150. (c) |
| 151. (a) | 152. (c) | 153. (a) | 154. (b) | 155. (b) | 156. (b) |
| 157. (d) | 158. (d) | 159. (c) | 160. (a) | 161. (b) | 162. (c) |
| 163. (b) | 164. (c) | 165. (d) | 166. (c) | 167. (d) | 168. (a) |
| 169. (b) | 170. (b) | 171. (b) | 172. (b) | 173. (c) | 174. (c) |
| 175. (a) | 176. (b) | 177. (a) | 178. (b) | 179. (c) | 180. (b) |
| 181. (a) | 182. (a) | 183. (a) | 184. (b) | 185. (c) | 186. (b) |
| 187. (b) | 188. (c) | 189. (c) | 190. (b) | 191. (a) | 192. (c) |

| | | | | | |
|---|---|---|---|---|---|
| 193. (a) | 194. (a) | 195. (a) | 196. (b) | 197. (b) | 198. (b) |
| 199. (d) | 200. (c) | 201. (a) | 202. (c) | 203. (a) | 204. (d) |
| 205. (a) | 206. (c) | 207. (a) | 208. (c) | 209. (a) | 210. (a) |
| 211. (b) | 212. (a) | 213. (b) | 214. (a) | 215. (c) | 216. (d) |
| 217. (a) | 218. (a) | 219. (b) | 220. (a) | 221. (a) | 222. (b) |
| 223. (a) | 224. (a) | 225. (b) | 226. (a) | 227. (b) | 228. (a) |
| 229. (c) | 230. (b) | 231. (c) | 232. (b) | 233. (d) | 234. (a) |
| 235. (a) | 236. (b) | 237. (c) | 238. (a) | 239. (c) | 240. (c) |
| 241. (a) | 242. (b) | 243. (a) | 244. (c) | 245. (a) | 246. (a) |
| 247. (c) | 248. (b) | 249. (a) | 250. (b) | 251. (c) | 252. (c) |
| 253. (d) | 254. (a) | 255. (c) | 256. (b) | 257. (d) | 258. (a) |
| 259. (d) | 260. (a) | 261. (c) | 262. (b) | 263. (b) | 264. (b) |
| 265. (a) | 266. (c) | 267. (b) | 268. (a) | 269. (a) | 270. (a) |
| 271. (a) | 272. (a) | 273. (b) | 274. (a) | 275. (d) | 276. (c) |
| 277. (a) | 278. (d) | 279. (a) | 280. (c) | 281. (a) | 282. (a) |
| 283. (b) | 284. (b) | 285. (b) | 286. (a) | 287. (b) | 288. (c) |
| 289. (d) | 290. (b) | 291. (c) | 292. (d) | 293. (a) | 294. (b) |
| 295. (d) | 296. (a) | 297. (b) | 298. (c) | 299. (d) | 300. (a) |

# 4

# Same Title, Different Authors

*The Double* by Fyodor Dostoyevsky
*The Double* by Jose Saramago
*The Double* by Greg Boyd

*The Cave* by Tim Krabbe
*The Cave* by Jose Saramago

*Wonder...* by Robert C. Fuller
*Wonder* by Rachel Vail

*Don't Tell* by Karen Rose
*Don't Tell* by Elizabeth Chandler

*Forever* by Judy Blume
*Forever* by Karen Kingsbury
*Forever* by Pete Hamill

*Cat's Eye* by Andre Norton
*Cat's Eye* by Margaret Atwood

*Holes* by Louis Sachar

*The Hole* by Guy Burt

*Twilight* by Stephenie Meyer
*Twilight* by Meg Cabot
*Twilight* by Elie Wiesel
*Twilight* by Cate Tiernan

*Aphrodite* by Pierre Louÿs,
*Aphrodite* by Isabel Allende

*Play Dead* by Peter Dickinson
*Play Dead* by Harlan Coben

*Time and Again* by Clifford D. Simak
*Time and Again* by Jack Finney

*The Devil's Advocate* by Morris West
*The Devil's Advocate* by Taylor Caldwell

*The Advocate's Devil* by Alan M. Dershowitz

*Son of York* by Julia Hamilton
*Son of York* by Margaret Abbey

*History of the Life and Reign of Richard the Third* by James Gairdner
*History of the Life and Reign of Richard the Third* by George Buck

*Death of a Salesman* by Arthur Miller
*Death of a Salesperson* by Robert Barnard

*Snow* by Orhan Pamuk
*Snow* by Nigel Frith

*Sanctuary* by William Faulkner
*Sanctuary* by Edith Wharton

*The Homecoming* by Harold Pinter
*The Homecoming* by Ray Bradbury

*Matisse* by Rene Percheron
*Matisse* by Pierre Schneider

*Ovid* by David Wishart
*Ovid* by Sara Mack

*Ruddy Gore* by Kerry Greenwood
*Ruddigore* by William Gilbert (in The Complete Gilbert and Sullivan)

*The Siege* by Peter David
*The Siege* by Troy Denning

*The Gold Coast* by Nelson DeMille
*The Gold Coast* by Kim Stanley Robinson

*The Legacy* by R.A. Salvatore
*The Legacy* by Lynda LaPlante

*The Fury* by John Farris
*The Fury* by Colin Forbes

*Final Frontier* by Diane Carey
*Final Frontier* (series) by Peter David

*The Night Watch* by Sarah Waters
*Night Watch* by Terry Pratchett
*Night Watch* by Sean Stewart

*Wizard at Large* by Terry Brooks (a Magic Kingdom of Landover novel)
*Wizard at Large* by Jim Butcher (a book club omnibus of some of the Dresden Files books)

*The Touch* by F. Paul Wilson
*The Touch* by Brian Lumely

*Haunted* by Kelley Armstrong
*Haunted* by Tamara Thorne

*Lost World* by Arthur Conan Doyle
*Lost World* by Michael Crichton

*The Lady and the Unicorn* by Tracy Chevalier
*The Lady and the Unicorn* by Isolde Martyn

*Night* by Elie Wiesel
*Night* by Francis Pollini

*Personal History* by Vincent Sheean
*Personal History* by Katharine Graham

*The Prince of Darkness* by P Doherty
*The Prince of Darkness* by Jean Plaidy
*The Prince of Darkness* by Sharon Penman

It's impossible to even estimate the number of people who have entitled a book *Collected Poems*. Just a very partial list would include: Zbigniew Herbert, T.S. Eliot, Robert Lowell, Sylvia Plath, Ted Hughes (I wonder if he stole the idea from her), William Blake, A.E Housman, Stanley Kunitz, Blind Lemon Jefferson, Philip Whalen, I could go on!

*Blood Ties* by David Adams Richards
*Blood Ties* by C.C. Humphreys

*The Innocent* by Harlan Coben
*The Innocent* by Posie Graeme-Evans
*The Innocent* by Ian McEwan

*The Winter's Tale* by William Shakespeare

*Winter's Tale* by Mark Helprin
*Winter's Tale* by Isak Dineson

*Dead Wrong* by J.A. Jance
*Dead Wrong* by William X. Kienzle

*The Painted Veil* by W. Somerset Maugham
*The Painted Veil* by Susan Carroll
There are several *Emma's* also. Jane Austen, Charlotte Bronte, Kaoru Mori

*Vanishing Point* by Michaela Roessner
*Vanishing Point: A Novel* by David Markson

*Imperium: A Novel of Ancient Rome* by Robert Harris
*Imperium* by F. Yockey

*Night Shift* by Stephen King
*Night Shift* by Jessie Hartland
*Night Shift* by Nora Roberts
*Night Shift* by Rick Kirkman and Jerry Scott
*Night Shift* by Valerie Sinason
*Night Shift* by Brad Curtis
*Night Shift* by Henry Brewis
*Night Shift* by David Belbin
*Night Shift* by Carl Hanni
*Night Shift* by Greg Biehle and Martha Moore
*Night Shift* by Maria Gitin
*Night Shift* by Dermot Bolger
*Night Shift* by Maritta Wolff and George Salter
*Night Shift* by Mark Murphy
*Night Shift* by Margot J. Fromer
*Night Shift* by Dave Shive and Michelle Lovric
*Night Shift* by John F. Kirch
*Night Shift* by Mike Staier

*Night Shift* by Inez Holden
*Night Shift* by Zondervan
*Night Shift* by Lowell Ganz
*Night Shift* by Marc Blitzstein

*The Duke* by Gaelen Foley
*The Duke* by Catherine Coulter
*The Duke* by Philip Guedalla

*Love Among the Ruins: A Novel* by Robert Clark
*Love Among the Ruins: A Novel* by Angela Mackail Thirkell
*Love Among the Ruins: A Romance of the Near Future* by Evelyn Waugh

*Book of the Dead* by Douglas Preston
*Book of the Dead* by Patricia Cornwell
*Book of the Dead* by Tanith Lee
*Book of the Dead* by Robert Richardson
*Book of the Dead* by Ashley McConnell

*Yankee Wife* by Pat Pritchard
*Yankee Wife* by Linda Lael Miller

*Kiss and Tell* by Cherry Adair
*Kiss and Tell* by Suzanne Brockmann

*The Orchid Hunter* by Jill Marie Landis
*The Orchid Hunter* by Sandra K. Moore

*Tell Me Lies* by Jennifer Crusie
*Tell Me Lies* by Claudia Dain

*Out of Control* by Suzanne Brockman
*Out of Control* by Shannon McKenna
*Out of Control* by Candace Schulyer

*Over the Edge* by Suzanne Brockmann
*Over the Edge* by Jeannie London

*On Thin Ice* by Cherry Adair
*On Thin Ice* by Susan Andersen

*One Way Out* by Michele Albert
*One Way Out* by Wendy Rosnau

*Every Waking Moment* by Meryl Sawyer
*Every Waking Moment* by Brenda Novak

*Trust No One* by Meryl Sawyer
*Trust No One* by Christianne Hegan

*A Kiss in the Dark* by Meryl Sawyer
*A Kiss in the Dark* by Tiffany White

*Tempting Fate* by Meryl Sawyer
*Tempting Fate* by JoAnn Ross

# 5

# Miscellaneous Questions with Answers

1. Choose the correct pairs:

| | |
|---|---|
| (A) Richard Steel | 1. John Fletcher |
| (B) Dr. S. Johnson | 2. S.T. Coleridge |
| (C) William Wordsworth | 3. Joseph Addison |
| (D) Francis Beaumont | 4. James Boswell |

   (a) Richard Steel–Joseph Addison
   (b) Dr. S. Johnson–James Bosewell
   (c) William Wordsworth–S.T. Coleridge
   (d) Francis Beaumont–John Fletcher
2. The following line occurs in

   "To travel hopefully is a better thing than to arrive".
   (a) R.L. Stevenson's *E.L. Dorado*
   (b) Joh Bunyan's *Pilgrim's Progress*
   (c) Thomas Moore's *Utopia*
   (d) Rousseau's *Confessions*
3. "Squire Allworthy" is a character in
   (a) Dickens's *Oliver Twist*
   (b) Henry Fielding's *Tom Jones*
   (c) William Thackeray's *Vanity Fair*
   (d) Jane Austen's *Pride and Prejudice*
4. Michael Henchard is the hero of
   (a) George Orwell's *1984*
   (b) Jules Verne's *Round the World in Eighty Days*
   (c) Thomas Hardy's *Mayor of Casterbridge*
   (d) Walter Scott's *Guy Mannering*
5. Kimbal O' Hara is the hero of
   (a) Jane Austen's *Sense and Sensibility*
   (b) Emily Bronte's *Wuthering Heights*
   (c) James Joyce's *Ulysses*
   (d) Rudyard Kipling's *Kim*
6. What is common between John Dryden, William Wordsworth, Robert Bridges, and Lord Tennyson?
   (a) All of them were Romantic poets
   (b) They were rich poets
   (c) They were Poet Laureates
   (d) They were famous both as poets and playwrights
7. In which of the following does this line occur?

   They also serve who only stand and wait.
   (a) John Milton's Sonnet *On His Blindness*
   (b) Henry Vaughan's *The World*
   (c) William Wordsworth's *Intimations of Immorality*
   (d) Pope's *Essay on Man*
8. The following lines occur in

   I arise and go now, for always night and day
   I hear lake water lapping with low sounds by the shore
   (a) William Wordsworth's *Tintern Abbey*
   (b) W.B. Yeats's *Lake Isle of Innisfree*
   (c) John Keats's *Endymion*
   (d) P.B. Shelley's *Ode to the Westwind*

9. The following lines occur in

   I grow old ......... I grow old .......
   I shall wear the bottom of my trousers rolled

   (a) W.B. Yeats's *Lake Isle of Innisfree*
   (b) T.S. Eliot's *The Love Song of J. Alfred Prufrock*
   (c) W.H. Auden's *The Diaspora*
   (d) C.D. Lewis's *A Time to Dance*

10. The following lines occur in

    A crowd flowed over London Bridge, so many,
    I have not thought death had undone so many.

    (a) W.H. Anden's *The Witnesses*
    (b) W.B. Yeats's *When You are Old*
    (c) T.S. Eliot's *The Wastle Land*
    (d) William Wordsworth's *Lines Composed upon Westminster Bridge*

11. The following lines occur in

    Was he free? Was he happy? The question is absurd:
    Had anything been wrong, we should certainly have heard.

    (a) W.B. Yeats's *No Second Troy*
    (b) W.H. Auden's *The Unknown Citizen*
    (c) T.S. Eliot's *Ash Wednesday*
    (d) Dylan Thomas's *A Grief Ago*

12. The following lines have been taken from

    Life, like a dome of many-coloured glass,
    Stains the white radiance of Eternity

    (a) Pope's *Essay on Man*
    (b) Shakespeare's *Macbeth*
    (c) John Keats's *Ode on Melancholy*
    (d) P.B. Shelley's *Adonais*

13. Which of the following pairs is not correct:

    (a) *Something of Myself* — 1. Rudyard Kipling
    (b) *The Way of All Flesh* — 2. Samuel Butler
    (c) *Confessions of an English Opium Eater* — 3. H.G. Wells
    (d) *A Sentimental Journey* — 4. Lawrence Sterne

14. Who is the author of the following lines:

    Her feet beneath her petticoat,
    Like little mice, stole in and out,
    As if they fear'd the light.

    (a) Sir John Suckling (b) John Donne
    (c) Jonathan Swift (d) Robert Bridges

15. The following lines have been written by

    I sing of brooks, of blossoms, birds and bowers:
    Of April, May, of June, and July flowers.

    (a) Sir John Suckling
    (b) William Wordsworth
    (c) Robert Herrick
    (d) John Burgon

16. The following lines occur in

    But at my back I always hear
    Time's winged chariot hurrying near:
    And yonder all before us lie
    *Deserts of vast eternity*

    (a) Walter Savage Lander's *Dying Speech on an Old Philosopher*
    (b) John Milton's *Lycidas*
    (c) P.B. Shelley's *Adonais*
    (d) Andrew Marvell's *To His Coy Mistress*

17. The following lines have been taken from:

    Stone walls do not a prison make,
    Nor iron bars a cage.

    (a) Richard Lovelace's *To Althea*
    (b) Leigh Hunt's *A Thought of the Nile*
    (c) John Keat's *Bright Star*
    (d) Lord Tennyson's *Audley Court*

18. Match the characters with the novels:

    (A) Edmund Tressilian 1. *The Black Dwarf*

(B) Caleb Balderstone 2. *Guy Mannering*
(C) Dominie Sampson 3. *Kenilworth*
(D) Grace Armstrong 4. *The Bride of Lammermoor*

(a) 3, 1, 4, 2 (b) 3, 4, 2, 1
(c) 1, 2, 4, 3 (d) 2, 4, 3, 1

19. Who, among the following, said about Chaucer:
He was the 'morning star of song'
(a) Tennyson (b) Matthew Arnold
(c) Dr. S. Johnson (d) P.B. Shelley

20. What is common between the following books?
(A) Edmund Spenser's *The Fairy Queen*
(B) Jonanthan Swift's *Tale of a Tub*
(C) Addison's *Vision of Mirza*
(D) Bunyan's *Pilgrim's Progress*
(a) Satires (b) Religious books
(c) Allegories (d) Fairy Tales

21. Choose the correct pair:
(a) *Black Beauty* W.H. Hudson
(b) *The Scarlet Letter* John Buchan
(c) *In the Key of the Blue* Nathaniel Hawthorne
(d) *The White Devil* John Webster
(*Black Beauty* was written by Anna Swell; *The Scarlet Letter* by Nathaniel Hawthorne and *In the Key of Blue* by J.A. Symonds)

22. Who is the most famous Interlude Writer?
(a) John Heywood
(b) Delaune Michel
(c) Karen Russell
(d) None of the above

23. When was the first theatre established in England?
(a) 1574 (b) 1576
(c) 1577 (d) 1578
(The first theatre was established at Shoreditch)

24. What is the main contribution of Seneca to the drama?
(a) Comedy (b) Tragedy
(c) Revenge Play (d) None of the above

25. Which one of the following plays is not a revenge play?
(a) *Hamlet*
(b) *The Spanish Tragedy*
(c) *The White Devil*
(d) *Romeo and Juliet*

26. Which one of the following is a Greek playwright?
(a) Aeschylus (b) Seneca
(c) Plautus (d) Terence

27. Which one of the following is not a Roman playwright?
(a) Plautus (b) Terence
(c) Seneca (d) Sophocles

28. Who was the first Soneteer in England?
(a) Shakespeare (b) Wyatt
(c) Surrey (d) None of the above

29. Which one of the following is not the rhyme scheme of the sestet of a Petrarch Sonnet?
(a) cde, cde (b) cdc, dcd
(c) cde, dce (d) ced, ced

30. Who, among the following, is not an English Sonneteer?
(a) Petrarch (b) Shakespeare
(c) Milton (d) Keats

31. Petrarch belonged to
(a) England (b) France
(c) Italy (d) Spain

32. Who introduced blank verse in England?
(a) Shakespeare (b) Marlowe
(c) Surrey (d) Wyatt

33. Match the locale of the following novels:
(a) *Romola* 1. London Clerkenwell district

(b) *Finnegans Wake* 2. Florence
(c) *Angel Pavement* 3. Dublin
(d) *Riceyman Steps* 4. London
(a) 2, 3, 4, 1 (b) 3, 2, 1, 4
(c) 1, 2, 4, 3 (d) 1, 4, 3, 2

(*Ronola* was written by George Eliot, *Finnegans Wake* by James Joyce, *Angel Pavement* by J.B. Priestley and *Riceyman Steps* by Arnold Bennett)

34. Charles Dickens's novel *A Tale of Two Cities* was published in
(a) 1851 (b) 1854
(c) 1856 (d) 1859

35. Daniel Defoe's *Robinson Crusoe* was published in
(a) 1719 (b) 1721
(c) 1823 (d) 1725

36. What was the most favourite branch of literature in the Renaissance period?
(a) Epic (b) Novel
(c) Drama (d) None of the above

37. Who, among the following, is called the first child of the Renaissance?
(a) Shakespeare (b) Spenser
(c) Marlowe (d) Ben Jonson

38. The Spenserian Stanza consists of
(a) 8 lines (b) 7 lines
(c) 6 lines (d) 9 lines

39. Who has been called the 'spoilt child of the Renaissance'?
(a) William Shakespeare
(b) Edmund Spenser
(c) Christopher Marlowe
(d) Robert Greene

40. Who, among the following, is not a University Wit?
(a) John Lyly
(b) Thomas Kyd
(c) Robert Greene
(d) Edmund Spenser

41. Who is considered the father of English Tragedy?
(a) Christopher Marlowe
(b) John Dryden
(c) Thomas Kyd
(d) William Shakespeare

42. Who was the first practitioner of the English dramatic blank verse?
(a) William Shakespeare
(b) John Dryden
(c) Edmund Spenser
(d) Christopher Marlowe

43. The theme of John Galsworthy's play *Strife* (1909) is the struggle between
(a) The rich and the poor
(b) Capital and labour
(c) Landlords and peasants
(d) None of the above

44. Which Marlowe's play contains the following lines:

Was this the face that launch'd a thousand ships
And burnt the topless towers of Ilium?

(a) *Dr. Faustus*
(b) *The Jew of Malta*
(c) *Tamburlaine the Great*
(d) *Edward the Second*

45. Shakespeare was indebted to John Lyly for
(a) Tragedy (b) Blank Verse
(c) Romantic Comedy (d) History plays

46. Which Shakespeare's play contains the following lines:

All the world's a stage
And all the men and women merely players,
They have their exists and entrances,
And one man in his time plays many parts

(a) *The Merchant of Venice*
(b) *As You Like It*
(c) *A Midsummer Night's Dream*
(d) *The Tempest*

(These lines have been spoken by Jaques, the metancholy philosopher)

47. Which Shakespeare's play contains the following lines?

    Cowards die many times before their deaths;

    The Valiant taste of death but only once.

    (a) *Henry IV, Part I* (b) *Hamlet*
    (c) *Julius Caesar* (d) *Coriolanus*

48. In which of Ben Jonson's plays do the following lines occur?

    Strip the ragged follies of the time
    Naked as their birth ................
    ............. and with a whip of steel
    Print Wounding lashes in their iron ribs.

    (a) *Everyman Out of His Humour*
    (b) *Everyman in His Humour*
    (c) *Volpone*
    (d) *The Alchemist*

49. Who said about Shakespeare, "He was not of an age, but for all time"?

    (a) Dr. Johnson (b) John Dryden
    (c) Alexander Pope (d) Ben Jonson

50. Which Shakespeare play contains the following line?

    The devil can cite scripture for his purpose

    (a) *As You Like It*
    (b) *Othello*
    (c) *The Merchant of Venice*
    (d) *Measure for Measure*

51. Caliban is a character in

    (a) *Troilus and Cressida*
    (b) *The Alchemist*
    (c) *The Tempest*
    (d) *Caesar and Cleopatra*

52. Who was the first great English essayist?

    (a) Steele (b) Bacon
    (c) Addison (d) Charles Lamb

53. Who was the first writer to use the word 'Essay'?

    (a) Bacon (b) Addison
    (c) Montaigne (d) Steele

54. About whom did Alexander Pope say that he was the 'wisest, brightest, meanest of mankind'?

    (a) Bacon (b) Spenser
    (c) Marlowe (d) Kyd

55. Who is regarded as the father of English criticism?

    (a) Dr. Johnson
    (b) Sir Philip Sidney
    (c) John Dryden
    (d) Alexander Pope

56. Who, among the following, is not a post-Shakespearean dramatist?

    (a) George Chapman
    (b) Thomas Nashe
    (c) John Martson
    (d) Middleton

57. *Atlanta and Calydon* is a lyrical drama by

    (a) A.C. Swinburne
    (b) John Dryden
    (c) William Shakespeare
    (d) James Shirley

58. Which of the following bears the title of a novel as well as a poem?

    (a) *The Rape of Lucrece*
    (b) *Gone with the Wind*
    (c) *Ulysses*
    (d) *Promethens Unbound*

    (*Ulysses* (1922) is a famous novel by James Joyce, while Tennyson's poem *Ulysses* deals with the wanderings and adventures of Ulysses (also called Odysseus).

59. In which poem of Dryden do the following lines occur?

    Great wits are sure to madness near allied
    And thin partition do their bounds divide;

    (a) Absalom and Achitophel

(b) The Medal
(c) Mac Flecknoe
(d) The Hind and the Panther

(In these lines Dryden satirises Earl of Shaftesbury. He wanted to exclude James from the succession and favoured Monmouth.)

60. In which of Pope's work do the following lines occur?

Know then thyself, presume not God to scan,
The proper study of mankind is man.

(a) *The Rape of the Lock*
(b) *Essay on Man*
(c) *Epistle to Dr. Arbuthnot*
(d) *Dunciad*

61. In which Pope's work do the following lines occur?

Damn with faint praise, assent with civil leer,

x x x x

Willing to wound, and yet afraid to strike.

(a) *The Rape of the Lock*
(b) *Dunciad*
(c) *Epistle to Dr. Arbuthnot*
(d) None of the above

62. The following line occur in Alexander Pope's

Fools rush in where angels fear to tread

(a) *Epistle to Arbuthnot*
(b) *Dunciad*
(c) *The Rape of the Lock*
(d) *An Essay on Criticism*

63. The following lines occur in

The mind is its own place, and in itself
Can make a Heaven of Hell, a Hell of Heaven

(a) *Paradise Lost*
(b) *Paradise Regained*
(c) *The Fairie Queene*
(d) *Promethens Bound*

64. The following line occurs in

Better to reign in Hell than serve in Heaven.

(a) *The Fairy Queen*
(b) *Paradise Lost*
(c) *Macbeth*
(d) None of the above

65. *Visible darkness* is an example of

(a) Hyperbole
(b) Synecdoche
(c) Oxymoron
(d) None of the above

66. Which one of the following is the odd book?

(a) *Murder in the Cathedral*
(b) *Strife*
(c) *Hard Times*
(d) *The Spanish Tragedy*

67. In which Shakespeare's play does the following line occur?

To be, or not to be: that is the question

(a) *Hemlet* (b) *Othello*
(c) *Macbeth* (d) *King Lear*

68. Which one of the following is the correct chronological order of Shakespeare's plays?

(a) *The Merchant of Venice, Coriolanus, Othello, Love's Labour Lost*
(b) *Love's Labour Lost, The Merchant of Venice, Othello, Coriolanus*
(c) *Othello, The Merchant of Venice, Coriolanus, Love's Labour Lost*
(d) *Coriolanus, Love's Labour Lost, The Merchant of Venice, Othello*

69. About whom has it been said, "You cannot ignore him any more than you can ignore Alexander the Great, or Cromwell, or Napoleon"?

(a) William Shakespeare
(b) Edmund Spenser
(c) John Milton
(d) Dr. S. Johnson

(This is by E.M.W. Tillyard)

70. Give the correct chronological order of the following art movements:
    (a) Expressionism, Imagism, Dadaism, Surrealism
    (b) Imagism, Dadaism, Surrealism, Expressionism
    (c) Surrealism, Imagism, Dadaism, Expressionism
    (d) Dadaism, Expressionism, Imagism, Surrealism
71. Which of the following books inspired Nelson Mandela when he was incarcerated?
    (a) *The Man who would be King* (Rudyard Kipling)
    (b) *Invictus* (Ernest Henley)
    (c) *The Riddle of the Sands* (Erskine Childer)
    (d) *The Scarlet Pimpernel* (Emma Orczy)
72. Who, among the following, is the creator of Peter Pan?
    (a) *Rudyard Kipling*
    (b) *Anthony Hope*
    (c) *J.M. Barrie*
    (d) None of the above
73. Which, among the following, is regarded as a children classic?
    (a) *The Jungle Book*
    (b) *King Solomon Mines*
    (c) *Alice in wonderland*
    (d) *The Wind in the Willows*
74. In which play of Shakespeare occurs the following line?

    Never, never, never, never, never!

    (a) *Macbeth* (b) *King Lear*
    (c) *Othello* (d) *Hamlet*

    (The repetition of 'never' five times has great dramatic significance. It expresses King Lear's deep anguish and agony whose daughter, Cordelia, has just died in front of him. This repetition for emphasis is a rhetorical device called *epizeuxis*.)

Choose the correct option which the given statement belongs to. (Q 75-84)

75. 'He likes bananas, mangoes, watermelons, strawberries'.
    (a) Asyndeton (b) Litotes
    (c) Chiasmus (d) Anaphora

    (Asyndeton consists of omitting conjunctions between words, phrases, or clauses)
76. 'She walked and wept and ran and stumbled'—
    (a) Hyperbole (b) Litotes
    (c) Chiasmus (d) Polysyndeton

    (*Polysyndeton* is the use of conjunction between each word, phrase, or clause and is the opposite of asyndeton)
77. 'Success makes man proud; failure makes them wise'.
    (a) Understatement (b) Paradox
    (c) Antithesis (d) Anaphora
78. 'Gido' is the best of all Alsatians, nay of all dogs'.
    (a) Distinctio (b) Metanoia
    (c) Oxymoron (d) Diacope

    (*Metanoia* qualifies a statement by recalling it and expressing it in a better, milder, or stronger way. A negative is often used to do the recalling.)
79. 'I will speak daggers to her. (Hamlet)
    (a) Catachresis (b) Synecdoche
    (c) Metonymy (d) Hyperbole

    (*Catachresis* is an extravagant, implied metaphor using words in a unusual way. Here Hamlet uses *daggers* instead of *angry words*)
80. 'He replied him with an eloquent silence'
    (a) Eponym (b) Zeugma
    (c) Oxymoron (d) Antithesis

    (Oxymoron is a paradox reduced two words, usually in an adjective-noun.)

81. 'The ploughman homeward plods his weary way'.
   (a) Transferred Epithet
   (b) Mixed Metaphor
   (c) Epithet
   (d) None of the above

82.'We will do it, I tell you; we will do it'.
   (a) Antiphrasis (b) Hyperbole
   (c) Diacope (d) Hyperbaton

   (*Diacope* is the repetition of a word or phrase after an intervening word or phrase as a method of emphasis.)

83. What do you see? Trees, trees, trees.
   (a) Enumeratio (b) Epizeuxis
   (c) Hypotaxis (d) Parataxis

   (*Epizeuxis* is the repetition of words for emphasis.)

84. 'I love her eyes, her hair, her nose, her cheeks, her lips'.
   (a) Epizeuxis (b) Parataxis
   (c) Enumeratio (d) Hypotaxis

   (*Enumeratio* is detailing the parts, causes, effects, or consequences to make a point forcefully.)

85. "It is a despair that nothing cannot be
   Flares in the mind that leaves a smoky mark of dread
   Look upward. Nothing firm or free
   Purposeless matters hover in the dark."
   These lines occur in Thom Gunn's poem.
   (a) The Annihilation of Nothing
   (b) The Man with Night Sweat
   (c) A School of Resistance
   (d) None of the above

   (In these lines, Thom Gunn explores modern anxieties.)

86. Seamus Heaney, an Irish poet and playwright, won the Nobel Prize in Literature in
   (a) 1990 (b) 1992
   (c) 1995 (d) 1997

87. The following lines are by

   Then poetry arrived in that city—
   I would abjure all cant and self-pity—
   And poetry wiped my brow and sped me.
   Now they will say I bite the hand that fed me.

   (a) Ted Hughes (b) R.S. Thomas
   (c) Thom Gunn (d) Seamus Heaney

88. Who, among the following, are known as the 'Thirties Poets'?
   (a) W.H. Anden, C.D. Lewis, Stephen Spender, Louis MacNeice
   (b) Seamus Heaney, W.H. Auden, Thom Gunn, Stephen Spender
   (c) C.D. Lewis, Thom Gunn, Kingley Amis, Philip Larkin
   (d) Stephen Spender, Louis MacNeice, Thom Gunn, Kingley Amis

89. *The Corrections* is a novel by
   (a) Isabel Allende
   (b) Philip Roth
   (c) Jonathan Franzen
   (d) None of the above

   (*The Corrections* is a 2001 American novel revolving around the troubles of an elderly Midwestern couple and their three adult children.)

90. *The House of Spirits* (1982) was written by
   (a) Margaret Atwood
   (b) Jonathan Franzen
   (c) Isabel Allende
   (d) David Mitcell

   (*The House of Spirits* is Allende's debut novel. The novel deals with the life of the Trueba family, spanning four generations. It traces the post-colonial, social and political upheavals of Chile. It incorporates elements of magical realism. It was named the Best Novel of the Year (1982) in Chile.)

91. Who, among the following, wrote the novel *Amsterdam*?
   (a) David Mitchell
   (b) Ian McEwan
   (c) Jonathan Franzen
   (d) None of the above

   (*Amsterdam* is a 1998 novel by British writer McEwan, who was awarded the Booker Prize for this novel. It is the story of a strange euthanasia pact between two friends, a composer and a newspaper editor, whose relationship spins into disaster.)

92. Which one of the following books by Margaret Atwood whose central themes include the perspectives of story-telling, double standards between the sexes and the classes, and the fairness of justice?
   (a) *The Penelopiad*
   (b) *Driver's Seat*
   (c) *Oryx and Crake*
   (d) None of the above

93. *Big Breasts and Wide Hips* (1996) is a novel written by
   (a) Toni Morrison
   (b) Margaret Atwood
   (c) Isabel Allende
   (d) Mo Yan

   (Mo Yan, whose real name is Guan Moye, is a Chinese novelist. He was awarded the Nobel Prize in Literature in 2012 for his work as a writer "who with hallucinatory realism merges folk tales, history and the contemporary". The novel tells the story of a mother and her eight daughters and one son, and explores Chinese history through the 20th century.)

94. *Everyman* (2006) is a novel written by
   (a) Philip Roth (b) John Updike
   (c) Zadie Smith (d) None of the above

95. *White Teeth* is a novel written by
   (a) John Updike (b) Philip Roth
   (c) Zadie Smith (d) David Mitchell

   (James Wood, literary critic, coined the term 'hysterical realism' in 2000 to describe Zadie Smith's debut novel, *White Teeth*. Smith agreed that it was a "painfully accurate term for the sort of overblown, manic prose to be found in novels like my own *White Teeth*".)

96. Identify the novel which did not win the Pulitzer Prize.
   (a) Edith Warton's *The Age of Innocence* (1920)
   (b) Willa Cather's *One of Ours* (1922)
   (c) Sinclair Lewis's *Arrowsmith* (1925)
   (d) Ernest Hemingway's *A Farewell to Arms* (1929)

97. Identify the chronological sequence of the following novels by Henry Miller:
   (a) *Tropic of Cancer, Tropic of Capricorn, The Colossus of Maroussi, The Air-conditioned Nightmare*
   (b) *Tropic of Capricorn, The Air-conditioned Nightmare, The Colossus of Maroussi, Tropic of Cancer*
   (c) *The Colossus of Maroussi, Tropic of Cancer, The Air-conditioned Nightmare, Tropic of Capricorn*
   (d) *The Air-conditioned Nightmare, Tropic of Capricorn, The Colossus of Maroussi, Tropic of Cancer*

   (*Tropic of Cancer* (1934); *Tropic of Capricorn* (1939); *The Colossus of Maroussi* (1941); *The Air-conditioned Nightmare* (1945).)

98. *The Red Badge of Courage* (1895) was written by
   (a) Theodore Dreiser
   (b) Stephen Crane
   (c) Hamlin Garland
   (d) Frank Norris

(*The Red Bed of Courage* is about the American Civil War. The story is about a young soldier of the Union Army, Henry Fleming, who flies from the field of battle. Overcome with shame, he longs for a wound—a 'red bed of courage'—to counteract his cowardice.)

99. Who, among the following, wrote the novel *The Jungle*?
 (a) Stephen Crane
 (b) Frank Norris
 (c) Upton Sinclair
 (d) Edward Bellamy

100. Which one of the following novels is an innovative work of fiction influenced by the author's familiarity with cubism, jazz, and other movements in contemporary art and music?
 (a) Theodore Dreiser's *Sister Carrie*
 (b) Edward Bellamy's *Looking Backward*
 (c) Stephen Crane's *Maggie: A Girl of the Streets*
 (d) Gertrude Stein's *Three Lives*

101. Who, among the following, demonstrate the growth of an international perspective in American literature?
 (a) Gertrude Stein (b) Ezra Pound
 (c) Henry James (d) All of the above

102. John Steinback was awarded the Nobel Prize in Literature in
 (a) 1960 (b) 1962
 (c) 1964 (d) 1965

103. Who, among the following, is regarded as the key figure of the surrealistic New York School of Poetry?
 (a) John Ashbery
 (b) Ezra Pound
 (c) Elizabeth Bishop
 (d) None of the above

 (Ashbery's celebrated *Self-Portrait in a Convex Mirror* won the Pulitzer Prize for Poetry in 1976.)

104. Who, among the following American poets, won the Pulitzer Prize twice for his collection of poems?
 (a) Richard Wilbur (b) John Berryman
 (c) W.S. Merwin (d) Rita Dove

 (W.S. Merwin's *The Carrier of Ladders* won the Pulitzer Prize in 1971 and *The Shadow of Sirius* in 2009.)

105. Who, among the following American novelists, has a novel bearing a title with a single letter?
 (a) Toni Morrison
 (b) William Faulkner
 (c) Thomas Pynchon
 (d) Ernest Hemingway

 (One of Thomas Pynchon's novel has the title *V.* (1963). His other notable novels are *Mason and Dixon* (1997), *Gravity's Rainbow* (1973), *Vineland* (1990) *The Crying of Lot* (1966), and *Against the Day* (2006).)

106. The novels *The Bluest Eye* (1970), *Song of Solomon* (1977) and *Beloved* (1987) have been written by
 (a) Toni Morrison
 (b) Thomas Pynchon
 (c) William Faulker
 (d) William Gaddis

 (Toni Morrison's novel *The Bluest Eye* won widespread critical acclaim. Coming on the heels of the signing of the Civil Rights Act of 1965, the novel includes an elaborate description of incestuous rape and explores the conventions of beauty established by a historically racist society. It paints the portrait of a self-immolating black family in search of beauty in whiteness. The novel is widely studied in American schools.)

107. Who, among the following, wrote the Pulitzer-Prize winning novel *The Road* (2007)?

(a) William Faulkner
(b) Cormac McCarthy
(c) Toni Morrison
(d) John Steinback

(McCarthy's other novels are *The Orchard Keeper* (1965), *Suttree* (1979), *Blood Meridian* (1985), *Border Trilogy* (1992-98) and *All the Pretty Horses* (1992).)

108. Which one of the following Don DeLillo's novels chronicles American life through and immediately after Cold War and examining with equal depth subjects as various as baseball and nuclear weapons?
(a) *Underworld* (1977)
(b) *American* (1971)
(c) *Libra* (1988)
(d) *Falling Man* (2007)

(Don DeLillo's novel *Mao II* was written in 1991.)

109. Which one of David Foster Wallace's novels gives a futuristic portrait of America and is a playful critique of the media-saturated nature of American life?
(a) *The Broom of the System* (1987)
(b) *Infinite Jest* (1997)
(c) *The Pale King* (2011)
(d) *Girl with Curious Hair* (1989)

110. Who, among the following, wrote *The Amazing Adventures of Kavalier and Clay* (2000)?
(a) Jonathan Franzen
(b) Thomas Pynchon
(c) Michael Chabon
(d) Denis Johnson

(*The Amazing Adventures of Kavalier and Clay* tells the story of two friends, Joe Kavalier and Sam Clay, as they rise through the ranks of the comics industry in its heyday.)

111. Natty Bumpo is a famous character in
(a) Mark Twain's *A Tramp Abroad*
(b) James Fenimore Cooper's *The Pathfinder*
(c) Nathaniel Hawthorne's *The Marble of Faun*
(d) None of the above

112. *Let us, then, be up and doing,*
With a heart for any fate;
Still achieving, still pursuing,
Learn to labour and to wait.
These lines occur in
(a) H.W. Longfellow's *Psam of Life*
(b) Walt Witman's *Leaves of Grass*
(c) Robert Frost's *Road Not Taken*
(d) W.H. Auden's *The Unknown Citizen*

113. Which one of the following Harriet Beecher Stowe's works helped lay the groundwork for the civil war in America?
(a) *Oldtown Folk*
(b) *The Pearl of Orr's Island*
(c) *Uncle Tom's Cabin or The Man that was a Thing*
(d) *Pink and White Tyranny*

114. Who is the first American to win the Nobel Prize in Literature?
(a) Sinclair Lewis (b) Edgar Allan Poe
(c) Walt Whitman (d) Henry James

115. Dorris Lessing won the Nobel Prize in Literature in
(a) 2004 (b) 2006
(c) 2007 (d) 2009

116. Stephen Kumalo is a protagonist in one of the following Alan Paton's novels. Which is that novel?
(a) *Cry, the Beloved Country* (1948)
(b) *Too Late in Phalarope* (1953)
(c) *Ah, But your Land is Beautiful* (1981)
(d) None of the above

117. As flies to wanton boys, are we to the gods.
They kill us for their sport.
These lines occur in

(a) *The Duchess of Malfi*
(b) *Hamlet*
(c) *King Lear*
(d) *Arms and the Man*

118. The real name of Voltaire was
(a) Fraz Grillparzer
(b) Hermann Broch
(c) Adalbert Stifter
(d) Francois-Maria Arouet

119. Who wrote the play *Oedipus*?
(a) Sophocles (b) Voltaire
(c) Aeschylus (d) Sartre

120. In which of the following plays by Voltaire is there a satire specifically at government authority and organized religion?
(a) *Mahomet* (b) *Mariamme*
(c) *Socrates* (d) *Irene*

121. *Confessions* by Rousseau is often published with the title
(a) *The Confessions*
(b) *The Confessions of Rousseau*
(c) *The Confessions of Jean-Jacques Rousseau*
(d) *Confessions of Rousseau*

122. Which of the following works by Rousseau deals with the nature of education?
(a) *Emile*
(b) *Julie*
(c) *The Social Contract*
(d) *On the Origin of Language*

123. The story of Victor Hugo's novel *The HunchBack of Notre-Dame* is centred on
(a) A young man with a hump on his back
(b) A girl with a hump on her back
(c) The Notre Dame Cathedral in Paris
(d) None of the above

124. Victor Hugo's novel *Les Miserables* (1862) comprises
(a) 2 volumes (b) 3 volumes
(c) 4 volumes (d) 5 volumes

125. Andre Braton, the French writer, is well-known for
(a) *The First Surrealist Manifesto*
(b) *Cubism*
(c) *Dadaism*
(d) None of the above

126. Who, among the following, coined the term 'Modernity'?
(a) T.S. Eliot
(b) Charles Pierre Baudelaire
(c) F.R. Leavis
(d) Paul Verlaine

127. Whom did Victor Hugo described as "an infant Shakespeare"?
(a) Paul Verlaine
(b) Francois Villon
(c) Arthur Rimbaud
(d) Baudelaire

128. Which one of the following is not a novel by Graham Greene?
(a) *The Power and the Glory*
(b) *The Heart of the Matter*
(c) *The Human Factor*
(d) *Brave New World*

(*Brave New World* is a novel by Aldous Huxley.)

129. *The Mayor of Casterbridge* is subtitled
(a) *An Unfortunate Man*
(b) *A Miserable Man*
(c) *The Life and Death of a Man of Character*
(d) *An Arrogant Man*

130. Susan Henchard is the heroine of
(a) *Far from the Maddling Crowd*
(b) *The Mayor of Casterbridge*
(c) *A Pair of Blue Eyes*
(d) *The Well-Beloved*

131. In his novels, Henry James generally deals with
(a) The American Civilization

(b) The European Culture
(c) The contrast between the American civilization and the European culture
(d) The American Dream

132. In which year did Patrick White, an Australian author, won the Nobel Prize in Literature, "for an epic and psychological narrative art, which has introduced a new continent into literature"?
(a) 1971 (b) 1973
(c) 1975 (d) 1977

133. *How Late it was, How Late* (1994) was written by
(a) James Kelman (b) J.M. Coetzee
(c) Patrick White (d) A.L. Kennedy

134. Who, among the following, wrote *Day* (2007)?
(a) Alasdair Gray (b) Patrick White
(c) A.L. Kennedy (d) None of the above

135. Point out which of the following novels is written by Leonard Cohen.
(a) *The Story of An African Farm*
(b) *The Good Terrorist*
(c) *Under the Net*
(d) *Beautiful Losers*

136. Rastignac in an important character in one of the following novels by Balzac.
(a) *The Old Goriot*
(b) *Eugenie Grandet*
(c) *Lost Illusions*
(d) *The Harlot High and Low*

137. Who, among the following, does not belong to the Kailyard School of Scottish writers?
(a) J.M. Barrie
(b) J.J. Bell
(c) George MacDonald
(d) J.M. Synge

138. "Inklings" is
(a) a literary magazine
(b) the title of a novel
(c) an informal literary group associated with Oxford University
(d) None of the above

139. Who, among the following, does not belong to the "Inklings"?
(a) J.R.R. Tolkien (b) C.S. Lewis
(c) David Cecil (d) Ian Fleming

140. Who created the character James Bond 007?
(a) Ian Fleming (b) David Cecil
(c) Balzac (d) John Buchan

141. *Casino Royale* is a novel written by
(a) J.R.R. Tolkien (b) Ian Fleming
(c) David Cecil (d) John Buchan

142. Kenneth Grahame's *The Wind in the Willows* (1908) is a
(a) realistic novel (b) romantic novel
(c) children classic (d) bildungsroman

143. *The Lord of the Rings* is written by
(a) J.R.R. Tolkien
(b) J.M. Barrie
(c) Ian Fleming
(d) None of the above

(*The Lord of the Rings* is an epic high fantasy novel. The story began as a sequel to Tolkien's 1937 children's fantasy novel *The Hobbit*.)

144. C.S. Lewis is especially known for
(a) *Live and Let Die*
(b) *Dr No*
(c) *The Riddle of the Sands*
(d) *The Chronicles of Narnia*

(*The Chronicles of Narnia* is a series of seven high fantasy novels. It is considered a children's classic. It was written by Lewis between 1949 and 1954. It has been adapted several times, complete or in part, for radio, television, the stage and film.)

145. J.K. Rowling is best known for his
   (a) *Harry Potter series*
   (b) *Charlie and the Chocolate Factory*
   (c) *His Dark Materials*
   (d) *James and the Giant Peach*

   (*His Dark Materials* is a trilogy by Philip Pullman, While *Charlie and the Chocolate Factory* and *James and the Giant Peach* are fantasy novels by Ronald Dahl.)

146. A *Space Odyssey* was written by
   (a) Alan Moore
   (b) Neil Gaiman
   (c) Michael Moorcock
   (d) Arthur C. Clarke

   (A *Space Odyssey* (2001) belongs to the genre of Science fiction.)

147. Which of the following novel revolves round the Bigtree family?
   (a) *A Dog's Purpose*
   (b) *Swamplandia*
   (c) *The Lovely Bones*
   (d) None of the above

   (*Swamplandia,* a 2011 novel, is written by Karen Russell.)

148. *A Dog's Purpose* (2011), an American novel, is written by
   (a) Karen Russell
   (b) W. Bruce Cameron
   (c) Alice Seabold
   (d) Andy Andrews

149. The novel *The Lovely Bones* by Alice Seabold was written in
   (a) 2002 (b) 2004
   (c) 2005 (d) 2007

   (The novel is the story of a teenage girl who, after being raped and murdered, watches from her personal Heaven as her family and friend struggle to move on with their lives.)

150. Which of the following novels was written by Andy Andrews?
   (a) *Room*
   (b) *Seabiscuit*
   (c) *The Traveller's Gift*
   (d) *Free Culture*

   (*The Traveller's Gift—Seven Decisions That Determine Personal Success* (2002) weaves a fictional tale about a man who loses his job and money, but finds his way after he is magically transported into seven key points in history.)

151. *Life of Pi* (2001) is written by
   (a) Yann Martel
   (b) Ian McEwan
   (c) Lawrence Lessing
   (d) None of the above

152. Who, among the following, has written *Atonement* (2001), a family saga novel?
   (a) Andy Andrews
   (b) Ian McEwan
   (c) Lawrence Lessing
   (d) None of the above

153. *Middlesex* (2002) was written by
   (a) Andy Andrews
   (b) Alice Seabold
   (c) Jeffrey Eugenides
   (d) Roberto Bolano

   (*Middlesex* is a Pulitzer Prize—winning novel, whose characters and events are loosely based on the aspects of Eugenides' life and observations of his Greek heritage.)

154. *Everything is Illuminated*, the first novel by Jonathan Safran Foer, was published in
   (a) 1998 (b) 2001
   (c) 2002 (d) 2003

155. Who, among the following, has written *2666* (2004)?
   (a) W. Bruce Cameron
   (b) Robert Balano

(c) Jonathan Safran Foer
(d) Lawrence Lessing

(The novel explores 20th century degeneration through a wide array of characters, locations time periods, and stories within stories.)

156. *A Thousand Splendid Suns* (2007) is written by
(a) Khaled Hossieni
(b) Yann Martel
(c) Lawrence Lessing
(d) Robert Bolano

(This novel is Hosseini's second novel, following his best-selling 2003 debut, *The Kite Runner*. The book focuses on the tumultuous life of two Afghan women and how their lives cross each other, spanning from the 1960s to 2003.)

157. *EFL* stands for
(a) English for Learners
(b) English for Learning
(c) English as a Foreign Language
(d) English as a Foreigners' Language

158. I am a man more sinned against than sinning.
This line in *King Lear* is spoken by
(a) Gloucester (b) Edgar
(c) Edmund (d) King Lear

159. In which of the following plays by Shakespeare does Sir John Falstaff, a comic character, make his appearance?
(a) *Henry IV, Part I*
(b) *Henry IV, Part II*
(c) *The Merry Wives of Windoor*
(d) All of the above

160. There is nothing either good or bad, but thinking makes it so occurs in
(a) *Hamlet*
(b) *The White Devil*
(c) *Twelfth Night*
(d) *The School for Scandal*

161. Identify the work which is not written by Shakespeare.
(a) *Titus Andronicus*
(b) *Caesar and Cleopatra*
(c) *Taming of the Shrew*
(d) *Much Ado about Nothing*

162. Identify the play which is not a comedy.
(a) *She Stoops to Conquer*
(b) *The Country Wife*
(c) *The Rivals*
(d) *Pericles*

163. Which one of the following is the correct chronological order?
(a) William Wycherley, George Etherege, William Congreve, John Vanbrugh
(b) William Congreve, John Vanbrugh, George Eherege, William Wycherley
(c) George Etherege, William Wycherely, John Vanbrugh, William Congreve
(d) John Vanbrugh, William Congreve, George Etherege, William Wycherley

164. Which, one of the following, is a ten-act play?
(a) *Of Human Bondage*
(b) *The Iceman Cometh*
(c) *The Rat Trap*
(d) *Long Day's Journey into Night*

165. The following lines are by

Oh you oppressed brothers, get up!
Get up and be ready
to break the centuries-old slavery,
Get up brothers!
Get up brothers for learning.

(a) Rabindranath Tagore
(b) Sarojini Naidu
(c) Mahatma Phule
(d) None of the above

166. The word 'Dalit' was first used in the
(a) 1920s (b) 1930s
(c) 1940s (d) 1950s

167. Who used the term 'Dalit' for the first time?
   (a) Mahatma Jyotirao Phule
   (b) Dr. B.R. Ambedkar
   (c) Mahatma Gandhi
   (d) None of the above

168. The 'Dalit' literature is also called
   (a) Second World Literature
   (b) Third World Literature
   (c) Oppressed Literature
   (d) Fourth World Literature

169. Who substituted Bheemasmriti for Manusmriti?
   (a) Dr. B.R. Ambedkar
   (b) Mahatma Gandhi
   (c) Mahatma Phule
   (d) None of the above

170. Who, among the following, said?

   We need to pull away the nails which hold the framework of caste-bound Hindu Society together, such as those of intermarriage...otherwise untouchability cannot be removed.

   (a) Mahatma Gandhi
   (b) Pandit Jawaharlal Nehru
   (c) Dr. B.R. Ambedkar
   (d) Mahatma Phule

171. The play *Kanyadaan* is written by
   (a) Badal Sircar
   (b) Vijay Tendulkar
   (c) Mohan Rakesh
   (d) Girish Karnad

   (The play deals with the theme of inter-caste marriage between a Brahmin girl, Jyoti, and a dalit youth, Jayaprakash.)

172. Who is the central figure of the *Prakalpana Movement*?
   (a) Sheila Murphy
   (b) Don Webb
   (c) Vattacharja Chandan
   (d) None of the above

   (The Prakalpana Movement symbolizes India's experimental and avant-garde counter culture.)

173. When was the term 'Dalit Literature' first used?
   (a) 1948 (b) 1950
   (c) 1954 (d) 1958

   (The term came into use when the first conference of *Maharashtra Dalit Sahitya Sangh* was held at Mumbai in 1958.)

174. Who is regarded as the pioneer of Dalit writings in Marathi?
   (a) Baburao Bagul
   (b) Bandhu Madhav
   (c) Arjun Dangle
   (d) Shankarrao Kharat

175. Who, among the following, is the founder of Dalit Panther?
   (a) Bandhu Madhav
   (b) Kanwal Bharti
   (c) Namdeo Dhasal
   (d) None of the above

176. Baburao Bagul's first collection of short stories *Jevah Mi Jat Chorali* (When I had Concealed My Caste) was published in
   (a) 1958 (b) 1960
   (c) 1962 (d) 1963

   (The collection created a stir in Marathi literature with its passionate depiction of a crude society and thus brought in a new momentum to Dalit literature in Marathi. Today it is seen by many critics as the epic of the Dalits, and was later made into a film.)

177. Who, among the following, is known for his autobiography *Joothan*?
   (a) Om Parkash Valmiki
   (b) Sheoraj Singh Bechain
   (c) K. Nath
   (d) A.R. Akela

178. *The Dalit Diary* (1999) was written by
(a) Om Parkash Valmiki
(b) Kanwal Bharti
(c) Chandra Bhan Prasad
(d) K. Nath

179. Who founded DS-4?
(a) Kanshi Ram (b) Mayawati
(c) A.R. Akela (d) None of the above

180. Who, among the following, has written *Bheem Gyan Gitanali*?
(a) Om Parkash Valmiki
(b) A.R. Akela
(c) Anita Bharti
(d) Kanwal Bharti

181. *Baba Saheb Ne Khaha Tha* was written by
(a) Suraj Parkash Chauhan
(b) Devendra Chaubey
(c) A.R. Akela
(d) K. Nath

182. Who, among the following, is associated with *Vachana Sahitya*?
(a) Madara Chennaiah
(b) Mohandas Nemishray
(c) Dev Kumar
(d) Bandhu Madhav

183. Who, among the following, was awarded *The Prabuddha Ratna Puraskar*?
(a) A.R. Akela (b) Arun Kamble
(c) Raja Dhale (d) Daya Pawar

184. Who, among the following Marathi Dalit writers, was awarded the Padam Sri for Literature in 1999?
(a) Arjun Dangle
(b) Namdeo Dhasal
(c) Bandhu Madhav
(d) Madara Chennaiah

185. Who, among the following, wrote *The White Tiger* (2008)?
(a) Chitra Bannerjee
(b) Kumal Basu
(c) Aravind Adiga
(d) Santa Ram Rau

(The novel examines issues of religion, caste, loyalty, corruption and poverty in India. It tries to catch the voice of the colossal underclass. It won the 2008 Booker Prize.)

186. Give me to drink each joy and pain
Which Thine eternal hand can mete,
For my insatiate soul would drain
Earth's utmost bitter, utmost sweet.
These lines occur in
(a) *Songs of Radha—The Quest*
(b) *The Soul's Prayer*
(c) *Soul-weariness*
(d) *Spirit of Light*

187. When, finally, we reached the place
We hardly knew why we were there,
The trip had darkened every face,
Our deeds were neither great nor rare.
Home is where we have to gather grace.
These lines occur in Nissim Ezekiel's
(a) *Night of the Scorpion*
(b) *Marriage*
(c) *Enterprise*
(d) None of the above

188. I don't know politics but I know the names
Of those in power, and can repeat them like
Days of week, or names of months ........
These lines occur in Kamala Das's poem
(a) *An Introduction*
(b) *The Dance of Eunuchs*
(c) *In Love*
(d) *Ghanshyam*

189. They took their time to die this dynasty
Falling in slow motion from Aurangzeb's time.
These lines occur in A.K. Ramamjan's poem
(a) *History*

(b) *The Last of the Princess*
(c) *Small Scale Reflections on a Great House*
(d) *Obituary*

190. I know I can never come alive

If I refuse to consecrate at the actor of my origins ..........

These lines occur in Jayant Mahapatra's poem

(a) *Indian Summer Poem*
(b) *A Missing Person*
(c) *The Logic*
(d) *Relationship*

(The poem won Mahapatra the prestigious Sahitya Akadami Award in 1981.)

191. destiny lies

in parting of hair
in the parting of grasses
in the parting of thighs

These lines occur in K.N. Daruwalla's poem

(a) *Love among Pines*
(b) *Migrations*
(c) *The Unrest of Desires*
(d) *Ruminations*

192. Who, among the following poets, has written these lines?

Hereafter, I should be content
I think, to go through life
With the small change of uncertainities.

(a) K.N. Daruwalla
(b) R. Parthasarthy
(c) Jayant Mahapatra
(d) None of the above

(These lines occur in *Homecoming*.)

193. The following lines occur in Arun Kolatkar's poem

The roof comes down on Maruti's head
Nobody seems to mind.

(a) *Heart of Ruia* (b) *Hills*
(c) *Scartch* (d) *The Butterfly*

194. These lines occur in Gieve Patel's poem

It makes sense
to have the body
seamless,
hermetically sealed, a
non-official box of incorruptible

(a) *Urban* (b) *Public Hospital*
(c) *It Makes* (d) *Post Mortem*

195. Who, among the following, wrote *Palace of Illusions* (2008), *Mistress of Spices* (1997) and *Arranged Marriage* (1995)?

(a) Chitra Banerjee Divakruni
(b) Upamanyu Chatterjee
(c) Rama Mehta
(d) Suraj Pal Chauhan

196. *English August: An Indian Story* (1988) is written by

(a) Ruth Prawer Jhabvala
(b) Upamanyu Chatterjee
(c) Rama Mehta
(d) Santa Ram Rau

197. Who, among the following, has written *The Yellow Emperor's Cure* (2011)?

(a) Rama Mehta (b) Vikas Swarup
(c) Kiran Nagarkar (d) Kunal Basu

(Other novels written by Basu are *The Opium Clerk* (2001), *The Miniaturist* (2003), *Racists* (2006).)

198. Who wrote the novel *Remember the House*?

(a) Kiran Nagarkar (b) Vikas Swarup
(c) Santa Ram Rau (d) None of the above

199. *Inside the Haveli* (1977) was written by

(a) Rama Mehta
(b) Ruth Prawer Jhabvala
(c) Kamala Markandaya
(d) Santa Ram Rau

(The novel is a modern classic. It is about an independent young woman's struggle to hold on to her identity.)

200. Ruth Prawer Jhabvala's novel *Heat and Dust* won the Booker Prize in
   (a) 1971 (b) 1973
   (c) 1975 (d) 1977

   (The novel is about a woman who travels to India, to find out more about her step-grandmother, Olivia.)

201. Githa Hariharan's novel *The Thousand Faces of Night* was written in
   (a) 1990 (b) 1992
   (c) 1993 (d) 1995

   (The novel articulates the problems of women with the help of Indian Mythology)

202. The novel *Cuckold* (1997) is written by
   (a) Chitra Banerjee Divakaruni
   (b) Upamanyu Chatterjee
   (c) Kunal Basu
   (d) Kiran Nagarkar

   (Kiran Nagarkar was awarded the 2001 Sahitya Akademi Award for this novel. His other novels are *Seven Sixes are Forty Three* (1974) and *Ravan and Eddie* (1994).)

203. *Q & A* (2005) is written by
   (a) Vikas Swarup (b) Santa Rama Rau
   (c) Rama Mehta (d) None of the above

204. Who, among the following, wrote *Six Suspects* (2008)?
   (a) Santa Rama Rau
   (b) Vikas Swarup
   (c) Upamanyu Chatterjee
   (d) Rama Mehta

205. *Interdisciplinary Studies in Literature and Environment* is
   (a) an essay (b) a book
   (c) a journal (d) None of the above

   (It is a journal brought out by Association for the Study of Literature and Environment (ASLE).)

206. Who, according to Barry, may be the first critic to use the term *ecocriticism*?
   (a) William Rueckert (b) Lawrence Buell
   (c) Cheryll Glotfelty (d) Harold Fromm

   (Rueckert coined the term in 1978.)

207. Which of the following terms can be used for *ecocriticism*?
   (a) Ecopoetics
   (b) Environmental Literary Criticism
   (c) Green Cultural Studies
   (d) All of the above

208. Glen A. Love's *Practical Ecocriticism* defines eco-criticism as a literary inquiry that
   (a) encompasses non-human as well as human contexts and considerations
   (b) deals with the practical aspects of both man's life and nature
   (c) we should have a practical attitude to nature
   (d) None of the above

209. *Revaluating Nature: Toward an Ecological Criticism* is written by
   (a) Lawrence Buell
   (b) Glen A. Love
   (c) Thomas J. Lyon
   (d) Edward Abbey

   (It is one of the most influential essays of the current ecocritical movement.)

210. Which of the following are the traits of 'Deep Ecology'?
   (a) Deep Ecology demands a return to a monistic, primal identification of humans and the ecosphere.
   (b) It means an equal and egalitarian identification of all forms of the ecosphere.

(c) It blames the anthropocentric dualism of humanity versus nature as the ultimate source of all anti-ecological beliefs and practices.
(d) All of the above.

('Deep Ecology' is a contemporary ecological and environmental philosophy characterized by its advocacy of the inherent worth of living beings regardless of their instrumental utility to human needs, and advocacy for a radical restructuring of modern human societies according to such ideas.)

211. *Turtle Island* (1974) is written by
(a) Gary Synder (b) Barry Lopez
(c) Rachel Carson (d) Mary Austin

212. *Silent Sprint* (1962) is written by
(a) Barry Lopez (b) Rachel Carson
(c) Aldo Leopold (d) Annie Dillard

213. *The Land of Little Rain* (1903) is written by
(a) Mary Austin (b) Aldo Leopold
(c) Harold Fromm (d) Lynne Cherry

214. Who, among the following, wrote *A Sand Country Almanac*?
(a) Mary Austin (b) Gary Syndey
(c) Aldo Leopold (d) None of the above

(Aldo Leopold (1887-1948) is considered the father of modern environmental ethics.)

215. Who, among the following said, "Asking a working writer what he thinks about critics is like asking a lamp–post what it thinks about dogs"?
(a) Ezra Pound
(b) J.M. Synge
(c) George Orwell
(d) Christopher Hampton

## ANSWERS

| | | | | | |
|---|---|---|---|---|---|
| 1. (a) | 2. (a) | 3. (b) | 4. (c) | 5. (d) | 6. (c) |
| 7. (a) | 8. (b) | 9. (b) | 10. (c) | 11. (b) | 12. (d) |
| 13. (c) | 14. (a) | 15. (c) | 16. (d) | 17. (a) | 18. (b) |
| 19. (a) | 20. (c) | 21. (d) | 22. (a) | 23. (b) | 24. (c) |
| 25. (d) | 26. (a) | 27. (d) | 28. (b) | 29. (d) | 30. (a) |
| 31. (c) | 32. (c) | 33. (a) | 34. (d) | 35. (a) | 36. (c) |
| 37. (b) | 38. (d) | 39. (c) | 40. (d) | 41. (a) | 42. (d) |
| 43. (b) | 44. (a) | 45. (c) | 46. (b) | 47. (c) | 48. (a) |
| 49. (d) | 50. (c) | 51. (c) | 52. (b) | 53. (c) | 54. (a) |
| 55. (c) | 56. (b) | 57. (a) | 58. (c) | 59. (a) | 60. (b) |
| 61. (c) | 62. (d) | 63. (a) | 64. (b) | 65. (c) | 66. (c) |
| 67. (a) | 68. (b) | 69. (c) | 70. (a) | 71. (c) | 72. (c) |
| 73. (d) | 74. (b) | 75. (a) | 76. (d) | 77. (c) | 78. (b) |
| 79. (a) | 80. (c) | 81. (a) | 82. (c) | 83. (b) | 84. (c) |
| 85. (a) | 86. (c) | 87. (d) | 88. (a) | 89. (c) | 90. (c) |
| 91. (b) | 92. (a) | 93. (d) | 94. (a) | 95. (c) | 96. (d) |

| | | | | | |
|---|---|---|---|---|---|
| 97. (a) | 98. (b) | 99. (c) | 100. (d) | 101. (d) | 102. (b) |
| 103. (a) | 104. (c) | 105. (c) | 106. (a) | 107. (b) | 108. (a) |
| 109. (b) | 110. (c) | 111. (b) | 112. (a) | 113. (c) | 114. (a) |
| 115. (c) | 116. (a) | 117. (c) | 118. (d) | 119. (b) | 120. (c) |
| 121. (c) | 122. (a) | 123. (c) | 124. (d) | 125. (a) | 126. (b) |
| 127. (c) | 128. (d) | 129. (c) | 130. (b) | 131. (c) | 132. (b) |
| 133. (a) | 134. (c) | 135. (a) | 136. (a) | 137. (d) | 138. (c) |
| 139. (d) | 140. (a) | 141. (b) | 142. (c) | 143. (a) | 144. (d) |
| 145. (a) | 146. (d) | 147. (a) | 148. (b) | 149. (a) | 150. (c) |
| 151. (a) | 152. (b) | 153. (c) | 154. (c) | 155. (b) | 156. (a) |
| 157. (c) | 158. (d) | 159. (d) | 160. (a) | 161. (b) | 162. (d) |
| 163. (c) | 164. (b) | 165. (c) | 166. (b) | 167. (a) | 168. (d) |
| 169. (a) | 170. (c) | 171. (b) | 172. (c) | 173. (d) | 174. (a) |
| 175. (c) | 176. (d) | 177. (a) | 178. (c) | 179. (a) | 180. (b) |
| 181. (c) | 182. (a) | 183. (b) | 184. (b) | 185. (c) | 186. (b) |
| 187. (c) | 188. (a) | 189. (b) | 190. (d) | 191. (a) | 192. (b) |
| 193. (a) | 194. (c) | 195. (a) | 196. (b) | 197. (d) | 198. (c) |
| 199. (a) | 200. (c) | 201. (b) | 202. (d) | 203. (a) | 204. (b) |
| 205. (c) | 206. (a) | 207. (d) | 208. (a) | 209. (b) | 210. (d) |
| 211. (a) | 212. (b) | 213. (a) | 214. (c) | 215. (d) | |

# 6

# Winners of Nobel Prize in Literature

2012
Mo Yan

2011
Tomas Tranströmer

2010
Mario Vargas Llosa

2009
Herta Müller

2008
Jean-Marie Gustave Le Clézio

2007
Doris Lessing

2006
Orhan Pamuk

2005
Harold Pinter

2004
Elfriede Jelinek

2003
John M. Coetzee

2002
Imre Kertész

2001
Sir Vidiadhar Surajprasad Naipaul

2000
Gao Xingjian

1999
Günter Grass

1998
José Saramago

1997
Dario Fo

1996
Wislawa Szymborska

1995
Seamus Heaney

1994
Kenzaburo Oe

1993
Toni Morrison

1992
Derek Walcott

1991
Nadine Gordimer

1990
Octavio Paz

1989
Camilo José Cela

1988
Naguib Mahfouz

1987
Joseph Brodsky

1986
Wole Soyinka

1985
Claude Simon

1984
Jaroslav Seifert

1983
William Golding

1982
Gabriel García Márquez

1981
Elias Canetti

1980
Czeslaw Milosz

1979
Odysseus Elytis

1978
Isaac Bashevis Singer

1977
Vicente Aleixandre

1976
Saul Bellow

1975
Eugenio Montale

1974
Eyvind Johnson, Harry Martinson

1973
Patrick White

1972
Heinrich Böll

1971
Pablo Neruda

1970
Aleksandr Isayevich Solzhenitsyn

1969
Samuel Beckett

1968
Yasunari Kawabata

1967
Miguel Angel Asturias

1966
Shmuel Yosef Agnon, Nelly Sachs

1965
Mikhail Aleksandrovich Sholokhov

1964
Jean-Paul Sartre

1963
Giorgos Seferis

1962
John Steinbeck

1961
Ivo Andric

1960
Saint-John Perse

1959
Salvatore Quasimodo

1958
Boris Leonidovich Pasternak

1957
Albert Camus

1956
Juan Ramón Jiménez

1955
Halldór Kiljan Laxness

1954
Ernest Miller Hemingway

1953
Sir Winston Leonard Spencer Churchill

1952
François Mauriac

1951
Pär Fabian Lagerkvist

1950
Earl (Bertrand Arthur William) Russell

1949
William Faulkner

1948
Thomas Stearns Eliot

1947
André Paul Guillaume Gide

1946
Hermann Hesse

1945
Gabriela Mistral

1944
Johannes Vilhelm Jensen

1939
Frans Eemil Sillanpää

1938
Pearl Buck

1937
Roger Martin du Gard

1936
Eugene Gladstone O'Neill

1934
Luigi Pirandello

1933
Ivan Alekseyevich Bunin

1932
John Galsworthy

1931
Erik Axel Karlfeldt

1930
Sinclair Lewis

1929
Thomas Mann

1928
Sigrid Undset

1927
Henri Bergson

1926
Grazia Deledda

1925
George Bernard Shaw

1924
Wladyslaw Stanislaw Reymont

1923
William Butler Yeats

1922
Jacinto Benavente

1921
Anatole France

1920
Knut Pedersen Hamsun

1919
Carl Friedrich Georg Spitteler

1917
Karl Adolph Gjellerup, Henrik Pontoppidan

1916
Carl Gustaf Verner von Heidenstam

1915
Romain Rolland

1913
Rabindranath Tagore

1912
Gerhart Johann Robert Hauptmann

1911
Count Maurice (Mooris) Polidore Marie Bernhard Maeterlinck

1910
Paul Johann Ludwig Heyse

1909
Selma Ottilia Lovisa Lagerlsöf
1908
Rudolf Christoph Eucken
1907
Rudyard Kipling
1906
Giosuè Carducci
1905
Henryk Sienkiewicz
1904
Frédéric Mistral, José Echegaray y Eizaguirre
1903
Bjørnstjerne Martinus Bjørnson
1902
Christian Matthias Theodor Mommsen
1901
Sully Prudhomme

# 7

# NET Examination Paper II, June 2012 with Answers

1. To refer to the unresolvable difficulties a text may open up, Derrida makes use of the term
   (a) Aporia (b) Difference
   (c) Erasure (d) Supplement
2. Who, among the following English playwrights, scripted the film *Shakespeare in Love*?
   (a) Harold Pinter (b) Alan Bennett
   (c) Caryl Churchill (d) Tom Stoppard
3. Arrange the following in the chronological order:
   1. Mary Wollstonecraft's *Vindication of the Rights of Women*
   2. *Lyrical Ballads*
   3. *French Revolution*
   4. *Percy's Reliques of Ancient English Poetry*

   (a) 4, 3, 1, 2 (b) 3, 2, 1, 2
   (c) 1, 2, 4, 3 (d) 2, 1, 3, 4
4. Which of the following employs a narrative structure in which the main action is relayed at second hand through an enclosing frame story?
   (a) *Sons and Lovers*
   (b) *Ulysses*
   (c) *The Power and the Glory*
   (d) *Heart of Darkness*
5. The Irish Dramatic Movement was heralded by such figures as
   (a) W.B. Yeats, Lady Gregory and Edward Martyn
   (b) Jonathan Swift and his contemporaries
   (c) H. Drummond, Edward Irving and John Ervine
   (d) Oscar Wilde and his contemporaries
6. Which poem by Chaucer was written on the death of Blanche, wife of John of Gaunt?
   (a) "Troilus and Criseyde"
   (b) "The House of Fame"
   (c) "The Book of Duchess"
   (d) "The Legend of Good Women"
7. *The Tragedy of Ferrex and Porrex* is the other title of
   (a) *Gorboduc*
   (b) *Ralph Roister Doister*
   (c) *Damon and Pythias*
   (d) *Lamentable Tragedy*
8. Who of the following poets is Australian?
   (a) Austin Clarke (b) Judith Wright
   (c) Edwin Muir (d) Derek Walcott
9. "He found it [English] brick and left it marble", remarked one great writer on another. Who were they?
   (a) Milton on Shakespeare
   (b) Dryden on Milton
   (c) Johnson on Dryden

(d) Jonson on Shakespeare

10. Who, among the following, is a Nobel Laureate?
    (a) Tony Morrison
    (b) Seamus Heaney
    (c) Ted Hughes
    (d) Geoffrey Hill

11. **List I**
    I. "Because I could not stop for death..."
    II. "O Captain ! My Captain!"
    III. "Two roads diverged in a wood...."
    IV. "So much depends/upon"

    **List II**
    A. Robert Frost
    B. William Carlos Williams
    C. Emily Dickinson
    D. Walt Whitman

    The correctly matched series would be
    (a) I-D; II-C; III-B; IV-A
    (b) I-A; II-B; III-C; IV-D
    (c) I-B; II-A; III-D; IV-C
    (d) I-C; II-D; III-A; IV-B

12. The predominant tone and thrust of Jonathan Swift's *A Modest Proposal* are
    (a) Comic (b) Solemn
    (c) Hortatory (d) Irony

13. I sit in one of the *dives*
    On Fifty Second Street,
    Uncertain and afraid
    As the clever hopes expire
    Of a low dishonest decade.
    So begins Auden's "September 1, 1939". What is the meaning of the word in italics?
    (a) Bench (b) Night club
    (c) House (d) Park

14. C.K. Ogden and I.A. Richards were reputed in the 1930s for introducing
    (a) Practical Criticism
    (b) New Criticism
    (c) Standard English Project
    (d) Basic English Project

15. In which of the following works does Mrs. Malaprop appear?
    (a) *The Rivals*
    (b) *She Stoops to Conquer*
    (c) *The Mysteries of Udolpho*
    (d) *The Way of the World*

16. Which of the following statements about Christopher Marlowe are true ?
    I. *Edward II* was written in the last year of Marlowe's life.
    II. Many critics consider *Doctor Faustus* to be Marlowe's best play.
    III. His *Spanish Tragedy comes* a close second.
    IV. Marlowe was less educated than Shakespeare.
    (a) I and II are true.
    (b) II and III are true.
    (c) II and IV are true.
    (d) III and IV are true.

17. *"Art for Art's Sake"* became a rallying cry for
    (a) the Aesthetes
    (b) the Symbolists
    (c) the Imagists
    (d) the Art Noveau School

18. *Confessions of an English Opium Eater* is a literary work by
    (a) S.T. Coleridge
    (b) P.B. Shelley
    (c) Thomas De Quincey
    (d) Lord Byron

19. Which of the following statements about *The Canterbury Tales* is true?
    (a) "The General Prologue' is appended to *The Canterbury Tales*.
    (b) In all, Chaucer tells thirty tales in this

work.

(c) *The Canterbury Tales* remained unfinished at the time of its author's death.

(d) The Wife of Bath, The Clerk, Sir Gawain and The Franklin are characters and tale-tellers in this work.

20. Who, among the following, was a Catholic novelist, an Intelligence Officer, a film critic and set his fictions in far-away places wrecked by political conflicts ?

(a) Anthony Powell
(b) Evelyn Waugh
(c) William Golding
(d) Graham Greene

21. **List I**

A. Good sense is the body of poetic genius.
B. Poetry is the breath and a finer spirit of all knowledge.
C. Literary criticism is a description and evaluation of its object.
D. Nature never set forth the earth in as rich a tapestry as diverse poets have done.

**List II**

1. Brooks, "The Formalist Critic"
2. Sidney, Defence/An Apology for Poetry.
3. Wordsworth, *Preface to Lyrical Ballads.*
4. Coleridge, *Biographia Literaria*

| | A | B | C | D |
|---|---|---|---|---|
| (a) | 4 | 3 | 1 | 2 |
| (b) | 2 | 4 | 3 | 1 |
| (c) | 3 | 2 | 1 | 4 |
| (d) | 4 | 2 | 1 | 3 |

22. In which of the following travel books does Mark Twain give an account of his visit to India?

(a) *A Tramp Abroad*
(b) *Roughing It*
(c) *The Innocents Abroad*
(d) *Following the Equator*

23. William Blake's famous poems such as "London", "The Sick Rose", and "The Tyger" appear in

(a) *Songs of Innocence*
(b) *Songs of Experience*
(c) *The Marriage of Heaven and Hell*
(d) *Vision of the Daughters of Albion*

24. Who among the following English artists illustrated the novels of Dickens and Scott?

(a) Richard Hogarth
(b) Joshua Reynolds
(c) George Cruishank
(d) John Tennial

25. The last of *Gulliver's Travels* is to

(a) The Land of the Houyhnhnms
(b) The Land of Homosapiens
(c) The Land of the Hurricanes
(d) The Newfound Land

26. Madam Merle is a character in

(a) *The Great Gatsby*
(b) *The Portrait of a Lady*
(c) *The Jungle*
(d) *The Heart is a Lonely Hunter*

27. In which of the following scenes of *The Waste Land* do we have a departure from Standard English?

(a) The typist scene
(b) The pub scene
(c) The hyacinth garden scene
(d) The Chapel Perilous scene

28. The words "If it were done when tis done, then twere well/ It were done quickly..." are uttered by

(a) Hamlet (b) Lear
(c) Othello (d) Macbeth

29. John Dryden's *Absalom and Achotophel* a

(a) Religious tract

(b) Political allegory
(c) Comic verse epic
(d) Comedy

30. The term 'the comedy of menace' is associated with the early plays of
(a) Arnold Wesker
(b) John Arden
(c) Harold Pinter
(d) David Hare

31. Examine the following statements and identify one of them which is not true.
(a) Rudyard Kipling died in the year 1936.
(b) He was born in India but schooled in England.
(c) He returned to India as a police constable in Burma.
(d) He is the author of *Jungle Book* and *Barrack Room Ballads.*

32. What is the correct combination of the following?
I. Balachandra Rajan
II. R.K. Narayan
III. Kamala Markandaya
IV. Romen Basu
A. *The Tamarind* Tree
B. *The Coffer* Dams
C. *The Dark Dancer*
D. *The Dark Room*
(a) I-C; II-D; III-B; IV-B
(b) I-D; II-A; III-B; IV-C
(c) I-C; II-A; III-D; IV-B
(d) I-D; II-C; III-A; IV-B

33. Name the poet who chooses his successor and the successor-poet whom Dryden satirises in his famous poem.
(a) James Shirley and Chris Shirley
(b) Henry Treece and Charles Triesten
(c) Richard Flecknoe and Thomas Shadwell
(d) Thomas Percy and Samuel Pepys

34. "If ____ comes, can ____ be far behind?" (Shelley, "Ode to the West Wind")
(a) winter, spring
(b) autumn, summer
(c) wind, rains
(d) spring, winter

35. The following passages are the very first lines of well-known works. Match the lines and the works :
I. Let us go then, you and I.....
II. Call me Ishmael.....
III. When shall we three meet again ?
IV. He disappeared in the dead of winter
V. I wish either....begot me .....
A. *Moby Dick*
B. *Macbeth*
C. "The Love Song of J. Alfred Prufrock"
D. *Tristram Shandy*
E. "In Memory of W.B. Yeats"
(a) I-C; II-A; III-B; IV-E; V-D
(b) I-E; II-B; III-A; IV-C; V-D
(c) I-B; II-A; III-D; IV-E; V-C
(d) I-B; II-E; III-D; IV-C; V-A

36. Which of the following is not a revenge tragedy?
(a) *Hamlet*
(b) *The Duchess of Malfi*
(c) *Volpone*
(d) *Gorboduc*

37. What is a neologism?
(a) A word with roots in a native language.
(b) A word whose meaning changes with every renewed use.
(c) A word newly coined or used in a new sense.
(d) An obsession with new words and phrases.

38. Which of the following is not true of Edward Said's *Orientalism*?
(a) Makes use of Foucault's concept of discursive formulation.

(b) Is one of the founding texts of postcolonial theory.
(c) Makes use of Barthes's concept of writerly text.
(d) Utilises the Gramscian notion of hegemony.

39. Thomas Love Peacock classified poetry into four periods. They are
(a) carbon, gold, silver and brass
(b) brass, silver, gold and diamond
(c) iron, gold, silver and brass
(d) gold, platinum, silver and diamond

40. Which among the following novels has more than one ending?
(a) *Lucky Jim*
(b) *The Prime of Jean Brodie*
(c) *The French Lieutenant's Woman*
(d) *The Clockwork Orange*

41. "You have seen how a man was made a slave; you shall see how a slave was made a man" is an example of
(a) Bathos (b) Epistrophe
(c) Chiasmus (d) Anti-climax

42. Which of the following statements is not correct?
(a) Chaucer used the rhyme royal, a stanzaic form in some of his major poems.
(b) Chaucer was the author of *The Legend of Good Women.*
(c) Chaucer wrote in English when the court poetry of his day was written in Anglo-Norman and Latin.
(d) Chaucer wrote *The Book Named the Governor.*

43. Material feminism studies inequality in terms of
(a) only gender
(b) only class
(c) both class and gender
(d) only patriarchy

44. Who among the following is not an Irish writer?
(a) Oscar Wilde
(b) Oliver Goldsmith
(c) Edmund Burke
(d) Thomas Gray

45. Entries in *The Diary of Samuel Pepys* begins after
(a) The Restoration
(b) The Glorious Revolution
(c) The Reformation
(d) The French Revolution

46. In a poem, a line may either be *endstopped* or
(a) Rhymed (b) Broken
(c) Accented (d) Run-on

47. Which of the following poets wrote the essay "Naipaul's India and Mine"?
(a) Kamala Das
(b) R. Parthasarthy
(c) A.K. Ramanujam
(d) Nissim Ezekiel

48. Match the following :

| | |
|---|---|
| A. *James Joyce* | 1. Peter Ackroyd |
| B. *T.S. Eliot* | 2. James Boswell |
| C. *Life of Johnson* | 3. Samuel Johnson |
| D. *Lives of Poets* | 4. Richard Ellman |

(a) A-3, B-4, C-1, D-2
(b) A-4, B-1, C-2, D-3
(c) A-1, B-2, C-3, D-4
(d) A-2, B-3, C-1, D-4

49. "The pen is mightier than the sword" is an example of
(a) Simile (b) Image
(c) Conceit (d) Metonymy

50. An epilogue is
(a) prefixed to a text which it introduces.
(b) suffixed to a text which it sums up or extends.

(c) a piece of writing or speech that formally begins a book.

(d) a piece of writing or speech that bears no relation to the text at hand.

## ANSWERS

| | | | | | |
|---|---|---|---|---|---|
| 1. (a) | 2. (d) | 3. (a) | 4. (d) | 5. (a) | 6. (c) |
| 7. (a) | 8. (b) | 9. (c) | 10. (b) | 11. (d) | 12. (d) |
| 13. (b) | 14. (c) | 15. (a) | 16. (a) | 17. (a) | 18. (c) |
| 19. (a) | 20. (d) | 21. (a) | 22. (d) | 23. (b) | 24. (c) |
| 25. (a) | 26. (b) | 27. (b) | 28. (d) | 29. (b) | 30. (c) |
| 31. (c) | 32. (a) | 33. (c) | 34. (a) | 35. (a) | 36. (c) |
| 37. (c) | 38. (c) | 39. (c) | 40. (c) | 41. (c) | 42. (d) |
| 43. (c) | 44. (d) | 45. (a) | 46. (d) | 47. (d) | 48. (b) |
| 49. (d) | 50. (b) | | | | |

# 8

# English Paper III, June 2012 with Answers

1. In Ben Jonson's *Volpone*, the animal imagery includes
   1. the fox and the vulture
   2. the fly and the cockroach
   3. the fly, the crow and the raven
   4. the fox, the vulture and the goat

   (a) 1 and 2 are correct.
   (b) 4 is correct.
   (c) 2 and 4 are correct.
   (d) 1 and 3 are correct.

2. Salman Rushdie's "Imaginary Homelands" is _______.
   (a) a discussion of imperialist assumptions
   (b) an essay that propounds an antiessentialist view of place
   (c) an existential lament on triumphant colonialism
   (d) an orientalist description of his favourite homelands

3. Identify the incorrect statement below:
   1. BASIC was an experiment initiated by C.K. Ogden and I.A. Richards from 1926 to about 1940.
   2. Expanded, BASIC read: Broadly Ascertained Scientific International Course.
   3. BASIC English was an attcmpt to reduce the number of essential words to 850.
   4. While keeping to normal constructions, BASIC failed as an experiment because its documents were far too complicated and technical to understand.

   (a) 1 and 2 (b) 2 and 4
   (c) 1 and 3 (d) 3 and 4

4. Items in a published book appear in the following order:
   (a) Index, Copyright Page, Bibliography, Footnotes
   (b) Copyright Page, Bibliography, Index, Footnotes
   (c) Copyright Page, Footnotes, Bibliography, Index
   (d) Bibliography, Copyright Page, Index, Footnotes

5. Match the following:
   A. James Thomson, Oliver Goldsmith, William Cowper, George Crabbe
   B. George Herbert, Henry Vaughan, Andrew Marvell, Abraham Cowley, John Donne
   C. Rupert Brooke, Wilfred Owen, Siegfried Sassoon, Edmund Blunden, Robert Graves
   D. W.H. Davies, Walter de la Mare, John Drinkwater, Rupert Brooke

   1. Metaphysical poets
   2. Transitional Poets
   3. War Poets
   4. Georgians

| | A | B | C | D |
|---|---|---|---|---|
| (a) | 4 | 1 | 3 | 2 |
| (b) | 4 | 2 | 4 | 1 |
| (c) | 2 | 1 | 3 | 4 |
| (d) | 1 | 3 | 4 | 2 |

6. The following phrases from Shakespeare have become the titles of famous works. Identify the correctly matched group.

| | |
|---|---|
| A. *Pale Fire* | 1. Thomas Hardy |
| B. *The Sound and the Fury* | 2. Somerset Maugham |
| C. *Rosencrantz and Guildenstern are Dead* | 3. William Faulkner |
| D. *Under the Greenwood Tree* | 4. Tom Stoppard |
| E. *Of Cakes and Ale* | 5. Vladimir Nabokov |

| | A | B | C | D | E |
|---|---|---|---|---|---|
| (a) | 5 | 4 | 3 | 1 | 2 |
| (b) | 4 | 5 | 2 | 3 | 1 |
| (c) | 5 | 3 | 4 | 1 | 2 |
| (d) | 3 | 4 | 2 | 5 | 1 |

7. Identify the statement that is not true among those that explain "stage directions" in drama.
   (a) Stage directions inform readers how to stage, perform or imagine the play.
   (b) The place, time of action, design of the set and at times characters' actions or tone of voice are indicated by stage directions.
   (c) Stage directions are often italicized in the text of a play in order to be spoken aloud.
   (d) Stage directions may appear at the beginning of a play, before a scene or attached to a line of dialogue.

8. The emergence of the concept of "World literature" is associated with
   1. Friedrich Schiller
   2. Johann Wolfgang von Goethe
   3. Johann Goltfried Herder
   4. Immanuel Kant

   (a) 1 and 2 (b) 3 and 4
   (c) 2 and 3 (d) 1 and 4

9. Günter Grass's Tin Drum is part of a trilogy known as the *Danzig trilogy*.
   The other two novels are
   (a) *The Flounder* and *Dog Years*
   (b) *The Rat* and *Cat and Mouse*
   (c) *Cat and Mouse* and *Dog Years*
   (d) *Crabwalk* and *The Rat*

10. The hostess proudly announces that the family can afford a servant and her daughters have nothing to do with the kitchen. Who is the proud mother in this Jane Austen novel?
    (a) Mrs. Morland
    (b) Lady Catherine de Burgh
    (c) Mrs. Bennet
    (d) Mrs. Dashwood

11. When Keats writes about the "beaker full" of "The blushful Hippocrene", Hippocrene is
    (a) the fountain of the horse.
    (b) a spring sacred to the Muses.
    (c) Mount Helicon produced from a blow of Pegasus.
    (d) Both (a) and (b).

12. Which of the following statements on The Prelude by William Wordsworth is/are not true?
    1. The Prelude was published posthumously.
    2. In this poem, Wordsworth records his development as a poet.
    3. The poem runs to 14 books; at crucial stages the poet celebrates the sublime natural scenery in developing his spiritual, moral and imaginative nature.

4. Poems like "Michael", "The Old Cumberland Beggar", "She dwelt among the untrodden ways", "Nutting" etc. are the highlights of this volume.

(a) 1 to 4 are true.
(b) 1 is not true.
(c) 4 is not true.
(d) 3 is true.

13. **Assertion (A) :** At the end of Heart of Darkness, Marlow tells a lie to the Intended about Kurtz when he tells her "The last word he pronounced was—your name".

**Reason (R) :** Marlow tells this lie because he is secretly in love with the Intended and tells her what she wants to hear.

(a) Both (A) and (R) are true, (R) is the correct explanation.
(b) Both (A) and (R) are true, but (R) is not the correct explanation.
(c) (A) is true, but (R) is false.
(d) (A) is false, but (R) is true.

14. Ear-training in ELT is easily achieved by :

1. composition
2. dictation
3. cloze tests
4. listening exercises
5. précis writing

(a) 3 and 5 (b) 1, 3 and 5
(c) 2, 3 and 4 (d) 2 and 4

15. William Shakespeare's *Julius Caesar*, *Antony and Cleopatra* and *Coriolanus* are based on _______.

(a) Holinshed's Chronicles
(b) Folk-tales and legends
(c) Older Roman Plays
(d) Plutarch's Lives

16. The basic concept that creation was ordered, that every species exists in a hierarchy of status, from God to the lowest creature, was prevalent in the Renaissance. In this hierarchical continuum, man occupies the middle position between the animal kinds and the angels.

This world view is known as

(a) Humanism
(b) The Enlightenment
(c) The Great Chain of Being
(d) Calvinism

17. In Virginia Woolf's *To the Lighthouse*, the lighthouse does not symbolize :

(a) permanence at the heart of change.
(b) change in the unchanging world.
(c) celebration of life in the heart of death.
(d) celebration of order in the heart of chaos.

18. "Can one imagine any private soldier, in the nineties or now, reading Barrack-Room Ballads and feeling that here was a writer who spoke for him? It is very hard to do so. [....] When he is writing not of British but of 'loyal' Indians he carries the 'Salaam, Sahib' motif to sometimes disgusting lengths. Yet it remains true that he has far more interest in the common soldier, far more anxiety that he shall get a fair deal, than most of the 'liberals' of his day and our own. He sees that the soldier is neglected, meanly underpaid and hypocritically despised by the people whose incomes he safeguards".

(a) This is E.M. Forster's "India, Again".
(b) This is Malcolm Muggeridge on E.M. Forster's India.
(c) This is T.S. Eliot on Rudyard Kipling.
(d) This is George Orwell on Rudyard Kipling.

19. In the well-known poem "To His Coy Mistress", the word coy means

(a) Shy (b) Timid
(c) Voluptuous (d) Sensuous

20. From the following list, identify "backformation":

Sulk, bulk, stoke, poke, swindle, bundle.

(a) Sulk, bulk, stoke, poke
(b) Stoke, poke, swindle, bundle
(c) Sulk, stoke, bundle
(d) Bulk, poke, bundle

21. "It blurs distinctions among literary, non-literary and cultural texts, showing how all three intercirculate, share in, and mutually constitute each other." What does it in this statement stand for?

(a) Marxism
(b) Structuralism
(c) Formalism
(d) New Historicism

22. For, though, I've no idea.

What this accoutred frowsty ___ is worth,
It pleases me to stand in silence here. (Fill in the blank)

(a) bar (b) barn
(c) attic (d) alcove

23. Which of the following novels is not a Partition novel?

(a) *Azadi*
(b) *Tamas*
(c) *Clear Light of the Day*
(d) *That Long Silence*

24. Of the following characters, which one does not belong to *A House for Mr. Biswas*?

(a) Raghu (b) Ralph Singh
(c) Dehuti (d) Tara

25. In English literature, the trope of the vampire was used for the first time by

(a) Matthew Gregory Lewis
(b) John Polidori
(c) John Stagg
(d) Bram Stoker

26. Why is "Universal grammar" so called?

(a) It is a set of basic grammatical principles universally followed and easily recognized by people.
(b) It is a set of basic grammatical principles assumed to be fundamental to all natural languages.
(c) It is a set of advanced grammatical principles assumed to be fundamental to all natural languages.
(d) It is a set of universally respected practices that have come, in time, to be known as "grammar".

27. Identify the novel with the wrong subtitle listed below

(a) *Middlemarch, A Study of Provincial Life*
(b) *Tess of the D'Urbervilles, A Pure Woman*
(c) *The Mayor of Casterbridge, A Man of Character*
(d) *Felix Holt, the Socialist*

28. Match List I with List II.

| List I | List II |
|---|---|
| A. David Malouf | 1. *The Solid Mandala* |
| B. Patrick White | 2. *Wild Cat Falling* |
| C. Peter Carey | 3. *Remembering Babylon* |
| D. Colin Johnson | 4. *True History of the Kelly Gang* |

| | A | B | C | D |
|---|---|---|---|---|
| (a) | 1 | 3 | 2 | 4 |
| (b) | 3 | 1 | 4 | 2 |
| (c) | 2 | 3 | 1 | 4 |
| (d) | 3 | 4 | 2 | 1 |

29. The opening sentence of Tolstoy's Anna Karenina, "Happy families are all alike, every unhappy family is unhappy in its own way." The specific cause of the

unhappiness in Oblonsky's house was the husband's affair with

(a) a kitchen-maid
(b) an English governess
(c) a French governess
(d) a socialite

30. This periodical had the avowed intention "to enliven morality with wit and to temper wit with morality...to bring philosophy out of the closets and libraries, schools and colleges, to dwell in clubs and assemblies, at tea-tables and coffee houses". It also promoted family, marriage and courtesy.

The periodical under reference is

(a) *The Tatler*
(b) *The Spectator*
(c) *The Gentleman's Magazine*
(d) *The London Magazine*

31. **Assertion (A) :** "Tam O' Shanter" by John Clare is about the experience of an ordinary human being and became quite popular during that time.

**Reason (R) :** John Clare, having suffered bouts of madness, could really feel for the misery of common man.

In the context of the two statements, which of the following is correct?

(a) Both (A) and (R) are true and (R) explains (A).
(b) Both (A) and (R) are true, but (R) does not explain (A).
(c) (A) is true but (R) is false.
(d) (A) is false but (R) is true.

32. Alexander Pope's *An Essay in Criticism*

1. purports to define "wit" and "nature" as they apply to the literature of his age.
2. claims no originality in the thought that governs this work.
3. is a prose essay that gives us such quotes as "A little learning is a dangerous thing!"
4. appeared in 1701.

(a) 3 and 4 are incorrect.
(b) 1 and 2 are incorrect.
(c) 1 to 4 are correct.
(d) 1 and 4 are correct.

33. What is register?

(a) The way in which a language registers in the minds of its users.
(b) The way users of a language register the nuances of that language.
(c) A variety of language used in social situations or one specially designed for the subject it deals with.
(d) A variety of language used in non-professional or informal situations by professionals.

34. Jeremy Collier's *Short View of the Immorality and Profaneness of the English Stage* (1698) attacked ______.

(a) the practice of mixing tragic and comic themes in Shakespeare's plays
(b) the bawdiness of "low" characters in Shakespeare's plays
(c) the coarseness and ugliness of Restoration Theatre
(d) irreligious themes and irreverent attitudes in the plays of the seventeenth century

35. One of the most important themes the speakers debate in *Dryden's An Essay on Dramatic Poesy* is ______.

(a) European and non-European perceptions of reality
(b) English and non-English perceptions of reality
(c) the relative merits of French and English theatre
(d) the relative merits of French and English poetry

36. Identify the correctly matched pair
   (a) Amitav Ghosh — *All About H. Halterr*
   (b) Anita Desai — *Inheritance of Loss*
   (c) Shashi Deshpande — *A Bend in the Ganges*
   (d) Salman Rushdie — *The Enchantress of Florence*

37. Match the following correctly :

| | |
|---|---|
| A. Langue/Parole | 1. Noam Chomsky |
| B. Competence/ Performance | 2. C.S. Pierce |
| C. Ieonic/Indexical | 3. Ferdinand de Saussure |
| D. Readerly/ Writerly | 4. Roland Barthes |

| | A | B | C | D |
|---|---|---|---|---|
| (a) | 3 | 2 | 1 | 4 |
| (b) | 3 | 1 | 2 | 4 |
| (c) | 1 | 3 | 4 | 2 |
| (d) | 2 | 3 | 1 | 4 |

38.

| | |
|---|---|
| A. Joy Kogawa | 1. *Bloody Rites* |
| B. M.G. Vasanjee | 2. *Obasan* |
| C. Sky Lee | 3. *The Gunny Sack* |
| D. Arnold Itwaru | 4. *Disappearing Moon Café* |

| | A | B | C | D |
|---|---|---|---|---|
| (a) | 4 | 1 | 2 | 3 |
| (b) | 1 | 4 | 3 | 2 |
| (c) | 2 | 3 | 4 | 1 |
| (d) | 1 | 2 | 3 | 4 |

39. Why does Jean Baudrillard adopt Disneyland as his own sign?
   (a) Disneyland is by far the most eminently noticeable cultural sign in the post modern world.
   (b) Disneyland captures 'essences' and 'non-essences' of Reality more convincingly than other cultural venues.
   (c) Disneyland is an artefact that so obviously announces its own fictiveness that it would seem to imply some counter balancing reality.
   (d) Disneyland is both 'appearance' and 'reality' in the post modern visual game of handy-dandy.

40. Which of the following statements is not true of Dante Gabriel Rossetti?
   (a) D.G. Rossetti was a Londoner, the son of an Italian refugee who taught Italian at King's college.
   (b) Rossetti formed the Pre-Raphaelite Brotherhood with Holman Hunt, Ford Madox Brown and Painter Millais.
   (c) He married Christina Georgina who was a poet in her right.
   (d) Rossetti's "Blessed Damozel" displays his remarkable gifts as a poet and painter.

41. Goethe's Faust (Part I , Scene 1) opens in
   (a) Heaven (b) Hell
   (c) Forest (d) Faust's study

42. "Is it their single-mind-sized skulls or a trained
Body, or genius, or a nestful of brats
Gives their days this bullet and automatic purpose...."
(Thrushes)

In the above lines what does 'their' refer to and what quality of 'their' does the poet speak of?
   1. Human beings and their intelligence.
   2. The thrushes and their concentration in achieving what they set out for.
   3. The efficiency of the thrushes in getting at their prey.
   4. All of the above.
   (a) 3 is correct.
   (b) 4 is correct.
   (c) 1 and 2 are correct.
   (d) 2 and 3 are correct.

43. Find the odd (wo)man out:

Belladonna – Engenides – The Typist – Marie – Madame Sosostris – the ruinbibber – Tiresias – the Youngman Carbuncular

(a) Belladonna
(b) Madame Sosostris
(c) Tiresias
(d) The ruin bibber

44. Wilkie Collins's novel, *The Moonstone* (1868) tells the story of ______.

(a) a detective's exploits in Victorian England
(b) a doctor's adventures in a Middle-Eastern Suburb
(c) a fabulous yellow diamond stolen from an Indian shrine
(d) illegal mining of diamonds in eastern U.P. during British rule

45. Identify the correctly matched group:

| | |
|---|---|
| A. "Because I could not stop for death...." | 1. Walt Whitman |
| B. "O Captain ! My Captain!" | 2. William Carlos Williams |
| C. "Two roads diverged in a wood...." | 3. Emily Dickinson |
| D. "So much depends upon...." | 4. Robert Frost |

| | A | B | C | D |
|---|---|---|---|---|
| (a) | 1 | 2 | 3 | 4 |
| (b) | 3 | 1 | 4 | 2 |
| (c) | 1 | 3 | 2 | 4 |
| (d) | 3 | 1 | 2 | 4 |

46. "Now stop your noses, readers, all and some,
For here's a tun of midnight – work to come,
Og, from a treason-tavern rolling home.
Round as a globe and liquor'd e'vry chink,
Goodly and great he rails behind his link".

In the above passage from Absalom and Achitophel, link means

(a) a connection in the court.
(b) a hired servant who carries a lighted torch.
(c) a social tie.
(d) a rich patron.

47. Which among the following is not a typical "Indian English Poem" by Nissim Ezekiel?

(a) "How the English Lessons Ended"
(b) "The Railway Clerk"
(c) "Goodbye Party for Miss Pushpa T.S."
(d) "The Patriot"

48. Match the correct pair:

| | |
|---|---|
| A. George Eliot | 1. Ellis Bell |
| B. Saki | 2. Mary Anne Evans |
| C. Emily Bronte | 3. Samuel Langhorne Clemens |
| D. Mark Twain | 4. H. H. Munro |

| | A | B | C | D |
|---|---|---|---|---|
| (a) | 2 | 3 | 1 | 4 |
| (b) | 2 | 4 | 1 | 3 |
| (c) | 1 | 3 | 4 | 2 |
| (d) | 3 | 2 | 1 | 4 |

49. In Canto 17 of the *Inferno*, the monster Geryon represents ______.

(a) fraud (b) usury
(c) sloth (d) gluttony

50. I.A. Richards's famous experiment with poems and his Cambridge students is detailed in *Practical Criticism: A Study of Literary Judgement* (1929). Richards was astonished by

(a) the poor quality of his students' "stock responses".
(b) the very astute remarks made by his students.
(c) the non-availability of poems, worthy of classroom attention.
(d) the success of his experiment.

51. Based on the following description, identify the text in reference :

This is a play in which no one comes, no one goes, nothing happens. In its opening scene a man struggles hard to remove his boot. The play was originally written in French, later translated into English. It was first performed in 1953.

(a) *Look Back in Anger*
(b) *Waiting for Godot*
(c) *The Zoo Story*
(d) *The Birthday Party*

52. One of the following *Canterbury Tales* is in prose, identify.

(a) *The Pardoner's Tale*
(b) *The Parson's Tale*
(c) *The Monk's Tale*
(d) *The Knight's Tale*

53. In his distinction between imagination and fancy, Coleridge identifies the following:

1. it dissolves, diffuses, dissipates, in order to recreate.
2. it has aggregative and associative power.
3. it plays with fixities and definites.
4. it has shaping and modifying power.

The correct combination reads

(a) 1 and 2 for fancy; 3 and 4 for imagination.
(b) 1 and 3 for fancy; 2 and 4 for imagination.
(c) 2 and 3 for fancy; 1 and 4 for imagination.
(d) 3 and 4 for fancy; 1 and 2 for imagination.

54. Julia Kristeva's 'Intertextuality' derives from

1. Saussure's signs
2. Chomsky's deep structure
3. Bakhtin's dialogism
4. Derrida's difference

(a) 1 and 4 (b) 1 and 3
(c) 3 and 4 (d) 1 and 2

55. Ralph Ellison enjoys subverting myths about white purity through characters like

1. Norton 2. Bledsoe
3. Rhinehart 4. all of the above

(a) 1 and 2 (b) 1, 2 and 3
(c) 2 and 3 (d) 1 and 3

56. Which of the following is not true of Ralph Waldo Emerson?

(a) He wrote essays on New England scenery, woodcraft and plantations.
(b) He was an eloquent pulpit orator, a member of the Unitarian Church under William Chawming.
(c) In essays like *Nature*, he elaborates on the importance of seeing familiar things in new ways.
(d) His famous "American Scholar" was delivered as an address before the Phi Beta Kappa Society at Cambridge in 1837.

57. "Exorcism" is the title of Act III of who's *Afraid of Virginia Woolf?*

What is the significance of 'exorcism' in the context of the play?

(a) The casting out of evil spirits
(b) Deconstructing of myths involving marriage, fertility and sons
(c) Facing life without illusions
(d) Exposing all attempts at illusionmaking

58. "Womanist is to feminist as purple is to lavender". This is an important statement

defining the womanist perspective advanced by
(a) Toni Morrison
(b) Zora Neale Hurston
(c) Alice Walker
(d) Bell Hooks

59. Identify the mismatched pair in the following where characters in Golding's *Lord of the Flies* fit the allegorized pattern of virtues and vices.
(a) Ralph - rationality
(b) Piggy - pragmatism
(c) Jack - pity
(d) Simon - innocence

60. A subaltern perspective is one where
(a) power-structures define and determine your command of language and language of command in an uneven world.
(b) the politically dispossessed could be voiceless, written out of the historical record and ignored because their activities do not count for "Cultural" or "Structured".
(c) you don't know what your 'story' is, how to deal with a 'story' and therefore you are forced to put stereotyped situations in it to please your listeners.
(d) you begin to see how we live, how we have been living, how we have been led to imagine ourselves, how our language has trapped as well as liberated us.

61. 1. "Interlanguage" is a term we owe to M.A.K. Halliday.
2. Interlanguage develops an autonomous and self-contained grammatical system.
3. It is a distinct stage in a learner's progress in the study of a second language.
4. It owes nothing at all either to the learner's native or target/second language.
(a) 4 is correct.
(b) 2 is correct.
(c) 1 and 3 are correct.
(d) 3 and 4 are correct.

62. In a classic statement that inaugurated feminist thought in English, we read: "A woman writing thinks back through her mothers". Where does this occur?
(a) Virginia Woolf's *A Room of One's Own*
(b) Kate Millet's *Sexual Politics*
(c) Gertrude Stein's *Three Lives*
(d) Mary Hiatt's *The Way Women Write*

63. Identify the correctly matched pair of translators and translations.

| | |
|---|---|
| A. A.K. Ramanujan | 1. *The Ramayana* |
| B. Manmathanath Dutt | 2. *The Bhagavad Gita* |
| C. Mohini Chatterjee | 3. *Speaking of Shiva* |
| D. Romesh Chandra Dutt | 4. *The Mahabharata* |

| | A | B | C | D |
|---|---|---|---|---|
| (a) | 3 | 4 | 2 | 1 |
| (b) | 4 | 3 | 1 | 2 |
| (c) | 4 | 1 | 2 | 3 |
| (d) | 2 | 1 | 4 | 3 |

64. **Assertion (A) :** In The Power and the Glory, Greene shows how the Whisky Priest transcends his weakness for drink and his human fears, moving towards martyrdom.

**Reason (R) :** Transcendence in Greene's novels is generally an outcome of love for humanity, but pride is also an essential ingredient in the Priest's character.
(a) (A) is true, but (R) is false.
(b) (A) is false, but (R) is true.

(c) Both (A) and (R) are true, but (R) is not the correct explanation for (A).
(d) Both (A) and (R) are true and (R) is the correct explanation for (A).

65. Which of the following statements on John Dryden is incorrect ?
    1. John Milton and John Dryden were contemporaries.
    2. Dryden was a Royalist, while Milton fiercely opposed monarchy.
    3. Dryden wrote a play on the Mughal Emperor Humayun.
    4. Dryden was appointed the Poet Laureate of England in 1668.

    (a) 1 is incorrect.
    (b) 4 is incorrect.
    (c) 3 is incorrect.
    (d) 2 and 3 are incorrect.

66. "Like walking, criticism is a pretty nearly universal art; both require a constant intricate shifting and catching of balance; neither can be questioned much in process; and few perform either really well. For either a new terrain is fatiguing and awkward, and in our day most men prefer paved walks and some form of rapid transportsome easy theory or overmastering dogma." (R.P. Blackmur, *A Critic's Job of Work*)
    1. Blackmur compares walking with criticism because he considers both to be "arts" of a similar kind that call for attention to detail and utmost care.
    2. Blackmur admits that some people do however manage to be good critics and good walkers.
    3. Critics prefer tried and tested approaches for much the same reason as Walkers would look for paved walks and rapid transport.
    4. Blackmur does not quite give us the equivalents of "Some paved walks and some form of rapid transport" in order to press his comparison.

    (a) 1 and 4 are correct.
    (b) 1 and 3 are correct.
    (c) 4 is correct.
    (d) 2 is correct.

67. The world dominated by cold and hypocritical materialists is represented by William Blake in the mythological figure of ________ .

    (a) Urizen (b) Albion
    (c) Geryon (d) Satan

68. Identify the correctly matched group:

| | | |
|---|---|---|
| (a) | Third Space | Wolfgang Iser |
| | Hybridity | Edward Soja |
| | Reception aesthetics | Ferdinand de Saussure |
| | Langue | Homi Bhabha |
| (b) | Third Space | Ernst Bloch |
| | Hybridity | Edward Said |
| | Reception aesthetics | Eve K. Sedgwick |
| | Langue | G.S. Frazer |
| (c) | Third Space | Edward Soja |
| | Hybridity | Homi Bhabha |
| | Reception aesthetics | Wolfgang Iser |
| | Langue | Ferdinand de Saussure |
| (d) | Third Space | G.S. Frazer |
| | Hybridity | Eve K. Sedgwick |
| | Reception aesthetics | Edward Soja |
| | Langue | Edward Said |

69. Which of the following can be best described as: (i) the first statement of Bernard Shaw's idea of Life Force; (ii) a play dealing with a woman's pursuit of her mate; and (iii) a play whose third act called "Don Juan in Hell" is both unconventional and hilarious?

(a) *The Devil's Disciple*
(b) *Man and Superman*
(c) *Candida*
(d) *Arms and the Man*

70. Identify the untrue statement on the Contact Zone below:
(a) "The contact zone" is a space where disparate cultures meet, clash and grapple with each other.
(b) In postcolonial societies "contact" suggests the historical moment when settler and indigenous cultures first met.
(c) The idea of the Contact Zone was first proposed and defined by Mary Louise Pratt's *Imperial Eyes : Travel Writing and Transculturation* (1992).
(d) It is believed that the Contact Zone was largely instrumental in spearheading nationalist movements across the world.

71. Name the novel in which
I. the protagonist is a war veteran called Tayo.
II. Tayo returns from World War II, thoroughly disillusioned and haunted by his violent actions of war time.
III. Tayo seeks consolation and counsel from old Betonie.
IV. The protagonist realizes the importance of harmonizing humanity and the universe.
(a) *Beloved*
(b) *Ceremony*
(c) *Daisy Miller*
(d) *Enter, Conversing*

72. One of the following poems in *Men and Women* is addressed to Elizabeth Barrett Browning by the poet. Identify it.
(a) "In Three Days"
(b) "By the Fireside"
(c) "One Way of Love"
(d) "One Word More"

73. Match List I with List II according to the codes given below :

| List I | List II |
|---|---|
| A. Tennessee Williams | 1. *Emperor Jones* |
| B. Eugene O'Neill | 2. *A Streetcar Named Desire* |
| C. Lorraine Hansberry | 3. *After the Fall* |
| D. Arthur Miller | 4. *A Raisin in the Sun* |

| | A | B | C | D |
|---|---|---|---|---|
| (a) | 3 | 1 | 4 | 2 |
| (b) | 1 | 3 | 2 | 4 |
| (c) | 4 | 2 | 3 | 1 |
| (d) | 2 | 1 | 4 | 3 |

74. Match the correct pair :

| | |
|---|---|
| A. Theatre of Cruelty | 1. Safdar Hashmi |
| B. Theatre of the Oppressed | 2. Georg Kaiser |
| C. Expressionist Theatre | 3. Jerzy Grotowsky |
| D. Agitprop | 4. Augusto Bal |

| | A | B | C | D |
|---|---|---|---|---|
| (a) | 1 | 2 | 4 | 3 |
| (b) | 3 | 4 | 2 | 3 |
| (c) | 2 | 3 | 1 | 4 |
| (d) | 4 | 1 | 3 | 2 |

75. Bertolt Brecht's Epic Theatre
1. turns the spectator into an observer.
2. wears down the spectator's capacity for action.
3. relies on argument.
4. presents man as a process.
(a) 1 and 4 are correct; 2 and 3 are incorrect.
(b) 1, 3 and 4 are correct; 2 is wrong.
(c) 2 and 4 are correct; 1 and 3 are incorrect.
(d) 1, 2 and 3 are correct; 4 is incorrect.

## ANSWERS

| | | | | | |
|---|---|---|---|---|---|
| 1. (d) | 2. (b) | 3. (b) | 4. (c) | 5. (c) | 6. (c) |
| 7. (c) | 8. (c) | 9. (c) | 10. (c) | 11. (d) | 12. (c) |
| 13. (b) | 14. (d) | 15. (d) | 16. (c) | 17. (b) | 18. (d) |
| 19. (a) | 20. (d) | 21. (d) | 22. (b) | 23. (d) | 24. (b) |
| 25. (c) | 26. (b) | 27. (d) | 28. (c) | 29. (c) | 30. (b) |
| 31. (b) | 32. (d) | 33. (c) | 34. (c) | 35. (c) | 36. (d) |
| 37. (b) | 38. (c) | 39. (c) | 40. (c) | 41. (d) | 42. (d) |
| 43. (d) | 44. (c) | 45. (b) | 46. (b) | 47. (a) | 48. (b) |
| 49. (a) | 50. (a) | 51. (b) | 52. (b) | 53. (c) | 54. (b) |
| 55. (a) | 56. (a) | 57. (d) | 58. (c) | 59. (c) | 60. (b) |
| 61. (c) | 62. (a) | 63. (a) | 64. (c) | 65. (c) | 66. (b) |
| 67. (a) | 68. (c) | 69. (b) | 70. (d) | 71. (d) | 72. (d) |
| 73. (d) | 74. (b) | 75. (b) | | | |

# 9

# NET Examination Paper II, December 2012 with Answers

1. Identify the work below that does not belong to the literature of the eighteenth century:
   (a) *Advancement of Learning*
   (b) *Gulliver's Travels*
   (c) *The Spectator*
   (d) *An Epistle to Dr. Arbuthnot*
2. Which, among the following, is a place through which John Bunyan's Christian does not pass?
   (a) The Slough of Despond
   (b) Mount Helicon
   (c) The Valley of Humiliation
   (d) Vanity Fair
3. The period of Queen Victoria's reign is
   (a) 1830–1900
   (b) 1837–1901
   (c) 1830–1901
   (d) 1837–1900
4. Which of the following statements about *The Lyrical Ballads* is not true?
   (a) It carried only *one* ballad proper, which was Coleridge's *The Rime of the Ancient Mariner.*
   (b) It also carried pastoral and other poems.
   (c) It carried a "Preface" which Wordsworth added in 1800.
   (d) It also printed from Gray's *Elegy Written in a Country Churchyard.*
5. One of the following texts was published earlier than 1955. Identify the text:
   (a) William Golding, *The Inheritors*
   (b) Philip Larkin, *The Less Deceived*
   (c) William Empson, *Collected Poems*
   (d) Samuel Becket, *Waiting for Godot*
6. Who among the poets in England during the 1930s had left-leaning tendencies?
   (a) T.S. Eliot, Ezra Pound, Richard Aldington
   (b) Wilfred Owen, Siegfried Sassoon, Rupert Brooke
   (c) W.H. Auden, Louis MacNeice, Cecil Day Lewis
   (d) J. Fleckner, W.H. Davies, Edward Marsh
7. Match the following:

| | |
|---|---|
| 1. The Sage of Concord | 5. Emily Dickinson |
| 2. The Nun of Amherst | 6. R.W. Emerson |
| 3. Mark Twain | 7. T.S. Eliot |
| 4. Old Possum | 8. Samuel L. Clemens |

   (a) 1–6; 2–5; 3–8; 4–7
   (b) 1–5; 2–6; 3–7; 4–8
   (c) 1–8; 2–7; 3–6; 4–5
   (d) 1–7; 2–8; 3–5; 4–6
8. Name the theorist who divided poets into "strong" and "weak" and popularized the practice of misreading:

(a) Alan Bloom
(b) Harold Bloom
(c) Geoffrey Hartman
(d) Stanley Fish

9. In *The Rape of the Lock* Pope repeatedly compares Belinda to
(a) the sun
(b) the moon
(c) the north star
(d) the rose

10. Which of the following awards is not given to Indian-English writers?
(a) The Booker Prize
(b) The Sahitya Akademi Award
(c) The Gyanpeeth
(d) Whitbread Prize

11. Identify the correct statement below:
(a) *Gorboduc* is a comedy, while *Ralph Roister Doister and Gammer Gurton's Needle* are tragedies.
(b) *Gorboduc* is a tragedy, while *Ralph Roister Doister and Gammer Gurton's Needle* are comedies.
(c) All of them are problem plays.
(d) All of them are farces.

12. W.M. Thackeray's *Vanity Fair* owes its title to
(a) Browning's *Fifine at the Fair*
(b) Shakespeare's *Merchant of Venice*
(c) Goldsmith's *Vicar of Wakefield*
(d) Bunyan's Pilgrim's *Progress*

13. The Puritans shut down all theaters in England in
(a) 1642 (b) 1640
(c) 1659 (d) 1660

14. Who of the following was not a contemporary of Wordsworth and Coleridge?
(a) Robert Southey
(b) Sir Walter Scott
(c) William Hazlitt
(d) A.C. Swinburne

15. Which of the following statements about *Waiting for Godot* is not true?
1. It carries a subtitle: "a tragicomedy in two acts".
2. It carries a subtitle: "a tragicomedy in two scenes".
3. It carries a subtitle: "a tragicomedy in two parts".
4. It does not carry a subtitle.
(a) 4 (b) 2
(c) 3 (d) 1

16. The Bloomsbury Group included British intellectuals, critics, writers and artists. Who among the following belonged to the Bloomsbury Group?
I. John Maynard Keynes, Lytton Strachey
II. E.M. Forster, Roger Fry, Clive Bell
III. Patrick Brunty, Paul Haworth
IV. Thomas Hardy, Henry James, Walter Pater
(a) I and II (b) I
(c) II and III (d) IV

17. Who, among the following is credited with the making of the first authoritative *Dictionary of the English Language*?
(a) Bishop Berkeley
(b) Samuel Johnson
(c) Edmund Burke
(d) Horace Walpole

18. In Dryden's *Essay of Dramatic Poesy* (1668), who opens the discussion on behalf of the ancients?
(a) Lisideius (b) Crites
(c) Eugenius (d) Neander

19. The term *invective* refers to
(a) the abusive writing or speech in which there is harsh denunciation of some person or thing.
(b) an insulting writing attack upon a real person, in verse or prose, usually involving caricature and ridicule.

(c) a written or spoken text in which an apparently straightforward statement or event is undermined in its context so as to give it a very different significance.
(d) the chanting or reciting of words deemed to have magical power.

20. Which of the following novels depicts the plight of the Bangladeshi immigrants in East London?
(a) *How Far can You Go*
(b) *The White Teeth*
(c) *An Equal Music*
(d) *Brick Lane*

21. The year 1939 proved to be a crucial year for two important writers in England. Identify the correct phrase below:
(a) For Yeats who died, for Auden who left England for the U.S.
(b) For Eliot who started publishing verse-drama, for Hardy whose *Wessex Poems* were published.
(c) For Evelyn Waugh and Graham Greene, each for publishing his first novels.
(d) For Eliot who won the Nobel Prize and Orwell who published his *Animal Farm.*

22. The Enlightenment was characterized by
(a) accelerated industrial production and general well-being of the public.
(b) a belief in the universal authority of reason and emphasis on scientific experimentation.
(c) the Protestant work ethic and compliance with Christian values of life.
(d) an undue faith in predestination and neglect of free will.

23. Which Shakespearean play contains the line: "...there is a special providence in the fall of a sparrow"?
(a) *King Lear* (b) *Hamlet*
(c) *Coriolanus* (d) *Macbeth*

24. Match the following pairs of books and authors:

| | **Books** | **Authors** |
|---|---|---|
| I. | *Condition of the Working Class in England* | i. John Ruskin |
| II. | *London Labour and the London Poor* | ii. Henry Mayhew |
| III. | *Past and Present* | iii. Thomas Carlyle |
| IV. | *The Unto This Last* | iv. Friedrich Engels |

| **Codes:** | **I** | **II** | **III** | **IV** |
|---|---|---|---|---|
| (a) | iv | i | ii | iii |
| (b) | iv | ii | iii | i |
| (c) | ii | iv | i | ii |
| (d) | iii | ii | iv | iv |

25. In which of the following texts do Aston, Davies and Mick appear as characters?
(a) Wyndham Lewis's *Enemy*
(b) Harold Pinter's *Caretaker*
(c) Katherine Mansfield's "Life of Ma Parker"
(d) Graham Greene's *Brighton Rock*

26. What is common to the following writers? Identify the correct description below:
William Congreve
George Etherege
William Wycherley
Thomas Otway
(a) All of these were Restoration playwrights
(b) All of them were critics of Orwell's regime
(c) All of them edited Shakespeare's plays
(d) All of them wrote tragedies in the same age

27. In which Jane Austen novel do you find the characters Anne Elliott, Lady Russell, Louisa Musgrove and Captain Wentworth?
   (a) *Emma*
   (b) *Mansfield Park*
   (c) *Persuasion*
   (d) *Northanger Abbey*

28. In which of his essays does Homi Bhabha discuss the 'discovery' of English in colonial India?
   (a) "Signs taken for Wonders"
   (b) "Mimicry"
   (c) *Nation and Narration*
   (d) "The Commitment to Theory"

29. ______ was the first Sonnet Sequence in English.
   (a) Edmund Spenser's *Amoretti*
   (b) Philip Sidney's *Astrophel and Stella*
   (c) Samuel Daniel's *Delia*
   (d) Michael Drayton's *Idea's Mirror*

30. Which is the correct sequence of the novels of V.S.Naipaul?
   (a) *The Mystic Masseur–Miguel Street–The Suffrage of Elvira–A House for Mr. Biswas.*
   (b) *Miguel Street–The Mystic Masseur–A House for Mr. Biswas–The Suffrage of Elvira.*
   (c) *The Suffrage of Elvira –Miguel Street–The Mystic Masseur–A House for Mr. Biswas.*
   (d) *The Mystic Masseur–The Suffrage of Elvira, Miguel Street–A House for Mr, Biswas.*

31. "Kubla Khan" takes an epigraph from
   (a) Samuel Purchas' *Purchas His Pilgrimage*
   (b) Hakluyt's *Voyages*
   (c) *The Book Named the Governour*
   (d) Sir Thomas More's *Utopia*

32. Which of the following author-theme is correctly matched?

| | | |
|---|---|---|
| (a) | *The Battle of the Books* | Tribute to "The rude forefathers of the hamlet". |
| (b) | *The Rape of the Lock* | Quarrel between ancient and modern authors. |
| (c) | *Gray's "Elegy"* | Accumulation of wealth and the consequent loss of human lives and values. |
| (d) | *The Deserted Village* | Quarrel between two families caused by Lord Petre. |

33. Which among the following titles set a course for academic literary feminism?
   (a) *Nostromo*
   (b) *From Ritual to Romance*
   (c) *A Room of One's Own*
   (d) *A Dance to the Music of Time*

34. In which play do we see a reworking of E.M. Forster's *A Passage to India* as a camaeo?
   (a) *The Birthday Party*
   (b) *A Resounding Tinkle*
   (c) *Indian Ink*
   (d) *Amadeus*

35. Shakespeare's sonnets
   (a) do not carry a dedication.
   (b) are dedicated to James I of England.
   (c) are dedicated to Mary Arden.
   (d) are dedicated to an unknown "Mr. W.H."

36. Which of the following poems uses *terza rima*?
   (a) John Keats's "Ode to a Nightingale"
   (b) P.B. Shelley's "Ode to the West Wind"
   (c) William Wordsworth's "The Solitary Reaper"
   (d) Alfred Tennyson's "Ulysses"

37. When one says that "someone is no more" or that "someone has breathed his/her last", the speaker is resorting to
   (a) euphism (b) euphony
   (c) understatement (d) euphemism

38. Which of the following are "companion poems"?
   (a) "Gypsy songs" and "Songs and Sonnets"
   (b) "L'Allegro" and "II Penseroso"
   (c) "The Good Morrow" and "The Sun Rising"
   (d) "Full Fathom Five" and "Hark, Hark! the Lark"

39. What does the term *episteme* signify?
   (a) Knowledge (b) Archive
   (c) Theology (d) Scholarship

40. Which of the following is a better definition of an *image* in literary writing?
   (a) A reflection
   (b) A speaking picture
   (c) A refraction
   (d) A reflected picture

41. Whom did Keats regard as the prime example of 'negative capability'?
   (a) John Milton
   (b) William Wordsworth
   (c) William Shakespeare
   (d) P.B. Shelley

42. Charles Dickens's *A Tale of Two Cities* begins with the sentence
   (a) It was the best of times, it was the worst of times.
   (b) It was the brightest of times, it was the darkest of times.
   (c) It was the richest of times, it was the poorest of times.
   (d) It was the happiest of times, it was the saddest of times.

43. The works of Gerard Manley Hopkins were published posthumously by
   (a) Edwin Muir
   (b) Edward Thomas
   (c) Robert Bridges
   (d) Coventry Patmore

44. Which of the following is the correct chronological sequence?
   (a) A Poison Tree – The Deserted Village – The Blessed Damozel – Ozymandias
   (b) The Deserted Village – A Poison Tree – Ozymandias – The Blessed Damozel
   (c) The Blessed Damozel – A Poison Tree – The Deserted Village – Ozymandias
   (d) The Deserted Village – The Blessed Damozel – Ozymandias – A Poison Tree

45. The term *homology* means a correspondence between two or more structures. Who of the following developed a theory of relations between literary works and social classes in terms of homologies?
   (a) Raymond Williams
   (b) Christopher Caudwell
   (c) Lucien Goldmann
   (d) Antonio Gramsci

46. F. Turner's famous hypothesis is that
   (a) the Frontier has outlived its ideological utility in American civilization.
   (b) the Frontier has posed a challenge to the American creative imagination.
   (c) the Frontier has been the one great determinant of American civilization.
   (d) the Frontier has been the one great deterrent to American progress.

47. Which statement(s) below on the Spenserian Stanza is/are accurate?
   I. a quatrain, unrhymed, but alliterative
   II. a stanza of four lines in iambic pentameter
   III. an eight-line stanza in iambic pentameter followed by a ninth in six iambic feet

IV. an eight-line stanza with six iambic feet followed by a ninth in iambic pentameter

(a) I and II (b) II

(c) III (d) IV

48. Match the following texts with their respective themes:

| | |
|---|---|
| I. *Areopagitica* (Milton) | i. Fashion, courtship, seduction |
| II. *Leviathan* (Hobbes) | ii. The liberty for unlicensed printing |
| III. *Alexander's Feast* (Dryden) | iii. Absolute sovereignty |
| IV. *The Way of the World* (Congreve) | iv. The power of music |

| **Codes:** | **I** | **II** | **III** | **IV** |
|---|---|---|---|---|
| (a) | i | ii | iii | iv |
| (b) | ii | iii | iv | i |
| (c) | iii | iv | i | ii |
| (d) | iv | iii | i | ii |

49. The preliminary version of James Joyce's *Portrait of the Artist as a Young Man* was called

(a) *Stephen Hero*

(b) *Bloom's Blunder*

(c) *A Day in the Life of Stephen Dedalus*

(d) *The Dead*

50. (i) A *pastiche* is a mixture of themes, stylistic elements or subjects borrowed from other works.

(ii) It is distinguished from parody because not all parody is pastiche.

(iii) A pastiche is also known as a 'purple passage'.

(iv) A pastiche is given to an elevated style, especially in its use of figurative language.

(a) (i) and (ii) are correct.

(b) only (i) is correct.

(c) (iii) and (iv) are correct.

(d) only (iv) is correct.

## ANSWERS

| | | | | | |
|---|---|---|---|---|---|
| 1. (a) | 2. (b) | 3. (b) | 4. (d) | 5. (c) | 6. (c) |
| 7. (a) | 8. (b) | 9. (a) | 10. (c) | 11. (b) | 12. (d) |
| 13. (a) | 14. (d) | 15. (d) | 16. (a) | 17. (b) | 18. (b) |
| 19. (a) | 20. (d) | 21. (a) | 22. (b) | 23. (b) | 24. (b) |
| 25. (b) | 26. (a) | 27. (c) | 28. (a) | 29. (a) | 30. (d) |
| 31. (a) | 32. (a) | 33. (c) | 34. (c) | 35. (d) | 36. (b) |
| 37. (d) | 38. (b) | 39. (a) | 40. (b) | 41. (c) | 42. (a) |
| 43. (c) | 44. (b) | 45. (a) | 46. (c) | 47. (d) | 48. (b) |
| 49. (a) | 50. (a) | | | | |

# 10

# English Paper III, December 2012 with Answers

1. Which of the following book by V.S. Naipaul is subtitled *The Caribbean Revisited*?
   (a) *In a Free State*
   (b) *A Bend in the River*
   (c) *The Middle Passage*
   (d) *An Area of Darkness*
2. 'Fluency' in language is the same as
   (a) the ability to put oneself across comfortably in speech and/or writing.
   (b) the ability to command language rather than language commanding the user.
   (c) glibness
   (d) accuracy
3. Which of the following statements on *Pathetic Fallacy* is not true?
   (a) This term applies to descriptions that are not true but imaginary and fanciful.
   (b) Pathetic Fallacy is generally understood as human traits being applied or attributed to non-human things in nature.
   (c) In its first use, the term was used with disapproval because nature cannot be equated with the human in respect of emotions and responses.
   (d) The term was originally used by Alexander Pope in his *Pastorals* (1709).
4. Identify the correctly matched group :

| List – I | List – II |
|---|---|
| i. 'L' Allegro and 'Il Pensoro so' | 1. Pastoral elegy |
| ii. 'Lycidas' | 2. Masque |
| iii. *Comus* | 3. Sonnet |
| iv. 'On His Blindness' | 4. Prose tract |
| v. Areopagitica | 5. Companion poems in octo-syllabic couplets |

| Codes: | i | ii | iii | iv | v |
|---|---|---|---|---|---|
| (a) | 1 | 2 | 3 | 4 | 5 |
| (b) | 5 | 1 | 2 | 3 | 4 |
| (c) | 1 | 3 | 2 | 4 | 5 |
| (d) | 5 | 1 | 2 | 4 | 3 |

5. The Pre-Raphaelite brotherhood – The University Wits – The Rhymers' Club – The Transitional Poets – The Scottish Chaucerians. The right chronological sequence would be
   (a) The Scottish Chaucerians – The University Wits – The Transitional Poets – The Pre- Raphaelite brotherhood – The Rhymers' Club.
   (b) The Rhymers' Club, The University Wits – The Scottish Chaucerians – The Transitional Poets, The Pre-Raphaelite brotherhood.
   (c) The Pre-Raphaelite brotherhood – The Rhymers' Club – The Transitional

Poets, The Scottish Chaucerians – The University Wits.

(d) The University Wits, The Scottish Chaucerians – The Pre-Raphaelite brotherhood, The Transitional Poets – The Rhymers' Club.

6. 'Aucitya' refers to:
   I. Decorum
   II. Propriety
   III. Proportion
   IV. Accuracy
   (a) I and IV are correct.
   (b) I and III are correct.
   (c) II is correct.
   (d) II and IV are correct.

7. In the closing paragraph of *The Trial* two men accompany Joseph K to a part of the city to eventually execute him. The place is
   (a) a Public Park
   (b) a Church
   (c) a Quarry
   (d) an Abandoned Factory

8. Match List – I with List – II according to the code given below:

| List – I (Character) | List – II (Work) |
|---|---|
| i. Telemachus | 1. Notes from underground |
| ii. Anya | 2. Old Goriot |
| iii. Zverkov | 3. The Cherry Orchard |
| iv. Rastignac | 4. The Odyssey |

| Codes: | i | ii | iii | iv |
|---|---|---|---|---|
| (a) | 4 | 1 | 2 | 3 |
| (b) | 3 | 1 | 4 | 2 |
| (c) | 2 | 4 | 1 | 3 |
| (d) | 4 | 3 | 1 | 2 |

9. This renowned German poet was born in Prague and died of Leukemia. When young he met Tolstoy and was influenced by him. The titles of his last two works contain the words "sonnets" and "elegies". He is
   (a) Herman Hesse
   (b) Heinrich Heine
   (c) Joseph Freiherr Von Eichendorff
   (d) Raine Marie Rilke

10. Which of the following plays gained notoriety for its caricature of the philosopher Socrates?
    (a) *The Birds* (b) *The Wasps*
    (c) *The Clouds* (d) *The Frogs*

11. Raskolnikov murders the old lady:
    I. to get her money and achieve his ambition in life.
    II. to achieve his political goal as an extremist and a nihilist
    III. to prove his superiority over other young men of the time.
    IV. All of the above Find the correct combination according to the code:
    (a) I and II are correct.
    (b) I and III are correct.
    (c) II and III are correct.
    (d) I, II and III are correct.

12. In his preface to *The Order of Things*, Foucault mentions being influenced by a Latin American writer and his work.

    Choose the correct answer:
    (a) Marquez – "The Solitude of Latin America"
    (b) Borges – "Chinese Encyclopaedia"
    (c) Juan Rulfo – *Pedro Paramo*
    (d) Alejo Carpentier – "On the Marvelous in America"

13. Here is a list of Partition novels which have 'violence on the woman's body' as a significant theme. Pick the odd one out:

(a) *The Pakistani Bride*
(b) *What the Body Remembers*
(c) *Train to Pakistan*
(d) *The Ice-Candy Man*

14. Match the translators in List – I with the English translations of Indian Literature texts in List – II according to the code given below:

| List – I | List – II |
|---|---|
| i. K.B. Vaid | 1. *Says Tuka* |
| ii. O.V. Vijayan | 2. *The Diary of a Maid Servant* |
| iii. Dilip Chitre | 3. *Samskara* |
| iv. A.K. Ramanujan | 4. *Saga of Dharmapuri* |

| Codes: | i | ii | iii | iv |
|---|---|---|---|---|
| (a) | 4 | 1 | 2 | 3 |
| (b) | 3 | 2 | 1 | 4 |
| (c) | 2 | 4 | 1 | 3 |
| (d) | 1 | 2 | 3 | 4 |

15. In his poem "A Morning Walk" Nissim Ezekiel talks about a 'Barbaric City sick with slums/ Deprived of seasons, blessed with rains/ Its hawkers, beggars, ironlunged/ Processions led by frantic drums.' Identify the city:
(a) Calcutta (b) Banares
(c) Bombay (d) Agra

16. *In Practical Criticism* I.A. Richards links four kinds of meanings in most human utterances to four aspects. These are
(a) Sense, Feeling, Tone, Intention
(b) Sound, Feeling, Nuance, Intention
(c) Sense, Voice, Emotion, Intention
(d) Sense, Image, Tone, Intention

17. In 'Christabel' after Geraldine enters Sir Leoline's castle on her way to Christabel's chamber there are several ill omens which warn the reader about Geraldine. Pick out the phrase which does not serve as an omen:
(a) the 'angry moan' of the ailing mastiff bitch
(b) 'The Owlet's Scritch'
(c) 'The Moaning Wind'
(d) 'a tongue of light, a fit of flame'

18. The word resurrect is
(a) an abbreviation
(b) a spurious verb
(c) a back-formation
(d) a disguised compound

19. Match List – I with List – II according to the code given below:

| List – I | List – II |
|---|---|
| i. Annie John | 1. Picaresque |
| ii. Tom Jones | 2. Bildungsroman |
| iii. The Sorrows of Young Werther | 3. Gothic |
| iv. Vathek | 4. Epistolary |

| Codes: | i | ii | iii | iv |
|---|---|---|---|---|
| (a) | 1 | 2 | 3 | 4 |
| (b) | 2 | 1 | 4 | 3 |
| (c) | 4 | 3 | 2 | 1 |
| (d) | 3 | 4 | 1 | 2 |

20. Ted Hughes's poem "The Thought-Fox" is
I. About Thought as Fox
II. About the Fox as Thought
III. About the process of writing poetry.
IV. About Thought entering the poet's brain like the Fox emerging from darkness.
Find the most appropriate combination according to the code :
(a) I and II are correct.
(b) I and III are correct.
(c) I and IV are correct.
(d) I, III and IV are correct.

21. In Aristotle's *Poetics* we read that *it* is the imitation of an action that is complete and whole, and of a certain magnitude...

having a beginning, a middle, and an end'.

What is 'it'?

(a) tragedy (b) epic
(c) poetry (d) farce

22. According to Matthew Arnold, 'touchstones' help us test truth and seriousness that constitute the best poetry. What are the 'touchstones'?
    (a) The purple passages of lyric poetry
    (b) Passages from ancient poets
    (c) The lines and expressions of the great masters
    (d) Passages of epic strength and vigour

23. 'An extremely simplified form of language used for oral, verbal contact among a community whose members speak different languages but do not share a common language in order to fulfill the essential needs of communication.'

    Which of the following is best described by this definition?

    (a) Creole (b) Pidgin
    (c) Dialect (d) *Lingua franca*

24. What do the prosodic features of a language tell us?
    (a) The speaker's native language and its cognate languages.
    (b) The speaker's age, emotional state, social class, educational background, geographical provenance etc.
    (c) The speaker's self-confidence or lack of it.
    (d) The speaker's command of the resources of the language spoken by him/her and their deployment.

25. What novel answers to the following descriptions?

    This was a 1990 best-seller by a British writer. The work incorporates many genres such as letters, diaries and poetry as also third-person narratives. The plot here involves two time-periods – contemporary and Victorian. The work is subtitled *A Romance*.

    (a) *The Virgin in the Garden*
    (b) *Possession*
    (c) *The Girl in the Polka Dot Dress*
    (d) *The Sea Lady*

26. The following words and phrases, 'peace makers', 'help-meet', 'the fat of the land', 'a labour of love', 'the eleventh hour' and 'the shadow of death' were made current by
    (a) the British Greek scholars like Roger Ascham
    (b) the fifteenth century British prelates
    (c) the Puritan tractarians
    (d) the sixteen-century translators of the Bible

27. Who among the following writers asserted 'Commonwealth Literature' does not exist?
    (a) Amitav Ghosh
    (b) Sulman Rushdie
    (c) V.S. Naipaul
    (d) Nirad Chaudhari

28. Identify the one in correct chronological sequence:
    (a) The Norman Conquest – The Death of Geoffrey Chaucer – William Tyndall's *New Testament* – The Birth of William Shakespeare
    (b) The Death of Geoffrey Chaucer – William Tyndall's *New Testament* – The Birth of William Shakespeare – The Norman Conquest
    (c) The Norman Conquest –William Tyndall's *New Testament* – The Death of Geoffrey Chaucer – The Birth of William Shakespeare
    (d) William Tyndall's *New Testament* – The Norman Conquest – The Death

of Geoffrey Chaucer – The Birth of William Shakespeare

29. Which of the following arrangements is in the correct chronological sequence?
    (a) Mary Wellstone Craft's *A Vindication of the Rights of Woman* – *Lyrical Ballads* by Wordsworth and Coleridge – *Lyrical Ballads* with 'Preface', second edition by Wordsworth and Coleridge – Edmund Burke's Reflections on the Revolution in France.
    (b) Edmund Burke's *Reflections on the Revolution in France* – Mary Wollstone Craft's *A Vindication of the Rights of Woman* – *Lyrical Ballads* by Wordsworth and Coleridge – *Lyrical Ballads* with 'Preface', second edition by Wordsworth and Coleridge.
    (c) *Lyrical Ballads* with 'Preface', second edition by Wordsworth and Coleridge – *Lyrical Ballads* by Wordsworth and Coleridge – Edmund Burke's *Reflections on the Revolution in France* – Mary Wollstone Craft's *A Vindication of the Rights of Woman.*
    (d) *Lyrical Ballads* by Wordsworth and Coleridge – *Lyrical Ballads* with 'Preface', second edition by Wordsworth and Coleridge – Edmund Burke's *Reflections on the Revolution in France* – Mary Wollstone Craft's *A Vindication of the Rights of Woman.*

30. Who is John Keats's 'Sylvan Historian'?
    (a) Fanny Brawne
    (b) Nightingale
    (c) The Grecian Urn
    (d) The Bridge of Quietness

31. This periodical was started in 1709 with a motive 'to expose the false arts of life, to pull the disguise of cunning, vanity and affectation, and to recommend a general simplicity in our dress, our discourse and our behaviour.' The founder of the periodical wrote under the pseudonym of Isaac Bickerstaff.

    The periodical described above is
    (a) *The Tatler*
    (b) *The Spectator*
    (c) *The Critical Review*
    (d) *The Rambler*

32. Arrange the following in the order in which the details of a research article/essay appear in your bibliography.
    (a) Page numbers, the title of the essay, the title of the journal, volume & issue numbers, year of publication
    (b) The title of the essay, page numbers, the title of the journal, volume and issue numbers, year of publication
    (c) The title of the journal, the title of the essay, page numbers, volume and issue numbers, year of publication
    (d) The title of the essay, the title of the journal, volume & issue numbers, the year of publication, page numbers

33. From the following indicate the work which is not a Dystopia:
    (a) Aldous Huxley – *A Brave New World*
    (b) George Orwell – *1984*
    (c) Yevgeny Zamyatin – *We*
    (d) Evelyn Waugh – *Brideshed Revisited*

34. 'Unless wariness be used, as good almost kill a man as kill a good book. Who kills a man kills a reasonable creature, God's image, but he who destroys a good book, kills reason itself, kills the image of God as it were in the eye. Many a man lives a burden to the earth; but a good book is the precious life-blood of a master spirit....'

    Where is the passage from?

(a) Milton's *Areopagitica*
(b) Sidney's *Apologie for Poetry*
(c) Dryden's 'Preface to the Fables'
(d) Marvell's *The Rehearsal Transposed*

35. Virginia Woolf rubbished the idea of character and the understanding of realism of writers like Arnold Bennett, John Galsworthy and H.G. Wells. Her famous essay is called 'Mr. Bennet and Mrs. Brown'. Who is Mrs. Brown ?
(a) The name Woolf gives a woman whom she happens to meet in a train.
(b) A servant in Mr. Bennett's household.
(c) A character in a Bennett story.
(d) Mr. Bennett's neighbour who happens to be a writer.

36. E.M. Forster uses some recurrent images in *A Passage to India*. Pick the odd one out:
(a) Wasp (b) Stone
(c) Thunder (d) Echo

37. 'Now stop your noses, readers, all and some,
For here's a tun of midnight-work to come,
Og, from a treason-tavern rolling home.
Round as a globe, and liquor'd ev'ry chink
Goodly and great he rails behind his link'.

In the above extract from *Absalom and Achitophel* Og is
(a) Elkanah Settle
(b) Lord Harvey
(c) Thomas Shadwell
(d) Joseph Addison

38. D.H. Lawrence uses the expression 'a bright book of life' to describe
(a) the novel
(b) the dramatic monologue
(c) the Bible
(d) the short lyric

39. Identify the correctly matched group:

| | List – I | List – II |
|---|---|---|
| i. | *Where Angles Fear to Tread* | 1. Malay |
| ii. | *A Portrait of the Artist as a Young Man* | 2. Russia |
| iii. | *The Plumed Serpent* | 3. Italy |
| iv. | *An Outcast of the Islands* | 4. Mexico |
| v. | *Under Western Eyes* | 5. Dublin |

| Codes: | i | ii | iii | iv | v |
|---|---|---|---|---|---|
| (a) | 3 | 5 | 4 | 1 | 2 |
| (b) | 4 | 3 | 5 | 2 | 1 |
| (c) | 5 | 4 | 3 | 2 | 1 |
| (d) | 2 | 1 | 3 | 4 | 5 |

40. Given below are two statements, one labelled as Assertion (A) and the other labelled as Reason (R).

**Assertion (A):** Chaucer describes 'Madame Eglentyne' thus: 'She was so charitable and so pitous, She wolde wepe, if that she sawe a mous caught in a trappe'

**Reason (R):** On her 'broche of gold full shene' was written *Amor Vincit Omnia*.
In the context of the two statements, which one of the following is correct?
(a) Both (A) and (R) are true and (R) is the correct explanation of (A).
(b) Both (A) and (R) are true but (R) is not the correct explanation of (A).
(c) (A) is true but (R) is false.
(d) (A) is false but (R) is true.

41. Identify the correct statements on *Langue* and *Parole* below:
1. *Langue* is the abstract language system, the grammar of a language.
2. *Parole* is the language actually produced by its user following langue.

3. *Langue* is the language actually produced by its users following parole.
4. *Parole* is the abstract language system, the grammar of a system.

(a) 1 and 3 are correct.
(b) 1 and 2 are correct.
(c) 2 and 3 are correct.
(d) 2 and 4 are correct.

42. In Monica Ali's *Brick Lane* which among the following characters has 'a face like a frog'?

(a) Nazneen (b) Chanu
(c) Hasina (d) Karim

43. 'The grey-eyed morn smiles on the frowning night, Check'ring the eastern clouds with streaks of light; And flecked darkness like a drunkard reels From forth day's path and Titan's burning wheels.'

(*Romeo and Juliet* II 3, 1 – 4)

The speaker describes

(a) The Setting Sun
(b) The Return Home of a Drunkard
(c) The Drawing of a New Day
(d) The Rising Sun

44. 'How noble in reason! how infinite in faculty! in form and moving how express and admirable! In action how like an angel! in apprehension how like a God!'

What does Hamlet marvel at in this passage?

(a) His own self (b) His father
(c) Man (d) Woman

45. Said identifies Orientalism as:

I. What an Orientalist does.
II. A style of thought based on an ontological and epistemological distinction made between the Orient and the Occident.
III. a discourse dealing with the Orient
IV. a fact of nature rather than one of human production In the light of the statement above:

(a) II and III are correct, I and IV are wrong.
(b) I and III are correct, II and IV are wrong.
(c) I, II and III are correct and IV is wrong.
(d) IV is correct and I, II and III are wrong.

46. Identify the period during which the Puritans under the rule of Oliver Cromwell and his Commonwealth shut down all English theatres on religious and moral grounds:

(a) 1640-1660 (b) 1649-1660
(c) 1649-1659 (d) 1640-1659

47. "To tell the truth Shug act more manly than rest, men. I mean she upright, honest, speak her mind..."

What light does the quotation throw on Shug Avery?

(a) She is a manly woman.
(b) She is upright and honest in asserting her lesbian identity.
(c) She is bent on self-assertion
(d) Both (b) and (c)

48. 1. A content word is not a function word.
2. A content word has lesser meaning than a function word.
3. A content word has no function.
4. A content word bears lexical meaning whereas a function word just about means functionally.

Which of these statements are correct?

(a) 1 and 4 are correct.
(b) 1 and 2 are correct.
(c) 3 and 4 are correct.
(d) 2 and 4 are correct.

49. The year 1828 is a landmark in the history of American language and literature. Identify the reason from the following:

(a) Mark Twain's *The Adventures of Huckleberry Finn* was published in that year.
(b) The Southern Literary Messenger gained wide circulation since that year.
(c) Washington Irving was adjudged the nation's greatest writer in that year.
(d) Noah Webster published An American Dictionary of the English Language in that year.

50. What alternative title to her *Frankenstein* did Marry Shelley give?
(a) A Gothic Tale
(b) A Gothic Romance
(c) The Modern Prometheus
(d) A Modern Parable

51. Which of the following statements on George Lamming's *In the Castle of My Skin* [1953] is not true?
(a) On one level this is a coming of-age story.
(b) It is an elegiac account of a village's growth into awareness in the late colonial period.
(c) Its themes parody *The Tempest*.
(d) This was George Lamming's first novel.

52. We are likely to misunderstand an Emily Dickinson poem if we take her famous dashes to be...
(a) quite specific and unambiguous
(b) ambiguous and indeterminate
(c) suggestive of both forward and backward movements in terms of sense
(d) suggestive of links but equivocally

53. Readers of Tayeb Salih's *Seasons of Migration to the North* will undoubtedly notice its parallels with the story/stories of:
I. *Death in Venice*
II. *Othello*
III. *Bartleby the Scrivener*
IV. *Heart of Darkness*

Of the above:
(a) I and II are correct.
(b) Only IV is correct.
(c) II and III are correct.
(d) II and IV are correct.

54. Which statement is not true of Benedict Anderson's *Imagined Communities*?
(a) It is a prosaic response to the myth of El Dorado.
(b) It is subtitled *Reflections on the Origin and Spread of Nationalism*.
(c) In this book, Anderson advances the view that nations are not natural entities but narrative constructs.
(d) In Anderson's view, modern nationalism was basically a consequence of the convergence of capitalism, the new print technology and the fixity that resulted from print extending to 'Vernacular' languages.

55. 'By swaggering could I never thrive, For the rain it raineth everyday.' These lines from *Twelfth Night* occur in the novel:
(a) *Middlemarch*
(b) *Vanity Fair*
(c) *Our Mutual Friend*
(d) *Far From the Madding Crowd*

56. What is a mock-heroic poem? A mock-heroic poem
(a) mocks at heroic pretensions in poets and critics
(b) mocks heroism, an exaggerated virtue in all epics
(c) uses a heroic style to deride airs and affectations
(d) uses a mocking style to deride heroes and hero-worship

57. Which of the following statements is not true of Laurence Sterne's *Tristram Shandy*?

(a) It has a linear plot.
(b) It opens and ends with the theme of birth.
(c) It contains a trip to France.
(d) It contains a marbled page.

58. In drama, an aside is addressed...
(a) to an audience by an actor; the words so spoken are not meant to be heard by other actors on the stage.
(b) to other actors on the stage; the words so spoken are not meant to be heard by the audience.
(c) by the playwright to the audience.
(d) by the protagonist to his/her antagonist

59. Match List – I with List – II according to the code given below:

| **List – I** (Novels) | **List – II** (Last Lines) |
|---|---|
| i. *The Mayor of Casterbridge* | 1. 'He walked towards the faintly humming, glowing town, quickly.' |
| ii. *Sons and Lovers* | 2. 'In their death, they were not divided.' |
| iii. *The Great Gatsby* | 3. 'Happiness was but the occasional episode in a general drama of pain.' |
| iv. *The Mill on the Floss* | 4. 'So we beat on, boats against the current, borne back ceaselessly into the past.' |

| **Codes:** | **i** | **ii** | **iii** | **iv** |
|---|---|---|---|---|
| (a) | 1 | 2 | 3 | 4 |
| (b) | 2 | 1 | 3 | 4 |
| (c) | 4 | 3 | 2 | 1 |
| (d) | 3 | 1 | 4 | 2 |

60. "There is nothing outside the text," is a statement by
(a) Victor Shklovsky
(b) Jacques Derrida
(c) Roland Barthes
(d) Ferdinand de Saussure

61. Here is a list of women abandoned by their lovers in Hardy's novels.
Pick the odd one out:
(a) Fanny Robin
(b) Tess D'Urberville
(c) Marty South
(d) Bathsheba Everdene

62. What is the following a description of? 'a loose sally of the mind; an irregular indigested piece'
(a) Essay
(b) Autobiography
(c) Epistolary Fiction
(d) Diary

63. From the following indicate the critic who is not a New Critic:
(a) Allen Tate
(b) Robert Penn Warren
(c) Cleanth Brooks
(d) Claude Levi-Strauss

64. From the following list, pick out a woman character who does not belong to Amitav Ghosh's novels:
(a) Ila (b) Urvashi
(c) Sonali (d) Piyali

65. Pick the odd man out of the following members of the subaltern group:
(a) Ranajit Guha
(b) Partha Chatterjee
(c) Dipesh Chakrabarty
(d) Sumit Sarkar

66. **Statement (S):** "Our birth is but a sleep and forgetting."

**Interpretation (I):** The human soul never tires in the course of life, it never dies. Therefore, the human life is a long sleep and ephemeral events are better forgotten.

(a) (S) is a view and (I) is not correct.
(b) (S) is a view and (I) is correct.
(c) (S) is a poetic view, the (I) does not suit it.
(d) (S) is a poetic view and bears no relationship to (I).

67. 'The parish of rich women, physical decay,/Yourself...'

What do these make of W.B. Yeats in W.H. Auden's view?

(a) Proud (b) Vainglorious
(c) Avaricious (d) Silly

68. Who among Charles Dickens's characters is 'umble' and who 'willin'?

(a) Mr. Pickwick, Mrs. Gamp
(b) Master Humphrey, Nicolas Nickleby
(c) Martin, Little Nell
(d) Uriah Heep, Barkis

69. "Fourth World Literature" refers to

I. the works of native people living in a land that has been taken over by non-natives.
II. the works of black people in the United States.
III. the literature of the marginalized.
IV. refers to the works of nonheterosexuals

Of the above :

(a) I and II are correct.
(b) I and III are correct.
(c) II and IV are correct.
(d) I, III and IV are correct.

70. **Assertion (A):** In *The Duchess of Malfi* Ferdinand sets a whole group of mad men on the Duchess and they dance and sing in a crazy manner.

**Reason (R):** His desire was to provide a strange entertainment to drive the Duchess mad. In the context of the two statements, which one of the following is correct?

(a) (A) is correct, but (R) is wrong.
(b) Both (A) and (R) are correct.
(c) (A) is wrong, but (R) is correct.
(d) Both (A) and (R) are wrong.

71. Why is *The Signifying Monkey* of Henry Louis Gates JR. a notable contribution to the study of African-American literature?

(a) It focuses on largely neglected African-American novelists and poets.
(b) It offers a theory of African- American criticism that draws upon rhetorical and signifying practices.
(c) It offers a theory of African- American films and dramatic arts that signify Black ethos.
(d) It departs from critical theory of autobiographical narratives involving Black lives and cultural traditions.

72. This influential critic

I. wrote influential commentaries on such poets as Shelley, Blake and Yeats.
II. published such titles as *The Anxiety of Influence, A Map of Misreading, Poetry and Repression and The Western Canon.*
III. asserted that most literary criticism is but slightly disguised religion and
IV. is, arguably, the most widely known and contrarian among his American peers in the English Academy.

Identify the critic

(a) Edward Said
(b) Geoffrey Chaucer
(c) Harold Bloom
(d) Sven Birkrets

73. According to the Italian Marxist theorist Antonio Gramsci:
   (a) hegemony is synonymous with domination
   (b) hegemony involves a degree of consent on the part of subject people.
   (c) hegemony involves a degree of coercion on the part of a dominant political entity.
   (d) hegemony is synonymous with subjugation

74. Match the following:

| | |
|---|---|
| i. George Peele, Robert Greene, Thomas Lodge, Thomas Kyd | 1. The Rhymers' Club / The Decadents of the 1890's |
| ii. William Congreve, William Wycherley George Eltherege, George Farquhar | 2. The Pre-Raphaelite Brotherhood |
| iii. John Everett Millais, James Collinson, Ford Madox Brown, Dante Gabriel Rossetti | 3. The University Wits |
| iv. Ernest Dowson, Lionel Johnson, W.B. Yeats | 4. The Restoration Playwrights |

| **Codes:** | i | ii | iii | iv |
|---|---|---|---|---|
| (a) | 3 | 2 | 1 | 4 |
| (b) | 1 | 4 | 3 | 2 |
| (c) | 2 | 1 | 4 | 3 |
| (d) | 3 | 4 | 2 | 1 |

75. Combine the statements correctly:
   According to Homi Bhabha ________
   1. mimicry is not mere copying or emulating the colonizer's culture, behaviour and manners.
   2. but it is further aimed at perfection and excess.
   3. mimicry is mere copying the colonizer's culture, behaviour and manners...
   4. but is informed by both mockery and a certain menace.
   (a) 1 and 4 (b) 1 and 2
   (c) 3 and 4 (d) 3 and 2

## ANSWERS

| | | | | | |
|---|---|---|---|---|---|
| 1. (c) | 2. (a) | 3. (d) | 4. (b) | 5. (a) | 6. (c) |
| 7. (c) | 8. (d) | 9. (d) | 10. (c) | 11. (b) | 12. (b) |
| 13. (c) | 14. (c) | 15. (c) | 16. (a) | 17. (c) | 18. (c) |
| 19. (b) | 20. (d) | 21. (a) | 22. (c) | 23. (b) | 24. (b) |
| 25. (b) | 26. (d) | 27. (b) | 28. (a) | 29. (b) | 30. (c) |
| 31. (a) | 32. (d) | 33. (d) | 34. (a) | 35. (a) | 36. (c) |
| 37. (c) | 38. (a) | 39. (a) | 40. (b) | 41. (b) | 42. (b) |
| 43. (c) | 44. (c) | 45. (c) | 46. (b) | 47. (d) | 48. (a) |
| 49 (d) | 50. (c) | 51. (c) | 52. (a) | 53. (d) | 54. (a) |
| 55. (a) | 56. (c) | 57. (a) | 58. (a) | 59. (d) | 60. (b) |
| 61. (d) | 62. (a) | 63. (d) | 64. (b) | 65. (d) | 66. (b) |
| 67. (d) | 68. (d) | 69. (c) | 70. (b) | 71. (b) | 72. (c) |
| 73. (b) | 74. (d) | 75. (a) | | | |

11

# NET Examination Paper II, June 2013 with Answers

1. In Pinter's *Birthday Party*, Stanley is given a birthday present. What is it?
   (a) A toy (b) A piano
   (c) A drum (d) A violin
2. How does *Lord Jim* end?
   (a) Jim is shot through the chest by Doramin
   (b) Jim kills himself with a last unflinching glance
   (c) Jim answers "the call of exalted egoism" and betrays Jewel
   (d) Jim surrenders himself to Doramin
3. "Where I lacked a political purpose, I wrote lifeless books." To which of the following authors can we attribute the above admission?
   (a) Graham Greene
   (b) George Orwell
   (c) Charles Morgan
   (d) Evelyn Waugh
4. Modernism has been described as being concerned with "disenchantment of our culture with culture itself". Who is the critic?
   (a) Stephen Spender
   (b) Malcolm Bradbury
   (c) Lionel Trilling
   (d) Joseph Frank
5. "Only that film, which fluttered on the grate,
   Still flutters there, the sole unquiet thing."
   The above lines are quoted from
   (a) "Tintern Abbey Revisited"
   (b) "Michael"
   (c) "Frost at Midnight"
   (d) "This Lime-Tree Bower, My Prison"
6. Which one of the following modern poems employs ottava rima?
   (a) "Among School Children"
   (b) "In Praise of Limestone"
   (c) "The Wild Swans at Coole"
   (d) "The Shield of Achilles"
7. John Dryden in his heroic tragedy *All for Love* takes the story of Shakespeare's
   (a) *Troilus and Cressida*
   (b) *The Merchant of Venice*
   (c) *Antony and Cleopatra*
   (d) *Measure for Measure*
8. Arrange the following works in the order in which they appear. Identify the correct code:
   I. *No Longer at Ease*
   II. *Things Fall Apart*
   III. *A Man of the People*
   IV. *Arrow of God*
   The correct combination according to the code is:
   **Codes:**
   (a) III, IV, II, I (b) IV, III, I, II
   (c) II, I, IV, III (d) I, II, III, IV
9. Samuel Pepys kept his diary from
   (a) 1660 to 1669 (b) 1649 to 1660
   (c) 1662 to 1689 (d) 1660 to 1689

10. In the *Defence of Poetry*, what did Sydney attribute to poetry?
    (a) A magical power whereby poetry plays tricks on the reader
    (b) A divine power whereby poetry transmits a message from God to the reader
    (c) A moral power whereby poetry encourages the reader to evaluate virtuous models
    (d) A realistic power that cannot be made to seem like mere illusion and trickery
11. *An Epistle to Dr. Arbuthnot* presents portraits of the following contemporary individuals.
    (a) Addison and Lord Hervey
    (b) Dryden and Rochester
    (c) Swift and Steele
    (d) Smollett and Defoe
12. Match the following authors with their works:

    **List A (Authors)**
    I. Alice Walker
    II. Ralph Ellison
    III. Richard Wright
    IV. Zora Neale Hurston

    **List B (Works)**
    1. *Invisible Man II*
    2. *The Color Purple I*
    3. *Their Eyes Were Watching God*
    4. *Native Son*

    Which is the correct combination according to the code:

| Codes: | I | II | III | IV |
|---|---|---|---|---|
| (a) | 2 | 1 | 3 | 4 |
| (b) | 3 | 4 | 2 | 1 |
| (c) | 4 | 3 | 1 | 2 |
| (d) | 1 | 2 | 4 | 3 |

13. Which of these plays by Shakespeare does *not* use 'cross-dressing' as a device?
    (a) *As You Like It*
    (b) *Julius Caesar*
    (c) *Cymbeline*
    (d) *Two Gentlemen of Verona*
14. Which of the following works cannot be categorised under postcolonial theory?
    (a) *Nation and Narration*
    (b) *Orientalism*
    (c) *Discipline and Punish*
    (d) *White Mythologies*
15. Locke's *Essay Concerning Human Understanding* is a classic statement of _____ Philosophy.
    (a) Aesthetic (b) Empiricist
    (c) Nationalist (d) Realist
16. "Power circulates in all directions, to and from all social levels, at all times." Who said this?
    (a) Edward Said
    (b) Michel Foucault
    (c) Jacques Derrida
    (d) Roland Barthes
17. Which one of the following is not written by an Australian Aboriginal writer?
    (a) Kath Walker (b) Peter Carey
    (c) Robert Bropho (d) Jack Davis
18. Sir Thomas Wyatt and the Earl of Surrey jointly brought out *Tottel's Miscellany* during the Renaissance. Identify the name of the Earl of Surrey from the following:
    (a) Thomas Lodge
    (b) Thomas Nashe
    (c) Thomas Sackville
    (d) Henry Howard
19. Match the following lists:

    **List I (Novelists)**
    I. Margaret Laurence
    II. Margaret Atwood
    III. Sinclair Ross
    IV. Thomas King

    **List II (Novels)**
    1. *Surfacing*

2. *The Stone Angel*
3. *Medicine River*
4. *As for Me and My House*

Which is the correct combination according to the code:

| Codes: | I | II | III | IV |
|---|---|---|---|---|
| (a) | 1 | 4 | 3 | 2 |
| (b) | 3 | 2 | 1 | 4 |
| (c) | 4 | 3 | 2 | 1 |
| (d) | 2 | 1 | 4 | 3 |

20. The dramatic structure of Restoration comedies combines in it the features of
    I. The Elizabethan Theatre
    II. The Neoclassical Theatre of Italy and France
    III. The Irish Theatre
    IV. The Greek Theatre

    The correct combination according to the code is:

    **Codes:**
    (a) I and IV are correct
    (b) III and IV are correct
    (c) II and III are correct
    (d) I and II are correct

21. Which American poet wrote: "I sound my barbaric yawp over the roofs of the world"?
    (a) Robert Lowell
    (b) Walt Whitman
    (c) Wallace Stevens
    (d) Langston Hughes

22. The etymological meaning of the word "trope" is
    (a) gesture (b) turning
    (c) mirror (d) desire

23. Who among the following English poets defined poetic imagination as "a repetition in the finite mind of the eternal act of creation in the infinite 'I AM'"?
    (a) Blake (b) Wordsworth
    (c) Coleridge (d) Shelley

24. Little Nell is a character in Dickens'
    (a) *David Copperfield*
    (b) *The Old Curiosity Shop*
    (c) *Bleak House*
    (d) *Great Expectations*

25. Match the following:

    **List A (Schools/Concept of Criticism)**
    I. Formalism
    II. New Critics
    III. Psychological Theory of the Value of Literature
    IV. Literary art as archetypal image

    **List B (Critics)**
    1. John Crow Ransom
    2. The Jungians
    3. Victor Shklovsky
    4. I.A. Richards

    The correct combination according to the code is:

| Codes: | I | II | III | IV |
|---|---|---|---|---|
| (a) | 3 | 1 | 4 | 2 |
| (b) | 2 | 4 | 1 | 3 |
| (c) | 4 | 1 | 2 | 3 |
| (d) | 3 | 2 | 1 | 4 |

26. In the late seventeenth century a "Battle of Books" erupted between which two groups?
    (a) Cavaliers and Roundheads
    (b) Abolitionists and Enthusiasts for slaves
    (c) Champions of Ancient and Modern Learning
    (d) The Welsh and the Scots

27. "Everything that man esteems
    Endures a moment or a day
    Love's pleasure drives his love away..."

    In the above quote the last line is an example of
    (a) allusion (b) pleonasm
    (c) paradox (d) zeugma

28. Match the author with the work:

    **List I (Authors)**
    I. Kingsley Amis

II. Allan Silletoe
III. Doris Lessing
IV. Jean Rhys

**List II (Works)**

1. *Saturday and Sunday Morning*
2. *The Golden Note Book*
3. *The Left Bank*
4. *Lucky Jim*

Which is the correct combination according to the code:

| Codes: | I | II | III | IV |
|---|---|---|---|---|
| (a) | 3 | 4 | 1 | 2 |
| (b) | 4 | 1 | 2 | 3 |
| (c) | 2 | 3 | 1 | 4 |
| (d) | 1 | 2 | 3 | 4 |

29. In which of Hardy's novels does the character Abel Whittle appear?
(a) *Far from the Madding Crowd*
(b) *The Return of the Native*
(c) *A Pair of Blue Eyes*
(d) *The Mayor of Casterbridge*

30. The phrase "dark Satanic mills" has become the most famous description of the force at the centre of the industrial revolution. The phrase was used by
(a) William Wordsworth
(b) William Blake
(c) Thomas Carlyle
(d) John Ruskin

31. "Five miles meandering with a mazy motion
Through wood and dale the scared river ran."
Where does this 'sacred river' directly run to?
(a) A lifeless ocean
(b) The caverns measureless
(c) A fountain
(d) The waves

32. Who is the twentieth century poet, a winner of the Nobel Prize for literature who rejected the label "British" though he has always written in English rather than his regional language?
(a) Douglas Dunn
(b) Seamus Heaney
(c) Geoffrey Hill
(d) Philip Larkin

33. Which of the following statements best describes Sir Thomas Browne's *Religio Medici*?
(a) It is a story of conversion or providential experiences
(b) It emphasizes Browne's love of mystery and wonder
(c) It is full of angst, melancholy and dread of death
(d) It reports the facts of Browne's life

34. Which of the following characters from Eliot's *Waste Land* is not correctly mentioned?
(a) The typist
(b) Madam Sosostris
(c) The Merchant from Eugenides
(d) The Young Man Carbuncular

35. Which one of the following best describes the general feeling expressed in literature during the last decade of the Victorian era?
(a) Studied melancholy and aestheticism
(b) The triumph of science and morbidity
(c) Sincere earnestness and Protestant zeal
(d) Raucous celebration combined with paranoid interpretation

36. Which poem by Shelley bears the alternative title, "The Spirit of Solitude"?
(a) *Mont Blanc*
(b) "Hymn to Intellectual Beauty"
(c) "Adonais"
(d) *Alastor*

37. Which tale in *The Canterbury Tales* uses the tradition of the Beast Fable?
(a) *The Knight's Tale*

(b) *The Monk's Tale*
(c) *The Nun's Priest's Tale*
(d) *The Miller's Tale*

38. At the end of *Sons and Lovers* Paul Morel
(a) sets off in quest of life away from his mother
(b) considersthe option of committing suicide
(c) joins his elder brother William in London
(d) embraces a Schopenhauer-like nihilism

39. When you say "I love her eyes, her hair, her nose, her cheeks, her lips" you are using a rhetorical device of
(a) Enumeration (b) Antanagoge
(c) Parataxis (d) Hypotaxis

40. The following are two lists of plays and characters. Match them.

**List I (Plays)**
I. *Women Beware Women*
II. *The Malcontent*
III. *The City Madam*
IV. *The Changeling*

**List II (Characters)**
1. Malevole 2. Beatrice
3. Bianca 4. Doll Tearsheet

Which is the correct combination according to the code:

| **Codes:** | I | II | III | IV |
|---|---|---|---|---|
| (a) | 3 | 1 | 4 | 2 |
| (b) | 2 | 1 | 3 | 4 |
| (c) | 1 | 2 | 3 | 4 |
| (d) | 4 | 3 | 2 | 1 |

41. With Bacon the essay form is
(a) an intimate, personal confession
(b) witty and boldly imagistic
(c) the aphoristic expression of accumulated public wisdom
(d) homely and vulgar

42. Evelyn Waugh's Trilogy published together as *Sword of Honour* is about
(a) The English at War
(b) The English Aristocracy
(c) The Irish question
(d) Scottish nationalism

43. Who coined the phrase "The Two Nations" to describe the disparity in Britain between the rich and the poor?
(a) Charles Dickens
(b) Thomas Carlyle
(c) Benjamin Disraeli
(d) Frederick Engels

44. Milton introduces Satan and the fallen angels in the Book I of *Paradise Lost.* Two of the chief devils reappear in Book II. They are
I. Moloch II. Clemos
III. Belial IV. Thamuz
The correct combination according to the code is
**Codes:**
(a) I and IV are correct
(b) I and III are correct
(c) I and II are correct
(d) II and III are correct

45. When Chaucer describes the Friar as a "noble pillar of order", he is using
(a) irony (b) simile
(c) understatement (d) personification

46. John Osborne's *Look Back in Anger* is an example of
(a) drawing room comedy
(b) kitchen-sink drama
(c) absurd drama
(d) melodrama

47. Which character in Jane Eyre uses religion to justify cruelty?
(a) Blanche Ingram
(b) Mr. Brocklehurst
(c) Sir John Rivers
(d) Eliza Reed

48. Which Romantic poet defined a slave as 'a person perverted into a thing'?
    (a) Blake (b) Coleridge
    (c) Keats (d) Shelley
49. John Suckling belongs to the group of
    (a) Metaphysical poets
    (b) Cavalier poets
    (c) Neo-classical poets
    (d) Religious poets
50. Sir Thomas More creates the character of a traveller into whose mouth the account of Utopia is put. His name is
    (a) Michael (b) Raphael
    (c) Henry (d) Thomas

**ANSWERS**

| | | | | | |
|---|---|---|---|---|---|
| 1. (c) | 2. (a) | 3. (b) | 4. (c) | 5. (c) | 6. (a) |
| 7. (c) | 8. (c) | 9. (a) | 10. (c) | 11. (a) | 12. (a) |
| 13. (b) | 14. (c) | 15. (b) | 16. (b) | 17. (b) | 18. (d) |
| 19. (d) | 20. (d) | 21. (b) | 22. (b) | 23. (c) | 24. (b) |
| 25. (a) | 26. (c) | 27. (c) | 28. (b) | 29. (d) | 30. (b) |
| 31. (b) | 32. (b) | 33. (b) | 34. (c) | 35. (a) | 36. (d) |
| 37. (c) | 38. (a) | 39. (a) | 40. (a) | 41. (c) | 42. (a) |
| 43. (c) | 44. (b) | 45. (a) | 46. (b) | 47. (b) | 48. (b) |
| 49. (b) | 50. (b) | | | | |

12

# English Paper III, June 2013 with Answers

1. Match the following:

   **List I (Browning's poems)**

   I. Abt Vogler
   II. Andrea del Sarto
   III. Childe Ronald to the Dark Tower Came
   IV. Cleon

   **List II (Type of Character)**

   1. A Medieval Knight
   2. A Musician
   3. A Poet
   4. An Artist

   The right combination according to the code is:

| **Codes:** | I | II | III | IV |
|---|---|---|---|---|
| (a) | 4 | 2 | 3 | 1 |
| (b) | 2 | 4 | 1 | 3 |
| (c) | 3 | 1 | 2 | 4 |
| (d) | 1 | 3 | 4 | 2 |

2. All forms of feminism posit that:

   **Codes:**

   I. The relationship between the sexes is one of inequality and oppression.
   II. There should be an end to all wars.
   III. Women need financial independence.
   IV. All men are prone to violence.

   The correct combination according to the code is:

   (a) I and II are correct
   (b) III and IV are correct
   (c) I and III are correct
   (d) II and IV are correct

3. Which one of Brecht's works was intended to lampoon the conventional sentimental musical but the public lapped up the work's sentiment and missed the humour?

   (a) *Man is Man*
   (b) *Three Penny Opera*
   (c) *The Mother*
   (d) *Life of Galileo*

4. Ostensibly a musical treatise, *The Anatomy of Melancholy* is a reflection on human learning and endeavour published under the pseudonym

   (a) Vox Populi
   (b) Epicurus Senior
   (c) Democritus Junior
   (d) Jesting Pilate

5. Horace Walpole's novel *The Castle of Otranto* tells the story of

   (a) A defiant and heartless tyrant who kills his own son mercilessly
   (b) An usurper and a tyrant who kills his own daughter by mistake
   (c) A castle that collapses and crushes the young and sickly prince to death
   (d) A tyrant who retires to a monastery at the end and lives happily ever after with his queen

6. In the Literature of Romanticism there was a widespread frustration with visions

experienced in dreams, in nightmares and other altered states. The following list contains poems which illustrate this theme, with one exception. Identify the exception.
(a) "Kubla Khan"
(b) "Confessions of an English Opium Eater"
(c) "The Ruined Cottage"
(d) "The Fall of Hyperion"

7. The book was for many years banned for obscenity in Britain and the United States. The central character is a Catholic Jew in Ireland. The author claimed that the book is meant to make you laugh. Which is this book?
(a) *The Picture of Dorian Grey*
(b) *Herzog*
(c) *Portnoy's Complaint*
(d) *Ulysses*

8. A.S. Byatt in her famous award winning novel of 1990 contrasts past and present involving a search for a Victorian poet's past illuminating a contemporary university researcher's life and times. Which is the novel?
(a) *The Virgin in the Garden*
(b) *Possession*
(c) *Babel Tower*
(d) *Still Life*

9. Which of the following statements best describes J.M. Coetzee's *Disgrace*?
(a) It is a murder mystery set in post-apartheid South Africa
(b) It is a complex narrative of sin and redemption which involves both White and Black South Africans
(c) The protagonist David Lurie is a priest who brings disgrace to his calling
(d) Coetzee has a schematic and reductive view on the relations between Whites and the Blacks in South Africa

10. Which of the following statements is not true of Mahesh Dattani's *Final Solutions*?
(a) The play centres around a middle class Hindu family during a communal riot
(b) It challenges communalism
(c) It is concerned with homosexual relationship
(d) It promotes religious pluralism in South Asia

11. According to Bakhtin the idea of the Carnivalesque represents the following characteristics *except*:
(a) a liberation from the prevailing truth and established order
(b) a harking back to the past
(c) emphasis on play, parody, pleasure and the body
(d) the suspension of all hierarchical rank, principles, norms and prohibitions

12. Which of the following statements is not true of Patrick White?
(a) He is remembered today for his epic and psychological narrative art
(b) He is the only Australian to receive the Nobel Prize in literature
(c) He pioneered a new fictional landscape and introduced a new continent in literature
(d) His style is noted for lucidity and simplicity

13. Conventional scholarship dates 'Early Modern English' as beginning around
(a) 450 (b) 1066
(c) 1500 (d) 1800

14. "Every demon carries within him unknown to himself, a tiny seed of self-destruction and goes up in thin air at the most unexpected moment." To which of R.K. Narayan's characters the above statement applies?
(a) Raju – *The Guide*

(b) Jagan – *The Sweet Vendor*
(c) Vasu – *Man Eater of Malgudi*
(d) Margayya – *The Financial Expert*

15. Which of the following is not true of post-structuralism?
(a) It seeks to undermine the idea that meaning pre-exists its linguistic expression
(b) There can be no meaning which is not formulated and no language formulation reaches anywhere beyond language
(c) There is no a-textual 'origin' of a text
(d) Every sign refers to every other sign adequately

16. Which of the following statements is not true of Wole Soyinka's *The Swamp Dwellers*?
(a) It talks about the family, the extended family in the African society
(b) It is a confrontation between the traditional and modern society
(c) It talks about the migration of people, crossing of borders and diasporic anguish
(d) It is a comment about the city, urban, modern and the country rural, the swamp, the ancient

17. Arrange the following English literary periods in the order in which they appeared. Use the codes given below:
**Codes:**
I. Elizabethan II. Caroline
III. Anglo Norman IV. Early Tudor

The correct combination according to the code is
(a) III, II, IV, I (b) III, IV, II, I
(c) II, III, IV, I (d) III, IV, I, II

18. Which of the following plays is not written by Rabindranath Tagore?
(a) *Sacrifice* (b) *Chandalika*
(c) *Muktadhara* (d) *Eknath*

19. Given below are two statements, one is labelled as Assertion (A) and the other labelled as Reason (R):
**Assertion (A):** A quarto refers to a text in which each leaf was a quarter the size of the original sheet.
**Reason (R):** Because eight pages of text were printed on large sheets of paper, which were then folded four times to produce four leaves.

In the context of the above statements, which one of the following is correct:
(a) (A) is correct but (R) is wrong
(b) Both (A) and (R) are correct
(c) (A) is wrong but (R) is correct
(d) Both (A) and (R) are wrong

20. The purpose of the Pre-Raphaelites was primarily to promote
(a) complexity and ambivalence in art and literature
(b) simplicity and naturalness in art and literature
(c) symbolic and classical modes in art and literature
(d) psychological and mythic modes in art and literature

21. Which one of the following plays does not use the device of "the play within the play"?
(a) *Hamlet*
(b) *Women Beware Women*
(c) *The Spanish Tragedy*
(d) *A Midsummer Night's Dream*

22. Given below are two statements, one is labelled as Assertion (A) and the other labelled as Reason (R):
**Assertion (A):** In the Absurd plays of Pinter and Beckett, lack of communication seems to be a predominant theme.

**Reason (R):** Existentialist philosophy had a tremendous influence on the dramatists of the period, nihilism and meaninglessness of life taking a front seat.

In the context of the above statements, which one of the following is correct:

(a) Both (A) and (R) are true and (R) is the correct explanation of (A)
(b) Both (A) and (R) are true but (R) is not the correct explanation of (A)
(c) (A) is true but (R) is false
(d) (A) is false but (R) is true

23. Which of the following observations are true about Beatrice Culleton's *April Raintree*?
    I. It is a fictional account of the lives of two metis sisters growing up in Winnipeg.
    II. April has a darker complexion and identifies herself with Metis population.
    III. The two sisters have been removed from their parents home and placed with a series of foster families.
    IV. Cheryl has a lighter complexion and identifies herself with white population.
    (a) I and III are correct
    (b) I and II are correct
    (c) II and III are correct
    (d) III and IV are correct

24. "She dwells with beauty—Beauty that must die",—wrote Keats in one of his odes, referring to
    (a) Indolence (b) Autumn
    (c) Melancholy (d) Psyche

25. Kafka's *Trial* has all the following characteristics except:
    (a) Vivid yet surreal
    (b) Dystopian
    (c) The use of historical details of setting
    (d) The depiction of totalitarian society

26. Match the following lists:
    **List I (Phrases from poems)**
    I. "Sound of stick upon the floor"
    II. "Hade's bobbin bound in mummy cloth"
    III. "With beauty like a tightened bow"
    IV. "A tattered coat upon a stick"
    **List II (Titles of poems)**
    1. "Byzantium"
    2. "Sailing to Byzantium"
    3. "Coole and Ballylee, 1931"
    4. "No Second Troy"

    The right combination according to the code is:

| Codes: | I | II | III | IV |
|---|---|---|---|---|
| (a) | 4 | 1 | 3 | 2 |
| (b) | 3 | 2 | 1 | 4 |
| (c) | 4 | 3 | 2 | 1 |
| (d) | 3 | 1 | 4 | 2 |

27. Given below are the two statements, one is labelled as Assertion (A) and the other labelled as Reason (R).
    **Assertion (A):** The literature of the Jacobean Age is dominated by works revealing symptoms of melodrama and sensationalism.
    **Reason (R):** The Jacobean Age is generally ruled by the spirit of decadence.

    In the context of the two statements which one of the following is correct explanation of (A).
    (a) Both (A) and (R) are true and (R) is the correct explanation of (A)
    (b) Both (A) and (R) are true and (R) is not the correct
    (c) (A) is true but (R) is false
    (d) (A) is false but (R) is true

28. Which of the following statements best describes the term 'deconstruction'?
    (a) It seeks to expose the problematic nature of 'centered' discourses
    (b) It advocates 'subjective' or 'free' interpretation
    (c) It emphasizes the importance of historical context
    (d) It is a method of critical analysis

29. Which of these authors is not a writer of African American slave narratives?
    (a) Solomon Northrop
    (b) Frederick Douglass
    (c) Phillis Wheatley
    (d) Sojourner Truth

30. "For nature then
    The courser pleasures of my boyish days,
    And their glad animal movements all gone by
    To me was all in all".
    In these lines from "Tintern Abbey Revisited", Wordsworth is talking about:
    (a) the second stage in his relationship with Nature
    (b) the first stage in his relationship with Nature
    (c) both the first and second stages in his relationship with Nature
    (d) the third stage in his relationship with Nature

31. **Assertion (A):** One of Flaubert's main motivations in writing the novel *Madam Bovary* was his antipathy for the bourgeoisie.
    **Reason (R):** Flaubert strongly believed that bourgeoisie are those who think, feel and act in terms of utilitarianism and who reject the humanity and uniqueness of the individual person.
    (a) Both (A) and (R) are true and (R) is the correct explanation of (A)
    (b) Both (A) and (R) are true but (R) is not the correct explanation of (A)
    (c) (A) is true, but (R) is false
    (d) (A) is false but (R) is true

32. "A Tun of Man in thy large Bulk is writ,
    But sure thou'rt but a Kilderkin of wit".
    In the above lines what does Dryden mean by 'Kilderkin'?
    (a) a trivial instance
    (b) a small barrel of wine
    (c) kith and kin
    (d) a small amount, as contrasted with 'tun'

33. Which of the following statements is not true of Kazuo Ishiguro's *Remains of the Day*? The novel
    (a) uses a butler as a pivotal character
    (b) uses the classic English detective story form
    (c) refers to England in the 1930s
    (d) became a very successful film

34. "From a Second Space perspective city space becomes more of a mental and ideational field, conceptualised in imagery, reflexive thought and symbolic representation, a conceived space of the imagination or what I will henceforth describe as the urban imagery."
    (Edward Soja, *Postmetropolis*)
    Which of the following statements cannot be applied to Soja's proposition on the Second Space?
    (a) Second Space perspective tends to be more subjective
    (b) Second Space perspective is concerned with symbolic representation of reality
    (c) Second Space perspective is concerned with the fundamentally materialist approach
    (d) Second Space perspective deals with 'thoughts about space'

35. "Lightly, O lightly, we bear her along,
    She sways like a flower in the wind of our song;
    She skims like a bird on the foam of a stream,
    She floats like a laugh from the lips of a dream....."
    These lines occur in the poem
    (a) "Palanquin bearers"
    (b) "The Illusion of Love"
    (c) "Indian Love Song"
    (d) "Cradle Song"

36. Which among the following novels of Anita Desai is a children's book?
    (a) *Fire and The Mountain*
    (b) *Fasting, Feasting*
    (c) *The Zig Zag Way*
    (d) *The Village by the Sea*

37. Who among the following writers describes novels as "not form which you see but emotion which you feel"?
    (a) D.H. Lawrence
    (b) Jean Rhys
    (c) Virginia Woolf
    (d) Joseph Conrad

38. In *Paradise Lost,* Milton invokes his 'Heav'nly Muse', 'Urania' at the beginning of:

    **Codes:**

    I. Book one  II. Book four
    III. Book nine  IV. Book seven

    The right combination according to the code is
    (a) I and II are correct
    (b) I, III and IV are correct
    (c) II and III are correct
    (d) I and IV are correct

39. Which one of the following best describes the basic principle of New Criticism?
    (a) an emphasis on the distinctive style and personality of the authors
    (b) stressing the virtues of discipline, order and the ethical mean
    (c) locating the meaning of a literary work in the internal relations of the language that constitute a text
    (d) evaluating a literary text against a backdrop of historical

40. Who among the following figures give a preview of Aschenbach's fatal end in *Death in Venice?*
    I. The Graveyard Stranger
    II. The Governess
    III. The barber
    IV. The Gondolier

    The right combination according to the code is:
    (a) III and IV are correct
    (b) I and IV are correct
    (c) II and III are correct
    (d) I and III are correct

41. Jacques Lacan posits three 'orders' which structure human existence. In the list that follows: Identify the one that is not included by Lacan:
    (a) Imaginary  (b) Unconscious
    (c) Real  (d) Symbolic

42. Given below are two statements, one labelled as Assertion (A) and the other labelled as Reason (R).

    **Assertion (A):** Deconstructive reading is apolitical.

    **Reason (R):** Because it focuses exclusively on language. It primarily holds that all texts or linguistic structures contain within them a principle of destabilisation and hence it is difficult to pin down meaning. Such a reading, therefore, is unable to assign historical agency.

    In this context above statements, identify which one of the following is correct?
    (a) (A) is correct but (R) is wrong
    (b) Both (A) and (R) are correct
    (c) (A) is wrong but (R) is correct
    (d) Both (A) and (R) are wrong

43. Match the following lists:

    **List I (Title of poem)**
    I. "I hear a fly Buzz"
    II. "Birches"
    III. "Sunday Morning"
    IV. "A Supermarket in California"

    **List II (Poet)**
    1. Wallace Stevens
    2. Emily Dickinson
    3. Allen Ginsberg
    4. Robert Frost

The correct combination is:

| **Codes:** | I | II | III | IV |
|---|---|---|---|---|
| (a) | 2 | 4 | 3 | 1 |
| (b) | 2 | 1 | 3 | 4 |
| (c) | 2 | 4 | 1 | 3 |
| (d) | 3 | 2 | 1 | 4 |

44. 'Lexis' refers to
   (a) all word forms having meaning or grammatical functions
   (b) the history of words
   (c) study of select word forms
   (d) the selection of words

45. The following writers are involved in social activism in addition to their practice of creative writing:
   **Codes:**
   I. Mahasweta Devi
   II. Shashi Deshpande
   III. Arundhati Roy
   IV. Shobha De

   The correct combination according to the code is
   (a) I and II are correct
   (b) III and IV are correct
   (c) I and III are correct
   (d) II and IV are correct

46. In relation to Spenser's *Faerie Queene* which of the following character virtue link is rightly matched?
   (a) Justice-Artegall; Courtsey-Guyan; Temperance-Calidore
   (b) Chasity-Britomart; Justice-Guyan; Temperance-Talus
   (c) Courtsey-Calidore; Temperance-Guyon; Justice-Artegall
   (d) Courtsey-Calidore; Temperance-Artegall; Justice-Britomart

47. *The Divine Comedy* is divided into three canticas, each consisting of
   (a) 30 cantos (b) 33 cantos
   (c) 24 cantos (d) 28 cantos

48. *The Modern Promethean* is the alternative title of
   (a) *Dracula* (b) *Frankenstein*
   (c) *Caleb Williams* (d) *The Italian*

49. In *Words Upon Words*, Saussure says, "The actual birth of a new language has never reported in the world" because "we have never known of a language which was not spoken the day before or which was not spoken in the same way the day before". What does he mean?
   (a) Old languages die making way for new ones
   (b) The birth and death of a language are not subject to human laws
   (c) Languages do not get borne, they evolve out of previously existing linguistic situations
   (d) Old speech patterns trigger the birth of a new language

50. What did Henry James describe as "Loose Baggy Monsters"?
   (a) Novels (b) The Spaniards
   (c) Epic Poems (d) His trousers

51. "High above the north pole, on the first day of 1969, two professors of English literature approached each other at a combined velocity of 1200 miles per hour."
   This is the opening of David Lodge's
   (a) *Nice Work*
   (b) *Changing Places*
   (c) *Small World*
   (d) *The British Museum is Falling Down*

52. At the end of *The Portrait of a Lady* Isabel Archer
   I. Goes back to the house from the Garden
   II. Accepts the proposal of Casper Goodwood
   III. Straightaway refuses the offer of Goodwood

IV. Probably goes back to Rome and Osmond

Which is the correct combinations according to the code?

**Codes:**

(a) I and II are correct
(b) III and IV are correct
(c) I and IV are correct
(d) I and III are correct

53. "I will put myself in poor and mean attire And with a kind of umber smirch my face." The word umber means:
(a) a dusty yellow or brown pigment
(b) a dark brown pigment
(c) light brown powder
(d) yellow paste

54. Which of the following psychoanalysts rewrote Descarte's dictum: "I think therefore I am" as "I am not where I think, and I think where I am not"?
(a) Lacan (b) Freud
(c) Jung (d) Cixous

55. By the end of *In Memorium* the speaker
(a) re-embraces a Christian vision of after life
(b) re-asserts religious doubts and scientific scepticism
(c) reiterates the Darwinian view of social life
(d) reaffirms his faith in universal brotherhood

56. The system of social rules that a speaker knows about language and uses it is called
(a) grammar (b) morphology
(c) orthography (d) pragmatics

57. The term 'ecological imperialism' was coined by
(a) Vandana Shiva (b) Laurence Buell
(c) Paulo Freire (d) Alfred Crosby

58. Emotional ties and personal relationships play a minor part in Defoe's works. The following protagonists of Defoe have no family except one who leaves family at an early age. Which is that character?
(a) *Moll Flanders*
(b) *Colonel Jacque*
(c) *Robinson Crusoe*
(d) *Captain Singleton*

59. Match the following lists:

**List I (Novels)**

I. *The Power and the Glory*
II. *The Quiet American*
III. *The Honorary Consul*
IV. *The Comedians*

**List II (Settings)**

1. Vietnam 2. Haiti
3. Paraguay 4. Mexico

The right combination according to the code is:

| Codes: | I | II | III | IV |
|---|---|---|---|---|
| (a) | 4 | 1 | 3 | 2 |
| (b) | 1 | 2 | 3 | 4 |
| (c) | 4 | 3 | 2 | 1 |
| (d) | 3 | 4 | 1 | 2 |

60. "......every other stone
is god or cousin
there is no crop
other than god
and god is harvested here
around the year."

This extract is from:
(a) Jayanta Mahapatra's "Konarak"
(b) Arun Kolatkar's *Jejuri*
(c) P. Lal's "Being Very Simple, God"
(d) R. Parthasarathy's "Under Another Sky"

61. In E.M. Foster's *A Passage to India* some of the major symbols are associated with:

**Codes:**

I. Mountains II. Tigers
III. Echoes IV. Clouds

The right combination according to the code is:
(a) I and II are correct
(b) I, II and IV are correct
(c) I and III are correct
(d) II and IV are correct

62. Which of the following features are present in Dostoevsky's *Crime and Punishment*?
I. Nihilism
II. Utilitarianism
III. Rationalism
IV. Christian Symbolism

The correct combination according to the code is:
(a) I and II are correct
(b) I and IV are correct
(c) III and IV are correct
(d) I and III are correct

63. "Count no man happy until he dies, free of pain at last", is the last line of
(a) *Oedipus at Colonus*
(b) *Agamemnon*
(c) *Oedipus the King*
(d) *Orestes*

64. What characteristics of 17th century metaphysical poetry sparked the enthusiasm of modernist poets and critics?
**Codes:**
I. its intellectual complexity
II. its uncompromising engagement with politics
III. its religious fervour
IV. its union of thought and passion

The right combination according to the code is
(a) I and III are correct
(b) I and IV are correct
(c) II and III are correct
(d) I and II are correct

65. Th' inferior Priestess, at her Altar's side,
Trembling, begins the sacred Rites of Pride.
In this description of Belinda at the dressing table, what does the word Pride refer to?
(a) Vanity
(b) Pride as the first of man's sins
(c) Both (a) and (b)
(d) Complacency

66. "Cover her face; mine eyes dazzle; she died young.... She and I were twins: And should I die this instant, I had liv'd her time to a minute."
In the light of the above quotation which of the following interpretations is not correct?
(a) The beauty and youth of the Duchess become obvious to Ferdinand when he sees her dead body
(b) Only when he identifies himself with her, does he realize the enormity of his crime
(c) When he compares the age of the Duchess with his own and puts himself in her position does he realize his guilt
(d) He wants her face to be covered because it reminds him of her infidelity

67. All except one of the following scholars have come up with models which aim to characterise world Englishes within one conceptual set. Identify the lone exception.
(a) Tom McArthur
(b) Noam Chomsky
(c) Braj Kachru
(d) Manfred Gorlach

68. In the very opening scene of *Volpone*, the protagonist says, "Open the shrine, that I may see my Saint," By the word 'Saint', Volpone is referring to
(a) The Sun (b) Saint Arthur
(c) Gold (d) Apollo

69. A close friend of Dickens objected to the original ending of *Great Expectations* in which Estella remarries and Pip remains single. Dickens accordingly revised to a more conventional ending which suggests that Pip and Estella will marry. Who was the friend?
    (a) Wilkie Collins
    (b) Thomas Beard
    (c) Thomas Carlyle
    (d) Richard Bentley

70. Which of the following statements best describes an example of the influence of an affective factor on second language acquisition?
    (a) A second language learner makes educated guesses about word meanings in a text by recognizing cognates
    (b) A second language learner uses familiar vocabulary to mentally form sentences before speaking
    (c) An adult second language learner finds it impossible to form second language sounds that do not occur in his first language
    (d) A second language learner employs several words from the first language when speaking the second language but not when writing it

71. Marvell's "The Coronet" seeks to explore the human condition in terms of the conflict between
    (a) body and soul
    (b) war and peace
    (c) nature and grace
    (d) flesh and spirit

72. Which of the following is not true of post-structuralism?
    (a) It seeks to undermine the idea that meaning pre-exists its linguistic expression
    (b) There can be no meaning which is not formulated and no language formulation reaches anywhere beyond language
    (c) There is no a-textual 'origin' of a text
    (d) Every sign refers to every other sign adequately

73. Which of the following second-language learners would most likely acquire the second language more easily?
    (a) A high school student who has been enrolled in mandatory classes in the second language since elementary school
    (b) A visitor to a country where the second language is spoken; he interacts with hotel and restaurant personnel using the second language
    (c) A business person for whom fluency in the second language may lead to career advancement
    (d) An immigrant living in a country where the second language is spoken; he feels accepted by speakers of the second language

74. In *Wuthering Heights*, Cathy appears in a dream beating at a window, wailing "Let me in", blood running down her wrist. Who dreams her?
    (a) Lockwood (b) Nelly
    (c) Heathcliffe (d) Edgar Linton

75. Who among the following characters in Thomas More's *Utopia* did not correspond in biographical background to an actual historical person?
    (a) Morton (b) Hythloday
    (c) Giles (d) More

## ANSWERS

| | | | | | |
|---|---|---|---|---|---|
| 1. (b) | 2. (c) | 3. (b) | 4. (c) | 5. (b) | 6. (c) |
| 7. (d) | 8. (b) | 9. (b) | 10. (c) | 11. (b) | 12. (d) |
| 13. (c) | 14. (c) | 15. (d) | 16. (c) | 17. (d) | 18. (d) |
| 19. (a) | 20. (b) | 21. (b) | 22. (a) | 23. (a) | 24. (c) |
| 25. (c) | 26. (a) | 27. (b) | 28. (a) | 29. (c) | 30. (c) |
| 31. (a) | 32. (b) | 33. (b) | 34. (c) | 35. (a) | 36. (d) |
| 37. (c) | 38. (d) | 39. (c) | 40. (b) | 41. (b) | 42. (b) |
| 43. (c) | 44. (a) | 45. (c) | 46. (c) | 47. (b) | 48. (b) |
| 49. (c) | 50. (a) | 51. (b) | 52. (c) | 53. (a) | 54. (a) |
| 55. (a) | 56. (d) | 57. (d) | 58. (c) | 59. (a) | 60. (b) |
| 61. (c) | 62. (b) | 63. (c) | 64. (b) | 65. (c) | 66. (d) |
| 67. (b) | 68. (c) | 69. (a) | 70. (b) | 71. (c) | 72. (d) |
| 73. (d) | 74. (a) | 75. (b) | | | |

13

# NET Examination Paper II, December 2013 with Answers

1. ____ the very word is like a bell
To toll me back from thee to my sole self!
Which word?
(a) Bird (b) Immortal
(c) Forlorn (d) Fancy

2. In poems like "The Altar" and "Easter Wings" _______ exploits _______.
(a) John Donne, alliteration
(b) Robert Herrick, trimetre
(c) G.M. Hopkins, sprung rhythm
(d) George Herbert, typographic space

3. No, no thou hast not felt the lapse of hours!
For what wears out the life of mortal men?
'Tis that repeated shocks, again, again,
Exhaust the energy of strongest souls
And numb the elastic powers....
Who does the poet address here?
(a) The Scholar Gipsy
(b) Telemachus
(c) The Nightingale
(d) The Poet's Sister, Dorothy

4. The *roman a clef* (French for "novel with a key") uses contemporary historical figures as its chief characters. They are of course given fictional names. One example is Aldous Huxley's *Point Counter Point.* Its Mark Rampion is modelled on
(a) D.H. Lawrence (b) E.M. Forster
(c) Wyndham Lewis (d) Arnold Bennett

5. She was a worthy woman al hir lyve,
Housbondes at chirche-dore she hadde fyve,
In the 'Prologue' Chaucer represents the Wife of Bath as:
I. crude and vulgar
II. outspoken and boastfully licentious
III. a witness to masculine oppression
IV. bubbling with vitality

Find the correct combination according to the code:
(a) I, II and III are correct.
(b) I, II and IV are correct.
(c) I, III and IV are correct.
(d) II, III and IV are correct.

6. The novel tells the story of twin brothers, Waldo, the man of reason and intellect, and Arthur, the innocent half-wit, the way their lives are inextricably intertwined. Which is the novel?
(a) *The Tree of Man*
(b) *Voss*
(c) *The Solid Mandala*
(d) *The Vivisector*

7. Who among the following was not a member of the Scriblerus Club?
(a) Thomas Parnell (b) Alexander Pope
(c) Joseph Addison (d) John Gay

8. _______ is a theological term brought into literary criticism by _______.
(a) Entelechy, St. Augustine

(b) Ambiguity, William Empson
(c) Adequation, Fr Walter Ong
(d) Epiphany, James Joyce

9. _______ the Almighty Power Hurled headlong flaming from th' Ethereal Sky,
With hideous ruin and combustion down
To bottomless perdition, there to dwell
In Adamantine Chains and penal Fire
Who durst defy th' Omnipotent to Arms.
(*Paradise Lost*, I.44-49)
Choose the appropriate word:
(a) Him (b) He
(c) Satan (d) The Fiend

10. Which of the following works does not have a mad woman as a character in it?
(a) *The Yellow Wallpaper*
(b) *The Mad Woman in the Attic*
(c) *Jane Eyre*
(d) *Wide Sargasso Sea*

11. Which of the following is not a quest narrative?
(a) Shelley's *Alastor*
(b) Byron's *Manfred*
(c) Coleridge's *Christabel*
(d) Keats's *Endymion*

12. The novel has a scene where African American students are made to compete and fight with each other as they rush for the gold coins tossed on an electric blanket. Identify the novel.
(a) Richard Wright : *Native Son*
(b) James Baldwin : *Another* Country
(c) Ralph Ellison : *Invisible Man*
(d) Toni Morrison : *Bluest Eye*

13. G.M. Hopkins's "Windhover" is dedicated:
(a) To Christ, our Lord
(b) To Christ our lord
(c) to no one
(d) to Christ, the Lord

14. Match List I with List II according to the code given below:

| List I (Authors) | List II (Poems) |
|---|---|
| I. Ted Hughes | 1. "The Otter" |
| II. Seamus Heaney | 2. "Snake" |
| III. W.H. Auden | 3. "Ghost Crabs" |
| IV. D.H. Lawrence | 4. "Prevent the Dog from Barking with a Juicy Bone" |

| Codes: | I | II | III | IV |
|---|---|---|---|---|
| (a) | 1 | 2 | 4 | 3 |
| (b) | 2 | 3 | 1 | 4 |
| (c) | 3 | 1 | 4 | 2 |
| (d) | 3 | 2 | 1 | 4 |

15. His cooks with long disuse their trade forgot;
Cool was his kitchen, though his brains were hot.
Who is this character whose stinginess passed into a proverb?
(a) Corah (b) Shimei
(c) Zimri (d) Achitophel

16. "The story and the novel, the idea and the form, are the needle and thread, and I never heard of a guild of tailors who recommended the use of the thread without the needle, or the needle without the thread."
This famous passage describing the relation of idea to form is found in
(a) Sir Philip Sidney, *An Apology for Poetry*
(b) Samuel Taylor Coleridge, *Biographia Literaria*
(c) Henry James, *The Art of Fiction*
(d) I.A. Richards, *Principles of Literary Criticism*

17. Identify the correctly matched set below:
(a) The Norman Conquest – 1066
William Caxton and the introduction of printing – 1575

The King James Bible – 1611
Dr. Johnson's *English Dictionary* – 1755
The Commonwealth Period/ the Protectorate – 1649-1660

(b) The Norman Conquest – 1066
William Caxton and the introduction of printing – 1475
The King James Bible – 1611
Dr. Johnson's *English Dictionary*- 1755
The Commonwealth Period/the Protectorate – 1649-1660

(c) The Norman Conquest – 1016
William Caxton and the introduction of printing-1475
The King James Bible – 1564
Dr. Johnson's *English Dictionary* - 1780
The Commonwealth Period/the Protectorate – 1649-1660

(d) The Norman Conquest – 1013
William Caxton and the introduction of printing – 1575
The King James Bible – 1627
Dr. Johnson's *English Dictionary* – 1746
The Commonwealth Period/the Protectorate – 1624-1660

18. Leopold Bloom in *Ulysses* is
   (a) a Great War veteran
   (b) a Dublin bar owner
   (c) a Jewish advertising agent
   (d) an Irish nationalist

19. "Late capitalism", by which is meant accelerated technological development and the massive extension of intellectually qualified labour, was first popularised by
   (a) Terry Eagleton
   (b) Ernst Mandel
   (c) Raymond Williams
   (d) Stanley Fish

20. Which of the following arrangements is in the correct chronological sequence?
   (a) *Native Son* by Richard Wright – *Invisible Man* by Ralph Ellison – *Their Eyes Were Watching God* by Zora Neil Hurston – *Another Country* by James Baldwin
   (b) *Their Eyes Were Watching God* by Zora Neil Hurston – *Native Son* by Richard Wright – *Invisible Man* by Ralph Ellison – *Another Country* by James Baldwin
   (c) *Invisible Man* by Ralph Ellison – *Native Son* by Richard Wright – *Another Country* by James Baldwin – *Their Eyes Were Watching God* by Zora Neil Hurston
   (d) *Their Eyes Were Watching God* by Zora Neil Hurston – *Another Country* by James Baldwin – *Native Son* by Richard Wright – *Invisible Man* by Ralph Ellison

21. Metaphor is so widespread that it is often used as an umbrella term to include other figures of speech such as metonyms which can be technically distinguished from it in its narrower usage.
   Identify the *metaphorical phrase* in this sentence:
   (a) narrower usage
   (b) technically distinguished
   (c) figures of speech
   (d) umbrella term

22. Along the shore of silver streaming Thames;
Whose rutty bank, the which his river hems,
Was painted all with variable flowers,
...
Fit to deck maidens' bowers
And crown their paramours
Against their bridal day, which is not long;

Sweet Thames ! run softly till I end my song.

(Spenser's *Prothalamion*)

Another poet fondly recalls these lines but cannot conceal their heavily ironic tone in:

(a) Marianne Moore's "Spenser's Ireland"
(b) Sylvia Plath's "Morning Song"
(c) W.H. Auden's "In Praise of Limestone"
(d) T.S. Eliot's *Waste Land*

23. The tramp in Pinter's first big hit, *The Caretaker*, often travels under an assumed name. It is

(a) Bernard Jenkins (b) Roly Jenkins
(c) Jack Jenkins (d) Peter Jenkins

24. Here is a list of early English plays imitating Greek and Latin plays. Pick the odd one out:

(a) *Gorboduc*
(b) *Tamburlaine*
(c) *Ralph Roister Doister*
(d) *Gammer Gurton's Needle*

25. Where does Act I Scene 1 of William Congreve's *Way of the World* open?

(a) A Chocolate-House
(b) A Pub
(c) A Carrefour
(d) The drawing room of Sir Willfull's mansion

26. While "a well-boiled bicicle" for "a well-oiled bicycle" is an example of Spoonerism, someone saying "Congenital food" for 'Continental food' is an example of

(a) Malaproprism (b) Pleonasm
(c) Neologism (d) Archaism

27. It is unimaginable that all the following events happened in one year:

1. Arthur Evans discovered the first European civilization; his excavations in Crete revealed a culture that was far older than either Attic Greece or Ancient Rome.
2. Sir Arthur Quiller-Couch published the *Oxford Book of English Verse*.
3. Pablo Picasso stepped off the Barcelona train at Gare d' Orsay, Paris.
4. Max Planck unveiled the Quantum Theory.
5. Hugo de Vries identified what would later come to be called genes.
6. Sigmund Freud published *The Interpretation of Dreams*.
7. Coca-cola arrived in Britain.

Identify the year:

(a) 1899 (b) 1900
(c) 1901 (d) 1903

28. *Brother to a Prince and fellow to a beggar if he be found worthy.*

This is the epigraph to

(a) T.S. Eliot's "The Hollow Men"
(b) Rudyard Kipling's "The Man Who Would be the King"
(c) George Eliot's *Silas Marner*
(d) E.M. Forster's *Howard's End*

29. Robert Graves's "In Broken Images" ends thus:

He in a new confusion of his understanding;
I in a new understanding of my confusion.

The figure of speech here is

(a) Chiasmus (b) Catachresis
(c) Inversion (d) Zeugma

30. The phrase "leaves dancing" is an example of

(a) pathetic fallacy (b) hyperbole
(c) pun (d) conceit

31. At the end of *The Great Gatsby*, the narrator Nick Carraway observes: "They were careless people". Who were they?

(a) Tom and Daisy
(b) The Wilsons
(c) Gatsby and his friends
(d) The people of East Egg

32. William Wordsworth's statement of purpose in publishing the *Lyrical Ballads* carries the following phrase. (Complete the phrase correctly).
"to choose incidents from common life and to relate or describe them, throughout, as far as possible, ______."
(a) in a selection of language really used by men
(b) in a relation to language really used by men
(c) in a selection of language really used by common man
(d) in deference to language actually used by men

33. Match List I with List II according to the code given below:
**List I (Novels)**
I. *Lord Jim*
II. *To the Lighthouse*
III. *A Passage to India*
IV. *A Portrait of the Artist as a Young Man*
**List II (Last lines)**
1. 'It was done; it was finished. Yes, she thought laying down her brush in extreme fatigue, I have had my vision.'
2. 'April 27. Old father, old artificer, stand me now and ever in good stead...'
3. 'He feels it himself and says often that he is "preparing to leave all this; preparing to leave,...", while he waves his hands sadly at his butterflies.'
4. '"No not yet," and the sky said, "No, not there".'

| **Codes:** | I | II | III | IV |
|---|---|---|---|---|
| (a) | 2 | 4 | 3 | 1 |
| (b) | 3 | 2 | 4 | 1 |
| (c) | 3 | 1 | 4 | 2 |
| (d) | 2 | 3 | 1 | 4 |

34. Identify the incorrect description/s of "Sprung Rhythm" from the following:
1. This rhythm causes ideas to spring in our minds—hence Sprung Rhythm.
2. In Sprung Rhythm the feet are of equal length.
3. A foot may have one to four syllables in Sprung Rhythm.
4. Its metre is derived from the metre of Anglo-Saxon poetry which was based on accent and linked by alliteration.
(a) 4 is incorrect.
(b) 1 and 4 are incorrect.
(c) 3 is incorrect.
(d) 1 is incorrect.

35. Who among the following proposes that the unconscious comes into being only in language?
(a) Sigmund Freud (b) Jacques Lacan
(c) Stuart Hall (d) Paul de Man

36. The Elizabethan Settlement established during the reign of Elizabeth I
I. ensured the supremacy of the Church of England.
II. allowed Christians to acknowledge the authority of the Pope.
III. allowed the extremer Protestants to be part of the Anglican church.
IV. created a group known as the Roundheads.
The correct combination according to the code is:
(a) I and III are correct.
(b) I and II are correct.
(c) II and III are correct.
(d) III and IV are correct

37. Which of the following poems by Tennyson does not speak of old age and death?
(a) "The Beggar Maid"

(b) "The Lotus-Eaters"
(c) "Ulysses"
(d) "Tithonus"

38. One English poet addressing another:
Thy soul was like a Star, and dwelt apart;
Thou hast a voice whose sound was like the sea:
Pure as the naked heavens, majestic, free,
So didst thou travel on life's common way,
In cheerful godliness....
Whose lines are these? To whom are they addressed?
(a) W.H. Auden – W.B. Yeats
(b) P.B. Shelley – William Blake
(c) William Wordsworth – John Milton
(d) Ben Jonson – William Shakespeare

39. Samuel Johnson's *Lives of Poets* (1781) was originally a series of introductions to the poets he wrote for a group of London publishers.
They were collected as:
(a) *Lives of English Poets : Critical and Biographical Essays.*
(b) *Prefaces, Biographical and Critical, to the Works of English Poets.*
(c) *Notes, Biographical and Critical, on the Works of English Poets.*
(d) *Lives of English Poets: Biographical and Critical Notes.*

40. Which of the following is not mentioned in Northrop Frye's four 'generic plots'?
(a) The comic (b) The tragic
(c) The lyric (d) The ironic

41. Arrange the sections of *The Waste Land* in the order in which they appear in the poem:
1. The Fire Sermon
2. Death by Water
3. A Game of Chess
4. What the Thunder Said
5. The Burial of the Dead
(a) 3, 2, 1, 5, 4 (b) 5, 1, 2, 3, 4
(c) 5, 2, 3, 1, 4 (d) 5, 3, 1, 2, 4

42. Sir Plume is a character in
(a) Dryden's *Absalom and* Achitophel
(b) Congreve's *The Way of the* World
(c) Pope's *The Rape of the Lock*
(d) Farquhar's *The Beaux' Strategem*

43. Steeling herself to the murder, Lady Macbeth calls on ______ to "unsex me here". (*Macbeth* I.5.39)
Choose the right option to fill in the blank:
(a) God
(b) the spirits of hell
(c) the angels in heaven
(d) no one in particular

44. You will find the following lines in an English poem:
Thou by the Indian Ganges' side
Shouldst rubies find; I by the side
Of Humber would complain.
Which poem? Who is the poet?
(a) "Lonely Hearts." Wendy Cope
(b) "Holy Thursday." William Blake
(c) "Tiger Mask Ritual." Chitra Banerjee Divakaruni
(d) "To His Coy Mistress." Andrew Marvell

45. Teach me half the gladness
That thy brain must know,
Such harmonious madness
From my lips would flow
The world should listen then, as I am listening now.
Whose lines are these? To whom are they addressed?
(a) John Keats. The Nightingale
(b) P.B. Shelley. The Skylark
(c) William Wordsworth. The Wye Valley
(d) Robert Browning. The Grammarian

46. Match List I with List II according to the code given below:

**List I (Novel)**

I. *Dombey and Son*
II. *The Return of the Native*
III. *Bleak House*
IV. *Tess*

**List II (Major symbol)**

1. fog 2. train
3. heath 4. mist

| Codes: | I | II | III | IV |
|---|---|---|---|---|
| (a) | 2 | 3 | 1 | 4 |
| (b) | 4 | 2 | 3 | 1 |
| (c) | 2 | 3 | 4 | 1 |
| (d) | 1 | 3 | 4 | 1 |

47. The following postmodernist novel has an unusual protagonist whose gender is not revealed. So much so, that we keep wondering whether that person's relationships are homo-/hetero-sexual:
(a) *The French Lieutenant's Woman*
(b) *English Music*
(c) *Written on the Body*
(d) *Enduring Love*

48. Which novel of Graham Greene in the following list does not end in some form of suicide by the protagonist?
(a) *The Heart of the Matter*
(b) *England Made Me*
(c) *Brighton Rock*
(d) *The Power and the Glory*

49. Who among the following gave a happy ending to *King Lear*?
(a) James Quin
(b) Nahum Tate
(c) Peg Woffington
(d) Charles Macklin

50. Jane Austen's *Pride and Prejudice* starts with the famous statement : "It is a truth universally acknowledged that a single man in possession of a good fortune must be in want of a life."
As we get to read the novel this statement seems to be made from the point of view of:
I. the surrounding families
II. Mrs Bennet
III. Mr Bennet
IV. The women of Jane Austen's age and society
Find out the correct combination according to the code:
(a) I, II and III are correct.
(b) I, II and IV are correct.
(c) II, III and IV are correct.
(d) I, III and IV are correct.

## ANSWERS

| | | | | | |
|---|---|---|---|---|---|
| 1. (c) | 2. (d) | 3. (a) | 4. (a) | 5. (b) | 6. (c) |
| 7. (c) | 8. (d) | 9. (a) | 10. (b) | 11. (c) | 12. (c) |
| 13. (b) | 14. (c) | 15. (b) | 16. (c) | 17. (b) | 18. (c) |
| 19. (b) | 20. (b) | 21. (d) | 22. (d) | 23. (a) | 24. (b) |
| 25. (a) | 26. (a) | 27. (b) | 28. (b) | 29. (a) | 30. (a) |
| 31. (a) | 32. (a) | 33. (c) | 34. (d) | 35. (b) | 36. (a) |
| 37. (a) | 38. (c) | 39. (b) | 40. (c) | 41. (d) | 42. (c) |
| 43. (b) | 44. (d) | 45. (b) | 46. (a) | 47. (c) | 48. (b) |
| 49. (b) | 50. (b) | | | | |

# 14

# English Paper III, December 2013 with Answers

1. In which of the following novels *Harikatha* is strategically used as a medium of 'consciousness raising'?
   (a) *Waiting for the Mahatma*
   (b) *The Serpent and the Rope*
   (c) *A Bend in the Ganges*
   (d) *Kanthapura*

2. Identify the text in the following list which offers a fictionalized survey of English Literature from Elizabethan times to 1928:
   (a) E.M. Forster, *The Eternal Moment*
   (b) Virginia Woolf, *Orlando*
   (c) Robert Graves, *Goodbye to All That*
   (d) David Jones, *In Parenthesis*

3. Match List I with List II according to the code given below:

| List I | List II |
|---|---|
| I. John Ruskin | 1. *London Labour and the London Poor* |
| II. Henry Mayhew | 2. *The Golden Bough* |
| III. Sir Charles Lyell | 3. *Unto The Last* |
| IV. Sir James George Frazer | 4. *The Principles of Geology* |

| Codes: | I | II | III | IV |
|---|---|---|---|---|
| (a) | 3 | 2 | 1 | 4 |
| (b) | 2 | 1 | 3 | 4 |
| (c) | 2 | 3 | 4 | 1 |
| (d) | 3 | 1 | 4 | 2 |

4. Which of the following poems does not begin in the first person pronoun?
   (a) Shelley's "Adonais"
   (b) Byron's "Don Juan"
   (c) Keats's "Lamia"
   (d) Coleridge's "The Aeolian Harp"

5. In his *Anatomy of Melancholy* Robert Burton proposes the following two principal kinds:
   I. Love II. Death
   III. Spiritual IV. Religious
   The correct combination according to the code is:
   (a) I and II are correct.
   (b) I and III are correct.
   (c) I and IV are correct.
   (d) II and IV are correct.

6. Listed below are some English journals widely read by professionals:
   *Screen, Critical Quarterly, Review of English, Wasafiri.*
   One of the above founded by C.B. Cox, and now being edited by Colin MacCabe, carries not only critical and scholarly essays in English Studies but reviews film, culture, language and contemporary political issues. Identify the journal:
   (a) *Wasafiri*
   (b) *Screen*
   (c) *Critical Quarterly*
   (d) *Review of English Studies*

7. In Marvell's "A Dialogue between Soul and Body", who/which of the following has the last word?
   (a) Body (b) God
   (c) Soul (d) Satan
8. In Blake's poem "A Poison Tree" the speaker's anger grows and becomes
   (a) a cherry (b) an apple
   (c) an orange (d) a rose
9. Given below are two statements, one labelled as Assertion (A) and the other as Reason (R):
   **Assertion (A) :** For deconstructive critics how human beings read and interpret signs they receive will determine their modes of knowing and being, whether those signs come in the form of literary texts or bank statements.
   **Reason (R) :** The fact of the matter is that human beings use signs to function in the world and are always likely to do so.
   In the context of the two statements, which one of the following is correct?
   (a) Both (A) and (R) are true and (R) is the correct explanation of (A).
   (b) Both (A) and (R) are true and (R) is not the correct explanation of (A).
   (c) (A) is true, but (R) is false.
   (d) (A) is false, but (R) is true.
10. Ian McEwan's *Saturday* spans one day in the life of
    (a) a divorce lawyer
    (b) an ageing pianist
    (c) a London neurosurgeon
    (d) a famous poet
11. "Open Forum" as applied to poetry, is the same as ________. It is poetry that is not written according to traditional fixed patterns. (Fill up)
    (a) Blank verse
    (b) Concrete poetry
    (c) Language poetry
    (d) Free verse
12. The author of the book observes "I have attempted, through the medium of biography, to present some Victorian visions to the modern eye". The four main characters in this book are Cardinal Manning, Florence Nightingale, Dr. Arnold and General Gordon. Who is this author?
    (a) Mathew Arnold
    (b) Robert Browning
    (c) Lytton Strachey
    (d) Oscar Wilde
13. In his attack delivered on the theatre in *A Short View of the Immorality and Profaneness of the English Stage*, Jeremy Collier specially arraigned _____ and _____.
    (a) Congreve and Vanbrugh
    (b) Farquhar and Vanbrugh
    (c) Wycherley and Farquhar
    (d) Congreve and Etherege
14. I.A. Richards' *Practical Criticism* (1929) inaugurated a new phase in the history of English critical thought. What was this book's subtitle?
    (a) *Studies in Poetry*
    (b) *A Study in Literary Judgement*
    (c) *Essays and Studies*
    (d) *A Theoretical Guide*
15. Which of the following arrangements is in the correct chronological sequence?
    (a) *The Castle of Otranto – Melmoth the Wanderer – The Monk – The Mysteries of Udolpho*
    (b) *The Castle of Otranto – The Mysteries of Udolpho – The Monk – Melmoth the Wanderer*
    (c) *The Mysteries of Udolpho – The Castle of Otranto – The Monk – Melmoth the Wanderer*
    (d) *Melmoth the Wanderer – The Castle of Otranto – The Mysteries of Udolpho – The Monk*

16. Select from among the following plays, the one that best suits the description below:
    I. Alyque Padamsee invited its author to write it.
    II. The play had communalism as its theme.
    III. This play was banned from the Deccan Herald Theatre Festival for dealing with a sensitive issue.
    IV. The play, however, was produced by Play pen in Bangalore on July 1993.

    The play is
    (a) *Dance Like a Man*
    (b) *Where There's a Will*
    (c) *Final Solutions*
    (d) *The Wisest Fool on Earth*

17. I have known three generations of John Smiths. The type breeds true. John Smith II and III went to the same school, university and learned profession as John Smith I. Yet John Smith I wrote pseudo-Swinburne; John Smith II wrote pseudo-Brooke; and John Smith III is now writing pseudo-Eliot. But unless John Smith can write John Smith, however unfashionable the result, why does he bother to write at all? Surely one Swinburne; one Brooke, and one Eliot are enough in any age?
    (Robert Graves, "The Poet and his Public")
    1. Graves is critical of blind adulation and imitation of successful poets.
    2. Graves is critical of blind conformity to standards set by Swinburne, Brooke, and Eliot.
    3. Swinburne, Brooke, and Eliot represent the movements: Decadence, the Georgian, and Modernist respectively.
    4. The poets in question are Algernon Charles Swinburne, Stopford Brooke, and Thomas Stearns Eliot.

    (a) Only 1 and 2 are correct.
    (b) Only 4 is incorrect.
    (c) Only 3 and 4 are correct.
    (d) Only 3 is incorrect.

18. During the colonial era, the British used to call the Indian Languages *vernaculars*. We do not use this word for our *bhashas* because:
    I. we consider English to be equally vernacular.
    II. *verna* is, literally a home-born slave.
    III. not all Indian languages are languages of the Indo-european family, and therefore not all vernacular.
    IV. the natives of India were never slaves.

    (a) IV (b) II and IV
    (c) III (d) I and III

19. More's *Utopia* displays strong influence of
    I. The Arthurian legends
    II. Plato's *Republic*
    III. Amerigo Vespucci's account of the travels
    IV. The teachings of John Wycliffe

    The correct combination according to the code is
    (a) I and III are correct.
    (b) II and III are correct.
    (c) II and IV are correct.
    (d) I and IV are correct

20. By 'language transfer' is meant
    (a) Knowledge generated in the development of a learner on account of other domains of knowledge.
    (b) The carryover of rules of the mother tongue syntax, phonology, or semantic system to the Second language in question.
    (c) The carryover of rules of the Second language syntax, phonology, or semantic system to the mother tongue in question.
    (d) The vocabulary and sentencestructure transferred haphazardly during Second

language acquisition from any other language accessed by the learner.

21. Which of the following descriptions is not true of Peter Carey's *The True History of the Kelly Gang*?
    (a) It is an epistolary novel.
    (b) It has such characters as Edward Kelly, his mother, and his wife.
    (c) It is also about the Bush and the frontier.
    (d) The novel is dedicated to Edward Kelly's father.

22. Identify the poem that opens with the lines:
    I walk through the long schoolroom questioning;
    A kind old nun in a white hood replies;
    The children learn to cipher and to sing
    ...
    (a) "Among the Schoolchildren"
    (b) "Among School Children"
    (c) "A Man Young and Old"
    (d) "The Man Young, and Old"

23. Which of the following statements is not true of Foucault's position in *History of Sexuality*?
    (a) Modern sexuality is produced through and as discourse.
    (b) The proliferation of modern discourses of sexuality is more striking than their suppression.
    (c) To write historically about sexuality involves increasingly direct, immediate knowledge or understanding of an unchanging sexual essence.
    (d) Modern sexuality is intimately entangled with the historically distinctive contexts and structures now called 'knowledge'.

24. The following is an exchange between two characters, husband and wife, in a famous play. The lines appear at the very end of an emotionally-charged sequence of the last scene:
    "... I've stopped believing in miracles."
    "But I'll believe. Tell me !
    Transform ourselves to the point that ....?"
    "That our living together could be a true marriage."
    (*She goes out down the hall.*)
    Which play? Name the characters.
    (a) *Othello*. Othello, Desdemona
    (b) *Sure Thing*. Bill, Betty
    (c) *A Doll's House*. Helmer, Nora
    (d) *Death of a Salesman*. Willy, Linda

25. The following statements relate to the early history of the English language. Identify the set that gives incorrect statements:
    1. English has borrowed words such as *sky, give, law,* and *leg* from Norse.
    2. English has also borrowed some pronouns like *they, their, them* from Norse.
    3. In grammar, Modern English is much more highly inflected than Old English.
    4. After the Norman Conquest, French became the language of the court, the language of nobility and polite society, and literature.
    5. Following the Norman Conquest, French virtually replaced English as the language of the people.
    6. Among the French words that came into English are: study, logic, grammar, noun, etc.

    (a) 1, 2, 3 (b) 3, 5
    (c) 4, 5, 6 (d) 2, 4

26. Choices of linguistic forms in using a language, or how a language is actually spoken/written, especially one that differs from its prescribed grammar, is called
    (a) Utterance (b) Use
    (c) Usage (d) Deviation

27. Jamaica Kincaid's narrative *A Small Place*
    (a) is all about learning Farsi and meeting young people in modern Iran.
    (b) is an essay that discusses the politics of tourism and other neo-colonial modes of foreign intervention.
    (c) is a collection of tiny narratives about gender relations and includes stories concerning the Sumerian goddess Inanna.
    (d) a novella that looks unblinkingly at marital ceremonies and maternity in Antigua.

28. Identify the correctly-matched poets and their works from the following:
    (a) Nissim Ezekiel-*Hymns in Darkness*, Kamala Das – *The Sirens,* R. Parthasarthy – *Rough Passage*, A.K. Ramanujan – *The Striders*
    (b) Nissim Ezekiel – *The Striders,* Kamala Das – *Rough Passage*, R. Parthasarthy – *Hymns in Darkness*, A.K. Ramanujan – *The Sirens*
    (c) Nissim Ezekiel – *The Sirens,* Kamala Das – *Hymns in Darkness*, R. Parthasarthy – *The Striders,* A.K. Ramanujan – *Rough Passage*
    (d) Nissim Ezekiel – *Rough Passage,* Kamala Das – *The Striders,* R. Parthasarthy – *The Striders,* A.K. Ramanujan – *Hymns in Darkness*

29. William Wordsworth had a deep influence on Thomas Hardy. According to Hardy a particular poem by Wordsworth was his 'best cure for despair'. Which is that poem?
    (a) "Michael"
    (b) "Tintern Abbey Revisited"
    (c) "The Idiot Boy"
    (d) "The Leechgatherer"

30. In Henry James's *Ambassadors*, there is a character who never appears in the novel. We get to know about this significant person, however, from the other characters. Who is this character?
    (a) Maria Gostrey
    (b) Madame de Vionette
    (c) Mrs. Newsome
    (d) Mrs. Sarah Pocock

31. Why are Scott's novels called "Waverley Novels"?
    (a) His novels are all set in Waverley.
    (b) The Waverley Castle has a significant role in his novels.
    (c) Waverley (in his first novel of that name) is a model hero for the protagonists of Scott's novels.
    (d) Scott started his novel-writing career in his 43rd year with the novel, *Waverley*.

32. Which of these descriptions/statements best suits the idea of the 'Renaissance Man'?
    I. A fop, a scoundrel, who enjoys enormous power in Renaissance courts and aristocratic families.
    II. A near-mythical figure : a knight, courtier, musician, poet, scholar and statesman.
    III. One who ploughs a lonely furrow and keeps away from politicking and scandals.
    IV. Someone like Sir Philip Sydney best suits the ideal of the Renaissance Man.
    (a) I (b) IV
    (c) I and III (d) II and IV

33. Maxim Gorky, the great Russian writer of fiction and drama, was in real life a man called
    (a) Goliardic Kreshkov
    (b) Ronsardo Felixikov
    (c) Malthias Serpieri
    (d) Aleksei Peshkov

34. After the prediction of the oracle that he was destined to kill his father, Oedipus could have avoided patricide
    I. had he not determined in horror never to return to the only parents he knew.
    II. had he been a man of unusual self-control.
    III. had he remembered the prediction and had he been more cautious having recognized that possibly after all Polybos was not his father.
    IV. had he never struck any man who was older than himself saying at the moment of provocation 'This insolent man is grey-haired; let him have the road'.

    Find the correct combination according to the code:
    (a) I, II and III are correct.
    (b) I, II and IV are correct.
    (c) I, III and IV are correct.
    (d) II, III and IV are correct.
35. Identify the Post-Apartheid novel by Nadine Gordimer.
    (a) *The Conservationist*
    (b) *The House of Gun*
    (c) *The Lying Days*
    (d) *Burger's Daughter*
36. The Duchess of Malfi married her steward, Antonio. For the Elizabethan audience her marriage was a triple offence. Which of the following is not one?
    (a) She was a widow marrying a second time.
    (b) She married on her own outside the Church.
    (c) She married beneath her status in disregard of 'degree'.
    (d) She married against the wishes of her brothers who almost acted like her guardians.
37. Who among the following has written the essay, "The Indian Jugglers"?
    (a) Charles Lamb
    (b) William Hazlitt
    (c) Thomas de Quincey
    (d) Thomas Love Peacock
38. How would you best describe George Meredith's *Modern Love* (1862)?
    (a) A ballad
    (b) A lyric travelogue
    (c) A verse romance
    (d) A sonnet sequence
39. The play was written in 1881 when its author was in Italy. This is considered to be his most remarkable intellectual effort. The softening of the brain as a result of a disease inherited from his father is the subject. Which is the play?
    (a) *An Enemy of the People*
    (b) *Ghosts*
    (c) *Rhinoceros*
    (d) *Six Characters in Search of an Author*
40. In many ways, grammatical categories remain mysterious. What does it mean to speak a language that in every sentence requires you to locate yourself in time, or specify your source of knowledge, or the shape of what you are talking about? We still don't know. But putting the question like this suggests a clear and limited way of interpreting the idea that different languages represent different worlds. Which of the following statements on this passage interprets it most accurately?
    (a) The passage reflects the unreliability of grammatical categories of a language generally.
    (b) The passage concedes that the Sapir-Whorf hypothesis cannot be discounted entirely.
    (c) The passage upholds the reliability of grammatical categories of a language generally.
    (d) The passage suggests that the Sapir-Whorf hypothesis is largely discredited today.

41. Tolstoy's *War and Peace* carries a lengthy discussion of determinism and free will in
    (a) its prologue
    (b) an exchange between Pierre and Natasha
    (c) an exchange between Nikolai Rostof and Princess Bezukhoi
    (d) its epilogue

42. Which from among the following is not true of *Nagmandala*?
    (a) It does not have multiple narratives.
    (b) It is open-ended.
    (c) It combines conventional and subversive modes.
    (d) Story is personified in the play.

43. Arrange the following literary journals chronologically:
    (a) *The London Magazine*
        *The Quarterly Review*
        *Blackwood's Magazine*
        *The Saturday Review*
        *The Tatler*
    (b) *The Tatler*
        *The Saturday Review*
        *Blackwood's Magazine*
        *The Quarterly Review*
        *The London Magazine*
    (c) *The Quarterly Review*
        *Blackwood's Magazine*
        *The Tatler*
        *The Saturday Review*
        *The London Magazine*
    (d) *The Tatler*
        *The London Magazine*
        *The Quarterly Review*
        *Blackwood's Magazine*
        *The Saturday Review*

44. Pick out the two relevant and correct descriptions of Caryl Churchill's *Serious Money* (1987):
    1. This play proposes the foundation of a monastery for the education of British gentlewomen.
    2. This narrative deals with children who are sick of their "enforced idleness."
    3. This play is subtitled "City Comedy."
    4. In this play, the state of the British economy is symbolized by a takeover bid by an international cartel.
    5. This narrative details the adventures of an Anglo-Indian orphan.
    6. Money is the only criterion for success for the players in this play's share-market.

    (a) 1 and 6 are correct.
    (b) 2 and 5 are correct.
    (c) 4 and 6 are correct.
    (d) 5 and 6 are correct.

45. Identify from among the following false statements:
    1. Eric Arthur Blair became the famous British novelist, George Orwell.
    2. Orwell was conversant in Hindustani and fond of Indian food.
    3. Young Eric Blair lived in Myanmar's trading town, Katha.
    4. This town gave him the model for the fictional district of Kyauktada in *Burmese Days*.
    5. Orwell was born on June 25, 1903 in Motihari, Bihar.
    6. The Orwell Commemorative Committee in Motihari has been demanding a restoration of Orwell's birthplace as a heritage site.
    7. Orwell never returned to his birth place.
    8. The British journalist Ian Jack was mainly responsible for our knowledge of Orwell's antecedents relating to Katha and Motihari.

    (a) 2, 4, 8 are false.
    (b) 7 and 8 are false.
    (c) 3, 6 and 8 are false.
    (d) All statements above are true.

46. Virginia Woolf borrowed the idea of the common reader from Dr. Johnson. To which particular work of Johnson's does she remain indebted?
   (a) *The Lives of the Most Eminent English Poets;* the essay on Milton
   (b) *The Lives of the Most Eminent English Poets;* the essay on Gray
   (c) *Preface to Shakespeare*
   (d) *The Patriot*

47. J.M. Coetzee was the first writer to be awarded the Booker Prize twice. He won the prize for
   (a) *Life and Times of Michael K.* and *Disgrace*
   (b) *Dusklands* and *Disgrace*
   (c) *Foe* and *Elizabeth Costello*
   (d) *Age of Iron* and *Disgrace*

48. After the Norman Conquest England became a three-language nation for at least two centuries. The three languages were
   (a) English, French and German
   (b) English, Latin and German
   (c) English, French and Latin
   (d) English, French and Greek

49. Here are sentences labelled Assertion (A) and Reason (R):
   **Assertion (A):** In *Who's Afraid of Virginia Woolf?* George and Martha's blue and green-eyed son is a myth.
   **Reason (R):** He is a creation of the couple's imagination originating from their sense of sterility and vacuum in life.
   In the light of (A) and (R), which of the following is correct?
   (a) Both (A) and (R) are true and (R) is the correct explanation of (A).
   (b) Both (A) and (R) are true, but (R) is not the correct explanation of (A).
   (c) (A) is true, but (R) is false.
   (d) (A) is false, but (R) is true.

50. In the word *rapidly*, 'ly' is an adverbial suffix indicating manner while *rapid* is a ______, ly is a ____.
   (a) Word, wordling
   (b) Morpheme, morpheme-bit
   (c) Free morpheme, bound-morpheme
   (d) Full morpheme, half-morpheme

**Question Nos. 51 to 55** are based on a poem. Read the poem carefully and pick out the most appropriate answers.

**It's Your Own Fault**

Of course you can play with them.
There's no harm in them.
They are only words.
Words alone are certain good, said someone.
And someone also said
Unlike sticks and stones
Words will never break your bones.

(That is called rhyme. A rhyme is nice to play with too from time to time.)

What? They've turned nasty?
They've clawed you and bitten you?
Dear me, there's blood all over the place.
And broken bones.

They were perfectly tame when I left them.
Something they ate might have
disagreed with them.
You mean you fed them on meaning?
No wonder then.

– D.J. Enright

51. The poet's remark on 'rhyme' is
   (a) put in parenthesis
   (b) put in parentheses
   (c) framed rhetorically
   (d) put in apposition

52. The poem is cast in the form of a clyric
   (a) romantic lyric

(b) verse epistle
(c) dramatic monologue
(d) dialogue

53. What is the "fault" to which the speaker refers here?
(a) Playing with words
(b) Using only words
(c) Taking words too seriously
(d) Reading meanings into words

54. What tone is most appropriate for reading this poem?
(a) Evasive (b) Plaintive
(c) Ironic (d) Sarcastic

55. "No wonder then." Explain.
(a) No wonder that the words here begin to mean.
(b) No wonder that you now find the words menacing.
(c) No wonder that the words find you menacing.
(d) No wonder the words still mean and are tame.

56. "Nothing odd will do long. ______ did not last long."
Dr. Johnson had this to say about one of the eighteenth century novels.
Identify it from the following list:
(a) *Tom Jones*
(b) *The Female Quixote*
(c) *Tristram Shandy*
(d) *Clarissa*

57. Identify the sonnet upon sonnet by William Wordsworth:
(a) "London, 1802"
(b) "The world is too much with us..."
(c) "Friend ! I know not which way..."
(d) "Nuns fret not at their convent's narrow room..."

58. Who among the following women writers has written *Novel on Yellow Paper*?
(a) Elizabeth Smither
(b) Stevie Smith
(c) Zulu Sofola
(d) Gita Mehta

59. In most people, the first language/dialect acquired is 'mother tongue'.
Among the commonly used terms for mother tongue, one of the following is avoided. Identify the one term not applied to mother tongue:
(a) First language
(b) Prime language
(c) Native language
(d) Primary language

60. Identify the group of critical concepts that parenthetically aligns them with their respective theorists:
(a) The Carnivalesque (Jean Baudrillard), *Habitus* (Pierre Bourdieu), *Flaneur* (Walter Benjamin), *Chora* (Gayatri C. Spivak), Simulacrum/Simulacra (Antonio Gramsci),The Subaltern (Mikhael Bakhtin), Metahistory (Walter Benjamin), Aura (Julia Kristeva), Polyphony (Mikhael Bakhtin), Hegemony (Antonio Gramsci)
(b) *Habitus* (Pierre Bourdieu), *Flaneur* (Walter Benjamin), *Chora* (Julia Kristeva), Simulacrum/Simulacra (Jean Baudrillard), The Subaltern (Gayatri C. Spivak) Metahistory (Hayden White), Polyphony (Mikhael Bakhtin), Hegemony (Antonio Gramsci)
(c) *Habitus* (Julia Kristeva), *Flaneur* (Walter Benjamin), *Chora* (Pierre Bourdieu), Simulacrum/Simulacra (Hayden White), The Subaltern (Gayatri C. Spivak), Metahistory (Jean Baudrillard), Polyphony (Mikhael Bakhtin), Hegemony (Antonio Gramsci)
(d) *Habitus* (Pierre Bourdieu), *Flaneur* (Antonio Gramsci), *Chora* (Julia Kristeva), Simulacrum/Simulacra (Jean

Baudrillard), The Subaltern (Gayatri C. Spivak), Metahistory (Hayden White), Polyphony (Mikhael Bakhtin), Hegemony (Walter Benjamin)

61. What was the mandate of the Stationer's Company incorporated in London in 1557?
    (a) To oversee the affairs of the Royal Registry.
    (b) To oversee authors' and printers', or printer-publishers' rights.
    (c) To oversee authors' and printers' or printer-publishers' use of stationery.
    (d) To oversee the quality of stationery harnessed by the Royal Registry.

62. One of the following was described by its author as "a poem including history." Identify the poem.
    (a) Robert Lowell, *Life Studies*
    (b) William Carlos Williams, *Paterson*
    (c) Elizabeth Bishop, *Questions of Travel*
    (d) Ezra Pound, *The Cantos*

63. Arrange the following groups of English writers in chronological order:
    (a) The Metaphysical poets
    The High Modernists
    Transitional poets
    The Georgians
    The Aesthetes
    The University Wits
    (b) The University Wits
    The Metaphysical poets
    Transitional poets
    The Aesthetes
    The Georgians
    The High Modernists
    (c) The High Modernists
    The Georgians
    The Aesthetes
    Transitional poets
    The Metaphysical poets
    The University Wits
    (d) The University Wits
    The Metaphysical poets
    The Aesthetes
    Transitional poets
    The Georgians
    The High Modernists

64. Which Bible is the earliest English version printed with verse divisions?
    (a) Tyndale's Translation
    (b) The Geneva Bible
    (c) The Douay-Rheims Version
    (d) King James Version

65. E.M. Forster's *Passage to India* begins with a description of the city of Chandrapore. It has an old Indian part and a new part consisting of the British civil station. Which of the following descriptions of the city is not found in the text?
    (a) The streets are mean, the temples ineffective.
    (b) It is a city of gardens.
    (c) It is a tropical pleasaunce washed by a noble river.
    (d) The new civil station is not sensibly planned and not modern.

66. In which of the following books would you find the following arguments/observations?
    Escapist fiction lacks serious fiction's apocalyptic experience of finality. The two versions of literary experience are qualitatively different; every novel fits one category or the other, not both. Serious fiction, however, compels our attention by representing improvements (the "world of potency") as being achieved (a "world of act") and by showing narrative movement "through time to an end, an end, we must sense even if we cannot know it."

(a) *Sincerity and Authenticity*
(b) *The Sense of an Ending : Studies in the Theory of Fiction*
(c) *Beyond the Apocalypse*
(d) *The Rhetoric of Fiction*

67. Philip Larkin's "The Whitsun Weddings"
I. describes a long train journey
II. establishes a 'we' voice of collective outlook
III. traces the disfigurement of a sunny landscape on an advertising poster
IV. gives an account of a drug pusher

The correct combination according to the code is:
(a) I and III are correct.
(b) I and II are correct.
(c) I and IV are correct.
(d) II and III are correct.

68. Match the last lines of the poems with their correct titles:

**List I (Last lines of poems)**

I. And we are here as on a darkling plain
Swept with confused alarms of struggle and flight,
Where ignorant armies clash by night.

II. Thus, though we cannot make our sun
Stand still, yet we will make him run.

III. One short sleep past, we wake eternally,
And death shall be no more; death, thou shalt die.

IV. This one last gift I give : that after men
Shall know, and later lovers, far-removed,
Praise you, "All these were lovely;" say,
"He loved."

**List II (Titles of poems)**
1. "Death, be not proud..."
2. "The Great Lover"
3. "Dover Beach"
4. "To His Coy Mistress"

| **Codes:** | I | II | III | IV |
|---|---|---|---|---|
| (a) | 3 | 4 | 1 | 2 |
| (b) | 4 | 3 | 2 | 1 |
| (c) | 2 | 1 | 4 | 1 |
| (d) | 1 | 2 | 3 | 4 |

69. The *Oxford Companions* are handy reference volumes for teachers and students of English. Identify the one volume that has not yet appeared in this series:
(a) *The Oxford Companion to Twentieth-Century Literature in English*
(b) *The Oxford Companion to Canadian Literature*
(c) *The Oxford Companion to American Literature*
(d) *The Oxford Companion to Indian Literature in English*

70. While writing or printing, scholarly use prefers titles in italics. Which of the following is the correct way of writing/printing?
(a) Charles Dicken's *Tale of Two Cities*
(b) *Charles Dickens'* Tale of Two Cities
(c) Charles Dickens' *A Tale of Two Cities*
(d) Charles Dicken's *A Tale of Two Cities*

**Questions from 71 to 75** are based on the following passage. Read the passage carefully and select the most appropriate option:

Somewhere, on the edge of consciousness, there is what I call a *mythical norm,* which each one of us within our hearts knows "that is not me". In America, this norm is usually defined as white, thin, male, young, heterosexual, Christian, and financially secure. It is with this mythical norm that the trappings of power reside within the society. Those of us who stand outside that power often identify one way in which we are different, and we assume that to be the primary cause of all oppression, forgetting other distortions around difference, some of which we ourselves may be practising. By and large within the women's movement today, white women focus upon their oppression as women and ignore differences of race, sexual preference, class, and age. There is a pretense to a homogeneity of experience covered by the word *sisterhood* that does not in fact exist.

(Audre Lorde)

71. A *mythical norm* is endemic to societies:
    1. where racial myths are prevalent and widely respected and perpetuated through utterances that establish 'we' and 'they' groups.
    2. where the superiority of one's own culture and nation no longer emphasized openly or straight-forwardly.
    3. where 'difference' has been a preoccupation in the representation of people who are racially, ethnically, and in terms of gender and sexual preference different from an assumed majority.
    4. that believe that the norm is part of their right to defend the ways of life enjoyed by a dominant group, their traditions and customs against outsiders—not because these outsiders are inferior, but because they belong to other cultures.

    (a) 1 and 4 are correct.
    (b) 2 and 3 are correct.
    (c) Only 4 is correct.
    (d) Only 3 is correct.

72. How does the author mark her difference from other writers on similar issues and underscore her radical style typo-graphically?
    1. By her use of parataxis
    2. By italicizing 'mythical norm' and 'sisterhood'
    3. By using lowercase for proper and common nouns
    4. By using phrases like 'Those of us who stand outside...'

    (a) 1 and 4 are correct.
    (b) 2 is correct.
    (c) 3 is correct.
    (d) 2 and 3 are correct.

73. That there are levels and grades of powerlessness in societies entertaining 'a mythical norm' is indicated
    1. by the overall tone and tenor of the passage.
    2. by the suggestion that 'a mythical norm' is responsible for the unequal distribution of power among people.
    3. by referring to 'other distortions around difference'.
    4. by referring to white women who narrow down oppression directed only at white women.

    (a) 4 is correct.
    (b) 1 and 2 are correct.
    (c) 3 is correct.
    (d) 2 is correct.

74. Why is the author dismissive about 'sisterhood'?
    1. Because it is italicised.
    2. Because it does not exist in principle.
    3. Because it assumes that all 'sisters' are alike.
    4. Because it assumes that all 'sisters' are unique.

    (a) 3 is correct (b) 1 is correct
    (c) 4 is correct (d) 2 is correct

75. Does the author absolve all women from the 'distortions around difference'?
    1. Yes.
    2. No.

3. Not sure.
4. Yes, in a qualified manner though.

(a) 1 is correct (b) 2 is correct
(c) 3 is correct (d) 4 is correct

## ANSWERS

| | | | | | |
|---|---|---|---|---|---|
| 1. (d) | 2. (b) | 3. (d) | 4. (c) | 5. (c) | 6. (c) |
| 7. (a) | 8. (b) | 9. (a) | 10. (c) | 11. (d) | 12. (c) |
| 13. (a) | 14. (b) | 15. (b) | 16. (c) | 17. (b) | 18. (b) |
| 19. (b) | 20. (b) | 21. (d) | 22. (b) | 23. (c) | 24. (c) |
| 25. (b) | 26. (c) | 27. (b) | 28. (a) | 29. (d) | 30. (c) |
| 31. (d) | 32. (d) | 33. (d) | 34. (d) | 35. (b) | 36. (d) |
| 37. (b) | 38. (d) | 39. (b) | 40. (b) | 41. (d) | 42. (a) |
| 43. (d) | 44. (c) | 45. (d) | 46. (b) | 47. (a) | 48. (c) |
| 49. (a) | 50. (c) | 51. (a) | 52. (c) | 53. (d) | 54. (c) |
| 55. (b) | 56. (c) | 57. (d) | 58. (b) | 59. (b) | 60. (b) |
| 61. (b) | 62. (d) | 63. (b) | 64. (b) | 65. (d) | 66. (b) |
| 67. (d) | 68. (a) | 69. (d) | 70. (b) | 71. (b) | 72. (c) |
| 73. (c) | 74. (a) | 75. (b) | | | |

15

# NET Examination Paper II, June 2014 with Answers

1. "The just man justices. What kind of foregrounding do you find in the above lines?
   (a) Syntactic (b) Semantic
   (c) Collocation (d) None of the above

2. Match the items in List–I with items in List–II according to the code given:

| List–I | List–II |
|---|---|
| I. Lambic | 1. An unstressed syllable followed by a stressed syllable |
| II. Anapaestic | 2. A stressed is followed by two unstressed syllables |
| III. Dactylic | 3. An unstressed syllable is followed by a stressed syllable |
| IV. Trochaic | 4. A stressed syllable is followed by an unstressed syllable |

| Codes: | I | II | III | IV |
|---|---|---|---|---|
| (a) | 2 | 1 | 3 | 4 |
| (b) | 3 | 2 | 1 | 4 |
| (c) | 4 | 1 | 2 | 3 |
| (d) | 3 | 1 | 2 | 4 |

3. The separation of styles in accordance with class appears more consistently in _____ than in medieval works of literature and art.
   (a) Ben Jonson (b) Shakespeare
   (c) Philip Sidney (d) Edmund Spenser

4. "Had we but world enough, and time, This coyness, lady, were no crime." This statement is an example of
   (a) Irony (b) Paradox
   (c) Hyperbole (d) Euphemism

5. A Spenserian stanza has
   (a) four iambic pentameters
   (b) six iambic pentameters
   (c) eight iambic pentameters
   (d) ten iambic pentameters

6. Match the items in List–I with items in List–II according to the code given below:

| List–I (Critic) | List–II (Theory) |
|---|---|
| I. Cleanth Brooks | 1. Ambiguity |
| II. William Empson | 2. Paradox |
| III. Mark Schorer | 3. Archetypal patterns in poetry |
| IV. Maud Bodkin | 4. Techniques as discovery |

| Codes: | I | II | III | IV |
|---|---|---|---|---|
| (a) | 2 | 1 | 4 | 3 |
| (b) | 3 | 2 | 1 | 4 |
| (c) | 1 | 2 | 3 | 4 |
| (d) | 2 | 3 | 4 | 1 |

7. "The artist may be present in his work like God in creation, invisible and almighty, everywhere felt but nowhere seen." Henry James is talking here about the artist's

(a) impersonality (b) absence
(c) presence (d) creativity

8. Match the items in List–I with items in List–II according to the code given below:

| List–I (Theorist) | List–II (Book) |
|---|---|
| I. Michel Foucault | 1. *Gender Trouble* |
| II. Judith Butler | 2. *Epistemology of the Closet* |
| III. Alan Sinfield | 3. *History of Sexuality* |
| IV. Eve Kosofsky Sedgwick | 4. *Cultural Politics-Queer Reading* |

Which is the correct combination according to the code:

| Codes: | I | II | III | IV |
|---|---|---|---|---|
| (a) | 3 | 1 | 2 | 4 |
| (b) | 3 | 1 | 4 | 2 |
| (c) | 4 | 2 | 1 | 3 |
| (d) | 4 | 3 | 1 | 2 |

9. "The greatness of a poet", Arnold says, "lies in his powerful and beautiful application of ideas to life". But a critic pointed out it was "not a happy way of putting it, as if ideas were a lotion for the inflamed skin of suffering humanity". Who was this critic?
(a) T.S. Eliot (b) F.R. Leavis
(c) David Lodge (d) Allen Tate

10. Derrida's American disciples were
(a) Geoffrey Hartman, Paul de Man, J. Hills Miller
(b) Gertrude Stein, Barbara Johnson, Michael Ryan
(c) Barbara Johnson, Michael Ryan, Mary Ellman
(d) Jean Baudrillard, Gilles Deleuze, Felix Guattari

11. Identify the correct group of playhouses in late sixteenth century London from the following groups:
(a) Curtain, Rose, Swan, Globe, Hope
(b) Curtain, Rose, Swan, Globe, Sejanus
(c) Hope, Curtain, Rose, Swan, Globe
(d) Swan, Curtain, Rose, Globe, Thames

12. "Keep up your bright swords, for the dew will rust them.

Good Signior, you shall more command with years.

Than with your weapons." The above lines are addresses by Othello to
(a) Roderigo and officers
(b) Brabantio, Roderigo and Officers
(c) The Duke and Senators
(d) Montano and Cassio

13. Act V of Marlowe's *Edward the Second* shows the murder of the king. Where does it take place?
(a) Westminster, a room in the palace
(b) A room in Berkeley Castle
(c) A room in Killingworth Castle
(d) Within the Abbey of Neath

14. Identify the correctly matched set:
(a) "*The Shepheards Calender*" – 1579
*Tottels Miscellany* – 1557
*Astrophel and Stella* – 1591
*The Spanish Tragedie* – about 1585
(b) "*The Shepheards Calender*" – 1559
*Tottels Miscellany* – 1579
*Astrophel and Stella* – 1585
*The Spanish Tragedie* – about 1591
(c) "*The Shepheards Calender*" – 1585
*Tottels Miscellany* – 1591
*Astrophel and Stella* – 1579
*The Spanish Tragedie* – about 1557
(d) "*The Shepheards Calender*" – 1579
*Tottels Miscellany* – 1591
*Astrophel and Stella* – about 1585
*The Spanish Tragedie* – about 1557

15. Match the items in the List–I with items in List–II according to the code given below:

| | List–I (Authors) | | List–II (Works) |
|---|---|---|---|
| I. | Lucy Hutchinson | 1. | *The Life and Death of Mr. Badman* |
| II. | John Bunyan | 2. | *Sylva : or a Discourse of Forest Trees* |
| III. | John Evelyn | 3. | *Natures Pictures* |
| IV. | Margaret Cavendish | 4. | *Memoirs of the Life of Colonel Hutchinson* |

| Codes: | I | II | III | IV |
|---|---|---|---|---|
| (a) | 2 | 3 | 1 | 4 |
| (b) | 4 | 3 | 2 | 1 |
| (c) | 4 | 1 | 2 | 3 |
| (d) | 4 | 2 | 1 | 3 |

16. "But deeds, and language, such as men do use;

    And persons, such as comedy would choose,

    When she would show an image of the time, and sport with human follies, not with crime."

    In the above lines Jonson
    I. Opposes the artificiality of the romantic tragic-comedy.
    II. Initiates the use of realism.
    III. Considers analysis of moral short comings more important.
    IV. Encourages the use of farce with melodrama.

    Find out the correct combination according to the code:
    (a) I, II and III are correct
    (b) I, II and IV are correct
    (c) I, III and IV are correct
    (d) II, III and IV are correct

17. "And if no peece of chronicle we prove, We'll build in _______ pretty roomes."
    (a) lyrics (b) epics
    (c) sonnets (d) stanzas

18. "That glory never shall his wrath or might extort from me." (*Paradise Lost*, Book I)

    What 'glory' is being referred to by Satan?
    (a) The courage never to submit or yield
    (b) To reign in Hell
    (c) To defeat God
    (d) To spread evil

19. It has been described as a "novel without predecessors", the product of an original mind and became immediately popular. It is a peculiar blend of pathos and humour, though the pathos is sometimes overdone to the point of becoming offensively sentimental.

    The novel was published in 1760.

    What is the name of the novel?
    (a) Gulliver's Travels
    (b) The Castle of Otranto
    (c) Tristram Shandy
    (d) A Tender Husband

20. The son of a joiner, he was apprenticed as a printer. He remained a printer throughout his life. He was asked to prepare a series of modern letters for those who could not write for themselves. This humble task taught him the art of expressing himself in letters. Who is the novelist?
    (a) Daniel Defoe
    (b) Samuel Richardson
    (c) Henry Fielding
    (d) Tobias Smollett

21. "Where ignorance is Bliss Tis folly to be wise." Who wrote the following lines?
    (a) Pope (b) Gray
    (c) Collins (d) Southey

22. Which of the following works is not actually a prose essay?

(a) *Essay of Dramatic Poesy*
(b) *Essay on Man*
(c) *An Essay Concerning Human Understanding*
(d) *An Essay Towards a New Theory of Vision*

23. Whom does Mirabell deceive into believing that he loves her in *The Way of the World*?
(a) Millamant
(b) Lady Wishfort
(c) Mrs. Marwood
(d) Mrs. Fainall

24. "Competence to age is supplementary to youth, a sorry supplement indeed, but I fear the best that is to be had. We must ride where we formerly walked: live better and be softer and shall be wise to do so—than we had means to do in the good old days you speak of."

Who speaks these words and to whom?
(a) Lamb to Bridget
(b) Wordsworth to Dorothy
(c) Dorothy to Bridget
(d) Lamb to Dorothy

25. *The Prelude* although begun as early as 1799 and finished in its first version in 1805, was not published until ________.
(a) 1815 (b) 1820
(c) 1830 (d) 1850

26. "A rosy sanctuary will I dress/ With the wreathed trellis of a working brain." The above lines are quoted from
(a) 'Adonais'
(b) 'Ode to Psyche'
(c) 'Eve of St. Agnes'
(d) 'Endymion'

27. "Love seeketh only self to please, To bind another to its delight." This selfish and possessive nature of love is illustrated in Blake's
(a) 'The Clod and the Pebble'
(b) 'The Sick Rose'
(c) 'A Poison Tree'
(d) 'Ah Sunflower'

28. ho is the author of *Mary*, and the unfinished *The Wrongs of Woman*?
(a) Mary Wollstonecraft
(b) William Godwin
(c) Mary Hay
(d) Elizabeth Inchbald

29. Identify the incorrect factor in Henry James' theory of the novel.
(a) It should be sentimental
(b) It should be objective
(c) It should be realistic
(d) It should be viewed as an artistic form

30. Match the items in List–I with items in List–II according to the code given below:

| | List–I (Novels) | List – II (Characters) |
|---|---|---|
| I. | *Ulysses* | 1. Mrs. Moore |
| II. | *A Passage to India* | 2. Molly Bloom |
| III. | *To the Lighthouse* | 3. Gerald Crich |
| IV. | *Women in Love* | 4. Lily Briscoe |

| Codes: | I | II | III | IV |
|---|---|---|---|---|
| (a) | 3 | 1 | 2 | 4 |
| (b) | 2 | 1 | 4 | 3 |
| (c) | 4 | 2 | 1 | 3 |
| (d) | 1 | 3 | 2 | 4 |

31. Which among the following novels was not written in 1922?
(a) *Ulysses*
(b) *Jacob's room*
(c) *Aaron's Rod*
(d) *A Passage to India*

32. "A sudden blow: the great wings beating still

Above the staggering girl, her thighs caressed
By the dark webs, her nap caught in his bill,
He holds her helpless breast upon his breast."

Who is the author of the above lines?

(a) W.B. Yeats (b) T.S. Eliot
(c) W.H. Auden (d) D.H. Lawrence

33. "Consume my heart away; sick with desire
And fastened to a dying animal."

The above lines are taken from

(a) "Felix Randal"
(b) "Sailing to Byzantium"
(c) "Coole and the Ballylee, 1931"
(d) "The Second Coming"

34. Who among the following is not a surrealist poet?

(a) Hugh Sykes Dykes
(b) David Gascoyne
(c) Kenneth Allot
(d) C. Day Lewis

35. The protagonist returns with an admonition, the diamond sent to him for smuggling out a packet of diamonds as bribe.

This scene occurs in one of the novels of Graham Greene—Identify the novel.

(a) *The End of the Affair*
(b) *The Heart of the Matter*
(c) *The Ministry of Fear*
(d) *Our Man in Havana*

36. Samuel Beckett's trilogy published together in London in 1959 under the English titles is

(a) *More Pricks than Kicks, Murphy, Molloy*
(b) *B. Molloy, Malone Dies, The Unnamable*
(c) *Molloy, Murphy, Malone Dies*
(d) *The Unnamable, More Pricks than Kicks, Murphy*

37. Among the following playwrights, who was awarded the Pulitzer Prize in 1920?

(a) Eugene O'Neill
(b) Sean O'Casey
(c) William Somerset Maugham
(d) J.B. Priestly

38. D.H. Lawrence popularized the concept of ________ in his novels.

(a) Realism (b) Naturalism
(c) Primitivism (d) Expressionism

39. Who among the following is not an American modernist poet?

(a) William Carlos Williams
(b) Ezra Pound
(c) William Ellery Channing, the younger
(d) Marianne Moore

40. An important poet and playwright who in the 1960s led the Black Arts Movement, in the spirit of negritude, posited a 'Black Aesthetic' that expressed a pan-African, organic and whole sensibility.

(a) Henry Louis Gates Jr.
(b) Amiri Baraka
(c) Ishmael Reed
(d) Bell Hooks

41. Match List–I with List–II according to the code given below:

| List–I (Authors) | List–II (Books) |
|---|---|
| I. V.S. Naipaul | 1. *Foe* |
| II. Jean Rhys | 2. *Indigo or Mapping the Waters* |
| III. Marina Warners | 3. *Wide Sargasso Sea* |
| IV. J.M. Coetzee | 4. *Mimic Men* |

| Codes: | I | II | III | IV |
|---|---|---|---|---|
| (a) | 4 | 2 | 3 | 1 |
| (b) | 4 | 1 | 2 | 3 |
| (c) | 4 | 3 | 2 | 1 |
| (d) | 1 | 3 | 4 | 2 |

42. Yasmine Gooneratne's *The Pleasures of Conquest* termed as a postcolonial novel of the nineties is ironically enough set in the tropical island nation of
    (a) Sri Lanka (b) Fiji
    (c) The Caribbean (d) Amnesia

43. Which of the following is not an Asian-Canadian writer?
    (a) Shauna Singh Badlwin
    (b) Himani Banerjee
    (c) Joy Kogawa
    (d) Meena Alexander

44. Which of the following is true?
    (a) 'Aurora Leigh' is a poem in nine books
    (b) 'Aurora Leigh' is a collection of sonnets from the Portuguese
    (c) 'Aurora Leigh' is a nursery rhyme book
    (d) 'Aurora Leigh' is "the Seeds and Fruits of English Poetry"

45. "The old order changeth yielding place to new,
    And God fulfils himself in many way."
    In which of the following poems do these lines appear?
    (a) "Locksley Hall" (b) "Two Voices"
    (c) "Morte d'Arthur" (d) "Ulysses"

46. George Eliot's attempt to write a historical novel of the Italian Renaissance was not successful.

    Which was this novel?
    (a) *Adam Bede*
    (b) *Felix Holt*
    (c) *Silas Marner*
    (d) *Romola*

47. In which novel, does the hero, driven by passion and revenge, add a new dimension to the concept of suffering?
    (a) *Wuthering Heights*
    (b) *Jude the Obscure*
    (c) *Mill on the Floss*
    (d) *Hard Times*

48. From the following women characters in Hardy's novels choose the odd one out.
    (a) Bathsheba Everdene
    (b) Eustacia Vye
    (c) Elizabeth Jane
    (d) Lucetta

49. "Out of the gosple he tho wordes caughte
    And this figure he added eek therto,
    That if gold ruste, what shal iren do?"
    In the Prologue the Parson is represented as a man:
    1. who loved money
    2. who criticized the corrupt clergy
    3. who practiced what he preached
    4. who was a poor but honest clerk

    Find the correct combination according to the code:
    (a) 1, 2 and 3 are correct
    (b) 1, 2 and 4 are correct
    (c) 2, 3 and 4 are correct
    (d) 1, 3 and 4 are correct

50. Match the items in List–I with items in List–II according to the code given below:

| List–I (Plays) | List–II (Characters) |
|---|---|
| I. *White Devil* | 1. Hieornimo |
| II. *Maids Tragedy* | 2. Old Knowell |
| III. *Every Man in his Humour* | 3. Vittoria Corombona |
| IV. *The Spanish Tragedie* | 4. Aspatia |

| Codes: | I | II | III | IV |
|---|---|---|---|---|
| (a) | 4 | 3 | 1 | 2 |
| (b) | 2 | 1 | 3 | 4 |
| (c) | 3 | 4 | 2 | 1 |
| (d) | 4 | 3 | 2 | 1 |

## ANSWERS

| | | | | | |
|---|---|---|---|---|---|
| 1. (a) | 2. (d) | 3. (b) | 4. (a) | 5. (c) | 6. (a) |
| 7. (a) | 8. (b) | 9. (a) | 10. (a) | 11. (a) | 12. (b) |
| 13. (b) | 14. (a) | 15. (c) | 16. (a) | 17. (c) | 18. (a) |
| 19. (c) | 20. (b) | 21. (b) | 22. (b) | 23. (b) | 24. (a) |
| 25. (d) | 26. (b) | 27. (a) | 28. (a) | 29. (a) | 30. (b) |
| 31. (d) | 32. (a) | 33. (b) | 34. (d) | 35. (b) | 36. (b) |
| 37. (a) | 38. (c) | 39. (c) | 40. (b) | 41. (c) | 42. (d) |
| 43. (d) | 44. (a) | 45. (c) | 46. (d) | 47. (a) | 48. (c) |
| 49. (c) | 50. (c) | | | | |

# 16

# English Paper III, June 2014 with Answers

1. Where Sir Thomas Wyatt adapted Petrarch and Petrarchanism to English sounds and metres, Survey's verse tends to look back beyond Petrarch to the
   (a) French verse (b) Italian verse
   (c) Spanish verse (d) Latin verse
2. Here are some characteristics of Morality Plays:
   1. They are dramatized allegories of the life of man.
   2. They depict man's temptation and sinning, his quest for salvation and his confrontation with Death.
   3. Though the hero represents Mankind, the other characters are by no means personifications, of virtues, vices and death.
   4. A character known as the Vice often plays the role of the hero, a predecessor of the Villainhero in Elizabethan drama.

   Find the correct combination according to the code:
   (a) Only 1 and 2 are correct.
   (b) Only 1 and 3 are correct.
   (c) Only 1 and 4 are correct.
   (d) Only 2 and 3 are correct.
3. In Spenser's *Re Faerie Queene* there are the allegorized moral and religious virtues with their counterparts in the vices. Identify the correctly matched set:
   (a) Una – Truth
   Guyon – Temperance
   Duessa – Deceit
   Orgoglio – Pride
   (b) Una – Pride
   Guyon – Deceit
   Duessa – Temperance
   Orgoglio – Truth
   (c) Una – Deceit
   Guyon – Pride
   Duessa – Temperance
   Orgoglio – Truth
   (d) Una – Temperance
   Guyon – Truth
   Duessa – Pride
   Orgoglio – Deceit
4. "Fop at the toilet, flatt'rer at the board
   Now trips a lady, a now struts a lord."
   The above lines are quoted from
   (a) *McFlecknoc*
   (b) *The Rape of the Lock*
   (c) *Epistle to Dr. Arbuthnot*
   (d) *Absalom and Achitrphel*
5. Which of the following arrangements is in the correct chronological sequence?
   (a) *Every Man in His Humour*
   *The Shoemaker's Holiday*
   *Antonio's Revenge*
   *The Changeling*

(b) *The Shoemaker's Holiday*
*Every Man in His Humour*
*The Changeling*
*Antonia's Revenge*

(c) *The Changeling*
*Antonio's Revenge*
*Every Man in His Humour*
*The Shoemaker's Holiday*

(d) *Antonio's Revenge*
*Every Man in His Humour*
*The Changeling*
*The Shoemaker's Holiday*

6. Though Coleridge refers to "Motive-hunting of a motiveless malignity", the "human villain" Iago is far from "motiveless". His motives are
   I. He has been disappointed of military promotion.
   II. He suspects Othello of cuckolding him.
   III. He has been in love with Desdemona.
   IV. He wants to become Othello.

   Find the most appropriate combination according to the code:
   (a) I and II are correct
   (b) I and III are correct
   (c) I and IV are correct
   (d) II and IV are correct

7. In 'The Prologue' to *Dr. Faustus*, the chorus proposes that the theme should be:
   I. "cursed necromancy"
   II. "audacious deeds"
   III. "dalliance of love"
   IV. "self-conceit"

   The correct combination according to the code is
   (a) I and II are correct
   (b) II and III are correct
   (c) I and IV are correct
   (d) III and IV are correct

8. The centre of his plays is a proud character on Marlowe's model, with a bold licence in speech and action, full of elaborate metaphors, phrase tumbling after phrase, as he asserts himself in the French Court. Dryden unjustly described his style as "a dwarfish thought, dressed up in gigantic words". Who is this Jacobean playwright?
   (a) John Fletcher
   (b) John Webster
   (c) George Chapman
   (d) John Marston

9. In *Paradise Lost* BK IX Milton writes that Adam was overcome with ______ and so ate the forbidden fruit against his "better knowledge".
   (a) "female charm"
   (b) "exceeding love"
   (c) "faithful love"
   (d) "taste so divine"

10. In which poem of Donne's is the lover's face reflected in the eyes of his beloved?
   (a) "The Good Morrow"
   (b) "The Canonization"
   (c) "The Apparition"
   (d) "A Valediction : Forbidding Mourning"

11. Match List–I with List–II according to the code given below:

| | **List–I (Dramatists)** | | **List–II (Plays)** |
|---|---|---|---|
| I. | Thomas Otway | 1. | *The Provok'd Husband* |
| II. | William Wycherley | 2. | *The Recruiting Officer* |
| III. | Colley Cibber | 3. | *The Country Wife* |
| IV. | George Farquhar | 4. | *The Orphan, or the Unhappy Marriage* |

| Codes: | I | II | III | IV |
|---|---|---|---|---|
| (a) | 4 | 3 | 1 | 2 |
| (b) | 3 | 2 | 1 | 2 |
| (c) | 4 | 2 | 3 | 1 |
| (d) | 3 | 1 | 2 | 4 |

12. "Thou wast no born for death immortal Bird."

    In what sense is the Bird "immortal" as compared to mortal man?

    I. Here man as an individual is unfairly compared to a bird as a species.

    II. The word "Bird" stands for the nightingale's song.

    III. When considered as a species man is equally "immortal" as the "Bird".

    IV. The "Bird" is "Immortal" because songs of birds have given pleasure to man through the ages.

    Find the correct combination according to the code:

    (a) Only I and III are correct
    (b) Only IV is incorrect
    (c) Only II and IV are correct
    (d) Only I and IV are incorrect

13. Coleridge's "The Rime of the Ancient Mariner" is a poem in ________.

    (a) 8 parts (b) 9 parts
    (c) 7 parts (d) 6 parts

14. Scott is known for the creation of mad, irrational witch-like women characters. From the following list pick the odd one out.

    (a) Madge Wildfive
    (b) Meg Murdockson
    (c) Euphemia Deans
    (d) Meg Merrilees

15. Joseph Addison called him "The Miracle of the present age" and Alexander Pope wrote the epitaph for the monument erected in his memory. Who is he?

    (a) John Locke
    (b) Isaac Newton
    (c) Ashley Cooper
    (d) Christopher Wren

16. The play was first performed in 1773. The author asked a friend "Did it make you laugh?" and getting the answer "Exceedingly" said then that was all he required. He used for plot a reputed experience of his own as a schoolboy when he lost his way and asked to be directed to an inn but was shown the gateway to the local squire's house. Which play is this?

    (a) Sheridan's *The Rivals*
    (b) Sheridan's *The School for Scandal*
    (c) Goldsmith's *She Stoops to Conquer*
    (d) Goldsmith's *The Good Natured Man*

17. What is Johnson's opinion regarding the "Violation" of the three unities in the plays of Shakespeare?

    I. Shakespeare should have followed the Unities.

    II. Shakespeare followed the important Unity of Action satisfactorily.

    III. Shakespeare's plays suffered because they did not follow the Unities.

    IV. Unity of Time and Place arise from false assumptions.

    The correct combination according to the code is

    (a) I and II are correct.
    (b) II and IV are correct.
    (c) III and IV are correct.
    (d) I and III are correct.

18. *The Tatler* appeared thrice a week

    (a) On Tuesdays, Thursdays and Saturdays
    (b) On Sundays, Tuesdays and Thursdays
    (c) On Mondays, Wednesdays and Fridays
    (d) On Wednesdays, Thursdays and Fridays

19. "No man is truly great, who is great only in his lifetime. The test of greatness is the page of history. Nothing can be said to be great that has a distinct limit, or that borders on something evidently greater than itself. Besides, what is shortlived and pampered into mere notoriety, is of a gross and vulgar quality in itself."

    This passage describing the quality of greatness is taken from
    (a) "Of studies" by Francis Bacon
    (b) "The Indian Jugglers" by William Hazlitt
    (c) *Preface to Shakespeare* by Samuel Johnson
    (d) *An Essay of Dramatic Poesy* by John Dryden

20. In Blake's "The Human Abstract", the fragmented world of Experience is symbolized in the image of the
    (a) Caterpillar (b) Fly
    (c) Raven (d) Fruit of Deceit

21. Here are sentences labelled Assertion (A) and Reason (R):

    **Assertion (A):** While referring to Charlotte Bronte's claim that she has excluded public interest from her novels Graham Greene writes: "Public interest in her day was surely more separate from public life... with us, however consciously unconcerned we are, it obtrudes through the cracks of our stories terribly persistent like grass through cement".

    **Reason (R):** The decade of the "thirties was bristling with recurring economic and political crisis like the Great Depression, Wall Street Crash, Unemployment, rise of Hitler and Mussolini, series of murders, invasions and tensions; writers could not remain unaffected.

    In the light of (A) and (R) which of the following is correct?
    (a) Both (A) and (R) are true and (R) is the correct explanation of (A).
    (b) Both (A) and (R) are true, but (R) is not the correct explanation of (A).
    (c) (A) is true but (R) is false.
    (d) (A) is false, but (R) is true.

22. Match the titles of the books with their authors:

| List–I | List–II |
|---|---|
| I. *Psychology and Art Today* | 1. John Strachey |
| II. *Revolution in Writing* | 2. W.H. Auden |
| III. *The Coming Struggle for Power* | 3. C. Day Lewis |
| IV. *Arrow in the Blue* | 4. Arthur Koestler |

| Codes: | I | II | III | IV |
|---|---|---|---|---|
| (a) | 3 | 1 | 2 | 4 |
| (b) | 4 | 2 | 3 | 1 |
| (c) | 2 | 3 | 1 | 4 |
| (d) | 1 | 2 | 4 | 3 |

23. George Meredith's first novel was banned by Mudie's Circulating Library for its supposed moral offence.
    Identify the novel:
    (a) *The Egoist*
    (b) *Evan Harrington*
    (c) *Diana of the Crossways*
    (d) *The Ordeal of Richard Feverel*

24. Match the titles of the following poems by Tennyson with their opening lines according to the code given below:

| List–I (Titles of Poems) | List–II (Opening Lines) |
|---|---|
| I. "Tithonus" | 1. "'Courage' he said, and pointed |

| | | | |
|---|---|---|---|
| | | | towards the land. The mounting wave will roll us shoreward soon." |
| II. | "The Lotos-Eaters" | 2. | "The woods decay, the woods decay and fall, The vapours weep their burthen to the ground." |
| III. | "Ulysses" | 3. | "On either side the river lie Long fields of barley and of rye." |
| IV. | "The Lady of Shalott" | 4. | "It little profists that an idle king, By this still hearth, among these barren crags, Matched with an aged wife, I mete and dole Unequal laws unto a savage race." |

| Codes: | I | II | III | IV |
|---|---|---|---|---|
| (a) | 2 | 1 | 4 | 3 |
| (b) | 3 | 2 | 1 | 4 |
| (c) | 4 | 3 | 2 | 1 |
| (d) | 2 | 4 | 3 | 1 |

25. Why are Elizabeth Barrett Browning's Sonnets called "From Sonnets from the Portuguese"?
    (a) She wrote the whole in Portugal.
    (b) The sonnets were translated from the Portuguese.
    (c) She presented it under the guise of a translation from the Portuguese language.
    (d) The sonnets were narrated by a Portuguese.

26. Yeast's "Sailing to Byzantium" is about
    (a) Irish Culture
    (b) The art and culture of Byzantium in general
    (c) Irish revolutionaries
    (d) Regenerating the art and culture that existed in Byzantium

27. "She had _______ lilies in her hand

    And the stars in her hair were ______."

    (Rossetti's "The Blessed Damozel")
    (a) 7 and 3 (b) 3 and 7
    (c) 6 and 4 (d) 4 and 6

28. Which of the following arrangements is in the correct chronological sequence?
    (a) *Adam Bede – Wuthering Heights – North and South – Villette*
    (b) *Wuthering Heights – Villete – North and South – Adam Bede*
    (c) *Villettee – North and South – Wuthering Heights – Adam Bede*
    (d) *North and South – Wuthering Heights – Adam Bede – Villette*

29. In which of the following novels by canrod do the Gould couple and Decoud appear as characters with Costaguana as the setting?
    (a) *Victory*
    (b) *Under Western Eyes*
    (c) *Nostromo*
    (d) *The Nigger of the Narcissus*

30. Match the following plays with their authors according to the code given below:

| | List–I (Plays) | | List–II (Authors) |
|---|---|---|---|
| I. | *Heartbreak House* | 1. | John Galsworthy |
| II. | *Loyalties* | 2. | Bertolt Brecht |
| III. | *In the Jungle of Cities* | 3. | T.S. Eliot |
| IV. | *The Family Reunion* | 4. | George Bernard Shaw |

| Codes: | I | II | III | IV |
|---|---|---|---|---|
| (a) | 3 | 4 | 2 | 1 |
| (b) | 1 | 2 | 3 | 4 |
| (c) | 2 | 1 | 4 | 3 |
| (d) | 4 | 1 | 2 | 3 |

31. In November 1910 in an exhibition organized by Roger Fry, the paintings of three painters were displayed. Identify the painters:
   (a) Duncan Grant, Vanessa Bell, Clive Bell
   (b) Cezanne, Van Gogh, Gauguin
   (c) Matisse, Picasso, Braque
   (d) Cezanne, Van Gogh, Matisse

32. Why did Phaedra, wife of Theseus, commit suicide by hanging herself?
   (a) Theseus hated her
   (b) Her stepson, Hippolytus rejected her love
   (c) Hippolytus wanted to marry her
   (d) She was lonely and depressed

33. Identify the poet in whose verse rural Ulster figures prominently
   (a) Tony Harrison
   (b) Ted Hughes
   (c) Seamus Heaney
   (d) Louis MacNeice

34. Match the pairs of authors and their works according to the code given:

| List–I (Authors) | List–II (Works) |
|---|---|
| I. Alexander Dumas | 1. Remembrance of Things Past |
| II. Honore de Balzac | 2. Madame Bovary |
| III. Gustav Flaubert | 3. The Human Comedy |
| IV. Marcel Proust | 4. The Count of Monte Christo |

| Codes: | I | II | III | IV |
|---|---|---|---|---|
| (a) | 4 | 3 | 2 | 1 |
| (b) | 1 | 2 | 3 | 4 |
| (c) | 2 | 1 | 4 | 3 |
| (d) | 3 | 4 | 1 | 2 |

35. Which of the following statements best applies to Anna Karenina?
   1. Among her most prominent qualities are her passionate spirit and determination to live life on her own terms.
   2. She accepts the exile to which she has been condemned.
   3. She is a victim of Russian patriarchal system.
   4. Anna is deeply devoted to her family and children.
   (a) 1 and 2 are correct
   (b) 2 and 3 are correct
   (c) 1 and 3 are correct
   (d) 1, 3 and 4 are correct

36. Match the pairs of authors and their works according to the code given:

| List–I (Authors) | List–II (Works) |
|---|---|
| I. Vladimir Nabokov | 1. *Germinal* |
| II. Italo Calvino | 2. *Foucault's Pendulum* |
| III. Umberto Eco | 3. *If on a Winter's Night a Traveller* |
| IV. Emile Zola | 4. *Lolita* |

| Codes: | I | II | III | IV |
|---|---|---|---|---|
| (a) | 3 | 1 | 4 | 2 |
| (b) | 4 | 3 | 2 | 1 |
| (c) | 1 | 2 | 3 | 4 |
| (d) | 2 | 4 | 1 | 3 |

37. Which among the following plays by Aristophanes is an attack on 'modern' education and morals as imparted and taught by the radical intellectuals known as The Sophists?

(a) *Clouds* (b) *Wasps*
(c) *Acharnians* (d) *Knights*

38. In which novel of Virginia Woolf does a painter in the act of painting actually figure as a character?
(a) *The Voyage Out*
(b) *The Waves*
(c) *Jacob's Room*
(d) *To the Lighthouse*

39. Religious controversies in England particularly during the 15th century led to the promotion of
(a) English prose
(b) The British Empire
(c) Naval power
(d) The Missionary Movement

40. Fill in the blanks with a suitable word from the list below:

In his fiction, Ian McEwan more than often suggests the ________ of love.
(a) Fragility (b) Madness
(c) Completeness (d) Security

41. Match List–I with List–II according to the code given below:

| **List–I (Dramatists)** | **List–II (Plays)** |
|---|---|
| I. Arnold Wesker | 1. *Jumpers* |
| II. Harold Pinter | 2. *What the Butler Saw* |
| III. Joe Orton | 3. *The Room* |
| IV. Tom Stoppard | 4. *Roots* |

| **Codes:** | **I** | **II** | **III** | **IV** |
|---|---|---|---|---|
| (a) | 3 | 2 | 4 | 1 |
| (b) | 1 | 2 | 4 | 3 |
| (c) | 4 | 3 | 2 | 1 |
| (d) | 4 | 3 | 1 | 2 |

42. Modern English emerged from the
(a) South Midland dialect
(b) East Midland dialect
(c) French language
(d) Northumbrian dialect

43. Most culinary terms in English are derived from
(a) Exotic cooking
(b) French cooking
(c) Native sources
(d) Arabic cooking

44. "Blended learning" is a mode of instruction/learning in which
(a) the learner's mother tongue and the target language are blended
(b) learning is accessed through the mother tongue
(c) a variety of instructional modes are integrated
(d) learning of a language is mediated by humanistic approaches

45. 'Risk-taking' is one of the traits of a good
(a) language learner
(b) language teacher
(c) teacher of grammar rules
(d) printer of books and authors

46. A teaching method advocated by Dr. Georgia Lozanav which is based on the principle of 'joy and easiness' is called
(a) Suggesto paedia
(b) Total physical response
(c) The Direct Method
(d) The audio-lingual method

47. Albert Camus, in his essay, "The Myth of Sisyphus" conveys:
1. The concept of Naturalism
2. The Absurdity of Human Existence
3. The Futility of all Human Endeavour
4. The concept of Existentialism
(a) 1, 2 and 3 are correct
(b) 2, 3 and 4 are correct
(c) 1, 2 and 4 are correct
(d) 1, 3 and 4 are correct

48. *In The Portrait of a Lady* Gilbert Osmond marries Isabel Archer because

1. Osmond wanted to get hold of Isabel's property.
2. He loved her.
3. Though he did not like her moral ideas about many things in life, he had hoped to win her over.
4. He realized that her moral ideas were quite deep-rooted.

Find the correct combination according to the code:

(a) only 1 and 2 are correct
(b) only 1, 2 and 3 are correct
(c) only 3 and 4 are correct
(d) only 1 is correct

49. Pick out the two relevant and correct descriptions of U.R. Ananthamurthy's *Samskara*.
 1. The novel is written in English.
 2. The novel is concerned with the progressive ideas of the times.
 3. The novel is set in Malgudi.
 4. The novel is a satire on the representatives of a decadent Brahmin society.
 5. *Samskara* is a regional novel.
 6. Praneschacharya does not atone for his sin.

 (a) 4 and 5 are correct
 (b) 1 and 4 are correct
 (c) 5 and 6 are correct
 (d) 3 and 2 are correct

50. Willy in Arthur Miller's play *Death of a Salesman* compares Biff and Happy to the mythic characters/figures
 (a) Venus and Adonais
 (b) Adonais and Hercules
 (c) Jupiter and Hercules
 (d) Venus and Hercules

**Question Nos 51 to 55** are based on a poem. Read the poem carefully and pick out the most appropriate answers.

**A Valediction Forbidding Mourning**

My swirling wants, your frozen lips.
The grammar turned and attacked me.
Themes, written under duress.
Emptiness of the notations.

They gave me a drug that slowed the healing of wounds.

I want you to see this before I leave:
the experience of repetition as death
the failure of criticism to locate the pain
the poster in the bus that said:
my bleeding is under control

A red plant in a cemetary of plastic wreaths.

A last attempt : the language is a dialect called metaphor.
These images go unglossed : hair, glacier, flashlight.
When I think of a landscape I am thinking of a time.
When I talk of taking a trip I mean forever.
I could say : those mountains have a meaning
but further than that I could not say.

To do something very common, in my own way.

—Adrienne Rich

51. How does the poet suggest that the lover has not left?
 (a) The words "a last attempt" indicate that she is trying her best to leave.
 (b) The words "before I leave" suggest that the speaker has not left yet.
 (c) The speaker talks of a trip 'forever' which means she will never return.
 (d) A drug she takes slows the healing of her wounds perhaps indicating that she may be able to leave sometime in future.

52. Why does the speaker/lover in Rich's poem plan to leave?
 I. Because her love has not been returned.

II. Because of the pain she has suffered in the relationship.
III. Because the lover has criticized her so much.
IV. Because though the pain has been located, the bleeding continues.

The right combination according to the code is

(a) I and II are correct
(b) I and IV are correct
(c) I, II and III are correct
(d) I and III are correct

53. What does Rich imply when she says "The grammar turned and attacked me"?
(a) Language that has been used to hurt her.
(b) Her lover has beaten her.
(c) The person she is leaving is not the source of pain but something else.
(d) The pain she has herself inflicted through language.

54. How would you compare Rich's poem and Donne's poem with the same title?
(a) Rich is recreating Donne's poem
(b) Rich is eulogising Donne's poem
(c) Rich's poem is a scathing attack on Donne's poem
(d) Rich is defining Donne's concept of love

55. What is the theme of the poem? Identify the false statement in the list below:

It is
(a) about the difficulty of actually saying goodbye.
(b) about not having the strength to leave though one might want to.
(c) about the pain suffered in relationship.
(d) a Classical love poem like Donne's where the speaker dominates the addressee.

56. Why does Girish Karnad base his play *Hayavadana* on Thomas Mann's *Transposed Heads*?
(a) It is a mock-heroic transcription of the original Sanskrit tales.
(b) It is concerned with materialism.
(c) It deals with domestic strife.
(d) It deals with ancient times.

57. *The Collected Poems of A.K. Ramanujan* has been divided into four sections. Arrange them in their chronological order:
(a) *The Striders – The Relations – Second Sight – The Black Hen*
(b) *The Relations – The Striders – The Black Hen – Second Sight*
(c) *Second Sight – The Relations – The Black Hen – Striders*
(d) *The Black Hen – Second Sight – The Striders – The Relations*

58. In one of her novels, Margaret Atwood demonstrated the potentially 'Cannibalistic' nature of human relationships. Identify the novel:
(a) *Surfacing*
(b) *Lady Oracle*
(c) *Life Before Man*
(d) *The Edible Woman*

59. Match the characters with the novels of Amitav Ghosh in which they appear according to the code given below:

| **List–I (Characters)** | **List–II (Novels)** |
|---|---|
| I. Fakir | 1. *The Glass Palace* |
| II. Tridip | 2. *The Hungry Tide* |
| III. Rajkumar | 3. *The Calcutta Chromosome* |
| IV. Murugan | 4. *Shadow Lines* |

| **Codes:** | **I** | **II** | **III** | **IV** |
|---|---|---|---|---|
| (a) | 2 | 4 | 1 | 3 |
| (b) | 2 | 4 | 3 | 1 |
| (c) | 1 | 3 | 1 | 4 |
| (d) | 3 | 2 | 4 | 1 |

60. Which of the following is not a play by Badal Sircar?
   (a) *Bhooma*
   (b) *Evam Indrajeet*
   (c) *That Other History*
   (d) *Agra Bazar*

61. Who is the protagonist of Shashi Deshpande's *That Long Silence*?
   (a) Mohan (b) Jaya
   (c) Rati (d) Kamat

62. In Derek Walcott's *Dream on Monkey Mountain*, Makak's vision of freedom for his people is
   (a) through money
   (b) through violence
   (c) through black power
   (d) through a decolonisation of the mind

63. Given below are two statements, one labelled as Assertion (A) and the other as Reason (R).

   **Assertion (A):** To give a text an author is to impose a limit on that text, to furnish it with a final signified, to close the writing.

   **Reason (R):** A text is made up of multiple meanings drawn from many sources, and this multiplicity is focused on the reader.

   In the context of the two statements, which one of the following is correct:
   (a) Both (A) and (R) are true and (R) is the correct explanation of (A).
   (b) Both (A) and (R) are true and (R) is not the correct explanation of (A).
   (c) (A) is true but (R) is false.
   (d) (A) is false but (R) is true.

64. Given below are two statements, one labelled as Assertion (A) and the other as Reason (R).

   **Assertion (A):** Spivak sees the project of colonialism as characterized by what Foucault had called 'epistemic violence', the imposition of a given set of beliefs over another.

   **Reason (R):** Spivak suggests that participation in the political process—access to citizenship, becoming a voter—will help to mobilize the subaltern on "the long road to hegemony."

   In the context of the two statements, which one of the following is correct:
   (a) Both (A) and (R) are true and (R) is the correct explanation of (A).
   (b) Both (A) and (R) are true and (R) is not the correct explanation of (A).
   (c) (A) is true but (R) is false.
   (d) (A) is false but (R) is true.

65. Match the following authors with their works from the given below:

| | List–I (Authors) | | List–II (Works) |
|---|---|---|---|
| I. | Buchi Emecheta | 1. | *Burger's Daughter* |
| II. | Ama Ata Aidoo | 2. | *Joy of Motherhood* |
| III. | Nadine Gordimer | 3. | *Devil on the Cross* |
| IV. | Ngugi Wa Thiong'o | 4. | *Our Sister Killjoy* |

   Find the correct combination according to the code:

| Codes: | I | II | III | IV |
|---|---|---|---|---|
| (a) | 1 | 2 | 3 | 4 |
| (b) | 2 | 4 | 1 | 3 |
| (c) | 3 | 1 | 4 | 2 |
| (d) | 4 | 3 | 2 | 1 |

66. Match the following authors with their plays from the lists given below:

| | List–I (Authors) | | List–II (Plays) |
|---|---|---|---|
| I. | Langston Hughes | 1. | *Dutchman* |
| II. | Lorraine Hansberry | 2. | *Clara's Ole Man* |

III. Ed Bullins 3. *Don't You Want to be Free*

IV. Amiri Baraka 4. *Raisin in the Sun*

Find the correct combination according to the code:

| **Codes:** | I | II | III | IV |
|---|---|---|---|---|
| (a) | 3 | 4 | 2 | 1 |
| (b) | 1 | 2 | 3 | 4 |
| (c) | 2 | 1 | 4 | 3 |
| (d) | 4 | 3 | 1 | 2 |

67. Identify the critics and their respective works:
    - (a) Horace – *Ars Poetica*; Aristotle – *Poetics*; Quintillian – *Institutio Oratoria*; Ben Jonson – *Discoveries*; Sidney – *An Apology for Poetry*; Dryden – *An Essay of Dramatic Poesy*
    - (b) Horace – *Poetics*; Aristotle – *Ars Poetica*; Quintillian – *On the Sublime*; Longinus – *Discoveries*; Ben Jonson – *Institutio Oratoria*; Sidney – *An Essay of Dramatic Poesy*; Dryden – *An Apology for Poetry*
    - (c) Horace – *On the Sublime*; Aristotle – *Poetics*; Quintillian – *Discoveries*; Longinus – *Institutio Oratoria*; Ben Jonson – *An Essay of Dramatic Poesy*; Sidney – *Ars Poetica*; Dryden – *An Apology for Poetry*
    - (d) Horace – *Ars Poetica*; Aristotle – *Poetics*; Quintillian – *Institutio Oratoria*; Longinus – *On the Sublime*; Ben Jonson – *An Apology for Poetry*; Sidney – *An Essay of Dramatic Poesy*; Dryden – *Discoveries*

68. Which of the following is not true of Imagist poetry?
    - (a) The poet spreads his language across the page as though language were sensation, to reproduce the mental effect of 'image'.
    - (b) The image is itself an instrument of vision, or lens, as well as an expression of imagination.
    - (c) The imagist like a scientist learns from history and uses it, and like a scientist does not deal in emotions.
    - (d) The new artist as scientist focuses vision through image as against the symbol which resorts to reduction to simplicity.

69. Who among the following is not a myth critic?
    - (a) Robert Graves
    - (b) Raymond Williams
    - (c) Francis Fergusson
    - (d) Northrop Frye

70. According to Northrop Frye there are four main narrative genres associated with the seasonal cycle of spring, summer, autumn and winter. They are comedy, ________, tragedy and irony (satire). Which is the second one?
    - (a) Romance (b) Epic
    - (c) Fiction (d) Novel

Questions No. 71–75 are based on the following passage:

Read the passage carefully and select the most appropriate option.

The town belonging to the colonized people, or at least the native town, the negro village, the medina, the reservation, is a place of ill fame, peopled by men of evil repute. They are born there, it matters little where or how; they die there, it matters not where, nor how. The native town is a hungry town, starved of bread, of meat, of shoes, of coal, of light. The native town is a crouching village, town on its knees, a town wallowing in the mire. The look that the native turns on the settler is a look of lust, of envy.... The colonized man is an envious man. And this the settler knows very well.... It is true, for there is no native who does not dream atleast once a day of setting himself up in the settler's place.

(From Frantz Fanon's *The Wretched of the Earth*)

71. To Frantz Fanon, the 'Negro' village is
    1. the worst face of apartheid
    2. a protected area
    3. a place of moral and physical degradation
    4. a special village with its own amenities.
    (a) 1 and 3 are correct
    (b) 1 and 2 are correct
    (c) only 3 is correct
    (d) only 4 is correct

72. Why is the 'native town' a hungry town?
    1. it did not have agricultural farms
    2. it did not have markets
    3. the blacks were steeped in poverty
    4. they were denied their fundamental rights by the Whites.
    (a) 1 and 2 are correct
    (b) 3 and 4 are correct
    (c) only 1 is correct
    (d) only 4 is correct

73. What does the term 'crouching village' indicate?
    1. The latent aggressiveness of the blacks
    2. The defenselessness of the people
    3. Hopelessness and despair
    4. Overflowing filth
    (a) 1 and 2 are correct
    (b) 2 and 3 are correct
    (c) only 1 is correct
    (d) only 2 is correct

74. Why does the native look at the settler's town with envy?
    1. it arises from a sense of desperation
    2. he has no other option in his life
    3. he wants to occupy a position of power
    4. he wants to be the colonizer instead of the colonized
    (a) only 1 is correct
    (b) 3 and 4 are correct
    (c) only 2 is correct
    (d) 1 and 4 are correct

75. What is the settler's attitude towards the blacks?
    1. the settler is not afraid
    2. the settler considers the blacks to be harmless
    3. the settler is contemptuous of the blacks
    4. the settler feels resentment because he knows that his position is never safe
    (a) only 1 is correct
    (b) 2 and 3 are correct
    (c) only 4 is correct
    (d) 3 and 4 are correct

## ANSWERS

| | | | | | |
|---|---|---|---|---|---|
| 1. (d) | 2. (a) | 3. (a) | 4. (c) | 5. (a) | 6. (a) |
| 7. (c) | 8. (c) | 9. (a) | 10. (a) | 11. (a) | 12. (c) |
| 13. (c) | 14. (c) | 15. (b) | 16. (c) | 17. (b) | 18. (a) |
| 19. (b) | 20. (d) | 21. (a) | 22. (c) | 23. (d) | 24. (a) |
| 25. (c) | 26. (d) | 27. (b) | 28. (b) | 29. (c) | 30. (d) |
| 31. (b) | 32. (b) | 33. (c) | 34. (a) | 35. (d) | 36. (b) |

| | | | | | |
|---|---|---|---|---|---|
| 37. (a) | 38. (d) | 39. (a) | 40. (a) | 41. (c) | 42. (b) |
| 43. (b) | 44. (c) | 45. (a) | 46. (a) | 47. (b) | 48. (b) |
| 49. (a) | 50. (b) | 51. (b) | 52. (c) | 53. (a) | 54. (a) |
| 55. (d) | 56. (a) | 57. (a) | 58. (d) | 59. (a) | 60. (d) |
| 61. (b) | 62. (d) | 63. (a) | 64. (b) | 65. (b) | 66. (a) |
| 67. (a) | 68. (c) | 69. (b) | 70. (a) | 71. (a) | 72. (b) |
| 73. (b) | 74. (b) | 75. (c) | | | |

17

# NET Examination Paper II, December 2014 with Answers

1. Two of the following list are "Angry Young Men" of the 1950's British literary scene.

   I. John Osborne II. C.P. Snow
   III. Anthony Powell IV. Kingsley Amis

   The right combination, according to the code:

   (a) I & II (b) II & IV
   (c) I & IV (d) I & III

2. Laurence Sterne's *Tristram Shandy* contains

   (a) Six volumes (b) Nine volumes
   (c) Ten volumes (d) Four volumes

3. Which of the following statement is not true of Areopagitica?

   (a) It was published in 1644.
   (b) It argues for the liberty of Unlicensed Printing.
   (c) It pleads for British privileges regarding Free Trade.
   (d) It is a speech addressed to the Parliament of England.

4. Thomas Hardy's last major novel was ______.

   (a) *Tess of the D'urbervilles*
   (b) *Jude the Obscure*
   (c) *The Return of the Native*
   (d) *The Trumpet Major*

5. *The Hind and the Panther Transvers'd to the Story of the Country Mouse and the City Mouse* is a satire on

   (a) Alexander Pope (b) Jonathan Swift
   (c) John Dryden (d) Samuel Butler

6. Match the columns:

| Terms | Theorists |
|---|---|
| I. Apollonian – Dionysian | 1. Matthew Arnold |
| II. Fancy – Imagination | 2. Friedrich Nietzsche |
| III. Hellenism – Hebraism | 3. G.H. Hopkins |
| IV. Inscape – Instress | 4. S.T. Coleridge |

| Codes: | I | II | III | IV |
|---|---|---|---|---|
| (a) | 2 | 4 | 1 | 3 |
| (b) | 2 | 4 | 3 | 1 |
| (c) | 1 | 4 | 2 | 3 |
| (d) | 4 | 2 | 1 | 3 |

7. In *King Lear* who among the following speaks in the voice of Poor Tom?

   (a) Kent (b) Edgar
   (c) Edmund (d) Gloucester

8. In Wordsworth's *Prelude* the Boy of Winander is affected by

   (a) Blindness (b) Deafness
   (c) Muteness (d) Lameness

9. Which of the following is not mentioned as part of the London locale in *The Waste Land*?

   (a) St. Magnus Martyr
   (b) King Arthur Street

(c) St. Mary Woolnoth
(d) Lower Thames Street

10. Which of the following novels is not written by Jean Rhys?
(a) *After Leaving Mr. Mackenzie*
(b) *Good Morning, Midnight*
(c) *The Quiet American*
(d) *Wide Sargasso Sea*

11. The first official royal Poet Laureate in English literary history was ______.
(a) Ben Jonson
(b) William Davenant
(c) John Dryden
(d) Thomas Shadwell

12. Who does Alexander Pope refer to in the following lines?

"Born to no pride; inheriting no strife,
Nor marrying discord in a noble wife,
Stranger to civil and religious rage,
The good man walked innoxious through his age."

(a) Pope's father
(b) Pope himself
(c) Dr. Arbuthnot
(d) The Duke of Marlborough

13. The Theory of Natural Selection is attributed to _______.
(a) Arthur Schopenhauer
(b) Charles Darwin
(c) A.N. Whitehead
(d) Aldous Huxley

14. Which character in William Golding's *Lord of the Flies* maintains, "Life is scientific"?
(a) Simon (b) Piggy
(c) Ralph (d) Jack

15. Match the authors under List–I with the titles under List–II:

| List–I | List–II |
|---|---|
| I. Claude Levi-Strauss | 1. *Of Grammatology* |
| II. Jacques Derrida | 2. *The Archaeology of Knowledge* |
| III. Northrop Frye | 3. *Structural Anthropology* |
| IV. Michel Foucault | 4. *Anatomy of Criticism* |

| Codes: | I | II | III | IV |
|---|---|---|---|---|
| (a) | 1 | 3 | 4 | 2 |
| (b) | 3 | 1 | 2 | 4 |
| (c) | 3 | 1 | 4 | 2 |
| (d) | 2 | 1 | 3 | 4 |

16. How did Chaucer's Pardoner make his living?
(a) By selling stolen cattle from the neighbourhood ottery
(b) By selling indulgences to those who committed sins
(c) By pardoning those who stole property or committed other crimes
(d) By assisting the Friar in Church services

17. From among the following, identify Coleridge's companion in a fanciful scheme to establish a Utopian community of free love on the banks of the Susquehaina river?
(a) Lord Byron
(b) Robert Southey
(c) William Hazlitt
(d) William Wordsworth

18. Which of the following novels by H.G. Wells is about the condition of England as Empire?
(a) *The Island of Dr. Moreau*
(b) *The War of the Worlds*
(c) *Tono-Bungay*
(d) *The Invisible Man*

19. *Joothan* by Om Prakash Valmiki is
(a) a collection of poems
(b) a play
(c) an autobiography
(d) a novel

20. Listed below are some English plays across several centuries:

    *Twelfth Night, She Stoops to Conquer, The Importance of Being Earnest, Pygmalion and Blithe Spirit.*

    What is common to them?
    (a) All problem plays; scheming and intrigue
    (b) All tragedies; sin and redemption
    (c) All ideologically framed; class and gender
    (d) All romantic comedies; love and laughter

21. Who among the following wrote a poem comparing a lover's heart to a hand grenade?
    (a) John Donne (b) Abraham Cowley
    (c) Wilfred Owen (d) Robert Graves

22. The Uncertainty Principle is attributed to
    (a) William James
    (b) John Dewey
    (c) Werner Heisenberg
    (d) Charles Darwin

23. "Jabberwocky" is a creation in _______.
    (a) Edward Lear's poetry
    (b) Lewis Carroll's work
    (c) Charles Dickens's *Martin Chuzzlewit*
    (d) Thomas Hardy's *Woodlanders*

24. Who are Didi and Gogo?
    (a) They are two characters in *Endgame*.
    (b) They are nicknames, respectively, for Lucky and Pozzo.
    (c) They are nicknames, respectively, for Vladimir and Estragon.
    (d) They are two characters in *Breath*.

25. Who among the following theorists talks about "the circulation of social energy"?
    (a) Raymond Williams
    (b) Stephen Greenblatt
    (c) Antonio Gramsci
    (d) Haydon White

26. How many legends of good women could Chaucer complete in his *The Legend of Good Women*?
    (a) Six (b) Seven
    (c) Eight (d) Nine

27. *The Round Table* is a collection of essays jointly written by _______.
    (a) Charles Lamb and William Hazlitt
    (b) Charles Lamb and Leigh Hunt
    (c) William Hazlitt and Leigh Hunt
    (d) William Hazlitt and Thomas de Quincey

28. Dylan Thomas is associated with the group _______.
    (a) The New Apocalypse
    (b) The Black Artsa
    (c) The Movement
    (d) Deep Image Poetry

29. Which of the following writers writes from Canada?
    (a) V.S. Naipaul (b) Margaret Atwood
    (c) Derek Walcott (d) James Joyce

30. "The boast of heraldry, the pomp of power,
    And all that beauty, all that wealth e'er gave,
    Awaits alike the inevitable hour
    The paths of glory lead but to the grave."

    What is the subject of awaits?
    (a) Hour
    (b) The things mentioned in the first 2 lines.
    (c) "And all that beauty, all that wealth e'er gave"
    (d) Grave

31. "Heav'n has no rage, like love to hatred turn'd/ Nor Hell a fury, like a woman scorn'd."

    Identify the text in which the above quote occurs:
    (a) *The Double-Dealer*

(b) *The Way of the World*
(c) *The Mourning Bride*
(d) *Love for Love*

32. *A Young Lady's Entrance into the World* is the sub-title of ______.
(a) *Belinda* (b) *Cecilia*
(c) *Evelina* (d) *Camilla*

33. "The old order changeth, yielding place to new" is from ______.
(a) "Morte d'Arthur"
(b) "Idylls of the King"
(c) "Paracelsus"
(d) "Asolando"

34. Which of the following cannot be classified as fantasy fiction?
(a) *The Inheritors* (William Golding)
(b) *The Magus* (John Fowles)
(c) *The Lord of the Rings* (J.R.R. Tolkein)
(d) *The History Man* (Malcolm Bradbury)

35. *Philosophy of Symbolic Forms* is a work associated with ______.
(a) Wilhelm von Humboldt
(b) Ernst Cassirer
(c) Immanuel Kant
(d) Battista Vico

36. Which of the following facts is not true of Spenser?
(a) He is a kind of English Homer, telling stories of heroic confrontations.
(b) He fashioned an original verse form : The Spenserian Stanza.
(c) He opposed England's break with the Roman Catholic Church.
(d) He is a Christian poet.

37. William Blake developed the ideas of "Prolifics" and "Devourers" in
(a) *Jerusalem*
(b) *Milton*
(c) *Marriage of Heaven and Hell*
(d) *Songs of Innocence and Songs of Experience*

38. Surrealism is associated with
(a) Ernst Cassirer (b) Tristan Tzara
(c) Henrik Ibsen (d) Andre Breton

39. "And miles to go before I sleep" is a line from a poem by
(a) Emily Dickinson
(b) Walt Whitman
(c) Ralph Waldo Emerson
(d) Robert Frost

40. What common link do you find among
"The Disquieting Muses" by Sylvia Plath,
"The Starry Night" by Anne Sexton,
"Mourning Picture" by Adrienne Rich, and
"Musee des Beaux Arts" by W.H. Auden?
(a) They inspired paintings.
(b) They are confessional poems.
(c) They are all inspired by paintings.
(d) They are all inspired by Van Gogh's paintings.

41. "All Rising to *Great Place* is by a ______ staire." (Francis Bacon)
(a) Murky (b) Winding
(c) Crooked (d) Sinister

42. In Jeremy Collier's 1698 pamphlet attacking the immorality and profaneness of the English stage, who among the following was the principal target?
(a) William Congreve
(b) John Dryden
(c) John Vanbrugh
(d) William Wycherley

43. Charles Dickens's visit to the United States produced ______.
(a) *Hard Times*
(b) *Nicholas Nickleby*
(c) *Martin Chuzzlewit*
(d) *Oliver Twist*

44. Who among the following is a working-class poet?

(a) John Betjeman (b) Tony Harrison
(c) Thom Gunn (d) Robert Graves

45. *New Science* is a work associated with ______.
(a) Ernest Cassirer
(b) Wilhelm von Humboldt
(c) G. Battista Vico
(d) Immanuel Kant

46. Identify Petrarch's sonnet sequence from among the following:
(a) *Rine Sparse* (b) *Astrophel and Stella*
(c) *Amoretti* (d) *Delia*

47. The island setting of Latmos figures in Keats's
(a) *Endymion* (b) *The Eve of St. Agnes*
(c) *Lamia* (d) *Hyperion*

48. The Artist Hero is a theatrical creation emphasized by ______.
(a) W.B. Yeats (b) Charles Baudelaire
(c) Oscar Wilde (d) Andre Gide

49. Which of the following African writers won the Nobel Prize for Literature?
(a) Chinua Achebe
(b) Nadine Gordimer
(c) Ngugi wa Thiong'o
(d) Bessie Head

50. "My lute, be as thou wert when thou didst grow

With thy green mother in some shady groove" – William Drummond

The above quote is an example of ______.
(a) End-stopped rhyme
(b) Alliteration
(c) Run-on line
(d) Tercet

## ANSWERS

| | | | | | |
|---|---|---|---|---|---|
| 1. (c) | 2. (b) | 3. (c) | 4. (b) | 5. (c) | 6. (a) |
| 7. (b) | 8. (c) | 9. (b) | 10. (c) | 11. (c) | 12. (a) |
| 13 (b) | 14. (b) | 15. (c) | 16. (b) | 17. (b) | 18. (c) |
| 19. (c) | 20. (d) | 21. (b) | 22. (c) | 23. (b) | 24. (c) |
| 25. (b) | 26. (d) | 27. (c) | 28. (a) | 29. (b) | 30. (a) |
| 31. (c) | 32. (c) | 33. (b) | 34. (d) | 35. (b) | 36. (c) |
| 37. (c) | 38. (d) | 39. (d) | 40. (c) | 41. (b) | 42. (c) |
| 43. (c) | 44. (b) | 45. (c) | 46. (a) | 47. (a) | 48. (a) |
| 49. (b) | 50. (c) | | | | |

# 18

# English Paper III, December 2014 with Answers

1. This work was a satire in Ottava rima, attacking George III and Robert Southey. Identify the poem:
   (a) *Dunciad*
   (b) *The Vision of Judgment*
   (c) *Childe Harold's Pilgrimage*
   (d) *Alastor*
2. Here's a famous exchange from Arthur Conan Doyle's *Silver Blaze*:

   'Is there any point to which you would wish to draw my attention?'

   'To the curious incident of the dog in the night-time.'

   'The dog did nothing in the night-time.'

   What was Sherlock Holmes' response?
   (a) 'Nothing? Nothing at all? Rather unbelievable.'
   (b) 'That was the curious incident.'
   (c) 'Anything else, at all?'
   (d) 'That sounds rather curious, don't you think?'
3. "The shrill, demented choirs of waiting shells,

   And bugles calling for them from sad shires."

   These lines are from Wilfred Owen's:
   (a) "Strange Meeting"
   (b) "Futility"
   (c) "Anthem for Doomed Youth"
   (d) "Duke et Decorum Est"
4. In Aphra Behn's *Oronooko*, how does the titular character die?
   (a) He disembowels himself.
   (b) He is whipped to death.
   (c) He is hanged in the public square.
   (d) He is cut to pieces slowly by the executioner.
5. The narrative of this novel is a meticulous, present-tense account of a woman with a death-wish who plots the circumstances of her own violent murder. Identify the novel.
   (a) Iris Murdoch's *A Fairly Honourable Defeat*
   (b) Muriel Spark's *The Driver's Seat*
   (c) Doris Lessing's *Children of Violence*
   (d) Angela Carter's *The Passion of the New Eve*
6. The library where the "Battle of Books" takes place is _______.
   (a) St. James' Library
   (b) King's Library
   (c) Sir William's Library
   (d) Christ Church Library
7. In Sophocles' *Oedipus Rex* the first scene finds Oedipus
   (a) in conversation with a priest
   (b) in consultation with a general
   (c) giving audience to an ambassador
   (d) in consultation with a minister

8. Who among Shakespeare's contemporaries did not write tragedies?
   (a) Thomas Kyd
   (b) John Lyly
   (c) Christopher Marlowe
   (d) Ben Jonson
9. *The Kite Runner*, a novel by Khaled Hosseini tells the story of ________.
   (a) Ahmed (b) Nadira
   (c) Amir (d) Amourrah
10. Thomas Babington Macaulay, the writer of the infamous Minute of 1835, finds a mention in Salman Rushdie's
   (a) *Midnight's Children*
   (b) *Shame*
   (c) *The Moor's Last Sigh*
   (d) *Fury*
11. The issue of privileging speech over writing was taken up for discussion in Plato's:
   (a) *Ion*
   (b) *Republic Book III*
   (c) *Republic Book X*
   (d) *Phaedrus*
12. 'The Medium is the Message' is a concept given by
   (a) Ernest Hemingway
   (b) Sylvia Plath
   (c) Seymour Hersh
   (d) Marshal McLuhan
13. Seamus Heaney's famous poem "Digging" forms a part of his celebrated collection called
   (a) *North* (b) *Death of a Naturalist*
   (c) *Field Work* (d) *Door into the Dark*
14. The first major report on *The Teaching of English* in England was published in 1921. It is known as ________, named after the Chair, Board of Education, _______.
   (a) the Newbolt Report; Sir Henry Newbolt
   (b) the Wood's Despatch; Charles Wood, Lord Halifax
   (c) the Chatham Report; Earl John Chatham
   (d) the Landow Document; Sir George Landow
15. Who first developed the notion of 'competence' in language studies?
   (a) Dell Hymes
   (b) Noam Chomsky
   (c) Leech and Svartvik
   (d) Henry Sweet
16. The fruit *was eaten.*

   The fruit *is ripening.*

   Which of the following statement(s) is/are correct?
   (1) English has two kinds of participle: the present and the past.
   (2) English has three kinds of participle: the present, the past and the future.
   (3) The first sentence here is an example of a verb in past participle.
   (4) The first sentence here is an example of a verb in the perfect tense.
   (5) The second sentence here is an example of a verb in present participle.
   (6) The second sentence here is an example of a verb in the continuous tense.
   (a) 2, 4, 6 are correct.
   (b) 1, 5, 6 are correct.
   (c) 1, 3, 5 are correct.
   (d) 3, 4, 5 are correct.
17. In 1722 the Crown awarded a certain English merchant a patent to manufacture copper coins for Ireland. Jonathan Swift intervened by way of composing a series of letters in response, better known as *The Drapier's Letters*. Who was the merchant?
   (a) Isaac Bickerstaff
   (b) William Bickerstaff

(c) William Wood
(d) William Sacheverell

18. "While the world moves
In appentency on its metalled way
Of time past and time future"

These lines are from:
(a) "Little Gidding" (b) "Dry Salvages"
(c) "Burnt Norton" (d) "East Coker"

19. The following is the stage-description of an opening scene of a famous modern play:

*A basement room. Two beds, flat against the back wall. A serving hatch, closed, between the beds. A door to the kitchen and lavatory, left. A door to a passage, right.*

Identify the play:
(a) The Importance of Being Earnest
(b) Travesties
(c) The Dumb Waiter
(d) Look Back in Anger

20. 'Homonyms' are words that _______
(a) are pronounced differently but have the same meaning.
(b) refer to both the male and female of the human species.
(c) are spelt similarly but have different meanings.
(d) refer to people who live in houses with similar structures.

21. Match the columns:

| Shakespearean Actors | Period |
|---|---|
| I. David Garrick | 1. The 19th century |
| II. John Gielgud | 2. The 18th century |
| III. Henry Irving | 3. The Restoration |
| IV. Thomas Betterton | 4. The 20th century |

| Codes: | I | II | III | IV |
|---|---|---|---|---|
| (a) | 2 | 4 | 1 | 3 |
| (b) | 4 | 2 | 1 | 3 |
| (c) | 3 | 4 | 1 | 2 |
| (d) | 2 | 3 | 4 | 1 |

22. In his "Structure, Sign, and Play in the Discourse of the Human Sciences," Derrida is all praise for the *bricoleur* whom Levi-Strauss sees as a supreme methodologist, "someone who uses 'the means at hand'."

Who does Levi-Strauss contrast *bricoleur* with in terms of method and approach?
(a) The Botanist
(b) The Anthropologist
(c) The Engineer
(d) The Semiotician

23. Heinrich Böll has something to say, and not of course merely something about the Germans. He says it several times. A common weakness of writers with something to say is their inability to understand that saying it four times is not necessarily four times as effective as saying it once. But to have something to say—how rare this is!

– D.J. Enright, "Three New Germans".

From a reading of the above, the reader can deduce:

I. Enright mildly disapproves of Heinrich Böll's saying not merely something about Germans.
II. Enright is disappointed that Heinrich Böll has practically nothing to say about people other than Germans.
III. Enright agrees that Heinrich Böll shares a weakness with writers who prefer saying something four times to saying it once.
IV. Enright does not believe that saying something four times will necessarily make the same effective.

The right combination, according to the code, is

(a) I and II (b) II and III
(c) III and IV (d) I and IV

24. Michel Foucault's earlier "archaeological" study is found in
(a) Power/Knowledge
(b) Social Theory and Transgression
(c) The Birth of the Clinic
(d) Beyond Structuralism and Hermeneutics

25. *Invisible Man* by Ralph Ellison is widely recognized as a masterpiece. It is also one of the finest examples of
(a) science fiction
(b) picaresque novel
(c) coming-of-age novel
(d) crime thriller

26. Match the following correctly:

| | List–I | | List–II |
|---|---|---|---|
| I. | Mulk Raj Anand | 1. | *Premashram* |
| II. | Raja Rao | 2. | *The Cat and Shakespeare* |
| III. | Prem Chand | 3. | *Coolie* |
| IV. | Girish Karnad | 4. | *Nagamandala* |

| Codes: | I | II | III | IV |
|---|---|---|---|---|
| (a) | 3 | 2 | 4 | 1 |
| (b) | 2 | 3 | 1 | 4 |
| (c) | 3 | 2 | 1 | 4 |
| (d) | 4 | 3 | 2 | 1 |

27. From which of Sheridan's plays the following extract is taken?

Lady Sneerwell: Why truly Mrs. Clackitt has a very pretty talent and a great deal of industry.

Snake: True, Madam, and has been tolerably successful in her day. To my knowledge she has been the cause of six matches being broken off and three sons disinherited, of four forced elopements ....

Lady Sneerwell : She certainly has talents but her manner is gross.

(a) *The Rivals*
(b) *The School for Scandal*
(c) *St. Patrick's Day*
(d) *The Critic*

28. Who, from among the following, has not been discussed by Simone de Beauvoir in "The Myth of Woman in Five Authors" in *The Second Sex*?
(a) Montherlant (b) Lawrence
(c) Stendhal (d) Kafka

29. In a collection of essays Orhan Pamuk shares how he writes his novels, tells about his friendship with his daughter, talks about his loneliness and happiness.

Identify the text:
(a) *Other Colors*
(b) *The Silent House*
(c) *The Black Book*
(d) *The White Castle*

30. Two of the following plays won the Sultan Padamsee Prize for Indian plays in English:
I. Princes
II. Where There's a Will
III. Larins Sahib
IV. Doongaji House

The right combination according to the code is:
(a) III and IV (b) I and III
(c) II and III (d) I and IV

31. Who among the following is not an Australian writer?
(a) Morris West (b) Patrick White
(c) Thomas Keneally (d) Bill Pearson

32. After Independence, Mulk Raj Anand, wrote a number of semi-autobiographical works to narrate chunks of his own life through a fictional persona. The name he gave this persona is _______.
(a) Lal Singh (b) Krishan Chander
(c) Puran Singh (d) Rahul Singh

33. What a mockery this.
Of history, the past and that to come!
Now do I feel how all men are deceived,
Reading of nations and their, in faith,
Faith given to vanity and emptiness ...
*The Prelude*

The above extract is from
(a) Book 9 Residence in France
(b) Book 7 Residence in London
(c) Book 3 Residence in Cambridge
(d) Book 4 Summer Vacations

34. While foregrounding the marginal presence of women in history in *A Room of One's Own*, Virginia Woolf refers to ______ *History of England.*
(a) Campbell's (b) Trevelyan's
(c) Sander's (d) Carter's

35. *Salomé* is a play written by Oscar Wilde written in
(a) English (b) Irish
(c) French (d) Italian

36. In More's *Utopia*, the fictional traveller Raphael Hythloday's second name in Greek means
(a) Dispenser of Justice
(b) Dispenser of Nonsense
(c) Dispenser of Grace
(d) Dispenser of Mercy

37. "You do not dwell in me nor I in you
however much I pander to your name"
These lines from Geoffrey Hill's "Lachrimae" address
(a) Christ
(b) The Devil
(c) The poet's beloved
(d) The poet's enemy

38. The author of *Black Skin, White Masks* is
(a) Ngugi wa Thiong'o
(b) Frantz Fanon
(c) Richard Wright
(d) Martin Luther King (Jr.)

39. Match the following:

| | **Poet** | | **Bird** |
|---|---|---|---|
| I. | John Keats | 1. | Hawk |
| II. | P.B. Shelley | 2. | Falcon |
| III. | G.H. Hopkins | 3. | Skylark |
| IV. | Ted Hughes | 4. | Nightingale |

| **Codes:** | **I** | **II** | **III** | **IV** |
|---|---|---|---|---|
| (a) | 4 | 3 | 2 | 1 |
| (b) | 4 | 3 | 1 | 2 |
| (c) | 3 | 4 | 2 | 1 |
| (d) | 3 | 4 | 1 | 2 |

40. Who of the following has written the novel *The Return*?
(a) Bapsi Sidhwa (b) V.S. Naipaul
(c) K.S. Maniam (d) Pankaj Mishra

41. Who among the following is a well-known Neo-Aristotelian critic?
(a) R.P. Blackmur
(b) John Crowe Ranson
(c) R.S. Crane
(d) Lionel Trilling

42. **Assertion (A):** The act of reading a text is both determinate and indeterminate.

**Reason (R):** Since our reading includes both a sense of the unity of the narrative held in place at the end and the different wishes and guesses made along the way.
(a) Both (A) and (R) are true and (R) is the true explanation of (A).
(b) Both (A) and (R) are true, but (R) is not the true explanation of (A).
(c) (A) is true, but (R) is false.
(d) (A) is false, but (R) is true.

43. Girish Karnad's *Hayavadana*, originally in Kannada, has been translated into English by
(a) U.R. Ananthamurthy
(b) By the playwright himself
(c) G.S. Amur
(d) A.K. Ramanujan

44. Edward Said's well-known book *Orientalism* was published in
   (a) 1978 (b) 1968
   (c) 2008 (d) 1988

45. "To the Memory of my Beloved, the Author Mr. William Shakespeare: And What He Hath Left Us" is an ode composed by
   (a) John Milton (b) Ben Jonson
   (c) Andrew Marvell (d) John Suckling

46. *Call Me Ishmail Tonight* is written by
   (a) A.K. Ramanujan (b) Agha Shahid Ali
   (c) Saleem Peeradina (d) Nissim Ezekiel

47. "All fiction for me is a kind of magic or trickery—a confidence trick." The statement has been made by
   (a) Angus Wilson (b) Anthony Powell
   (c) John Fowles (d) George Orwell

48. Here is a list of American words and word-makers. Match the following:

| | |
|---|---|
| I. H.L. Mencken | 1. Babbit |
| II. Philip Wylie | 2. Yes man |
| III. Jack Conway | 3. Bible belt |
| IV. Sinclair Lewis | 4. Monism |

| Codes: | I | II | III | IV |
|---|---|---|---|---|
| (a) | 4 | 3 | 2 | 1 |
| (b) | 3 | 4 | 1 | 2 |
| (c) | 3 | 4 | 2 | 1 |
| (d) | 4 | 3 | 1 | 2 |

49. Which of the following in Jacques Derrida's epigraph to his "Structure, Sign and Play in the Discourse of the Human Sciences"?
   (a) More body, hence more writing. ....... Helene Cixous.
   (b) We need to interpret interpretations more than to interpret things. ......... Michel Eyquem de Montaigne.
   (c) But unlike philosophical reflection, ...the reflections we are dealing with here concern rays whose only source is hypothetical. .... Claude Levi-Strauss
   (d) If Cleopatra's nose had been shorter the whole history of the world would have been different. ......... Blaise Pascal.

50. In Mann's *Death in Venice*, death of the protagonist occurs
   (a) in a bar (b) in a beach
   (c) in a church (d) on the highway

51. Two among the following poets wrote the "Village" poems that address the perennial theme of rural poverty:
   I. Oliver Goldsmith II. William Collins
   III. Samuel Johnson IV. George Gabbe

   The right combination according to the code is
   (a) I and III (b) II and III
   (c) I and IV (d) I and II

52. In which of the following works Yeats developed his theory of 'gyres'?
   (a) "A Vision"
   (b) "The Secret Rose"
   (c) "John Sherman and Dhoya"
   (d) "The Celtic Twilight"

53. Mystery and Miracle plays in English were based on ______.
   (a) English folklore
   (b) English legends
   (c) Biblical stories
   (d) Anglo-Saxon myths

54. When we rewrite a piece of discourse from one script into another, it is called ________.
   (a) Translation (b) Transliteration
   (c) Transcreation (d) Transformation

55. "No wonder then." Explain.
   (a) No wonder that the words here begin to mean.
   (b) No wonder that you now find the words menacing.
   (c) No wonder that the words find you menacing.

(d) No wonder the words still mean and are tame.

56. The term "womanism" was first used by
(a) Helene Cixous (b) Gayatri Spivak
(c) Kate Millet (d) Alice Walker

57. Two among the following critics have dealt with the reproduction of motherhood in feminist theory:
I. Nancy Chodorow
II. Judith Fetterley
III. Catherine R. Stimpson
IV. Carol Gilligan

The right combination according to the code is
(a) I and II (b) II and IV
(c) I and IV (d) III and IV

58. *Flowers* is a short play written by
(a) Mahesh Dattani (b) Asif Currimbhoy
(c) Girish Karnad (d) Paoli Sengupta

59. Match the columns:

| Character | Novel |
|---|---|
| I. Lady Dedlock | 1. *Vanity Fair* |
| II. Lady Bertram | 2. *Wives and Daughters* |
| III. Lady Harriet | 3. *Mansfield Park* |
| IV. Lady Jane | 4. *Bleak House* |

| Codes: | I | II | III | IV |
|---|---|---|---|---|
| (a) | 4 | 2 | 3 | 1 |
| (b) | 3 | 2 | 1 | 4 |
| (c) | 4 | 3 | 2 | 1 |
| (d) | 3 | 4 | 1 | 2 |

60. "The Books You Needn't Read, the Books Made For Purposes Other Than Reading, Books Read Before You Open Them Since They Belong To The Category of Books Read Before Being Written...."

The above extract is taken from
(a) Jorge Luis Borges's "The Library of Babel"
(b) Italo Colvino's *If on a Winter's Night a Traveller*
(c) Umberto Eco's *The Name of the Rose*
(d) Francis Bacon's "Of Studies"

61. Listed below are the titles of novels and the sources to which they are aligned by readers.

Match them appropriately:

| List–I | List–II |
|---|---|
| I. Peter Carey's *Jack Maggs* | 1. Daniel Defoe's *Robinson Crusoe* |
| II. J.M. Coetzee's *Foe* | 2. Charlotte Bronte's *Jane Eyre* |
| III. Jean Rhys's *Wide Sargasso Sea* | 3. R.M. Ballantyne's *The Coral Island* |
| IV. William Golding's *Lord of the Flies* | 4. Charles Dickens's *Great Expectations* |

| Codes: | I | II | III | IV |
|---|---|---|---|---|
| (a) | 4 | 1 | 3 | 2 |
| (b) | 4 | 3 | 1 | 2 |
| (c) | 4 | 1 | 2 | 3 |
| (d) | 4 | 2 | 1 | 3 |

62. Identify the right chronological sequence:
(a) *The Game of Chess – Volpone – The Duchess of Malfi – The City Madam*
(b) *The City Madam – The Duchess of Malfi – Volpone – A Game of Chess*
(c) *Volpone – The Duchess of Malfi – A Game of Chess – The City Madam*
(d) *The Duchess of Malfi – Volpone – A Game of Chess – The City Madam*

63. 'Nasal tone' in speech is a distinguishing feature of _______.
(a) British English
(b) Scottish English
(c) Australian English
(d) American English

64. Which of the following writers did not receive the Nobel Prize for Literature?

(a) Wole Soyinka (b) Chinua Achebe
(c) J.M. Coetzee (d) Nadine Gordimer

65. *The Decline and Fall of the Roman Empire* by Edward Gibbon is a significant work in ______ volumes.
(a) 3 (b) 4
(c) 5 (d) 6

66. The first novel written by Graham Greene is
(a) *Stamboul Train*
(b) *England Made Me*
(c) *The Heart of the Matter*
(d) *The Man Within*

67. From among the Canterbury pilgrims, which group would qualify as the 'upper class'?
(a) The Pardoner, The Miller, The Nun's Priest
(b) Franklin, Parson, Wife of Bath
(c) The Knight, The Squire, The Prioress
(d) The Reeve, The Manciple, The Clerk

68. Plagiarism is a well-known word and concept in academic circles. The word *plagiarius* in Latin, however, meant
(a) a trickster, a cheat
(b) a quack, a swindler
(c) a loafer, a lout
(d) a torturer, a plunderer

69. What superstition around the Eve of St. Agnes is crucial to an understanding John Keat's famous poem?
(a) If a virgin performed the proper ritual on St. Agnes' Eve, she would dream of her future husband.
(b) If a virgin performed the proper ritual on St. Agnes' Eve, she would marry her lover.
(c) If a married woman performed the proper ritual on St. Agnes' Eve, she would be reunited with her husband.
(d) If a woman performed the proper ritual on St. Agnes' Eve, she would dream of her future lover.

70. Identify the person who sets himself up as the 'Knight' with a pestle rather than a sword in the play *The Knight of the Burning Pestle*:
(a) Ralph (b) Tim
(c) George (d) Squire

71. Works like *The Earthly Paradise, Dante and His Circle, Goblin Market and Other Poems* and the journal, *The Germ* are associated with ________.
(a) the Pre-Raphaelites
(b) Higher Criticism
(c) the Cavalier Poets
(d) the Pre-Romantics

Read the following poem and answer questions (72 to 75):

A Bird came down the Walk –
He did not know I saw –
He bit an Angleworm in halves
And ate the fellow, raw,
And then he drank a Dew
From a convenient Grass –
And then hopped sidewise to the Wall
To let a Beetle pass –
He glanced with rapid eyes
That hurried all around –
They looked like frightened Beads, I thought –
He stirred his Velvet Head
Like one in danger, Cautious,
I offered him a Crumb
And he unrolled his feathers
And rowed him softer home –
Than Oars divide the Ocean,
Too silver for a seam –
Or Butterflies, off Banks of Noon
Leap, plashless as they swim.

72. Is "a convenient Grass" an example of "transferred epithet"?
    (a) Yes, it is. The "convenience" of grass is transferred from the bird to the poet who finds grass convenient of access.
    (b) Yes, it is. The grass is not "convenient", but is transferred from the bird who finds the grass convenient of access.
    (c) No. It is a regular epithet.
    (d) No. It is not an epithet in the strict sense.

73. Which of the following is not an example of kinetic imagery?
    (a) "unrolled his feathers"
    (b) "hopped sidewise"
    (c) "Velvet Head"
    (d) "rowed him"

74. The poem stages an encounter between:
    (a) the human and the non-human
    (b) distrust of the non-human about the humans
    (c) two old friends
    (d) two old enemies

75. "Like one in danger...." Who is in danger?
    (a) The Bird (b) The Poet
    (c) The Angleworm (d) Frightened Beads

## ANSWERS

| | | | | | |
|---|---|---|---|---|---|
| 1. (b) | 2. (b) | 3. (c) | 4. (d) | 5. (b) | 6. (b) |
| 7. (a) | 8. (b) | 9. (c) | 10. (c) | 11. (d) | 12. (d) |
| 13. (b) | 14. (a) | 15. (b) | 16. (c) | 17. (c) | 18. (c) |
| 19. (c) | 20. (c) | 21. (a) | 22. (c) | 23. (c) | 24. (c) |
| 25. (c) | 26. (c) | 27. (b) | 28. (d) | 29. (a) | 30. (a) |
| 31. (d) | 32. (b) | 33. (a) | 34. (b) | 35. (c) | 36. (b) |
| 37. (a) | 38. (b) | 39. (a) | 40. (c) | 41. (c) | 42. (a) |
| 43. (b) | 44. (a) | 45. (b) | 46. (b) | 47. (a) | 48. (c) |
| 49. (b) | 50. (b) | 51. (c) | 52. (a) | 53. (c) | 54. (b) |
| 55. (b) | 56. (d) | 57. (c) | 58. (c) | 59. (c) | 60. (b) |
| 61. (c) | 62. (c) | 63. (d) | 64. (b) | 65. (d) | 66. (d) |
| 67. (c) | 68. (a) | 69. (a) | 70. (a) | 71. (a) | 72. (b) |
| 73. (c) | 74. (b) | 75. (a) | | | |

19

# NET Examination Paper II, June 2015 with Answers

1. Matthew Arnold's "touchstones" were "short passages, even single lines" of classic poetry beside which the lines of other poets may be placed in order to detect the presence or absence of high poetic quality. In his "Study of Poetry" Arnold cited "touchstones" from such non-English poets as Homer and Dante and also from the English poets, Shakespeare and Milton. Which English poet did he disapprovingly call "not one of the great classics" in the list below?
   (a) Chaucer (b) Sidney
   (c) Spenser (d) Donne
2. Samuel Pepys began his diary on
   (a) New Year's Day 1660
   (b) All Saints' Day 1662
   (c) Thanksgiving Day 1665
   (d) New Year's Day 1667
3. On which of the following authors has Peter Ackroyd not written a biography?
   (a) Charles Dickens (b) William Blake
   (c) T.S. Eliot (d) W.B. Yeats
4. Which group of the following poets was called the Auden Group because they developed a style and viewpoint similar to that of W.H. Auden?
   (a) Louis MacNeice, C.D. Lewis, Stephen Spender
   (b) John Masefield, Edwin Muir, Norman McCaig
   (c) MacDiarmid, G.M. Hopkins, Edwin Muir
   (d) W.H. Davies, Robert Bridges, John Masefield
5. When one line of poetry runs into the next, with no punctuation to slow the reading, it is a case of
   (a) caesura (b) consonance
   (c) enjambment (d) hyperbole
6. Which of the following is not a characteristic of the Victorian Age?
   (a) The rise of a highly competitive industrial technology
   (b) An emphasis on strictly controlled social behaviour
   (c) A romantic focus on home and family
   (d) The growth of rural traditions and movement from large cities
7. In *The Heart of Midlothian*, Walter Scott deals with real political and personal details, but notable among his characters is the depiction of
   (a) Queen Anne (b) Queen Victoria
   (c) Queen Caroline (d) Queen Elizabeth
8. Chaucer's first work, *The Book of the Duchess* is a dream poem on the death of
   (a) Duchess of Malfi
   (b) Duchess of Lancaster
   (c) Duchess of Scotland
   (d) Duchess of Paris

9. What was Charles Lamb's connection with India?
   (a) He was fascinated by the Indian jugglers and trades-people in London and wrote an essay on them
   (b) He was fascinated by Eastern mystical religions, especially Buddhism
   (c) He was a clerk for thirty-three years in the East India Company
   (d) He was clerk in South Sea House that prepared patents and documents for British trading companies in India
10. Find the odd one among the Marxist critics below
    (a) Georg Lukacs
    (b) Louis Althusser
    (c) Raymond Williams
    (d) Northrop Frye
11. In the lines "With gold jewels cover every part,/ And hide with ornaments their want of art" (*Essay on Criticism*), Pope rejects
    (a) the 'Follow Nature' fallacy
    (b) artificiality
    (c) aesthetic order
    (d) poor taste
12. The opposite of hyperbole is
    (a) meiosis (b) inversion
    (c) anagnorisis (d) synecdoche
13. What significance do we attach to the publication of *I Am an Indian* in Canada?
    (a) The title refers to the autobiography of an unknown Indian writer longing for the South Asian countryside
    (b) The first ever account of ethnic conflicts within Canada
    (c) The first anthology of Native Canadian writing following the Civil Rights Movement of the 1960s
    (d) The first anthology of writers afflicted by class and gender differences in Canada of the late 1970s
14. What is the moral of "The Nun's Priest's Tale"?
    (a) Slow and steady wins the race.
    (b) Greed is the root of all evil.
    (c) Beauty lies within.
    (d) Never trust a flatterer.
15. The author of the essay "Silly Novels by Lady Novelists" is
    (a) George Eliot (b) Henry James
    (c) Oscar Wilde (d) Richard Steele
16. The unquenchable spirit of Robinson Crusoe struggling to maintain a substantial existence on a lonely island reflects
    (a) man's desire to return to nature
    (b) the author's criticism of colonization
    (c) the ideal of rising bourgeoisie
    (d) the aristocrat's disdain for the harsh social reality
17. Who is the author of the collection *The Celtic Twilight*?
    (a) J.M. Synge (b) Sean O'Casey
    (c) W.B. Yeats (d) Lady Gregory
18. In medieval England a _________ was understood to be a trained craftsman, one who worked under a master who owned the business.
    (a) pardoner (b) summoner
    (c) journeyman (d) manciple
19. Christopher Marlowe's heroes are said to be larger than life, exaggerated both in their faults and in their qualities. They have a desire for everything in extreme. In one of his plays the hero wants to conquer the whole world. The name of the play is
    (a) *The Jew of Malta*
    (b) *Doctor Faustus*
    (c) *Tamburlaine the Great*
    (d) *Edward II*
20. With what does the speaker claim to be half in love in "Ode to a Nightingale"?

(a) the nightingale's haunting melody
(b) the scented flavour of early summer
(c) the night sky and all the stars
(d) the peace that comes with death

21. In which chapter of *Poetics* does Aristotle use the word 'catharsis' in his definition of tragedy?
(a) Chapter IV (b) Chapter VI
(c) Chapter III (d) Chapter V

22. Match the following

| | |
|---|---|
| (A) "The Function of Criticism" | (i) Terry Eagleton |
| (B) "The Function of Criticism at the Present Time" | (ii) Richard Ohmann |
| (C) *The Function of Criticism: From The Spectator to Poststructuralism* | (iii) Matthew Arnold |
| (D) "The Function of English at the Present Time" | (iv) T.S. Eliot |

The right matching according to the code is:

| | (A) | (B) | (C) | (D) |
|---|---|---|---|---|
| (a) | (iv) | (iii) | (i) | (ii) |
| (b) | (i) | (ii) | (iii) | (iv) |
| (c) | (iii) | (iv) | (i) | (ii) |
| (d) | (ii) | (iii) | (iv) | (i) |

23. Identify the TRUE statement on Thomas More's *Utopia*.
(a) *Utopia* is divided into four parts, each dealing with Raphael Hythloday's adventures in the four suburbs of Antwerp.
(b) *Utopia* is divided into two parts; the first records a conversation between Thomas More and Raphael Hythloday, and the second is Hythloday's discourse on the institutions and practices of Utopia.
(c) *Utopia* is divided into two parts; the first is Thomas More's discourse on the institutions and practices of Utopia, and the second a conversation between More and Hythloday.
(d) *Utopia* is divided into four parts, each dealing with the ordered patterns of towns and cities in Antwerp.

24. In "The Rime of the Ancient Mariner" what disaster befalls the ship and the crew?
(a) The ship is caught in ice and breaks into pieces.
(b) A fierce storm batters the ship and drowns the crew.
(c) "Slimy things with legs" attack the ship and kill many of the crew.
(d) The ship is becalmed and the crew dies of thirst.

25. Falstaff is a character in
(A) *Henry IV Part I*
(B) *The Merry Wives of Windsor*
(C) *The Comedy of Errors*
(D) *Titus Andronicus*

The right combination according to the code is:
(a) (A) and (B) (b) (A) and (C)
(c) (C) and (D) (d) (A) and (D)

26. In her essay "Professions for Women" Virginia Woolf finds an analogy between the act of writing and
(a) driving a motor car
(b) riding a horse
(c) fishing
(d) gardening

27. The ascension of King James I in ________ inaugurated the Jacobean age.
(a) 1600 (b) 1601
(c) 1603 (d) 1609

28. Which of the following is not true of the Byronic hero?

(a) moody (b) passionate
(c) repentant (d) remorse-torn

29. Like many other novelists, Hardy employed language variation (dialect and standard) with a purpose. In this respect which of the following statements is correct?
   (a) His major characters such as Tess and Jude always speak in local dialects, as per their social positions.
   (b) His major characters such as Tess and Jude rarely speak in local dialects, in spite of their social positions.
   (c) His major characters such as Tess and Jude rarely speak in standard language in spite of their social positions.
   (d) His major characters such as Tess and Jude rarely speak in a mixture of a dialect and standard.

30. "It used to be said," began a famous English writer, "everyone had a novel in them.... Just now, though, in 1999, you would probably be obliged to doubt the basic proposition What everyone has in them, these days, is not a novel but a memoir". Identify the source
   (a) Martins Amis, *Experience*
   (b) Michel Butor, *Passing Time*
   (c) John Fowles, *The French Lieutenant's Woman*
   (d) Julian Barnes, *Flaubert's Parrot*

31. The opening sixteen lines of *Paradise Lost* comprise:
   (a) One sentence (b) Two sentences
   (c) Three sentences (d) Four sentences

32. Who among the following poets compared human tears to "love's wine"?
   (a) Ben Jonson (b) John Donne
   (c) Andrew Marvell (d) John Suckling

33. Ernest Pontifex is a character in
   (a) *Tono Bungay*
   (b) *The Man of Property*
   (c) *The Way of All Flesh*
   (d) *Nostromo*

34. In which of the following stories does Rudyard Kipling present a newspaper editor who recounts his dealings with a couple of "loafers"?
   (a) "His Chance in Life"
   (b) "Thrown Away"
   (c) "Lispeth"
   (d) "The Man Who Would Be King"

35. Trying to capture the upbeat mood of 1964-65, the poet Thom Gunn said: "They stood for a great optimism, barriers seemed to be coming down all over, it was as if World War II had finally drawn to close, there was an openness and high-spiritedness and relaxation of mood". Who were "they"?
   (a) The Beatles
   (b) The Rolling Stones
   (c) The New Left
   (d) The Arts Council folks

36. In *Paradise Lost* Milton presents the action of the fall of man in two stages in Books
   (a) IV and IX (b) IV and VIII
   (c) III and IX (d) V and X

37. In *Gulliver's Travels* Struldbruggs are
   (a) people replete with abstract learning.
   (b) people exempt from natural death.
   (c) people persecuted by pets and servants.
   (d) people lured by a new ideal.

38. Margaret Atwood has tried a revisionist writing of a crucial scene in Hamlet called "Gertrude Talks Back". The scene in Atwood opens with a reference to the name of an implied listener. Who is this implied listener?
   (a) Hamlet (b) Ophelia
   (c) Polonius (d) Claudius

39. Samuel Johnson wrote *London* in imitation of

(a) Horace (b) Ovid
(c) Juvenal (d) Moschus

40. Which of the following is not written by Buchi Emecheta?
(a) *The Joys of Motherhood*
(b) *Second-Class Citizen*
(c) *A Question of Power*
(d) *Kehinde*

41. Samuel Johnson's use of the term "metaphysical" in a piece of criticism was
(a) approving (b) disapproving
(c) positive (d) accidental

42. "I am not an angel ... and I will not be one till I die: I will be myself." This is
(a) Maggie Tulliver in *Mill on the Floss*
(b) Aurora Leigh in the eponymous poem
(c) Jane Eyre in the eponymous novel
(d) Betty Higdon in *Our Mutual Friend*

43. Who among the following playwrights was the son of a gardener?
(a) Harold Pinter (b) Joe Orton
(c) Tom Stoppard (d) Edward Bond

44. "He is the very pineapple of politeness!" This sentence is an example of
(a) paronomasia (b) spoonerism
(c) malapropism (d) anaphora

45. Ferdinand de Saussure argued that meaning is generated through
(a) a system of structured differences in language
(b) a system of random differences in language
(c) a system of structured references in language
(d) a system of random references in language

46. Identify the group known as "The Wesker Trilogy"?
(a) *The Growth of the Soil, Game of Life, In the Grip of Life*
(b) *Chicken Soup with Barley, Roots, I'm Talking about Jerusalem*
(c) *The Four Seasons, Chips with Everything, Golden City*
(d) *Lunatics and Lovers, The Patriots, Dead End*

47. Who is the central character of Derek Walcott's *Dream on the Monkey Mountain*?
(a) Diana Guinness, one of the Mitford Sisters
(b) Jordan, a fantasist
(c) Makak, a charcoal burner
(d) Eva Smith, a seamstress

48. The phrase "darkness visible" (*Paradise Lost*, 1.63) is an example of
(a) periphrasis (b) pun
(c) oxymoron (d) transposition

49. What is common to writers such as Sam Selvon (*The Lonely Londoners*), Timothy Mo (*Sour Sweet*), and Hanif Kureishi (*The Black Album*)?
(a) All of them are brilliant writers of autobiographies who tell stories and write poetry.
(b) They use Standard English with some Creole inflections peculiar to the Caribbean.
(c) They are diasporic writers who depict postcolonial London very different from its colonial representations.
(d) They contrast the 'First Nations' with local populations of their respective countries.

50. F.R. Leavis and Q.D. Leavis launched a critical journal devoted to the moral centrality of English Studies. Name the Journal.
(a) *The English Historical Review*
(b) *The Criterion*
(c) *Scrutiny*
(d) *The Edinburgh Review*

## ANSWERS

| | | | | | |
|---|---|---|---|---|---|
| 1. (c) | 2. (a) | 3. (c) | 4. (c) | 5. (a) | 6. (b) |
| 7. (c) | 8. (a) | 9. (a) | 10. (c) | 11. (d) | 12. (b) |
| 13. (b) | 14. (c) | 15. (b) | 16. (c) | 17. (c) | 18. (c) |
| 19. (d) | 20. (d) | 21. (a) | 22. (c) | 23. (b) | 24. (b) |
| 25. (d) | 26. (d) | 27. (b) | 28. (c) | 29. (b) | 30. (d) |
| 31. (b) | 32. (b) | 33. (d) | 34. (c) | 35. (b) | 36. (b) |
| 37. (c) | 38. (c) | 39. (b) | 40. (c) | 41. (b) | 42. (d) |
| 43. (c) | 44. (b) | 45. (d) | 46. (b) | 47. (b) | 48. (b) |
| 49. (b) | 50. (a) | | | | |

# 20

# English Paper III, June 2015 with Answers

1. When Luigi Pirandello's *Six Characters in Search of an Author* opens the audience find the producer attempting to stage a play. What is the title of this play?
   (a) "Rites of Performance"
   (b) "Rules of the Game"
   (c) "Tonight We Stage a Play"
   (d) "Modes of Acting"
2. Which Canterbury pilgrim carries a brooch inscribed with the Latin words meaning "Love Conquers All"?
   (a) The Prioress (b) The Monk
   (c) The Wife of Bath (d) The Squire
3. In his Introduction to *The Oxford Book of Twentieth-Century English Verse* (1973), Philip Larkin underlines the importance of a native tradition with _________ seen as the major poet of the Modern Period.
   (a) William Butler Yeats
   (b) T.S. Eliot
   (c) Thomas Hardy
   (d) D.H. Lawrence
4. Philip Sidney defended poetry against such descriptions of it as "the mother of lies" and "the nurse of abuse." His main argument here is
   (a) The poet is no conjuror or illusionist and represents a world.
   (b) The poet cannot lie because he is not claiming to tell us the truth.
   (c) The poet cannot speak the truth because he is not representing the real world.
   (d) The poet is a philosopher for whom truth is a lie, and lie truth, in an imaginary world.
5. Chapter III of *Oliver Twist* opens with a narratorial remark about Oliver being punished for "the commission of the impious and profane offence of asking for more." What did Oliver ask for more?
   (a) More time to play
   (b) More food to eat
   (c) More books to read
   (d) More money to spend
6. Edmund Spenser's *Epithalamion* is a carefully structured poem carrying corresponding to the
   (a) twelve stanzas; months of the year
   (b) three hundred and sixty-five lines; days of the year
   (c) fourteen stanzas; two week-long bridal ceremonies
   (d) eleven stanzas; eleventh month, November
7. Choose the right chronological sequence below:
   (a) Victorian Period - Jacobean Period - Tudor Period - Restoration Period
   (b) Edwardian Period - Tudor Period - Jacobean Period - Victorian Period

(c) Tudor Period - Jacobean Period - Restoration Period - Edwardian Period
(d) Jacobean Period - Tudor Period - Restoration Period - Edwardian Period

8. "That woman's days were spent
In ignorant good-will,
Her nights in argument
Until her voice grew shrill" (W.B. Yeats "Easter 1916")

Who is the poet referring to?
(a) Maud Gonne
(b) Lady Augusta Gregory
(c) Kathleen Pilcher
(d) Constance Gore-Booth Markievicz

9. Which of the following was replaced by Communicative Language Teaching?
(a) Motivational Approach
(b) Situational Language Teaching
(c) Natural Language Processing
(d) Structural Approach

10. To whom does Francis Bacon offer the following piece of advice?

"Let him sequester himself from the Company of his Countrymen, and diet in such Places, where there is good company of the Nation... Let him upon his Removes, ... procure Recommendation, to some person of Quality, residing in the Place, whither he removeth..."

(a) The Beaux (b) The Peddler
(c) The Traveller (d) The Stationer

11. In his masterpiece, *Of the Lawes of Ecclesiasticall Politie*, Richard Hooker affirmed the Anglican tradition as that of a "threefold cord not quickly broken." He specifically referred to the following except
(a) tradition (b) scripture
(c) community (d) reason

12. Match the following:

**List - I**
(A) Christina Rossetti: *Goblin Market*
(B) Matthew Arnold: *Sohrab and Rustom*
(C) Robert Browning: *The Ring and the Book*
(D) Arthur Hugh Clough: *The Bothie of Tober-na-Vuolich*

**List - II**
(i) The tale of a father who inadvertently destroys his son
(ii) Gently satiric account of an Oxford student on vacation
(iii) Story of pleasure-seeking Laura and the conventionally moral Lizzie who resists temptations
(iv) A sensational 17th century murder presented through multiple dramatic monologues

The right matching according to the code is:

| | (A) | (B) | (C) | (D) |
|---|---|---|---|---|
| (a) | (iii) | (iv) | (i) | (ii) |
| (b) | (ii) | (iv) | (iii) | (i) |
| (c) | (iii) | (i) | (iv) | (ii) |
| (d) | (iv) | (ii) | (iii) | (i) |

13. "Beneath them sit the aged men, wise guardians of the poor;

Then cherish pity, lest you drive an angel from your door."

These concluding lines of William Blake's *Innocence* poem called "Holy Thursday" allude to a Biblical passage. Identify the passage.
(a) The angel of the Lord encampeth round about those who fear Him and delivereth them. Psalms 34.7
(b) Suffer not thy mouth to cause thy flesh to sin; neither say thou before the angel, that it was an error. Ecclesiastes 5.6

(c) And they said unto her, Thou art mad. But she constantly affirmed that it was even so. Then said they, It is his angel. The Acts 12.15
(d) Be not forgetful to entertain strangers for thereby some have entertained angels unawares. Hebrews 13.2

14. Direct Method of Language Teaching involves:
(A) the use of Target Language only
(B) repetition of exercises
(C) linguistic correctness
(D) problem solving exercises

In relation to the above which of the following is correct?
(a) (C) and (D) only
(b) (A), (B) and (D)
(c) (A), (B) and (C)
(d) (A), (B), (C) and (D)

15. In which of the following works does the narrator proclaim, "either I'm nobody, or I'm the nation"?
(a) George Lamming's *In the Castle of My Skin*
(b) Derek Walcott's "The Schooner Flight"
(c) Jamaica Kincaid's "Girl"
(d) Kamau Braithwaite's "Nation Language"

16. Like Cordelia, the Fool in *King Lear* is
(a) killed by Goneril's troops.
(b) referred to by Lear as his child.
(c) disliked by Regan and Cornwall.
(d) punished for not telling the truth.

17. Sindi Oberoi, the narrator hero in Arun Joshi's *The Foreigner* says: "My foreignness lay within me and I couldn't leave myself behind wherever I went." Identify the countries which Sindi Oberoi went to.
(a) Kenya, Uganda, England, America, India
(b) Kenya, Uganda, New Zealand, England, India
(c) Kenya, England, Canada, India
(d) Kenya, America, England, Australia, India

18. **Assertion (A):** The world does not become raceless or will not become unracialized by assertion. The act of enforcing racelessness in literary discourse is itself a racial act.

**Reason (R):** Pouring rhetorical acid on the fingers of a black hand may indeed destroy the prints, but not the hand. Besides, what happens, in that violent, self-serving act of erasure, to the hands, the fingers, the fingerprints of the one who does the pouring? Do they remain acid-free? The literature itself suggests otherwise.

In the context of the statements above,
(a) (A) makes complete sense in the light of (R).
(b) (A) makes complete sense regardless of (R).
(c) Neither (A) nor (R) makes complete sense.
(d) (R) challenges the view advanced in (A).

19. A poet laureate said: "I do not think that since Shakespeare there has been such a master of the English language as I." Who is the poet?
(a) Stephen Spender
(b) John Dryden
(c) Alfred Lord Tennyson
(d) Ted Hughes

20. Who among the following was a contemporary of John Milton and wrote *The Worthy Communicant*? It is said that his prose "can be read easily, when Milton's must be studied."
(a) Jeremy Taylor (b) John Bunyan
(c) Andrew Marvell (d) George Herbert

21. In 1668, Dryden wrote *Of Dramatic Poesie*: An Essay which uses _________ separate characters to dramatise the conflicting viewpoints which new theatrical activity had produced.
    (a) three (b) two
    (c) four (d) six

22. Writing his most influential play, August Strindberg called it "My most beloved drama, the child of my greatest suffering." The play is:
    (a) *A Dream Play*
    (b) *Miss Julie*
    (c) *The Bridal Crown*
    (d) *The Dance of Death*

23. In which essay does Virginia Woolf observe that "if a writer were a free man [sic] and not a slave" to the conventions of the literary marketplace, there would be "no plot, no comedy, no tragedy, no love interest, or catastrophe in the accepted style, and perhaps not a single button sewn on as the Bond Street tailors would have it"?
    (a) "How it Strikes a Contemporary"
    (b) "Modern Fiction"
    (c) "The Russian Point of View"
    (d) "Mr. Bennett and Mr. Brown"

24. In his famous letter to Benjamin Bailey (November 22, 1817) John Keats wrote: "I am certain of nothing but the holiness of the Heart's affections and the truth of Imagination—What the imagination seizes as Beauty must be truth." Which of the following sentences follows this passage?
    (a) Now I am sensible all this is a mere sophistication, however it may neighbour to any truths, to excuse my own indolence...
    (b) The Imagination may be compared to Adam's dream—he woke and found it true.
    (c) This however I am persuaded of, that nothing beside Imagination can give us sweet sensations and pleasurable thoughts.
    (d) My pains at last some respite shall afford, while I behold the battles Imagination maintains.

25. Which of the following pair best describes the characteristic features of Marlowe's portrait of Tamburlaine?
    (A) ambition (B) apathy
    (C) cruelty (D) sympathy

    The right combination according to the code is
    (a) (A) and (B) (b) (A) and (D)
    (c) (A) and (C) (d) (B) and (C)

26. Who is the author of the statement: "The nineteenth century dislike of Realism is the rage of Caliban seeing his own face in the glass"?
    (a) Arthur Symons
    (b) Benjamin Disraeli
    (c) W.B. Yeats
    (d) Oscar Wilde

27. Which of the following statements about Thomas Mann's novels is true?
    (A) *Buddenbrooks* is a family saga set in the early decades of the twentieth century.
    (B) Aschenbach, the writer protagonist in *Death in Venice*, is preoccupied with classicism, especially with classical ideals of male beauty.
    (C) In his second winter at the sanatorium, Hans Castorp, protagonist of *The Magic Mountain* gets lost in a blizzard during a solitary skiing expedition.
    (D) Adrian Leverkuhn, the modern-day Faustus in Mann's *Doctor Faustus* is a musician.

    The right combination according to the code is:

(a) Only (A) and (C) are correct
(b) Only (B) and (D) are correct
(c) (B), (C) and (D) are correct
(d) (A), (B) and (D) are correct

28. To whom did Raja Ram Mohan Roy write in 1823 his letter seeking the introduction of English education in India?
(a) Lord Amherst (b) Lord Bentinck
(c) Lord Cunningham (d) Lord Hastings

29. Listed below are the seemingly friendly characters in *The Pilgrim's Progress* who give Christian dangerous advice. Among them is one who does not belong to this group. Identify this odd character.
(a) Mr. Worldly Wiseman
(b) Evangelist
(c) Ignorance
(d) Talkative

30. Aristotle argued that poetry provides a/an ________ outlet for the release of intense emotions.
(a) safe (b) dangerous
(c) uncertain (d) unreliable

31. The direct French influence on the English language during the Middle English period was in the form of
(a) loss of inflections.
(b) intake of French words into English.
(c) both the loss of inflections and intake of French words into English.
(d) addition of inflections.

32. A significant development in 1662 was the establishment of The Royal Society in England.
The main purpose of the society was
(a) to set the rules for the royal court and governance
(b) to guide and promote the development of science and scientific exploration
(c) to set norms for civil society
(d) to promote theatre

33. William Cowper wrote in *The Task* (IV. 681-82) about those who "Build factories with blood, conducting trade/ At the sword's point..." These lines allude to:
(a) Turkish militant traders across Europe
(b) Nordic conquerors across East Asia
(c) West Indian slave-plantation owners and the East India Company 'nabobs'
(d) Exploiters of child labour in the London suburbs

34. The *commedia dell'arte* originated in Italy in the sixteenth century. Which of the following descriptions are the most appropriate?
(A) Tears alternating with crude laughter
(B) Comedy of the guild or by the professionals in the "art"
(C) Plautine comedy alternating with ritualistic manoeuvres
(D) Improvised comedy that follows a scenario rather than written dialogue
The right combination according to the code is
(a) (A) and (B) (b) (B) and (D)
(c) (A) and (C) (d) (B) and (C)

35. "Nature and Nature's Laws lay hid in Night,
God said Let Newton be! And all was Light."
Alexander Pope's famous couplet impressively captures
(a) Newton's confirmation of the Genesis passage where God ordains Light
(b) Newton's empirical observations of *Philosophiae Naturalis Principia Mathematica*
(c) Newton's application of principles of motion to account for many natural phenomena
(d) Newton's discovery that all colours are contained in white light

36. What was the name of the experimental theatre group founded in 1915 by Susan Glaspell, Eugene O'Neill and other dramatists in order to challenge Broadway's control over American drama?
   (a) The Wall Street Theatre Group
   (b) The Washington Square Players
   (c) The Actor's Studio
   (d) The Provincetown Players

37. After his return from the land of Houyhnhnms, Gulliver refused to let his wife and children
   (a) show disrespect to English horses.
   (b) ride horse-drawn carriages.
   (c) touch his bread, or drink out of his cup.
   (d) communicate with him in English tongue.

38. In which of the following volumes do you find a charming appreciation of the Wordsworth household by Thomas de Quincey?
   (a) *The Confessions of an English Opium-Eater*
   (b) *Lives and Letters, Far Away and Long Ago*
   (c) *Notes on My Lake Country Evenings*
   (d) *Reminiscences of the English Lake Poets*

39. One of the most highly revered, scholarly, and passionate interpreters of English and world literatures, he was appointed the Lord Northcliffe Professor of Modern English Literature at University College, London in 1967, and later as King Edward VII Professor of English Literature at Cambridge in 1974, an appointment made by the Crown at the suggestion of the Prime Minister of the United Kingdom. He was knighted by Queen Elizabeth in 1991. Entitled to designate himself as "Sir," he never did, but wrote and autobiography entitled *Not Entitled* in 1995. The epigraph to this book came from *Coriolanus*: "He was a kind of nothing, titleless."
   Who among the following is this writer/critic?
   (a) F.R. Leavis (b) I.A. Richards
   (c) Frank Kermode (d) David Lodge

40. Which of the following provided theoretical basis for Audio-Lingual Method of Language Teaching?
   (a) Transformational Generative Linguistics
   (b) Congnitive Psychology and Structural Linguistics
   (c) Behaviourist Psychology and Bloomfieldian Structural Linguistics
   (d) Systemic Functional Linguistics

41. Who among the following characters of *The Cherry Orchard* by Anton Chekhov dies in the final scene?
   (a) Anya (b) Firs
   (c) Varya (d) Lopakhin

42. In tracing the history of English poetry, Thomas Gray's "Progress of Poesy" invokes a major poet as follows:
   "Nor second He, that rode sublime
   Upon the seraph-wings of Extasy,
   The secrets of th' Abyss to spy."
   Who is "He"?
   (a) William Shakespeare
   (b) Edmund Spenser
   (c) John Milton
   (d) John Dryden

43. "I suffered from impaired eye-sight, depression and poverty and left Oxford without a degree. After a period as a teacher and my marriage to a widow twice my age, I left for London, to begin writing for a magazine, I produced my own journal." Choose the correct answer,

identifying the writer, the magazine and the journal.

(a) John Milton, *The Examiner's Magazine, London Magazine*
(b) Joseph Addison, *The Freeholder, The Tatler*
(c) Richard Steele, *The Guardian, The Spectator*
(d) Samuel Johnson, *The Gentlemen's Magazine, The Rambler*

44. Which of the American novelists is associated with the series of five books about Natty Bumppo, an old hunter, also called Leatherstocking?
(a) Stephen Crane
(b) James Fennimore Cooper
(c) Herman Melville
(d) Jack London

45. In John Dryden's *Essay on Dramatic Poesy* Neander defends the English invention of
(a) romantic comedy
(b) action tragedy
(c) tragi-comedy
(d) morality plays

46. Who wrote *The History of Australian Literature* in 1961?
(a) Randolph Stow
(b) H.M. Green
(c) Handel Richardson
(d) Francis Adam

47. Match the following:

| Theorist | Theories |
|---|---|
| (A) Bharata | (i) Vakrokti |
| (B) Kuntaka | (ii) Riti |
| (C) Bhamaha | (iii) Dhvani |
| (D) Anandavardhana | (iv) Rasa |

The right matching according to the code is:

| | (A) | (B) | (C) | (D) |
|---|---|---|---|---|
| (a) | (i) | (iv) | (ii) | (iii) |
| (b) | (ii) | (iii) | (i) | (iv) |
| (c) | (iv) | (i) | (ii) | (iii) |
| (d) | (iii) | (ii) | (iv) | (i) |

48. What is "Forster Collection"?
(a) Memorabilia and documents related to the Scottish War of Independence (1296-1328) housed in Glasgow Museum
(b) The special collection of E.M. Forster effects housed in King's College, Cambridge
(c) The largest collection of Charles Dickens manuscripts and proofs curated by John Forster
(d) The collection of political and military documents named after the liberal M.P., W.E. Forster reputed for the Forster Education Act

49. What was remarkable about the poet F.T. Marinetti's first Futurist Manifesto in *Le Figaro*?
(a) It resounded like the monotonous beating of a big drum that filled the air with muffled shocks and lingering vibration.
(b) It proclaimed that someone must go on writing for those who were still convinced of the future for which they had taken up arms.
(c) It blasted the dead weight of "museums, libraries, and academics," glorifying "the beauty of speed."
(d) It declared that man, the individual, is an infinite reservoir of possibilities; and if man can so rearrange society by the destruction of oppressive disorder, then the possibilities have a future.

50. How would one best describe Thomas Carlyle's *Sartor Resartus* (1833)?
(a) A combination of journal, fashion-book, and tips for advertisers
(b) A lyrical novel *à la* Marcel Proust
(c) A combination of novel, autobiography, and essay

(d) A satire on sartorial fashions and feibles of medieval Europe

51. An Indian English poet once remarked that his discipline and education gave him his "outer" whereas his Indian origin gave him "inner" form. Reflecting a part of this claim is a famous essay he called
   (a) "Is There a Native Way of Thinking?"
   (b) "Can the Subaltern Speak?"
   (c) "Where Do We Go from Here: Some Speculations"
   (d) "Is There an Indian Way of Thinking?"

52. In the remarkably crucial courtroom scene of *Their Eyes were Watching God*, Janie is called upon to speak. Whose voice do we hear in the narrative?
   (a) Tea Cake's voice
   (b) Janie's first-person voice
   (c) Pheoby's voice
   (d) The omniscient third-person voice

53. Who is the author of the statement "A prophet is a Seer, not an Arbitrary Dictator"?
   (a) Salman Rushdie (b) Kahlil Gibran
   (c) William Blake (d) Oscar Wilde

54. The word order in Modern English became relatively fixed because
   (a) it developed its inflectional system.
   (b) it lost its highly developed inflectional system.
   (c) it lost its derivational system of word formation.
   (d) it developed its derivational system of word formation

55. Julia Kristeva's 'intertextuality' derives from
   (A) Noam Chomsky's deep structure
   (B) Mikhail Bakhtin's dialogism
   (C) Jacques Derrida's differance
   (D) Ferdinand de Saussure's sign

   The right combination according to the code is:
   (a) (A) and (B) (b) (B) and (C)
   (c) (C) and (D) (d) (A) and (D)

56. Dylan Thomas's famous poem "Fern Hill," is named after
   (a) a countryside in Austria to which he paid occasional visits.
   (b) a childhood haunt of the poet's family in Devonshire.
   (c) the Welsh farmhouse where the poet spent summer holidays as a boy.
   (d) The Welsh Anglican church to which the young poet used to be taken by his mother.

57. "In the seventeenth century," writes T.S. Eliot in "The Metaphysical Poets," "a dissociation of sensibility set in, from which we have never recovered; and this dissociation, as is natural, was aggravated by the influence of the two most powerful poets of the century, and
   (a) Ben Jonson and Abraham Cowley
   (b) George Herbert and Henry Vaughan
   (c) John Donne and Andrew Marvell
   (d) John Milton and John Dryden

58. The label 'material feminism' refers to the work of those thinkers who study inequality in terms of
   (a) gender differences.
   (b) class differences.
   (c) both gender and class differences.
   (d) female consumerism.

59. Who among the following displays in her best work the dual influence of feminism and magic realism?
   (a) Pat Barker (b) Muriel Spark
   (c) Angela Carter (d) J.K. Rowling

60. Identify the group of British poets who evidently draw upon new trends in literary

theory (such as poststructuralism) and wrote poems that reflect on themselves and the language used in/by them.

(a) Seamus Heaney, Michael Longley, Derek Mahon
(b) Medbh McGuckian, Denise Riley, Wendy Cope
(c) Christopher Middleton, Roy Fisher, J.H. Prynne
(d) Donald Davie, Charles Tomlinson, Thom Gunn

61. In Old English other grammatical classes also had the four cases that nouns had. Which were these grammatical classes?
(a) Pronouns and verbs only
(b) Pronouns and adjectives only
(c) Definite article and verbs only
(d) Pronouns, adjectives and definite article

62. Which of the following novels opens with the description of an accident to a hot-air balloon?
(a) John Fowles's *The Magus*
(b) Ian McEwan's *Enduring Love*
(c) James Kelman's *How Late It Was, How Late*
(d) Irvine Welsh's *Trainspotting*

63. Azizun, a courtesan from Kanpur in *A Tale from the Year 1857: Azizun Nisa* by Tripurari Sharma undergoing self-actualisation says: "Yes, I must complete what I've set out to do. I'm not a mere woman." In order to make her impact by her attitudinal shift, she
(a) challenges the codifiers of the Shariat.
(b) forsakes her profession to become a soldier.
(c) becomes a political leader.
(d) becomes a successful dancer.

64. The *hermeneutics of suspicion* is a term coined by Paul Ricoeur
(A) to designate the postcolonial tendency to see theory and related reading manoeuvres as a global conspiracy.
(B) to describe interpretive bids that challenge and seek to overcome compartmentalized cultural experiences.
(C) who, following Marx, Nietzsche, and Freud, held that textual appearances are deceptive and texts do not gracefully relinquish their meanings.
(D) to describe a mode of interpretation that adopts a distrustful attitude towards texts in order to elicit otherwise inaccessible meanings or implications.

The right combination according to the code is:
(a) (A) and (B) (b) (A) and (D)
(c) (C) and (D) (d) (B) and (C)

65. Which of the following is not a feminist novel?
(a) Ashapurna Debi's *Subarnalata*
(b) Rajam Krishnan's *Lamp in the Whirlpool*
(c) Chudamani Raghavan's *Yamini*
(d) Bani Basu's *The Enemy Within*

66. The term 'poetic justice' was coined by
(a) Samuel Taylor Coleridge
(b) Thomas Rymer
(c) Samuel Johnson
(d) William Wordsworth

67. Which of the following novels deals with the Biafran War?
(a) *July's People*
(b) *Waiting for the Barbarians*
(c) *Half of a Yellow Sun*
(d) *Arrow of God*

68. Which of the following is not true in Dalit aesthetics as given by Sharan Kumar Limbale?

(a) The agony, assertion, resistance, anger and protest of the dalits should be expressed.
(b) Dalit *anubhava* (experience) should take precedence over *anuman* (speculation).
(c) Sympathy for the dalits should be generated.
(d) Ungrammatical language, different from the standard norms of expression, should be used.

69. Which of the following is not a critical study by William Empson?
(a) *Seven Types of Ambiguity*
(b) *The Dyer's Hand*
(c) *Milton's God*
(d) *Some Versions of the Pastoral*

70. This was a path-breaking feminist essay written in the 1970s which used hybrid terms like "sext" and "chaosmos." Identify the author.
(a) Luce Irigaray
(b) Helene Cixous
(c) Julia Kristeva
(d) Simon de Beauvoir

**Read the poem and answer the questions that follow (71-75):**

**The Voice**

Woman much missed, how you call to me, call to me,
Saying that now you are not as what you were
When you had changed from the one who was all to me
But as first, when our day was fair

Can it be you that I hear? Let me view you, then
Standing as when I drew near to the town
Where you would wait for me yes, as I knew you then,
Even to the original air-blue gown!

Or is it only the breeze, in its listlessness
Travelling across the wet mead to me here,
You being ever dissolved to wan wistlessness
Heard no more again far or near?

Thus I; faltering forward,
Leaves around me falling,
Wind oozing thin through the thorn from norward
And the woman calling.

71. What suggestion does the opening stanza give of a woman won or a woman lost?
(a) The contrast between 'now' and 'then'
(b) The continuity between 'now' and 'then'
(c) The phrase "had changed"
(d) The phrase "our day was fair"

72. What is tantalizing about the speaker's experience in stanza 2?
(a) The disappearance of the lady and the echo of the voice
(b) The indistinct voice heard by the speaker and the absence of woman
(c) The uncertainty of the voice and the speaker's inability to see the woman
(d) The woman disappearing before her voice is fully heard

73. What phrase in the poem suggests the possibility of the woman as "dead"?
(a) "You had changed .... to me"
(b) "I knew you then"
(c) "You being ever dissolved"
(d) "Woman much missed"

74. Identify the special sound effect in the line given: Wind oozing thin through the thorn from norward...
(a) Alliteration
(b) Onomatopoeia
(c) Assonance
(d) The use of sibilants

75. What longing does the speaker voice?
   (a) Longing for reunion in the other world
   (b) Longing for physical union in the present
   (c) Longing for physical union in the town where they used to meet
   (d) Longing for a return to the town where they used to meet

## ANSWERS

| | | | | | |
|---|---|---|---|---|---|
| 1. (c) | 2. (d) | 3. (b) | 4. (c) | 5. (b) | 6. (d) |
| 7. (d) | 8. (b) | 9. (b) | 10. (a) | 11. (b) | 12. (a) |
| 13. (d) | 14. (d) | 15. (a) | 16. (c) | 17. (a) | 18. (b) |
| 19. (d) | 20. (c) | 21. (b) | 22. (d) | 23. (d) | 24. (c) |
| 25. (d) | 26. (a) | 27. (b) | 28. (d) | 29. (d) | 30. (a) |
| 31. (a) | 32. (d) | 33. (a) | 34. (c) | 35. (d) | 36. (b) |
| 37. (a) | 38. (a) | 39. (b) | 40. (c) | 41. (a) | 42. (c) |
| 43. (b) | 44. (d) | 45. (b) | 46. (d) | 47. (c) | 48. (b) |
| 49. (b) | 50. (c) | 51. (b) | 52. (c) | 53. (c) | 54. (c) |
| 55. (c) | 56. (a) | 57. (a) | 58. (a) | 59. (c) | 60. (b) |
| 61. (b) | 62. (a) | 63. (b) | 64. (a) | 65. (c) | 66. (b) |
| 67. (b) | 68. (a) | 69. (a) | 70. (b) | 71. (b) | 72. (b) |
| 73. (b) | 74. (d) | 75. (b) | | | |

21

# NET Examination Paper II, December 2015 with Answers

1. Who, among the following, advanced the theory that the mind is a *tabula rasa* at birth, and acquires all ideas by experience?
   (a) John Locke (b) John Wesley
   (c) Isaac Watts (d) Denis Diderot
2. Which of the following authors wrote *Studies in the History of the Renaissance*?
   (a) Walter Pater (b) Oscar Wilde
   (c) Thomas Carlyle (d) John Ruskin
3. Whom does Harriet Smith finally marry in one of Jane Austen's novels?
   (a) Knightley (b) Darcy
   (c) Collins (d) Mr. Martin
4. A poet once referred to an old man as "A tattered coat upon a stick". That is an example of
   (a) Metonymy (b) Sarcasm
   (c) Simile (d) Metaphor
5. Which of these is not a pastoral elegy?
   (a) *Lycidas* (b) *In Memoriam*
   (c) *Thyrsis* (d) *Adonais*
6. In Beckett's *Waiting for Godot* the characters often use dislocated, repetitious and cliched speech primarily to:
   (a) illustrate the essentially illogical, purposeless nature of the human condition
   (b) re-create the workings of the subconscious
   (c) mock the exaggerated dignity and wisdom of modern, self-professed intellectuals
   (d) reinforce the comic action of farcical plots
7. Which of the following sixteenth-century poets was not a courtier?
   (a) George Puttenham
   (b) Philip Sidney
   (c) Walter Raleigh
   (d) Thomas Wyatt
8. Patrick White published two novels in the 1950s giving the eras of pioneering and exploration in Australian history an epic, ironic and psychological dimension. The novels are:
   (A) *A Fringe of Leaves*
   (B) *The Tree of Man*
   (C) *Voss*
   (D) *The Aunt's Story*
   The right combination according to the code is:
   (a) (A) and (B) (b) (B) and (C)
   (c) (C) and (A) (d) (C) and (D)
9. In which of the following works did Bakhtin propose his widely cited concept of the 'Carnivalesque'?
   (a) "Discourse in the novel"
   (b) *Dialogic Imagination*

(c) *Rabelais and his World*
(d) "Forms of Time and of the Chronotope in the Novel"

10. Match the columns:

| | (Author) | | (Text) |
|---|---|---|---|
| (A) | Sebastian Faulks | (i) | *Amsterdam* |
| (B) | Peter Ackroyd | (ii) | *Changing Places* |
| (C) | Ian McEwan | (iii) | *Hawksmoor* |
| (D) | David Lodge | (iv) | *Birdsong* |

| **Codes:** | **(A)** | **(B)** | **(C)** | **(D)** |
|---|---|---|---|---|
| (a) | (i) | (ii) | (iii) | (iv) |
| (b) | (ii) | (iii) | (i) | (iv) |
| (c) | (iv) | (iii) | (i) | (ii) |
| (d) | (iii) | (iv) | (ii) | (i) |

11. In New Criticism, the key term 'tension' is associated with:
(a) Cleanth Brooks
(b) John Crow Ransom
(c) Austin Warren
(d) Allen Tate

12. While compiling what sort of book did Samuel Richardson conceive of the idea for his *Pamela or Virtue Rewarded?*
(a) An account of the plague in London
(b) An instruction manual for manners
(c) A book of devotion
(d) A book of model letters

13. Who among the war poets gained notoriety in 1917, when disenchanted with the way the war was being conducted he drafted his letter of "wilful defiance of the military authority" which captured attention in the House of Commons, and was forcibly admitted to the war hospital at Craiglockhart, primarily to avoid his being court-martialled?
(a) Rupert Brook
(b) Siegfried Sassoon
(c) Wilfred Owen
(d) Isaac Rosenberg

14. If you cannot understand an argument and remark, "It's Greek to me", you are quoting
(a) John Milton
(b) Samuel Johnson
(c) William Shakespeare
(d) John Donne

15. Which of the following works did Walter Scott compile?
(a) *The Lay of the Last Minstrel*
(b) *Marmion*
(c) *Ivanhoe*
(d) *The Minstrelsy of Scottish Border*

16. Which of the following is not written by Wole Soyinka?
(a) *Home and Exile*
(b) *Kongi's Harvest*
(c) *The Interpreters*
(d) *The Swamp Dwellers*

17. In the *Defense of Poesy* Sidney says: "Now as in geometry the oblique must be known as well as right and in arithmetic, the odd as well as the even, so in the actions of our life who seeth not the filthiness of evil wanteth a great foil to perceive the beauty of virtue". Which of the following forms of poesy offers a foil that helps us perceive the beauty of virtue?
(a) Pastorals (b) Parody
(c) Comedy (d) Tragedy

18. John Dryden described a major English poet as "a rough diamond, and must first be polished ere he shines....." Identify him.
(a) Geoffrey Chaucer
(b) John Gower
(c) George Herbert
(d) Robert Herrick

19. In a remarkably proleptic insight, a critic wrote the following, anticipating Benedict Anderson's definition of the nation as "an imagined political community":

"Most novels are in some sense knowable communities. It is part of a traditional method—an underlying stance and approach—that a novelist offers to show people and their relationships in essentially knowable and communicable ways".

Name the critic and the reference.

(a) Van Wyck Brooks, *The Writer in America*
(b) Raymond Williams, *The Country and the City*
(c) Joseph Wood Krutch, *The Modern Temper*
(d) T.S. Eliot, *Notes Towards a Definition of Culture*

20. "Fair is my love, and cruel as she's fair; Her brow-shades frown, although her eyes are sunny". The above lines are characterized by

(a) circumlocution (b) antithesis
(c) anticlimax (d) bathos

21. In his "Epistle to Dr. Arbuthnot" Pope tells us that as a poet he had benefited from "This saving counsel, 'keep your piece nine years'"—which enjoins on writer's patience and great care before they rush to print. Whose "counsel" is Pope referring to?

(a) Longinus's in *On the Sublime*
(b) Horace's in *Ars Poetica*
(c) Quintilian's *Institutio Oratoria*
(d) Aristotle's *Poetics*

22. An English architect and stage-designer—Beginning 1605, joined Jacobean court to design masques—contributed significantly to the spectacular theatre which succeeded the commonwealth after his death—the first designer to use revolving screens to indicate scene-changes on the English stage.

Identify this artist/designer.

(a) Henry Irving
(b) Inigo Jones
(c) Henry Arthur Jones
(d) William Inge

23. ________ may be defined as any departure from the rules of pronunciation or diction, for the sake of rhyme or metre, or an unjustifiable departure from fact.

(a) Poetic license (b) Poetic justice
(c) Poetic deviance (d) Poetic diction

24. That Humanities and the sciences were in fact "two cultures" was suggested by

(a) Aldous Huxley in his Oxford lectures on poetry
(b) W.H. Anden in his Oxford lectures on poetry
(c) F.R. Leavis in his book, *The Great Tradition*
(d) C.P. Snow in his Rede lecture

25. Chaueer satirizes the Monk because the Monk:

(a) is too concerned with courtesy and matters of etiquette
(b) cheats the poor peasants by selling them false religious relics
(c) courts favour of wealthy people but spends no time with poor people
(d) spends too much time hunting and too little time on religious duty

26. Divided into three sections this ground-breaking work published in 1953 uses as the frame of the spiritual and moral awakening of a fourteen-year-old during a Saturday night service in a Harlem church. Identify the work.

(a) Zora Neale Hurston's *Their Eyes are Watching God*
(b) James Baldwin's *Go Tell it on the Mountain*
(c) Toni Morrison's *Song of Solomon*
(d) Richard Wright's *Native Son*

27. Chartism, a political movement that took its name from the People's Charter had six points. Identify the one point on the following list that was not Chartist:
    (A) universal manhood sufferage
    (B) equal electoral districts
    (C) comprehensive insurance scheme for labour
    (D) vote by secret ballot
    (E) payment of MPs
    (F) no property qualifications for MPs
    (G) Annual parliaments

    **Codes:**
    (a) (E) (b) (G) (c) (C) (d) (D)

28. These beauteous forms,
    Through a long absence, have been to me
    As is a landscape to a blind man's eye...
    ("Tintern Abbey Lines")

    Which of the following rhetorical terms best suits these lines?
    (a) Apostrophe (b) Litotes
    (c) Hyperbole (d) Catachresis

29. The 'monster' in *Frankenstein* is not responsible for the death of:
    (a) Clerval
    (b) Justine
    (c) Elizabeth
    (d) Alphonse Frankenstein

30. Which of the following plays of William Shakespeare is not directly referred to in T.S. Eliot's *The Waste Land*?
    (a) *Hamlet* (b) *King Lear*
    (c) *Coriolanus* (d) *The Tempest*

31. Identify the group below which is known as the "Sons of Ben".
    (a) Noel Coward, E.G. Craig, William Macready, Matheson, Lang
    (b) John Dryden, the Earl of Rochester, Samuel Butler
    (c) William Cartwright, Richard Corbett, Thomas Randolph
    (d) William Holman Hunt, John E. Millais, D.G. Rossetti, William Morris

32. Christopher Marlowe was one of the first major writers to affirm what can be identified as a clearly homosexual sensibility. Which drama of his deals with it?
    (a) *Edward II*
    (b) *The Jew of Malta*
    (c) *Doctor Faustus*
    (d) *Dido, Queen of Carthage*

33. "When true silence falls we are still left with echo but are nearer nakedness. One way of looking at speech is to say that it is a constant stratagem to cover nakedness". Identify the playwright who underlines the significance of silence thus.
    (a) Samuel Beckett (b) Harold Pinter
    (c) Luigi Pirandello (d) Joe Orton

34. The determining feature of *syllabic verse* is neither ________ nor ________ but the number of syllables in a line.
    (a) number, numbers
    (b) sounds, silences
    (c) stress, quantity
    (d) gists, piths

35. In Robert Browning's dramatic monologue, which painter does Andrea del Sarto compare himself to? What does he find lacking in his own work in comparison?
    (a) Fra Lippo Lippi - humour
    (b) Raphael - Soul
    (c) Leonardo da Vinci - Verisimilitude
    (d) Botticelli - liveliness

36. In which of the following does Robert Southey detail the Indian superstitions as an idolatry to be suppressed by a civilizing protestant form of colonialism?
    (a) "Thalaba"
    (b) *The Curse of Kehama*
    (c) "Pitying the wolves"
    (d) *Country Horrors!*

37. The following is the classic ending of a celebrated novella in English:

    "I kept on creeping just the same, but I looked at him over my shoulder. 'I've got out at last'," said I, "in spite of you and Jane. And I've pulled off most of the papers, so you can't put me back!"

    Now why should that man have fainted? But he did, and right across my path by the wall, so that I had to creep over him every time!"

    (a) *Yellow Woman* (Leslie Mormon Silko)
    (b) *The Yellow Wallpaper* (Charlotte P. Gilman)
    (c) *Johny Panic and the Bible of Dreams* (Sylvia Plalth)
    (d) *Where Are You Going Where Have You Been?* (Joyce C. Oates)

38. Harriet B. Stowe had wanted to write a work based on the life of an Afro-American writer which was later published as:

    (a) *Uncle Tom's Cabin*
    (b) *Incidents in the Life of a Slave Girl*
    (c) *Cry, The Beloved Country*
    (d) *Narrative of the Life of Frederick Douglass*

39. Samuel Johnson's "Dissertation upon Poetry" is part of which of his following works?

    (a) The final section of his preface to Shakespeare
    (b) A chapter of his novel *Rasselas*
    (c) The epilogue of his *Lives of Poets*
    (d) One of his *Rambler* essays

40. A new series called "New Accents" was launched by Methuen in 1977. The first title to be published in the series was:

    (a) *Deconstruction : Theory and Practice*
    (b) *Formalism and Marxism*
    (c) *Structuralism and Semiotics*
    (d) *Making and Difference : Feminist Literary Criticism*

41. "Humble and rustic life was generally chosen, because, in that condition, the essential passions of the heart find a better soil in which they can attain their maturity, are less under restraint, and speak a plainer and more emphatic language.... The language, too, of these men has been adopted...because such men hourly communicate with the best objects from which the best part of language is originally derived". Which of the following groups of the author's poems in the *Lyrical Ballads* (1800) contradict this statement in the "Preface to the Lyrical Ballads", as pointed out by S.T. Coleridge?

    (a) "Ode on the Intimations of Immortality", *Prelude*.
    (b) *The Tasks, Seasons*.
    (c) "Michael", "Ruth", "The Brothers".
    (d) "Elegy Written in a country churchyard", "Ode on the Popular Superstitions of the Highlands".

42. A remarkable novelist of the English Modernist phase who wrote a short book on what the novel is (and why it matters) remarked, "Oh dear, yes—the novel tells a story". Identify the novelist.

    (a) Virginia Woolf (b) James Joyce
    (c) E.M. Forster (d) D.H. Lawrence

43. What is the name of the angel, who, of those who owed allegeance to Satan, dared to protest against his impious doctrine and left his company to return to God (*Paradise Lost*, Book V)?

    (a) Michael (b) Abdiel
    (c) Uriel (d) Gabriel

44. Which of the following is not a school associated with Romantic period in English literature?

(a) The Cockney School
(b) The Fireside School
(c) The Lake School
(d) The Satanic School

45. The idea of "new ethnicities" in post-war Britain was advanced by:
(a) Donald Hall (b) Stuart Hall
(c) Paul Gilroy (d) Hanif Kureishi

46. Virginia Woolf's *To the Lighthouse* begins in a piece of dialogue:
"Yes, of course, if it's fine tomorrow", said Mrs. Ramsay. "But you'll have to be up with lark", she added.
Present among the listeners of her remark is
(a) her father (b) her nephew
(c) her son (d) her driver

47. Match the phrase with character:
(A) "motiveless malignity" (i) Macbeth
(B) "Reason in Madness" (ii) Hamlet
(C) "Supp'd full of horrors" (iii) Lear
(D) "To be, or not to be" (iv) Iago

| Codes: | (A) | (B) | (C) | (D) |
|---|---|---|---|---|
| (a) | (i) | (iii) | (ii) | (iv) |
| (b) | (iv) | (ii) | (iii) | (i) |
| (c) | (iv) | (iii) | (i) | (ii) |
| (d) | (iii) | (i) | (ii) | (iv) |

48. In *Tristram Shandy* the narrator's presentation of his life and opinions is
(a) linear (b) digressive
(c) chronological (d) rounded

49. The famous sonnet of John Milton beginning "When I consider how my light is spent..." ends with
(a) Before me stares a wolfish eye, Behind me creeps a groan or sigh
(b) They also serve who only stand and wait
(c) And—which is more—you'll be a Man, my son!
(d) And bless him for the sake of him that's gone

50. Her vision was of several caves. She saw herself in one, and she was also outside it, watching its entrance, for Aziz to pass in. She failed to locate him. It was the doubt that had often visited her, but solid and attractive, like the hills. "I am not—" speech was more difficult than vision. "I am not quite sure".
The above extract from *A Passage to India* is about Adela's cave experience. Who is questioning Adela?
(a) Mrs. Moore (b) Mr. McBryde
(c) Fielding (d) Ronney Heaslop

## ANSWERS

| | | | | | |
|---|---|---|---|---|---|
| 1. (a) | 2. (a) | 3. (d) | 4. (d) | 5. (b) | 6. (a) |
| 7. (a) | 8. (b) | 9. (c) | 10. (c) | 11. (d) | 12. (d) |
| 13. (b) | 14. (c) | 15. (d) | 16. (a) | 17. (c) | 18. (a) |
| 19. (b) | 20. (b) | 21. (b) | 22. (b) | 23. (a) | 24. (d) |
| 25. (d) | 26. (b) | 27. (c) | 28. (Z) | 29. (d) | 30. (b) |
| 31. (c) | 32. (a) | 33. (b) | 34. (c) | 35. (b) | 36. (b) |
| 37. (b) | 38. (b) | 39. (b) | 40. (c) | 41. (c) | 42. (c) |
| 43. (b) | 44. (b) | 45. (b) | 46. (c) | 47. (c) | 48. (b) |
| 49. (b) | 50. (b) | | | | |

Z means no option is correct

22

# English Paper III, December 2015 with Answers

1. Thomas and Henrietta Bowdler's edition of *The Family Shakespeare* gave rise to the word "Bowdlerize". What does it mean?
   (a) The expurgation of indelicate language
   (b) The modernization of archaic vocabulary
   (c) The insertion of bawdy songs
   (d) The expansion of female characters
2. First follow _______ and your judgement frame. By her just ________, which is still the same. Supply the appropriate words to fill in the blanks.
   (a) wit, law (b) reason, rule
   (c) nature, standard (d) sense, criterion
3. Preparation of vocabulary list for the purpose of English language teaching was carried out by
   (a) Otto Jespersen (b) Noam Chomsky
   (c) N.S. Prabhu (d) Michael West
4. Michael Hardt and Antonio Negri prefer to use "Empire" rather than imperialism. According to them:
   (a) There is only one empire and we had better recognize it. Hence the Empire with E upper case.
   (b) There may be many empires but only one is patently visible and operational. That is denoted by Empire with E upper case.
   (c) The present-day empire does not have an identifiable location or centre. Hence we ought to differentiate this view of Empire with E upper case.
   (d) The culturally dominant global empire is the only one that really matters. We signify that Empire with E upper case.
5. Who among the following critics discerned in the Shelleyan Lyric the signs "of adolescence"?
   (a) F.R. Leavis (b) T.S. Eliot
   (c) Cleanth Brooks (d) I.A. Richards
6. Two among the following critical journals became strongly associated with New Criticism.
   (A) *Partisan Review* (B) *Southern Review*
   (C) *Kenyon Review* (D) *Hudson Review*
   The right combination according to the code is
   (a) (A) and (B) (b) (A) and (D)
   (c) (B) and (C) (d) (C) and (D)
7. Match the columns
   (A) Robert Burton (B) Richard Hooker
   (C) Thomas Browne (D) Thomas Nashe
   (i) *Urn Burial*
   (ii) *The Unfortunate Traveller*
   (iii) *The Anatomy of Melancholy*
   (iv) *Of the Laws of Ecclesiastical Politie*

|  | (A) | (B) | (C) | (D) |
|---|---|---|---|---|
| (a) | (iii) | (i) | (ii) | (iv) |
| (b) | (iv) | (ii) | (i) | (iii) |
| (c) | (iii) | (iv) | (i) | (ii) |
| (d) | (i) | (iii) | (iv) | (ii) |

8. Which of the following characters in *The White Devil* describes the glory of great men as: "Glories, like glow worms a far off shine bright/ But looked to near have neither heat nor light".
   (a) Vittoria (b) Lodovico
   (c) Flamineo (d) Cornelia
9. In which of Philip Larkin's poem does he refer to "long uneven lines" of men waiting to be enlisted for the war?
   ("Never such innocence again" concludes the poem)
   (a) "Mr. Bleaney" (b) "Mc MXIV"
   (c) "Ambulances" (d) "Sad Steps"
10. In Franz Kafka's *Metamorphosis*, Gregor Samsa one morning found himself changed in his bed to a monstrous kind of vermin. The most difficult thing for Samsa was:
    (a) to look at his image in the mirror
    (b) to remember what happened the day before
    (c) to communicate with anyone
    (d) to brush his teeth
11. Identify the individual who is a nihilist from the following:
    (a) Pechorin in *A Hero of Our Times*
    (b) Bazarov in *Fathers and Sons*
    (c) Levin in *Anna Karenina*
    (d) Oblomov in *Oblomov*
12. Which of these works in nineteenth-century Russian fiction originated the type of a Superfluous Man?
    (a) *The Diary of a Superfluous Man*
    (b) *A Hero of Our Own Times*
    (c) *Eugene Onegin*
    (d) *Dead Souls*
13. What is *Gilgamesh?*
    (A) A Babylonian epic poem
    (B) A series of gnomic verses
    (C) A classical play
    (D) The story of a harsh ruler
    (a) (A) and (B) (b) (C)
    (c) (A) and (B) (d) (B)
14. *American Dictionary of the English Language* was the work of _________ published in ___________.
    (a) Merriam Webster, 1903
    (b) H.L. Mencken, 1930
    (c) Noah Webster, 1828
    (d) Benjamin Franklin, 1768
15. Which of the following texts of Amitav Ghosh is based on the refugee occupation of an island in the Sundarvans?
    (a) Sea of Poppies
    (b) The Hungry Tide
    (c) River of Smoke
    (d) The Glass Palace
16. Which of the following is described by Robert Browning as "A Child's Story"?
    (a) "Bells and Pomegranates"
    (b) "Pauline"
    (c) "Fifine at the Fair"
    (d) "The Pied Piper of Hamelin"
17. Identify the New Critic who served as the cultural attaché at the American Embassy in London from 1964 to 1966:
    (a) John Crowe Ransom
    (b) Cleanth Brooks
    (c) Allen Tate
    (d) Robert Penn Warren
18. "*The Gilded Age*" refers to a period of American history between 1870 and the first decades of the twentieth century.
    Who among the following American writers is credited with the coining of the term?
    (a) F. Scott Fitzgerald
    (b) Mark Twain
    (c) William Dean Howells
    (d) Theodore Dreiser

19. *The Decline and Fall of the Roman Empire* in six volumes was a great achievement by Edward Gibbon. It was published between 1776 and 1788, two significant dates that.
   (a) Signalled the end of the Napoleonic wars and the rise of Feudalism.
   (b) Signalled the American Revolution and the French Revolution.
   (c) Covered the fall of peasantry and the rise of bureaucracy in England.
   (d) Suggest the period of Queen Anne's reign.

20. Being so caught up, so mastered by the brute _______ of the air, Did she put on his knowledge with his power, Before the _________ beak could let her drop.
   Yeats, "Leda and the Swan".
   Choose the right words for the blanks:
   (a) beast, shiny (b) force, animal
   (c) blood, indifferent (d) thrust, irate

21. Match the following:
   **Terms**
   (A) Ambiguity (B) Aporia
   (C) Intertextuality (D) Heteroglossia
   **Description**
   (i) A term coined by Julia Kristeva to refer to the fact that texts are constituted by a "tissue of citations".
   (ii) A term used by Mikhail Bakhtin to describe the variety of languages and voices within a novel.
   (iii) An irresolvable internal contradiction or logical disjunction in a text, usually associated with deconstructive thinking.
   (iv) A term made famous by William Empson to indicate that a word, phrase, or text can be interpreted in more than one way.

|  | (A) | (B) | (C) | (D) |
|---|---|---|---|---|
| (a) | (iv) | (i) | (ii) | (iii) |
| (b) | (ii) | (iii) | (iv) | (i) |
| (c) | (iv) | (iii) | (i) | (ii) |
| (d) | (iii) | (iv) | (i) | (ii) |

22. Did I request thee, Maker, from my clay
   To mould me man? Did I solicit thee
   From darkness to promote me?
   Which nineteenth-century work bears these lines from *Paradise Lost* as epigraph?
   (a) *Wuthering Heights*
   (b) *Frankenstein*
   (c) *Don Juan*
   (d) *Jude the Obscure*

23. A literary researcher now faced with choosing between a print text and its digital counterpart chooses the latter mostly to:
   (a) facilitate the consultation of an exhaustive bibliography
   (b) avoid the expense of buying books
   (c) look for specific words and phrases and lines
   (d) enhance his/her understanding of textual variants, if any, between the two media

24. Which of the following statements on *Hudibras* are true?
   (A) It is a novel written by Matthew Prior.
   (B) It is a satirical poem published in three parts.
   (C) *Hudibras* was written by Samuel Butler.
   (D) *Hudibras* discusses complex issues of justice, politics and religion.
   (a) (C) and (D) are true
   (b) (A) and (D) are true
   (c) (B) and (C) are true
   (d) (A) and (B) are true

25. The formalist critic _______ mocked the character-based criticism of _________ by posing a famous question, "How many children had Lady Macbeth"?

(a) F.R. Leavis, E.K. Chambers
(b) Cleanth Brooks, F.L. Lucas
(c) Monroe Beardsley, Kenneth Burke
(d) L.C. Knights, A.C. Bradley

26. Which of the following pair of words does not have two different vowel glides?
(a) Care, pure (b) Write, freight
(c) Caught, court (d) Eight, ate

27. **Assertion (A):** Arts will often work obliquely, by myth or symbol. They may make their best 'criticism of life' simply by being; they may best state by not stating.
**Reason (R):** It follows, if even only part of all this is true, that the arts do have an important social function. [...] Arts can give greater depth to a society's sense of itself. [...] A country without great art might be a powerful collection of thriving earthworms but would be a sorry society.
(a) Reason (R) is perfectly aligned with Assertion (A)
(b) Assertion (A) is unrelated to Reason (R)
(c) Assertion (A) hardly reflects Reason (R)'s elaboration
(d) Reason (R), in fact, contradicts Assertion (A)

28. Which of the following is not an example of derivational morpheme?
(a) friend - friendship
(b) courage - courageous
(c) rely - reliable
(d) climate - climactic

29. Which of these statements is incorrect about presentism and its basic premises?
(a) Hugh Grady is its principal proponent.
(b) Our knowledge of works from the past is conditioned by and dependent upon the ideologies of the present.
(c) Presentism does not contextualize cultural production in the same way or make use of the theorists that New Historicism does.
(d) Historicism itself necessarily produces an implicit allegory of the present in its configuration of the past.

30. "Where there is leisure for fiction, there is little grief", was Samuel Johnson's criticism of a famous poem. Which poem was it?
(a) P.B. Shelley's "Adonais"
(b) Philip Sidney's "Astrophel and Stella"
(c) Thomas Gray's "Elegy Written on a Country Churchyard"
(d) John Miltion's "Lycidas"

31. The story is grounded in the forbidden nature of Aschenbach's Obsession with a young boy; its author ultimately links the obsession with death, disease and esthetic disintegration.
The author of the story is:
(a) Goethe (b) Mann
(c) Borges (d) Proust

32. Which of the following novels of Joseph Conrad is set in Malay?
(a) *Nigger of the Narcissus*
(b) *Lord Jim*
(c) *Nostromo*
(d) *Heart of Darkness*

33. Nuruddin Farah's *Maps* tells the story of
(a) Abida (b) Abu
(c) Askar (d) Andy

34. One of the most quoted statements on poetry by John Keats is reproduced with blanks below. Complete the statement with correct words.
"If Poetry __________ as naturally as the leaves to a tree, it _________ at all".
(a) does not come; had better not come
(b) comes not; might come not
(c) come not; had better not come
(d) come not; did not come

35. Manohar Malgonkar was a hunter, a lieutenant colonel in the British army, and a tea-planter. He also wrote a memorable novel about the Sepoy Mutiny, especially Peshwa Baji Rao II. What is that novel?
    (a) *A Distant Drum*
    (b) *A Combat of Shadows*
    (c) *A Bend in the Ganges*
    (d) *The Devil's Wind*
36. Who wrote the screenplay for the film version of John Fowles's novel *The French Lieutenant's Woman*?
    (a) Harold Pinter (b) Tom Stoppard
    (c) David Mamet (d) Caryl Phillips
37. "How all their plays be neither right tragedies, nor right comedies, mingling kings and elowns, not because the matter so carrieth it, but thrust in the clown by head and shoulders to play a part in majestical matters".
    What term does Philip Sidney use to characterize such plays and which of the unities of Aristotle do they violate?
    (a) Mongrel tragicomedy; unity of action
    (b) Mixed tragedies; unity of action
    (c) Multi-plot drama; unity of time
    (d) Mingled yarn; unity of place
38. There is a large number of religious poems in Old English Poetry. One of the finest is the *Dream of the Rood*. The words 'the Rood' in the title means:
    (a) the Cross (b) the Christian
    (c) the Infidel (d) the Cardinal
39. Identify from among the following, the one *incorrect* statement on M. Anantanarayanan's *Silver Pilgrimage* (1961):
    (a) M. Anantanarayanan modelled this narrative on the well-known picaresque novels in English.
    (b) *The Silver Pilgrimage* is M. Anantanarayanan's only foray into fiction.
    (c) This novel is mainly an account of the adventures of Jayasurya, a Sri Lankan prince of the sixteenth century.
    (d) Among the literary texts quoted by the novel are lines from Shakespeare, Donne and Rilke and classical Tamil poets.
40. Listed below are the titles of some influential books by Frank Kermode. Identify which one of the titles that does not belong to the set.
    (a) *The Sense of an Ending*
    (b) *Not Entitled—A Memoir*
    (c) *The Genesis of Secrecy*
    (d) *The Great Code: The Bible and Literature*
41. Identify the one *erroneous* statement on Neoclassicism listed below:
    (a) Lodovico Castelvetro and Torquato Tasso greatly influenced English writers like Milton and Dryden.
    (b) Neoclassicism took its final form during the reign of Louis XIV (1638-1715).
    (c) Boilean's *L'Art poétique* influenced Pope's *Essay on Criticism*.
    (d) The English relation to Neoclassicism was one of dialogue. Most literally, this dialogue is effected in Addison's *An Essay on Dramatic Poesy*.
42. In his *Poems of Love and War*, a collection of classic Indian poems in English translation, A.K. Ramanujan sought to revive an ancient _______ poetic tradition. Choose the right word.
    (a) Tamil (b) Sanskrit
    (c) Kannada (d) Pali

43. Arrange the following sentences in the order in which they appear in Emerson's "Self-Reliance":
   (A) To be great is to be misunderstood.
   (B) Pythagoras was misunderstood, and Socrates, and Jesus, and Luther, and Copernicus, and Galileo, and Newton, and every pure and wise spirit that ever took flesh.
   (C) If it so bad then to be misunderstood!
   (D) It is a right fool's word.
   (E) Misunderstood!
   (a) (A), (E), (D), (C), (B)
   (b) (E), (A), (B), (C), (D)
   (c) (C), (D), (A), (B), (E)
   (d) (E), (D), (C), (B), (A)

44. X: Do you know it is nearly seven?
   Y: (irritably) Oh! it always is nearly seven.
   X: Well, I'm hungry.
   Y: I never knew you when you weren't...
   X: What shall we do after dinner? Go to a theatre?
   Y: Oh no! I loathe listening.
   X: Well, let us go to the club?
   Y: Oh no! I hate talking.
   X: Well, we might trot round to the Empire at ten?
   Y: Oh no! I can't bear looking at things. It is so silly.
   X: Well, what shall we do?
   Y: Nothing!
   X: It is awfully hard work doing nothing. However, I don't mind hard work where there is no definite object of any kind.

   Identify the speakers in this dialogue:
   (a) Aston (X) to Mick (Y) *The Caretaker*
   (b) Algernon (X) to Jack (Y) *The Importance of Being Earnest*
   (c) Lucky (X) to Pozzo (Y) *Waiting for Godot*
   (d) Man (X) to the Woman (Y) *The Waste Land*

45. Which of these Greek plays was a source for *The Winter's Tale?*
   (a) *Iphigeneia at Aulis*
   (b) *Alcestis*
   (c) *Medea*
   (d) *Iphigeneia at Tauris*

46. Sweet is the lore which nature brings;
   Our meddling intellect
   Mis-shapes the beauteous forms of things:
   We murder to dissect.
   —Wordsworth

   Which of the following best summarises the speaker's position?
   (a) Nature is incomplete without a human witness to attest to its beauty.
   (b) Human endeavours will succeed only if the laws of nature are taken into account.
   (c) Nature yields a pleasure superior to that derived from intrusive human inquiry.
   (d) The flaws inherent in human nature are also evident in the natural world.

47. (A) Jean Baudrillard tells us that postmodern societies are marked by simulacra.
   (B) By simulacra he means non-representations of reality.
   (C) Simulacra artificially produce a mediated world masquerading as authenticity.
   (D) It was not Jean Baudrillard but his interpreters who coined the term "simulacra".

   Which of the above statements are true?
   (a) (B), (C) and (D) (b) (A) and (C)
   (c) (C) and (D) (d) (B) and (C)

48. Which of the following is correct as the natural order of language acquisition?

(a) Listening - Reading - Speaking - Writing
(b) Writing - Reading - Listening - Speaking
(c) Listening - Speaking - Reading - Writing
(d) Reading - Listening - Speaking - Writing

49. Which of the following statements is not true regarding the poems of Derek Walcott?
(a) His poem "Goats and Monkeys" has an epigraph from Shakespeare's *Othello*
(b) In "The Sadhu of Couva" Walcott refers to Diwali, Hanuman and the Ramayana
(c) Walcott has written a poem entitled "Jean Rhys"
(d) In "A Far Cry From Africa" Walcott depicts his divided loyalties in the context of the Changuna Uprising

50. In Shakespeare's time who owned the rights to a theatrical script?
(a) the playwright(s)
(b) the patron of the acting company
(c) the printer
(d) the acting company

51. Which of the following sentences uses more than three cohesive devices?
(a) At that time a person could drive for miles without seeing a house.
(b) All of them could recite the poem yesterday.
(c) You can use a pencil, though not a pen, to write your name.
(d) As soon as Mohan entered the stadium the crowd cheered.

52. Match the columns:
**Indian Text**
(A) *The Love of Kamarupa and Kamalata*
(B) *Ramayana*
(C) *Upanishads*
(D) *Abhijnan Sakuntalam*
**English Translator**
(i) William Jones
(ii) Nathaniel Halhed
(iii) W. Franklin
(iv) T.H. Griffith

| | (A) | (B) | (C) | (D) |
|---|---|---|---|---|
| (a) | (iv) | (iii) | (ii) | (i) |
| (b) | (iii) | (iv) | (ii) | (i) |
| (c) | (ii) | (iv) | (iii) | (i) |
| (d) | (iv) | (ii) | (iii) | (i) |

53. Which of the following is not true of the New Bolt Report, "The Teaching of English in England"?
(a) It was commissioned in 1919.
(b) It urged the teaching of the national literature.
(c) It proposed the teaching of English Literature at the university level.
(d) It aimed at uniting divided classes after the war.

54. This revenge tragedy opens with the long soliloquy of the protagonist carrying the skull of his poisoned fiancé and swearing vengeance for the old Duke who has committed the vicious act. Identify the play.
(a) *The Spanish Tragedy*
(b) *The Revenger's Tragedy*
(c) *The Duchess of Malfi*
(d) *The Changeling*

55. What did Anthony Trollope seek to criticize through the character Mr. Slope?
(a) Methodism
(b) Low Churchmen
(c) High Church doctrine
(d) Anglicanism

56. "To refer to symbols as 'Lacanian symbols', to dub self-doubt as 'Lacanian self-doubt', and to call reflections in a

mirror 'Lacanian reflections' is not to read the mind from a perspective informed by Lacan. Nor do parenthetical references to Barthes' hermeneutic code and Foucault's analysis of sexual discourse constitute an interpretation necessarily different from that of traditional humanist criticism".

The author of the passage is objecting to critics who

(a) try to force a parallel between recent critical approaches and traditional humanist criticism.
(b) decoratively apply the names and terminology of recent critical theories without employing the methodology.
(c) attempt to reduce the study of literature to a hunt for coded messages and symbols.
(d) stubbornly maintain a traditional notion of the role of criticism while refusing to acknowledge new theoretical developments.

57. Peter Ackroyd's first novel, *The Great Fire of London*, picks up the historical echoes and artfully deploys a Dickens novel as an intertext. Identify the source Dickens text.
(a) *Great Expectations*
(b) *Little Dorrit*
(c) *Martin Chuzzlewit*
(d) *Old Curiosity Shop*

58. Which of the following plays by Henrik Ibsen deals with the perils that await the emancipated woman in a society which is not ready to accept her?
(a) *A Doll's House*
(b) *An Enemy of the People*
(c) *Hedda Gabler*
(d) *Pillars of Society*

59. "Yet it is the masculine values that prevail", observed a famous writer "Speaking cruelly", she continued, "football and sport are 'important', the worship of fashion, the buying of clothes 'trivial'."

Name the author and the text.
(a) Mary Wollstonecraft, *A Vindication of the Rights of Woman*
(b) Audre Lorde "Age, Race, Class..."
(c) Virginia Woolf, *A Room of One's Own*
(d) Jean Rhys, *After Leaving Mr. Mackenzie*

60. According to coleridge, the "secondary imagination" "dissolves, diffuses, _______, in order to recreate...".

Choose the right word for the blank.
(a) disintegrates (b) dissipates
(c) displaces (d) dissociates

61. Beginning 1996, an Indian publisher commenced the publication of a series of modern Indian novels in English translation. By 2003, it had published eighty novels of repute from almost all Indian languages. Identify the publisher.
(a) Asia Publishing House
(b) Macmillan India
(c) Jaico
(d) Arnold Heinemann

62. William Dunbar's *Lament for the Makers* is about
(a) kings (b) priests
(c) poets (d) peasants

63. Who among the following protagonists of Thomas Hardy feels his lot as akin to Job's?
(a) Clym Yeo bright (b) Angel Clare
(c) Jude (d) Troy

64. Edward Brathwaite's poem "Calypso" assumes that you are familiar with
(a) the business of Calypso during the Middle Passage
(b) the West Indian music in syncopated African rhythm

(c) the folk ways and mores of Trinidadian merchants
(d) the operatic performance of Banjos

65. Which of the modern plays by a British playwright actually puts Shakespeare as character on stage?
(a) Edward Bond's *Bingo*
(b) Harold Pinter's *Mountain Language*
(c) Terence Rattigan's *Inspector calls*
(d) Joe Orton's *Loot*

66. A famous challenge to the Neoclassical tenets of form and reason in aesthetic considerations came from Edmund Burke. His work was titled:
(a) *An Enquiry into the Philosophical Origin of, Our Ideas of the sublime and the Beautiful*
(b) *Philosophical Enquiry into the Origin of Our Ideas of the Sublime and the Beautiful*
(c) *An Enquiry into the Philosophical Origin of, Our Ideas of the Beautiful and the Sublime*
(d) *Philosophical Enquiry into Our Original, Ideas of the Beautiful and the Sublime*

67. Match the following

**List-A**
(A) The Grammar-Translation Method
(B) The Direct Method
(C) Total Physical Response
(D) The Natural Approach

**List-B**
(i) comprehensible input
(ii) strategic use of mother tongue
(iii) shuns mother tongue
(iv) oral input

| | (A) | (B) | (C) | (D) |
|---|---|---|---|---|
| (a) | (ii) | (iii) | (iv) | (i) |
| (b) | (ii) | (iv) | (i) | (iii) |
| (c) | (iv) | (ii) | (i) | (iii) |
| (d) | (iii) | (i) | (ii) | (iv) |

68. Which of these works by Indian writers does not have the Naxalite Movement as a background?
(a) *Mother of 1084*
(b) *The Lives of Others*
(c) *The Shadow Lines*
(d) *The Lowland*

69. "So when the last and dreadful hour
This crumbling pageant shall devour,
The trumpet shall be heard on high,
The dead shall live, the living die,
And music shall untune the sky."

These are the closing lines of a famous poem.

Identify the poem.
(a) *Il penseroso*
(b) "Song for St. Cecilia's Day"
(c) "The Good - Morrow"
(d) "Song: The Year's at the Spring"

70. This eighteenth-century English poem imitates spenser in stanza form and in allegorical narrative: passers-by are lured by an enchanter with promises of ease, luxury, and aesthetic delight, then consigned to a dungeon where they languish in apathy and impotence until the Knight of Arts and Industry dissolves the spell. Identify the poem.
(a) *The Vanity of Human Wishes*
(b) *The Seasons*
(c) *The Castle of Indolence*
(d) *The Task*

71. Which of the following statements on the Hogarth press is false?
(a) The Hogarth press was founded in 1917 by Leonard and Virginia Woolf
(b) Its location was their home, called Hogarth House
(c) The press was solely devoted to publishing international classics in translation

(d) The press published translations of Gorky, Chekhov, Tolstoy, Dostoevsky, Rilke, Svevo and others

**Read the below passage and answer questions 72 to 75 that follow:**

THE ANTIGUA THAT I knew, the Antigua in which I grew up, is not the Antigua you, a tourist, would see now. That Antigua no longer exists. That Antigua no longer exists partly for the usual reason, the passing of time, and partly because the bad-minded people who used to rule over it, the English, no longer do so. (But the English have become such a pitiful lot these days, with hardly any idea what to do with themselves now that they no longer have one quarter of the earth's human population bowing and scraping before them. They don't seem to know that this empire business was all wrong and they should, at least, be wearing sackcloth and ashes in token penance of the wrongs committed, the irrevocableness of their bad deeds, for no natural disaster imaginable could equal the harm they did. Actual death might have been better. And so all this fuss over empire—what went wrong here, what went wrong there—always makes me quite crazy, for I can say to them what went wrong: they should never have left their home, their precious England, a place they loved so much, a place they had to leave but could never forget. And so everywhere they went they turned it into England; and everybody they met they turned English. But no place could ever really be England, and nobody who did not look exactly like them would ever be English, so you can imagine the destruction of people and land that came from that. The English hate each other and they hate England, and the reason they are so miserable now is that they have no place else to go and nobody else to feel better than.)

72. To whom is the passage directly addressed?
    (a) Readers (b) Non-antiguans
    (c) Tourists (d) The English
73. The English feel extremely miserable because:
    (a) Their political supremacy is over
    (b) They do not have anyone else to feel superior to
    (c) They have been reduced to a state of non-entity
    (d) They have no lands to colonise
74. Do the British realize that colonizing countries was a bad practice, according to the narrator?
    (a) Yes; they do
    (b) No; they don't
    (c) The narrator is rather unsure they do
    (d) The narrator is rather unsure they don't
75. Which of the following best describes the content of the extract?
    (a) The speaker fervently desires better understanding between the English and the colonized people in post colonial times
    (b) The speaker is interested in nostalgic tours of emigre antiguans to their childhood home
    (c) The speaker whose childhood was spent in Antigua reports the great change currently evident in the pungent irony
    (d) The speaker is making a case for the penance of the English, the erstwhile rulers of Antigua.

## ANSWERS

| 1. (a) | 2. (c) | 3. (d) | 4. (c) | 5. (b) | 6. (c) |
|---|---|---|---|---|---|
| 7. (c) | 8. (c) | 9. (b) | 10. (c) | 11. (b) | 12. (c) |

| | | | | | |
|---|---|---|---|---|---|
| 13. (c) | 14. (c) | 15. (b) | 16. (d) | 17. (b) | 18. (b) |
| 19. (b) | 20. (c) | 21. (c) | 22. (b) | 23. (c) | 24. (c) |
| 25. (d) | 26. (d) | 27. (a) | 28. (d) | 29. (c) | 30. (d) |
| 31. (b) | 32. (b) | 33. (c) | 34. (c) | 35. (d) | 36. (a) |
| 37. (a) | 38. (a) | 39. (a) | 40. (d) | 41. (d) | 42. (a) |
| 43. (d) | 44. (b) | 45. (b) | 46. (c) | 47. (b) | 48. (c) |
| 49. (d) | 50. (d) | 51. (c) | 52. (b) | 53. (c) | 54. (b) |
| 55. (b) | 56. (b) | 57. (b) | 58. (c) | 59. (c) | 60. (b) |
| 61. (b) | 62. (c) | 63. (c) | 64. (b) | 65. (a) | 66. (b) |
| 67. (a) | 68. (c) | 69. (b) | 70. (c) | 71. (c) | 72. (c) |
| 73. (b) | 74. (c) | 75. (c) | | | |

23

# NET Examination Paper II, June 2016 with Answers

1. Which British University figures in William Wordsworth's *Prelude*?
   (a) Durham (b) Glasgow
   (c) Cambridge (d) Oxford
2. Who is the author of *A Woman Killed with Kindness*?
   (a) John Marston
   (b) Thomas Middleton
   (c) John Fletcher
   (d) Thomas Heywood
3. In William Congreve's *The Way of the World* identify the speaker of the line: "One's cruelty is one's power, and when one parts with one's cruelty, one parts with one's power."
   (a) Mirabell (b) Witwoud
   (c) Millamant (d) Mincing
4. T.S. Eliot found spiritual support in
   (a) Christianity (b) Hinduism
   (c) Buddhism (d) Judaism
5. By what name is Gulliver known in Brobdingnag?
   (a) Grildrig (b) Glumdalclitch
   (c) Splacknuck (d) Mannikin
6. Who among the following was born in India?
   (a) Paul Scott (b) Lawrence Durrell
   (c) E.M. Forster (d) V.S. Naipaul
7. What metaphor does Edmund Spenser employ (*Faerie Queene* Book 1 Canto 12) to frame his tale and to describe the relationship between the tale and its readers?
   (a) That of a caravan of lost souls, traversing a desert.
   (b) That of a stagecoach, which picks up diverse passengers along the way.
   (c) That of a ship filled with jolly mariners.
   (d) That of a riderless horse, following his own direction.
8. Who among the following is not associated with Russian formalism?
   (a) Roman Jakobson
   (b) Georges Poulet
   (c) Boris Eichenbaum
   (d) Victor Shklovsky
9. Which character in Dickens keeps on hoping that "something will turn up"?
   (a) Barkis
   (b) Micawber
   (c) Uriah Heep
   (d) Miss Havisham
10. What is the name of the boat that rescues Ishmael in Herman Melville's *Moby Dick*?
    (a) Pequod (b) Rachel
    (c) Hagar (d) Sphinx
11. *Northanger Abbey* is a parody of the _____ romance.

(a) Oriental (b) French
(c) Gothic (d) Popular

12. Who among the following authors were greatly influenced by Thomas Carlyle's writings?
I. Charles Dickens
II. Elizabeth Gaskell
III. Emily Bronte
IV. Oscar Wilde

The right combination according to the code is:
(a) I and II (b) II and III
(c) I and IV (d) I and III

13. Which of the following is another term to describe "art for art's sake"?
(a) Aestheticism (b) Didacticism
(c) Realism (d) Neo-realism

14. The statement that there are "none so credulous as infidels" is an illustration of
(a) Oxymoron (b) Antithesis
(c) Paradox (d) Metonomy

15. Who narrates *Heart of Darkness*?
(a) Marlow
(b) Director of Companies
(c) Kurtz
(d) An unnamed narrator

16. *The Mistakes of a Night* is the subtitle of
(a) *The Conscious Lovers*
(b) *The Good Natur'd Man*
(c) *She Stoops to Conquer*
(d) *The Rivals*

17. Identify the first novel written by Patrick White:
(a) *The Living and the Dead*
(b) *The Tree of Man*
(c) *Happy Valley*
(d) *The Aunt's Story*

18. In *King Lear* for what reason does Kent assume a disguise?
(a) To continue to serve Lear, though Lear has banished him.
(b) To spy on Edmund.
(c) To antagonize Goneril and Regan.
(d) To revenge upon Lear for banishing him.

19. What is a feminine rhyme?
(a) A rhyme on two syllables in which the last syllable is unstressed.
(b) A rhyme on two syllables.
(c) A rhyme on three syllables.
(d) A poem in which every third syllable rhymes.

20. Identify two of the following written by Christopher Fry:
I. *French Without Tears*
II. *The Lady's Not for Burning*
III. *Venus Observed*
IV. *The Deep Blue Sea*

The right combination according to the code is:
(a) II and III (b) I and III
(c) II and IV (d) I and IV

21. In "Tradition and Individual Talent", according to T.S. Eliot, the term "Traditional" usually means
(a) something positive
(b) something negative
(c) something historical
(d) something old

22. Who of the following is a Cavalier poet?
(a) George Herbert (b) John Donne
(c) Robert Herrick (d) Andrew Marvell

23. Which of the following is *not* Jacques Derrida's work?
(a) *Of Spirit: Heidegger and the Question*
(b) *The Transcendence of the Ego*
(c) *Of Grammatology*
(d) *The Work of Mourning*

24. In *Paradise Lost* which character narrates the story of the making of Eve from a rib in Adam's side?
(a) Adam (b) Eve
(c) Raphael (d) God

25. A.S. Byatt's *Possession* attempts the imitation of the work of two Victorian poets, loosely based on:
I. Alfred Tennyson
II. Robert Browning
III. Christina Rossetti
IV. William Morris

The right combination according to the code is:
(a) I and II (b) II and IV
(c) II and III (d) III and IV

26. *The Dark Lady of the Sonnets* is a short comedy by
(a) Bernard Shaw (b) W.B. Yeats
(c) J.M. Synge (d) John Osborne

27. John Milton's description of gold as a "precious bane" (*Paradise Lost*, Book II) is best described as
(a) a dactyl (b) an oxymoron
(c) enjambment (d) zeugma

28. There is a play on the name of Machiavelli in the prologue to Christopher Marlowe's
(a) *Doctor Faustus*
(b) *The Jew of Malta*
(c) *Tamburlaine, the Great*
(d) *Edward II*

29. Shakespeare famously neglects to observe Aristotle's rules concerning the three dramatic unities, and Samuel Johnson undertakes to defend Shakespeare from these criticisms in his *Preface to Shakespeare*. Which of the Aristotelian dramatic unities does Johnson believe Shakespeare to observe most successfully?
(a) Time
(b) Place
(c) Action
(d) Johnson does not feel that the Aristotelian dramatic unities are important

30. Who among the following was praised and patronized as a "Ploughman Poet"?
(a) John Clare (b) George Crabbe
(c) Robert Burns (d) Walter Scott

31. Which novel of Doris Lessing ends with a projection forward in time after a devastating atomic war?
(a) *The Grass is Singing*
(b) *The Golden Notebook*
(c) *The Four-Gated City*
(d) *A Proper Marriage*

32. Name the dominant meter of the following quatrain:

The curfew tolls the knell of parting day,
The lowing herd winds slowly o'er the lea,
The plowman homeward plods his weary way,
And leaves the world to darkness and to me.

(a) Iambic Hexameter
(b) Trochaic Pentameter
(c) Iambic Pentameter
(d) Terza Rima

33. Which two novels of Buchi Emecheta provide a fictionalized portrait of poor, young Nigerian women struggling to bring up their children in London?
I. *The Slave Girl*
II. *The Joys of Motherhood*
III. *Second Class Citizen*
IV. *In the Ditch*

The right combination according to the code is:
(a) I and II (b) II and III
(c) III and IV (d) I and IV

34. In John Bunyan's *Pilgrim's Progress* who keeps Christian's head above water in the River of Death?
(a) Hopeful (b) Helpful
(c) Faithful (d) Cheerful

35. *Childe Harold's Pilgrimage* is a
(a) religious allegory (b) fairy tale
(c) long poem (d) Utopian novel

36. In Thomas More's *Utopia* which of the following leisure pastimes is not a favourite among Utopians?
(a) Music (b) Public lectures
(c) Conversation (d) Dicing and cards

37. Which of the following statements does not describe Michel Foucault's position?
(a) In Foucault's work sexuality is literally written on the body.
(b) Power operates through discourse.
(c) There is connection between power and knowledge.
(d) Where there is power, it is possible to find resistance.

38. In which year did the Great Exhibition take place?
(a) 1851 (b) 1857
(c) 1861 (d) 1871

39. When Fidessa says, "O but I fear the fickle freakes ..../ Of fortune false, and oddes of armes in field" (*Faerie Queene*, Book I, Canto 5), this is a fine example of
(a) Alliteration (b) Allegory
(c) Assonance (d) Antithesis

40. Match the work with author:
**List I**
I. "The Excursion" II. "Christabel"
III. *Milton* IV. *Queen Mab*
**List II**
A. S.T. Coleridge
B. P.B. Shelley
C. William Wordsworth
D. William Blake

| | I | II | III | IV |
|---|---|---|---|---|
| (a) | C | A | B | D |
| (b) | C | A | D | B |
| (c) | B | C | A | D |
| (d) | B | A | C | D |

41. Which of the following phrases is not found in Thomas Gray's "Elegy written in a Country Churchyard"?
(a) "Far from the madding crowd"
(b) "A youth to Fortune and Fame unknown"
(c) "Full many a flower is born to blush unseen"
(d) "All nature is but art, unknown to thee"

42. Robert Browning's "Rabbi Ben Ezra" is a defence of
(a) youth against old age
(b) old age against youth
(c) power against knowledge
(d) knowledge against power

43. In Geoffrey Chaucer's *Canterbury Tales*, the pilgrims, like the medieval society of which they are a part, are made up of three social groups or "estates". What are the three estates?
(a) Nobility, church and commoners
(b) Royalty, nobility and peasantry
(c) Royalists, republicans and peasants
(d) Country, city and commons

44. Which novel of Toni Morrison tells the wrenching story of a protagonist who murders her child rather than to allow him/her to live as a slave?
(a) *Sula* (b) *Tar Baby*
(c) *Song of Solomon* (d) *Beloved*

45. Who among the following translated Homer?
(a) Thomas Gray
(b) Samuel Johnson
(c) Oliver Goldsmith
(d) Alexander Pope

46. Shyam Selvadurai's *Funny Boy* is a
    (a) Picaresque novel
    (b) Epistolary novel
    (c) Diary novel
    (d) Coming-of-age novel
47. When was the English ban on James Joyce's *Ulysses* lifted?
    (a) 1924 (b) 1945
    (c) 1936 (d) 1962
48. Who among the following is not an imagist?
    (a) Ezra Pound (b) W.B. Yeats
    (c) Amy Lowell (d) T.E. Hulme
49. Thomas Carew's *Poems* appeared in print in 1640 and contain a variety of amorous addresses to and reflections on, a fictional mistress known as
    (a) Celia (b) Julia
    (c) Anne (d) Melanie
50. Match the novelists with their work:
    I. William Golding A. *Grimus*
    II. Salman Rushdie B. *Hawksmoor*
    III. Graham Swift C. *Darkness Visible*
    IV. Peter Ackroyd D. *Waterland*

| | I | II | III | IV |
|---|---|---|---|---|
| (a) | D | A | C | B |
| (b) | C | A | D | B |
| (c) | B | C | A | D |
| (d) | B | A | C | D |

## ANSWERS

| | | | | | |
|---|---|---|---|---|---|
| 1. (c) | 2. (d) | 3. (c) | 4. (a) | 5. (a) | 6. (b) |
| 7. (c) | 8. (b) | 9. (b) | 10. (b) | 11. (c) | 12. (a) |
| 13. (a) | 14. (c) | 15. (d) | 16. (c) | 17. (c) | 18. (a) |
| 19. (a) | 20. (a) | 21. (b) | 22. (c) | 23. (b) | 24. (a) |
| 25. (c) | 26. (a) | 27. (b) | 28. (b) | 29. (c) | 30. (c) |
| 31. (c) | 32. (c) | 33. (c) | 34. (a) | 35. (c) | 36. (d) |
| 37. (a) | 38. (a) | 39. (a) | 40. (b) | 41. (d) | 42. (b) |
| 43. (a) | 44. (d) | 45. (d) | 46. (d) | 47. (c) | 48. (b) |
| 49. (a) | 50. (b) | | | | |

24

# English Paper III, June 2016 with Answers

1. Which of W.M. Thackeray's novel's closing sentence is this?
   "Which of us is happy in this world? Which of us has his desire? Or, having it, is satisfied?"
   (a) *The History of Henry Esmond*
   (b) *Vanity Fair*
   (c) *The Luck of Barry Lyndon*
   (d) *Pendennis*
2. Why does Lovewit in Ben Jonson's play *The Alchemist* leave his house, setting the stage for his servant Face, alongwith Subtle, a fake alchemist to fleece people?
   (a) To visit his father who left him long ago.
   (b) To find out new sources of minting money.
   (c) Because of an epidemic of plague.
   (d) To make a pilgrimage.
3. By the end of the nineteen fifties novelists like Stan Barstow, Sid Chaplin, Alan Sillitoe and David Storey were routinely lumped together as representatives of "Kitchen-sink realism". Who in 1954 wrote the article "The Kitchen Sink", calling attention to the gritty and direct realism?
   (a) Martin Harrison (b) Stan Smith
   (c) David Sylvester (d) Philip Callow
4. Which of the following is not an allegorical character in the play *Everyman*?
   (a) Kindred (b) Strength
   (c) Christian (d) Discretion
5. Who among the following translators is notable as the first translator of *Bhagavad Gita* into English?
   (a) Charles Wilkins
   (b) Nathaniel Halhead
   (c) William Jones
   (d) Barbara Stoler Miller
6. In *Biographia Literaria* S.T. Coleridge defines the imagination as the faculty by which
   (a) the soul perceives the phenomenal diversity of the universe.
   (b) the soul perceives the spiritual unity of the universe.
   (c) the mind acquires images by its associative power.
   (d) the mind separates images by its discriminatory power.
7. Why do the Houyhnhnms have so few words in their language?
   (a) Their wants and passions are fewer than human wants and passions, and they need fewer words.
   (b) They consider language to be morally corrupt and prefer to remain silent.
   (c) They find speech difficult because they are horses.
   (d) They prefer action to words.

8. Identify the title of A.D. Hope's first published book of poems.
   (a) *Native Companions*
   (b) *The Wandering Islands*
   (c) *A Midsummer Eve's Dream*
   (d) *The Cave and the Spring*
9. Which of the following is an incorrect assumption in language teaching?
   (a) Learners acquire language by trying to use it in real situations.
   (b) Learners' first language plays an important role in learning.
   (c) Language teaching should have a focus on communicative activities.
   (d) Language teaching should give importance to writing rather than speech.
10. The Bhasmasura myth is used in R.K. Narayan's __________.
   (a) *The Man-Eater of Malgudi*
   (b) *The Financial Expert*
   (c) *The English Teacher*
   (d) *The World of Nagaraj*
11. During the Middle English period, many words were borrowed from two languages:
   I. Celtic II. Latin
   III. French IV. Old Norse

   The right combination according to the code is:
   (a) I and II (b) II and III
   (c) II and IV (d) III and IV
12. Select the right chronological sequence of the date of Bible translations.
   (a) King James Version – Tyndale – Revised Standard Version – Holman Christian Standard Bible
   (b) Revised Standard Version – King James Version – Tyndale – Holman Christian Standard Bible
   (c) Tyndale – King James Version – Revised Standard Version – Holman Christian Standard Version
   (d) Revised Standard Version – Holman Christian Standard Bible – King James Version – Tyndale
13. The last word in James Joyce's *Finnegans Wake* is
   (a) No (b) The
   (c) Morning! (d) Jaysus
14. **Assertion (A):** In so far as we are taught how to read, what we engage are not texts but paradigms.

   **Reason (R):** We appropriate meaning from a text according to what we need or desire, or, in other words, according to the critical assumptions or predispositions that we bring to it.
   (a) Both (A) and (R) are true and (R) is the correct explanation of (A).
   (b) Both (A) and (R) are true but (R) is not the correct explanation of (A).
   (c) (A) is true, but (R) is false.
   (d) (A) is false, but (R) is true.
15. One of the key terms in Michel Foucault's work is discourse. This is best described as
   (a) the power of persuasion in all articulations.
   (b) the selective language powerful people use.
   (c) conceptual frameworks which enable some mode of thought and deny or severely constrain certain others.
   (d) the ability to suggest transcendental levels of meaning in an utterance.
16. The narrators of *Oroonoko* are:
   I. a woman
   II. Oroonoko

III. a purported eyewitness of the events described

IV. Trefy

The right combination according to the code is:

(a) I and IV (b) I and III
(c) II and III (d) II and IV

17. Which character of Henrik Ibsen speaks the following lines: "The life of a normally constituted idea is generally about seventeen or eighteen years, at the most twenty?"
   (a) Nora in *A Doll's House*
   (b) Dr. Thomas Stockman in *An Enemy of the People*
   (c) John Rosmer in *Rosmerscholm*
   (d) Oswald in *Ghosts*

18. In literary studies structuralism promotes
   (a) new interpretations of literary works.
   (b) the view that literature is one signifying practice among others.
   (c) a systematic account of literary archetypes.
   (d) unstable structures of systems of signification.

19. P.B. Shelley's *Julian and Maddalo* is a conversation between Julian and Count Maddalo. Who do these two characters represent?
   (a) Julian represents Keats and Count Maddalo, Byron
   (b) Julian represents Shelley and Count Maddalo, Byron
   (c) Julian represents Shelley and Count Maddalo, William Godwin
   (d) Julian represents Mary Shelley and Count Maddalo, William Godwin

20. What is practical criticism?
   (a) The close analysis of literary texts in such a way as to bring out their political meaning.
   (b) A movement which wished to make literary criticism more relevant.
   (c) The close analysis of poems without taking account of any external information.
   (d) The study of ambiguity.

21. Which of the following does not describe some of the practices/beliefs of feminist literary criticism?
   (a) Feminist criticism recuperates female writers ignored by the canon.
   (b) Feminist literary critics offer a criticism of the construction of gender.
   (c) Feminist literary critics argue that the traditional canon is justified.
   (d) Feminist literary critics mostly reject the essentialising of 'male' and 'female'.

22. Which work by Franz Kafka is also known as *The Man Who Disappeared*?
   (a) *The Castle*
   (b) "Metamorphosis"
   (c) "In the Penal Colony"
   (d) *Amerika*

23. Towards the end of Evelyn Waugh's *A Handful of Dust* the protagonist Tony Last is trapped in the jungle by the calculating crazy Mr. Todd who forces him to read and reread the novels of a particular author. Waugh has also written a short story dealing with Tony's singular experience in the jungle. Who is the novelist referred to and what is the title of the short story?
   (a) Rudyard Kipling, "Revisiting the Jungle"
   (b) Joseph Conrad, "Shadows of the Dark Trees"
   (c) Charles Dickens, "The Man Who Liked Dickens"
   (d) Henry Fielding, "Tom Jones's Journey into the Wild"

24. At the beginning of the Restoration period, there was a seismic shift in the social, political and religious attitudes of the English. Which of the following statements best describes that shift?
    (a) England shifted from an aristocratic Catholic monarchy to a parliamentary democracy.
    (b) England shifted from an atheistic oligarchy to a deistic squirearchy.
    (c) England shifted from a Republican Puritan Commonwealth to an aristocratic Anglican monarchy.
    (d) England shifted from a parliamentary democracy to an aristocratic Catholic tyranny.

25. The Grammar-Translation Method in English Language Teaching stresses on
    (a) Fluency (b) Accuracy
    (c) Appropriateness (d) Listening Skill

26. "[They] then heaved out,/ away with a will in their wood-wreathed ship." This line describing Beowulf's departure from Geatland, is typical of the poem's form and Old English poetic technique because
    I. it features alliteration
    II. it rhymes
    III. it features onomotopoeia
    IV. it has four strong stresses
    The right combination according to the code is
    (a) I and II (b) II and III
    (c) I and IV (d) II and IV

27. Identify the poet, translator, publisher and essayist who founded a press in the 1950s called Writers' Workshop and provided a publishing outlet for Indians writing in English.
    (a) P. Lal
    (b) A.K. Mehrotra
    (c) Vinay Dharwadkar
    (d) A.K. Ramanujan

28. Antagonised by what he considered to be the provinciality of the Lake Poets, Byron wrote the preface to which of his works as a rebuke to Wordsworth's own introduction to "The Thorn"?
    (a) *The Prisoner of Chillon*
    (b) *Don Juan*
    (c) *Childe Harold's Pilgrimage*
    (d) *The Vision of Judgement*

29. Which of the following theoretical movements claimed that "the device is the only hero of literature"?
    (a) Russian formalism
    (b) New Criticism
    (c) Phenomenology
    (d) Deconstruction

30. In Jean Francois Lyotard's works the term "language games", sometimes also called "phrase regimens" denotes:
    I. the multiplicity of communities of meaning.
    II. the breakdown of communities of meaning.
    III. the innumerable and incommensurable separate systems in which meanings are produced.
    IV. the singular system in which meanings are dispersed and displaced.
    The right combination according to the code is:
    (a) I and IV (b) I and III
    (c) II and IV (d) II and III

31. What part of Canada is Alice Munro most famous for depicting?
    (a) Vancouver (b) Montreal
    (c) Ontario (d) Quebec

32. In John Gay's *Beggar's Opera* what is Peachum's occupation?
    I. Pimp
    II. Lawyer

III. Fencer of stolen goods, and master of a gang of thieves
IV. Impeader of less powerful criminals

The right combination according to the code is:

(a) III & IV (b) II & III
(c) I & IV (d) II & IV

33. In the opening stanza of "Song of Myself", Whitman begins his spiritual awakening at the age of ______.
(a) 37 (b) 15
(c) 24 (d) 61

34. In which of the following poems does Tennyson describe and condemn the spirit of aestheticism whose sole religion is the worship of beauty and of knowledge for their own sake and which ignores human responsibility and obligations of one's fellowmen?
(a) "The Princess"
(b) "The Lady of Shalott"
(c) "The Palace of Art"
(d) "Tithonus"

35. Luigi Pirandello's *Six Characters in Search of an Author* deliberately blurs the boarder lines between the world of the theatre and the world of 'real life' by carefully chiselled dialogues like:
"Don't you feel the ground beneath your feet as you reflect that this 'you' which you feel today, all this present reality of yours, is destined to seem a mere illusion to you tomorrow?" Who is the speaker? Who is it addressed to?
(a) Stepdaughter to Father
(b) Father to Stage Manager
(c) Stage Manager to Director
(d) Mother to Director

36. In a poem in memory of Major Robert Gregory, Lady Gregory's son, W.B. Yeats mentions an Irish writer who had found his inspiration "In a most desolate stony place" that he came "Towards nightfall upon a race/ passionate and simple like his heart." Who is the writer?
(a) J.M. Barrie
(b) J.M. Synge
(c) Isaac Bickerstaffe
(d) Thomas More

37. Jacques Derrida's work received some criticism from analytical philosophers. Who below was a critic of Derrida?
(a) John Searle
(b) Jean-Francois Lyotard
(c) Emmanuel Levinas
(d) Paul de Man

38. Who among the following bought and renovated the house of the Anglican poet, George Herbert, near Salisbury, England, in 1996?
(a) Daljit Nagra (b) Vikram Seth
(c) Amitava Kumar (d) Arundhati Roy

39. Which pair of novels by Anita Desai take as their subject the suppression and oppression of Indian women?
I. *Where Shall We Go This Summer*?
II. *The Zigzag Way*
III. *Cry, The Peacock*
IV. *Baumgartner's Bombay*

The right combination according to the code is:

(a) I and II (b) I and III
(c) II and III (d) III and IV

40. From among the following identify the two Indian English authors who received appreciation and encouragement from their British counterparts:
I. R.K. Narayan, Graham Greene
II. Nirad C. Chaudhuri, Evelyn Waugh
III. Mulk Raj Anand, E.M. Forster
IV. Raja Rao, Iris Murdoch

The right combination according to the code is:

(a) I and II (b) II and IV
(c) I and III (d) III and IV

41. Match the character with the work:

I. Count Fosco II. Margaret
III. Lucy Snowe IV. Maggie Tulliver

A. *Villette*
B. *Adam Bede*
C. *The Woman in White*
D. *North or South*

| Codes: | I | II | III | IV |
|---|---|---|---|---|
| (a) | C | D | A | B |
| (b) | D | C | A | B |
| (c) | C | A | D | B |
| (d) | C | A | B | D |

42. This poet was accidently killed in Burma by a pistol shot in 1944. His posthumously published collection of poems *Ha! Ha! Among the Trumpets* is divided into three sections.
The first section describes a tense, waiting England and the second the voyage to the East. In the third section he uncomfortably comes to terms with the alien contours, the harsh light and the dry wastes of India as evident in poems like "The Maratta Ghats", "Indian Day" and "Observation Post: Forward Area". Who is the poet?

(a) Keith Douglas (b) Sidney Keyes
(c) David Gascoyne (d) Alun Lewis

43. As Adam and Eve leave Paradise, "hand in hand with wand'ring steps and slow" (Book XII, *Paradise Lost*) what is their consolation?

(a) They are comforted by their love for one another.
(b) They are comforted by their foreknowledge of the coming of Christ as Redeemer of mankind.
(c) They are comforted by God, who travels before them in the form of a pillar of fire.
(d) They are comforted by the angel, who holds each of them by the hand.

44. In *An Essay of Dramatic Poesy* to whom does Dryden refer with the phrase "he needed not the spectacles of books to read Nature"?

(a) Ben Jonson
(b) Ovid
(c) William Shakespeare
(d) Geoffrey Chaucer

45. Emily Dickinson's use of "open form" or "free verse" is comparable to her contemporary American poet,

(a) Anne Bradstreet (b) Robert Lowell
(c) Walt Whitman (d) Sylvia Plath

46. In "A Letter of the Authors" Edmund Spenser writes that two characters in *Faerie Queene* represent Queen Elizabeth. Who are they?

I. Britomart
II. Cynthia
III. Belphoebe
IV. The Faerie Queene

The right combination according to the code is:

(a) III and IV (b) I and IV
(c) I and III (d) II and III

47. Who among the following African novelists was a student of philosophy and literature in India?

(a) Nuruddin Farah
(b) Ben Okri
(c) Helon Habila
(d) Benjamin Kwakye

48. In particular William Blake was influenced by the religious writings of

I. Martin Luther
II. Jacob Boehme

III. Emanuel Swedenborg
IV. Confucious

The right combination according to the code is:

(a) I and IV (b) I and II
(c) II and III (d) III and IV

49. Which British King, having defeated the Viking invaders, consciously used the English language to create a sense of national identity and retain political control over independent countries?
(a) Alfred the Great
(b) Edward the Elder
(c) King Arthur
(d) Ethelbert of Kent

50. In "Politics and the English Language" George Orwell provides a list of rules to aid in curing the English language. What is the final rule?
(a) Never use a metaphor, simile or other figure of speech which you are used to seeing in print.
(b) Never use a long word where a short one will do.
(c) If it is possible to cut a word out, always cut it out.
(d) Break any of these rules sooner than say anything outright barbarous.

51. In his *Defence of Poesy* what is the "best and most accomplished kind of poetry" in Sidney's estimation?
(a) Heroical, or epic poetry
(b) Lyric poetry
(c) Pastoral poetry
(d) Elegiac poetry

52. Which writer of the Romantic period makes the following comment: "The poet is far from dealing only with these subtle and analogical truths. Truth of every kind belongs to him, provided it can bud into any kind of beauty, or is capable of being illustrated and impressed by poetic faculty"?
(a) Wordsworth in Preface to the *Lyrical Ballads*
(b) William Hazlitt in "On the Feeling of Immortality in Youth"
(c) Leigh Hunt in *What is Poetry*?
(d) Keats in one of his letters to his brother

53. In his poem "Whispers of Immortality" T.S. Eliot says that a dramatist "was much possessed by death/ And saw the skull beneath the skin" and a poet "knew the anguish of the marrow/ The ague of the skeleton." Who are the dramatist and the poet referred to by Eliot?
(a) Christopher Marlowe and Andrew Marvell
(b) John Webster and John Donne
(c) Seneca and Homer
(d) Thomas Kyd and Henry Vaughan

54. Functional Communicative Approach in English Language Teaching is in opposition to:
(a) Structural Approach
(b) Comprehensive Approach
(c) Translation and Grammar Method
(d) Functional Approach

55. According to Julia Kristeva, it is the eruption of the ______ within the _____ that provides the creative and innovative impulse of modern poetic language.
(a) individual, tradition
(b) specific, generic
(c) semiotic, symbolic
(d) particular, general

56. In *Crime and Punishment* which character speaks the following words. Who/what are they addressed to?
"I waited for you impatiently...all this blasted psychology is a double-edged weapon."

(a) Svidrigailov to the pistol with which he shoots himself
(b) Katherine Ivanovna to Marmeladov
(c) Porfiry Petrovich to Raskolnikov
(d) Raskolnikov to the Bible he finds in the prison cell in Siberia

57. What three Germanic tribes invaded Britons in the fifth century AD, bringing with them the roots of modern English?
(a) The Danes, Saxons and Celts
(b) The Celts, Jutes and Saxons
(c) The Saxons, Danes and Angles
(d) The Jutes, Angles and Saxons

58. Which of the following is not a part of the series of poems called *Jejuri*, written by Arun Kolatkar?
(a) "Yeshwant Rao" (b) "Chaitanya"
(c) "The Priest" (d) "An Old Man"

59. Bertolt Brecht's concept of alienation was a rejection of the idea that realism was the only mode of art a critique of capitalist society should produce. Alienation is best described as
(a) making the audience feel that they do not belong.
(b) distancing artistic conventions to prevent an emotional catharsis.
(c) scripting unnatural behaviour on stage.
(d) a rejection of capitalism or the market.

60. Ngugi wa Thiongo changed the medium of his writing from English to _______.
(a) Swahili (b) Yoruba
(c) Xhosa (d) Gikuyu

61. Which of the following ancient critics does Alexander Pope commend as exemplary in *Essay on Criticism*?
(a) Aristotle, Quintilian, Dryden, Dionysius, Horace
(b) Aristotle, Longinus, Quintilian, Durfey, Dryden
(c) Aristotle, Horace, Dionysius, Quintilian, Longinus
(d) Aristotle, Horace, Durfey, Quintilian, Longinus

62. Which of the following poems by Philip Larkin is best described as a self-elegy, anticipating the poet's death?
(a) "The Old Fools" (b) "Aubade"
(c) "Ambulances" (d) "Faith Healing"

63. In John Bunyan's *Pilgrims Progress* what is the first obstacle encountered by Christian on his progress?
(a) The Slough of Despond
(b) Vanity Fair
(c) The River of Death
(d) The Swamp of Despair

64. Identify the correct chronological sequence of publication of the four parts of *The Four Quartets*.
(a) Burnt Norton – The Dry Salvages – East Coker – Little Gidding
(b) Burnt Norton – Little Gidding – The Dry Salvages – East Coker
(c) Burnt Norton – East Coker – The Dry Salvages – Little Gidding
(d) Little Gidding – Burnt Norton – The Dry Salvages – East Coker

65. Which of the following is not true of the novels of Charles Dickens?
(a) They deal with the problems of the discontents of an urban civilization.
(b) The plots are strikingly tight-knit.
(c) They share a sense of fun and determining optimism.
(d) They incorporate elements of popular contemporary culture.

66. Published in 1604, the first monolingual English Dictionary was
(a) Nathaniel Bailey's *Universal Etymological Dictionary of the English Language*

(b) Samuel Johnson's *Dictionary of the English Language*
(c) Robert Cawdrey's *Table Alphabetical*
(d) Thomas Blount's *Glossographia*

67. Which of the following statements best describe the narrative perspective employed in Thomas More's *Utopia*?
    I. First-person narration by Raphael Hythloday
    II. Third-person narration by a narrator named Thomas More
    III. First-person narration by a narrator named Thomas More
    IV. Third-person narration by Raphael Hythloday

    The right combination according to the code is:
    (a) I and III (b) II and IV
    (c) II and III (d) I and II

68. In the opening pages of one of Thomas Mann's novels we can see space itself becoming a form of time: "Space, like time, engenders forgetfulness but it does so by setting us bodily free from our surroundings and giving us back our primitive unattached state." Which is the novel?
    (a) *Doctor Faustus*
    (b) *Death in Venice*
    (c) *The Confessions of Felix Krull*
    (d) *The Magic Mountain*

69. Match the lines with the titles of the poems:
    I. The boa-constrictor's coil/ Is a fossil
    II. My manners are tearing off heads/ The allotment of death
    III. More coiled steel than living
    IV. Time in the sea eats its tail
    A. "Thrushes"
    B. "The Jaguar"
    C. "Relic"
    D. "Hawk Roosting"

| Codes: | I | II | III | IV |
|---|---|---|---|---|
| (a) | A | D | B | C |
| (b) | B | D | A | C |
| (c) | C | D | B | A |
| (d) | D | B | C | A |

70. Which one of Joseph Conrad's novels expresses the contrast between the solidarity of shipboard life and the profound underlying loneliness of existence thus: "loneliness impenetrable and transparent, elusive and everlasting… that surrounds, envelops, clothes every human soul from the cradle to the grave, and perhaps beyond"?
    (a) *The Heart of Darkness*
    (b) *The Nigger of the Narcissus*
    (c) *Lord Jim*
    (d) *Nostromo*

71. John Dryden's two philosophico-religious poems are
    I. *Absalom and Achitophel*
    II. *A Layman's Faith*
    III. *Annus Mirabilis*
    IV. *The Hind and the Panther*

    The right combination according to the code is:
    (a) I and II (b) III and I
    (c) II and III (d) II and IV

Read the following poem and answer the questions, 72 to 75:

**Stray Cats**

They are not exactly homeless.
They are dissidents who have lost their faith in furnished interiors, morning walks, the cake and the cutlery.

When you have nine lives to live you learn to take things in your stride. You learn to stretch your body at full length and yawn at domestic fictions. And for this reason

you figure in horror films in the mandatory moment between the flash of lightning and the appearance of the ghost. The light is darkish blue and you see yourself in the iris of the burning eye. The horror is in the seeing. What you see is altered by the act of seeing. The mystery does not stop there. The seer is in turn altered by what he sees. Having known this, stray cats jump from roof to roof. They monitor the world from treetops and hold their weekly meetings in the graveyard, like wandering mendicants.

And when they walk out of the mirror of the sun and cross the crowded road in a flash, for a shining moment, they lurk in the light like a giant shadow of doubt. Ill-omens to those who cannot see beyond what they see.

72. The poem constructs its account of stray cats by way of a contrast with
    (a) wild cats (b) ominous cats
    (c) domestic cats (d) mysterious cats

73. In the overall context, what do "furnished interiors, morning walks,/ the cake and the cutlery" represent?
    (a) Ordinary life
    (b) "Domestic fictions"
    (c) "A giant shadow of doubt"
    (d) Creaturely comforts

74. The last two lines suggest that cats crossing the crowded road
    (a) is an unexceptionable superstition.
    (b) is not necessarily the ill-omen it is held out to be.
    (c) is an example of human obsession.
    (d) is indicative of the homelessness of stray cats.

75. From among the following select two words that help accentuate the enigmatic character of stray cats:
    I. Doubt II. Mandatory
    III. Faith IV. Mystery

    The right combination according to the code is:
    (a) I and II (b) I and IV
    (c) II and IV (d) III and IV

## ANSWERS

| | | | | | |
|---|---|---|---|---|---|
| 1. (b) | 2. (c) | 3. (c) | 4. (c) | 5. (a) | 6. (b) |
| 7. (a) | 8. (b) | 9. (d) | 10. (a) | 11. (b) | 12. (c) |
| 13. (b) | 14. (a) | 15. (c) | 16. (b) | 17. (b) | 18. (b) |
| 19. (b) | 20. (c) | 21. (c) | 22. (d) | 23. (c) | 24. (c) |
| 25. (b) | 26. (c) | 27. (a) | 28. (b) | 29. (a) | 30. (b) |
| 31. (c) | 32. (a) | 33. (a) | 34. (c) | 35. (b) | 36. (b) |
| 37. (a) | 38. (b) | 39. (b) | 40. (c) | 41. (a) | 42. (d) |
| 43. (b) | 44. (c) | 45. (c) | 46. (a) | 47. (a) | 48. (c) |
| 49. (a) | 50. (d) | 51. (a) | 52. (c) | 53. (b) | 54. (a) |

| | | | | | |
|---|---|---|---|---|---|
| 55. (c) | 56. (c) | 57. (d) | 58. (d) | 59. (b) | 60. (d) |
| 61. (c) | 62. (b) | 63. (a) | 64. (c) | 65. (b) | 66. (c) |
| 67. (a) | 68. (d) | 69. (b) | 70. (Z) | 71. (d) | 72. (c) |
| 73. (b) | 74. (b) | 75. (b) | | | |

Z means no option is correct.

25

# NET Examination Paper II, January 2017 with Answers

1. Identify from the following the work Nirad C. Chaudhuri called "the finest novel in the English language with an Indian theme".
   (a) *Kim*
   (b) *A Passage to India*
   (c) *Train to Pakistan*
   (d) *Private Life of an Indian Prince*
2. Who is the author of the poem "The Defence of Lucknow" dealing with the siege of Lucknow, one of the terrible incidents of the Indian Mutiny?
   (a) Rudyard Kipling
   (b) Edward Lear
   (c) Alfred Lord Tennyson
   (d) Robert Browning
3. Who among the following theorists holds that metaphor and metonymy are the two fundamental structures of language?
   (a) Ferdinand de Saussure
   (b) J.L. Austin
   (c) Roman Jakobson
   (d) Victor Shklovsky
4. From among the following, who are the Dashwood sisters in Jane Austen's *Sense and Sensibility*?
   I. Elinor    II. Marianne
   III. Mary    IV. Amanda
   The right combination according to the code is:
   (a) I and III    (b) I and II
   (c) II and III    (d) III and IV
5. Which among the following texts can be characterised as a lesbian Bildungsroman?
   (a) Angela Carter, *The Magic Toyshop*
   (b) Sylvia Plath, *The Bell Jar*
   (c) Jeanette Winterson, *Oranges Are Not the Only Fruit*
   (d) Ruth Pawar Jhabvala, *Heat and Dust*
6. Identify the correct chronological sequence of publication:
   (a) *Paradise Lost – The Advancement of Learning – An Essay Concerning Human Understanding – MacFlecknoe*
   (b) *The Advancement of Learning – An Essay Concerning Human Understanding – MacFlecknoe – Paradise Lost*
   (c) *The Advancement of Learning – Paradise Lost – MacFlecknoe – An Essay Concerning Human Understanding*
   (d) *Paradise Lost – MacFlecknoe – The Advancement of Learning – An Essay Concerning Human Understanding*
7. Poe's "The Raven" mourns the death of Poe's
   (a) lost Lenore    (b) lost Abigail
   (c) pet animal    (d) lost heritage
8. In Shakespeare's *Macbeth* who was "untimely ripped" from his mother's womb?

(a) Macbeth (b) Macduff
(c) Duncan (d) Malcolm

9. Alexander Pope revised *The Rape of the Lock* three times. In the final revision of the poem in 1717 he inserted a speech by
(a) Belinda (b) Clarissa
(c) Betty (d) Thalestris

10. Identify, from the following list, two plays written by John Webster:
I. *A Woman Killed with Kindness*
II. *The Revenger's Tragedy*
III. *The White Devil*
IV. *The Ducchess of Malfi*
The right combination according to the code is
(a) I and IV (b) II and IV
(c) III and IV (d) I and III

11. Which of the following works by David Malouf tells the story of the Roman poet, Ovid, during his exile in Tomis?
(a) *Remembering Babylon*
(b) *The Great World*
(c) *The Conversations at Curlow Creek*
(d) *An Imaginary Life*

12. In his *Defence of Poesy* which of the following works does Sidney commend as good examples of English Poesy?
I. *The Mirror of Magistrates*
II. *The Shepherd's Calendar*
III. *Lament for the Makers*
IV. *Ballad of Scottish King*
The right combination according to the code is
(a) I and III (b) I and IV
(c) I and II (d) II and III

13. Who among the following dismissed *Ulysses* as "a misfire"?
(a) Virginia Woolf (b) Wyndham Lewis
(c) E.M. Forster (d) D.H. Lawrence

14. Which of the following works Daniel Defoe offered his readers as a collection of "Strange Surprising Adventures"?
(a) *Moll Flanders*
(b) *Robinson Crusoe*
(c) *Roxana*
(d) *Captain Singleton*

15. In Charlotte Bronte's *Jane Eyre*, what does Mr. Brocklehurst accuse Jane of when he visits Lowood School?
(a) Laziness (b) Stealing
(c) Lying (d) Spying

16. William Faulkner's *As I Lay Dying* contains one of the shortest chapters in literary history. Which of these sentences is the chapter in its entirety?
(a) "For the love of God, where is my hat?"
(b) "My mother is a fish."
(c) "Addie Bundren was dead, to begin with."
(d) "Apricot jam is the worst sort of jam."

17. The prelude to *Middlemarch* makes a reference to the particular history of a remarkable woman, _____.
(a) St. Agnes (b) St. Theresa
(c) St. Joan (d) St. Carmel

18. "O, for a draught of vintage! that hath been
Cooled a long age in the deep-delved earth,
Tasting of Flora and the country green,
Dance, and Provencal song, and sunburnt mirth!"
The above description is an example of
(a) Paronomasia (b) Synaesthesia
(c) Aphaeresis (d) Synecdoche

19. The term, "poetic justice," to designate the idea that the good are rewarded and the evil punished, was devised by
(a) Aristotle (b) John Dryden
(c) Thomas Rhymer (d) Ben Jonson

20. ______ is the producer of the first complete printed English Bible.
    (a) Jerome (b) William Tyndale
    (c) Miles Coverdale (d) Bede

21. In *The Fall of Hyperion: A Dream,* Keats sees a ladder leading upwards and is addressed by a prophetess in the following words: "None can usurp this height.../ But those to whom the miseries of the world/ Are misery, and will not let them rest." Who is the prophetess?
    (a) Urania (b) Moneta
    (c) Melete (d) Mneme

22. Virginia Woolf's *To the Lighthouse* has a tripartite structure. The three parts are named the following EXCEPT:
    (a) The Sky (b) The Window
    (c) Time Passes (d) The Lighthouse

23. Which novel by Patrick White is based on the story of Ludwig Leichhardt, the Prussian naturalist who explored Australia in the mid-1840s, in which White's fictional hero says when asked about navigation—"The Map? I will first make it"?
    (a) *The Tree of Man*
    (b) *Voss*
    (c) *Riders in the Chariot*
    (d) *The Solid Mandala*

24. Who among the following is not a character in William Golding's *Lord of the Flies*?
    (a) Ralph (b) Piggy
    (c) Peter (d) Jack

25. Dante Gabriel Rossetti founded the Pre-Raphaelite Brotherhood which included
    I. Holman Hunt
    II. Arthur Hugh Clough
    III. Gerald Manley Hopkins
    IV. John Millais

    The right combination according to the code is
    (a) II and III (b) I and IV
    (c) I and III (d) II and IV

26. The seven deadly sins are sought to be portrayed in Chaucer's *Canterbury Tales.* Which of the following sins is not covered by Chaucer?
    I. Jealousy II. Envy
    III. Lust IV. Homicide

    The right combination according to the code is
    (a) I and II (b) I and III
    (c) I and IV (d) III and IV

27. Richardson's *Pamela* had its origin in
    (a) the real case of a woman born to lower-middle-class parents
    (b) an elementary letter-writing manual
    (c) the general plight of English women
    (d) the suggestion of a friend to defend middle-class values

28. *The Medall*, a poem written by John Dryden in 1681, is sub-titled
    (a) *A Satire against Sedition*
    (b) *A Satire against Tyranny*
    (c) *A Satire against Greed*
    (d) *A Satire against Apostasy*

29. "Full fathom five thy father lies" is an example of
    (a) assonance (b) alliteration
    (c) apostrophe (d) enjambment

30. What is a trochee?
    (a) A two syllable foot of verse with two heavy stresses
    (b) A two syllable foot of verse in which the stress falls on the first syllable
    (c) Three successive heavy stresses
    (d) A six line stanza in which the rhyme sounds are all identical

31. Keats's "La Belle Dame Sans Merci" combines two poetic forms
    I. Lyric
    II. Dramatic Monologue
    III. Ballad
    IV. Sonnet

    The right combination according to the code is
    (a) II and III (b) I and IV
    (c) I and III (d) II and IV
32. ______ narrator highlights the problem of narrative authority.
    (a) First person (b) Self-conscious
    (c) Third person (d) Participant
33. Who among the following modern writers is associated with the quote, "Only connect"?
    (a) D.H. Lawrence (b) Virginia Woolf
    (c) James Joyce (d) E.M. Forster
34. Which of the following images does not figure in Auden's "Musee des Beaux Arts"?
    (a) a boy falling out of the sky
    (b) children...skating on a pond at the edge of wood
    (c) ranches of isolation and the busy griefs
    (d) the dogs go on with their doggy life
35. Feste is a clown in
    (a) *Twelfth Night*
    (b) *As You Like It*
    (c) *The Taming of the Shrew*
    (d) *Much Ado About Nothing*
36. Which play by Tom Stoppard has a play within the play?
    (a) *Enter a Free Man*
    (b) *The Real Inspector Hound*
    (c) *Jumpers*
    (d) *Night and Day*
37. Which of the following is not true of free verse?
    (a) Characterised by short, irregular lines.
    (b) No rhyme pattern.
    (c) Written in iambic pentameter
    (d) A dependence on the effective and more intense use of pauses
38. James Thomson's long poem, *The Seasons*, revised and expanded all his life, began in the first instance as a poem entitled
    (a) *Spring* (b) *Summer*
    (c) *Winter* (d) *Autumn*
39. Two cantos from the seventh book of *The Faerie Queene* appeared posthumously. They are known as
    (a) Mutability cantos
    (b) Friendship cantos
    (c) Justice cantos
    (d) Courtesy cantos
40. Foucault believes that the facts of history will protect us from
    (a) repeating mistakes
    (b) totalitarianism
    (c) deconstructionism
    (d) historicism
41. What is the occupation of Max's son, Lenny, in Harold Pinter's *The Home Coming*?
    (a) Boxer (b) Butcher
    (c) Pimp (d) Cab driver
42. Which Byron poem begins in the following manner: "I want a hero: an uncommon want, when every year and month sends forth a new one"?
    (a) *Beppo*
    (b) *Childe Harold's Pilgrimage*
    (c) *Don Juan*
    (d) *The Vision of Judgement*
43. In the second ending of John Fowles's *The French Lieutenant's Woman* Charles Smithson's lawyer finds that Sarah has been living in the house of
    (a) William Morris
    (b) William Holman Hunt

(c) D.G. Rossetti
(d) James Collinson

44. In 1692 William Congreve published *Incognita*, a work of fiction which is dubbed a 'novel' on its title-page. What is the sub-title?
(a) *Love and Duty Reconcil'd*
(b) *Beauty in Distress*
(c) *Virtue Rewarded*
(d) *Love in Excess*

45. In "Tradition and the Individual Talent" T.S. Eliot uses the analogy of the catalyst to elucidate his theory of impersonal poetry. He cites the example of a filament of platinum and, in the poetic process this is equivalent to
(a) the language of the poet
(b) the mind of the poet
(c) the soul of the poet
(d) the life of the poet

46. Match the character with the work:

| | |
|---|---|
| A. Pip | I. *Middlemarch* |
| B. Causaubon | II. *Great Expectations* |
| C. Becky Sharp | III. *Wuthering Heights* |
| D. Heathcliff | IV. *Vanity Fair* |

The right combination according to the code is

| Codes: | A | B | C | D |
|---|---|---|---|---|
| (a) | II | III | IV | I |
| (b) | IV | I | III | II |
| (c) | II | I | IV | III |
| (d) | III | II | I | IV |

47. Samuel Johnson's *Lives of the English Poets* combines the following except
(a) analytical criticism
(b) literary history
(c) personal biography
(d) socratic dialogue

48. Which two works of JM Coetzee won Booker Prize on two occasions?
I. *In the Heart of the Country*
II. *Life and Times of Michael K.*
III. *Disgrace*
IV. *Waiting for the Barbarians*

The right combination according to the code is
(a) II and III (b) II and IV
(c) III and IV (d) I and III

49. Who among the following Greek Philosophers has a bearing on the composition of Shelley's "Adonais"?
(a) Miletus (b) Socrates
(c) Plato (d) Aristotle

50. Match the author with the work:

| | |
|---|---|
| A. John Locke | I. *A Short View of the Immorality and Profanity of the Stage* |
| B. William Dampier | II. *Two Treatises on Government* |
| C. Jeremy Collier | III. *A Short View of Tragedy* |
| D. Thomas Rhymer | IV. *Voyages* |

| Codes: | A | B | C | D |
|---|---|---|---|---|
| (a) | II | I | IV | III |
| (b) | III | IV | I | II |
| (c) | II | IV | I | III |
| (d) | IV | III | II | I |

## ANSWERS

| | | | | | |
|---|---|---|---|---|---|
| 1. (a) | 2. (c) | 3. (c) | 4. (b) | 5. (c) | 6. (c) |
| 7. (a) | 8. (b) | 9. (b) | 10. (c) | 11. (d) | 12. (c) |
| 13. (a) | 14. (b) | 15. (c) | 16. (b) | 17. (b) | 18. (b) |
| 19. (c) | 20. (c) | 21. (b) | 22. (a) | 23. (b) | 24. (c) |
| 25. (b) | 26. (c) | 27. (b) | 28. (a) | 29. (b) | 30. (b) |
| 31. (c) | 32. (b) | 33. (d) | 34. (c) | 35. (a) | 36. (b) |
| 37. (c) | 38. (c) | 39. (a) | 40. (d) | 41. (c) | 42. (c) |
| 43. (c) | 44. (a) | 45. (b) | 46. (c) | 47. (d) | 48. (a) |
| 49. (c) | 50. (c) | | | | |

26

# English Paper III, January 2017 with Answers

1. Who among the following is not a diasporic writer?
   (a) Beryl Bainbridge (b) Timothy Mo
   (c) Hanif Kureishi (d) Sam Selvon
2. "A text is not a line of words releasing a single 'theological' meaning (the 'message' of the Author-God) but a multi-dimensional space in which a variety of writings, none of them original, blend and clash. The text is a tissue of quotations drawn from the innumerable centres of culture."

   Which of the following best expresses the position stated above?
   (a) A text is a tissue of lies that has no referential and cultural validity.
   (b) A text is a communication from the Author-God with multiple meanings.
   (c) A text is a force field of ambiguity where meanings collapse in the face of opposition.
   (d) A text is a linguistic construct without any unity of meaning and is linked to multiple sources of language and culture.
3. In William Congreve's *The Way of the World* Fairall is Lady Wishfort's
   (a) Son (b) Son-in-law
   (c) Nephew (d) Servant
4. Match the periodical with the founder/s:

| List–I | List–II |
|---|---|
| A. *The Egoist* | I. Wyndham Lewis and Ezra Pound |
| B. *The English Review* | II. Harriet Monroe |
| C. *Blast* | III. Harriet Weaver and Dora Marsden |
| D. *Poetry: A Magazine of Verse* | IV. Ford Madox Ford |

| Codes: | A | B | C | D |
|---|---|---|---|---|
| (a) | II | III | I | IV |
| (b) | III | I | IV | II |
| (c) | III | IV | I | II |
| (d) | III | II | I | IV |

5. Which statement best expresses the theme of Coleridge's "The Rime of the Ancient Mariner"?
   (a) To kill a living creature is immoral.
   (b) People should honour and respect all living things.
   (c) Prayer can accomplish miracles.
   (d) True harmony is achieved only through cooperative effort.
6. "The Comprehensible Output Hypothesis" was proposed by
   (a) Stephen Krashen (b) M.A.K.Halliday
   (c) Merrill Swain (d) Gertrude Buck
7. In *Tristram Shandy* Corporal Trim's brother Tom describes the oppression of a

black servant in a sausage shop in Lisbon that he visited. This episode is inspired by a letter Laurence Sterne received from a black man. Sterne's reply became an integral part of 18th century abolitionist literature.

Name the person who wrote the aforementioned letter to Sterne.

(a) William Wilberforce
(b) Ignatius Sancho
(c) William Blackstone
(d) John Hawkins

8. In Bertolt Brecht's *Mother Courage and Her Children*, which song does Yvette sing to Mother Courage and Kattrin?
(a) "The Song of the Great Souls of the Earth"
(b) "The Fraternization Song"
(c) "The Song of the Great Capitulation"
(d) "The Memorial Song"

9. In Gustave Flaubert's *Madame Bovary*, under what pretext does Emma go every week for her clandestine meeting with Leon in Rouen?
(a) Under the pretext of going to the church for weekly confession.
(b) Under the pretext of meeting her blind friend who lives alone.
(c) Under the pretext of weekly shopping.
(d) Under the pretext of taking piano lessons.

10. Identify the two books by C.S. Lakshmi (Ambai) published in English translation:
I. *Astride the Wheel*
II. *Going Home*
III. *A Purple Sea*
IV. *In a Forest, A Deer*

The right combination according to the code is

(a) III and II (b) I and II
(c) I and IV (d) III and IV

11. Elizabeth Barrett Browning's *Sonnets from the Portuguese* is
I. a sequence of forty-four Petrarchan sonnets.
II. a rewriting of Popean didactic verse.
III. a depiction of a contemporary setting and small events of ordinary life.
IV. a scathing criticism of the British colonial enterprise.

The right combination according to the code is

(a) I and II (b) I and III
(c) II and IV (d) I and IV

12. In *The Story of My Experiments with Truth*, M.K. Gandhi covers the narrative of his life from early childhood through to
(a) 1925 (b) 1929
(c) 1921 (d) 1927

13. In a writing system the minimal unit that can cause a difference of meaning is called
(a) phoneme (b) grapheme
(c) morpheme (d) jargon

14. Nnu Ego is a character in
(a) Chinua Achebe's *Anthills of Savannah*
(b) Chimamanda Ngozi Adichie's *Half of a Yellow Sun*
(c) Buchi Emecheta's *The Joys of Motherhood*
(d) Ben Okri's *The Famished Road*

15. Match the word with definition:

| List–I | List–II |
|---|---|
| A. Etymon | I. Changing from one language variety to another in discourse |
| B. Code switching | II. Rules governing the social use of language |
| C. Cognate | III. Etymological source of a word |
| D. Pragmatics | IV. Words with a common ancestor |

| Codes: | A | B | C | D |
|---|---|---|---|---|
| (a) | IV | I | III | II |
| (b) | III | II | IV | I |
| (c) | III | I | IV | II |
| (d) | IV | I | II | III |

16. What would help a reader recognize Keats's "To Autumn" as a poem from the Romantic period?
    (a) Its logical succession of images
    (b) Its concise use of couplets
    (c) Its lavish natural imagery
    (d) Its use of iambic pentameter

17. Which of the following is an accurate description of 'heteroglossia'?
    (a) Heteroglossia makes the job of the novelist easier by incorporating diversity into the novelistic structure.
    (b) Heteroglossia functions in a novel in alliance with its stylistic system incorporating multiple voices inscribed in social language and differentiated components of a writer's ideological position.
    (c) Heteroglossia creates concrete conceptualisations through language in association with the singular view of the artistic effort resulting in the unified world of the novel.
    (d) Heteroglossia enters the linguistic universe of the novel to homogenize its multiple differences and voices in a singular vision of accomplished structure.

18. In *Ulysses* Leopold Bloom works for a Dublin
    (a) bar (b) park
    (c) newspaper (d) bank

19. Which pair of plays belongs to the early career of Harold Pinter?
    I. *The Caretaker* II. *One for the Road*
    III. *Celebration* IV. *The Room*
    
    The right combination according to the code is
    (a) I and III (b) II and III
    (c) I and IV (d) II and IV

20. Who among the following contemporaries of John Donne wrote the following lines on his death: "Here lies a king, that ruled as he thought fit/ The universal monarch of wit"?
    (a) George Herbert (b) Henry King
    (c) Thomas Carew (d) Henry Crashaw

21. In his poem "Australia" A.D. Hope says that
    I. Australia is "without songs, architecture, history".
    II. "Her five cities are like five dry rivers."
    III. The poet turns to her "to find/ The Arabian desert of the human mind/ Hoping if still from deserts prophets come."
    IV. "She is the first of lands, the warmest."
    
    **Codes:**
    (a) I and III (b) II and III
    (c) III and IV (d) I and IV

22. Basic English, a simplified and fundamental framework of English, was formulated by
    I. I.A. Richards II. Alastair Fowler
    III. William Empson IV. C.K. Ogden
    
    The right combination according to the code is
    (a) I and II (b) II and III
    (c) I and IV (d) I and III

23. "Britons will never be slaves!"—felt proud Britons in the eighteenth century. A great many Britons, though, had no qualms about owning slaves and profiting from them. Who among the following British authors self-consciously engaged with the issue of slavery in some poems?
    I. Hannah More II. Mary Collier
    III. Anna Seward IV. Anna Yearsley

The right combination according to the code is

(a) I and III (b) I and IV
(c) II and III (d) III and IV

24. Match the Novelist with the work:

| List–I | List–II |
|---|---|
| A. Anita Desai | I. *Rich Like Us* |
| B. Nayantara Sahgal | II. *The Nowhere Man* |
| C. Arun Joshi | III. *In Custody* |
| D. Kamala Markandaya | IV. *The Last Labyrinth* |

| Codes: | A | B | C | D |
|---|---|---|---|---|
| (a) | III | II | IV | I |
| (b) | III | I | IV | II |
| (c) | II | I | IV | III |
| (d) | III | IV | I | II |

25. Identify the right chronological sequence:
    (a) *The American Pastoral – Sister Carrie – The Great Gatsby – Beloved*
    (b) *The Great Gatsby – Sister Carrie – Beloved – The American Pastoral*
    (c) *Sister Carrie – The Great Gatsby – Beloved – The American Pastoral*
    (d) *Sister Carrie – The Great Gatsby – The American Pastoral – Beloved*

26. In which of the following senses did Marx and Engels originally use the term "ideology" in *The German Ideology*?
    (a) Something that mystifies the actual material conditions of society, a sort of false consciousness.
    (b) The elaborate structures and institutions that mark the bourgeoise society.
    (c) The concepts of base and superstructure that govern the economic relations of the society.
    (d) The fundamental class consciousness of the proletariat which leads to their awakening.

27. The plot of this Coetzee novel unravels the narrative of a poor man of colour trying to survive in a civil-war situation, never taking sides. Identify the novel.
    (a) *Disgrace*
    (b) *Age of Iron*
    (c) *Waiting for the Barbarians*
    (d) *Life and Times of Michael K.*

28. Which of the following lines of T.S. Eliot is used by Anita Desai as the epigraph for her novel, *Baumgartner's Bombay*?
    (a) "I will show you fear in a handful of dust," *The Waste Land*
    (b) "In my beginning is my end," "East Coker"
    (c) "Human kind cannot bear very much reality," "Burnt Norton"
    (d) "I have measured out my life with coffee spoons," "Love Song of J. Alfred Prufrock"

29. In the General Prologue to *The Canterbury Tales* which two characters are examples of deep Christian goodness?
    I. the Summoner II. the Parson
    III. the Ploughman IV. the Pardoner

    The right combination according to the code is
    (a) I and II (b) II and IV
    (c) II and III (d) I and IV

30. Identify Falstaff's first words in *Henry IV, Part I*:
    (a) "Now, Harry, what time of day is it, lad?"
    (b) "Now, Hal, what time of day is it, lad?"
    (c) "Now, Harry, what time of night is it, lad?"
    (d) "Now, Hal, what time of night is it, lad?"

31. Anna Barbauld, Laetitia Elizabeth London, Charlotte Smith, Mary Robinson and Felicia Hemans are

(a) first wave feminists
(b) women poets of the Romantic period
(c) Victorian writers of popular fiction
(d) nineteenth century stage artists

32. Ray Bradbury has titled one of his short story collections—*Golden Apples of the Sun*—after the last line of a W.B. Yeats poem. Which poem?
(a) "The Death of Cuchulain"
(b) "The Peacock"
(c) "The Hour Before Dawn"
(d) "The Song of Wandering Aengus"

33. Which play by Tom Stoppard set in Zurich during the First World War presents a character's interactions with James Joyce as he was writing *Ulysses*, Tristran Zara during the rise of Dadaism, and Lenin leading up to the Russian Revolution, all of whom were living in Zurich at that time?
(a) *After Magritte*
(b) *Dirty Linen*
(c) *Artist Descending a Staircase*
(d) *Travesties*

34. "Most blameless is he, centered in the sphere
Of common duties, decent not to fail
In offices of tenderness..."

In these lines from "Ulysses", what does Ulysses suggest about Telemachus?
(a) He shows heroic qualities.
(b) He is patient and selfless.
(c) He is very much like his father.
(d) He may be too tender-hearted to be king.

35. In Restoration comedies the following is true EXCEPT
(a) the London life of hedonistic young men is portrayed.
(b) names encapsulate traits.
(c) unchaste women, widows and cuckolds scarcely make an appearance.
(d) the heroines seek a say in the choice of a marriage partner.

36. What happens to the character Boy at the end of Luigi Pirandello's play *Six Characters in Search of an Author*?
(a) He drowns in the fountain.
(b) He is shot dead by the Father.
(c) He leaves the stage alone.
(d) He commits suicide.

37. Which of the following adjectives will not apply to Becky Sharp, a major character in *Vanity Fair*?
(a) ambitious (b) energetic
(c) wellborn (d) scheming

38. Which character in Anton Chekhov's play, *The Cherry Orchard*, first suggests the selling of the orchard?
(a) Trofimov (b) Yephikodov
(c) Lopakhin (d) Varya

39. Identify the correct chronological sequence of the founding of the following 18th century English periodicals:
(a) *Tatler – Spectator – The Gentleman's Magazine – Rambler*
(b) *Spectator – Tatler – The Gentleman's Magazine – Rambler*
(c) *Rambler – Tatler – Spectator – The Gentleman's Magazine*
(d) *Tatler – Spectator – Rambler – The Gentleman's Magazine*

40. Who identified "strangled articulateness" as a theme in Canadian writing?
(a) Margaret Atwood
(b) Northrop Frye
(c) Michael Ondaatjee
(d) Joy Kogawa

41. Identify the gynocritics in the following list:

I. Alice Jardine II. Elaine Showalter
III. Sandra Gilbert IV. Kate Millett

The right combination according to the code is

(a) I and II (b) II and IV
(c) II and III (d) III and IV

42. Identify the character who is not part of the group of three protagonists in Girish Karnad's *Hayavadana*:

(a) Padmini (b) Gautama
(c) Kapila (d) Devadatta

43. Aurobindo Ghosh, author of *Savitri*, taught for some time at Baroda College after his return from England in 1893. Which subject did he teach?

(a) English (b) French
(c) Sanskrit (d) Bengali

44. Christopher Marlowe's *Hero and Leander* can be classified as a/an

(a) complaint (b) stichomythia
(c) epyllion (d) pasturelle

45. Which among the following does not belong to Indo-European language family?

(a) English (b) German
(c) Scandinavian (d) Finnish

46. What, among the following, is ruled out by Longinus as a way of achieving the sublime?

(a) great thoughts
(b) immoderate emotion
(c) noble diction
(d) dignified and elevated word arrangement

47. Who among the following is not a beat writer?

(a) Jack Kerouac
(b) Allen Ginsberg
(c) Robert Lowell
(d) William Burroughs

48. This was a masque written by Ben Jonson, staged on Twelfth Night and it was the first masque in which Prince Charles took part.

(a) *Masque of Blankness*
(b) *The Masque of Queens*
(c) *Pleasure Reconciled to Virtue*
(d) *The Gypsies Metamorphed*

49. Elizabeth Bishop's poems are best remembered for their

(a) conversational intimacy
(b) intellectual tenor
(c) astringent satire
(d) urban topography

50. Which chilling novel of surveillance and entrapment had the alternative title *Things as They Are*?

(a) Horace Walpole's *Castle of Otranto*.
(b) Matthew Gregory Lewis's *The Monk*.
(c) Thomas Love Peacock's *Nightmare Abbey*.
(d) William Godwin's *Caleb Williams*.

51. In "My Last Duchess" which of the following is not one of the Duchess's misdemeanours, according to the Duke?

(a) She was flattered by compliments from Fra Pandolf.
(b) She enjoyed the sunset as much as she enjoyed her husband's favour.
(c) She wouldn't listen to her husband when he tried to correct her behaviour.
(d) She was equally grateful for all acts of kindness, regardless of their source.

52. In his essay "From Work to Text" Roland Barthes says the following about the text:

I. The text is singular.
II. The text can be held in the hand.
III. The text is held in language.
IV. The text is a methodological field.

The right combination according to the code is

(a) I and III (b) II and IV
(c) III and IV (d) II and III

53. Seamus Heaney's "Digging" in his first volume of poetry, *Death of a Naturalist*, illustrates all the following EXCEPT
   (a) his preoccupation with his roots
   (b) his obsession with Irish legend and folklore
   (c) his respect for the natural world of the farming community and the labour of his ancestors
   (d) his displaced vocation of digging with a pen

54. Here is a list of Indian writers who have translated their work into English. Match the writer with his source language:

| List–I | List–II |
|---|---|
| A. O.V. Vijayan | I. Kannada |
| B. Vilas Sarang | II. Malayalam |
| C. Krishna Baldev Vaid | III. Marathi |
| D. Girish Karnad | IV. Hindi |

| Codes: | A | B | C | D |
|---|---|---|---|---|
| (a) | II | IV | III | I |
| (b) | I | III | IV | II |
| (c) | II | III | IV | I |
| (d) | II | III | I | IV |

55. In Book 8, *Paradise Lost* Adam identifies his chief flaw or weakness to Raphael. What is this flaw?
   (a) gluttony
   (b) pride in his superiority to Eve
   (c) overconfidence in his free will
   (d) passion for Eve

56. Identify the correct chronological sequence of the following early English texts:
   (a) *Troilus and Criseyde – The Owl and The Nightingale – Utopia – Morte d'Arthur*
   (b) *Troilus and Criseyde – Utopia – Morte d'Arthur – The Owl and the Nightingale*
   (c) *The Owl and the Nightingale – Troilus and Criseyde – Morte d'Arthur – Utopia*
   (d) *The Owl and the Nightingale – Morte d'Arthur – Troilus and Criseyde – Uttopia*

57. In Sophocles's play *King Oedipus* Laius, the erstwhile ruler of Thebes, was murdered
   (a) at the edge of the forest on his way to Delphi
   (b) at the edge of the forest as he returned from Delphi
   (c) at the crossroads as he returned from Delphi
   (d) at the crossroads on his way to Delphi

58. The quintessentially metafictional novel, *If On a Winter's Night a Traveller* by Italo Calvino has alternate chapters with chapter numbers and titles. Which of the following are the titles of the chapters in the novel?
   I. Looks Down in the Gathering Shadow
   II. In a Network of Lines that Enlace
   III. In a Network of Lines that Interface
   IV. What Story there Awaits its End?

   The right combination according to the code is
   (a) I and II (b) I and IV
   (c) III and IV (d) II and IV

59. The novel *Maurice* by E.M. Forster appeared posthumously in 1971. It had a homosexual theme, so Forster considered its subject matter too indelicate for publication during his life time. It was influenced by a writer who was a socialist and open homosexual. Identify the writer.
   (a) Oscar Wilde
   (b) Edward Carpenter
   (c) W.H. Auden
   (d) E.F. Benson

60. Who among the following has elaborated on the "Indianisation" of English?
    (a) L.M. Khubchandani
    (b) B. Kumaravadivelu
    (c) B.B. Kachru
    (d) Rajendra Singh

61. These are four models of relating literature to history. Which of the following is associated with formalism?
    (a) Literary texts are universal and transcend history: the historical context of their production and reception has no bearing on the literary work which is aesthetically autonomous, having its own laws, being a world into itself.
    (b) The historical context of a literary work is integral to a proper understanding of it: the text is produced within a specific historical context but in its literariness it remains separate from that context.
    (c) Literary works can help us to understand the time in which they are set: realist texts in particular provide imaginative representations of specific historical moments, events or periods.
    (d) Literary texts are bound up with other discourses and rhetorical structures: they are part of a history that is still in the process of being written.

62. As Gunter Grass's novel *The Tin Drum* opens we find Oskar Matzerath
    (a) on the war front entertaining the soldiers as part of a band of dwarfs.
    (b) in a mental hospital writing his story.
    (c) admitted in a hospital after his fatal fall in the wine cellar.
    (d) watching a ball in which the young ladies ignore his presence.

63. D.H. Lawrence's 1926 novel *The Plumed Serpent* is set in which country?
    (a) Egypt (b) South Africa
    (c) Mexico (d) Peru

64. Which two writers can be described as writing historical novels?
    I. Sir Walter Scott
    II. Charlotte Bronte
    III. Maria Edgeworth
    IV. Jane Austen

    The right combination according to the code is
    (a) I and II (b) II and III
    (c) I and III (d) III and IV

65. Which of Kazuo Ishiguro's novels are set mostly in Japan?
    I. *The Unconsoled*
    II. *The Remains of the Day*
    III. *An Artist of the Floating World*
    IV. *A Pale View of Hills*

    The right combination according to the code is
    (a) I and III (b) II and III
    (c) III and IV (d) I and IV

66. In *The Advancement of Learning* Bacon noted the need for more studies of
    I. moral knowledge
    II. forbidden knowledge
    III. civil knowledge
    IV. spiritual knowledge

    The right combination according to the code is
    (a) I and III (b) I and IV
    (c) II and III (d) II and IV

67. Which among the following texts purports to be the autobiography of a mad German philosopher edited by an equally fictitious editor?
    (a) *Sartos Resartus*
    (b) *The Dream of Gerontius*
    (c) *The Professor*
    (d) *Felix Holf*

68. As Sidney argues in *A Defence of Poesy* which discipline is more useful and praiseworthy – history or poetry?
   (a) History "being captivated to truth" is more useful than poetry.
   (b) Poetry where man can see "virtue exalted and vice punished" is more useful than history.
   (c) History is more useful for poetry is "an encouragement to unbridled wickedness".
   (d) History and poetry are synonymous, and so both are useful.

69. In Bunyan's *Pilgrim's Progress* Christian and his friend faithful cause a commotion at the Vanity Fair for many reasons. Which of the following statements is not true of their appearance at the fair?
   (a) They are dressed differently than the other fair-goers.
   (b) They speak the language of the Bible at the fair.
   (c) They sample every entertainment at the fair.
   (d) They refuse to look at the merchandise at the fair.

70. What does the title *Morte d'Arthur* mean?
   (a) Arthur mortified (b) Death of Arthur
   (c) Castle of Arthur (d) Burial of Arthur

71. **Assertion (A):** Characters in novels are people whose secret lives are visible or might be visible. We are people whose secret lives are invisible.

   **Reason (R):** Even when novels are about wicked people, they can solace us; they suggest a more manageable human race, they give us the illusion of seeing clearly and of power.

   In the light of the statements above
   (a) Both (A) and (R) are correct and (R) is the correct explanation of (A).
   (b) Both (A) and (R) are correct but (R) is not the correct explanation of (A).
   (c) (A) is right, but (R) is wrong.
   (d) (A) is wrong, but (R) is right.

Read the following poem and answer the questions, 72 to 75:

**Dead Fox**

We pretended to know nothing about it.
I withdrew to my childhood training: stay out
of swampy undergrowth, choked edges.
This was around the time
we were too cruel to kill the mice we caught,
leaving them in the Have-a-Heart trap
under the sun-burning bramble of rugosa.
But moving up the trail, we caught a glimpse
right at the start: the fox just over the hillock
on the dune-side slope, spoiling
the grass-inscribed sand. Neither of us looked—
it seemed best to back away.
On the dune's steep side
we surveyed what we'd come for: ocean's
snaking blue beyond the meadow, the silvered
blade-like wands lying down. Lovely enough
to hold ourselves to that view.
But the currents of an odor wafted in and out,
until the sweep of smell grew wider, wilder.
The heat compounded, and ugliness
settled its cloud over us, profound as human speech,
although by then we were not speaking.

72. The "We" of the opening line indicates
   (a) a group
   (b) two persons
   (c) the speaker and an imaginary listener
   (d) an unspecified crowd

73. The dead animal was sighted
   (a) at the end of the trail
   (b) on the dune's steep side

(c) on the dune's sloping side
(d) in the swampy undergrowth

74. The reaction evoked in response to a glimpse of the dead fox is best described as
I. evasive
II. angry
III. bizarre
IV. muted

The right combination according to the code is
(a) I and II
(b) II and III
(c) I and IV
(d) III and IV

75. At the close of the poem, which of the following senses overpowers and renders the visitors speechless?
(a) sight
(b) touch
(c) sound
(d) smell

**ANSWERS**

| | | | | | |
|---|---|---|---|---|---|
| 1. (a) | 2. (d) | 3. (b) | 4. (c) | 5. (b) | 6. (c) |
| 7. (b) | 8. (b) | 9. (d) | 10. (d) | 11. (b) | 12. (c) |
| 13. (b) | 14. (c) | 15. (c) | 16. (c) | 17. (b) | 18. (c) |
| 19. (c) | 20. (c) | 21. (a) | 22. (c) | 23. (b) | 24. (b) |
| 25. (c) | 26. (a) | 27. (d) | 28. (b) | 29. (c) | 30. (b) |
| 31. (b) | 32. (d) | 33. (d) | 34. (b) | 35. (c) | 36. (d) |
| 37. (c) | 38. (c) | 39. (a) | 40. (b) | 41. (c) | 42. (b) |
| 43. (a) | 44. (c) | 45. (d) | 46. (b) | 47. (c) | 48. (c) |
| 49. (a) | 50. (d) | 51. (c) | 52. (c) | 53. (b) | 54. (c) |
| 55. (d) | 56. (c) | 57. (d) | 58. (a) | 59. (b) | 60. (c) |
| 61. (a) | 62. (b) | 63. (c) | 64. (c) | 65. (c) | 66. (a) |
| 67. (a) | 68. (b) | 69. (c) | 70. (b) | 71. (b) | 72. (b) |
| 73. (c) | 74. (c) | 75. (d) | | | |

27

# NET Examination Paper II, November 2017 with Answers

1. In Frances Burney's novel, *Evelina*, the eponymous heroine comes out in society in two locations. They are:
   (i) Bath (ii) Bristol
   (iii) Leeds (iv) London
   The right combination according to the code is:
   (a) (i) and (ii) (b) (ii) and (iii)
   (c) (i) and (iv) (d) (ii) and (iv)
2. Which of the following lines by Shakespeare is repeated several times in Virginia Woolf's novel *Mrs. Dalloway*?
   (a) "If music be the food of love, play on".
   (b) "Fear no more the heat of the sun, Nor the furious winter's rages".
   (c) "Those are pearls that were his eyes".
   (d) "There is a tide in the affairs of man".
3. Identify the important theatres of the Elizabethan period:
   (i) Peacock (ii) Globe
   (iii) Swan (iv) Grand
   The right combination according to the code is:
   (a) (i) and (ii) (b) (ii) and (iii)
   (c) (ii) and (iv) (d) (i) and (iv)
4. In which poem does Matthew Arnold express the dilemma of:
   "Wandering between two worlds, one dead, The other powerless to be born"?
   (a) "Self - Dependence"
   (b) "Stanzas from the Grande Chartreuse"
   (c) "To a Republican Friend"
   (d) "Dover Beach"
5. Who made the comment that, "All modern American literature comes from one book by Mark Twain called *Huckleberry Finn*"?
   (a) Henry James
   (b) William Faulkner
   (c) Jack London
   (d) Ernest Hemingway
6. The Emblem is a poetic genre containing a symbolic picture with a text and a verse exposition popular in the early 17th century. Who popularised this kind of poetry through the work *Emblems* [1635]?
   (a) Robert Southwell
   (b) Francis Quarles
   (c) John Davies
   (d) Joseph Sylvester
7. Which Byron work begins thus:
   "I want a hero: an uncommon want, when every year and month sends forth a new one........."?
   (a) Beppo (b) Cain
   (c) Manfred (d) Don Juan
8. The title of Sir Thomas Browne's famous treatise, *Religio Medici* means:
   (a) Religion of a Doctor
   (b) Religion of Magician

(c) Religion of Divinity
(d) Religion of Meditation

9. Which among the following recent novels is a retelling of Sophocles's *Antigone*?
(a) Kamila Shamsie, *Home Fire*
(b) Fiona Mozley, *Elmet*
(c) Zadie Smith, *Swing Time*
(d) Mohsin Hamid, *Exit West*

10. Identify the two important works of Paul de Man from the following list:
(i) *Blindness and Insight*
(ii) *Allegories of Reading*
(iii) *Theoretical Essays*
(iv) *Criticism and Ideology*
The right combination according to the code is:
(a) (i) and (ii) (b) (i) and (iii)
(c) (ii) and (iii) (d) (ii) and (iv)

11. Samuel Johnson denounced the metaphysical poets saying, "About the beginning of the seventeenth century appeared a race of writers that may be termed the metaphysical poets". In the biography of which of the following poets in his *Lives of Poets* did Johnson make this remark?
(a) John Dryden
(b) Thomas Parnell
(c) Abraham Cowley
(d) Alexander Pope

12. The terms of the contract are not disagreeable to me.
The above sentence contains an example of:
(a) enumeration (b) litotes
(c) anaphora (d) metonymy

13. Who is the author of the following lines?
"To see a World in a Grain of Sand
And a Heaven in a Wild Flower
Hold Infinity in the palm of your hand
And Eternity in an hour...".
(a) Thomas Gray
(b) William Blake
(c) William Collins
(d) William Cowper

14. In *Women in Love* what is Winifred's pekinese dog called?
(a) Bismarck (b) Looloo
(c) Lucky (d) Buddy

15. Which of the following New Critics put forward the idea of the 'heresy of paraphrase'?
(a) Allen Tate
(b) Cleanth Brooks
(c) W.K. Wimsatt
(d) Monroe C. Beardsley

16. Edmund Spenser's *Colin Clout's Come Home Again* is a fine example of:
(a) carpe diem
(b) sonnet sequence
(c) georgic poetry
(d) pastoral eclogue

17. In *An Essay of Dramatic Poesy* whom does John Dryden refer to as "the most learned and judicious Writer which any Theater ever had"?
(a) John Webster
(b) Christopher Marlowe
(c) Ben Jonson
(d) William Shakespeare

18. This Australian poet was raised in New South Wales and grew up in rural Australian landscape. In 1946 she published her first book of poems. In 1962, she became cofounder and president of the Wild Life Preservation Society of Queensland and served as its president several times thereafter. Identify the poet.
(a) Dorothy Hewett (b) Nettie Palmer
(c) Judith Wright (d) Amy Witting

19. Aphra Behn's *Oroonoko* is set in _____.
    (a) Surinam (b) Abyssinia
    (c) Egypt (d) Assyria

20. Who published the first collected edition of Gerard Manley Hopkins's poems in 1918?
    (a) Robert Bridges
    (b) Coventry Patmore
    (c) John Betjeman
    (d) Stephen Spender

21. Samuel Richardson named his heroine Pamela after one of the characters in ____.
    (a) Edmund Spenser's *Faerie Queene*
    (b) William Shakespeare's *Venus* and *Adonis*
    (c) Philip Sidney's *Arcadia*
    (d) Geoffrey Chaucer's *Canterbury Tales*

22. Pinter once admitted that he first became aware of the dramatic power of the pause from seeing a popular American comedian. Which one?
    (a) Bob Hope (b) W.C. Fields
    (c) Jack Benny (d) Charlie Chaplin

23. Charles Dickens's *Bleak House* is pointedly critical of England's:
    (a) Privy Council
    (b) Court of Appeal
    (c) Court of Chancery
    (d) Military courts

24. Which of the following is not true of the ideal state in Thomas More's Utopia?
    (a) Personal property, money and vice are effectively abolished.
    (b) The root causes of crime, ambition and political conflict, are eliminated.
    (c) There is only one religion guided by the principle of a benevolent Supreme Being.
    (d) Its priesthood, which includes some women, is limited in number.

25. Which character created by Coleridge makes the following account of her harrowing experience?
    "Five warriors seized me yestermorn,
    Me, even me, a maid forlorn:
    They choked my cries with force and fright,
    And tied me on a palfrey white".
    (a) Geraldine
    (b) Christabel
    (c) Christabel's mother
    (d) The maid who appeared in Christabel's dream

26. Which novel of Thomas Hardy begins with the sombre description of Egdon Heath?
    (a) *Jude the Obscure*
    (b) *The Return of the Native*
    (c) *Far from the Madding Crowd*
    (d) *Under the Greenwood Tree*

27. The metrical form of Gower's *Confessio Amantis* is:
    (a) iambic pentameter
    (b) anapestic trimeter
    (c) octosyllabic couplets
    (d) trochaic tetrameter

28. What happens to the lock of hair at the end of Alexander Pope's *The Rape of the Lock*?
    (a) It is given back to its rightful owner.
    (b) It is preserved in a monument.
    (c) It turns into a star.
    (d) It is presented to the poet as a token of gratitude

29. The Bard. The Iron Lady. The King.
    The above are examples of:
    (a) anacoluthon (b) aposiopesis
    (c) asyndenton (d) antonomasia

30. Which of the following novels by Margaret Atwood depicts the historical event of the notorious murders committed in 1843?

(a) *The Blind Assassin*
(b) *Alias Grace*
(c) *Cats Eye*
(d) *Oryx and Crake*

31. Which of the following poems by W.B. Yeats repudiates the sensual world in favour of "the artifice of eternity"?
(a) "Under Ben Bulben"
(b) "Among School Children"
(c) "Sailing to Byzantium"
(d) "After Long Silence"

32. Which of the following characters in *Moby Dick* falls overboard and turns insane as a result?
(a) Pip (b) Queequeg
(c) Starbuck (d) Tashtego

33. Which of the following poems by Seamus Heaney is dedicated to the Irish poet Paul Muldoon?
(a) "The Loaning" (b) "The Sandpit"
(c) "A Migration" (d) "Widgeon"

34. In William Golding's *Lord of the Flies* which of the following characters is put to death?
(a) Piggy (b) Ralph
(c) Simon (d) Jack

35. In *Canterbury Tales* who has a red face full of sores?
(a) the Summoner (b) the Shipman
(c) the Yeoman (d) the Reeve

36. The pace of speech is called:
(a) syllable (b) loudness
(c) tempo (d) pitch

37. Match the title with the author:
(A) *Sexual Politics* (i) Mary Ellman
(B) *A Literature of Their Own* (ii) Elaine Showalter
(C) *Thinking About Women* (iii) Helene Cixous
(D) *The Laugh of the Medusa* (iv) Kate Millet

| Codes: | (A) | (B) | (C) | (D) |
|---|---|---|---|---|
| (a) | (iv) | (iii) | (i) | (ii) |
| (b) | (iv) | (ii) | (i) | (iii) |
| (c) | (iii) | (iv) | (i) | (ii) |
| (d) | (iv) | (i) | (ii) | (iii) |

38. Which of the following historical events does Tennyson's poem "The Charge of the Light Brigade" describe?
(a) The Battle of Hastings
(b) The Wars of the Roses
(c) The Battle of Waterloo
(d) The Crimean War

39. Northrop Frye's influential work, *Anatomy of Criticism* includes, as the subtitle indicates, four essays. Which of the following is not one among them?
(a) "Archetypal Criticism: Theory of Myths"
(b) "Typological Criticism: Theory of Types"
(c) "Historical Criticism: Theory of Modes"
(d) "Ethical Criticism: Theory of Symbols"

40. In Robert Browning's "Andrea del Sarto", with which of the following painters does Andrea not compare himself with?
(a) Michelangelo
(b) Leonardo da Vinci
(c) Rembrandt
(d) Raphael

41. In Jonathan Swift's *Gullivers Travels* Gulliver refers to William Dampier, the famous writer of two voyages, as:
(a) master (b) brother
(c) cousin (d) uncle

42. Who among the following is not a character in *Pride and Prejudice*?
(a) Mr. Darcy (b) Miss Bingley
(c) Miss Bates (d) Mr. Collins

43. "All the world's a stage,

And all the men and women merely players",

occurs in Shakespeare's *As You Like It*. Which character says the line?

(a) Jacques (b) Celia
(c) Rosalind (d) Touchstone

44. Which of the following rivers are mentioned in Andrew Marvell's poem "To His Coy Mistress"?

(a) Thames and Rhine
(b) Thames and Ganges
(c) Ganges and Humber
(d) Thames and Humber

45. "The truth, the whole truth, and nothing but the truth".

The above is an example of:

(a) ploce (b) epizeuxis
(c) plurisignation (d) diaeresis

46. Which of the following images is not part of W.H. Auden's poem "In Memory of W.B. Yeats"?

(a) Mercury sinking in the mouth of the dying day
(b) Wolves running through evergreen forests
(c) Silence invading the suburbs
(d) Memory scattering like the beads

47. Who among the following is the author of *Steps to the Temple*?

(a) John Donne (b) RichardCrashaw
(c) George Herbert (d) Henry Vaughan

48. Match the character with the work:

(A) Jim Dixon (i) *Room at the Top*
(B) Jimmy Porter (ii) *Hurry on Down*
(C) Joe Lampton (iii) *Look Back in Anger*
(D) Charles Lumley (iv) *Lucky Jim*

| **Codes:** | **(A)** | **(B)** | **(C)** | **(D)** |
|---|---|---|---|---|
| (a) | (iv) | (iii) | (i) | (ii) |
| (b) | (iv) | (iii) | (ii) | (i) |
| (c) | (iii) | (iv) | (i) | (ii) |
| (d) | (iii) | (i) | (ii) | (iv) |

49. In the opening book of *The Prelude* Wordsworth mentions famously that he was "fostered alike by _____ and _____".

Pick out the right pair.

(i) nature (ii) fear
(iii) imagination (iv) beauty

The right combination according to the code is:

(a) (i) and (iii) (b) (iv) and (ii)
(c) (iv) and (iii) (d) (i) and (iv)

50. The title of Ngugi wa Thiong'o's *Petals of Blood* is derived from a poem by Derek Walcott. Identify the poem.

(a) "A Far Cry from Africa"
(b) "The Swamp"
(c) "Goats and Monkeys"
(d) "Midsummer"

## ANSWERS

| | | | | | |
|---|---|---|---|---|---|
| 1. (d) | 2. (b) | 3. (b) | 4. (b) | 5. (d) | 6. (b) |
| 7. (d) | 8. (a) | 9. (a) | 10. (a) | 11. (c) | 12. (b) |
| 13. (b) | 14. (b) | 15. (b) | 16. (d) | 17. (c) | 18. (c) |
| 19. (a) | 20. (a) | 21. (c) | 22. (c) | 23. (c) | 24. (c) |
| 25. (a) | 26. (b) | 27. (c) | 28. (c) | 29. (d) | 30. (b) |

| | | | | | |
|---|---|---|---|---|---|
| 31. (c) | 32. (a) | 33. (d) | 34. (b) | 35. (a) | 36. (c) |
| 37. (b) | 38. (d) | 39. (b) | 40. (c) | 41. (c) | 42. (c) |
| 43. (a) | 44. (c) | 45. (a) | 46. (d) | 47. (b) | 48. (a) |
| 49. (b) | 50. (b) | | | | |

# 28

# English Paper III, November 2017 with Answers

1. This Byron work revolves around a wife whose husband is presumed lost at sea and she takes a lover in his absence. Everybody behaves agreeably on the husband's return. Byron's technical skills in verse is in display here as the work counterpoints the colloquial and the formal. Identify the work:
   (a) *Manfred*
   (b) *Don Juan*
   (c) *Beppo*
   (d) *The Bride of Abydos*
2. Who is the author of the poem, "Our Casuarina Tree"?
   (a) Sarojini Naidu
   (b) Toru Dutt
   (c) Rabindranath Tagore
   (d) Kamala Das
3. In this Jacobean play the Black King and his men, representing Spain and the Jesuits, are checkmated by the White Knight, Prince Charles. This political satire drew crowds to the Globe Theatre until the Spanish ambassador protested and James I suppressed the play.
   Identify the play:
   (a) *The Wonderful Yeare*
   (b) *A Game at Chess*
   (c) *A King and No King*
   (d) *The Knight of the Burning Pestle*
4. Frederic Jameson associated postmodern culture with ______ capitalism.
   (a) market (b) monopoly
   (c) imperialist (d) multinational
5. Early in Evelyn Waugh's *A Handful of Dust*, while Tony and his young son, John Andrew, walk to the church, John tells his father a story he has heard from the stable manager, Ben about a mule "who had drunk his company's rum ration" in the First World War and subsequently died. What is the mule named?
   (a) Peppermint (b) Dopey
   (c) Dynamo (d) Pookey
6. *The Oxford English Dictionary* was published in twelve volumes with its current title in the year:
   (a) 1928 (b) 1930
   (c) 1933 (d) 1915
7. *The Life and Opinions of Tristram Shandy, Gentleman* is notorious for its many digressions across nine volumes and its failure to deliver a complete autobiography. In which volume does Tristram Shandy finally recount his birth?
   (a) Volume III (b) Volume V
   (c) Volume VIII (d) Volume IX
8. Miguel de Cervantes's inimitable *Don Quixote*, foreshadows metafictional moorings when the novelist,

(i) says that the first chapters of the narrative are recreated from the Archive of La Mancha
(ii) says that it is a faithful rendering of a Catalan text in Spanish
(iii) says that part of it has been translated from the Arabic by the Moorish author Cide Hamete Benengeli
(iv) says that he is rewriting the history of a medieval knight altering the heroic vein with a farcical mode

The right combination according to the code is:

(a) (i) and (ii) (b) (ii) and (iii)
(c) (i) and (iii) (d) (ii) and (iv)

9. In his theory of Mimesis, Plato says that all art is mimetic by nature; art is an imitation of life. To argue his case he gives the example of a:

(a) cloud (b) chair
(c) tree (d) river

10. The translation of *Geeta* into English in 1784 called *Bhagavad-Gita* marked, in William Jones's opinion, an "event that made it possible for the first time to have a reliable impression of Indian Literature". Who was the translator?

(a) Charles Wilkins
(b) H.J. Colebrooke
(c) Rammohan Roy
(d) Nathaniel Halhed

11. One of the plays among the following contains the characters Coll, Gib, Dan and Mak. Identify the play:

(a) *Everyman*
(b) *The Castle of Perseverance*
(c) *The Second Shepherd's Play*
(d) *The Marshals*

12. Tereza, in Milan Kundera's novel *The Unbearable Lightness of Being*, troubled by Tomas's promiscuity, falls an easy prey to jealousy, fear and nightmares. Which of the following are the terrible dreams she has?

(i) She dreams of cats attacking her.
(ii) She dreams of wolves attacking her.
(iii) She dreams that she is dead and buried in a common grave where she lies with the corpses of strangers.
(iv) She dreams that she is dead, stripped of her clothes and plagued by other naked corpses.

The right combination according to the code is:

(a) (i) and (iii) (b) (i) and (iv)
(c) (ii) and (iii) (d) (ii) and (iv)

13. The opening lines of Wordsworth's "Immortality Ode":

"There was a time when meadow, grove, and stream,
The earth, and every common sight,
To me did seem
Apparelled in celestial light
The glory and freshness of a dream",

closely resembles Coleridge's lines:

"There was a time when earth, and sea, and skies,
The bright green vale, and the forest's dark recess,
With all things, lay before mine eyes
In steady loveliness".

Identify the Coleridge poem:

(a) "Fears In Solitude"
(b) "The Mad Monk"
(c) "To William Wordsworth"
(d) "Dejection: An Ode"

14. Christina Rossetti's "Goblin Market", a rare blend of allegory and fairytale world presents the story of two sisters, Laura and Lizzie. Which of the following is not true about the enchanted world that the poem unravels?

(a) Laura buys fruits from the goblins in exchange of her "golden lock" of hair and a "tear more rare than pearl"
(b) Jeanie, a girl who ate the goblins' fruits, "pined away" and "sought them by night and day"
(c) Laura, who goes to the market again, does not see the goblins but hears only "their shrill cry piercing the air"
(d) Laura's hair "grew thin and grey" and she wanes like the full moon to "swift decay"

15. In which of these prisons is Defoe's character, Moll Flanders born?
(a) Gatehouse (b) King's Bench
(c) Newgate (d) Ludgate

16. In which poem does Judith Wright lament the erasure of native culture in the following lines?
"The song is gone; the dance
Is secret with the dancers in the earth,
The ritual useless, and the tribal story
Lost in an alien tale".
(a) "The Five Senses"
(b) "Legend"
(c) "Bullocky"
(d) "Bora Ring"

17. Years before, Winston Smith, the protagonist of George Orwell's dystopia, *Nineteen Eighty-Four* got an evidence of the party's dishonesty. What is it?
(a) Emmanuel Goldstein's confession that he is a party operative; not an enemy of the party.
(b) O' Brien's diary entry hinting at the non-existence of Big Brother.
(c) A photograph which proves that some citizen accused of a crime was out of the country while it was committed.
(d) A colleague's revelation that the Inner Party members have systematically destroyed all historical documents and created false documents.

18. *The Indian Queen* is
(a) a heroic tragedy in rhymed couplets by John Dryden
(b) a long poem in free verse by Keki Daruwalla
(c) an autobiography of an Indian princess in exile
(d) a fictional account of the Life of Maharani Gayatri Devi

19. In J.M. Coetzee's *Disgrace* David Lurie is working on an opera on the life of one of the Romantic poets. Who is the poet?
(a) Blake (b) Shelley
(c) Byron (d) Coleridge

20. **Assertion (A):** There is no unity or absolute source of the myth.
**Reason (R):** The focus or the source of the myth are always shadows and virtualities which are elusive, unactualizable, and nonexistent in the first place. Any search for the discursive unity in the myth is, therefore, misplaced.
In the context of the above statements:
(a) Both (A) and (R) are true and (R) is the correct explanation of (A)
(b) Both (A) and (R) are true but (R) is not the correct explanation of (A)
(c) (A) is true but (R) is false
(d) (A) is false, but (R) is true

21. Which of the following landscapes of England figures prominently in the poetry of Ted Hughes?
(a) Cornish cliffs (b) Dorset moors
(c) Yorkshire moors (d) Chesil Beach

22. The title of M.C. Chagla's autobiography is
(a) *Memoirs of my Working Life*
(b) *Without Fear or Favour*

(c) *Roses in December*
(d) *The Pen as My Sword*

23. Who/Which among the following gave the expression, "a leopard can't change its spots," to English language?
(a) The King James Bible
(b) Geoffrey Chaucer
(c) Shakespeare
(d) The Royal Society

24. Which of the following is not true about Albert Camus's novel, *The Plague*?
(a) Dr. Rieux describes the phenomenon of dying rats using the metaphors of disease, especially the bubonic plague.
(b) Paneloux interprets the plague in his first sermon as a sign of the Apocalypse.
(c) M. Michel is the first victim of the plague.
(d) Tarrou thinks that the plague symbolizes human indifference.

25. John Lydgate begins his *Siege of Thebes* with a prologue of 176 lines in which he imagines himself joining Chaucer's pilgrims in Canterbury, where he speaks with the Host and agrees to tell the first tale on homeward journey. The story that Lydgate tells as the pilgrims depart from Canterbury is meant to be a companion piece to:
(a) The Pardoner's Tale
(b) The Wife of Bath's Tale
(c) The Knight's Tale
(d) The Miller's Tale

26. Stephen Krashen's theory of second language acquisition consists of six main hypotheses. Which of the following is not one of them?
(a) The Input Hypothesis
(b) The Affective Filter Hypothesis
(c) The Monitor Hypothesis
(d) The Writing Hypothesis

27. Among Derek Walcott's plays, which one is an exploration of colonial relationships through the Robinson Crusoe story?
(a) *Pantomime*
(b) *Dream on Monkey Mountain*
(c) *Ti-Jean and His Brothers*
(d) *The Charlatan*

28. 'Anti-foundationalism' holds that:
(a) Every theory poses different questions and, therefore, what counts as 'fact' and 'truth' differs in every case.
(b) All truth claims can be judged true or false, usually against empirical facts.
(c) Causal statements about the relationship between dependent and independent variables can be made.
(d) Truth is the foundation of all representational experience.

29. The interaction hypothesis is a theory of second language acquisition which states that the development of language proficiency is promoted by face-to-face interaction and communication. The idea is usually credited to
(a) David Nunan
(b) Michael Long
(c) Alastair Pennycook
(d) Claire Kramsch

30. In Pinter's *Birthday Party* Stanley is terrorised by two visitors to a seaside boarding house. Identify the two:
(i) McGrath (ii) Goldberg
(iii) McCann (iv) Robinson
The right combination according to the code is:
(a) (i) and (ii) (b) (ii) and (iii)
(c) (i) and (iv) (d) (ii) and (iv)

31. Match the phrase to the ode:
(A) beechen green
(B) gathering swallows
(C) globed peonies
(D) green altar

(i) "Ode on a Grecian Urn"
(ii) "Ode on Melancholy"
(iii) "Ode to a Nightingale"
(iv) "To Autumn"

| Codes: | (A) | (B) | (C) | (D) |
|---|---|---|---|---|
| (a) | (iii) | (ii) | (iv) | (i) |
| (b) | (iv) | (ii) | (iii) | (i) |
| (c) | (iv) | (iii) | (ii) | (i) |
| (d) | (iii) | (iv) | (ii) | (i) |

32. Which 19th century novelist expressed a wish to "exterminate the race" of Indians following the 1857 Mutiny in India?
(a) William Makepeace Thackeray
(b) Charles Dickens
(c) George Eliot
(d) Anthony Trollope

33. The second part of *Pilgrim's Progress* deals with the pilgrimage of Christian's wife, Christiana. She has a companion and a guide in this journey. Pick out the pair's names from the following list.
(i) Patience (ii) Tenderheart
(iii) Mercy (iv) Greatheart
The right combination according to the code is:
(a) (iii) and (iv) (b) (ii) and (iii)
(c) (i) and (iv) (d) (ii) and (iv)

34. In which play by Eugene Ionesco do you find the grotesque image of the leg of a corpse thrusting onto the stage, and, which begins to grow larger as the play progresses in a menacing manner?
(a) *The Bald Soprano*
(b) *Amede or How to Get Rid of It*
(c) *Exit the King*
(d) *The Lesson*

35. Which of the following characters finds that complete happiness is elusive and that "while you are making the choice of life, you neglect to live"?
(a) Lovelace in Samuel Richardson's *Clarissa*
(b) Rasselas in Samuel Johnson's *Rasselas*
(c) Matthew Bramble in Tobias Smollett's *Humphry Clinker*
(d) Harley in Henry Mackenzie's *The Man of Feeling*

36. Arrange the following in the chronological order of publication:
(a) *In Memoriam-A Christmas Carol-Men and Women-Henry Esmond*
(b) *A Christmas Carol-In Memoriam-Men and Women-Henry Esmond*
(c) *A Christmas Carol-In Memoriam-Henry Esmond-Men and Women*
(d) *In Memoriam-A Christmas Carol-Henry Esmond-Men and Women*

37. Which one of Alice Munro's short stories is about the domestic erosions of Alzheimer's disease?
(a) "Dear Life"
(b) "Runaway"
(c) "The Bear Came Over the Mountain"
(d) "Dance of the Happy Shades"

38. What work begins thus: "It befell in the days of Uther Pendragon, when he was king of all England, and so reigned, that there was a mighty duke in Cornwall that held war against him long time"?
(a) *Sir Gawain and the Green Knight*
(b) *Le Morte D'arthur*
(c) *Confessio Amantis*
(d) *Piers Plowman*

39. ______is the subject of Asif Currimbhoy's play, *Inquilab*.
(a) The Naxalite movement
(b) The Freedom movement
(c) The Non-Cooperation movement
(d) The Khilafat movement

40. Tom Stoppard's play *Rosencrantz and Guildenstern are Dead*, being

metatheatrical, lays bare the constructed nature of theatrical performance. In referring to *Hamlet's* end and the Elizabethan stage conditions lacking curtains one of the characters of Stoppard's play says: "No one gets up after death- there is no applause-there is only silence and some second hand clothes, and that's death". Who makes this statement?

(a) Rosencrantz (b) Guildenstern
(c) The Player (d) Hamlet

41. Who among the following, has translated the classic Malayalam novel, *Chemmeen*?
   (a) A.K. Ramanujan
   (b) Anita Nair
   (c) Nandini Nopany
   (d) Gita Krishnankutty

42. Which Victorian poet is the author of the following lines?
   "God himself is the best Poet,
   And the Real is His song."
   (a) Lord Tennyson
   (b) Robert Browning
   (c) Matthew Arnold
   (d) Elizabeth Barrett Browning

43. "You are your words. Your listeners see
   Written on your face the poems they hear
   Like letters carved in a tree's bark
   The sight and sounds of solitudes endured".
   These are lines from a poem by ______ on the death of ______.
   (a) T.S. Eliot; Robert Frost
   (b) Siegfried Sassoon; Wilfred Owen
   (c) Stephen Spender; W.H. Auden
   (d) Dylan Thomas; Robert Bridges

44. Allen Ginsberg's "Howl", a key work of the Beat Movement, was dedicated to ______.
   (a) Lucien Carr
   (b) Carl Solomon
   (c) Herbert Huncke
   (d) Jack Kerouac

45. In his views on the death of Cordelia in *King Lear*, which is the ground not specifically cited by Samuel Johnson?
   (a) It is contrary to the natural ideas of justice
   (b) It is contrary to neoplatonic idea of decorum.
   (c) It is contrary to the hope of the reader.
   (d) It is contrary to the faith of chronicles.

46. Which of the following plays by David Hare is not part of a trilogy of 'state of the nation' plays?
   (a) *The Absence of War*
   (b) *Racing Demon*
   (c) *The Power of Yes*
   (d) *Murmuring Judges*

47. Chimamanda Adichie's last novel, *Americanah* (2013) centres on the romantic and existential struggles of a young Nigerian woman studying in the United States and finding success as a blogger. What is her blogging about?
   (a) poverty (b) development
   (c) race (d) religion

48. Why does Father Dolan punish Stephen with the pandybat in Joyce's *Portrait of the Artist as a Young Man*?
   (a) Stephen is talking to another student to get the answer to a Latin problem.
   (b) Stephen is not doing his work because his glasses are broken.
   (c) Stephen is looking out of the window towards the infirmary.
   (d) Stephen is lost in remembering his mother's farewell and cannot hear Father Dolan calling out his name.

49. Using a non-linear narrative, this American novel explores the psychic damage to a veteran of World War II and shows how a measure of healing is attained through his acceptance of Laguna myths and rituals. Identify the work:

(a) *Dred* (b) *Beloved*
(c) *Ceremony* (d) *End Zone*

50. What illusion does Lyuba Ranevsky in Anton Chekhov's play *The Cherry Orchard* have as she looks at the orchard?
 (a) She sees it gleaming with a bluish aura.
 (b) She sees her dead mother walking through the orchard.
 (c) She sees it full of ripe fruits without a trace of leaves.
 (d) She sees her childhood friends playing in the orchard.

51. From which source did Swift get the idea of writing "Verses on the Death of Dr. Swift"?
 (a) In a conversation with John Gay
 (b) After a reading of a maxim by la Rochefoucauld
 (c) While taking a walk near Dublin's St. James's graveyard
 (d) After reading Richard Burton's *Anatomy of Melancholy*

52. Two of the following words were borrowed from French after the Norman Conquest.
 (i) mutton (ii) pork
 (iii) sheep (iv) swine
 The right combination according to the code is:
 (a) (i) and (ii) (b) (i) and (iii)
 (c) (ii) and (iv) (d) (iii) and (iv)

53. Which of the following is not true regarding the *Oresteia* trilogy by Aeschylus?
 (a) Cassandra, cursed by Apollo predicts the death of Agamemnon, though her prophecy is ignored.
 (b) Aegisthus's vengeful feelings for Agamemnon results from their rivalry for the hand of Clytemnestra.
 (c) Orestes, who has come back with the intention of murdering Clytemnestra unexpectedly meets her, and pretending to be a stranger, tells her that Orestes is dead.
 (d) Orestes, pursued by the Furies, flees from them when they fall asleep. Then, Clytemnestra's ghost appears to wake them up.

54. The first instance of female cross-dressing with the disconcerting nuances of a boy actor dressing as a boy while playing the role of a woman in the dramatic world of Shakespeare occurs in ______.
 (a) *The Two Gentlemen of Verona*
 (b) *As You Like It*
 (c) *Twelfth Night*
 (d) *A Midsummer Night's Dream*

55. For Coleridge, our power to perceive symbols gleaned from the world about us is related to the category of:
 (a) primary imagination
 (b) secondary imagination
 (c) fancy
 (d) intuition

56. After independence, although English was not an Indian language, it was accorded the status of an:
 (a) Additional language
 (b) Ancilliary language
 (c) Associate language
 (d) Administrative language

57. Which English journal announced that it was "principally intended for the use of Politick Persons who are so publick-spirited as to neglect their own Affairs to look into Transactions of State" but failed to live up to this and amused readers with "accounts of Gallantry, Pleasure and Entertainment"?
 (a) *The Spectator*
 (b) *The Tatler*
 (c) *The Daily Courant*
 (d) *The Review*

58. The grammar-translation method of language teaching does not include:
    (a) focus on grammar rules
    (b) vocabulary memorization
    (c) inductive teaching
    (d) focus on written language

59. Who is the narrator in Kamala Markandaya's *Nectar in a Sieve*?
    (a) Premala (b) Saroja
    (c) Rukmani (d) Mira

60. How would a New Historicist critic interpret Derrida's statement, "there is nothing outside the text"?
    (a) historicist critics should restrict their attention to a culture's literary productions, all other data is irrelevant to the critic's task
    (b) language conditions the way we see the world, and there is no reality beyond the 'prison house' of language
    (c) there is no meaning outside of textual meaning (contrary to the mimeticist's position)
    (d) "literature" encompasses all cultural artifacts and all the values, power relations, and ways of seeing reflected in those artifacts; there is nothing outside of the "text" broadly conceived

61. Pick out two Austen heroines from the following list who are right-minded but neglected in the beginning but gradually are acknowledged to be correct by characters who have previously looked down on them.
    (i) Elizabeth Bennet
    (ii) Fanny Price
    (iii) Emma Woodhouse
    (iv) Anne Elliot

    The right combination according to the code is:
    (a) (i) and (iii) (b) (ii) and (iv)
    (c) (iii) and (iv) (d) (i) and (iv)

62. The variety of English used between non-native speakers who do not share a first language is called
    (a) English for specific purposes
    (b) English for basic purposes
    (c) English as a lingua Franca
    (d) English as a language tool

63. Identify the story for which E.M. Forster wrote the libretto for its opera version:
    (a) *Heart of Darkness*
    (b) *The Man Who Would Be the King*
    (c) *Billy Budd*
    (d) *Death in Venice*

64. Who, among the following Prem Chand translators has not translated Godan?
    (a) Jai Ratan
    (b) P. Lal
    (c) Gordon C. Roadarmel
    (d) Christopher R. King

65. "When Fred got into debt, it always seemed to him highly probable that something or other—he did not necessarily conceive what—would come to pass enabling him to pay in due time". Why is Fred Vincy in debt in *Middle March*?
    (a) He takes out a large loan to enable him to woo Mary Garth.
    (b) He is an inveterate gambler.
    (c) He is paying off a blackmailer.
    (d) He runs a charity that has got into trouble.

66. William Blake has a rare elan to provide telling images in arresting phrases. Match the phrases with the poems they belong to:

| | |
|---|---|
| (A) "mind forg'd manacles" | (i) "The Tyger" |
| (B) "eternal winter" | (ii) "The Sick Rose" |
| (C) "fearful symmetry" | (iii) "London" |
| (D) "crimson joy" | (iv) "Holy Thursday" |

| Codes: | (A) | (B) | (C) | (D) |
|---|---|---|---|---|
| (a) | (ii) | (iv) | (i) | (iii) |
| (b) | (iii) | (i) | (iv) | (ii) |
| (c) | (iii) | (iv) | (i) | (ii) |
| (d) | (iv) | (i) | (ii) | (iii) |

67. In the debate between the two birds in the Middle English poem *The Owl and the Nightingale* who acts as the arbiter?
   (a) Master Henry of Shrewsbury
   (b) Master William of Hereford
   (c) Master Freeman of Stamford
   (d) Master Nicholas of Guildford

68. In the first scene in which Goethe's Faust appears he is dejected by the study of Philosophy, Law, Medicine and Theology, turns to Magic art to acquire infinite knowledge. But he fails and in desperation attempts to commit suicide, but refrains at the final moment. What prevents Faust from committing suicide?
   (a) The intervention of archangel Gabriel
   (b) His attendant Wagner persuades him to revoke the decision
   (c) The chiming of the bells announcing Easter festivities
   (d) Mephistopheles appears and offers to initiate him into magic art

69. Which novel by Joseph Conrad presents a young captain who like Coleridge's Ancient Mariner is haunted by the "vision of a ship drifting in calm and swinging in light airs, with all the crew dying slowly about her decks" and who feels "the sickness of my soul...the weight of my sins...my sense of unworthiness"?
   (a) *Under Western Eyes*
   (b) *The Shadow Line*
   (c) *Victory*
   (d) *The Rescue*

70. "Our almost-instinct almost true:
What will survive of us is love."
Identify the poem by Philip Larkin that ends with the above lines:
   (a) "This Be the Verse"
   (b) "An Arundel Tomb"
   (c) "High Windows"
   (d) "Next, Please"

71. In the epilogue to Congreve's *Way of the World* there is a warning:
Others there are whose malice we'd prevent,
Such, who watch plays, with scurrilous intent
To mark out who by characters are meant.
. . . . . . . . . . . . . . . . . . . . . . . . . . . . .
These, with false glosses feed their own ill-nature,
And turn to libel, what was meant a *satire*.
What does this warning mean?
   (a) Critics should not be ill-natured and malicious.
   (b) Critics should not look for portrait of real people in the play's characters and remember that the play is a social satire.
   (c) Critics should avoid writing malicious reviews, lest they be charged with libel.
   (d) Critics should try to identify the real-life equivalent for each character.

72. Which of the following is an elegy on John Donne's wife, who died in 1617?
   (a) "Death, be not proud"
   (b) "Thou hast made me"
   (c) "Holy Sonnet 17"
   (d) "At the round earth's imagined corners"

**Read the following poem and answer questions, 73 to 75:**

**Bored**

Margaret Atwood

All those times I was bored
out of my mind. Holding the log

while he sawed it. Holding
the string while he measured, boards,
distances between things, or pounded
stakes into the ground for rows and rows
of lettuces and beets, which I then (bored)
weeded. Or sat in the back
of the car, or sat still in boats,
sat, sat, while at the prow, stern, wheel
he drove, steered, paddled. It
wasn't even boredom, it was looking,
looking hard and up close at the small
details. Myopia. The worn gunwales,
the intricate twill of the seat
cover. The acid crumbs of loam, the granular
pink rock, its igneous veins, the sea-fans
of dry moss, the blackish and then the graying
bristles on the back of his neck.
Sometimes he would whistle, sometimes
I would. The boring rhythm of doing
things over and over, carrying
the wood, drying
the dishes. Such minutiae. It's what
the animals spend most of their time at,
ferrying the sand, grain by grain, from their tunnels,
shuffling the leaves in their burrows. He pointed
such things out, and I would look
at the whorled texture of his square finger, earth under
the nail. Why do I remember it as sunnier
all the time then, although it more often
rained, and more birdsong?
I could hardly wait to get
the hell out of there to
anywhere else. Perhaps though
boredom is happier. It is for dogs or
groundhogs. Now I wouldn't be bored.
Now I would know too much.
Now I would know.

73. "All those times"—the opening words of the poem locate the speaker in:
    (a) a city suburb
    (b) a mountain resort
    (c) a natural environment
    (d) a highway motel

74. Which pair of words best describes the repetitive tenor of the speaker's unpretentious yet oppressive life?
    (i) details (ii) the car
    (iii) the wood (iv) the minutae
    The right combination according to the code is:
    (a) (i) and (ii) (b) (i) and (iv)
    (c) (ii) and (iii) (d) (iii) and (iv)

75. Which of the following approximates closely a thematic statement of the poem?
    (a) Dogs or groundhogs lead a better life than men or women
    (b) Irrespective of the place, the boring rhythm of doing things over and over in human life cannot be escaped
    (c) Myopia is the result if you live life in the lap of nature
    (d) Knowledge cures existential boredom

## ANSWERS

| | | | | | |
|---|---|---|---|---|---|
| 1. (c) | 2. (b) | 3. (b) | 4. (d) | 5. (a) | 6. (c) |
| 7. (a) | 8. (c) | 9. (b) | 10. (a) | 11. (c) | 12. (b) |
| 13. (b) | 14. (c) | 15. (c) | 16. (d) | 17. (c) | 18. (a) |
| 19. (c) | 20. (a) | 21. (c) | 22. (c) | 23. (a) | 24. (b) |
| 25. (c) | 26. (d) | 27. (a) | 28. (a) | 29. (b) | 30. (b) |

| | | | | | |
|---|---|---|---|---|---|
| 31. (d) | 32. (b) | 33. (a) | 34. (b) | 35. (b) | 36. (c) |
| 37. (c) | 38. (b) | 39. (a) | 40. (b) | 41. (b) | 42. (d) |
| 43. (c) | 44. (b) | 45. (b) | 46. (c) | 47. (c) | 48. (b) |
| 49. (c) | 50. (b) | 51. (b) | 52. (a) | 53. (b) | 54. (a) |
| 55. (a) | 56. (c) | 57. (b) | 58. (c) | 59. (c) | 60. (d) |
| 61. (b) | 62. (c) | 63. (c) | 64. (d) | 65. (b) | 66. (c) |
| 67. (d) | 68. (c) | 69. (b) | 70. (b) | 71. (b) | 72. (c) |
| 73. (c) | 74. (b) | 75. (b) | | | |

29

# NET Examination Paper II, July 2018 with Answers

1. Which narrative poem by Lord Tennyson presents the story of a fisherman turned merchant-sailor who, after a shipwreck, is marooned on a desert island?
   (a) "Crossing the Bar"
   (b) "Tithonus"
   (c) "Enoch Arden"
   (d) "Maud"
2. In "Memorial Verses" Matthew Arnold pays tribute to three great poets. Who are they?
   (a) Goethe, Shakespeare, Wordsworth
   (b) Goethe, Shakespeare, Milton
   (c) Shakespeare, Milton, Wordsworth
   (d) Goethe, Wordsworth, Byron
3. Who among the following English playwrights wrote screenplays on novels such as Marcel Proust's *In Search of Lost Time*, John Fowles's *French Lieutenant's Woman*, and Margaret Atwood's *Handmaid's Tale*?
   (a) John Arden (b) Edward Bond
   (c) Harold Pinter (d) David Hare
4. The years in English literary history between 1649 and 1660 are known as _______.
   (a) the Neo-classical period
   (b) the Commonwealth period
   (c) the Stuart period
   (d) the Jacobean period
5. In R.K. Narayan's *Swami and Friends*, which game offers Swami the best kind of emotional release from the strains and pressures of disagreeable circumstances?
   (a) cricket (b) football
   (c) tennis (d) hockey
6. William Blake expressed the importance of the particular when he said that "To Generalize is to be ______. To particularize is the alone Distinction of Merit." Fill in the blank.
   (a) an idiot (b) a poet
   (c) a dreamer (d) a skunk
7. Which of the following was not a dialect of Old English?
   (a) Irish (b) Northumbrian
   (c) Mercian (d) Kentish
8. Anthony Burgess's last novel, published in 1993, is called *A Dead Man in Deptford*. Who is the central character to whom the title refers?
   (a) Sir Walter Raleigh
   (b) Sir Philip Sidney
   (c) Christopher Marlowe
   (d) Earl of Southampton
9. Choose the correct chronological order:
   (a) William Caxton prints the first English book—William Shakespeare's First Folio—John Milton's *Areopagitica*—"Tottel's Miscellany" (*Songs and Sonnets*).

(b) "Tottel's Miscellany" (*Songs and Sonnets*)—William Shakespeare's First Folio—William Caxton prints the first English book—John Milton's *Areopagitica*.
(c) William Caxton prints the first English book—"Tottel's Miscellany" (*Songs and Sonnets*)—William Shakespeare's First Folio—John Milton's *Areopagitica*.
(d) William Shakespeare's First Folio—John Milton's *Areopagitica*—William Caxton prints the first English book—"Tottel's Miscellany" (*Songs and Sonnets*).

10. What does the phrase *ut pictura poesis* from Horace's *Art of Poetry* mean?
(a) "as in painting, so in poetry".
(b) "poetry beggars pictorial description".
(c) "as in poetry, so in painting".
(d) "picture above all poetry".

11. Who among the following is the author of *Account of the Augustan Age in England* (1759)?
(a) John Gay
(b) William Hazlitt
(c) Oliver Goldsmith
(d) Samuel Johnson

12. In how many parts did Cervantes publish his novel, *Don Quixote*?
(a) three (b) five
(c) two (d) twelve

13. Lytton Strachey's *Eminent Victorians* carries biographical sketches of writers and public figures. Identify the list below that correctly mentions those Eminent Victorians.
(a) Cardinal Manning, Florence Nightingale, Thomas Arnold and General Gordon.
(b) A.E.W. Mason, Sir Arthur Quiller Couch, Matthew Arnold, Robert Bridges.
(c) E.F. Benson, Cardinal Manning, Lord Tennyson, Beatrice Webb.
(d) George Harding, General Gordon, Robert Browning, Mrs Humphrey Ward.

14. One of the following statements about the eponymous saint of Dryden's "Song for St. Cecilia's Day" is incorrect. Identify that statement.
(a) St. Cecilia was a Roman lady, an early Christian martyr.
(b) St. Cecilia was an Armenian devotee of the Christian faith.
(c) St. Cecilia's festival is celebrated on 22 November in England.
(d) St. Cecilia was a patroness of music who was fabled to have invented the organ.

15. Which of the statements on Michael Roberts's *Faber Book of Modern Verse* (1936) is not true?
(a) His anthology canonized modern poetry and poets for quite some decades.
(b) The collection begins with the poems of Robert Bridges.
(c) Roberts omitted the Georgian poets in his anthology.
(d) Yeats, Eliot and Pound find a place in the *Faber Book* of 1936.

16. Who among the following proposed that the First Gulf War had never taken place, it was simply a hyperreal, media-generated spectacle?
(a) Richard Rorty
(b) Jean-Francois Lyotard
(c) Jean Baudrillard
(d) Umberto Eco

17. Sir Thomas Browne's *Urn Burial* was prompted by ______.
(a) the discovery of ancient burial-urns near Norwich.

(b) the contemporary researches on burial rites in Norway.
(c) the death of St. Francis of Assissi and his burial.
(d) the publication of the *English Book of Common Prayer*.

18. Identify from among the following list those that cannot be called War Fiction.
(i) *A Modern Instance*
(ii) *Catch - 22*
(iii) *The Age of Innocence*
(iv) *The Naked and the Dead*
(a) (i) and (iv) (b) (ii) and (iii)
(c) (i) and (iii) (d) (ii) and (iv)

19. Who among the following writers was not the one identified with The Movement of the 1950's England?
(a) Roy Fuller (b) Kingsley Amis
(c) Philip Larkin (d) Donald Davie

20. Which of the following novels does not belong to Nuruddin Farah's *Blood In the Sun* Trilogy?
(a) *Maps* (b) *Knots*
(c) *Gifts* (d) *Secrets*

21. In the following series, which one has all the poets correctly matched with their poems?
(a) Ezekiel, "Poet, Lover, Birdwatcher"; Ramanujan, "Small-scale Reflections on a Great House"; Dutt, "Sunset at Puri"; Mahapatra, "Our Casuarina Tree".
(b) Ezekiel, "Sunset at Puri"; Ramanujan, "Small-scale Reflections on a Great House"; Dutt, "Our Casuarina Tree"; Mahapatra, "Poet, Lover, Birdwatcher".
(c) Ezekiel, "Poet, Lover, Birdwatcher"; Ramanujan, "Sunset at Puri"; Dutt, "Our Casuarina Tree"; Mahapatra, "Small-scale Reflections on a Great House".
(d) Ezekiel, "Poet, Lover, Birdwatcher"; Ramanujan, "Small-scale Reflections on a Great House"; Dutt, "Our Casuarina Tree"; Mahapatra, "Sunset at Puri".

22. From among the following, identify the incorrect observation regarding Ferdinand de Saussure's seminal distinction between *langue* and *parole*.
(a) *Parole* is the particular language system, the elements of which we learn as children, and which is codified in our grammars and dictionaries, whereas *langue* is the language-occasion (what A says to B).
(b) A language consists in the interrelationship between *langue* and *parole*.
(c) Saussure made this crucial distinction in a study called *A Course in General Linguistics* (1916).
(d) *Langue* is the particular language-system, the elements of which we learn as children, and which is codified in our grammars and dictionaries, whereas *parole* is the language-occasion (what A says to B).

23. John Heywood wrote a farcical interlude called *The Four P's*.
Who were the Four P's?
(a) a Palmer, a Pedlar, a Pothecary, a Packer
(b) a Printer, a Pedlar, a Pothecary, a Palmer
(c) a Pedlar, a Parson, a Palmer, a Pothecary
(d) a Palmer, a Pardoner, a Pothecary, a Pedlar

24. In the mechanical drill method of second language acquisition:
(i) The learner has the freedom to choose from many responses.
(ii) The learner's response is totally controlled.

(iii) Comprehension of the item by the learner is not required.
(iv) Comprehension of the item by the learner is obligatory.

The right combination according to the code is:

(a) (i) and (iv) (b) (i) and (iii)
(c) (ii) and (iii) (d) (ii) and (iv)

25. Thou wilt not wake
Till I thy fate shall overtake;
Till age, or grief, or sickness must
Marry my body to that dust
It so much loves; and fill the room
My heart keeps empty in thy Tomb.
Stay for me there; I will not fail
To meet thee in that hollow Vale.
And think not much of my delay;
I am already on the way.

Which of the following readings do you find appropriate to the spirit of the lines above?

(a) In that interspace between the lines, the ending of one and the beginning of another, there is a silent internal language, the poem's language-within-language, tacitly signalled through the deployment of rhymed space.
(b) Ageing and dying are of course helplessly passive; but here love makes them as though they were now also willing things in the husband eager to join his dead wife. Through simple intimate tones of their shared earthly life—stay for me, wait for me, I will not fail—he not only imagines her but imagines her thinking of him.
(c) The lyric voice here can feel the poem speaking back to him—in the cold lineal stare of 'there was nothing in my belief'—even as his dead wife did not. It is as though the poem itself then demands his response, in order to be able to move from one line to another. To attempt that movement in keeping the poem's space alive, the lyric voice asserts, "I will not fail/ To meet there in that hollow Vale."
(d) My whole nature was so penetrated with grief and humiliation of such considerations, that, even now, famous and caressed and happy as I am, I often forget in my dream that I have a dear wife who died, leaving me alone in this world. Even that I am a man, and now I wander desolately back to that time of our lives when my wife and I shared moments of bliss.

26. Match the characters with the novels:

(A) Arthur Seaton (i) *Top Girls*
(B) Marlene (ii) *The Golden Notebook*
(C) Anna Wulf (iii) *The Swimming Pool Library*
(D) Beckwith (iv) *Saturday Night and Sunday Morning*

| Codes: | A | B | C | D |
|---|---|---|---|---|
| (a) | ii | iii | i | iv |
| (b) | iv | i | ii | iii |
| (c) | iii | iv | ii | i |
| (d) | ii | iv | iii | i |

27. The very last passage of a novel is given below. Identify the novel.

"Welcome, O life, I go to encounter for the millionth time the reality of experience and to forge in the smithy of my soul the uncreated conscience of my race.

April 27. Old father, old artificer, stand me now and ever in good stead."

(a) *To the Light House*
(b) *A Portrait of the Artist as a Young Man*
(c) *Maurice*
(d) *Almayer's Folly*

28. Francis Bacon's *New Atlantis* is about a utopian state called ______.
    (a) Asgard (b) Avalon
    (c) Bensalem (d) Baltia
29. The 1950's saw the rise of backlash against modernism and against New Romanticism that became known as The Movement. Which of the following little magazines came to be associated with The Movement?
    (i) *Departure*
    (ii) *New Verse*
    (iii) *London Mercury*
    (iv) *New Poems*

    The right combination according to the code is:
    (a) (i) and (ii) (b) (iii) and (iv)
    (c) (i) and (iv) (d) (ii) and (iv)
30. The error of interpreting a literary work by referring to evidence outside of itself, such as the design and purpose of the author is called ______.
    (a) Affective fallacy
    (b) Intentional fallacy
    (c) Authorial fallacy
    (d) Synecdochic fallacy
31. A.R. Ammons parodies a famous poem in his "Swoggled"

    I'd rather
    be
    suckled by
    an
    outworn pagan
    than
    get my horn
    wreathed in
    an
    old triton.

    Which poet, which poem?
    (a) John Keats, "On First Looking into Chapman's Homer"
    (b) John Milton, "On His Blindness"
    (c) William Wordsworth, "The World is Too Much with Us"
    (d) Elizabeth B. Browning, "How do I Love Thee...?"
32. Fanny Burney's *Evelina* carries the subtitle:
    (a) *or a Naive Lady's Entrance into the World*
    (b) *or a Young Lady's Entrance into the World*
    (c) *or a Young Lady's Exit from the World*
    (d) *or a Bold Lady's Entrance into the Hall*
33. What does Philip Sidney call poet-haters in his *Defence of Poesie*?
    (a) misogynists (b) misanthropes
    (c) misnomers (d) mysomousoi
34. Who, among the following, raises the following painful question of longing and belonging?

    "Where shall I turn, divided to the vein?
    I who have cursed
    The drunken officer of British rule, how choose
    Between this Africa and the English tongue I love?"

    (a) Derek Walcott
    (b) Louise Bennett
    (c) Kamau Brathwaite
    (d) Wole Soyinka
35. In the 1940's, a critic and a philosopher produced two influential and controversial papers called "The Intentional Fallacy" and "The Affective Fallacy".

    Identify them.
    (i) Cleanth Brooks
    (ii) Monroe C. Beardsley
    (iii) William K. Wimsalt Jr.
    (iv) R.P. Blackmur

    The right combination according to the code is:

(a) (i) and (ii) (b) (ii) and (iv)
(c) (ii) and (iii) (d) (iii) and (iv)

36. Philip Larkin's "Sad Steps" notices "The way the moon dashes through clouds that blow Loosely as cannon-smoke to stand apart...."

The poem alludes to:

(a) Coleridge's "Dejection: An Ode"
(b) The moonlit scenes in *A Midsummer Night's Dream*
(c) Philip Sidney's *Astrophel and Stella*
(d) T.S. Eliot's "Morning at the Window"

37. Match the following opening lines with their respective titles:

(A) "I leant upon a coppice gate"
(B) "A sudden blow: the great wings beating still...."
(C) "Among twenty snowy mountains"
(D) "I know what the caged bird feels, alas..."

(i) "Thirteen Blackbirds"
(ii) "Sympathy"
(iii) "The Darkling Thrush"
(iv) "Leda and the Swan"

| **Codes:** | **(A)** | **(B)** | **(C)** | **(D)** |
|---|---|---|---|---|
| (a) | (iv) | (iii) | (ii) | (i) |
| (b) | (iii) | (iv) | (i) | (ii) |
| (c) | (ii) | (i) | (iii) | (iv) |
| (d) | (i) | (ii) | (iv) | (iii) |

38. Identify the titles that were published in the 1920's.

(i) *Look, Stranger!*
(ii) *The Tower*
(iii) *The Waste Land*
(iv) *The Road to Wigan Pier*

**Codes:**

(a) (i) and (iii) (b) (ii) and (iii)
(c) (ii) and (iv) (d) (iii) and (iv)

39. This novel is dedicated "To the railroad of bones" and has as its epigraph the line, "I am the woman they give dead women's clothes to" from Christine Gelineau's "Inheritance". Identify the novel.

(a) *African Psycho* by Alain Mabanckou
(b) *The Chibok Girls* by Helon Habila
(c) *The Underground Railroad* by Colson Whitehead
(d) *The Book of Night Women* by Marlon James

40. An English poet couldn't help the excitement that an historical event caused in his life-time:

Bliss was it in that dawn to be alive,
But to be young was very heaven.

Which poet? What "dawn"?

(a) W.H. Auden; the Spanish Civil War
(b) Lord Tennyson; the Jubilee of Queen Victoria's reign
(c) William Wordsworth; the French Revolution
(d) William Blake; the Industrial Revolution

41. Which novel by John Banville tells the story of a group of travellers who arrive on a small island and stumble upon the house of Prof. Kreutznaer whose relationship to a painting entitled *The Golden World* by a fictional Dutch artist named Vaublin plays a central role?

(a) *Ghosts* (b) *The Sea*
(c) *The Ark* (d) *Eclipse*

42. Identify the two plays, usually paired for their critique of the politics of language and acts of police interrogation.

(a) *Earthly Powers, The Wanting Seed*
(b) *Chicken Soup with Barley, Roots*
(c) *Left-handed Liberty, The Hero Rises*
(d) *One for the Road, Mountain Language*

43. Semiotics originated mainly in the works of two theorists. They are:

(i) Charles Sanders Peirce
(ii) Mikhail Bakhtin
(iii) Ferdinand de Saussure
(iv) Valentin Voloshinov

The right combination according to the code is ________.

(a) (i) and (ii) (b) (ii) and (iii)
(c) (i) and (iii) (d) (iii) and (iv)

44. Robert Burton's *Anatomy of Melancholy* was published in 1621 and expanded and altered in _______ subsequent editions.
(a) two (b) four
(c) six (d) five

45. Which of the following magazines self-consciously created an identity for Vorticists, a group of painters, sculptors and writers?
(a) *Blast* (b) *The Egoist*
(c) *The Criterion* (d) *New Age*

46. "In every cry of every Man,
In every Infant's cry of fear,
In every voice, in every ban..."

The figure of speech characterized by repetition of words or group of words at the beginning of consecutive sentences is called _______.
(a) apostrophe
(b) anaphora
(c) incremental repetition
(d) alliteration

47. At whose behest does the Redcrosse Knight undertake his quest in *The Faerie Queene*?
(a) Gloriana's (b) Una's
(c) Duessa's (d) Prosperine's

48. In which city did John Ruskin see a paradigm for Victorian Britain?
(a) Vienna (b) Venice
(c) Rome (d) Paris

49. Which novel of Kazuo Ishiguro is narrated by a Japanese widow living in England and draws on the destruction and rehabilitation of Nagasaki?
(a) *An Artist of the Floating World*
(b) *The Unconsoled*
(c) *A Pale View of Hills*
(d) *When We Were Orphans*

50. Which novel opens thus:
"Whether I shall turn out to be the hero of my own life, or whether that station will be held by anyone else, these pages must show."
(a) *Tristram Shandy*
(b) *Lady Audley's Secret*
(c) *David Copperfield*
(d) *Fitz-Boodle's Confessions*

51. Traces of the Morality plays are discernible in a play like *Dr. Faustus*, traces such as______.
(a) vernacular songs adapting secular themes
(b) its soliloquizing protagonist, Good and Bad Angels and its final moral
(c) its refrains from the Corpus Christi Carol, the complaint of Christ, the lover of mankind
(d) its rhythmical prose, and the presence of a larger narrative rhythm in the Morality plays

52. The branch of philosophy that asks the question, 'How do we know what we know?' is _________.
(a) ontology (b) epistemology
(c) eschatology (d) phenomenology

53. The eighteenth century practice in England of bookselling was midway between direct patronage and impersonal sales. A patron paid half the cost of a book before publication and half on delivery. The author of the book received these payments directly. The patron's name appeared in the preface for the book published in this manner.

This practice was known as _____.

(a) Subscription (b) Contribution
(c) Pre-publication (d) Remaindering

54. Oxford India has published a volume of Premchand translations in English, *The Oxford India Premchand*. Who among the following is not one of the translators?
   (a) David Rubin
   (b) Alok Rai
   (c) Gillian Wright
   (d) Christopher King

55. Which of the two novels of Jane Austen have the spa town of Bath as a primary location?
   (i) *Emma*
   (ii) *Pride and Prejudice*
   (iii) *Northanger Abbey*
   (iv) *Persuasion*

   The right combination according to the code is:
   (a) (i) and (iv) (b) (ii) and (iii)
   (c) (iii) and (iv) (d) (i) and (ii)

56. In the communicative approach to ELT, the development of language learning or teaching involves a shift:
   (i) from form-based to a meaning-based approach.
   (ii) from an eclectic approach to a rigid method.
   (iii) from teacher-centred to learner-centred classes.
   (iv) from broad-based competence to specific needs.

   The right combination, according to the code is:
   (a) (ii) and (iv) (b) (i) and (iv)
   (c) (ii) and (iii) (d) (i) and (iii)

57. The four *Moral Essays* of Alexander Pope are addressed to carefully selected figures. Identify the correct group.
   (a) Timons, Newton, Martha Blount, Wellington
   (b) Lord Cobham, Robert Walpole, Houghton Hall, Chandos
   (c) Martha Blount, Lord Cobham, Bathurst, Burlington
   (d) William III, John Haydn, Joseph Addison, John Dennis

58. Bertolt Brecht's *Mother Courage and Her Children* presents the war-torn Europe as its protagonist as she follows troops with her canteenwagon.

   What is the real name of Mother Courage?
   (a) Paula Danckert (b) Anna Fierling
   (c) Jane Vanstone (d) Jani Lauzon

59. From among the following, identify the journal that publishes articles on English language teaching and learning.
   (a) *University of Toronto Quarterly*
   (b) *Agenda*
   (c) *TESOL Quarterly*
   (d) *English Language Notes*

60. Arrange the following elegies in English in chronological order.
   (a) "Elegy Written in a Country Churchyard"—"Adonais"—"Thyrsis"—"In Memoriam"
   (b) "Elegy Written in a Country Churchyard"—"Adonais"—"In Memoriam"—"Thyrsis"
   (c) "Elegy Written in a Country Churchyard"—"In Memoriam"—"Adonais"—"Thyrsis"
   (d) "Adonais"—"Elegy Written in a Country Churchyard"—"In Memoriam"—"Thyrsis"

61. Who is the only one of Milton's contemporaries to be mentioned by name in *Paradise Lost*?
   (a) Francis Bacon
   (b) Johannes Vermeer

(c) Gallileo
(d) King Charles 1

62. K.S. Maniam is a major writer of Indian origin, writing in English, born and living in Malaysia. Identify two of his novels from the following list.
(i) *The Rice Mother*
(ii) *The Return*
(iii) *Touching Earth*
(iv) *Between Lives*
The right combination according to the code is:
(a) (i) and (iv) (b) (ii) and (iii)
(c) (iii) and (iv) (d) (ii) and (iv)

63. What did Thomas Percy collect in his *Reliques*?
(a) medieval folklore and lyrics of the Midlands
(b) old songs, ballads, and romances in English and Scots
(c) Highland lore, mostly oral wisdom of the Scots
(d) Romantic idylls, sonnets and odes

64. Nirad Chaudhuri's *Autobiography of an Unknown Indian* concludes with an essay on the course of Indian history. But in the penultimate chapter Chaudhuri concludes the account of events in his life. How does this narrative end?
(a) Chaudhuri ties the knot with his childhood sweetheart and moves from Calcutta to Delhi.
(b) Chaudhuri obtains a job in the military accounts department and gives it up because he finds it soul-destroying.
(c) Chaudhuri joins the editorial team of a Calcutta newspaper and is upset over the drudgery of a reporter's life.
(d) Chaudhuri rushes to his ancestral village Bangram on receiving the news of the death of his uncle and recalls his past life.

65. In John Gower's *Confessio Amantis*, Amans, the lover makes his confession to the priest named _______.
(a) Verito (b) Genius
(c) Amor (d) Phoebe

66. In Eugene Ionesco's *Chairs*, the absurdity is not so much in the banal words that are uttered as ________.
(a) in the large scale use of frightening stage props and lightning effects.
(b) in the absurdist interpretation of them by character after character.
(c) in the fact that they are spoken to an ever-growing number of empty chairs.
(d) in the fact that they are spoken time and again by members of the audience.

67. A half-sentence in *Purchas his Pilgrimage* triggered off "Kubla Khan". Whose work was *Purchas his Pilgrimage*?
(a) Robert Herrick, the poet's
(b) John Hakluyt's, the collector of traveller's tales
(c) Samuel Purchas, the London Parson's
(d) Edward Purchas, the globe-trotter's

68. Based on the life of a thirteenth-century troubadour, from among the following identify the work, that marked a catastrophic failure in Robert Browning's poetic career, earning him a reputation for impenetrable difficulty?
(a) *Paracelsus*
(b) *Sordello*
(c) *The Ring and The Book*
(d) *Pauline*

69. In *Tristram Shandy*, the Author's preface
(a) is hawked to the highest bidder.
(b) appears in-between chapters 13 and 14 in Volume II.
(c) is printed in italics in all editions.
(d) appears in-between chapters 10 and 11 in Volume I.

70. Evelyn Waugh once complained that T.S. Eliot's *Poems, 1909-1925* was "marvellously good, but very hard to understand." The most pessimistic novel Waugh wrote was called ______ and he owed the title to ______.
(a) *Black Mischief*—"Sweeney among the Nightingales"
(b) *Scoop*—"Morning At the Window"
(c) *Prancing Nigger—Ash Wednesday*
(d) *A Handful of Dust—The Waste Land*

71. During the years 1830 to 1850, the illusion of peace in Victorian England was broken by such incidents as _______.
(a) the Revolution in France and the Chartist Movement in England
(b) the General Strike of 1835 and the Rail Tragedy of 1847
(c) the visionary libertarianism of poets and the lawless embodiment of revolution
(d) the disaster of the Indian Mutiny and the incompetent bungling of the Crimean War

72. Gulliver receives the following response when he boasts about his countrymen:
"...the most pernicious race of little odious vermin that nature ever suffered to crawl upon the face of the earth." Whose response?
(a) The King of Lilliput's
(b) The King of Brobdingnag's
(c) The Governor of Glubbdubrib's
(d) The first of the Houyhnhnms's he meets

73. In the *Inferno* Dante, as he travels through the various circles of the hell finds Judas who is unable to speak. What is the reason behind this?
(a) His tongue is transformed into a coiled snake.
(b) His head is battered and so he cannot open his mouth.
(c) Lucifer is chewing on his head.
(d) His tongue is pulled out and nailed on the tree of sin.

74. **Assertion (A):** Our reality is linguistic, a language mediated reality.
**Reason (R):** Our perception and understanding of reality are largely constructed by the words and other signs we use.
In the light of the statements above,
(a) Both (A) and (R) are true and (R) is the correct explanation of (A).
(b) Both (A) and (R) are true, but (R) is not the correct explanation of (A).
(c) (A) is true but (R) is false.
(d) (A) is false but (R) is true.

75. In his book, *In Theory*, Aijaz Ahmed works out the relations between the three entities:
(a) Classes, Nations, Literatures
(b) Regions, Nation, Languages
(c) State, Religions, Gender
(d) Literature, Print, Theory

76. In 1660, a group of 12 people including Robert Boyle and Christopher Wren formed what they called the Royal Society. In 1663, it became The Royal Society of London for Improving Natural Knowledge. What was the Society's motto?
(a) "In Him we trust"
(b) "In the words of no one"
(c) "Lighted to lighten"
(d) "Love conquers all"

77. Of whom did W.B. Yeats say that "We were the last Romantics"?
(a) The Pre-Raphaelite Brotherhood
(b) The Imagiste poets
(c) His Friends in the Irish Literary Revival
(d) Himself and his lady love, Maud Gonne

78. Who wrote *The Wandering Jew*, a poem in four cantos and the short lyric, "The Wandering Jew's Soliloquy"?
   (a) S.T. Coleridge (b) Lord Byron
   (c) Thomas Gray (d) P.B. Shelley
79. Where, according to T.S. Eliot, are we likely to find "not only the best, but the most individual parts of a poet's work"?
   (a) in the poet's juvenilia or rejected drafts.
   (b) in the best anthologies and scrap-books.
   (c) in those parts where the dead poets assert their immortality.
   (d) in those parts where the living poets depart from their ancestors.
80. Which of the following is true of *The Canterbury Tales*?
   (a) Chaucer, the pilgrim, narrates *Sir Thopas' Tale* only.
   (b) Chaucer, the pilgrim, narrates *The Tale of Melibee* only.
   (c) Chaucer, the pilgrim, narrates both *Sir Thopas' Tale* and *The Tale of Melibee*.
   (d) Chaucer, the pilgrim does attempt to narrate an unnamed tale but abruptly stops due to the intervention of the other pilgrims.
81. During the reign of Norman Kings, it was fashionable to speak _____ in upper-class circles in England.
   (a) Norse (b) Latin
   (c) Danish (d) French
82. Who, among the following, collaborated with Purohit Swami in translating the *Ten Principal Upanishads* into English?
   (a) Christopher Fry
   (b) Aldous Huxley
   (c) Lawrence Durrell
   (d) W.B. Yeats
83. What unique distinction does Ben Jonson's "To Penshurst" have in the English literary canon?
   (a) It is the only distinguished poem in English addressed to the Lords of Penshurst.
   (b) It celebrates Philip Sidney's elevation to knighthood, Sidney being the youngest scion of the family.
   (c) It is one of the first English poems celebrating a specific place, a forerunner to *Cooper's Hill* and *Windsor-Forest*.
   (d) It is the first poem in an elegiac series that late Elizabethan poets began on the demise of the Lord of Penshurst.
84. It is well known that in many of his plays, Tom Stoppard has consciously drawn upon earlier, often reputed, works. Match the following Stoppard plays with earlier works whose spirit seems to have informed them.

| | |
|---|---|
| (A) *Rosencrantz and Guildenstern Are Dead* | (i) *Hamlet* |
| (B) *Indian Ink* | (ii) *A Passage to India* |
| (C) *Inspector Hound* | (iii) *The Mousetrap* |
| (D) *Travesties* | (iv) *Importance of Being Earnest* |

| **Codes:** | **(A)** | **(B)** | **(C)** | **(D)** |
|---|---|---|---|---|
| (a) | (iii) | (ii) | (i) | (iv) |
| (b) | (i) | (ii) | (iv) | (iii) |
| (c) | (iv) | (iii) | (i) | (ii) |
| (d) | (ii) | (i) | (iv) | (iii) |

85. After discovering the truth about his heinous crimes committed in the past, what does Oedipus request as his punishment?
   (a) exile (b) castration
   (c) decapitation (d) blindness
86. How does *Women in Love* open?
   (a) Rupert Birkin, Lawrence's *alter ego*, is taking a walk in the English Countryside.

(b) The Brangwen sisters, Ursula and Gudrun, are "working and talking."
(c) The wedding party gathers at shortlands, the Criches's home.
(d) The last lesson is in progress, "peaceful and still" in Ursula's classroom.

87. Samuel Johnson has the following to say about an English poet:

"These images are marked by glittering accumulations of ungraceful ornaments: they strike, rather than please. The images are magnified by affectation: the language is laboured into harshness. The mind of the writer seems to work with unnatural violence—'Double, double, toil and trouble'. He has a kind of strutting dignity, and is tall by walking on tiptoe. His art and his struggle are too visible, and there is too little appearance of ease and nature."

Identify the poet.

(a) Thomas Gray (b) John Dryden
(c) John Milton (d) Thomas Wyatt

88. "Take the smoking disclaimer issue" begins Vishal Bharadwaj. "Putting a disclaimer every time somebody smokes on screen is not an answer. If M.F. Hussain had painted a man with a cigar, would you have asked him to put the disclaimer, 'Cigarette smoking is injurious to health' on the painting"?

The point Bharadwaj makes with his rhetorical question is the following:

(a) The smoking disclaimer is ineffectual because M.F. Hussain's painting wouldn't have carried it.
(b) The smoking disclaimer on objects perceived as 'art' is simply superfluous.
(c) The smoking disclaimer is ineffectual because 'art' entertains but does not instruct.
(d) The smoking disclaimer on screen or on an M.F. Hussain painting distracts us from enjoying art.

89. According to ______, certain verbs actually 'perform' an act when they are uttered.

(a) Speech Act theorists such as Austin and Searle.
(b) Russian Formalists such as Shklovsky and Propp.
(c) Language theorists such as Sapir and Whorf.
(d) Cognitive linguists such as Lakoff and Johnson.

90. Haunted castles, strange noises, and an acceptance of the supernatural with all its trappings mark ______.

(a) metafiction (b) fantasy fiction
(c) epistolary fiction (d) gothic fiction

91. .... sure it waits upon
Some god o' th' island. Sitting on a bank,
Weeping again the King my father's wrack,
This music crept by me upon the waters,
Allaying both their fury and my passion
With its sweet air. Thence I have followed it,
Or it hath drawn me rather....

Which of the following statements on this passage are true?

(i) These lines, spoken by Edgar in *King Lear*, are part of a long speech delivered on the heath.
(ii) These lines, spoken by Ferdinand in *The Tempest*, describe Ariel's music.
(iii) The passage reappears in an altered and ironic version in T.S. Eliot's *Waste Land*.
(iv) The passage reappears verbatim in W.H. Auden's *Sea and the Mirror*.

The correct answer according to the code is:

(a) (i) and (iv) (b) (ii) and (iii)
(c) (iii) and (iv) (d) (i) and (iii)

92. Arrange the following plays of Shakespeare according to their periods (early, middle, late...) of composition.

(a) *As You Like It, Love's Labours Lost, Antony and Cleopatra, The Tempest, Midsummer Night's Dream.*
(b) *Antony and Cleopatra, The Tempest, Midsummer Night's Dream, Love's Labours Lost, As You Like It.*
(c) *Love's Labours Lost, Midsummer Night's Dream, As You Like It, Antony and Cleopatra, The Tempest.*
(d) *Midsummer Night's Dream, Antony and Cleopatra, The Tempest, As You Like It, Love's Labours Lost.*

93. Who among the following is not a reader-response critic?
(a) Maud Bodkin
(b) Hans-Robert Jauss
(c) Stanley Fish
(d) Wolfgang Iser

94. Leo Tolstoy's *Anna Karenina's* closing lines present...
(a) a sad reflection on the unfortunate suicide of Anna which should have been averted.
(b) the enlivening freshness of a rain which has been threatening to break out.
(c) Levin's affirmation that whatever happens to him, life is not meaningless but unquestionably meaningful.
(d) Vronsky's lament over the death of Anna which ends on a positive note, affirming the human tendency to pass over the tragic events with hope.

95. Which of the following novels begins with a Prologue under the title "The Storming of Seringapatam", saying "I address these lines written in India—to my relatives in England"?
(a) *The Siege of Krishnapur* by J.G. Farell
(b) *The Moonstone* by Wilkie Collins
(c) *The Sign of Four* by Sir Arthur Conan Doyle
(d) *The Jewel in the Crown* by Paul Scott

96. In "Gerontion", T.S. Eliot says:
"________ has many cunning passages, contrived corridors/ And issues, deceives with whispering ambitions,/ Guides us by vanities."
What is Eliot's subject?
(a) History (b) Politics
(c) State (d) Religion

**Read the following poem and answer questions 97 to 100.**

THE MOUNTAIN

My students look at me expectantly.
I explain to them that the life of art is a life
of endless labor. Their expressions
hardly change; they need to know
a little more about endless labor.
So I tell them the story of Sisyphus,
how he was doomed to push
a rock up a mountain, knowing nothing
would come of this effort
but that he would repeat it
indefinitely. I tell them
there is joy in this, in the artist's life,
that one eludes
judgment, and as I speak
I am secretly pushing a rock myself,
slyly pushing it up the steep
face of a mountain. Why do I lie
to these children? They aren't listening,
they aren't deceived, their fingers
tapping at the wooden desks—
So I retract
the myth; I tell them it occurs
in hell, and that the artist lies
because he is obsessed with attainment,
that he perceives the summit
as that place where he will live for ever,
a place about to be
transformed by his burden: with every breath,

I am standing at the top of the mountain.
Both my hands are free. And the rock has added height to the mountain.

(Louise Gluck)

97. Whose poetic voice is triggered right from the beginning?
    (a) of student's (b) of teacher's
    (c) of critics' (d) of an observer's
98. The speaker brings up the story of Sisyphus specifically by way of glossing _________.
    (a) art in life
    (b) life in art
    (c) endless labor
    (d) poetic expectation
99. In its context, the words "their fingers/ tapping at the wooden desks", best represent the students' _______.
    (a) lack of protest
    (b) lack of interest
    (c) show of disrespect
    (d) show of impatience
100. Why does the speaker say that "the rock has added height to the mountain"?
    (a) because the speaker is already on the top of the mountain.
    (b) because both the hands of the speaker are now free.
    (c) because the mountain now seems largely incomprehensible.
    (d) because she feels that the immensity of the problem has grown.

## ANSWERS

| | | | | | |
|---|---|---|---|---|---|
| 1. (c) | 2. (d) | 3. (c) | 4. (b) | 5. (a) | 6. (a) |
| 7. (a) | 8. (c) | 9. (c) | 10. (a) | 11. (c) | 12. (c) |
| 13. (a) | 14. (b) | 15. (b) | 16. (c) | 17. (a) | 18. (c) |
| 19. (a) | 20. (b) | 21. (d) | 22. (a) | 23. (d) | 24. (c) |
| 25. (b) | 26. (b) | 27. (b) | 28. (c) | 29. (c) | 30. (b) |
| 31. (c) | 32. (b) | 33. (d) | 34. (a) | 35. (c) | 36. (c) |
| 37. (b) | 38. (b) | 39. (d) | 40. (c) | 41. (a) | 42. (d) |
| 43. (c) | 44. (d) | 45. (a) | 46. (b) | 47. (t) | 48. (b) |
| 49. (c) | 50. (c) | 51. (b) | 52. (b) | 53. (a) | 54. (c) |
| 55. (c) | 56. (d) | 57. (c) | 58. (b) | 59. (c) | 60. (b) |
| 61. (c) | 62. (d) | 63. (b) | 64. (b) | 65. (b) | 66. (c) |
| 67. (c) | 68. (b) | 69. (t) | 70. (d) | 71. (d) | 72. (b) |
| 73. (c) | 74. (a) | 75. (a) | 76. (b) | 77. (c) | 78. (d) |
| 79. (c) | 80. (c) | 81. (d) | 82. (d) | 83. (c) | 84. (t) |
| 85. (a) | 86. (b) | 87. (a) | 88. (b) | 89. (a) | 90. (d) |
| 91. (b) | 92. (c) | 93. (a) | 94. (c) | 95. (b) | 96. (a) |
| 97. (b) | 98. (c) | 99. (d) | 100. (d) | | |

t = The marks have been awarded to all the Candidates against the question(s).